Gabrielle

Other books by this author

In her previous name of
T J Henley or Terence J Henley

Sci-Fi

Miranda (1st in the trilogy)
The Miranda Gate (2nd in the trilogy)
Miranda Revealed (3rd in the trilogy)
Invasion of the Cycloves
The Game
The Death Zone
Galactic Conquerors

Teen Romance

Hazel's Pride

Under Sarah Henley

TG Romance

The Secret (1st of a trilogy TG strongly orientated)
Second Chance (2nd of trilogy TG strongly orientated)

Gabrielle

Sarah Henley

ISBN 9798841988335

I dedicate this book to Terry,
My Soulmate

FOREWORD

Gabrielle, formerly named Paul Grayson a billionaire, married his wife, famous author Lynda Hill, after falling head over heels in love with each other on their first meeting. After a sex change to help Lynda's mental condition through her abused past and to fulfil Paul's dreams, they now live their lives as wife and wife, lesbians, travelling through Europe, the USA and Australia where Gabrielle's sister Janet lives with her husband Tom both billionaires, looking after their airline flying Boing 747's across Australia, to the UK and Paris, while Gabrielle and Lynda look after their TG Charity in London and their shops, Hats, Bags & Wraps throughout the UK, Europe |and the USA.

With the sudden death of their father Neil, by a car bomb, Gabrielle and Lynda have been summoned to meet George Rainer, who was Ian Edgar's close friend and Lynda's husband, who was killed with George in their first timeline, by Paul.

George has been resurrected by Death to help Him win a bet He has made with Fate, using Gabrielle and Lynda as their test subjects, after Death gave Gabrielle, the perfect woman's body and promised them as they had wished to live forever together in love, Death gave them Immortality. Fate has given them the power of telepathy, telekinesis and teleportation for their tasks ahead.

George was shot in the leg and head by the police, in their second timeline, which Death has given Gabrielle and Lynda in their *Second Chance.* George escaped from the police van he was travelling in and through the wound to his head, he now thinks Lynda is his wife and whore to do with as he pleases, including cutting her body with a Stanley knife.

George has given Gabrielle and Lynda one month to grieve for their father but during this time, they have been ordered by the Queen and the UK Government to go to Rome and have peace talks with Marko Don the current head of the Mafia in Rome whose people have been used in London and other cities with the thugs from George to carry out raids on shops throughout the city and take a number of the Drug Lords captive to take over their areas of power. It is now left up to Gabrielle and Lynda to finally diffuse this event.

Previously, they have been chased throughout Europe by George's thugs trying to kill them and their armed bodyguards, where they have been in many gunfights and an air battle.

Due to Gabrielle having attempted suicide over ten times, and Lynda has been killed once and brought back to life, by Death they have both spoken to Death several times and Death has taken a great interest in their lives as too has Fate.

On their last encounter with Death, He suggested they could live for eternity if they agreed to carry out a bet between Himself and Fate.

If Death wins the bet, He takes all the souls on Earth for his own to do with as He pleases. If Fate wins the bet, Fate will destroy the Earth using the Sun's radiation and the souls will be given to The Omega. However, Gabrielle and Lynda will be able to save a hundred thousand people to live on Mars where they will populate the planet and eventually move into space.

The bet is to see if the two girl's living as wife and wife, can stop one or two elegant men splitting them up. Without the two Entities knowing, Lynda retrieved the bet from her memory, and they are both extremely happy with the Earth and its billions of souls, as it is, they are not about to lose it. It is up to Gabrielle to fight George for Lynda's life and soul and all the souls on Earth.

CHAPTER 1

Gabrielle and Lynda made their arrangements to visit Marco Don in Rome for peace talks, two days after their father's funeral. As he had been killed in a car bomb and burned so badly there was very little left to put into his coffin and buried in Christchurch cemetery London.

The entire Grayson family gathered at Gabrielle and Lynda's apartment in London. All Hats, Bags & Wraps shops were officially closed for the day in respect to the funeral of Neil Grayson. All the Grayson dress shops were also closed in respect of Neil and most of the managers and senior managers of their shops and larger stores were now filing into the church. Arrangements had been made for their stay at two, local five-star hotels. There were six large limousines ready to follow the coffin through London and a police escort had been given to them by the Prime Minister on orders from the Queen.

In the first limousine were Brenda, Neil's wife. Gabrielle, Lynda, Janet, Tom and their two children Charlotte 8 and Peter 6, Uncle Jack Grayson, Neil's brother, and his wife Doreen. Sarah Watts, Jenny Fletcher, three armed bodyguards, John Fletcher, Alan Watts and Mike Nicole's, Neil's former bodyguard who was severely injured in the car bomb, while he was collecting a cake for Neil when the explosion took place and attained severe glass injuries in his front and back.

In the rest of the cars were other relatives, aunts, uncles and cousins with their bodyguards, Lynda's parents Elaine and Ethan, her sister Makhila, brother-in-law David and their three children, Louise 8, Oliver 10 and Nancy. Some managers of Neil and Brenda's top shops in the UK and Paris.

Overhead, a drone, was watching the convoy of black limousines, with a host of vehicles following in their wake. The drone was being controlled by Simon in the third four wheeled drive police vehicle with several screens in the back and a large antenna on the roof to control the four-foot diameter drone with four cameras giving them 360° views of the surrounding area.

The bodyguards could see the views via their iPhones giving everyone a heads up if things turned bad, which is what nobody wanted on this specific day as they hoped George would at least leave them alone for a few hours.

The funeral cars left Grayson Mansion at 11.40 for the twenty-minute slow drive through London's outer boroughs to St. Christopher's Church for the service and burial in the graveyard after. As the cars pulled up outside the church, the four Pole Bearers, Tom, Jack, Mike and John, carried the exceptionally light coffin, draped in flowers and even more flowers were carried into the church by the funeral men and one woman.

Brenda was holding Janet's arm, as she walked directly behind the coffin and Gabrielle, holding Lynda's arm walked after them. All four women walked up to the coffin and placed their hand on it saying a silent short prayer at the time and looking at the large photo of their father and husband. Taking their seats at the front of the packed church, they picked up their hymn-sheets and stood for the first hymn, Abide with me.

Two more hymns and a set of prayers later, Brenda walked unsteady to the Rostrum flanked by both her daughters, Janet and Gabrielle. She placed the small piece of paper on the rostrum and holding both girl's hands, she started to read.

"Neil was taken from me by a horrendous car bomb which also injured his bodyguard, Mike Nicoles. It was a terrible way to die. We now know who is behind this and Gabrielle and Lynda will be travelling to Rome to try and bring peace between the Mafia and our people here.

"Neil was my husband, concierge, friend and lover. We had forty-eight glorious years together. I shall miss his humour, jokes especially and our times travelling around Europe together and the rest of the world. I know he is in a good place and will be waiting for me, at least that is what Gabrielle tells me and I believe her." She turned and looked into Gabrielle's green eyes seeing a look of peace behind the front she was putting on for her mother. She had to be strong and yet she felt so hurt deep inside.

Her father had died in her place, she wondered who had really orchestrated his death. which was so real and painful, not just too her, but her entire family. Tears started to fill her eyes and she squeezed her mother's hand harder wiping her tears with a white, lace, hanky. She didn't know if she could manage to get through the day as she really wanted too. Would Paul have been able to do this? She had no idea, but her female hormones were all over the place and she was not fully used to them acting in this way.

She looked at Lynda whose eyes were turning bright green giving Gabrielle her strength to get through this strenuous time of the proceedings.

A cold feeling travelled through her soul and she knew Death was with her.

"I took your father at the exact moment he would have died that day of a massive heart attack. The fact that Mike Nicoles was injured was incidental, I did not take his life, but I could easily have done so."

The ice-cold feeling that had put them out of time, was only spoken to Lynda and Gabrielle and now they both felt the normal warmth of their body and soul.

Both spoke to each other using telepathy, one of the gifts Fate had given them to get through the test they had to endure to decide the fate of the world and all humans living on it.

"That was good to know, it makes me feel a little better, but I hope he felt no pain," Gabrielle said to Lynda, out of time.

"I'm sure he didn't, Death would have kept His promise to us."

They re-joined the ceremony.

"I can only thank everyone for coming to Neil's Funeral." Brenda broke down in tears as Janet and Gabrielle helped their mother back to their seats.

The rest of the church ceremony went without further incident with Jack and Tom Grayson giving an epitaph for Neil. The burial was going fine until two men entered the churchyard from an unlocked gate. They crept under the cover of trees, bushes and tall gravestones towards the people gathered around the grave. The overhead drone was watching the two men as they made their way towards the large number of people who were at the grave.

As they were getting closer to the grave, so were four armed police officers who had been given the okay to fire if needed. As they looked through their telescopic sights there seemed nothing out of the ordinary with them, just two young men trying to see what was happening, but this was no ordinary funeral, a very wealthy man had been killed by a car bomb, so the police kept advancing, their fingers on their triggers ready to fire if necessary.

Due to the funeral, their guns had been fitted with silencers. Getting within twenty feet of the two men, the four men dressed all in black noticed a change in the young men's appearance, they pulled balaclavas over their faces and one man had pulled out a Polish machine gun.

The two men had their eyes trained on the group fifteen metres before them and didn't see the police advancing on them. All the bodyguards were being given an update as the police moved in on the two men.

The bodyguards were now forming a ring around their people and had got their guns ready to draw. The drone, still high up was searching for other people either by the gate of the graveyard that the men had entered through, or more men inside the graveyard.

From its position, the drone flew over the cars parked outside the graveyard and was just about to move on when the keen-eyed operator returned the drone over a Punto, with its engine running, its smoky exhaust coming from the rear of the car.

The funeral itself was nearing the end, Neil's coffin had been lowered into the ground and the last rights had been given; mourners were now circling the coffin either throwing a small handful of dirt or a rose onto the coffin.

The people were supposed to move to their cars, but they slowly moved to the walled area where Neil's main flowers were to the walled area. The bodyguards were updated about the car on the exterior of the graveyard. The bodyguards took the most vulnerable people from the graveside and got them to some form of safety behind the church wall.

Six police cars drove slowly down the road then speeded up and stopped right next to the suspect vehicle. Eight officers leapt from their cars to surround the car and had their weapons trained on the driver.

The senior officer, with his machine gun in his arm, walked cautiously up to the driver's side of the car. "Put your hands on the steering-wheel where I can see them. Right, no quick movements, turn off your engine and unlock the car." He ordered.

The officer watched as he turned off the engine and the man looked at him still not opening the door locks. He looked worried, very worried that he was about to die, but there was no reason for this, the police, although they had guns were not about to kill him without just cause. There appeared to be no danger here, but the police were still on their guard.

The man in the car looked at the police officer and opened his window fractionally.

"You tell Gabrielle this war is not over yet and we will kill all the Mafia and she will die as George has told her in three weeks' time, now quickly remove your men, I do not relish their blood on my hands."

"Run, car bomb!" the senior officer shouted, and everyone ran as fast as they could as the car exploded.

Three men were blown across the road into a wall, one man was sent flying in the air as the boot exploded into his face. The senior officer was hit in his chest and face as the driver's door burst open and the window. Now almost molten glass with the intense heat wrapped itself around the officer's face and with the car door pushing him backwards, he was pushed into the path of an oncoming car and his legs were hit beneath him, breaking all the bones in his legs and pushing him thirty yards down the road. The car that hit the senior officer was skidding to a halt being hit by the shockwave and the explosion, the Punto, engulfed in flames, was flying through the air. It landed on top of the car that hit the police officer and a car close behind was also hit by flying debris and a second or two later, the exploding full petrol tank hit the second car and with its deluge of burning petrol, covered the car, while the petrol tank flew straight through the car's side killing the passenger instantly, and setting on fire the driver who despite his burning body, pushed the automatic gearbox into park.

The Mercedes was a right off, but the driver didn't wish to run over the two policemen on the pavement who had been blown across the road. The third police officer was just coming around and was dragging one of the other downed officers along the pavement before the Mercedes blew up as well. The two children in the back were burned alive.

Their wails of pain and death coming from their car was a terrible sound to the people who had run from their houses to see if they could help anyone in the cars. There was silence for a moment, a loud silence where the burning cars were now finding their resting place, the children both dead, their parents dead. In the car which hit the police officer the driver was on fire, as too the passenger who was killed instantly when the burning Punto crashed on top of their car and with the extreme heat, incinerated the passenger in a few seconds.

Two fire engines and six ambulances were already heading down the road, having previously been put on standby. Six more police cars were racing into the road from each end swerving and blocking the road stopping any cars from escaping.

As one car moved out and tried to ram a police car, without managing to move the car away the driver leapt from his car, running as fast as his legs would carry him, down past the cemetery wall using it as cover running between the other parked cars which were also on fire, but the fires had not yet reached their petrol tanks.

The officer who had helped the officer on the pavement, ran back to try and get the third officer, a woman away from the carnage that was about to happen. He was just two seconds too late. As his hands grabbed the woman's unconscious body, her gun on her chest, as he pulled her away from the burning Mercedes it ran over her legs and pinned her under the burning car.

As her uniform caught fire with the dripping fuel and intense heat from the burning car, the bullets in her gun started to explode and fire. The female officer was for her, luckily killed as four of the twenty bullets in the clip entered her body and the remainder fired indiscriminately down the road and ricocheted off walls.

The officer who was now pulling the second officer further along the pavement as the tarmac started to melt due to the heat, looked across the road at the fleeing man.

Picking up the unconscious officer's gun, he took aim and hit the man in the right leg, as he turned and started to fall to the ground, he fired again and hit his right arm forcing him to drop the gun in his hand.

Three ordinary police officers who were chasing the man, got closer to him and the armed officer shouted a warning to them. "Watch out he may be carrying a bomb on himself or grenades."

The armed officer, despite his burns and injuries, limped across the road, down to the man on the ground and checked him over before allowing the three young officers to finally cuff and arrest the man. He was checked again for weapons and knives before being looked at by an ambulance technician as paramedics checked over the police officers and three members of the public who had been in the car behind the Mercedes, as it was hit by flying debris.

As this was happening outside the cemetery gates, the people at the grave were running for cover of the bricked building. Just as they started to run, the two young men who had crept up the cemetery, hoping their second getaway car was still intact and the driver not yet discovered, stood up.

The man furthest away pulled two pins from his grenades and was leaning back with his arms behind his head when the police officers heard a voice over their earphones.

"Kill both men! Kill both men before they cause more carnage," the senior police officer who was commanding this part of the operation shouted into their ears. The police officers were slow in responding as they were talking about what was happening on the road to their right. One man had his wife working there and was worried she might be killed in the incident.

Due to their three second delay, they did not hit the first man with the machine gun until he was stood and was trying to open fire with his machine gun which had luckily jammed. He was shot in the head twice and his gun shot from his hands.

The man with the grenades just managed to throw them weakly forward as he too was shot in the head, but it was too late to stop the grenades from turning end over end toward the remainder of the crowd. At least twenty people still had to get clear and of these were Brenda who didn't want to leave the graveside, Janet, Tom Lynda and Gabrielle. Jack and his bodyguard had managed to get as many people out of the way as possible and carried four children to the security of the walled section and helped to thin out the crowd as the two grenades got ever closer to the last group of people. John had his gun out as too did Simon, Tom's bodyguard. They both fired at the same instant, their bullets true and hit the grenades making them explode twenty feet from them.

Everyone left ducked to the ground but luckily nobody was injured, and the remainder of the people were now ushered to the walled section where they were all talking about what had happened.

The armed police were now checking both dead men, removing their weapons and a further eight grenades.

Behind the wall with just over two hundred people huddled together, shaking and wondering what was happening, how could this happen? so much death and destruction?

"If I could just have your attention please," Gabrielle called to everyone. As the people stopped talking between themselves, the noise quietened down.

"If all the drivers could move to the left; you will be given the address of the wake venue by John and Alan. Due to the events that have taken place here today, we have decided that it would be unwise for Lynda and myself to accompany you all to the wake as we do not wish to bring further problems with us," Gabrielle said sounding terribly upset that she had been forced into making this decision.

"Gabrielle," Jack Grayson replied. "We have all at times had to cope with people coming after us for money, a business take over and even to try and kill us just because we have money and therefore have to employ bodyguards who are licensed to kill and we do not enjoy having to go to these extremes, but such are the lives that we lead. I therefore suggest you both change your minds, it was after all your father, my brother who was killed and we would like you both there with us at his wake, what say you all, should they stay or go?" He shouted asking everyone.

"Stay!" came the reply.

"Well, thank you how can we refuse if you all agree, we would really love to accompany you to our father's wake?" Gabrielle replied. "We will just give the police time to sort out what is to happen with us and then we'll depart; thank you for your patience and support."

Gabrielle looked at John and Alan who had finished handing their cards out, walking back to meet with Gabrielle and Lynda.

"John, Alan, would you like to talk with the police and find out when we can leave and how they intend getting us past the bodies please?"

"Sure Gabrielle," John replied and with Alan went off to organise their escape from the church.

Fifteen minutes later they were back and talking with the other bodyguards before reporting back to Gabrielle. Even now, people were forming into groups and getting ready for their departure.

After explaining what would happen to Gabrielle, she spoke to everyone.

"Ladies and gentlemen, the police would like us to return to the main church where we will get into our groups and get ready to move to our cars. Uncle Jack, if you could get your car group ready and take mum, Mike and Penny with you. If you leave now, we'll meet you at the venue. The rest of us, give them a minute or two to get through the church and then make your way into the church. If the drivers could get their groups together, we'll then make our way to the cars and drive onto the venue. Is there anyone who does not have a lift?"

Four people put their hand in the air. "If you will stay behind, you'll accompany Lynda and myself in one of our cars and I'll arrange a lift for you to get you home after. the wake," Gabrielle said calmly.

With the final evening talks over, Gabrielle led the love of her life into their bedroom, they undressed and got into bed. They had previously watched the evening news where a person who had recorded the entire event in the road had uploaded the ten-minute film to U-Tube and had already had over a million hits. As they lay together, they knew the following morning they would be flying to Rome to talk over the final peace treaty with Marko from the Mafia. Many of their members were still in the UK looking for George, as they made their way slowly down the country to London and returned to Rome.

Although they had buried the remains of their father that day, they were both naked and holding each other close, their love for each other and their desire for each other as for the day they had both been through needed to repair their lives, a repair that would bring them closer together and knowing that their father was buried that day, he had died eight days ago.

As their bodies lay close together, their breasts touched, and both were crying for a short time. They had a special love between them and as the time passed, their bodies, touching, breasts touching each other, arms around each other's backs pulling each other close, their lips touched, and they kissed. Their tongues intertwined like snakes, licking and exploring each other's mouth, their mouths rotating about each other.

Lynda finally moved on top of her wife and they found themselves engulfed in each other's love.

Gabrielle's hand slowly moved down the front of Lynda's body and curved inwards. slowly playing at first with her clitoris and then three fingers entered her vagina. They moved slowly in and out, making her damp and moving in unison with Gabrielle's hand, her body was soon writhing with delight as Gabrielle found her G Spot.

"Oh Gabrielle, please don't stop, you know I'll have an orgasm any moment now."

"I know my love, lay on your back and enjoy yourself," Gabrielle sighed softly and slowly turned Lynda on her side then gently onto her back, her fingers deep inside her vagina, massaging her vagina walls, gently rubbing her G Spot.

"Ohh yesss, that's lovely, please, don't stop, come here,"

Lynda groaned as her hands held Gabrielle's face bringing it close to hers so she could kiss her as she had her first orgasm of the night.

Gabrielle slowly moved her fingers as the rush of Lynda's orgasm wet her vagina walls, seeping further down her vagina as Gabrielle's fingers were still inside her Lynda, felt some of her orgasm wet her clitoris as Gabrielle pulled her wet fingers out of Lynda's vagina, her fingers played with her wet clitoris until

Lynda was writhing again; feeling very sexy kissing Gabrielle's mouth, feeling her love for her, had her second orgasm.

Lynda turned the tables around, with their breasts touching, nipples hard, they kissed as Lynda ran her fingers down Gabrielle's stomach and started to play with her clitoris, inserting three fingers into her vagina, played with her swiftly bringing her to an orgasm.

"Let me lick you," Lynda said giggling.

"Only if I can lick you at the same time and we'll bring each other to a climax; let's see who can achieve it first," Gabrielle replied chuckling. As they turned, with Lynda on top of Gabrielle, Gabrielle started to tickle Lynda's feet, which started Lynda tickling Gabrielle's feet and they both burst into laughter.

This made them feel much happier inside after their long, awfully bad day. As soon as the tickling was over with, they both concentrated on the job at hand and both girls started to lick and kiss each other's clitoris. Their lips kissing long and hard against the extremely sensitive skin. Gabrielle was first to use her fingers on Lynda's clitoris thus making her enjoy the sensation she was getting even more randy.

Gabrielle was used to licking Lynda's clitoris and knew exactly where to stimulate her and as her tongue went into Lynda's vagina, her vagina walls were already getting wet with excitement.

"Mmmmmhhhhh! Mmmmmhhhhh!" Lynda moaned as Gabrielle's tongue twisted and thrust itself against the wet sides of her vagina. Lynda was already nearing an orgasm and could not stop it bursting from the depths of her vagina, scouring the already damp walls with her excitement.

Turning around they kissed, holding each other close, feeling each other and playing with each other's breasts until at last at almost three in the morning they fell asleep, as always, with Lynda laying on top of Gabrielle, their arms wrapped around each other, as they had lain on the cold pavement in London six years ago.

Chapter 2

Three hours later they were up showered and dressed, with Sarah already in their apartment getting their clothes packed for their mission to Rome for their peace talks. At eleven they left their apartment and headed for the airport under police escort and drone support. They were met by the Prime minister who spoke briefly to the two girls.

"Gabrielle, Lynda, please accept my personal respects for the loss of your father and I have been asked by The Queen to give you her condolences and hope your peace talks go well. The Queen Elizabeth Carrier group are currently in the Mediterranean Sea doing war exercises which also includes helicopter trips into Rome with English troops dressed in Italian police uniforms and Italian troop dress were dropped off in the darkness of night at the rendezvous point. They are safely integrated with the forces surrounding the countryside, and the police dogs for the protection of the people in Rome are on the ground, with their handlers. If the talks fail, then we will withdraw all our men and women immediately, they have been given their rendezvous points for pickups and we will be bombing the areas to safeguard our troops and if needed, in Rome itself.

"These are your diplomatic papers for yourselves, your bodyguards, John and Alan and of course, Sarah. I take it she will be accompanying you both?"

"Yes, she will, thankyou Prime Minister," Gabrielle said taking the papers and Passport Gate passes from his hand.

"Gabrielle, please, if you feel your lives are in danger then please do not take the situation any further and get yourselves out of Rome by any means and a call to any of the officers in the carrier group will get you all aboard one of our ships."

"Thank you for the offer but I'm sure it will not come to that," Gabrielle said smiling, holding Lynda's hand firmly in hers.

"Have no fear Prime Minister, we'll be out of Rome and onto one of the ships at the sound of the first gunshot," Ian, Minister of Homeland Security said standing close to his Private secretary Christine.

The Prime Minister looked at him as did Gabrielle and Lynda, there was always gunfire in Rome now, the Prime Minister wondered why he had ever made Ian, Minister of Homeland security if he was going to run home at the first gunshot. He was glad Gabrielle and Lynda were there in charge of the peace talks, they had been through many gun fights and came out the other side fine, getting on with their lives and helping those who had been shot and Lynda was used to getting her clothes and hands covered in other people's blood.

They all shook hands and boarded their jet. Within ten minutes they were in the air and off to Rome to commence peace talks with the Mafia.

Upon landing in Rome, the jet taxied to a private section and the door was opened to a red carpet on the floor and a group of representatives from the Mafia waited to greet them.

"Welcome, welcome to Rome," Lorenzo said and kissed Gabrielle on the cheek each side.

Next, he kissed Lynda the same way and the others as they deplaned. The last two people to deplane were two girls, Alice and Rebecca, both wearing a white dress, white bra and panties, with white ankle socks and black shoes. They each carried their own handbag with a purse, small brush for their hair, lipstick and compact mirror in their bags. Each girl had long, auburn hair, to just below their shoulders; one wore a wig, the other it was her real hair.

Both girls were kissed and welcomed to Rome as the others. The girls were from the Young Transgender Group in London who wanted to visit their friends and parents who had helped them get out of Rome but deserved a visit this time in their transition. Both girls spoke perfect Italian, Spanish and English and were now learning French and German, using Gabrielle's teaching method. They were taken to their hotel under a Mafia escort of six cars and when they arrived, Lorenzo ushered the porters to get their cases and trunk up to their rooms. Once inside the hotel lobby, Lorenzo took Gabrielle and Lynda with John, Alan, Ian and Christine into the restaurant and there had coffee, the Italian way.

"Gabrielle, Marko would like it if Lynda and yourself, would join him and his wife for meal at the Osteria Dei Mascalzoni Tavern, it is a very good place to eat."

"And a very good name for it, Tavern of the Scoundrels, and we are after all, scoundrels are we not?" Gabrielle asked laughing, holing Lynda's hand tightly in hers.

"Very true indeed Gabrielle, Sereniti will be in attendance and she is very well and six months pregnant."

"I hope Marco is treating her well."

"She walks on water, anything she needs she has, and the nursery is all ready for the new arrival.

"Well . . .what is the sex?"

"It is a girl, but he is not worried, he no longer wants his children to be a Don like himself. He has helped the Transgender group here and with your money He has added the same amount to the Transgender group's funds. With the builders you have given us to help with the building of the main accommodation complex. Your builders have often showed ours up by working in the heat.

"The main living accommodation for Transgender people is now open and filling up. I'm sure Stephney will wish to meet with you and show you what your investment has made and of course, while they started to build the apartments, the diggers dug out the foundations for the Train station and café."

"This is excellent news We will have to visit the place while we are here, and I hope for everyone involved that it goes well, and Marco will assist the Transgender people who live there."

"Do you think Marco would mind if the two girls came with us, they are off to see their friends and Rebecca, the youngest girl, will see her mother."

"How is Draco doing?" Lorenzo asked.

"He's doing fine. He has been started on the young person's drug to stop him from becoming a man and this will also stop him getting facial hair. He would have joined us, but he is in the middle of intense psychiatric treatment for his change with three other boys who are at the same stage and he does not wish to lose out. He said there would be other trips and he wanted to make his father proud."

"I suppose that makes sense and with the Peace Talks, Marco will have extraordinarily little time with his son, or daughter now. I presume she is happy now?" Lorenzo asked.

"Yes, I saw her four days ago, she is incredibly happy and made many friends and is showing everyone how to do the Argentine Tango. She is an excellent dancer, and her parents will be pleased to see what she has achieved in such a short time when she next comes to visit, which will be in a few more weeks. We have to come back for a Hat & Bag show."

"I will tell Marco what you have said, Sereniti will certainly wish to see her."

Ian was growing tired of their talking about transgender boys and girls. He didn't understand them or care for them, in his opinion they should all be shot and put out of their misery, all over the world they were not welcome here. The money would be better off used to make better hotels and put more police on the pavements in his opinion and he decided to mention this to the Prime Minister and the Queen and who was Sereniti? No doubt an elderly woman who cleaned Marco's shoes and why would he bring this elderly maid with him to the start of the peace talks? ` The faster they got out of here the better and he didn't like this Italian coffee. He heard a gunshot down the road and Lorenzo left the table for a moment. Ian was shaking when he finally returned.

"It's okay, someone was caught shoplifting and one of my men fired his gun so the man knew what would happen the next time he was caught shoplifting."

"Did he shoot him?" Ian asked.

"No, just frightened him," Lorenzo replied to Ian smiling.

That was it for Ian, Marco's men were killing people in the streets.

He would call the captain of the aircraft carrier tonight and arrange for their transfer to his ship and return home. You could not talk to these people, they were barbarians. Best to wipe them all out. And bomb Rome destroying it.

Thirty minutes later Gabrielle and Lynda were in their room laying on the bed, arms wrapped around each other, kissing, their lips rotating around each other, tongues in each other's mouth and building themselves up to a proper sex session, which they knew would have to wait for later.

They changed outfits, then called Alice and Rebecca into their room. When the two girls entered, followed by Sarah and Janet, Gabrielle went through with them what would happen that evening.

"Alice, you will sit next to Jenny, Rebecca you will sit next to Alice. Do not forget we will be speaking in fluent Italian this evening. Alice you will be introduced first. Rebecca next, I will be sitting next to Lynda.

"Are you both ready? I want this to be good, especially for you Rebecca, you look beautiful this afternoon, do not forget your manners. Sereniti is Mam, Marko, Sir, is that completely understood?"

"Yes Gabrielle," Rebecca replied in a very grown-up feminine voice.

"Alice?"

"Yes Gabrielle," she replied.

Half an hour later they were seated at their table waiting for Marco and Sereniti.

"Everyone; stand, here they come, John, Alan, eyes open," Gabrielle ordered.

There was a loud screech of chairs as they moved their seats Gabrielle's table moved back allowing the occupants to stand, some trembling as the armada of gun carrying bodyguards followed Marco into the centre of the establishment. People put down their cutlery and nodded in silence as Marko, Sereniti with her hand through her husband's arm, passed them and walked up to the large table which had been set up to accommodate the afternoon's two waring factors, The Italians on the left British on the right of the specially designed tablecloth.

Marko took Gabrielle's hand and kissed the back of it, then he kissed her on both cheeks and the same with Lynda. He introduced his wife Sereniti and she too embraced everyone. and the formalities of introductions to the people around the table, came to an end. Ian did not agree with men kissing each other on the cheek, neither did he like lesbians, Gabrielle and Lynda should not be here, this was a job for a man to do, not a woman and definitely-not lesbians. The talks were now ready to begin as both leaders sat at the table. Finally, Alice and Rebecca were introduced to Marko and Sereniti.

"Alice, this is Marko Don, the head of the Mafia in Rome and Italy," Gabrielle said.

Alice curtsied and smiled. "I am very pleased to meet you Sir," she said.

"Alice, it's a pleasure to meet you, I see Gabrielle and Lynda's team have done well in making a young woman of you," he replied.

"It is not an easy road to follow, to break away from the road that I was prepared for in my first seven years. Now I am happy and looking forward to attending university studying astronomy and pure maths.

"Wow, such high ambitions that I hope you will be able to achieve and if there is anything, I can do to assist you, please do let me know. We have noticeably clear skies most nights here and some large telescopes and radio telescopes, so if you and your fellow students need time on a major full size 100-inch reflector telescope, let me know and I will get you the time you need on it and of course, to be here and do the visual observations yourselves."

"Thank you very much indeed Sir,"

"Marko, please call me Marko."

"And last this is Rebecca, she is one of our younger girls Rebecca aged thirteen. Rebecca this is Marko Don."

She curtsied as Alice had done and looked up into his eyes.

"It is a pleasure to meet you in person, Sir," she said and looked at Sereniti. "I see you are with child; I hope you are both well."

"Thank you Rebecca. It is good of you to ask after us. We are both very well thank you."

"And do you yet know the sex of the child, or is it to be a mystery until it is born?"

"It is to be a girl and we are both extremely happy. Do you see anything of Draco at your place of residence?" Sereniti asked.

"It is now a big place and with help from Gabrielle and Lynda, they have managed to increase the numbers of younger people wishing to change their sex and way of life. We are asked to pick a feminine name upon arrival, and we never repeat our original name again under any circumstances. It is like being reborn, so I would never know Draco."

"He; or she now is a very good dancer especially at the Argentinian Tango."

"Ah, I think I know the girl you are talking about. She is demonstrating the dance this week at Regents Park and on Hampstead Heath. They hope to raise a lot of money for the homes and other children. She is doing exceptionally well for a young person. Do you know her?"

"Yes, he, she is . . . Never mind. Let's just say we know of her."

"I can take a letter to her if you wish to write one."

"I'll see what I can do. We have a number of talks over the coming days, but I will find time to send you a note."

"I will pass it on."

Sereniti looked at the young girl standing before her and wished it were her new daughter, but it sounded as if she was having a good time and enjoying herself. She would see her new daughter soon when they travelled to the UK in six weeks after their baby was born. Until then she would not be able to fly, but there were plenty of naval ships in the Mediterranean Sea, she was sure that one of them could take her there in an emergency; after all, she was the wife of the Don.

"Please take your seats, I think three of your men will be acceptable at the table. The remainder can take the table at the far end of the room by the entrance. We will not be leaving until the meal is ended and I do not wish there to be any gunfights this afternoon, do you Marco?"

"No Gabrielle, indeed, not. Antonio, Francesco, Piero, take a seat here, the rest, take the table where the waiter shows you, the meal is on me."

As they took their seats, Gabrielle looked over to Sereniti.

"Would you like it if Rebecca sat between yourself and Marko, it might give you time to talk with her and get to understand a little more of what we do for our younger children?"

"I think that would be a good idea a way to bring the peace talks to a start. What do you think Marco?" Sereniti asked her husband.

"Of course, yes, a very, good idea. Rebecca, please, sit here between us."

"Alice, would you like to take a seat between myself and Lynda?" Gabrielle asked.

"Of course," she replied.

When they were all seated and ordered their food, small talk commenced between Marco, Gabrielle, Lynda and Sereniti. It was a little later as their meals started to arrive that Rebecca looked at Sereniti and moved her hair slightly so that Sereniti saw the small mark on the side of her neck which her father had put there so that in the event of her being kidnapped, she would be identifiable by her parents and his men.

"Would you mind if I felt your tummy?" Rebecca asked Sereniti.

"Of course, put your hand here, the baby is kicking. That's strange

as she is usually sleepy this time of day."

"She must like the sound of my voice."

"Yes, she misses her brother, or big sister now. Draco has been gone for six months, maybe just a little longer and the last thing he did was put his hand where yours is now," Sereniti said.

"Yes, I know, you feel much bigger now, have you picked a name for her yet?"

Sereniti looked at the girl sat next to her and could hardly breathe as her hand touched her throat. She took in a loud quick breath realising who the person was sat next to her.

Marco turned on hearing his wife and seeing where Rebecca's hand was; he was just about to pull it away when Sereniti shouted, "NO!" and held Rebecca close to her bosom.

"What is it, do you need an ambulance?" he asked urgently thinking the baby was now about to come early.

"No, it's Rebecca, look here," Sereniti retorted.

He turned and looked at her neck and the mark he himself had put there with his knife.

"Rebecca, is it you, is it really you?" he asked praying for a positive reply.

Draco looked across at Gabrielle and asked her a question with his eyes.

"Put them out of their misery Rebecca," Gabrielle said grinning.

"Mum, dad, I'm Rebecca, do you mind?"

"Mind? Of course not, if this is the life you wish to lead, then continue. You look sensational. I had my suspicions about you of course, but you look so beautiful, I must be honest, I didn't recognise you.

"Gabrielle, Lynda, you have done so well with our son, no daughter. I am pleased you did not tell us first about her, but you must admit, for a young girl, she looks absolutely fabulous."

"Yes, she does, and I apologise for not explaining, but I wanted to see how well she stood up to your own scrutiny and next weekend she has dance lessons, or rather she will help with the instructor William, with her dance routine in London."

"Is she behaving well? I know it would have been a huge stress for her being pulled out of the routine here, rather she had here in Rome.

"Rebecca is extremely well behaved and is a model student. She now speaks four languages besides Italian and English. Those being, French, Greek, Spanish and Croatian. She speaks all of them fluently. Her maths, English, Geography and Italian History with art, music and cookery as extra lessons as they have a lot of free time, are excellent.

While the others talked among themselves Marco, Gabrielle, Sereniti and Lynda went through some of the finer points of their agreement for two hours.

"I think it is time to take a break, we will resume once again in the morning at 09.00 to go through and overview our agreement before we sign it. Are we all in agreement?" Marco asked.

Agreements came from everyone, and the meeting broke up.

On their way out of the building, Marco called out to Gabrielle.

"Gabrielle, Lynda, I know you have much to do but I would like to know if you would join me and Sereniti in a meal this evening? This maybe the last night you are in Rome for a while," Marco asked.

"I suppose we could; what time were you thinking?" Lynda asked holding Gabrielle's hand tightly.

"Eight pm our usual place?"

Ian was annoyed that he had to pretend to know what they were talking about as they were talking in Italian, even the two small girls, or rather boys. It made him shudder to think they were sat at their table. It was disgusting and he still didn't know who Sereniti was. He was holding Christine's hand as she took what she hoped were notes of what was said as she too didn't speak Italian. Ian thought it rude that he was not really involved in the peace talks. He would talk to Gabrielle this evening and get the talks spoken in English as they were supposed to be helping them not the other way around.

"We would be delighted to join you, thank you," Lynda replied, holding Gabrielle's hand tight.

The girls turned and left with Alan, John and everyone else in tow. Rebecca left with her parents for a few hours for them to catch up with each other.

When they were back in their room even though they had been inside buildings all day since they arrived they were both sweating and feeling like a shower. John was already in the shower while Alan stood guard.

The room phone rang, and Alan answered it, pressing the record button on the small recording unit.

"Dame Grayson's room, how may I help you?"

"Sir Ian Galaway here, could you please pass on to Gabrielle and Lynda, thank you for the invitation to attend the meal tonight, but Mrs Howard and myself will be dining at this hotel, then going out for some late-night shopping as we will be returning to the UK tomorrow and we both need to get a few gifts for our children."

"Of course, I will. Before you go out, tell your bodyguard Noah what you are planning to do, and he will accompany you both with Paul. The four of you remain together and I want to know of any problems as soon as possible," Alan replied.

"Of course, Alan, thank you for thinking of our safety."

"No problem," Alan replied and replaced the phone, stopping the recording.

Lynda and Gabrielle showered together then dressed each other in a beautiful strapless evening dress in red, with a front slit from the ankle to the top of the thigh in matching red and white hats, red court shoes. They each wore their diamond hearts, matching earrings and carried matching red purses. There was a loud knock at their door and Alan went to answer it. He had his gun in his hand as he opened the door and pushed his gun forward into the face of Ian Galaway.

"Put that gun away if you're nervous you shouldn't have a gun. I am sending Paul home on the next flight I don't like guns, especially in your hands. Now put it away and lock it in your safe. I don't want to see it in your hands again, comprehend? Now stand aside I need a stern word with Gabrielle and Lynda before we go down for dinner," Ian said abruptly. Very loud. "What's happening Alan?" Lynda called out and went to their door.

"Ian doesn't like guns and told me to holster it then he told me to lock it in my gun safe. Oh, and he has sent Paul home," Alan replied still holding his gun in his hand.

"Quite right, this idiot answered the door pushing his gun into my head. He could have killed me, then he would be in serious trouble. In a maximum hold prison for the rest of his life," Ian shouted at Lynda.

"What's all this shouting about my love?" Gabrielle asked quietly and calmly, putting her arm around her back, then holding her hand.

"Their eyes flared green for a moment as Lynda explained to Gabrielle what had taken place.

"We expect that of our bodyguards, they are here and accompany us for our protection. We pay their wages not the government. Lynda tells Alan what to do, he'll keep his gun in his hand for now and will not be putting it in his gun- case. You had no right to send Paul home, he was here for your and Christine's protection, now we are one man down and George's thugs are in Rome and Southern Italy."

"At last, the organ grinder," Ian retorted. "Don't walk away I want a word with you," he shouted.

"I was going to our lounge where we'll take this conversation, I'll not have you bellowing just inside our door and you practically stood on the landing, understand? If you don't come with us, I'll have John kill you, Comprehend?" She asked and continued walking to their lounge.

"Come on my love you too Alan, oh and kill the son of a Bitch if he doesn't follow us. I'll drop his body into the sea," Gabrielle said in Croatian. they all walked into the lounge with Ian slamming their door closed and entered their lounge.

"Take a seat Ian," Gabrielle told him. "Is this about the fact that we were speaking Italian this afternoon and you don't speak the language which is not our fault?" Gabrielle asked.

"How do you know about that? I haven't mentioned it before," he demanded to know.

"Lynda told me what you were thinking about while I spoke with Marco."

"Can she read minds?" Ian questioned.

"Among other things, yes." She replied and took Lynda's hand in hers "So what's your grievance?"

"I want all further talks in English I take it he can speak our language. Why did you bring those bloody kids and who the fuck is Sereniti?" he bellowed at Gabrielle.

"Her name is in your notes pack, but she is the wife of Marco."

"So, who's the pretty pregnant girl he was sitting with? His bit on the side no doubt and he's gone and got her up the spout, bloody idiot," Ian replied, looking disgusted.

"Read your information pack it's all in there, but the pretty pregnant lady is Marco's wife. The reason I brought the two girls is because Rebecca is their daughter, and I thought the talks would go better with someone they haven't seen in six months. It did help start of the last round of the peace talks. Oh, I have spoken with Captain Arther Hammond."

"Who's he?"

"His name and telephone number are in your pack, please read it thoroughly. He is Captain of HMS Queen Elizabeth, the aircraft carrier. I have cancelled your call to him for a helicopter to pick us all up later tonight because of the gunfire this afternoon."

"A man was killed by one of Marco's men."

"Nobody was killed, he just fired his gun so the man would know what would happen next time he was caught, and they usually shoot petty thieves in the leg or arm," Gabrielle informed him.

"Okay, but I don't agree with you bringing those two queers with us, no matter what relation they are to Marko and why do you keep talking about Transgender groups and building homes and hospital wings for them? It's a total waist of public money. I also don't agree with you two holding hands all the time and kissing each other, it's not natural or good for other people to see."

"Get off your high horse, you're insulting me as well as Lynda. No public money goes into our Transgender homes or the rebuilding of hospitals, putting private rooms in and operating theatres. We pay for most of it in the UK with two other billionaires who help our charity and Marco has put the same amount of money into the new Transgender homes and Train Station where our Transgender children and young adults can have a decent meal for free any time of the day and they always have a meal there when on their way home from school or university.

"They are safe, they are all the same and nobody else can get in without a Universal Transgender Card. The place is also guarded in the UK by police and some of our bodyguards which we pay for and here in Rome by Marco's men. The two groups are also bringing our relationship with Marco, much closer together and helping in our talks," Gabrielle said.

"Why, is Marco a queer as well?" he asked trying to upset her as he was upset over the language. Tomorrow it would be different, they would all talk in English and he would take control of the last meeting and sign the Peace Treaty himself with Marco leaving Gabrielle and Lynda out of it altogether. It would be him who would take all the credit for it no matter how many hours the girls had put into the Treaty. He could get another high medal from the Queen; the two girls wouldn't turn up to be rebuffed by the Queen for bringing their Transgender groups into the Peace Treaty.

"Why do you think Marco is a queer?" Lynda asked him.

"Well, he is, he holds men in a loving embrace and kisses them not once but twice on each cheek. I bet he gets a big hardon doing that, 'cause he's halfway there, kissing men like that."

"Marco isn't Gay or a queer. Talk to him like that and he'll kill you himself."

"Is that why you two girls have bodyguards because your open lesbians?" He asked.

"No, it's because of the jobs we do, being chased by George all over the UK and Europe and the money we have."

"How much can that be, you both don't do proper work?" Ian asked rudely again.

"We have our business Hats, Bags & Wraps, which takes up a great deal of our time and our charities, plus staying out of George and his thug's way, and yes we do have money and are multi billionaires.

"Really?"

"It's all."

"Don't tell me it's in my pack, I have no idea why I didn't get around to reading it?"

"May I suggest Christine? you hold hands, kiss when you can and run up to your room as soon as you've both finished your dinner and you lock your own doors and don't tell your bodyguards what you are doing, where you are going or how long you will be. What time you're leaving and think you'll be back.

"It's normal throughout Spain Rome and France to greet each other that way, it's just that we English are stuck up and think we are the best it doesn't hurt to show a bit of emotion.

"Now get out of here, read your pack and when you arrive at breakfast you better have a decent head on your shoulders, or I'll get John to blow it off."

"You can't threaten me like that, and John would go to prison for a very long time, I told you before."

"All our bodyguards are licensed to kill in any country and are known to the police here and the courts and let the police handle it as they often help the police out in a gunfight and kill people.

"It's all in your pack," Gabrielle added.

Ian stood up and looked at the girls who were holding hands as they kissed. Ian tutted and left the room, returning to his to look at his pack and talk through with Christine what the girls had said to him. He would still object to the Prime Minister and The Queen. A little later Christine and himself would enjoy a night of sex together.

"At the restaurant Gabrielle and her party arrived first. Lynda sat next to Gabrielle John and Alan on the outside of the girls and their wives on the outside of John and Alan. When Marco entered the restaurant with his wife Sereniti and four bodyguards with their guns showing, Alan, John, Tina and Noah stood allowing their jacket front flaps to open revealing they too were packing but did not need to withdraw their weapons yet.

As Marco's party approached the table, the room fell silent, and everyone turned to look at him and his wife. Everyone including the waiters were silent as they approached the table. The two stunning women stood their bodyguards gently pulled out their chairs so they could stand easily.

Before Marko sat, he kissed Gabrielle and Lynda's hands and only when they had taken their seats again, did he take his seat. It was now, when everyone could see there was not going to be a gunfight, that people started to consume their meals again and the waiters took food to their respective tables.

As soon as the wine and soft drinks for the bodyguards were poured, and they had ordered their meals, the first thing Marco wished to discuss was his new daughter, Rebecca.

"We are helping the younger Transgender girls This is because some of the younger girls aged twelve, should be having small breasts by now and they are being asked why they do not have them yet as the other girls do. We have talked with breast surgeons and with a few volunteers, we now have a programme that enable our twelve and thirteen-year-old girls to have small inserts that can be enlarged as they go through school to match the size of the average girl's breasts."

"Rebecca is having the same treatment and is also having female hormone replacement tablets that will stop her testosterone from starting to create a boy's facial hair from forming and will help with her voice. If the strength of the tablets is high enough, it will stop their voice from breaking so they will sound feminine," Gabrielle explained.

"I'm sure that you will see a huge difference when you see her again. You should also see Rebecca is much happier in her new body," Lynda added.

As Lynda looked at Marco, she could see he was undressing her with his eyes and she thought he would right now, be having an erection he would very soon no longer be able to control. Her nipples were hard and erect just like his cock.

"Tell me, when will you be showing off your latest editions of your new hats and bags here in Rome?" Sereniti asked.

"Two months' time, we'll all be here, and we hope you will join us, you should have had your baby by then," Gabrielle replied smiling.

It was then she remembered their time would be up and if they wanted to save all their shops from being destroyed, they would need to rely on Marco and his men and face George alone. There was no way Gabrielle could send her soulmate to face George, he would not know her and therefore, she would attend the meeting in Lynda's place.

Beneath the table, she held Lynda's hand tight, trying hard to keep her mind empty of the frightful thoughts that were currently filling it.

The evening ended with Marco and his party leaving first, then Gabrielle and her party left when their car was outside waiting for them.

When Gabrielle and Lynda stood beside their bodyguards, everyone in the restaurant stopped eating and applaud them for what they had achieved. Most of the smaller businesses no longer had to pay the Mafia protection money, they were asked instead, if they made enough profit they could contribute to the Transgender Clinic where there were now fifty boys living in the accommodation and another fifty old enough to attend the clinic.

Surgeons at hospital could only carry out four operations a week and with the extra money, new surgeons could be taught what to do and purchase the extra equipment they would need for the operation which also included a new blood bank which would help everyone in Rome. At the main hospital in Rome, where all the Transgender operations were carried out, plus breast operations, a new private wing was in the process of being built for Transgender patients to stay after their operation for up to ten days.

There was also a day clinic being finalised where the breast operations could be carried out and the patients discharged the same or next day. Behind this was a small after operation clinic where those who had had their breasts made larger would come and be checked' if there were problems, they could be treated at the same time.

As the applause got louder, Gabrielle held Lynda's hand, they raised their joint hands in the air and bowed. The applause died down and the room went quiet. A woman stood and smiled at the two ladies still standing before her.

"Dame Gabrielle, Dame Lynda, my name is Greta Romano, and I am one of the people who help collect the collection boxes daily from restaurants and take it to the bank. We here know what you have done for us and you have showed mercy to our children and loved ones who have the need to change their sex. It is not just boys and girls but men and women who have lived a lie all their lives not just to keep the peace, or are afraid of coming out, but because they love their family.

"We now know after talking with some of the new women, that there is still the family after the change and they often, return to their wife for help with clothes and how to act as a woman.

"Everyone in Rome and visitors donate money for the new hospital wing and blood bank. So far today we have raised with Marko's cheque for €50,000; €64,864. All this money will go into the bank tomorrow morning direct into the hospital appeal account. So, I would like to thank everyone who is here this evening and have donated money.

"I would like to add that all the builders give three hours a day free and work some weekends free to get the main build completed. All the electricians, plumbers, carpenters and heating engineers are also working up to three hours a day free."

"If I may say, we would also like to contribute this evening," Lynda said while Gabrielle got their cheque book from John.

"How much will you be putting into the pot John, Jenny included of course. Alan Sarah, Noah and Tina?" It was not a request to donate, but an order.

"Will fifty euros be adequate?" John replied.

"Yes, I think that's enough, you may if you wish add it to your expenses sheet. Alan what about you and Sarah?"

"The same, I have that on me."

"As do I," Tina added.

"I'll go halves with you," Noah said smiling at her.

"Thank you, Noah, it's very kind of you," Tina replied as their hands touched with the money and their eyes met, smiling at each other.

"Sarah, will you do the honours and give this cheque and cash to Greta please?"

"Of course, Gabrielle." She took the cheque and cash and walked over to Greta giving her the money then after a few quiet words returned to her seat.

Greta looked at the value of the cheque and gasped. "I must tell you all, Gabrielle and Lynda have donated two hundred thousand Euros. This is a huge help, but you have given so much to the main Transgender clinic and Train Station."

"We are pleased to help you," Lynda replied.

Everyone applauded them again and Lynda put her hands in the air to try and quieten the room "It is not just our donation, but with everyone donating money and time, and I've also heard that some companies are donating timber, cable and other commodities, it becomes a people's hospital wing and blood bank. You all made it happen and you should all be immensely proud of yourselves." Lynda started to applaud the people in the room with Gabrielle and the others joining in.

I'm afraid we must be leaving you now, there is still much to do this evening before the treaty signing tomorrow the treaty and unity bond between the UK Transgender groups and your own Transgender groups, will make a much stronger link between our two countries Thank you for everything you give to the community and I'm sure the hospital extension will be completed very soon. Thank you all once again." As Gabrielle stood, she led the group away from their table.

John moved in front of her, behind her Alan moved in front of Lynda, his jacket was also undone, his gun showing. Sarah was at the rear with Jenny and Tina who also had her gun showing. Noah was behind Tina with his gun showing. Everyone waited while John went outside, checked the road and car, then held the back door of the limousine open.

"When John says go, you get into the limo first and I'll follow you, it's okay, John will still protect me at the door," Gabrielle whispered to Lynda then kissed her on her lips.

Less than a minute later they were all in the limo and it was slowly moving off merging with the other traffic.

As soon as they arrived at their hotel, the porter asked Gabrielle and Lynda to come over to his desk.

"I have two large bouquets of flowers for Gabrielle and Lynda Grayson from no other than the head of the Mafia Marco Don." He produced two huge bouquets of flowers for Gabrielle and Lynda who were holding hands.

The girls looked at the flowers smelt them and wondered how Marco managed to get them here just before they arrived at the hotel.

"We are going to the bar for a late drink and discuss our evening with Marco. Could you have a porter take them to our room please? Have him or her place one vase by the phone and the other on the table in our drawing room," Gabrielle said with a voice of authority. "Get the porter to leave his name by the phone please."

"Of course, Dame Grayson." He nodded and looked around the reception area. "Guy, take these to suite 917 please, and leave your name by the phone." He knew what it was for and he would get half of the tip Guy got.

A moment later the flowers were gone as too were Gabrielle and Lynda with their bodyguards.

In the bar, they found a table in the corner and John went up to order their drinks. When their drinks arrived, they were discussing the new hospital wing and blood bank.

"It appears everyone is getting behind the new hospital wing and blood bank," Lynda said starting the conversation.

"That's because they don't have a big blood bank and when the theatres need blood, they call for people to come in and donate urgently," Alan informed everyone.

Tina and Noah were sat next to each other with his arm around her shoulder. Sometimes they kissed as Gabrielle and Lynda did, but they were both carrying their guns.

"What? They don't I was talking to someone about it the other day and they said the blood bank is an excellent idea and people would fill it up amazingly fast because it's what we need. When I questioned him further on the hospital wing, he said they needed that as well, their hospital needs a massive upgrade, they don't even have an MRI scanner and if someone needs an MRI scan, they have to go to Italy, usually Madrid," Lynda continued.

"MRI Scanners, that's our department dear, what do you think, we would have to build a new annex for it plus show them how to use it and a radiographer to show them how to read the scans," Gabrielle sighed.

"It might cost a lot dear but think of the relations it will build up between our two countries," Lynda said holding Gabrielle's hand and giving her a kiss on her cheek. She also sent her a thought which made Gabrielle smile, and turn her head to look at Lynda.

"Yes!" she said aloud, laughing and held Gabrielle's hand.

"I think after the talks and signing is completed tomorrow morning, which I hope goes through without a hitch, I suggest we ask Marco if we could have a look at the site and add the MRI scanner idea at the same time. If the Italians are putting in extra hours for free, I think we could bring in our team of builders who build the scanner rooms abroad for us."

"I agree my love and we might need another day for the arrangements to be made for us to see the hospital and during that time we could go and have a look at our own complex. The place should be completed, by now," Lynda suggested hoping everyone would agree.

"Would you be alright with that John, Alan? What about you two love birds sitting there quietly trying to blend in?"

"Of course, boss, as Lynda said, it should be finished by now."

Jenny put her hand in the air. "Once the people who want an operation to change their sex is converted in Rome, the extra rooms won't be needed until another person comes along who either didn't come out or was far too young.

"So, what if we invited people from Italy, Greece, Spain and other countries in the Mediterranean area? We could start looking in each country to see what they have and without spending further money on building a new hospital wing in each country, we bring the people here and we ask them to contribute to their stay in the complex and have the operation for a full sex change including giving them breasts.

"All we would need to do is find a small club, make them a charity and they could collect money to help those who couldn't afford it. They could also let it be known that we are doing the whole lot, the psychiatric profiling, the talks about transferring to be a woman, the clothes to buy and the jobs to look out for and if they have a job, could they go back to it as a woman? Is this going too far?"

"Too far Jenny? You have hit the nail on the head. You have had an incredible idea and with us having to do little work in each country, it will make the hospital, the Train Station and our accommodation complex worth the money we have invested. There is one other item that we could start tomorrow and that is making it a charity then they could start collecting money as we do. It they can come up with an emblem for the Mafia, they could add it to their web site and have big companies who back the charity as in the UK, they would have their monogram on the web site as well," Gabrielle quickly elaborated.

"Well done love an excellent idea that will work," John said to his wife, then hugged her and kissed her lips.

Gabrielle had been recording their discussions and knew this idea would give everyone in the Mediterranean area the chance to be what they want to be and come out, or start from a young age, just like they do in the UK.

"How much do you think the building and start up for the charity will cost?" Lynda asked Gabrielle.

"No more than thirty thousand Euros. They will need a hall to meet in, a few computers to sort out a Data Base for the club and printing costs for A4 posters telling people where they are and what they are doing. There will also be paperwork for the charity to get. That is about it, we will need someone to take charge, but I think if we start in one country and see how it takes off, we will learn from any mistakes we make," Gabrielle elaborated. "Do we all agree we should give this a try?" Lynda asked.

Everyone agreed and she noted it on her tablet. Noah put his hand in the air.

"Yes, Noah what do you wish to say?"

"First please don't take this the wrong way, it is just what I have noted. When I was working for the Government, I had to look after a lot of different men. Some of them worked on building sites working out costs for a total rebuild or a partial rebuild of a hospital, and the equipment the doctors and nurses would need to be replaced, as most men worked for the NHS.

"Tonight, you gave the hospital people another cheque for two hundred thousand Euros. Marco had given a cheque for fifty thousand Euros you have previously given the same people another cheque for a hundred thousand Euros. So where is all this money going? In London, you could build a brand-new hospital and kit it out including an MRI and CT scanner for what you have spent on that hospital.

"I think it might be a good idea to push this MRI scanner with the building and include a CT scanner. Have a quantity surveyor with our builders to have a look around the hospital to see how much it has so far cost and the time taken to build the extra wing and update the hospital. Then you will have a much better idea of how much more it will cost you or how money has not been needed. If they are collecting money every day, the hospital extra wing should have been finished by now. It's not a difficult build. Sorry, I just thought I should bring this matter to your attention."

Everyone was silent just looking at him. Tina held his hand and spoke to him quietly in his ear.

"I'm sorry Gabrielle, Lynda, do I still have a job with you?"

"I'm sorry Noah, you are damn well right, you still have a job with us. What you have said makes perfect sense. People see us as an open chequebook. We need to do this before we throw another Euro into the pot. What say you all?"

"Yesses" came from around the table. John stood up and looked down upon Noah.

"Well thought out Noah, Glad to have you aboard. Welcome to the family," John said then shook his hand.

"Noah, do you mind sharing a room back home until the top story is completed?" Gabrielle asked him.

"No that will be fine with me." He wondered who he would be sharing with as Lynda spoke.

"Tina, you have a double room despite it being downstairs in what we call the cellar. There are six double bedrooms down there all with a toilet and shower in each room, with built in wardrobes and chests of drawers. Each room also has a gun safe, spare bullets and clips for your Glock's.

"Tina, as we are low on space at home do you mind sharing your room with Noah until the upper floor is completed?"

"Yes!" Yes, yes, that will be lovely," she replied and smiled at Lynda; then looked into the loving eyes of Noah. They kissed each other their mouths rotating around each other's mouth.

"Okay you two, enough for now, or you'll be making love on the table here." Gabrielle said and joined everyone else as they laughed at Gabrielle's remark. "We will get this money side looked into and see how much they need and the medical equipment they will want. Some of it may have to come from the UK or Germany. Whatever the cost we will make it with Marco's helpers," Gabrielle said looking at Lynda, her eyes, flaring green. She made the glasses move on the table into an arrow which she pointed to the people at the bar.

"It's now 12.25 and we have to be up early plus there is another item to complete before we go to sleep. No doubt for the two love birds too." Gabrielle said laughing holding Lynda's hand firmly in hers.

"I'll just go to the loo a moment, Tina would you escort me please?" Lynda asked.

In the toilet Lynda emptied her bladder then her green eyes looked over the wall. She pointed to Tina and they both read the small note. They are signing the treaty tomorrow I will have sixty men at 08:30 outside the hotel.

"We will go out laughing and holding hands together, I might even kiss you, you have lovely lips."

"Whatever you say Lynda."

"I had better tell Gabrielle what we have found." Her eyes flared green for a second. "Come on, let's go," Lynda said.

They finished their drinks and John lead the way out of the room with Alan walking before Lynda. After John checked their room, Gabrielle and Lynda said goodnight to the others and with Sarah joining them, closed their door. As soon as Sarah unzipped each of their dresses, they were out of them and holding each other close, and now laying on their bed, kissing each other as if there were no tomorrow.

With the dresses costing over three thousand Euros each, she carefully hung them up, taking no notice of what the girls were up to. Sarah put the flowers into a better shape and placed the small card and envelope by the side of the vase. Her eyes turned to the couple who were deeply in love and showing it, turned out the main lights, leaving the room in total darkness for the girls to play undisturbed.

She knocked on the adjoining room and opened its door seeing John sitting on his bed polishing his gun and checking the bullets were all clear and would not jam in the magazine. She knew Alan would be doing the same thing, even if your gun was not fired, you clean it every night, it might just save your life one day, who knew what the future held.

"Their door is locked, and all is well with them, let's hope they can get up early in the morning," Sarah said laughing.

"I'll give them a shout if they haven't stirred by 06:30. It's a big day tomorrow and I do believe they are wearing suits, the red ones to sign the documents am I right Sarah?"

"Yes John, I've hung them out separate from their other clothes and it's the same with their white blouses," Sarah replied.

"Goodnight Jenny, night John, see you both in the morning," she said and entered her room through the other connecting internal door.

"'night Sarah," Jenny replied.

"'night Sarah," John added as she walked out of their adjoining door to her bedroom with Alan, who had now completed cleaning his gun and checking his bullets. His gun went under his pillow so he could get at it at a moment's notice. Sarah walked around the bottom of the bed and stepped out of her dress then hung it up.

Like Gabrielle's and Lynda's dress, her dress was also expensive. Alan was sat on his side of the bed doing the last checks with the clock and turning out the main lights then getting into bed. Sarah had been hoping for sex, especially after the late evening's talks. Her dress was strapless as well and as she pulled back the covers on her side of the bed, there was a very, short black silk nightie and a pair of petit black panties ready for her to put on. She turned to look at her husband and he smiled back at her, indicating the sexy nightie to put on for a few short minutes.

"We only have an hour, sorry, but we have to be up early, we'll have more time tomorrow night I'm sure," Alan said.

Sarah put the nightie on and was just about to. change her panties when Alan gently took hold of her arm.

"Don't worry about the panties, just get into bed and give me a big kiss and a hug. It's been an exceptionally long day." With the erotic display of Lesbians kissing, breasts touching each other and hands holding each other close, she was already close to an orgasm and had they asked her to join them, she would have locked the adjourning door to John's room and stripped off to make it a lesbian threesome. Instead, she was about to have a sexy night, if only for an hour with her husband. However, she couldn't get the lesbian couple out of her mind, which made her all the more randy.

Gabrielle and Lynda were kissing each other on their lips and face; their hands gently playing with each other's breasts. They were still hot, sweating and the sweat was making their bodies slippery, and they loved it.

Their tongues entered each other's mouth and their lips rotated about each other as they embraced, and Gabrielle pulled Lynda on top of her, and their naked legs wrapped themselves around each other as they tried to consume each other with their mouths kissing and sucking each other's breasts making their nipples hard and erect.

Gabrielle turned over putting Lynda on her back and slithered slowly down her body, gently kissing each breast and tantalising each erect nipple with her lips. As she moved slowly down the front of her body, she kissed every centimetre of her abdomen until she finally arrived at her clitoris. Her tongue licked it and her lips kissed it over and over. Finally, her tongue entered Lynda's vagina and commenced to lick her wet walls.

"Oh, that's lovely, how can you make me feel so sexy? It's wonderful, oh please don't stop, that's terrific," she cried. Her hands covered her breasts as her fingers tweeted her nipples making her body rise and gave Gabrielle a little more room to get her tongue deeper into her vagina.

"Put a finger or two into me, please, I'm almost there my love," Lynda cried as her body arched again.

Gabrielle pushed three fingers into her vagina and kissed her clitoris again. and again, "Oh yes my love, that's brilliant, I'm almost there I never want us to stop."

"Neither do I my love," Gabrielle replied and then inserted her tongue into Lynda's Vagina just as she had her orgasm and swallowed most of her orgasm juices.

Gabrielle moved slowly up Lynda's sweat-soaked body and kissed her breasts before they kissed each other again, their mouths rotating as they inserted their tongue into each other's mouth, like snakes they explored, touched and mingled, exciting both women. Their hands explored each other's hair, pulling their faces close together.

Lynda pushed Gabrielle onto her back and Lynda ran her hand down Gabrielle's body and inserted three fingers into her vagina; gently bringing her to an orgasm as they kissed and lay together, happy in each other's arms.

Thirty minutes later they were stepping out of the shower, drying each other off then got into bed, kissed each other again and as usual, Lynda slipped herself on top of Gabrielle and Gabrielle's arms held her body still, wrapped around her so she didn't fall from her. By four they were asleep, at six they woke, kissed, showered together again and started to slowly dress each other in a slow and sexy way.

Lynda heard an alarm clock go off in John's room and a movement, then the alarm stopped, and John got out of bed. He opened the adjoining door between their suites and looked at Lynda in her panties and bra.

"You're up early," he said in his usual tone of voice.

"We had some unfinished love making to do, we're okay now though," Lynda said as she made her body shudder from head to toe, smiling at John all the time getting his attention.

"Are we expecting any trouble today?" John asked.

"I hope not, I don't want anyone getting injured and I'm sorry John, but I think because of what is happening you should wear your bullet proof jacket which needs to be closed to give you as much protection as you can get, am I right Jenny?" Lynda asked aloud, bringing the poor woman to life after a short sleep but after a good night of sex.

"Yes, Lynda I also agree, as long as he can get to his gun to keep us all safe," she replied and kissed her husband.

"John, Lynda come here and look at this," Gabrielle said in a concerned voice. The next moment they were looking from their balcony window to the street below by the entrance to their hotel. There were at least six big TV vans with satellite dishes being raised into the air and commentators already starting to talk to each other and some commentators were talking to their TV Studios.

"What in the Hell is happening down there?" John asked the girls hoping for an answer, they had been watching them for the last ten minutes or more.

"I would say that is for us, we practically have the top floor on the front side of the hotel. These talks were supposed to be private so how did it leak out?" Gabrielle asked.

"Don't ask me and I know it wasn't anyone in our group, however, the two diplomats went for walk abouts last night," John suggested getting very annoyed with what Ian had done.

"It's six thirty, I suggest we all finish getting dressed, and we'll all go down to breakfast together. I will not be put off these talks by a few TV men," Gabrielle said sounding upset and tears started to fill her eyes.

Lynda put her arm around her wife's shoulder, hugged her close and kissed her face. "It may not be for us, there are other people in the hotel or who may have arrived last night," Lynda suggested and received Gabrielle's thoughts on the situation and replied in her mind's own words. "It can't be for us, we've been here a week, and nobody has noticed us."

"Yes, you could well be right, but it is better to be prepared for the press don't you agree?" Gabrielle asked her wife.

"Yes, my love, I suppose you're right. Lynda agreed."

"Then let's finish getting dressed and get something to eat I'm famished after last night and again this morning."

Gabrielle slipped her arm around Lynda's back, and they turned facing each other and their lips touched. Suddenly the street outside was alight with camera flashes and long lenses pointing in their direction. The kiss lasted a few more seconds before they parted and looked together at the large crowd of reporters below them with their cameras.

"This really is for us," Lynda said sounding happy they now knew what this was all about she quite liked the press.

They stood back from the window and John returned to his room. They remained together in their loving embrace like any other couple might do before they had to enter a crowd of reporters, who would be asking them questions?

Their lips rotated about each other, and their tongues entered each other's mouth; hands held each other's head in a loving embrace which they hoped would last for all time.

Time, that was something they had plenty of, thanks to Death and Fate; all they had to do was pass the test that could happen at any time in their lives.

As they parted, Gabrielle looked at Lynda, their heads were still, and their eyes met. "I love you Lynda, I love you so very much with all my heart and soul. There is nothing I wouldn't do for you and if you should happen to die, I would follow you so our souls would travel together into the afterlife," Gabrielle said to her wife.

"I love you too, with all my heart and soul, I will follow you to the ends of the earth and universe. You are my soulmate, and my soul is going nowhere without yours."

As they looked into each's other's green eyes, their eyes started to grow a brighter and brighter green until the entire room was filled with the glow of their eyes. They exchanged thoughts over the last week in Rome, the day ahead and the time they would spend in bed that night and the following day back to the UK and visit the Queen's Palace.

All this happened in a matter of seconds, then they were looking into each other's eyes again with the room still glowing green. Finally, after kissing and sending loving thoughts to each other, they parted and glared at each other.

"That was great," Lynda sighed.

"More than great, it was incredible," Gabrielle sighed as she hugged her wife again, kissing her lips and smiled at her.

"I suppose we had better finish getting dressed and make a start at putting on our makeup then brush our hair."

"Yes, and today, as we are signing the Treaty, we should wear our Dame Medals don't you think?" Lynda suggested.

"Sounds a good idea my love," Gabrielle replied.

They parted, but for a few more seconds their minds were held together with their green eyes.

Forty minutes later they were ready to go, except for putting on their jackets. When John entered their suite again, they were scanning through the documents they would be signing later that morning, ensuring everything they agreed was there and there was a way for the Mafia members to remain in the UK if they had a family who helped in this war.

"Well girls, are we ready to go?" John asked with Jenny closing the adjourning doors to their suites. "Have you finished kissing with your green eyes, I've already had four calls from people outside and from the hotel opposite concerned about the green lights and what do they represent?" John said sounding worried.

"John, you should have enough excuses by now for our green light. Just one more kiss to keep the people on their toes," Lynda replied and turned to fall into Gabrielle's open arms and their lips merged together as if they were one and their eyes were so bright John and Jenny had to shield their eyes.

When they completed their kiss, they parted smiling at each other, caressing each other with their eyes and then held hands, like they would never let go and they were protecting each other.

"Yes, we are ready to go John, where is Alan and Sarah?" There was a knock at their door, which John went to answer. A moment later Alan and Sarah joined the group.

"Alan," Lynda said calling him to her side. "Can you please ring Noah and ask him if Ian and Christine are ready to go down to breakfast yet? I think we should all go at the same time especially as I want a word with Ian."

"I'll get onto that right now Lynda." He picked up the phone and spoke with Noah, after the call he sighed deeply looking down at his bullet proof suit. He would need a quick word with John about the number of clips they had between them. A few minutes later he went to see Lynda. "Noah said they are ready to go, and we will meet them on the landing in two minutes, but I will need more time if I can please. I need to get a few more clips for my gun, as we are now one man down. Paul took a plane home yesterday at six pm. Noah said it was Ian who was bragging to the young man late last night as he talked to him about the Treaty, and he was in charge and you two were there to support him."

"Thank you, Alan, Go get your extra clips and tell John, Noah and Tina to do the same. I want you all fully armed today, there is a storm brewing in the wind, I'll tell John, you tell the others. John, can you come here please? Everyone else, we leave here in just under four minutes," Gabrielle said.

"Is everyone ready? Sarah, do you have all the documents we will need later?" Lynda asked.

"All in this briefcase, Lynda," Sarah replied quickly and held the briefcase in the air.

"Handbags," Lynda said to Gabrielle smiling.

John was back with all the clips he had. He was now just finishing making sure the girls medal from the Queen were in the right place and well secured. Alan returned, having told Tina and Noah what to do. He had emptied his secure gun safe of spare clips and a box of extra bullets.

"Are we all ready to leave?" John asked before he opened the door to the landing.

Yeses came from his group; he opened the door and looked outside. Noah was just doing the same. They acknowledged each other and everyone walked onto the landing and along to the lifts. Moments later they were sitting in the main restaurant ordering breakfast and drinks.

Ian, by any chance did you mention to anyone who you met last night that we are signing the Treaty today?" Gabrielle asked him while they were waiting for their order to arrive.

"As a matter of fact, we did. A young man stopped us as we were about to enter the hotel. He asked what you two were doing here actually. He said the Italian people in Rome are always interested in you and are wondering if you are about to do another Hat & Bag show? I naturally told them about the Treaty, and he thanked me, we are government officials, and we don't lie."

"Tell the Prime Minister that! It was a very stupid thing to do, do you see those TV reporters out the front? They are here for us. Any nut with a gun could have a go at us, why on earth do you think we have armed bodyguards?" Gabrielle retorted.

"I thought it was overrated and I've sent the other bodyguard Paul home. No need for two men with guns. As I say guns attract guns. I did leave strict instructions with Noah to leave his gun in his room safe," Ian said sternly.

Noah was at the self-service area getting another four slices of toast with a second cup of tea, even though he might regret it later. When he returned to the table Gabrielle looked at him and could see where his gun was so did not bother to question him. With breakfast over, they made their way to the inner reception area. Already photographers were taking their photos from across the road. Their limousine finally arrived, and a doorman opened the door for them. John left first, his jacket undone, ready for anything. The press was now coming across the road with their microphones, shouting questions at Gabrielle and Lynda.

Halfway across the pavement they were stopped by the press who were pushing microphones into their faces asking what they were doing here in Rome and was it true they were about to sign a Treaty between the Mafia and the UK Government to try and control protection money from small business and the people who work for them as outside workers in Rome?

"All Protection money has stopped for a number of small shops and all outworkers in Rome. The same will apply to the shops in the UK which are currently under Mafia Protection. As you know there are forces trying to bring a war between the Mafia here and in the UK; we must bring this to an end as swiftly as possible," Gabrielle explained to the press.

While Gabrielle was talking, Jenny and Sarah got into the back of the limousine. They made sure if anyone needed to get into the limo quickly, they could help pull them in. Lynda was holding Gabrielle's hand and several cameramen were looking at the two women.

Lynda talked to the press for a few minutes then one of the pressmen pushed his microphone into Ian's face and asked him what he was doing here in Italian. He had absolutely no idea what he was being asked and he looked at Christine for help. She had no idea either, they had been speaking in English all the time they were here at the talks.

Gabrielle translated the question for him before the reporter had the chance to change his question into English.

"I am here on behalf of Her Majesty's Government to ensure the Treaty is exactly what we want and that these two ladies do not mess it up," he replied with a grin.

"We hold Dame Gabrielle and Dame Lynda in the highest esteem here. They have managed to help both our countries save thousands of people from this person named George who is currently trying to infiltrate our city. They also do not insult us by leaving us to do the translation and learn your language. They speak Italian and many other languages fluently, you really should have had a go at learning something in Italian," the pressman retorted in fluent English.

Ian answered a few more questions in English, while Gabrielle and Lynda were also answering questions in fluent Italian on the other side of the limousine's open car door.

"We really must be leaving but thank you for your time and interest in us," Lynda said to the pressman.

She was just turning to face her wife when a shout rang out from the other side of the road. A man was holding a gun and pointing it in their direction.

"This is from George Rainer!" the gun went off, but Noah had his gun out and already had the man in his sights as he pulled his trigger. The gunman fired a second shot as Noah's bullet hit the man in his heart and he went down. The police who were watching the crowds of people, turned with their guns ready to fire and ran to the dead man on the floor.

Noah was also falling back against Ian as he was shot in the chest. Christine was screaming as Alan grabbed her arm and pulled her away from Ian and pushed her into the welcome arms of Sarah who pulled her into the safety of the limo as it had bullet proof glass and door panels.

"Bastards, that was my brother, take this from George," another man shouted from on top one of the TV Vans. He had a machinegun in his hands and was now taking aim at Gabrielle. The trigger was pulled and the first short burst of seven bullets were on their way to Gabrielle.

John's hand grabbed Gabrielle and pushed her to the left of his back as the first, second third fourth fifth six bullets hit John in the chest, left arm, stomach and chest, the seventh bullet was heading for his head as he lifted his right arm and covered his face. The bullet hit his wrist and was absorbed by his bullet proof suit, but the bullet still had enough kinetic energy to veer off the suit and hit John's forehead. Blood flew into the air as the next short round of seven bullets came towards him.

Gabrielle screamed "John" at the top of her voice and screamed his name again as he just stood in front of Gabrielle, holding her hand tightly with his left hand. This way he knew where Gabrielle was behind him.

A second round of seven shots were fired from the man's machinegun, one after another each shot was fired at John who took it in his stomach. He reached in his jacket with his hand, which was bleeding from one of the bullets hitting him. He pulled his Glock out of its holster and with a round of bullets hitting his chest, he raised his gun and fired six rounds of bullets in the region, he thought was where the man firing the gun was.

Gabrielle screamed again, "John," at the top of her voice as his blood was hitting her head.

Inside the car Jenny was screaming her husband's name then she was crying, her tears streaming down her face as she cried his name out again but he and Gabrielle were too far away from the car for them to get into it. Jenny heard her husband's Glock fire off another eight shots. She knew this time it was not going to be a quick gun fight. Noah was down, Alan now protecting Ian as he had pushed Christine into their car just in time.

John ejected the empty clip from his Glock, pushed his bleeding hand into his pocket and retrieved another twenty round clip and inserted it into the Glock's handle. The last bullet hit his chest as he raised his hand once again. Blood was running down his face as he heard the machinegun go off again. Now he had a general idea where the man was, and he moved his hand to the left as the first two bullets hit his chest. He raised his hand and fired his gun on automatic fire.

The entire twenty round clip was fired and ejected from the gun as the rest of the bullets hit John in the stomach and chest. He knew his suit would not last much longer, he had missed the gunman and heard the man insert another clip of bullets into his machine gun. John had done the same and was now holding another clip in his left hand.

The camera men had seen what had happened at the front and were now watching John absorb all the bullets and he was firing blind as blood covered his right eye. John had emptied his fourth clip into the area he thought the man might be.

John heard a man shout out that he'd been shot but was okay to carry on. In John's mind's eye, he had a good idea of where the shooter was. He raised his gun and using his mind's eye, he pointed the Glock to where the man should be, He heard the machinegun fire again, a short burst of seven bullets. He closed his eyes and fired the full clip. As soon as it was empty, another twenty-round clip, was inserted into his gun as he heard the machinegun let off another short burst. Not all the bullets hit him, in fact only two bullets got through.

Then John heard another Glock let off a full clip, he knew the gun belonged to Alan and he knew now they had been set up and lured into a trap. He would be having strong words with Ian when this mess was over.

The camera men were now filming Alan as he was shooting under some framework where eight men with machineguns were now attacking Alan who was stood up, protecting Ian who was now crying to be let go free from the hell trap they were in.

Then another Glock opened fire next to Alans and all of a sudden, there were forty bullets heading towards the men at the bottom of the cage. Tina and Alan inserted new twenty round clips into their guns, took aim and left their fingers on their triggers. It was a horrendous sound as the two Glocks fired together. Jenny was still crying hard, tears rolling down her face. She too heard the two Glocks firing further away from them. She suddenly realised the truth and screamed aloud.

"We've been set up; this is a trap. Do we have a spare Glock here? I need to help John, he'll die soon," Jenny cried. "Won't someone please help my husband?" she cried, and she felt Lynda's hand on her shoulder and her calm voice giving her reassurance help would eventually come to them.

"We cannot leave this car if we open the door any further, we will all be killed," Lynda said to everyone. Now calm down and pray, hard!" Lynda said to everyone in the car including the driver.

The cameramen knew what Alan could do and were now filming him as he drew his weapon. It appeared to everyone that he couldn't have aimed properly as his first shot hit the rifle from the man's hands and the second shot hit the gunman in the centre of his forehead, as there was little else of the man that anyone could see.

John managed to stay on his feet keeping Gabrielle behind him. "Gabrielle . . . are you hit?" John shouted.

"My right shoulder took a bullet, but I feel okay, the jacket was well worth the expense," she replied putting her left hand up to her right shoulder.

"Noah, how are you?" Alan shouted to him.

Noah was on the ground with Ian sat directly behind him holding his bleeding shoulder. "Just winded, I'll be fine in a minute or two, but my jacket has a hole in it."

"Ian, how are you?"

"I've been shot in the arm and I'm bleeding a lot. You should have protected me better," he retorted.

"We've been set up Ian, now we're in a trap so shut up; this is all your doing. I wouldn't like to be in your shoes if John survives, Gabrielle as well. Now pipe down."

Noah saw a man on the top of a TV van inch himself closer to the edge where he could open fire on them. He turned on his side, with his gun in his right hand he sent six bullets into the man and heard him cry out as he fell to the ground dead. Another man ran to take his place and Noah fired another round off again, killing the second man who fell to the ground dead.

Two more men ran to take his place. Ian saw Noah slip a new clip into his gun and realised he had already fired twenty bullets, no this could not be happening, he only said a few words, a bullet ricocheted off some rocks and flew past Ian's right arm. Noah raised his gun and fired a full clip into the two men who both fell to the floor dead.

Tina heard two machine guns open fire on John. She fired another full clip down the corridor and killed two men who were running to take over on the TV van roof.

"Alan, I'm going to help John, or he'll die soon Oh Death, he's been shot in the face and can't see, but he's still on his feet with Gabrielle right behind him. They'll kill them both. Can I go Alan?"

"No wait a minute and while you're waiting, fire another full round down the corridor."

"What am I waiting for?" she asked.

"My trousers, they are bulletproof, take them and if you get to John, put them over his head to save it getting hit again."

Tina emptied her Glock along the corridor then slammed another twenty-round clip into her gun. "Tina," Alan called "Tell Sarah I love her with all my heart, it's been great working with you, I'm so proud to know you, Tina. Now, go to John. Give him my love."

"I will, here is five twenty round clips," she said and handed the clips over to Alan. Then taking hold of his trousers, she ran with her gun in her right hand up towards John. A Man was waiting with his machinegun ready, to send Hell into the car and kill everyone inside. She knelt, took two deep breaths took aim and pulled her trigger. Six bullets hit the man in his chest and one more shot hit him right between his eyes.

Tina waited for another man to come and take his place. Sure enough, another man was running along the path right into five bullets from Tina's gun. As he fell down dead, another man was running behind him and into another five bullets from her gun. The man was dead as he hit the floor and another man ran to take his place. Tina wished she could talk with Alan who was firing his gun into the alley killing more of George's men. After killing four more men, nobody else wanted to take their place.

Tina put Alan's trousers on and said a prayer. She put her gun into its holster, picked up one of the machine guns took two full clips from the other guns on the floor put a bullet into the gun barrel then took a slow walk over the dead bodies.

She turned right hearing voices coming from that direction and quietly walked down a short alley then into a room filled with at least twenty men laughing and smoking. She opened fire on the men closest to her and they all fell to the ground dead. She had to eject the clip in the gun and insert another to kill more men at the back of the room who were starting to run along the alley right into Alan's bullets. Inside the room the last of the men were falling to the floor dead. She heard Alan fire his gun killing the men who decided to try and run away.

Tina walked into the alley and waved her gun in the air shouting to Alan. "Alan don't shoot, it's me Tina. I'm going to take a walk along the alley and see who is about."

"Not without me you're not," Noah shouted and holding his chest tightly with one hand ran along the alley to be with Tina. Noah picked up a machinegun and spare clip.

Then taking hold of Tina's hand they walked along the alley to the end, looked left, it was now clear of men, turning right they heard voices and walked together, hand in hand, guns ready to fire and entered another room with ten men inside and a few seconds later they were all dead.

Alan was now running with his jacket on and his shorts right up to John. They held hands for a moment as Alan asked him how he was feeling.

"I feel like I've been pummelled in my stomach and chest and I'm bleeding from my hand and head. I can't see, my eyes are covered in blood.

"Good, that means you're still alive," Alan said then turning around he saw a man coming out of the corridor that would get him up to the car without being seen. Alan raised his gun and fired off six rounds which killed the man and he fell to the floor dead. They heard the sound of two machine guns being loaded then they opened fire and two men fell backwards to the floor dead. They had been shot in their chests then six bullets hit their heads and that was it, they were both dead. Two people crawled out behind the dead two men and fired their guns into the air.

"Hello boys, Tina shouted to Alan, John and Gabrielle. Do you want your trousers back Alan?"

"Yes please, behind you," Alan shouted.

Tina and Noah turned and at the same time emptied their guns into the man who had already been shot in the chest and legs. He was now on the floor as ten bullets hit his head and four bullets hit his chest ripping his heart to shreds.

"We had better take a walk back through these tunnels and make sure nobody is left alive," Noah suggested.

"Good idea, make sure our backs are clear before we start clearing up," Alan replied. Noah and Tina disappeared down the holes they had come up from and ran through the alleys checking small openings where George's men had stayed, ready to start this fight which George hoped would put an end to Gabrielle and Lynda. He had sixty men here, they should be able to do the job.

As they got towards the last bend in the road, they both stopped and turned to face each other. They kissed, their mouth's rotating about each other, their tongues examined each other's mouth as they fell into each other's arms, holding each other tight. They kissed again as Noah whispered to Tina,

"I love you with all my heart. I've just literally fallen head over heels in love with you, now I know we must be together as much as possible. I know we will be apart when you must protect Sabrina on the catwalks. Will you marry me?" he boldly asked.

"Yes," Tina replied. "I love you too with all my heart." Tina wrapped her arms around his body pulling him close to her. Then her hand was on his Glock. Noah felt her slowly, pull his gun out of its holster and knew something was deadly wrong.

"Oh yes, very, nice, do you have a ring to give her? No? It doesn't really matter where you two are going to go now." The man stood back grinning and held his machinegun in his arms. That was as far as he got as Tina pulled the gun a little further from its holster and fired five bullets into the man killing him.

Noah put his finger to his lips and pointed behind him, then Tina heard a voice, talking to George or one of his men. They were about to take a step forward when Tina pulled him back and kissed his lips. "For luck," she whispered.

They walked quietly into the small room where a man was still talking on a radio to someone important, because the person on the other end was shouting at this poor man who was about to see his maker.

The man on the end of the phone was still shouting when Tina put her gun near the man's head then blew his brains all over the back wall. Noah kicked his body to the floor then picked up the phone.

"Hello who am I speaking to?" Noah asked.

"George, who are you?" he bellowed back.

"I'm Noah one of Gabrielle's new bodyguards what do you want George as we are in a hurry, people to kill you know what happens."

"What has happened to all my men?"

"They are all dead," Noah replied. "All of them," he added. "What!" George exploded. He threw the mobile phone against the nearest wall and smashed it to pieces.

The phone went dead, and Noah finished it off with two bullets through the phone. They turned around and left the room checking the paths again before taking another route they hoped would lead them out of here.

On their way out they stopped for another kiss, and they couldn't stop kissing for three long minutes which seemed like hours.

"We should tell John and Gabrielle how we feel about each other," Noah said into Tina's ear.

"Yes, as soon as possible," Tina added smiling.

They were soon outside the alley Tina had been shooting down earlier. Right before them was Ian, the very man who had got them into this mess. They got him on his feet and ushered him back up the path to meet with John. Ian could see where John had taken all the bullet hits, his bullet proof suit was covered in spots, some were breaking through the suit, so some bullets hit his chest as well. His head was bleeding still, blood covering his eyes and he had also been hit in his hand.

Two cars screeched to a halt and eight men from the Mafia jumped from their cars and with machine guns at the ready they surrounded Gabrielle's car and the people on the ground. "Alan, it's okay, we'll take over your protection. An ambulance is on its way with more police and a senior officer," Stefano, a man Alan had met before said.

Alan looked around at the mess where people had dropped glasses or cups when the shooting started, and the injured people fell to the ground. Alan allowed Lynda and Jenny out of the car and explained to Sarah what had happened to John's face and could she clean up his eyes?

"Can you give your husband a kiss? I've taken a few rounds of bullets as well and I need your love."

Sarah leaned forward laughing, her arms went around his neck and she kissed him profusely. Then looked at her husband again.

"Alan where are your trousers?"

"Ahh, Tina is wearing them, they should by now be on top of John's head, but she got side-tracked."

"Well get them off Tina and put them back on to cover your legs," Sarah told her husband, still holding his head close to her and kissing his lips, only glad he was still alive.

Just as Alan was going to leave Sarah. They heard machinegun fire and a loud cry of pain from a woman. "Gabrielle and Lynda are out there, and John can't see at the moment. I have to go," Alan insisted.

Sarah leaned forward and kissed her husband. "Go, but be careful," Sarah replied.

Alan was gone, his Glock in his right hand. He headed to Gabrielle and Lynda. "Over there," Lynda said as more machine gun fire started again. Lynda had looked at her wife and noticed she had taken a bullet in her right shoulder. Luckily, she too had a bullet proof jacket on and was just bruised.

Lynda opened her jacket and the top four buttons of her blouse. As her green eyes shone brighter, she heated up the area where the bullet would have hit her shoulder. She looked inside her shoulder and with her eyes, brought out the bruise and sealed off two small blood vessels before her hand now boiling hot, healed her broken skin by the bullet impact area.

"Now sit in the car next to Jenny, she'll help get you dressed," Lynda said to her wife. They kissed passionately before Gabrielle passed Sarah with a large first aid box in her hand and got into the car.

"My God John, you are in a mess, are you in any pain? Tell me because I am going to work on your face."

"Yes, some pain," he reluctantly replied.

"Bite on this and swallow the contents," Sarah replied and placed a small capsule between his teeth.

"What was that?" John asked.

"Morphine. I'm going to start cleaning up your face."

Five minutes later his eyes were clear of blood and the hole in his head was being worked on by Lynda. Her green eyes were very bright as she looked into the bullet hole, she repaired all the broken blood vessels and was now healing the skin on his forehead.

Lynda looked at John's face and placed her hot hand on top of the hole in his head. With the help of her bright green eyes, she stopped the healing process and looked at his face which was back too normal. "Now John, into the car, your wife wants to hold you close to her," Lynda ordered.

John breathed deep and carefully walked then stopped. "I need a pee," he said.

"Okay, I'll find you a spot," Alan said and put his arm around John's shoulder. Two minutes later they were looking at blood in his urine.

"Looks like you damaged your kidneys, that might be a hospital job unless Lynda can help you, she did a fine job on your forehead."

"Let's get you in the car first, I want us away from here as soon as possible. Let's get the agreement signed.

"Stefano," John called. He was soon at his side and waved to Noah with Tina in his arms walking slowly towards the safety of the car.

"What's happened to Tina?" John asked.

"She was raked by a machinegun, but its owner is now dead," Noah replied.

"Can you get her into the limo and lay her on the long seat,

Lynda will help her I'm sure. If not, we'll have her airlifted to the Carrier Group. We need to get out of here as soon as possible, can you give us an escort to Marco's residence?" John asked Stefano.

"Of course. An ambulance has just arrived, and a paramedic is checking Ian over. As soon as you are ready to go, my two drivers will get in front and behind you. I'll go and see how Ian is. Then we should get ready to leave."

The paramedic looked at Stefano. "He has a broken shoulder and a bullet in his arm, if he has his operation this morning, he will be back at his hotel later tonight."

"Where is my bodyguard?" Ian shouted.

"You have four bodyguards down Gabrielle has also taken a hit in her shoulder John received over sixty hits in the front of his body, a bullet hit him in his forehead. Tina has just had a machinegun raked across both her legs. Noah is also shot in the back and down. Now I must sort this mess out. You will be taken to the local hospital for your operation."

"Who will look after me if all my, our bodyguards are down?"

"Adelmo, you will be his bodyguard for today until I can sort this mess out and find out who has set us up. Now I must go, Adelmo is a first class shot," Stefano said and was gone retracing his steps back to the car.

John was now inside the car and Tina was laying on the right long car seat. Noah was just taking a seat by Tina's head. He had taken a bullet in his back as he tried to protect Tina. Alan got into the car and sat next to his wife.

"Stefano, we are ready to go now," Alan said and closed the door.

"Anton, follow Stefano's car and keep up with them," Alan ordered. The car started and a minute later they were on their way to Marco's Mansion. Gabrielle's phone rang and she put the call on loudspeaker.

"Hello Gabrielle, we've had a call from Ian again and he said there was lot of shooting going on and he has been shot in the arm and was now on the way to hospital for an operation. He is demanding an evac immediately with helicopter gunships and bombers overhead."

"Please David, don't do that, we are so close to signing this Treaty. Ian will be fine; he has one of Stefano's men with him. Anyway, it was him who accidentally set us up, loose lips sink ships. He needs his tongue cut out for the number of men that were killed and injured this morning. We are on our way to Marco's residence where we will hopefully be more protected," Gabrielle said.

"Is there anything we can help you with, like an air strike? You can't fool me Gabrielle, we've all been watching in slow motion and real time. How is John?"

"I'm fine now thank you David."

"Alan where are your trousers?"

"Oh no, surely, they didn't film me like this?"

"I'm afraid so. How is that delicious young girl Tina doing we saw her take the rake of bullets, good job she was wearing your trousers, never-the-less, a brave girl indeed, the Admiral is already writing you all up for medals."

"David, we are extremely low on ammo, we've never encountered a fight like this. We need about two hundred twenty shot clips for our Glocks then four short machineguns and twenty clips for those. Could one of your small helicopters and one man drop the ammo off, oh and another Glock for me please?"

"What time do you want it all delivered?" David asked.

John looked at his watch, they were already an hour late for the signing it was now ten thirty. "David, how about fourteen hundred at the rear of Marco's mansion? Only a small teeny-weeny helicopter, I don't want us all blown away by the downdraft." John laughed and David laughed as well.

"My God, I could certainly do with some more men and women like you. Bye for now John, I'll give you a call when we're on our way."

"Thanks' David." Gabrielle stopped the call and looked around at the women.

"Ladies, please touch up your makeup it looks like you've all been crying, which you have. We have a Treaty to sign then home," Gabrielle said. "Lynda can you please have a look at Tina for me so Alan can have his trousers back? Then Noah has a bullet in his back."

"Come and give me a hand," Lynda said to Gabrielle.

"Of course, my love," Gabrielle replied, and they both approached Tina and gently removed Alan's trousers. Her legs were covered with blood.

"How many shots did you take? I thought it was only one rake across your legs?" Lynda asked.

"The gun went back and forth twice before Noah killed him," Tina replied.

"Do you have any more morphine?" Lynda asked Sarah.

Sarah looked in her medical bag and pulled out a morphine capsule. "Here Tina, bite hard on this it's morphine and you will be in a lot of pain very soon," Sarah sighed and put another capsule in her pocket.

As they pulled Alan's trousers further down her legs there was a lot more blood and already tears were filling Tina's eyes. Noah leaned forward and kissed her lips, then started to kiss the tears from her face. I'll love you and look after you forever, no matter what mess your legs are in."

"Forever? Promise?" she tentatively asked.

"I promise, on my soul, I'll never leave except for work." He kissed her lips again then holding her hand in his and his right arm around her front. He talked love to her as Lynda and Gabrielle made a start on the top of her legs.

The back of the car was bright green as their eyes healed the bones in her legs and blood vessels that had been broken by the force of the bullets. By the time they arrived at Marco's mansion, they had managed to mend the top of both legs to her knees. They pulled the last few inches of Alan's trousers from her legs and they were tossed back to Alan who quickly put them on.

"I'm sorry about all the blood on the inside of your trousers Alan."

"That's alright Tina they saved your legs from a lot more damage, isn't that right Noah?" he asked smiling and placed his hand on his shoulder. Noah fell into Tina's lap. Alan pulled him upright and checked his body for any more hits. John moved forward and helped Alan remove his jacket and shirt. Now they could see what was happening.

"He's been hit four times in the back and once in his chest. These bullets need to come out now," Alan said. Lynda finished the last bullet hole in Tina's left leg and looked over to Noah.

"I bet his blood pressure has dropped to zero, do we have a blood pressure monitor?" She asked.

Sarah looked in her medical bag and pulled out a new blood pressure gauge for use in the field. She placed the machine on his arm, and it sucked itself onto his arm and pumped extremely fast. Ten seconds later it showed his blood pressure was rock bottom.

She helped push Noah onto Tina's lap then Lynda started to look for the bullets, Sarah had a pair of long bullet removers in her hand. Lynda took them from her and removed the first bullet then healed the blood vessels inside. She moved onto the next bullet as Gabrielle completed healing the hole the bullet had made. Five minutes later all the bullets were out, and his skin healed, although there would be scars.

Noah was sitting up and holding Tina close to him. Lynda and Gabrielle were talking fast to each other. Lynda then started to work on Tina's right leg.

"John, you look the worst for ware, take Jenny with you and explain to Marco what has happened and that we will need another ten minutes to deal with our injured bodyguards. Tell him we need the Treaty ready to sign when we come in, please."

"Of course, Gabrielle" They left the car and walked hand in hand up to the guards who took them to meet Marco. He was shocked when he saw John and the state of his suit.

"My God John, what in the Hell happened to you?"

"It wasn't just me; it was Alan, Tina and Noah. Even Gabrielle took a bullet in her shoulder. We were set up and caught in a trap that we couldn't escape from."

"How many men did you need to kill?"

"Over fifty, we were pinned down until Noah and Tina got in behind George's men, they picked up a machinegun each and extra clips from the dead men lying on the floor. Then they walked through the alleys and when they found George's men, they killed them all. Two chambers later they had killed fifty-seven men between them. Then they got Ian to a safer place until the ambulance arrived and took him to hospital for an operation." John's phone wrang. "Excuse me a moment please, it is Gabrielle. Ah, they are now on their way and may I ask if we can borrow a white shirt, please? Noah was shot in the back with a machinegun four times and once in his chest, Lynda and Gabrielle have just finished operating on him using their green eyes and a bullet extractor. He is still in severe pain and has taken another in-combat morphine capsule. Tina is the same and she too has taken a morphine capsule. Noah is only wearing his jacket which has also been shot apart."

"Roseli, get me a white shirt please. Medium and a large one for now." The woman ran off and soon returned with two shirts. When Noah arrived, Marco pointed to the lady with the shirts. "I hope something fits you."

"Thank you, Marco," Noah replied. He stood before the woman who went and got a damp cloth and wiped the blood from the bullet holes on his back then wiped clean the one hole in his chest.

"Let us try this one first, yes?" She helped put the shirt on him through his arms and rubbed her hand down the front of it and did the buttons up. She left the bottom four buttons undone so he could get his hand onto his gun if needed.

"Thank you," he said to the woman. In fluent Italian. He walked over to be by Tina and stood behind her. Tina's legs were bleeding still as the last three holes had not been healed yet, but she was anxious not to make them stay any later than they were. At least her bones were healed.

"Right Marco, I think we are ready to start, what do you think?" Gabrielle asked, holding Lynda's hand.

"Think?" he said allowed. "By what I have seen on TV this morning, I don't know how you all survived. I sent another eight men to assist you but both cars were hit by land mines, two men died I'm afraid, and it took a little longer than I thought to get more of my men to you. John, when you couldn't see, we all watched in wonder with your suit taking more hits, you fired one hundred and twenty rounds to the shooters and after another sixty rounds, you killed the last shooter. Congratulations to you all for keeping your ladies alive and out of danger." He kissed Gabrielle and Lynda on each cheek then welcomed the bodyguards, into his house.

"I see you are tired are you sure you wish to continue today?" Marco asked Gabrielle.

"Oh yes, let's get the Treaty signed," she replied.

After coffee, morning cakes and sandwiches to calm everyone's nerves, the press were allowed into the main hall where the talks had taken place. Marko and Gabrielle were seated at the top of a grand wooden table, highly polished which reflected the camera flashes. Before them was a red folder with the Peace Treaty inside which Marco and Gabrielle would very soon be signing.

Everything they had agreed was inside the ledger and Christine did the honours of checking their signatures and swapping the documents after they had been signed.

Everyone was quiet as Gabrielle signed her document first, then Marco signed his identical document. Christine checked their signatures and they had signed on the correct line. She swapped them over and Gabrielle signed first again.

The contracts were then taken to Lynda and Sereniti, who signed to say they too agreed with the Treaty and the top two signatures were correct. With both documents countersigned, each document was sealed with an imprint of HRH the Queens official seal of authority and the Mafia's seal of authority. The documents were then returned to the front of the table where they were checked once again by Christine and her own signature was added to represent the British Government on both papers.

Gabrielle and Marco stood, faced each other and shook hands before the press when they were photographed so that pictures could be added to the documents. They then kissed each other on the cheek and faced the cameras once again.

Two TV crews had been allowed to film the signing of the treaty and were now sending live images around the world. Gabrielle looked at Marco then the cameras.

"This Treaty between the UK Government which in this instance Lynda and I represent, and the Italian and Rome Mafia represented by Marco Don and his wife Sereniti, will bring peace to both countries from the rival clans in the UK and Rome, where protection money from shops and outworkers, went out of control. Now the Mafia has stopped taking protection money from the small shops and outworkers. They have also stopped taking money from many of the other shops which were striving to stay in business.

"The same will happen in London and other cities throughout the UK. There is a third organisation which has taken over two drug importers in London and killed their top people and others to gain control of the two organisations and at least twenty billion UK pounds.

"This new organisation is currently trying to overthrow the Mafia here in Rome and the UK's police force in London. It has been agreed between our two countries that Marines from HMS Queen Elizabeth will assist the Mafia in finding these men and stop them. The marines will be protected by gunships from HMS Queen Elizabeth," Gabrielle said to the cameras and the rest of the world.

"It is hoped with this new Treaty, we will both work in harmony to remove this third organisation from attacking Rome and the UK.

"This will bring about a joint coalition Mafia and UK police force to bring this third organisation down and put its leaders behind bars along with many of their operatives. You would have also seen earlier today a gunfight outside our hotel we are staying at where over fifty-two men from the third organisation were killed and six of us injured including myself.

"This is what we are up against, and these people will kill innocent children and adults who get in their way. With this Treaty signed, which we have worked hard and long hours at getting this right, peace will come to both our countries."

"Thank you, Gabrielle and Lynda, women go on a bit don't they," Marco said laughing and smiled at Gabrielle.

"Now I forgot what I wanted to say. Oh yes, we do not wish you people in the UK to think you are not wanted in Rome or the southern Italian border. You will not see much in the way of gunfights or this third organisation trying to take your hard-earned money from you.

"We are offering you twenty-five per cent off any hotel holiday booking and children under ten will go free, and that will be aboard any airlines that come to our country from the UK.

We look forward to seeing many of you come to visit our country and show this third organisation that you do not fear them, just as you go about your own business in the UK. There is one other announcement, that Gabrielle is slightly embarrassed to tell you all, is that when you come to Rome for your holiday, you can get twenty-five per cent off any of their Hats, Bags & Wraps in any of their shops.

"Gabrielle and Lynda Grayson who own Hats, Bags & Wraps worldwide, will be visiting our country many times in the future to show they too are not worried about these people who are trying to bring this country to its knees."

They both shook hands again and kissed each other on the cheek. As Gabrielle moved back to her position facing the cameras, she noticed something red from the corner of her eye.

Her head turned to Marko, and she shouted out at the top of her voice. "Laser light on Marco from a camera."

She stepped sideways and turned her body, so Marco and Gabrielle faced each other. She held him tight and moved to the right as a bullet sped past them hitting the wall behind them. Four machineguns opened fire on the man who was using a TV camera to cover up his gun. He just managed to get a second shot off before a dozen or more bullets entered his body killing him outright. Other Mafia men were now checking each man who was either holding a camera or operating one of the larger cameras for international countries and of course the UK.

Just as the bullet was about to hit Gabrielle's back, Lynda thought to her and instructed her to jump to her right one metre. Holding Marco tightly in her arms, Gabrielle thought to move her body and Marco's to the right. One second before the bullet was almost upon them, the next moment they had moved from its path and once again this bullet hit the wall behind them.

"How on earth did that bullet miss me and how did we get here?" Marco asked Gabrielle as he breathed hard on her face then fell into her arms and grabbed hold of her like he would never let her go?"

"I just moved myself and pulled you along with me or that bullet would have gone through me and hit you in the chest."

"But how did you move us so fast?" Marco asked again.

"An adrenalin rush let's just be glad I managed to move us and let that be the end of it, yes?" she asked him.

"I think that is an excellent answer. I also think my men put enough bullets into him to make a cullender out of him. That was very close, but you are still staying for lunch, everything is prepared in another room?" Marco asked.

"Yes, of course we are, we can't let one person ruin our day." They were still holding each other tight as Marco kissed Gabrielle on the lips.

"That's okay, I'll let you have that one kiss. No more though, cheeks fine, lips no, I'm a married woman and my wife can be very jealous."

"So is mine," Marco said laughing and let go of Gabrielle, feeling a little giddy for a moment, as he still wondered how he got to where he was with Gabrielle holding him tight.

With everyone in the room checked and cleared by Marco's men, four photographers took pictures of the dead man on the floor and his mockup camera with a smashed gun inside. He was then removed, and the blood cleared up by two of his men.

Gabrielle gave her document to Sarah who locked it in her briefcase. A few minutes later they were called into the next room where lunch had been laid out for them. This gave everyone a chance to talk.

Gabrielle found Marco and asked him about the hospital and how the building of the new wards was progressing? She asked if it would be possible to see it the following day?

"Of course, you can see the hospital, I was hoping to show you both around before you left. Are you going to look at your buildings and the Train Station, which is now completed, and can hold dinners for up to two hundred people at a time? I don't have the figures to hand, but we have young people attending local schools in the dress they feel comfortable in. Many of the twelve-year-old girls are on female hormone tablets which will help them in their later change and stop them growing a beard.

"Over three quarters of the people aged between 18 to 21 are at university and the rest are apprentices or studying other jobs which will give them a full-time job when they are fully changed.

"Those people over 21, who had to give up their job while they had their change; we have talked to their bosses, supported the person and either got them back into their job or have helped them get another job in the female work force."

"Do you visit the place much?" Gabrielle asked.

"At least once a week and I check on what they want and meet the new people there, so they are not afraid that the Mafia are involved in the group."

"That's excellent news, I'm looking forward to seeing it later this afternoon," Gabrielle said.

At two pm. a small helicopter landed at the back of Marco's Mansion and David stepped out and gave John and Alan the ammunician they asked for and the extra guns.

"If you need an extraction, just ring me and I'll have helicopters with you as soon as possible."

"Thank you, David, the Treaty is signed now, we killed a lot of George's men and I doubt he has many left in Rome to attack us again," John said and shook his hand before the helicopter lifted off into the clear sky. John handed out ten clips to each bodyguard, the remainder with the extra guns, were put into their limo by one of Marco's men. The extra Glock he put a full clip in it and handed it to his wife to look after for him.

With lunch over they took a short ride to their Transgender buildings, the offices, bedrooms, larger classrooms for photography, astronomy, art and cookery. The Train Station was last on their list.

When they arrived at the TG Centre, Stephney met them at the main reception area.

"Hello Gabrielle, Lynda," she said kissing them both on the cheek.

"You look well, how is Diago?" Lynda asked.

"He's fine, he will be back soon," she looked at her watch. "Well, another hour or so," she sighed. "He is picking up a boy aged fourteen, Pietra. He lives on the outskirts of Rome in one of the poorer areas and his father is against him becoming a girl, wearing a dress or even calling himself a girl's name. He is furious at him and beats him regularly. The problem is that fathers of a girl are supposed to pay for the wedding and the dress, it is not cheap. We have talked with him once and he was not letting his son go and said he would grow up a boy and become a man.

"We gave Pietra a couple of dresses, but his father has since torn them apart, so Diago rang him every day and Pietra has since gone on hunger strike. He said if he couldn't become a woman, then what is the sense in living? His father started to beat him hard, but he refused to eat and has eaten nothing for two weeks. His father has now agreed he will be allowed a trial period here to see by dressing as a girl all the time, he will hopefully change his mind."

"That sounds like a start," Lynda said holding Gabrielle's hand.

"Diago has taken a couple of dresses with him, some underclothes, shoes and short white socks. He will be changing in his home so his parents can see how he would like to be seen dressed and his mother can say goodbye properly as she always wanted a girl, and they have another two sons.

"It is going to be hard for him, his first trip out as a girl, Diago is taking her for a meal on the way here and go through what will be expected of her, which is nothing more than she won't want to do, and she has to attend school as a girl. I hope this is what he wants to do and is expecting to happen."

"Where will he be staying?" Gabrielle asked.

"In the main girl's rooms on the fourth floor for girl's aged 13 to 15. It will help her quickly get used to other boys who want to become girls. She then won't be so embarrassed attending school with the other girls and it's the fastest way to make friends and get help in becoming a girl by those who have been here a few months," Stephney said.

"As you know, we do the same as you for those who come from a family that practically disowns them. The girl's usually love the experience of going out for a meal for the first time as a girl," Gabrielle said.

"Is there anything else you need here?" Lynda asked.

"Some of the older girls have done a hairdressing and creative nail course at college so they can do some of the girl's hair, style others hair and they all love the long false nails now with different designs on them."

"Don't you have a ladies hairdresser shop in this locality?" Gabrielle asked.

"No, you have to go into the city we are on the outskirts if you remember, it was and is the safest place to put this many TG's," Stephney said.

"Of course, you're right, but there is a school here and the mothers all need to have their hair cut or permed at times," Gabrielle replied.

"Yes, I suppose they do," Stephney replied, not knowing what Gabrielle was getting at.

"Shall we go over and take a look at the Train Station?" Marco asked. "It is completely finished, and our bodyguards are sure to be hungry by now."

"Excuse me a moment, I need to use the loo," John said.

"Use the toilet on your right John," Stephney said and showed him where it was.

He was soon feeling a little better but there was a lot of blood in his urine. Then as he finished emptying his bladder, he collapsed to the floor. Gabrielle was the first to see the toilet door push hard closed. She went to investigate what had happened as John had not come out yet. Then she saw him on the floor on his back. "John," she screamed and flashed her green eyes speaking to Lynda.

Lynda grabbed Jenny's hand and pulled her to the toilet. She was already crying and when she saw her husband lying on the floor, she screamed "John, what's happened to you?"

"Anyone any ideas?" Lynda asked.

"He had blood in his urine but that was a couple of hours ago, I said he should be seen by a doctor on the carrier, and he said let's get on and get the Treaty signed, he was most insistent, you both know what John is like," Alan said.

"Kidney's then, it's always kidneys," Lynda said holding Gabrielle's hand. "There is a long seat out in the reception, can we get him onto that?" she asked Alan.

Alan called Noah over and with help from two of Marco's men, they moved John to the sofa. Lynda started straight away, as the room became bright green. Then Gabrielle looked at John where his kidneys would be and helped Lynda, sending her all her love giving Lynda the extra energy to heal John's kidney's and stop the internal bleeding.

"Twenty minutes later John was sitting up with Jenny holding onto him with all her might. She kissed him profusely, tears running down her face, then she held Lynda and kissed her on her cheeks and forehead and the same with Gabrielle.

"Now, I think he needs a strong cup of tea, it will help to flush the blood out of his body, and we won't leave here until he has emptied his bladder and I have seen what his stream is like. Just think of me as your doctor," Lynda said smiling.

"Dr, Lynda, can I stand up now?" John asked.

"Yes, stand up slowly, Jenny, hold him steady he may be wobbly on his feet," Lynda explained.

With John steady on his feet, they all walked across the road into the Train Station.

The doorman welcomed the people about to enter his domain and followed them in. "Ladies and gentlemen please welcome from the UK our gracious benefactors, Gabrielle and Lynda Grayson," the man said boldly.

Everyone stopped eating and stood up applauding the girls who were thanking everyone, but their words were not heard. Once the applause, shouts and whistles had calmed down, they managed to get their words heard and the people slowly took their seats again after Lynda managed to get her words heard. Eventually they made their way to the counter and looked at the food on display or what could be made special for anyone with a food allergy.

Making their choices of food, they sat down with people they knew a lot about and cared for. It was just like being home only speaking a different language.

All the way through their meal Gabrielle was thinking of how they could help the new girls further, then she had an idea and spoke to Lynda about it as they ate. They remained a further hour in the Train Station then went outside and looked at the site Gabrielle had been talking about. Gabrielle looked around, giving her expertise thought to the situation and finally made her decision to build a ladies, hairdressers and nail shop where the girls would cut and style the local women's hair and cut the boy's and men's hair. Those girls who had done a nail course, would be able to treat the young girls and ladies with false nails before they moved to the city to open their own nail shop with a grant from their charity. That evening they dined at the hotel after Ian had been operated on and was allowed out of hospital providing, he listened to his bodyguard. Christine helped him with his meal, and everyone could see a sparkle in their eyes.

"I expect she'll be helping him get undressed later this evening," Gabrielle said to Lynda.

"I can remember somebody else who needed help with their food, getting undressed and dressed," she added grinning and sent pictures of their early life together when Paul had just left hospital with his hands in bandages.

Gabrielle smiled at her wife and kissed her lips. They felt no embarrassment, just love for each other which everyone knew they loved to show.

As it was their last evening in Rome, they thought they would get an early night and asked Noah if he would mind being their bodyguard until John and Alan came up with their wives. Christine and Ian had already gone up on the pretence that his arm was aching, and he had missed his painkillers and needed them now. Ian agreed to at least have Noah check their rooms first then he could do as he liked as they would lock their doors.

Noah agreed, he had never looked after two beautiful women, who were in love with each other before. With his gun in hand, he checked their suite just as John would have done and opened the connecting door to John and Jenny's suite and checked that. "All okay, come in and I'll lock your door." While Noah secured their door and checked their windows, the girls were pouring themselves a drink. "I'll go into John's room. I have a report to write up on how Ian took a bullet and Christine has a few abrasions and will be putting in a claim for a new suit and shoes. Ian will do the same, but he needs me to explain why there will be hospital charges.

"What a day, but I must say, you both know how to handle yourselves in a situation and you did exactly as John and Alan told you to do, unlike my two; why did Ian send Paul home?" Noah asked.

"No doubt he will face a discipline hearing when he gets home," Lynda said smiling.

"No doubt. Now I'll say goodnight, ladies and I'll see you in the morning."

"Goodnight Noah." Gabrielle replied.

"Goodnight Noah," Lynda added, smiling at him.

Five minutes later with their lights out, both girls were in bed naked, their drinks unfinished on their bedside tables. They were kissing, tongues in each other's mouth as Gabrielle wrapped her right leg over Lynda's right leg, she pulled it towards her and slowly moving her righthand down Lynda's front, her fingers gently touching her nipple, over her breast and down to her vagina.

Her hands were tenderly moving her left thigh and leg to her left then three of her fingers entered her vagina, gently caressing her vagina wall and moving deeper in to find her G Spot. As her fingers moved in deeper, their mouths rotated, as they kissed more and more, while Gabrielle's left arm wrapped itself around Lynda's back holding her close, so their breasts touched as her fingers explored Lynda's vagina.

Lynda was moving her body to the actions of Gabrielle's fingers as she was getting nearer to her orgasm. Their bedcover had gone, sent to the floor during their exciting sexual play.

Next door, Noah had his laptop out and was writing up his report with the TV on, tuned into John's miniature camera that was set up to look along the landing. Everyone had a suite next to each other and the last suite on the landing was against the far wall where the landing turned left to go along the other side where the other suites were situated.

Forty-five minutes into writing his report, Noah noticed three men dressed in jeans and tee shirts walking slowly along the landing heading towards him. He put his computer down, picked up his gun and locked John's door. He had never been in a situation like this before, usually if someone wanted his charge killed, it would be in a quiet area, on a road and machinegun fire would rip through the car followed by a couple of grenades.

Usually just being a bodyguard on show was enough to put anyone off and he couldn't recall a time when a bodyguard had to use his gun, except in practice; apart from John and Alan as trouble seemed to follow them around. Then there was this morning, all that killing and trying to protect Ian and Christine at the same time. He thought George would have had enough killing for one day. Now he had to think, what did John say and what would John do? He touched his wireless switch on his earpiece and spoke to John in the restaurant with his wife.

"John, we have company, three men with machine guns and I can see two grenades on their belts, looks like they mean business."

"Damn! Lock my door, put my blue suit jacket on, it's in the wardrobe. Button it up, it's bullet-proofed or was after today, let's hope it protects you. Get the girls on the floor by the side of the bed and if their door opens, or appears to, pull the mattress over them, Gabrielle will help you. At all costs stay with the girls; we're on our way."

"I've got your jacket on and I'll protect them with my life."

"Don't shoot us if you need to get onto the landing."

"Okay; heading for the girl's room now."

Noah picked up his gun, checked there was a bullet up the spout and the clip was full. In John's pocket were ten clips, which would also fit his gun. Taking a deep breath, he opened the adjoining door to the girl's room, entered their lounge and made his way to their bedroom switching on the lights.

He was stuck for words for a brief second, then he got into action. He ran to the bed, held Lynda's leg and spoke quietly.

"Girls, we have trouble, both of you on the floor by the side of the bed, now!" he ordered. He found their bedcover and threw it over them like he was making a bed. We may be hit by a grenade if they drop one by the door, they have six grenades and three machineguns. John and Alan are on their way."

He ran around to the far side of the bed and moved the mattress so it could easily protect the girls. At the same time, he found their red silk nighties and returned to the other side of the bed. "Here," he said pushing the nighties beneath the cover and made sure the mattress would protect them.

He could hear what sounded like two very drunken men edging their way closer to the room and he hoped they would not be injured. He found a place where he could protect the girls and get shots off to kill the three men.

On the landing, the two drunken men, John and Alan, were staggering along the landing looking for their room.

"You idiot, we're on the wrong side, our room is at the bottom."

"We can still get to it by walking around the bottom corner and we're almost opposite our door. Do you have the key?"

"No, you have it."

They were now just a few feet from the three men who were looking frightened. John looked at the man closest to him then quickly glanced at the floor. The three men parted, standing each side of the girl's door. John brought the man by him to the floor and threw his machinegun further along the landing.

"Grenade," John shouted to Alan just as it exploded next to the door, breaking it apart and throwing sharp pieces of wood into the room. A few shards of wood had hit Noah's suit jacket but did not get through.

The grenade exploded and sent over a hundred ball bearings in all directions, but it was the main blast of the grenade that did most damage in breaking down the door and sending a number of pieces of metal and ball bearings into the man who dropped the grenade and was lying on the floor unconscious.

Noah slowly stood, his ears ringing from the grenade blast and he pulled bits of wood from his jacket. As he pulled out his gun, Noah shouted to the girls, "Stay exactly where you are, it's not over yet."

Noah raced past the king size bed, past the toilet and had his gun pointing at the second man. "Don't try anything," he shouted to the man. His ears were still ringing from the grenade exploding. Just then a machinegun was raised, and the man pulled its trigger. Noah pulled his trigger, and a bullet went through the man's hand and the gun stopped firing and fell to the floor.

Noah took six bullets in the chest and was knocked back a good metre. The assassin's other hand was trying to get to another grenade from his jeans when Alan fired his gun. The bullet hit the man's hand and the grenade fell to the floor. As the grenade fell to the floor, Noah could see a grenade pull ring.

"Live grenade!" Noah shouted and fired his gun twice. Each bullet hit the man in the back of his knees forcing him to bend his knees forward and sending him falling to the floor.

Alan heard what Noah had shouted and knew exactly where the grenade had come from. He also heard the two shots from Noah's gun and for a moment he wondered why he had fired again; then he saw the man buckle and start his fall on top of the grenade.

Alan jumped into the air and did four forward somersaults with his gun in his hand. There was a loud thump; then blood and parts of a man's body started to fall from the air onto the landing.

John heard the call as well and used the first man's body to hide behind. Once again, he took a few pieces of metal while blood and body parts hit him hard in the back. When everything settled down, John turned his man over and removed the other two grenades then frisked him from head to foot, finding a small Barrette gun, twenty spare clips for the machinegun and two eight-inch knives. Finding any weapons on the other man by the door was going to be hard so they left him alone.

The second man still on the landing started to get up as Noah walked out of the broken door, seeing the man raise his machine gun and point it at Alan. Noah pulled out his gun and shot him in the back of the head twice, pushing his brains out of his eyes. Outside were the sound of police cars and ambulances; already four police officers were running up the stairs while two ambulance paramedics were going up in the lift with three black bags and a spinal board.

Noah staggered through the missing door with his gun in his hand. "John, Alan, are you both alive?" he shouted.

"Yes, I'm fine," John replied as he stood up covered in blood.

"I survived without being hit by a bullet, but a leg hit me in the chin and what is all this blood? I thought we only had eight pints, this bloke must have had twenty," he joked as he walked to the girl's room.

"That was bloody good thinking and shooting Noah, you probably saved our lives or at least time in hospital."

"Excuse me a moment, I just have to check on my two girls. Get it John? My girls and aren't they bloody sexy and extremely good looking in the flesh," Noah said grinning then his eyes fell on Tina who was holding her Glock in her hand.

"Everything is alright my love, I'm still alive, thanks to John's suit jacket," Noah said, wondering how much she had heard.

"I'm so glad Noah," Tina replied and grabbed hold of his neck, kissing him profusely. "You better talk like that about me later," she told him quietly and kissed him again.

"Ah yes, I forgot to tell you they would be naked and probably having sex of some kind," John replied smiling.

Noah retraced his steps back to the bed and looked under the bedcover. The girls had put their nighties on and were waiting for Noah to give them the all-clear.

"Where are your dressing gowns and slippers. There are a lot of men outside and waiting to come in here, especially the manager of the hotel. The floor is covered with glass and shards of wood. Oh, one other thing, I shot one of the men in the back of his knees so he would collapse onto his grenade and now there are parts of his body in here as well."

"Well done for protecting us Noah, our dressing gowns are just inside the lounge in one of the chairs and our slippers are there as well," Lynda said.

He was gone and back with the clothes, Gabrielle emerged first, took the dressing gown and slipped it on, then Lynda followed." With slippers on their feet, they looked at the mess the room was in as John entered the room and examined how Noah had protected the girls, just as he told him to do."

"Oh John, I'm sorry but your suit jacket has taken a number of wooden shards and at least six bullets, other than that, it saved my life."

"You had better keep it on until this mess is all over and the police let us get to bed."

"Thanks!"

It took an hour for the police to take statements from the three men and two women. During this time, Alan talked to Ian and Christine, who he found arm in arm in Christine's bed.

"As you are both cuddled up nicely together. You may as well stay here for the rest of the night," he said sternly.

"Alan, Christine was naturally upset hearing the bombs go off and the gunfire."

"It wasn't bombs, it was two hand grenades and there were not many shots fired. Noah will sleep in your room Ian with Tina, no doubt. You can get your clothes in the morning."

"I bet Noah didn't help you at all, he was a last-minute man as the first-grade officer had to protect someone else."

"Noah alerted John and me to the three men and described what guns and grenades they had. He protected Gabrielle and

Lynda and made sure they could make themselves respectable as they were both naked. He then walked into the path of an exploding door, fired twice and took six bullets in the chest and abdomen. Finally, on seeing the pin removed from the second, hand grenade, he shot the man once in each knee, so he folded backwards and fell onto the grenade which exploded under him, killing him, then he killed another man shooting him twice in his head forcing his brain out of his eyes, checked we were fine and finally, got the two girls into their dressing gowns and slippers so they looked respectable for the police and hotel manager.

"Your bodyguard is a first-class man and today has killed his first twenty-nine men. Don't you dare think about putting him down in your reports, because I'll make sure your wife and your husband know about your love for each other."

Ian and Christine looked at Alan in silence, knowing that is exactly what he would do. They had better make the most of it, later this morning, it would be another day.

John went to the lounge and found his wife, kissed her then looked to Sarah. "Alan's fine, just needs a shower like me."

"John, what is all this red over your suit?" Jenny asked.

"Noah shot the second man in his knees, so he fell on top of his grenade, and it blew up under his back sending blood and parts of his body everywhere," John replied.

"Will we pass the gore?" Sarah asked grinning.

"No, I'll take you down the other side of the landing and we are all moving rooms, one room towards Ian and Christine's room.

"Well, they have been sleeping together since we arrived."

A short time later the girls were in their new room and managed to get just a few things they would need for the morning. They could move rooms to apply their makeup.

The manager was shouting at the police to see how long it would take them to clear the mess up. He was also demanding to know who would pay for the damage as he was not covered for a gunfight in his hotel.

Gabrielle decided to calm the manager down after talking the situation over with Lynda. In her nightie and dressing gown, cheque book and pen in hand, with John in tow, they walked through the connecting door into what was left of their suite.

"It's certainly a mess John, it looks like those three men were out to get both of us."

"It certainly does but I don't think the man I took down will make it through the night. Apparently, he has two pieces of shrapnel in his brain, he'll be no use to us, it's a shame. Now we have to deal with this mess," John said looking around the room. How much are you thinking of offering him?"

"The room will be out of service for at least three days so too the room below us, if it has suffered damage, we will need to see it before we leave."

They met Mr Romano by the broken door. He was just about to start protesting when Gabrielle held her hand up for silence.

"Mr Romano, I profoundly apologise for the mess and destruction the three assassins have caused, I am so pleased they didn't kill me or my wife. I have nothing but praise for Noah, John and Alan, our bodyguards; they saved our lives and a lot more damage to this room, the three men would have killed some of your staff with their machine guns on their way out and you may have had a police gun fight in the lobby, and they still had six grenades on them. Think of the damage they would have caused.

"I think three excellent carpenters could have the door hung on a new frame and patch up the floor, make repairs to the wooden areas that the bullets have hit and have a glazier replace the broken glass.

"The room is seven thousand Euro's a night; I will pay you for three nights and I will start with thirty thousand Euros for the damage."

"That is very gracious of you, I do not think there will be damage to the room below, I have already had a porter check the room for damage and there is none. There is a one point five metre gap between floors for the air conditioning. Any damage to floor or main joists, which are steel, will need to be investigated by the carpenters."

"I suggest for now, you get your maids to clean the room up as best they can. Captain Rosso, do your men have any other work to do here?"

"No Dame Grayson, I have a special police crew arriving shortly to clear up the body parts and the blood from around this area. It should take no more than an hour."

"Thank you, Captain Rosso. Mr Romano, here is your cheque, so I suggest you start getting your people working on this room now and calling your carpenters to see what they will need. John, turn around please." He looked at her confused.

She held the cheque book in her hand, and he got the idea. Gabrielle wrote the cheque and handed it to Mr Romano. He looked at it and nodded his head.

"Thank you, it is extremely thoughtful of you."

"I would like the receipt for the cheque before we leave in the morning. It is now . . ." She looked at John's watch. "It is now 4:07 am, we will try to get some sleep, but do not worry if your people make any noise, we understand, but please keep it to a minimum. My complete party will have breakfast in the dining room, then return up here to finish packing.

"Lynda and I have an early meeting, at 10:00 with Marco Don, I will be asking him if he can keep an eye on your carpenters and other workmen in case they are slacking. If it takes longer than three days, I will send in my own people and your people will not get paid by me."

"Of course, Dame Grayson, I completely understand," he replied, recalling how powerful this woman was. She had been the only person with her wife to stop the Mafia collecting on shops and hotels in Rome and Italy. So far, he had saved several thousand Euros from Mafia funds.

"I will ensure everything is ready for you and your party, I shall wish you good night, what is left of it."

"Thank you for your understanding in this matter," Gabrielle said and held out her hand for him to kiss, which he did. Gabrielle smiled at him and heard women's voices coming along the landing. As John and Gabrielle entered her bedroom, the women were climbing over the black plastic bag that covered the remains of the assassin.

John locked the internal joining door and bade the girls goodnight. They got into bed still wearing their nighties and matching panties. Lynda lay her head on her pillow thinking, while Gabrielle gingerly pulled the bedcover up over them, and tucked it in behind Lynda's back. She lay down slipping her left arm around Lynda's back and pulled Lynda into her.

Lynda looked at Gabrielle with tears rolling down her face. "Do you think they will continue to come after us? Last night was horrendous and Noah could have been killed, so could John or Alan. Perhaps we should move to another country where we are not so well known?"

"There, there my love, George is not going to ruin our lives and we have a long time to live and people to choose. As soon as George is dead, the money will dry up to the assassins over here and the marines have killed many of his men and taken over fifty prisoners. They think there are no more than three cells left and yesterday we killed sixty men.

"I won't let George get to you and if Marco can find these last few cells, that will be the end of it in Rome. Don't worry my love, you won't have to go back to his service or be with him again."

Gabrielle softly stroked Lynda's face, as Lynda cried herself to sleep. Fearing another episode where Lynda was so frightened of George and Ian, she was trying to run away from them in the night. She put her arm over Lynda's side and pulled Lynda on top of her, pulling her close so their breasts and bodies touched, so Lynda would feel her love.

When Gabrielle woke an hour later, Lynda was not in their bed. She panicked recalling the time when Lynda had that nightmare in their home. She was up and ran to the front door, it was still locked and sealed, so she must be still in the suite unless she had jumped somewhere and right now Gabrielle was searching for her as she ran through the suite then found her in the bathroom staring into the bathroom mirror, as if hypnotised by an image a long way in her past.

"What's up? I felt your thoughts looking for me. I was just about to reply when you found me. Did you miss me in bed?" Lynda asked.

"Miss you? I thought you had gone and jumped somewhere and was wandering around, lost and almost naked," she replied. Gabrielle walked forward and gave her a huge hug and kiss. "Please don't worry about the past I'm sure we can overcome the obstacles that lay before us.

"I'll make you this promise, whatever happens no matter what with George, I'll be right by your side holding your hand with all my love encompassing you. That's a long word for this time of morning and the little sleep we've had. Fancy a shower together?" They turned towards each other, embraced and kissed each other on the lips, rotating their heads, tongues in mouths and love pouring from them.

Their bags, makeup and shoes were already packed by the interlocking door by the maids and John had taken their safe into his room before they finally managed to get to bed. As they walked past their old door to their suite, they could see the amount of damaged that had been done by the grenades and already two carpenters were working on getting the old doorframe off and pulling up part of the floor to get beneath it to see the damage.

Later in the morning they met up with Marco then went to the hospital. Before leaving, Gabrielle discussed another project she had in mind with Marco, and he insisted on taking them to lunch.

At 3:30, they left their hotel and headed to the airport with two of Marco's cars and eight of his men giving them an escort to their private jet. At 4:10, they were heading home, flying over Italy. At the rear of the plane, Gabrielle and Lynda had reclined their seats to a bed position and with a blanket over them, got some shuteye before landing at Heathrow.

Chapter 3

Only half an hour after arriving home, the doorbell rang and Alan went to answer it with John watching from the main office doorway. Two men were standing there: packing weapons but not on display.

"George said to give this letter to Gabrielle, and this letter to Lynda. They should not forget the date they have to meet him. For every hour they are late, he will destroy one of their shops in the UK. Once all these shops are gone, he will start again in France, throughout Europe and Rome will be the last to feel his wroth.

"Marco will not survive the onslaught he is preparing. He asked me to tell Gabrielle he now has more money than her and her mother combined since the change in the drug laws to legalise Cannabis.

"It's not just Cannabis, it's everything, morphine, Coke, Crack, Cocaine, Heroin, Smack, Dope, LSD, Acid, Ketamine, Ecstasy, Crystal Meth, Ice, Glass, OxyContin, Angel Dust, Magic Mushrooms, Speed Ritalin and everything in between plus all the stuff you need to take it including syringes and fresh needles, these are free.

"Of course, George helped to get the drug law changed while you were out of the country and that dumb idiot Ian what's his surname? Galaway, that's it, the bloke who went with you and has now lost his job, well, he'll resign in two weeks."

"Do you mind waiting here a moment I'll just close the door?" John went to the lounge where Lynda and Gabrielle had been listening to the conversation at the front door.

"Here are your letters from George," he said handing them out.

"Did you hear what they said about the drugs?" he continued anxiously.

"Yes, we did, but surely it can't be true, we were only gone ten days. Ian's in charge of Homeland security and I would have thought they would need his agreement before legalising every drug there is. I'll tell you what, I'll come to the door with you and keep your hand on your gun. Let's see what has really happened or at least as much as they know."

John escorted Gabrielle to the front door while Alan protected Lynda. Tina kept her gun on the front door.

"Right, what is going on now; should I be concerned?" Gabrielle asked the tall man before her. "And what's your name?" she continued.

"Stuart!" the tall man replied in a strong northern accent. "This is Todd he added, "and you must be the infamous Gabrielle Grayson, I didn't think Lynda would have the balls to come and speak to us."

"Well, she's a woman and doesn't have any balls, neither do I, but she's close enough to hear what you say. This is John, one of my bodyguards and I've told him if either of you or the man over there in the car goes to draw his gun, he is to shoot you, to kill. He also has his hand on his gun, ready to use it."

"You'll have no trouble from us I promise," Stuart replied.

"Will this take long to explain?" Gabrielle asked.

"About twenty minutes," Stuart replied.

"You had better come in then, all your guns on the table there," Gabrielle ordered.

There was quite a lot of noise as both men placed several guns and long knives on the table, waited patiently for John to check them out and let them into the lounge. As Stuart passed Gabrielle, he handed her the previous week's Daily Mirror. She looked at the front page in horror, then turned to pages 3,4,5,6,7, 8, 9,10. She was still reading the paper as she took a seat on the sofa next to Lynda.

"Wow, so can you tell us in short what has transpired over the last week?" Gabrielle asked.

"After you left, George sent a message to the Prime Minister if he did not declare all drugs legalised and would be accessible through his special drug shops within twelve hours, he would send a rocket into 10 Downing Street then another an hour later to 11 Downing Street, then another at 9 Downing Street.

"If he would still not agree, then George would wait until Parliament was full and blow the entire building up with as many rockets as it took. He's in a right mess with his body and he has only now got help with his leg.

"The PM was in his Cobra shelter beneath 10 Downing Street when it was hit by six Trogon bombs. They are still trying to clear up the mess as he said no to George's idea saying he was quite mad. He destroyed 9,10 and 11 Downing Street in one go, not giving them more time to wait, Parliament has been closed and we have a new Prime Minister, Mrs Margaret Stevens; she was the only one person who would take the job."

"So, she caved in?" Lynda asked.

"Not quite, she has given George what he wants, all drugs will be made legal when his first drug shop opens, and it is to be inspected by the NHS first. He is currently going through, with a small committee on drugs control how his idea is to be put into service. All syringes and needles must be put in a yellow container which will be issued to the prescribed user on the first time.

"Nobody is allowed to shoot up in the street or in a close proximity to a school. It must be done in a club, a new drug club which is being run by George's men and the Government Committee. George has also donated five billion pounds to the NHS to build four new super hospitals, give them all the equipment they need, build another large children's hospital with a parents' room on each floor. The five billion has already been donated to the NHS as a show of good faith," Stuart explained.

"What do you and other people who now work for George think of his drug shops?"

"We are not in favour of them; we prefer the old way, when we can keep the number of drugs hitting the street under our control. Although George's idea is good, the country will be saturated with drugs and we'll get no work done and the suppliers will have problems getting the drugs out of their country to ours to put in the shops."

"Do you understand why he is coming after us?" Lynda asked.

"He said he's legally married to Lynda, and you should not have married Gabrielle and also that you are his whore."

"Well, we are not married; I was married to Ian before Paul, now Gabrielle, killed him and if I were anyone's whore, I would have been Ian's whore. George and Ian were just close mates and George killed his wife and her parents because he thought she told the police on him when she didn't. It was just his paranoia."

"How long have you been with him?" Lynda asked.

"Two months, the guy in the car, four months, but we all fear for our lives. If anyone says anything against him, he kills them and hires a new guy, paying them thousands of pounds to basically agree with him. A few months ago, he killed five men and two women for just suggesting he get his leg and head seen too.

"When Joanne and Stacy who have been caring for his head, both agreed it should be looked at by a proper doctor, he just got his gun out and shot them in a frenzy putting a full clip into each woman to ensure she was dead."

"Crikey the man sounds perfectly insane," Gabrielle sighed. "How is he getting his men if he's like this?"

"Ken Mattingly is the man is getting people to do jobs. He's just hired another hundred people to do some work and he pays them a lot of money. We were paid two grand each to come here and deliver the letters and give you the warning. We are then on standby for when you arrive and he has a load of people ready to do work for him, they are all in training now and still getting paid," Todd butted in excitedly.

Stuart looked at Todd with anger showing on his face. "Todd, say no more." They now looked at each other as Gabrielle read their minds and smiled to herself.

"That's a lot of money he paid you, was there a risk we might kill you?"

"He said you had a couple of gunslingers with you, and he was right by the looks of it."

"We always have our bodyguards wherever we go. It's been a part of our lives for twelve years now. We go to dangerous places and face people like you or George or Marco. We also wear expensive jewellery, and our insurance company asks that we have people with us to fight off thieves," Gabrielle replied.

"Just what is George going to use all these men for?" Lynda asked Stuart, as he appeared to be the lead man.

"I know exactly what they are going to do as I have been training with them," he retorted smugly.

"Okay what is it you've been training for?" she continued. He smiled showing his brilliant white teeth which were veneers and he had obviously just had them done.

"We are going to blow up your shops if you don't turn up and then blow up one shop for every hour you are late. But as you don't have that many shops in the UK and we want you to take the blame, we'll blow up other shops as well. We might even blow up two shops at the same time in different cities. You'll never be able to get insurance again," he said leaning back and laughing.

"Would you like me to kill them both here and now boss?" Alan asked Lynda.

"Not yet Alan, but they will not leave here alive unless they answer my questions," Lynda replied calmly. She was talking to Gabrielle at the same time using telepathy.

Gabrielle leaned forward and looked at Stuart. "Well Stuart, you do realise you need a lot of explosives to completely destroy a shop. One grenade, even two or three, will do no more than burn clothes and destroy a few display rails or shelves."

"Yes, but there will be a lot of water damage from the shop sprinkler system which will come on automatically as soon as the grenades explode."

"It won't be grenades, but high explosive in four packs. The men will enter the shop walk around and deploy their explosives at the same instant and activate the timer giving them thirty seconds to get out and into the getaway car. The last man to leave will close the door and drop a block of explosive with a ten second delay timer. That will stop people running from the shop and if the shop has handles on the doors, they will drop a bar through them so they cannot be opened by anyone from the inside," he replied with a smirk on his face.

"Now get out of that, you don't know when we'll come or what shops will be hit. Even if you managed to kill George, we have orders to continue for a few hours until we have used up all the explosive, we have on us. If George needs to escape, the same thing will happen, keeping the police busy with traffic and trying to identify bodies while the fire brigade put out the fires.

"You will also be in police custody due to the statement we will leave for the police saying this is all your idea. Turn around and say we are lying; we'll have proof left in each shop that it's your doing," Stuart continued in his monolog, unaware of what he was saying or that Tod was prodding him, trying to get him to shut up.

"Tell me Stuart, what form of statement will it be?" Gabrielle asked forcing him to speak.

"In the case of your shops, a statement to the police from George saying you are blowing up your own shops for the insurance money. In the case of other shops, a letter will be left for the police telling them you wanted to buy their shop and they refused to sell it to you. If you can't have it, then no one will have it. There will also be receipts from some of our Italian friends for monies paid to them in cash to do the job. All our Italian friends have of course returned home except four men who will lead the assault on your shops in London because of the men you have had killed in Rome and Italian border skirmishes with the Royal Navy Marines and helicopter gunships," he added in the same monotonous voice.

"Do you know when the attacks on our shops will start?" Gabrielle asked, still leaning forward, her eyes looking through his, drawing the answers she wanted out into the room.

John had pulled out his gun and pointed it at Todd. "Touch him again in these talks and I'll blow your head off." Todd sat back on the sofa and said nothing else, looking at John with his gun pointing at him and he knew John was not joking.

"When will this campaign against us commence?" Gabrielle asked Stuart.

"You have just returned from Rome and have meetings with the government and Queen over the next few days and it should have been next Friday, but I'll give you an extra two weeks so you two love birds can enjoy your last moments on Earth.

"I'll expect to see you both in three weeks at midday at this reference. Would you care to write it down, so you don't forget it?"

"I'm ready," Gabrielle replied with pen and notepad in her hand."

"It's LP4 6NY the Priory. No bodyguards allowed with you; they will remain in the car at this point. You will then be driven in a Rolls Royce to a secret location where you will meet George and he will decide what he is to do with you. I am looking forward to meeting the two of you as well. I have paid a handsome price for you Gabrielle and I have you to myself for two whole hours before he more than likely kills you."

"What is to happen to me?" Lynda asked, drawing more answers from him.

"You will be his bride again, and his whore, you will do exactly what whores do, bring in money for your man and take all the drugs you like to take your mind away from the degradation you'll feel as more and more men pay for your body and beat you as they like and have sex with you.

"I'm sure you remember what that feels like. I was one of your last paying customers to have you when Ian and George stole all my money; over ten-grand. George stopped me from slashing your tits up and both of your wrists. I suppose I did go a bit too far, but it was well worth it even managing to finally get a last kick into your head, then George threw me out into the street after he took all my money except for a donkey to get me home.

"Now I have the pleasure of getting my final reward, after George has had you one or two or three times, if he can keep it hard enough by then. He's in a bad mental and physical shape. I would say more mental than physical, but it's his head, that's the problem. Two new girls, Kathleen and Bella care for him now. It's like looking at a horror film. The heating is on full and the girls wear bikinis while they apply pulses and bandages to his leg and head. His leg should have been amputated weeks ago and I have no idea how he is still alive with the green muck coming out of his head.

"No matter when he dies. I'll take good care of you both and sell Gabrielle at least six times a day and you; you Lynda, will be mine to do what I like with. It would be worth trying to kill him just to have you both in my care and I could, look after you have both been abused all day, to make love to each other, naked of course."

There was suddenly a loud bang at the front door and a repetitive ring of the doorbell. John went to answer the door and with his right hand holding his gun roughly level to where he expected the man's head to be, he opened the door and pushed his gun into the man's temple.

"I want to know if Stuart and Todd are okay?"

"Want to know? That's a demand and you don't knock on this door and demand something. Now, ask me again, this time more politely."

"I apologise. Could you please tell me if Stuart and Todd are okay and how much longer they will be?" he asked.

"Neither man is dead . . .. yet. They will be a little longer but no more than ten minutes. Have no fear they will not be harmed in this house. When they get out, that may change. I see your driver has a rifle with a scope, is he thinking of trying to kill me?"

"No, it's for my safety really."

"Now you know the answer to your question, you may leave. If you go to pull a gun on me, you die first, the man in the car second, Stuart third and Todd last, all within a few seconds of each other. There is a police car a quarter of a mile away and it will be here in a matter of a few minutes and blast Hell out of your car."

"Yes John!"

"I did not give you my name."

"Everybody in George's team know you and Alan. We all fear you because you do not fear Death or protecting your boss, even though she is not royalty or a President or Prime Minister.

"Once the girls are in his care, he would like Alan and yourself to join him and take care of the girls when they are working, but they have to work so don't get any ideas of saving them; they will be fitted with a remote explosive that will blow their heads off and the same goes for you. The offer is made and there is work, to be done. The police car, is it still waiting for a gun shot or does it move around the block?"

"Why do you wish to know?"

"It will make my life easier."

"What do you mean?"

"George has been listening to their conversation and he is not a happy man with what Stuart has said and he should be dealt with."

"Well, not on our turf. I can keep their guns if that will help?"

"That would help. Okay, keep their guns and knives if you have them. We'll take care of them on the way home. Did they give you the Postcode?"

"Yes!"

"Thank you send them out at your convenience. Don't mention this to Stuart because he can hear your words as well."

"They'll be out soon."

He smiled and turned around, put his gun in its holster and walked back to the car. John closed the door, looked at the guns and knives on the table, the larger guns, four knives and put them in a drawer. Entering the room, he looked at everyone and noticed Gabrielle had Stuart in her trance and was getting more information from him. He took the notepad and pen from Lynda and started to write on it.

He first showed the notepad to Gabrielle and Lynda, then the two men and the room fell silent.

George can hear what is being said. You two men are to be killed on your way home. I am keeping all your knives and guns. However, to give you a fair chance, you may keep the smaller guns. Stuart you will be sat in the back of the car; you Todd will be sat in the front.

"All I can say is good luck on your way home. Shoot each other on a road near a cliff." John said laughing and looked for their microphones which he soon found pulling them apart.

"Gabrielle, do you have enough information from him only I don't want those two blokes outside causing us trouble?"

"I suppose I'm finished with him," she replied.

"Right boys, time to go. Your coats are by the front door. Thanks for the visit, tell George the girls will be there on time, and I'll be needing a new job," John said with a smile.

Both men stood and looked at both girls. "Thank you for your time and cooperation. "We'll see you both again very soon," Stuart said.

"Yes, I suppose we will," Gabrielle replied wondering what was happening. The idea was to get as much information from the man as possible, but here was John turning them away.

"Here are your coats," John said, then showed them two guns he had left on the table. They each picked up a gun and put it in their coat pocket.

John opened the front door and looked across the road at the car. There was another man in the back and two men in the front, something he had missed in the two seconds he had to glance at the car before.

Sam; the driver and Bob; the man in the back had with Stuart and Todd kidnapped a bobby on his beat nearer the main shopping area so they had someone to bargain with if the police cornered them. Right now, Bob was getting himself into position with his rifle.

"Turn around," Bob said to the police officer in a rough tone. He took a pair of wire cutters from his front door pocket and cut the plastic bonds that held his arms in place behind his back.

"Here is your hat, I suggest you put it on and shout out "police officer" when you see their car as they will be shooting wild. The people they are guarding have just returned from Rome and have made a Peace Treaty with the Mafia. So, if you don't wish to die, make yourself known.

"Stay in the car until Stuart and Todd come out of the house. Here they come, open the door, and get out, wait until I tell you to run understand?"

"Yes! But why did you kidnap me just for a few hours?"

"Don't ask questions, get ready to run."

"Ummmm, which way do I run?" he asked as he got out of the car and picked up his helmet.

"I'm heading into town, you run away from it because that is where the police are coming from. Now, walk away for ten paces then run, the gunfire is about to start." Bob leaned over and pulled the door closed. "Go!" he said sounding annoyed.

As Stuart and Todd left the house, John looked over and saw the police officer getting out of the car, walking towards where the police car would come from.

"Thanks for the assistance, goodnight," John said politely and closed the door, locking it with the four locks.

It was late at night and there was little traffic about in their area. Sam had his rifle out of the backdoor window. He trained it first on Stuart.

"Come on guys, the police will be here soon," Bob said as he started the engine.

Todd ran ahead of Stuart while he was checking the road. Sam wasn't happy, but one or the other had to die here. Sam took aim and pulled the trigger four times and then another three times as he altered his aim. Todd fell to the road, dead.

As Stuart looked around to see who had fired, he felt something warm hit his chest. Then another and another bullet he now realised entered his chest and he was bleeding heavily and finding it hard to breathe.

He thought for a moment it was John and he had decided to kill them both for threatening Gabrielle and Lynda. He then saw a bright flash with his right eye come from the rear car window and he knew it was his own friends. That was the last thing the eye saw as the bullet entered his eye and went straight into his brain. He felt two more bullets hit his face; then he was on the cold road and his left eye closed; he was dead.

"Go, go, go!" Bob shouted to Sam. Bob left his favourite rifle on the back seat and clambered into the front passenger seat. As he did so, he transferred his handgun from his jacket pocket to his trouser pocket.

As the police car slowed down approaching the police officer, the car stopped. The officer in the passenger's seat had his window down.

"What's the problem officer?" Officer Frank Cole asked the man out of breath standing by their car.

"The two men down there are both dead. I was captured by the four men and kept in their car for about six hours. They let me go just before they killed their own men. Something to do with George. They are now driving off in a white BMW. I saw them walk into that house," he said pointing to the house. "I was then released from the car as the two men left the house. The people in the house may be with this gang too," he suggested out of breath.

"That I very much doubt. The people inside were trying to get information from the men but Gabrielle and Lynda Grayson are the good girls, don't you listen to the news and your morning briefings? They just returned from Rome in their own private jet after getting a Peace Treaty signed with Marco Don."

"Can I grab a lift, they took my radio and ID, in fact everything and I bought my own Stab Vest, and they are not cheap. Can I get a lift to a local station or in town to be with another officer on the beat?" he asked confused.

"Yes sure, jump in the back, you can help identify the car," officer Cole said.

As they approached the two bodies, John was examining them without touching them and kicking their guns out of the way.

"Hello John," Officer Collin Daily said. "I'll call in people to work on the dead and ensure they are all cleared up by the morning. What time are you off to see Her Majesty?"

"We need to be there by ten thirty, let your guys know Alan and myself will be keeping an eye on the bodies until reinforcements arrive. These two aren't going anywhere."

"Frank, give me that roll of police tape please." He handed it over to Collin.

"Here you are John, this will keep you happy for a while," Collin said handing him the roll of blue and white tape.

John took it from his hands, "Thanks, now go and get those two men, Sam and Bob. Sam had a rifle on the back seat, and he looks to be an excellent shot on a moving target. They both have handguns."

"Thanks for the update, we'll be off, shooters to catch." He switched his red and blue lights on then joined the traffic. Adding his siren, he was now travelling at 70mph through the snow-covered streets of London.

John and Alan put up the blue and white police tape and soon four police cars arrived, a police Hurst, a Paramedic car with a doctor on board to confirm both men were dead and could be removed to the police morgue.

Forty miles further up the road, people were reporting gunfire and a crashed car. Three hours later John received a phone call from Collin telling him the two men who shot George's men, had a shootout in the car while it was travelling at 100mph. He was in his bedroom when he got the call and was thinking of telling

Gabrielle. At three thirty in the morning, he decided not to bother her at this time of night and anyway, if he heard right the girls were still having fun.

In their bedroom, Gabrielle and Lynda were still having fun, giving each other all the love, they could. They were both naked beneath the duvet, the heating on keeping the large apartment warm after the hot country they had just come from.

They both knew Lynda would have to encounter George in three weeks' time. Despite being able to jump from one place to another, George would not rest until he found her, and he would destroy all their shops and kill the people inside them. They could not be responsible for that! Gabrielle thought, she could not allow the love of her life to die at George's hands. However, he may take her in exchange for Lynda, to be his whore, be kicked, cut and beat up, raped by one man after many men some evenings.

As Gabrielle was kissing and sucking Lynda's breasts, she felt Lynda's arms wrap around her back and one arm moved up to her head, holding her as close to her body as she could.

"I will not allow you to go through that for me and we will not be separated, we yet have a test to overcome," Lynda said.

"Perhaps this is the test," Gabrielle whispered.

"No, this is not it, Fate said two men would try and split us up. As for George, we will have to come up with an answer between the four of us."

"Four of us?" Gabrielle questioned.

"Alan and John of course, and you, the love of my life silly. Now come up here and kiss my lips like you have been kissing my tits," Lynda said laughing then realised what the time was and was quiet.

Gabrielle slithered up Lynda's body and their lips touched, so gently, tenderly, as if they were made of glass about the crack. Their tongues intertwined as their lips made contact, with remnants of expensive lipstick; their lips slipped together, rotating around and around each other as they breathed through their noses, not wishing the kiss to stop, and it didn't. Their lips were still touching, sometimes they looked into each other's green eyes, passing thoughts of pure love and adoration to each other.

"I think my love," Lynda said smiling.

"And what are you thinking about my sweetheart?" Gabrielle closed her eyes and kissed the woman she could not part from, not for a thousand or million years, they wanted to live together to see the end of the world or perhaps travel through the universe and see the stars the Omega watched over.

"I think we should get a little sleep if we are to see the Queen later this morning. We don't want to be yawning in front of her and there is so much to say and go through and what we plan to do."

"Only if, you're sure. Would you like me to make love with you once more this morning?"

"Yes, I would, but I'll settle for a kiss and sleep in your arms."

"If that's the case my love, we will do exactly as you say."

They turned over to their favourite position where Lynda felt loved, cared for and wanted. Lynda pushed her fingers through Gabrielle's long light brown hair and Gabrielle reciprocated. A soft goodnight, or good morning kiss followed. Gabrielle waited until Lynda fell asleep, her thoughts turning into dreams, then nightmares of George beating her to death, but she knew Death, or thought she did.

Her nightmare continued until a thought entered her nightmare, a soothing thought that pulled her away from the Demon and into a loving and caring person, somebody she could rely on and Gabrielle was working hard to keep Lynda's mind on her until the Demon finally dispersed and her dream state changed to calmer dreams and only then would Gabrielle allow herself to have a light snooze until 6:00am when once again it would be time to get up and get ready for work.

After breakfast, they put on their final pieces of jewellery and perfume. Put their paperwork in the briefcase, locked it and handed it to Alan.

Their car parked outside the apartment and the four people got into the back of the black limousine. Their driver closed the door, and they were seen off by Sarah, Jenny and Tina, Jenny's bodyguard who were now doing other work to get ready for the next Hats & Bags show in Italy and then in Rome, where they would remain for one week before going to the USA and opening four new shops in New York, if they managed to get over the George problem.

At Buckingham Palace, the small party wearing their medals presented to them by the Queen, were joined by the new Prime Minister, Mrs Austin, the third in a matter of weeks and they still had to get a Deputy Prime Minister who would accept the job. She was joined by Ian Galway and Philip Stanford Minister for Internal Security. Noah was standing behind them with John and

Alan who was still carrying the briefcase under command of the Queen. after a short wait they were shown into a small morning room where coffee tables and easy chairs had been arranged for everyone.

"Please sit everyone, make yourselves welcome. My dear Gabrielle and Lynda, a gunfight seems to follow you wherever you go. I have had the Palace Guards change from rifles to machine guns with live ammunition. We have two tanks at the side of the palace with instructions not to allow any vehicle through the main gates now you are here," the Queen said, trying to put everyone in a calmer mood.

Everyone laughed, knowing what they had gone through in Rome.

"No, I mean it, they have cameras and undercover armed men in the crowds. This Palace is on its highest alert and that only happens when we have State Dinners."

"We feel deeply honoured your majesty," Gabrielle replied.

"Now to business, but first, what is it I heard from my Captain David Anderson? You arrive in Rome and on the first evening Ian, you contact him asking for an extract because you said one of Marko's men killed a man in the street, then Gabrielle had to ring Captain Arthur Hammond and tell him, Ian, was frightened by the gunshot, nobody was killed a petty thief was caught and Marko's man was showing him what would happen next time to him. The men shoot small time criminals in their leg. Justice is served immediately, and the punishment given. Hence there is no shop lifting in Rome or Italy, perhaps we should do the same.

"Lynda and Gabrielle don't have a problem with guns so why do you? You then sent one of your bodyguards home foolish man, you showed my government up and myself with your stupid acts of fear. You put the team in danger, they needed an extra gun by what I saw on television.

"Now Lynda, Gabrielle do we have an agreement between the

UK and the Mafia?"

"Yes, Your Majesty," Ian said with a smile.

"Let's hear what Gabrielle and Lynda have to say, after all, it was them who set this up and did all the groundwork." The Queen rebuffed. Ian fell silent and his smile faded from his face. He had hoped to take the limelight and steal the occasion, but it had backfired on him.

"Yes, indeed we do your Majesty, despite the small battle which Marco helped us out with by adding his own men to guard us and give us an escort to the airport, we did get what we wanted and more." Gabrielle started.

"Marco has agreed to remove all his people from the UK as swiftly as possible and I have asked my sister who you have met to allow one of her Boeing 747's take those people and their families back to Rome. This will happen in two weeks' time on the 18th. On this day we will need to arrange for several coaches to pick up the men women and families and take them to Luton Airport where the plane will be waiting for them. We request that there be no customs search of bags or checks on passports as several of them do not possess a passport. Prime Minister, will that be okay with your departments?" Gabrielle asked, her green eyes looking at the Prime Minister's thoughts.

"If Your Majesty agrees then yes," Rebecca Austin replied.

"In agreement to this which we have already agreed upon, there will be no further pressure put on the shops, pubs and clubs for "Private Protection Money" to be paid to the Mafia in the UK. In Italy and Rome, this will also cease, and any new shops opened by UK or Italian people, will also not be charged these protection fees. However, if shops wish to donate money to the new hospital wing which we have helped Marco get built or the new TG Centre which now has fifty residents, mainly children aged 10 to 15 that is fine.

"These children are having guidance and psychiatric treatment to ensure this is the right way they wish to go. It is based on the system we have here, and they even have a Train Station for a restaurant, two large group rooms, a games room and parent's room for those parents interested in how their children are coping.

The children go to a local school and for their discretion is allowing our children to dress as girls or some girls as boys, we have donated a hundred computers for the secondary school.

"The new girls who attend secondary school, will have small breast implants which can be increased in size as normal girls develop. Marco has also added money to this building fund, a million Euros. Lynda and I have done the same. This has helped the situation greatly in Rome and with the Mafia. To have Marco behind us like this, and his men guarding the Train Station and buildings we use, just like our police do here in London, it is keeping his men away from our shops."

"When was all this added to the Treaty? I was not made aware of it I object to this addition, and I do not agree to our public money helping these queers." Ian burst out making the Queen and Prime Minister look at him astonished.

"Pardon me Ian, but this is your signature is it not?" Lynda retorted, showing him the official Treaty Folder.

"Yes, but what you said was added later."

"If you look at pages118 Section E, it is all there. You will find it on your signed copy as well. And Ian if I hear you call our children that horrendous name again, I will boil you alive, is that understood?" Lynda asked as her eyes turned bright green and Ian felt his stomach getting hot.

"Yes, Yes," he answered. "Your Majesty please," Ian begged.

"Ian you will never use that word again unless you want me to exile you to the North Pole. If you listened to Gabrielle, you would have heard her say Marko put in a million Euros and Gabrielle and Lynda put in a million UK pounds. How much did you put in?" the Queen demanded to know.

"Nothing, I don't agree with them living here or in Rome, they should have been put out of their misery when they reached the age of seven, then they wouldn't be a burden on us the taxpayer." he added.

"I will be informing the treasury you wish to donate your last year's salary to Gabrielle and Lynda's charity here and you will repay the treasury," The Queen insisted.

"Yes, Your Majesty," he replied.

"Thank you, Ian, Your Majesty," Gabriele replied.

"You're welcome Gabrielle, he deserved it." The Queen replied smiling.

Ian was frantically flipping through the pages of his copy of the Treaty, there seemed to be so many more pages than the last time he had looked at it and what had he signed for?

It was now Thursday, and they had returned yesterday, he didn't read anything Tuesday evening or Monday night, in fact, he had hardly read the Treaty, just the first and second pages. So, what had he been up to? Then it dawned on him, it was Christine, sharing his bed. It was the only time they had to be alone and alone they were each night as soon as the evening meal was over or an evening out with Gabrielle and Lynda had come to an end. He looked at Lynda then Gabrielle knowing he had not only let them down, but the government and the Queen.

"I do apologise Lynda, these pages had slipped my mind, of course you are correct," he said putting his papers back into his shaking hands, upset what the Queen had done to him for the words he had said about the transgender children.

"I think you have all done a grand job and I am very happy with the way you have, what shall we say, curved the Mafia's appetite to help your organisation rather than take money from shops and other venues," The Queen said looking at Gabrielle and Lynda.

"I agree that the rest of the Mafia in this country will have a safe passage back to Italy or Rome when they can all be contacted. It would be favourable if you could let the Mafia know this as the last job for the Treaty. Once they have left, we will in due course invite The Don and his family here for a Treaty Banquet which you and your team will also be expected to attend as Peace Officers, not you Ian, your dismissed from your current post." The Queen explained.

"Thank you, Your Majesty, of course we will attend and sort out the final Mafia in this country," Gabrielle replied.

The meeting continued for a further half an hour before they all stood, bowed and walked out of the morning room. Getting into their limo, Noah joined them then they drove off heading towards their main shop on Kensington High Street.

They talked with their staff giving them hope for the future that their shop would not be targeted by George and his armed men. From there they travelled to the Shard where they had a light meal and the three bodyguards discussed what would happen when the time came to visit George.

"I for one do not think either of you should attend this meeting. He will I am sure, kill both of you and have his men find us after," Alan said firmly, thinking only of Lynda and Gabrielle.

"He will not kill us outright Alan," Lynda replied as the soft drinks arrived at their table. They paused talking for a moment as the plates of food were dispensed and the soft drinks poured into their wine glasses. They needed clear heads lives were indeed at stake.

Two hours later, after discussing their plans for the following three-weeks to the date they were to meet George, they returned home and got down to talking with their wives, husbands and partners. Noah had to move in with Tina and get to know the large apartment. The builders were still working on the second floor which would also accommodate the large thirty- inch reflector telescope.

During the early evening, Gabrielle left the family and walked briskly to her office where she looked up the position of all their eight stores in New York and three in Texas. They had already signed a lease for a further three stores in Washington DC and six in Washington. In the spring they would expand to the hotter climates of the USA to be ready for the hot summer, but with George on their backs, had decided to not open them until the battle was finally over.

Looking at the map of New York, she noticed there was another store they could lease and perhaps draw George there in Manhattan. She returned to the lounge twenty minutes later with an idea in her head which she sent to Lynda as she walked through the hallway to the lounge.

Upon entering the lounge, everyone looked at her wondering where she had been and what she had been up to.

"I like the idea," Lynda said as soon as she saw her wife.

Nobody else had any idea of what Lynda was talking about.

"There is a store we could lease in Manhattan, 66th street, Lincoln Centre. It's on the ground floor and it would be a good place to put another store as we don't have one in Manhattan and the other stores are doing very well. The thing is by taking the fight to the USA, we don't have so many stores to protect as we do in the UK alone.

"Then there is Europe. We have shops scattered throughout the place in most countries now, we have at least three shops, it's a lot to protect. If we say we are in the US, then we don't have so many stores and the police all carry guns. No disrespect John, Alan, Noah and Tina, but they are all over the place and a shootout is quite common for them. We will stand a better chance and the Mafia are not there, at least those we have made a treaty with.

"All George can do is take his men with him and fly or go by boat to the US and set up a camp where we hope will be by the new store and there we can put in just two ladies who know what they are supposed to be doing to sell our Hats and Bags, and the rest will be trained marksmen and women who are capable of disarming a homemade bomb in a few seconds, because that is all they may well have.

"All the staff, including the trained shooters, will always wear bulletproof vests and have bomb protection gear near them, I mean the clear shields and a hard hat so they can also protect customers and many of them will be our own staff who will also be wearing bulletproof vests.

"It will be a store we can control, have the police watching and maybe have a few of them as customers as well. Well, what do you all think of my idea, it has to be a team agreement as we are all in it together and Lynda and myself will be the main targets that he will be looking for?" Gabrielle asked everyone in the room including her mother.

"Dear, it's very, dangerous for you both and George is a nasty piece of work, especially since he's basically insane. He must be in extreme pain with his head and if he has gangrene in his leg, then he will be in terrible pain with that and flying from the UK to the US, it's an eight-hour flight if the wind is behind the plane. He could well get blood clots in his legs which could move up to his lungs or heart," her mother said smiling.

"I would go along with you on your idea, but tell us, how do you intend to get George and his men away from the UK and travel to the States?" Alan asked Gabrielle.

"This is where it gets tricky. When we left the hospital after Mike had been injured, one of the reporters who works for the London Press newspaper; didn't recognise me in my latest form and I had to speak to him before he recognised me, and we had only seen each other a few days previously.

"Since George has not seen me lately, I was thinking of going myself to see him and pretend I'm another woman and down-dress myself. John will be with me as a curtesy to Angela, who will be my other self and give him a message personally that we are both in New York and at the same time I tell him, Lynda will call him from our new shop and that if he wants her then he will need to come to New York as that is where we are living now, and we have left the UK for good because of his threats.

"If he goes to attack me, I can jump out of his grasp and I have been testing this idea with John, I can take him with me, only a short distance so far, but it will be far enough away from George's grasp. John will not leave my side the whole time; we only have to be close to each other and hold hands and we're off," Gabrielle explained.

"How far can you jump then?" her mother asked, not really knowing what her daughter was talking about. She had never seen her daughter jump or knew very, little of her latest discussions with Death and Fate.

"We can jump together for about two miles, which is where Alan will be with our car ready to go at a moment's notice."

"I didn't realise you could jump that far, I thought it was just a few metres away, like running very, fast in ultra-slow-motion movements. I did see you move fast or jump in France some time ago, but that is the only time I've seen you do anything like that," Brenda replied, smiling at her daughter.

"And how far can you jump Lynda?" Brenda asked.

"Further than Gabrielle by myself, about six thousand miles, but I'm working on it with Alan. I can jump further, by thinking of a place I know. I could jump to the US and arrive in one of our stores, or on top of the Empire State Building. It's a case of thinking hard of the place you wish to end up and as long as I or we have been there before, then I can travel that far in an instant," Lynda explained.

"For Gabrielle's idea to work, I will travel with her to find George and then while she is talking to him, I'll jump to our shop in the States and call George on my phone. Once he can confirm I'm in New York, and the conversation is over, I'll jump back to Alan in his car and tell them what is happening and if Alan needs to be ready to move in a hurry; by the time Gabrielle has jumped with John, the car will be started and ready to move off in any direction Gabrielle tells us while she is jumping," Lynda replied, making some of the people think this was all science fiction.

"I think it's a better plan than we came up with this afternoon," John said, thinking it through.

"The only one aspect of this plan that is not good is that Lynda will be alone in the States while we are all here and there will be nothing any of us can do to help her," Alan said also thinking the plan through more thoroughly than John had.

"If I may say something?" Noah asked.

"Go ahead Noah, anything to help we'll listen to," Gabrielle replied holding Lynda's hand firmly in hers sending her all the love she had for her into her mind and heart.

"We are all concerned about Lynda, she will have no one with her, but, what if Brenda were in the back of the shop with Mike, out of the way. Penny could be looking in through the shop window or walking past the shop showing interest in it. She will call Mike as soon as she sees George's men. Brenda is primarily there in case something goes wrong.

"Lynda might fall on the floor and bang her head, so you are unconscious. You may get hit by one of George's men and you're in shock for a few minutes. Brenda can help you get on your feet. Brenda could call Alan and let him know what is happening. If she needs more medical help you take her to the nearest hospital. We don't want you passing out and fall into the Atlantic Ocean on your way home.

"It might help if you had Jack with you. He's been in the US for a few years now and is known in all your stores. He could kill George's men if they find the place. Mike would protect Brenda and the back of Linda if George's men come in through the back of the store. I would suggest Brenda and her people fly out a few days before to get themselves acquainted with the store. Lynda would jump into the store before any of George's men arrive," Noah suggested and paused looking around at the faces staring at him.

"I hope I haven't gone too far and Lynda, take your passport with you in case you have to fly home. Gabrielle, you would need your Passport if you were to jump there yourself to be with

Lynda," Noah said.

Tina was holding his hand as silence filled the room. Everyone was stunned and looking at each other wondering what Gabrielle or Lynda might say in reply to him.

"I'm sorry Lynda, Gabrielle, I have gone too far and insulted Lynda." The girl's eyes turned bright green as they talked to each other. Then their eyes darkened, and they both smiled at Noah.

"Noah, this is the second time you have come up with an idea we did not even think about and now you come up with this brilliant plan to have someone there with Lynda we can all rely on. It's a brilliant idea. I like it," Gabrielle replied.

"I think it's an outstanding idea. You have given me, mum to help me if something goes wrong and I know Mike is a first-class bodyguard. You have covered all angles as best you can, not knowing what George will have up his sleeve and you have even remembered everyone's name, here and in the States," Lynda added and shook Noah's hand.

"Thank you, Noah an excellent idea, are you like this all the time?" Gabrielle asked.

"Sometimes being a bodyguard, you have to think of your next move on the run," he replied.

"We don't want many people to know what we can do, but I think mum could tell Jack your plan when she arrives in New York," Lynda said smiling at Noah. Mum what do you think of Noah's plan?" Lynda asked her mother.

"I'm glad you asked, when do we leave? It's a far better plan to keep Lynda safe and you will all know there is someone to take care of her if something goes wrong." Brenda said with a smile on her face.

"I agree," added Gabrielle, holding Lynda's hand firmly in hers.

"Yes, me too," Lynda added.

"I suggest we find a hotel for you," Gabrielle started to say. Her mother put her hand in the air.

"We have our own apartment, we'll stay there. Jack has his apartment, and he will sleep there. I can say to the staff, I have just come to look at the stores we are thinking of opening. And if all goes well, we'll stay a few extra days so I can do a little shopping, I need a new dress for when I go to the TG Office and go through the paperwork that is piling up and six young boys have been asking for our help," Brenda said.

"If you are sure mum, then we'll go with Noah's plan, Well done Noah, keep coming up with your ideas, we would all love to hear more from you," Gabrielle said and shook his hand. "Now, I think we need a good cup of coffee with some biscuits, what say you all?" Gabrielle asked, smiling at Noah.

Both girl's eyes were flashing bright green again, as they spoke quickly to each other. "I forgot to say, you'll leave five days before the meeting with George; this will give you time to be looking around our shops and you and Penny wear a nice hat and carry a matching bag," Gabrielle said smiling. Yeses were heard around the table as Wendy got up to make the coffee. Sarah and Penny also stood and followed Wendy into the kitchen despite her objections.

Gabrielle and Lynda moved their heads together and gave each other a kiss, just a quick one, but it was noticed by everyone and they all knew they were deeply in love and still thrilled by the fact they had their whole lives together and when George was out of the way, their future could be mapped out quite easily.

With the plan now firmly in everyone's head, they all settled down to watch a film.

When the two girls eventually climbed, tired into bed, Gabrielle turned out her bedside light and slipped her arms around the person she loved more than anyone else in the world. She knew in her head the plan was dangerous and there would be times when both their lives could change in an instant if George, in chronic pain with his head and leg, pulled the trigger of his gun, or threw a knife at Gabrielle, or had one of his henchmen kill Gabrielle and John when their backs were turned.

Lynda snuggled into Gabrielle's breasts and looked up into her green eyes and kissed her lips.

"I love you," she whispered.

"I love you too," Gabrielle replied instantly, and their bodies commenced to increase in movement.

Lynda's body moved to the right, and she lowered the thin straps of her silk nightie and Gabrielle pulled it down over her body as their legs intertwined, holding each other in place.

They were both breathing deeply as their arms moved up, down and around each other's backs. Their lips rotated around each other as their tongues slithered into each other's mouth and gently fondled the inside.

Lynda slithered off Gabrielle's front while they were kissing passionately, her right hand rippled down the front of her body and she inserted three fingers into Gabrielle's wet vagina,

Gabrielle was soon squirming with delight as they continued to kiss, and Gabrielle tried to take in deep breaths and squirm with delight. Gabrielle was just about to lower her hand over Lynda's body when Lynda stopped her and parted her lips.

"You can play with me in a few minutes, right now I want to bring you to an orgasm . . . or more," she whispered into Gabrielle's ear.

"Oh, if you insist my love," Gabrielle replied, feeling Lynda's fingers get deeper into her vagina and finding her 'G' Spot, Gabrielle was soon turning her body this way and that as feelings of pure delight flowed through her body and her juices started to flow down her vagina walls over Lynda's fingers and into her hand.

Lynda withdrew her fingers from Gabrielle's vagina and rubbed her wet hand over Gabrielle's left breast and commenced to lick it dry and kissed her breasts, sucking her nipples bringing Gabrielle to another orgasm.

"Oh yes, don't stop, it's brilliant," Gabrielle sighed, she kissed

Lynda's forehead then her face and finally lips.

As they continued to kiss, Gabrielle put her hand under her pillow and brought out one of her special vibrators that Lynda loved being used on her.

As Gabrielle brought it down behind her, Lynda squirmed with delight and her green eyes lit up the room as she felt the vibrator enter her vagina.

Gabrielle worked the vibrator in and out of her vagina wetting her walls and touching her 'G' Spot. At the same time, she was kissing Lynda's breasts and playing with her nipples with her tongue. Lynda's breasts were very wet now as Gabrielle licked and kissed them while her right hand worked the vibrator in and out of her,

Slowly, Gabrielle left Lynda's breasts and licked her way down the front of her body and when she got to her vagina, she removed the vibrator, licked and kissed her clitoris then pushed her tongue inside her vagina and started to lick her saturated walls and removing her tongue, she inserted two fingers into her to find her 'G' Spot and for the following five minutes Lynda was all Gabrielle's as she played and rubbed her 'G' Spot while she licked her clitoris.

When Lynda had an orgasm for the fifth time, Gabrielle slowly kissed the front of her body and worked her way up to her head and they kissed on their lips once again.

"I love you so much," Lynda whispered.

"I love you just as much and I'll never stop loving you; ever," Gabrielle whispered back.

The house was silent, everyone asleep except for the fire and burglar alarm system. Gabrielle looked at the bedside clock."

"Crikey love, it's five to three and we need to be up early in the morning to start getting the lease sorted and the store fitted out and ready for George.

"It's your fault we're awake so late my love, you shouldn't have gone down on me for the last time."

"Nonsense, you needed to have the last orgasm after what we have had to discuss today, and I only hope you liked it."

"Liked it? Gabrielle, it was the best, ever. I love how you make me feel and you're, so feminine with it as well. I don't ever want to be with another man ever again. Just you my love, just you and nobody else. My life is fulfilled now, and I met you just at the right time."

"We met each other at the right time, or you would have died at the hands of Ian," she replied pulling Lynda close to her, so their breasts touched. "I think it's time for sleep now or you'll be up late in the morning," Gabrielle replied and kissed Lynda on her lips. “Just lay on top of me and drop off to sleep, sweetheart, the love of my life,” Gabrielle suggested.

“I’ll take you up on that, Lynda replied and gently moved her body on top of Gabrielle, wrapping her legs around Gabrielle’s legs feeling sexy and tired at the same time but by the time Lynda had kissed Gabrielle good night, Lynda had dropped off to sleep and Gabrielle put her arms around her body holding her close and safe on top of her. Lynda was now fast asleep and once she was in the position Gabrielle loved, held her firmly in place, a few minutes later Gabrielle was herself asleep dreaming of her wife.

Chapter 4

When the time finally came for the girls to meet George, Gabrielle, in a white floral dress, no gold except her wedding ring sat in the back of the car with John which had arrived outside their apartment. Lynda and Alan were ready to follow at a distance behind.

Lynda was keeping in touch with Gabrielle telepathically, a gift from Fate to both girls for agreeing to a bet between Himself and Death. They raced up the M1 onto the A50 then joined the M6 to Liverpool.

"I told you before, I am not at all happy about this I'm sure that lunatic George will kill me because I only have one of you. He has already killed two drivers because they refused to collect you both. Now I only have one of you," Alfred their driver said to Gabrielle in the back seat.

"I told you, all will be explained to George when we get there but I thank you for your warning. We will help you if we can," Gabrielle replied.

"It would not be so bad, if it were not for that car now following us. We picked it up as we came off the motorway. I could lose it and drop you both here and say you were not at home if you wish?"

"No Alfred. I thank you for your offer of help, but George will only kill you by the sound of it and he may try and destroy my shops."

"Oh yes, he'll do that alright, he's been hoping you would not come but he will only kill you anyway. I'm sorry to say especially you and John, as you were the instigation of all this. Had you allowed Lynda to die and not rescue her even fight Ian and George off not once but twice in two different timelines but the first time, you showed great courage. I have seen a lot of fights where men were fighting for their lives, but never like you did the first time around.

"You were not only fighting for your life, but that of Lynda and that copper. How you managed to throw Ian's knives at George was insane girl. I was standing around the corner supposedly guarding the cameraman in silence. I didn't want you to see me, I thought I would be dead in a few seconds. But I watched you take on his sword which was double edged and razor sharp. I know that because it was I who sharpened it.

"I watched that sword as it cut your hands to shreds and then he thrust it into your stomach. I thought that was it for you but no, you were a man then and a man to contend with. How you managed to pull that sword out of you I'll never know or understand why you did it. What drove you on? Poor Lynda was looking at you, sure you were dead or going to die.

"I watched almost as if it was in slow motion as you withdrew the sword pushed it away from Ian and did an impossible turn to the back of Ian, so you were back-to-back. I thought you were going to fall to the floor behind him, but you didn't, you grabbed his last knife in your shredded hands, tossed it from one bloody hand to another then turned and put the knife to Ian's throat.

"You slit it, ear to ear, just like he would have done to you had he had the opportunity. You then thrust the knife into his heart not once but twice, just to make sure he was dead. You must almost had had enough as you looked to Lynda, eye to eye, sending a million thoughts to her which you thought you would never get a chance to do in real life. You fell to the floor into a pool of blood from the copper's severed leg.

"I was sure you were going to die there and then but no; you unbuckled your belt in excruciating pain, pulled it through your trousers and tied it as tight as you could around that copper's stump to stop the bleeding and then after talking to him you finally passed out.

"Lynda was on top of you as you passed out and she could see Ian and George were dead, in the first fight for life. She was kissing your face all over screaming for the paramedics to come down, but they were stopped by that dumb Police Commander who was dishonourably fired, and his name was mentioned in every paper in the world so he could never get a job in the police at any rank again.

"She must have kissed you a hundred times and blew into your mouth trying to bring you back to life before she ran screaming her head off down the central aisle and around the two children Ian had killed when all he had to do was send them out of the bookshop. He was insane with jealously and all he wanted was Lynda and to do what he wanted with her; to kill her for what she had done to him.

"Lynda absolutely flew into the ranks of police officers and grabbed the green bag from the paramedic, God alone knows what she was going to do with it. The paramedic of course pushed his way through the ranks of police and ran after Lynda and together they kept Paul alive for a few extra minutes before the Dr arrived and started to cut you open and stitch up your stomach. I can remember the fear in his voice as he called for help and blood. As far as I recall he didn't shut up until another Dr arrived and luckily, he was a heart surgeon.

"Your wife, now, in this timeline, remained by your head, speaking in tongues constantly while the heart surgeon opened your chest pulled out your heart and Lynda held it, praying over you or talking to someone all the time while she held your heart in her hands then she started it again. I saw you open your eyes for a split second and look at Lynda.

"Before you closed them, your eyes sent a thousand words to her eyes, but I don't know if she understood you. That Dr worked a miracle on you as he stitched your chest up then wrapped your stomach in medical clingfilm.

"He was shouting his head off for a medical extract by helicopter. Despite the snow the entire road was closed for police and medical helicopters that were rushing all the patients to hospital trauma centres.

"I would say most of the police who broke ranks and helped the hospital staff, even just holding bags of liquid or blood in the air were crying their eyes out, because it was their fault it had gone like this.

"The copper was taken first because you had put a tourniquet around his stump. You were next and in such a state the Surgeon went with you, but Lynda was not allowed in the helicopter, she was taken by a fast police car with your mother father and John to hospital and the police car didn't stop all the way while it was traveling at 80mph through the streets of London in the snow.

"It was as if I was everywhere in the shop and outside watching young girls and boys being carried to ambulances which took them under police escort to hospital. I was to be your witness for this time of what happened. The Nighting-Gale nurses were working hard trying to keep young girls alive.

"They had already discovered Ian had used a knife or sword on the girls and one boy, who needed a splenectomy. Because Dr Reynolds was so far behind them, the Nightingale nurses, with his permission gave the girl's a splenectomy without any anaesetic." Alfred had tears in his eyes now and had to wipe them so he could continue driving.

"Those poor girls, it should never have got that far, there was no need for the endless death and almost death inside that bookshop. I watched this nurse, it was like I was standing over her, my penance for being there I suppose. This one nurse went to the doctor and without even asking she took what she needed and ran two aisles down from where Dr Reynolds was working on another girl.

"She knelt down by a motionless girl, took her pulse, used the scissors she had to cut her dress apart looked at the girl again and used the scalpel cutting deep into the girl's skin, put the scalpel down in a blue dish opened her up and pushed her hand inside her and pulled out what I now know was her spleen, used the clamps to cut off the supply of blood in and out and cut out the spleen, put it in a small plastic bag then looked again at her as the girl opened her eyes.

"They talked and then the girl passed out again as the nurse turned her over and checked from where she had been stabbed twice in the stomach. As the girl turned in horror at what was happening to her. The scalpel again was in her hand went deep through the knife lines and she used her head torch to see where the blood was coming from. She saw where the two knife wounds were in the girls' stomach, liquid, stomach acid, and blood were oozing out of the cuts which the nurse, made, Angela was her name, the girl was awake again, Angela looked down at her and spoke, quietly and calmly. Then she took hold of a police officers' hand. He had knelt and was now holding the bag of saline in the air, keeping fluids going into her body.

"The copper was talking quietly with the girl, asking her name that sort of thing while Angela stitched up her stomach in two places. As she was awake Angela checked her legs and feet and the poor girl felt nothing. She turned the girl slowly over again and looked at her back. A moment later she found it, a small cut to the lumbar region of her spine. She pressed it and blood came out together with a small piece of metal.

"Angela asked if she could move her toes and the girl said yes and she could feel her legs. It was just that small piece of metal that broke off from the tip of the small knife Ian was using as well. There was a small bleed but that would be looked at in hospital.

"She called Dr Reynalds to her, but he was now checking what the other nurse had done to her girl. When he came down a minute later, he was amazed to see the girl wide awake. He checked her over and allowed Angela to call for an evac. The Dr checked the paperwork, and signed it at the bottom above Angela's signature, the person who carried out the operation and the temporary stomach repair as she would need an operation in hospital.

"There were still instruments protruding from the girls' stomach as she was strapped to a helicopter bed and then transferred with a helicopter paramedic taking over her care. He too was amazed to see the girl wide awake and as he looked at her notes, he saw that so far, she had no pain relief which he quickly gave to her.

"As soon as the girl was taken away, Angela's gloves came off and a new pair went on as she moved to another isle to start on another girl who was down and hardly breathing.

"Originally, I was there to stop Lynda getting away and nothing more. I killed no one, I think I was there as an observer and recall the timeline when it was needed.

"I saw you, your other self, with the book in your hands and I thought is this an idiot trying to get himself killed to show off to Lynda at the back of the room. I thought you were going to try and hit Ian on the back of the head, I had no idea you were going for his knife so you could get closer to the maniac. You would need an incredibly good reason to attack Ian, I never knew you loved the girl with all your heart, especially as you only met midmorning. It was a romance made in Heaven and you were soulmates right from the start.

"I will remind you that the love of your life is not with you now and you technically have nothing here to fight for. Insane George will kill you, be assured of that. I just hope that he will not kill me as well," Alfred finally said with tears rolling down his face.

"Thank you, Alfred for sharing that time with us, I must admit I didn't know what had happened, my mind was on other things. I didn't realise what it was like for the nurses and Dr's trying to save everyone, they did a fine job. They did a good job on me as well; I saved Lynda's life then it was her turn to save mine.

"If George recalls the first timeline, then why is he so insistent that Lynda was or is his wife?" Gabrielle asked.

"That's his head injury, he's all mixed up now; not knowing one timeline from another. His right leg is almost black now and he must be in horrendous pain with it, he's taking cocaine for the pain, I suppose it's the best drug he could take," Alfred replied. Gabrielle knew at once that neither George nor Alfred should be able to recall the first timeline as they didn't recall it when it changed to the second time around. She guessed this was another little test Death had thrown in to see if they could get out of it without injury, not that they could die, they were both protected by Death, but others around them could.

"May I ask where Lynda is?" Alfred asked.

"Lynda is in New York opening our new store."

"That's not good if she is by herself. George sent four men to New York yesterday to check out your new store. They are carrying guns and have an injection that will put her to sleep for a few days so that George can get his monies worth out of her while she is sleeping. She'll be in a right mess once she wakes, but that is just part of it, after they have patched her up, they intend to bring her back to the UK for a gang bang celebration and finally to be recoupled to George who will take over from where he left off and if he can get you as well, then it will be a double whammy if you get my drift?"

Gabrielle knew Lynda was safe in the car behind, but she didn't like the idea of her going to the States without her. Her mum was already in the shop with Mike and Jack hidden in the room at the back which would become their storeroom. Jack would exit the door of the future storeroom and silently walk up behind Lynda when she needed him.

"Lynda my love," She paused a moment to listen to John.

"You were talking aloud, tell Jack to use his silencer and no hostages or people left alive. Put their bodies in the store we'll dispose of them when we get to the States late tomorrow," John said and smiled at Gabrielle. He held her hand and pulled a key chain from his pocket and made a whoof sign with his hands. Gabrielle nodded in reply then a reply came from Lynda.

"It's alright my love, Jack is here with some friends, and he's carrying as well and has already put a silencer on his barrel. They will be standing inside the store by the window looking out for anyone British, apparently, we stand out a mile when we're there."

"You two take care in there, no mishaps and don't get caught, he's vile and needs to meet Death right now, if You're listening that is."

"I'm sure He is," Gabrielle replied.

Alfred turned and grinned, then looked back to the road. Ten minutes later they headed up to the richer part of the city and before them was a grand house, at the head of the cul-de-sac. It was a large ten-bedroom house, over three stories. Top two floors the bedrooms, all en-suite, large enough for a king size bed, sofa, table, and chairs for morning coffee looking out over the neighbourhood.

Downstairs, two very, large reception rooms, a library and large office. Basement, kitchens, laundry room and six bedrooms for the staff. Infront of a games room, swimming pool and wine cellar, which by now had been ransacked and consumed.

Gabrielle was getting worried, but she tried desperately not to let it show. She shifted in her seat from the side window next to John. Her jump gift was still working but she knew Death could be cunning, whereas Fate was more sincere and kept to His promises.

Gabrielle sent a message to Lynda not to jump but she was a second too late, Lynda was gone and, in the States. The link she had with her was still there and Gabrielle warned her to be extremely careful, Death was playing a game with us and He was right here in the car.

"Death, what is it you want to see from me?" Gabrielle asked.

"I want to see if you will fight for Lynda like you did the first time around. Do you still have all that love for her because if you don't, then what is the point of continuing the bet. I may as well tell Fate the bet is over; I have won. Every soul will come to me and I will be the judge of who goes up and who goes down, but the world will end as soon as I lose interest and see you failing her love and her passion for you.

"Once you get into the house, your jump power will be temporarily . . . disabled, go and complain to Fate when this is over, for I know I will win the game which will be finished in the next thirty minutes."

Death turned to show Himself to Gabrielle, He was driving slower now, but still going and John seemed to be unaware of what was taking place. She looked into Death's black eyes and knew this was going to be a fight like no other and they had very, little between them, much like the first timeline.

"I'll let you stay in touch with Lynda, and you can use your power of telekinesis but use it wisely. You will still at least have to fight knife to knife not with George, but one of his best assassins."

"Death, I'm wearing four-inch high-heels, can you at least give

me flat shoes like I had in the first timeline?"

"Agreed!"

Gabrielle was now wearing female flat shoes, but they could still slip off her feet and if they did, well she would fight barefoot.

"What if I lose the fight?"

"Then the Game is over, but have no fear, Lynda and yourself;

will spend eternity together . . . in my domain."

"Will Lynda be able to see the fight?"

"I will stop time in New York, so Lynda will be able to see you and the way things work out. She will not be able to call out to you as she did before because that only gave you more love in your heart to win, even if it caused your death."

"I thought you said we couldn't die and that was the main rule in this gamesmanship, or gameswomanship?"

"You are quite right." Came a booming voice into the car. Fate appeared in His red cape and took over the front passenger seat.

"Gabrielle is quite right, and I will not be taken for a ride Death. We had a deal, and the deal still stands. By what I have seen, there is still a great deal to see in New York and it will be far better than giving Gabrielle a one-sided fight, not that she would lose mind you, there is a great deal of love between these two girls, far more than You give them credit for.

"You could be missing out on a far better ending than you have tried to create here with practically a no-win scenario. Gabrielle, you are back in your favourite shoes and the gifts I gave you are back in use, all of them.

"Come my friend, let Alfred drive these two-good people into the jaws of Death and let us see how they get out of this mess and if I may say, as humans often do, into another."

Death laughed and put his arm around Fate and a second later both disappeared. Fate winked his eye at Gabrielle and the bonds that had been around their hands were gone.

John's Glock was on the front passenger seat and as they pulled up, Gabrielle pulled the gun to her hand then handed it to John and he slipped it into its holster.

Two men opened the back doors and ordered Gabrielle and John out of the car. They both walked to the front of the car, walking slowly and holding hands so that if needed they could get out of the building in an instant.

Two men holding guns on them, followed behind and as they entered the building two more men took the lead as they turned right and entered a large reception room. It was grand that was for sure. Pictures by famous artists adorned the walls, there was even a Picasso. Fine furniture filled the room, and, in the middle, a large chair decorated in red velvet with a high back in gold decoration.

Sat in the chair, looking to be in considerable pain was George dressed in an expensive suit, and wearing a loose fitting red and gold decorated robe. A man stood either side of him with a gun in their hand. The man on the right was preparing three lines of cocaine and put his gun in his pocket. When he was ready, he offered it up to George who snorted the three lines.

A moment later he sat upright and obviously was not in so much pain and under the influence of the cocaine.

"Sit down Gabrielle, John, take the weight off your feet," George said feeling slightly better now the pain was abating. They sat side by side in the middle of a four-seater comfortable sofa. As they sat, John removed the miniature smoke grenade from his pocket and held it in his right hand.

"It seems I am in the presence of the great Gabrielle Grayson and her bodyguard John; licenced to kill no doubt. I hold no grudge for you John, in the first timeline you were not there and in the second, well you gave me the opportunity to escape, so I thank you.

"But you Gabrielle, first you put a knife through my hand then a minute later you put another through my heart and killed me and I spent I don't know how long in a place; well, it definitely wasn't Heaven. Then you go and marry my wife and have her all to yourself and then you change into a woman, now how is that? Didn't she want you as a man?" George shouted at her and grinned.

"No, she didn't and that was because of all the abuse she had gone through with you and Ian. The multiple rapes, gang bangs, cuts to her body and breasts. After you killed your own wife and her family you raped Lynda every night of the week, watched other men beat the living daylights out of her, beat her to the brink of death. Yes, there were times you helped her, stopped some men beating her to death, but you let them use their knives on her, slicing her body apart, watching her almost bleed out. Was it your intent to kill her as well as your wife?

"Did she ever do anything towards you that was aggressive? She couldn't, you had permission to do what you liked with her from her husband Ian.

"Lynda was Ian's wife until I killed him, and he was shot in the second timeline by John. You managed to put her off men completely and I saved her from the Hell you and Ian, who was supposed to protect and love her, put her through. It is no wonder she loves me, and I love her with all my heart, man or woman, it makes no difference.

"I would and will give my life and soul for her, would you?"

"No, all I want is the money I should have made from her, and she is my wife no matter what you may say and where is the bitch?"

"Safe and far away from you. She's in New York looking over the new store we are going to open soon. I can ring her if you like and you'll see her for yourself, in New York."

"Yes, I would like to see her, call her now, video call, you can afford the call no matter how long it takes."

In New York, at the store, four men came in through the open door and crept into the empty store. All they knew was that Lynda would be here by herself and they were supposed to get hold of her, put her to sleep and take her to their hotel where they would all have her while she was asleep, and they could do whatever they liked with her. They had a photo of her, and she did look gorgeous, almost like an angel, they were all looking forward to fucking her, front and back and both together.

As they moved further into the store Lynda walked forward and they saw a girl who looked so beautiful their sexual desires were taking over their minds.

"Hello, are you Lynda?" one of the men asked with a huge grin on his face.

"Yes, I am she, what do you want here and why have you come into my store? We are closed."

"We've come for you, George sent us, he wants you back, but we'll take our time with that." The man held a syringe in his hand and started to laugh. Then Jack stepped forward and stood in front of Lynda.

"I think you're all intruding in this store. But you're here now. Put down the syringe and tell me if there are any more of George's men here in New York right now?" Jack asked.

"Just us, how many men do you think it will take to put the girl to sleep then take her to our place? Now stand aside boy and let us men get on with our job. We don't want to hurt you and after all, it is four against one."

Just then they heard the door close loudly and the locks engaged. They turned around to see two more young men standing behind them.

"Is this some kind of joke, did Gabrielle send some young boys to do a man's job?" the man with the syringe asked as he turned back to see Jack holding his gun at them.

"Now look kid, put the gun down and we'll take the girl and leave it at that. I bet it isn't even loaded, but this gun is," he added and pulled his gun from his trousers and went to point it at Jack.

There was a puff of smoke from the end of Jack's Glock and the man dropped the gun and syringe to the floor holding his bleeding hand close to his chest.

"Kill him, then his friends, then we take the girl," the man shouted in pain.

As the three men started to remove their guns, Jack looked at them.

"Excellent idea." Without aiming, he shot each of the three men between their eyes, then an extra bullet through their heart just to be sure they were dead.

The man left standing looked left to right, seeing his men on the floor dead. "George will ensure he gets her. He'll send more and more men here until he does," he seethed.

"I'll be waiting for them, and you won't see them. Sorry!" he added, then raised his gun and shot him between the eyes and again in the heart before he fell to the floor.

"Well done, Jack, I'm so proud of you, have you been shooting somewhere?"

"The local police force let me use their shooting range and enter competitions, I nearly always come first. I have to let them win at times," he said laughing. His Glock was already back in its holster as he smiled at Lynda. "You okay, they haven't hurt you have they by any chance?" he asked looking into her green eyes which were shinning like mirrors. He could see his friend behind him with a gun and the syringe.

Before he had a chance to go for his gun, it was gone from its holster and in the hand of Lynda. She pulled the trigger twice; the first bullet went between the man's eyes and the second through his heart.

"Let's get rid of that damn syringe, shall we?" Lynda asked and pointed Jack's gun at it and fired again, breaking the syringe apart and spilling the contents all over Jack's so-called friend. She handed the Glock back to Jack and he slipped a new clip in it before putting it away.

"You been practicing as well?" Jack asked.

"You know me Jack, I just have the knack. I'm going to like the States. I'll get myself a gun as well, plenty of bad people to shoot. We could go into business together 'Have Guns Will Travel'. Only joking but I'm sure John would like to join in, Alan too." Lynda joked.

"No, they wouldn't and you're not having a gun either, we employ people to look after us even if you can use your power to get a good aim. Now, concentrate on this phone call," Gabrielle said into her head.

"Spoilsport, right, I'm ready, ring me when you like," she replied.

"Right George, I'll ring her right now and you can see for yourself where she is," Gabrielle said taking out her phone and fast dialling her number.

"Hello love, George doesn't think you're in New York," she said putting the phone on loudspeaker.

She walked up to George and despite his guards, handed him her phone. He looked at the phone and straight into the face of Lynda.

"Prove to me you're in New York, you could be anywhere in the UK."

She panned the phone over the bodies of his men, then played the video of the killing and the remains of the syringe. "Here is my current New York bodyguard Jack, while Alan is still in the UK. Good shot isn't he, one after another, one shot right between the eyes, the second right through his heart. John, you should be proud of Jack," she said louder so that she knew George could hear her.

"Right, you're in New York that's for sure but I can send more men there to bring you back to me."

"No George, I'm not your wife or your whore. I'm married to Gabrielle, and we are extremely happy after what you did to me. You raped me every night and had your mates come in to pay for me. Then you go and threaten to kill my parents if I go to the police or try and escape.

"I escaped when my parents were away, but Ian was my husband, and we had an agreement that if I paid the mortgage and gave him five hundred pounds a week for his beer money I could write and get better.

"I had two hundred stitches and a hundred staples across my stomach, due to that last bastard you got. You didn't care how he sliced my body and breasts open, just that he had his time down to the last second when you managed to stop him and between you and Ian, robbed him of all his money. I was three weeks in hospital, and I needed an operation to have my breasts and upper torso stitched up inside and out and I still didn't tell on you.

"George I was never your wife, you killed your wife and her family, try and remember then all this can go away."

"You are my wife and I'm alive, so your marriage is nulled."

"If you try anything, the police will arrest you and you will go to prison for the rest of your life. I am not returning to the UK, we are starting in the USA now, and anyway, I like it here, lots of nasty gangsters to kill, I love it," she said grinning at George. "If you want me, then come and find me. Now hand the phone back to Gabrielle I need to tell her something which might help you make a decision."

He threw the phone at Gabrielle and she caught it in her right hand and looked at Lynda.

"Just to say I love you and I'll see you tomorrow afternoon. Love you!"

George heard what she said and grinned at Gabrielle. "You my girl are going nowhere, a life for a life and I want yours, after I have turned you into my whore for a few months or until I get tired of you. Guards; hold her and do not let her go. If you do, I'll kill you myself." He removed a large six gun from his chair and glared at Gabrielle.

The two guards by his side holstered their guns and moved forward taking hold of Gabrielle. Two more men who were standing behind the sofa ran forward to help their colleagues seeing how mad George was getting. They held her arms as well from behind.

"George, I don't care what you do to our shops in the UK, they're, all shut, and the stock and staff gone. We're packing up in the UK and moving to the USA. We intend to open six stores in every state," Gabrielle said.

"And I will be joining my wife no matter what you say or do tomorrow afternoon when we fly into John F. Kennedy airport," Gabrielle added.

"I have already made arrangements for all my staff who wish to join us there to be aboard the aircraft I have hired tomorrow. All our stock will be flown out in the next few days, so you see, you cannot beat us in the UK. No matter what your goons do to our shops they are heavily insured and that includes, for fire and bombs.

"If you really want to fight me, then you will do it in the USA not here and I will not be your whore, even for one night and you will never have me. Neither will you have Lynda. She is my wife, and I think the world of her, she knows that. I will fight you to the death for her and I mean it. You may bring two thugs with you for the fight, better odds than when I was fighting Ian, and let's be honest, he fought hard and the way he sliced off the coppers leg, rather good work if I don't say so myself.

"I did not have the heart to allow you to kill him and it wasn't really his fault he misread what I was trying to do. Had he not intervened you and Ian would have been alive and went to prison for a long time. Lynda would have got a divorce and she would still be my wife and I would still kill for her. I would take not one but a hundred bullets for her, that is how much I love her. Would you take a bullet for her, one bullet?" Gabrielle demanded to know making up for time, she knew John still had to get into position and anyway, she was enjoying herself. "Well!"

"I wouldn't take half a bullet for her, she isn't worth it, and I don't love her, I just know she's my wife and Whore. I want my monies worth from her. I could have made a fortune from her, and I've lost all that money."

"Did you get another girl to get money from and abuse her like you love to do?"

"Of course, I have to keep money flowing in and they must do as I say and take it like she did. Otherwise, they will get a bullet in their head for their misbehaviour. I've killed at least ten girls and you will go too when I've finished with you."

"Like I said, I will be leaving here today and flying to the US tomorrow where we will start our new company and look for a decent mansion for us all to live in. We have our lives mapped out and I'm afraid you don't come into it.

"If you don't come to the USA, then we will presume that you have come to terms with your life and have recalled what really happened in the first timeline. However, I'll give you a final solution, meet me on top of the Empire State Building in a month, you carry the same as you did on that day in the first timeline, except no gun, I will arrive with four KA-Bar knives. You may bring two men Lynda will be there as on the day. I'll meet you as I was dressed on the day. Let us see how the cards fall and that will be the end of it. Do you agree?"

"What time if you do escape my clutches today?"

"Six-fifteen, pm. Same time as the fight started."

"That sounds like the perfect end for you and the start of a beautiful and very welcome income for me. Yes, let us see where the cards lie, I like that idea.

"Should you get away, which I very much doubt, then I will come to the USA to find you and my wife and I'll bring you both back here to play out my games in chains and you won't like what will happen to you both one little bit," George seethed through black teeth.

With Gabrielle walking forward to shout at George it gave John the chance to change the mini smoke bomb to his left hand and remove his Glock and stand up. He took one step forward and placed his gun at the head of the first man he came to.

"Let go of Gabrielle's arm," he ordered.

"Piss off, there are still two men behind you, you can't kill us all and survive, plus George has a gun and he'll kill you himself." The man with John's gun at his head said boasting and hoped George would save his life.

"Wrong answer!" There was the sound of thunder as the Glock went off with no silencer and the man's brains went flying all over Gabrielle and the man in front.

John pulled his trigger again and the man in front of the man who was now slowly slipping to the ground, went the same way. He turned around and shot both men behind him and then pointed his gun at the man still holding Gabrielle's arm. He put a bullet between his eyes and the last man had his brains come out of the front of his head.

"We'll see you in New York, if you have the guts," Gabrielle shouted as a plume of grey smoke rose above their heads.

Gabrielle reached out and held John's hand and pulled him towards her, so she held him close to her body and they both jumped out of the mansion and into the back of Alan's car.

"Lynda, jump back now, we must move, we only have a few minutes before George's other men start looking for us and open fire on this car," Gabrielle thought to her wife.

"Five seconds later she appeared in the front passenger seat with a huge smile on her face. While she was putting her seat belt on, Alan was driving away from the mansion as fast as possible. He knew if they did run into trouble, then both girls would jump home. However, Alan had one last trick up his sleeve. He opened the middle storage container and removed a small blue police light.

He opened his window and switching it on, placed it on the car's roof and the magnetic bottom in the lamp ensured it didn't move no matter what speed they got up to.

"This is a sort of police car which the chief of the Met police has arranged for us to have. CB and everything, but if we're going to the States then it will have to go back. Let's see how fast it goes shall we?" Alan asked and put on the sirens.

"Blue pulsating small lights flashed non-stop across the front of the car and red pulsating lights ran across the boot.

"Pull down the middle backseat have a look, John." He did as he was told and looked in the lit boot. There was an arsenal of weapons including machine guns and a snipper's rifle.

"Do they think we are going to fight an army without any help?" John asked Alan.

"No, we have a special Call Name GL1 I insert my gun ring into the receptor, the police track us instantly and all police cars are sent to us and every armed car has priority."

"Well done, when did you arrange all this?" John asked as they sped through the streets, Alan driving as he had been taught by the Met police for his Royal Protection Duty.

"The car arrived yesterday while you were out with Gabrielle making the final arrangements for today. I take it all your shops are still open Gabrielle?"

"Yes, all earning money and with the threat on a lot of shops more relaxed, more people are coming in. We have a woman armed bodyguard standing guard outside each of our shops and after what was said today, I'm hoping that will be relaxed," Gabrielle explained.

"Will we be flying to New York dear?" Lynda asked, already knowing the answer, but she thought she needed to talk normally for the sake of Alan and John.

"No, I need a little time to make some arrangements and sort out with you what we intend to do in New York and the USA as regard to our shops and how we expand. What if we take the yacht? would you like that, take time to relax and give John and Alan a break?" Gabrielle asked Lynda.

"We need to take Sarah, get her to start putting all our clothes together and I would like to do a Hat & Bag show as well. Jenny will have to come of course; she will be our number one girl on the catwalk. What would you like to see her in. Do you like her in short dresses for the catwalk John?"

"I don't mind work, it is what it is, but a little longer dress when we're together or going shopping, but when we do get the chance to go out to a club, then the shorter the better," he replied smiling.

"Here we are, roundabout for the M1 south, no red lights for us." Alan put his foot down as he drove around the large roundabout and took the exit south. In a few seconds he was in the outside lane, siren blazing and lights flashing, he drove the car like he had when he was in the Royal Protection team, fast and hard.

"Let's see how fast this bird will fly," Alan said aloud as he put his foot down on the accelerator, his left foot hovering over the brake in case he needed it in a hurry.

The following day Gabrielle, Lynda, Jenny and Sarah were going through all the clothes they would need in the US, especially for the catwalks. Jenny agreed she would go shopping for some more shorter dresses that would help show off the Hats & Bags and her long, gorgeous legs.

She took six pair of six-inch high heels and Gabrielle packed the same while Lynda packed eight pairs of four-inch-high heels and four pair of two-inch high heels. Gabrielle and Jenny also packed more sensible shoes for shopping.

They packed four large trunks for the catwalks and another trunk each for their different dresses and outfits they would need to wear in New York. They were now representing Hats & Bags, they had to look good.

"That's the main packing done. Your main hats I'll have boxed up later, can these go to the yacht now?" Sarah asked Gabrielle.

"Yes, no, one other item I need," she replied and ran down into the basement and retrieved one of her expensive three thousand-pound suits, still in its sterile bag. She took it upstairs and went into their bedroom and showed Lynda.

"Do you think I should try it on?" Gabrielle asked.

"What's it for?" Lynda asked.

"The battle for you at the top of the Empire State Building like I told you."

"Do you really have to? Why not let John or Alan just kill him? I could have Jack shoot him between the eyes from a mile away; he's a first class shot with a Glock or a rifle, I don't know what make it is, but John would."

She was frightened, she didn't want her wife to have to go through this fight all over again. Once was bad enough and she knew she couldn't actually die; Fate would see to that. They were both still needed for their bet. However, Gabrielle could be cut up and it would be up to her to make her better if needed. This was all up to Death and Death wanted this little scenario to play itself out and let the cards fall as they would. This was a test for Gabrielle to show her love for Lynda, but how far was Gabrielle willing to go to save her once again?

Lynda would have Alan standing somewhere either with her or in the distance as he was there at the time, and he had his gun with him. She would make sure Alan's gun worked and if things looked as if they were going wrong, she would order Alan to kill George. Then she thought of Jack, she would put him on a rooftop a long way off but in sightline of the Empire State Building. On her signal he would open fire and kill George if anything were happening that shouldn't be.

This she knew would not be a fair fight and Death was certain to be close at hand to try and alter the show so it panned out for as long as He wanted until He was satisfied that Gabrielle could show her love for Lynda.

She came out of her deep thought looking at the love of her life before her. She stepped forward and gave her a huge hug and they started to kiss, mouths rotating, their tongues entered each other's mouth and explored as they always did, but this time it held more meaning for both.

It was love, deep and long-lasting; they would and could get through this together, but they were holding each other now breast to breast, tummy to tummy, their hands moving over each other's back, pulling their bodies closer and closer, tighter and tighter to each other.

They could have made love there and then, but kissing was enough for now to show their deepest feelings for each other. They parted their lips for a moment, and Gabrielle spoke quietly to Lynda.

"I love you with every part of me and I'll fight George to the death if I need to. You are my soulmate and I want to live with you forever, share our lives, travel the universe together when our people come up with a ship with a light drive."

"That sounds like a brilliant idea, I'd love to join you with all my heart and soul. You're my soulmate and I love you so much, my heart aches for you and I don't want anything to happen to you. I don't want your beautiful body to be cut apart like mine was. I don't want you cut up like our first timeline, I think Death would make you pay with pain.

"We both know what pain is like and I don't ever want us to have to go through it again. Now, kiss me like you did just now, like you always do," Lynda asked. They closed their eyes and their mouths met, they formed a circle and their mouths pressed harder and harder together, rotating and showing their love for each other. Sarah was just about to enter their bedroom and saw what they were doing and turned just in time to stop Jenny entering the room as well. She quietly closed their door and tip toed along the landing back to where they were packing clothes.

Gabrielle and Lynda were locked together, kissing, holding, touching each other until their kisses turned erotic, wanting each other so much their hearts and desires for each other were overflowing and they knew they still had a lot to do if they were going to leave the following lunchtime on the high tide.

Fifteen minutes later, they started to slow down, their rotating mouths slowing to a slow, long, passionate kiss, with their arms holding each other close, recalling a time when they first met in their first timeline, up in the air, falling back to the ice-covered pavement, with their arms rapped around each other and Paul, at the time, made sure he landed on his back and Lynda was on top of him.

They looked into each other's green eyes and instantly fell in love. Their lips touched but did they kiss or didn't they? she wasn't sure, but she knew she could have kissed him for an age on the ice- cold pavement. She was sure Paul would not have worried. The magic was happening right there and then, their hearts were melting, their souls mating, they would be soulmates forever. As they breathed into each other's open mouth, enclosed by their faint kiss, they were passing trillions of pieces of data to each other that would make them relax into each other's arms and love each other unconditionally.

Their green eyes were getting brighter and looking into each other's soul where they found love and understanding, romance and sexual desires for each other and the billions of pictures they would share together and take them together when the time came for them to meet their maker.

They could have been holding each other and on the ice for an eternity, they wouldn't have known, they wouldn't have cared, all that mattered was that they had finally met and instantly fell in love. A deep love that proved later that day, Paul would fight to the death for her and if needed, die himself. All he knew was that she was his girl and nobody else was going to have her because she may be broken and abused, she was still the woman for him, and nobody was going to hurt her ever again.

Paul didn't know what would happen to him just seven- hours later, but they had already spent a lifetime together and they knew each other inside and out and their hearts were now joined in harmony forever, nothing would or could break their romantic bond.

When Paul helped her up from his laying position, he held her again, hard, like he never wanted to let her go and then she held out her hand and helped him to stand, turned and brushed the ice and snow from his jacket and trousers. They entered the coffee shop a minute later already so deeply in love.

They talked for so long, talking was easy and so too was the second drink they had together. They didn't need spirits, or larger, they were so high on love they were reaching the sky.

Paul took her to his Hats & Bags shop and gave her a thirteen-hundred-pound hat and eight-hundred-pound handbag so she would look in character while signing her books in the bookshop where so many lives would be lost later that afternoon and the man who she didn't think had an ounce of fight in him would turn around and save her life.

As she hurried to the bookshop, looking the part of her new book that was at number one, she passed over a hundred people waiting for her to sign their book and was flying, on top of the world. Five hours later, she looked up into the eyes of her soulmate. His green eyes were shining for her as she looked into his eyes, hers grew brighter and once again they were trapped in time as their hands touched.

They smiled at each other, and she watched his lips speak the words I Love You. Her heart skipped a beat as she mouthed the words, I Love You Too. She signed two books for him and had their photo taken together, their bodies touching, his arm around her back, she could have melded with his body, she was so happy as they held the hardback cover between them.

Her cameraman took at least twenty pictures of them as they moved together in love. His head touched hers, she felt it, she wanted more, and he was going to take her to dinner after the signing was completed; she was looking forward to it. They would be together and able to talk about their future and hold hands.

She would steal a kiss and hold it in her mouth for all eternity, they would make love with their eyes. They would spend the night together she didn't know where, but they would spend the night together of that she was certain. She wasn't worried about the massive scars she had on her body, she knew he would understand and love her all the more.

He was wearing his expensive three-piece suit; she knew good material when she saw it. As he walked away, she saw him talk to her photographer and hand him his business card. He held himself well, like any businessman and he had given her the hat and bag and it was hers, to keep.

She was so happy as she took her seat, then she saw a hardback book slam onto the table and she looked up into the eyes of her husband Ian and just behind him, George, both men armed to the teeth with his knives and double-edged sword on their backs. This she knew was going to get ugly and her man of the moment was gone, probably out of the shop by now. Could she rely on him? She didn't know but she hoped deep down he had seen the men behind him and stayed to see what was going to happen and what they wanted from her.

She imagined what he might say to them, "excuse me but you can't talk to Lynda like that in this bookshop, it's her day and her book signing. Have your grievance with her tomorrow or through your solicitor. Please act civil, you're in a bookshop, nothing bad happens in a bookshop." But it already had.

Ian would look at him, draw his sword and split him in two, head down and George would laugh and then they would start on her as the sword was meant for her and she had nobody to protect her now, the love of her life was dead and gone. Yes, they would be together tonight, on a cold mortuary slab once the police had sorted them out, if they could. Once started, the two of them would fight cat and nail to save their lives.

I had no idea they had already started their killing spree killing staff in the aisles and in the Managers' office, they were all dead and so too, a mother and her two girls three years old, left bleeding out in the main aisle.

After thirty seconds of shouting and pointing to a book contract they wanted her to sign transferring all the Royalties to them. A fat lot of good that would do them in prison, she thought to herself on that horrendous day.

Her book manager was frightened, but he did try and calm them down only to be threatened with an eight-inch army KA-Bar knife. He was frightened now, Ian was threatening him, saying he knew where his family lived and they were going there next to rape his wife, then kill their two children and finally after raping her again, she would die. He was terrified and who wouldn't be? He was her book agent, not her bodyguard and he had no idea how to fight, especially a maniac like Ian.

While Ian was threatening my book manager, George was attacking my photographer, pushing his camera and tripod to the ground and my photographer was being attacked by George, he was grappling with his camera. He was already cut in his hand by George's KA-Bar knife, and he was also carrying a double-edged sword on his back and a gun in his jacket.

While the photographer was laying on the ground, he switched his camera from photo to record so the police would have some idea of what had happened and how he died. George was on the ground and getting ready to cut his bleeding hand off. He had looked along the book aisle and saw Paul holding a Star Wars Manual, he thought he was an idiot, what was he going to do with the book get Ian and George to sign it?

However, he was the only hope he had, or he would lose his hand and probably his life. He gazed at Lynda, showing he could not help her demise and said a silent prayer, thinking of his wife at home who would, without knowing very soon become a widow.

He heard Ian shouting at the book manager again he must have been waving a knife around similar to what he was about to meet his end with. Paul was gone, he heard a loud thud and then silence. George had turned his head to see what was happening and he thought he might have hit Ian on the back of the head so hard he knocked him out for a minute and that is all he needed to disarm him. One minute that is all he needed and now he was thinking he just might get out of this alive.

I was amazed to see Paul, I was sure he was gone, but no, here he was armed with a book. What do they say, the book is mightier than the sword? This book went right to the hilt of the knife Ian was holding which he was getting ready to kill my book manager with. I was proud of him but knew Ian would swiftly defeat Paul. Ian was mad and mad men do things without thinking and Paul looked like he couldn't do much more than hold Ian's knife hand down for a few seconds. I heard Paul shout "Run!"

I felt my manager's hand grab mine, but I was seated and wearing three-inch high heels and I fell to the ground. He left me and ran past Ian to freedom. I knew I was about to die at the hands of Ian and Paul would either go first or just after me.

Paul moved so fast I hardly saw him, one moment he was holding the book the next second a knife was being, in my slow-motion sight, turning end over end as it flew through the air. The next second George was screaming his head off that a knife was through the back of his hand and had pinned it to the wooden floor.

I saw the knife fly through the air at great speed and then with great accuracy the knife, blade first went right through the back of George's hand and pinned it to the wooden floor I pulled my bleeding hand away from George giving me the time to get to my feet and run down the far aisle into the street and hopefully some police.

As I ran down the aisle, I started to glance at the book aisles to my left. There were bodies lying on the floor and not moving with blood seeping out of their bodies. Some looked dead and as I glanced over to the far book aisle, there it was the same, young girls and a few boys, dead or hardly alive they would need help, but I was not a medic, I could do nothing for them but escape this madness and get the police and ambulances, lots of them.

As I passed the manager's office, I could see blood, lots of it running down the step and as I looked through the window, there were at least four or five dead bodies inside. Nothing could be done for them except to pray for salvation.

Near the end I saw a girl kneeling on the floor crying her heart out and talking to an unconscious boy who was bleeding badly from three or four knife wounds. I stopped and told her I would get help. Then in the next isle there was a woman at the end bleeding profusely or had been. Her arm was outstretched as if trying to grab something. Then I saw them, two little girls lying dead on the floor. Their throats had been cut and they died instantly thank goodness.

There were bodies still across in the far aisles, what were these crazed men doing and why did they want Lynda? I saw a police officer hurry down the central aisle ignoring the dead and dying, not letting any emotion show on his face. He could see a bigger picture.

Paul had managed to disarm Ian and held one of his knives to his throat. The copper got the end of the picture, he didn't listen to the people telling him what was happening, all he could see was Paul holding a sharp knife to a man's throat. He didn't see the sword because Paul's head was in the way.

The copper started to arrest Paul as he managed to move Paul to the right, so the knife was not at the man's throat. He must have seen the sword then; it wasn't on Ian's back for long. The sword came out of its scabbard like lightning and came down hard on the copper's thigh, I watched as his leg fell to the floor and then the copper was on the floor and all Hell broke loose.

I moved to the far aisle so I could witness what I saw. Ian had the sword in his hand, and he had ordered George to decapitate the copper who was awake and shaking like a leaf, probably from shock and hearing he was about to lose his head. There was no one to help him except the man who he tried to arrest but he wanted to save the girl.

Paul had one knife in his hand, it was either for Ian or George, but he could only save one life at a time and Paul was now deciding what to do.

George had managed to draw the knife out of the floor, but it was still through his hand as he withdrew his sword and took a step forward. The copper was about to die but Paul was about to pay a very heavy price for his decision to save him.

Paul turned left, the knife was in his right hand and then it was gone, flying through the air so fast and hit George in the heart killing him as he fell to the floor, dead. This is where Paul would pay dearly for saving the copper.

I watched Paul as he turned back to face Ian once again. He had nothing but his hands, I glanced at my watch I couldn't believe it was only two minutes, a few seconds less, one man was legless, another dead and Lynda was now facing death by Ian's sword.

I heard Lynda scream as the tip of the sword went through the thin material of her dress and scrape the skin of her belly, Ian was going to skin her alive. For me, I saw Paul grab the sword with his right hand and pull it towards himself. Then his left hand joined his right as he tried desperately to stop Ian pushing the sword into his stomach.

His left hand was bleeding profusely now as the sword cut through the skin down to the bone of both of his hands. He was losing the fight with the sword; then it entered his stomach and I saw the blood squirt out of his body. It was turning his white crisp shirt red, and a pool of blood was in his shirt and top of his trousers.

The sword went in deeper and up then down and across, cutting his body so easy. There was a grin on Ian's face, he had killed the stupid man who thought he could outsmart him; now he would take his revenge on Lynda. She would die here and now.

Another fifteen seconds. The photographer watching what transpired. I thought he would drop to the floor as soon as the sword was withdrawn. But Ian was holding the sword inside him, trying to do more damage. "My God!"

Paul had grabbed hold of the sword with his almost skinless hands and was pushing it out of his stomach. "Death: he's still alive," I cried.

The sword was out of his stomach and Paul had full command of it. One moment the sword was straight on at him then it was almost facing Lynda as Paul rolled along the sword and pulled the last knife from Ian's back pocket. I watched Paul miraculously throw the knife from his left hand to his right bloody hand then turn, holding Ian to stay upright and he cut his throat.

I watched as my lover's hand came over Ian's shoulder and the look of horror on Ian's face as he felt the cold steel of his own knife cut through his skin and arteries as Paul pulled the knife from one side of his throat to the other. He gurgled for a few seconds then the knife went deep into his heart not once but twice.

My former husband's favourite sword fell from his hand and onto the floor making a clattering sound, it would do him no good now and a lot of people would be glad he was dead, including myself. I had suffered a lot by his hands and George's, I was glad they were both dead but what of my lover? I needed his love I needed his soul. We said we were soulmates. Death told me I would meet Paul and Death told Paul he would meet a woman with green eyes, and he would love her all his life.

Paul had also talked with Death a number of times as he had attempted suicide ten times and often spent a lot of time with Death as his body grew cold on a trolly and his mother had prayed in tongue to Death to release her son's soul and allow him to live and she would do all she could to stop his meetings with Death, but Death wanted to see Paul suffer, to get him ready for this moment, he would need all his strength to stay alive and a meeting with Death may well take place.

As Ian collapsed to the floor dead, Paul also fell to the floor next to the copper. I could see Lynda run forward to Paul as she looked over him, she saw his last act of kindness. I couldn't believe it. Paul half sat up, looking at the copper's leg and unbuckled his belt and pulled it through the tabs of his trousers. Then put it with his raw hands around the copper's thigh, what was left of it and pulled the belt as tight as it would go then secured it off.

As I looked down on my lover he was talking to the copper.

"Tell her I love her, and I'll take her to the Shard for dinner when I can. I love Lynda with all my heart and soul, and we only just met at eleven this morning but it's like I've known her all my life and in the next life we were lovers, giving us another chance at love. It's the name of the game and what we're here for."

"You can tell her yourself; she's standing right over you and thanks for saving my life, I'll never forget what you did for me after what I did to you." I heard the copper say to Paul.

I knelt by Paul and pulled his body into the light. I knew I shouldn't have moved him, but there was no help yet. I pulled his waistcoat apart then the buttons on his shirt were ripped off as I parted his shirt and saw the size of the hole Ian had made in Paul's chest.

She put her hands over the hole to try to stop the bleeding, but blood was still flowing with another liquid, but I didn't know what it was.

My hands were covered in his blood as I looked at the police officer.

"It's okay he's just passed out; he's still breathing for now hurry and tell them the fight is over," the copper said to me in a soft reassuring voice.

I ran, as fast as I could down the central aisle and around the two dead girls with tears rolling down my face as the realisation of what happened in three minutes fifty seconds, was it really that fast for Paul to kill two men, save the life of her book manager and cameraman, then he saved the life of the constable.

My cameraman was now trying to push his way through the police cordon crying his eyes out that the killing and fight was over there was nobody left to kill unless we save two lives down there.

The officer in charge was ordering his men to form a strong line to let nobody in until the Met armed officers arrived.

I saw a young man in an expensive suit, he held up his official armed bodyguard licensed to kill card and at the same time he showed his Glock under his suit jacket.

"I am over this officer I order all you police to assist the injured and dying inside the shop. This is your duty, not to stay here. Break up this barricade, let the ambulance crews, paramedics and doctors in. Help the ambulance staff and paramedics. Sergent!" the man shouted above the commotion, "Help take charge and arrange your men properly.

"Listen to this man," he shouted to the rest of the police.

"Contact your station and request another senior officer to take over here. I want one small cordon to keep the public out and I want this road closed left and right. We'll need room for the emergency helicopters to land. By what the cameraman said we'll need at least another eight ambulances, paramedics doctors and surgeons. Can you organise that?" he asked.

"Yes Sir!" he replied and then added, "Thanks for taking over, that idiot hasn't even called the Met, I tried to tell him."

"That's okay, we'll sort it all out and it'll be a very long night."

"That was Alan, who was to be my bodyguard a few weeks later."

"I pushed my way through the police cordon screaming my head off for medical help, but nobody was moving, I guess the orders from Alan hadn't got this far down the line. There were two rows of police officers forming the cordon and I pushed my way through, tore the green bag from the paramedic's hand and started to run back to Paul. I had no idea what to do with the bag of medical equipment, but I could at least look for clean padding to stop the bleeding.

I heard shouting from Alan giving orders getting people organised. The Paramedic started to push his way through the cordon and caught me up, taking the green bag from my hand and running alongside me.

I was crying my eyes out begging him to hurry and save Paul's life, but he said we needed a doctor. Then a GP knelt beside Paul and took over ordering this and that to be done and bloods to be taken for cross matching.

Then he recognised me and then Paul. He was shocked and told me if he let him die his wife would kill him. She shops in his shops. He explained, "I said at least a dozen times who I was and what relationship we had."

I heard the first medical helicopter land close by and a minute later a senior heart surgeon was with us. With him he had a full operating kit for in the field. He cut Paul's chest open with a bonesaw, then spread it wide with special spreaders, I suppose that's what they were called.

Finally, after carrying the boy who had four knife wounds to an ambulance and his girlfriend who was in deep shock, Alan told the ambulance driver to move it, or he would come back and kill him himself and showed the handle of his gun to him.

As soon as the back doors were closed the Ambulance was off with its lights flashing and siren sounding into the falling snow. Alan came down and introduced himself to me and said John would be here soon. I thought he was going to tell me to move on and let the surgeon work on with caring for Paul. But he was genuinely nice to me and made sure I could stay with Paul and be at his head, talking quietly to him. Then he said, "Welcome to the family, we'll look after you, well most of the time and this is not a usual time, is it?"

He held my hand, placed it on Paul's head and he was gone checking on those dead and those still alive. He returned to the main doors, ordering more ambulances and Nighting Gale nurses from Kings Cross Hospital, the nearest hospital which also had a helipad on the roof. Alan had taken full control of the police and ambulance crews. Girls with knife and sword wounds were now being put into ambulances and with a police escort, taken to Kings Cross Hospital. Then an ambulance arrived with six Nighting Gale Nurses, scrub nurses who helped surgeons in surgery. They were not afraid of a scalpel and seeing men and women opened top to bottom for operations.

But this was different, they were in the field, the girls and boys had all been stabbed at least four times and every one of them had been stabbed in their spleen. They were bleeding out internally.

When a top officer arrived from the Met Police, he saluted Alan, and Alan returned his salute, then quickly gave him an assessment of what had taken place inside, where all the dead bodies were, so far ten of them.

By now there was a TV crew here, several TV crews and Pressmen and women were all hoping to get a picture of the police officer who Paul had saved and of course, the great Paul Grayson who was known for his Hats & Bags around the world. When the TV crew got through the police rank's they found Paul and were filming him, and all his parents could do was watch on their car television like the rest of the world as John put his foot down to get them to their dying son and the woman who would join their family that very night. Alan at last returned to Lynda, got her coat and bag and placed her coat around her shoulders, with a warm hand on the back of hers. He smiled and talked to her constantly for a while as Paul's stomach was finally stitched up and some of the internal bleeding stopped and clamped off, ready to work on when they got him to hospital.

Just a short thirty minutes later, with Paul's heart hardly beating, Mr Muhammed had his heart out of Paul's body and was examining it with a small headlamp when a nurse saw where the blood was coming through. He placed Paul's heart in my hands and said, "look after it." Then his heart stopped but Mr Muhammed was not concerned, he was used to these problems, he was a heart surgeon after all. Paul was officially dead, again, and now he was standing on the shelf that Death had made just for him, his soul able to feel the pull of other souls behind the black curtain. His body in the living world, was getting colder as Paul was looking down upon himself and talking with Death for some time, much longer than his heart had stopped beating for, there was a lot to get through.

When Mr Muhammed had completed repairing Paul's heart, he asked me to gently squeeze it to get it going again. All the time he was scanning the heart for further problems until on the tenth squeeze it started again, and Paul left Death standing on the shelf looking down on Paul's body. He would indeed go through Hell now Death knew. He had planned it with Fate so this would happen, and their love would deepen. Paul would need Lynda's love and he would change his life for me and be like he had always wanted to be.

Alan had left me, as he made, arrangements for Paul to be taken to hospital by helicopter. He also arranged for me to be taken to hospital by a fast police car so I could meet Paul outside the surgery.

Nobody was going against Alan now they knew who he was and who he was bodyguard to on this shift anyway. He walked briskly around the shop counting those being worked on, mainly by Nighting Gale Nurses, operating on girls with no anaesthetic. Girls were arriving in the Trauma unit asking how many sets of instruments, were inside them? and Talking with the doctors and general surgeons who would patch them up until a theatre was available. Some were operated on completely and stitched up in the Trauma Unit. It was a long night for everyone in the hospital as nurses were called from wards and other nurses, doctors and surgeons were being called in and some even arrived by police helicopter or a fast police car.

Mr Muhammed had put Paul's heart back in his chest, and as he was doing this, a nurse was finishing wrapping up Paul's hands and then cutting off all his top clothes. A police officer with gloved hands was bringing down a new roll of medical clingfilm so that Paul could be transferred to hospital without getting any more germs in his open chest and stomach. As he was sat up, he opened his eyes, he too had had no anaesthetic.

He spoke, only a few words but he spoke to me. "Hi Lynda, sorry about the meal this evening, I'll take you to the Shard when I'm a bit better. Are you okay? Ian didn't hurt you, did he? I tried my best, but I had to save the officer's life before I saved yours."

"Yes, Paul I'm fine, it's you I'm worried about." I kissed his lips and they felt warm and soft, I would get used to kissing his and her lips and never want to kiss another person for the rest of my life."

Next thing he's being evaced by helicopter and Mr Muhammed is going with him to operate on him again as soon as he is in theatre.

I was led by Alan to the police car I was going to hospital in. My hands were covered in Paul's blood, my dress and coat covered in his blood, his bag had survived the fight, but it was covered in his blood as I held it in my hand it was all I had of Paul.

John arrived with Paul's parents, and they hugged and kissed me even though I was new to them. They looked into my green eyes and knew I was The One. The three of us got into the back and John took over and sat in the front. He just looked at the driver showed his gun and said drive, as fast as you can. I would like to be there when the chopper arrives. The car started and with four police cycle outriders, with snow on the road we were driving at 80 mph all the way there and we didn't stop.

We were rushed by a nurse up to level 5 and taken along a corridor, brightly lit by florescent lights through another set of doors and we sat outside the operating theatre that Paul was already in. Although he was being prepped for surgery, he insisted I see him one more time for a few minutes before he went under. I was taken into the theatre where scrub nurses were ready to help operate. There were very bright operating lights over him with monitors and three TV screens. John was holding my coat and bag and I had given John Paul's wallet. I looked at his body, still open and wrapped up. I leaned forward and kissed him again and again, my lips pressing against his.

"I love you with all my heart," I said.

"I love you too, and you've had my heart in your hands, don't ever forget that. I was watching you and I had a long talk with Death all about us and what we'll do and get up to. I'll see you later in my suite."

"You have a suite here?" I asked smiling.

"Oh yes, it's all the rage nowadays. I'll explain everything to you when I wake up if I can talk then."

"You'll be able to talk to Lynda later, one more kiss, then you have to go, he will be operated on by several surgeons tonight. I will warn you that his hands are the worst problem by what I saw.

He'll have the very, best care I can assure you," Mr Muhammed explained.

"Can I wait outside on the seats there?"

"That is what they are there for. Try and get some sleep the night will go faster. He will be taken to his personal suite, John and Alan know where it is, they will take you up there."

"He has his own medical suite?" I asked.

"Yes, well he paid for it and the twelve large private rooms which when they have his people in, he pays for all their medical needs and operations. You have fallen in love with a particularly important man, which I will allow him to explain all about. You have been through enough today, get some rest and ask a nurse for a sandwich and coffee."

I kissed Paul's forehead again, he was fast asleep, and a nurse was now cutting the rest of his clothes off and cutting the surgical clingfilm that had protected his stomach and heart on the way to hospital. Mr Muhammed smiled at me as I turned and left the operating theatre. As I left the room there were two other surgeons getting ready to go in and help save his life, scrubbing their hands and there was another scrub nurse, scrubbing her hands and talking to the surgeons.

In the corridor, John was waiting for me and put my coat around my shoulders. He had already ordered coffee and sandwiches for both of us.

"As we sat together, John told me a little about the man I just fell head over heels in love with. He had saved my life, and I had brought him back from the dead and held his heart in my hands. No love could be any stronger.

"He told me about his business Hats & Bags, and I recalled the awfully expensive hat was still in the bookshop on the floor, covered in blood and ruined. He explained that he had three shops in London and more in France, Spain, Italy and Holland. Paul spoke eleven languages all fluent. His mother and father spoke twelve and had their own empire in clothes shops across the UK and Europe, even a few in Australia which is where his sister lives with her husband. They have their own airline with twelve Boeing 747's. flying all over Australia, and routes to France and the UK, with the occasional flight to the US.

His parents were billionaires almost multi-billionaires but always gave a lot to charities, something I would have to think about in the not-too-distant future. Paul too was almost a billionaire and extremely good looking with a slim body and looked good in his expensive suit.

"John kept looking into my green eyes and when I asked him why?" he said.

"I was The One. He knew quite a bit about me from the continuous phone calls from Paul during the afternoon while I was signing books and getting closer to that fateful moment. I sighed, deeply, thinking of those three minutes and fifty seconds. It all happened so fast, and the speed was all Paul's, he had no time to stop, he must have been considering his options on the go."

"John told me a little about one of his charities but was not coming forward as to what his main charity was and why Paul's main charity had spent over ten million on the new wing of the hospital with state-of-the-art operating theatres with all the very latest equipment. It was the same operating theatre he was in now and Mr Muhammed was still operating on him, and two other surgeons had commenced to work on his stomach and hands. Bloods were sent direct to the lab in a room on another floor which also had all the latest technology supplied by Paul's main charity.

Brenda was escorted along the same corridor I had walked along, I looked at my watch, three hours ago and they were still working on him. Mr Muhammed had come out and spoke to me, saying his heart was fine now and back to normal.

A man was with her who I had not seen before, but he walked with his expensive suit coat open, and I saw the handle of his gun and guessed this was her armed bodyguard. She told me who she was again, but I couldn't forget her name, I had a thing like that, a bit of a photographic memory for faces and names, it helped with my writing.

She introduced Mike to me, and I put his face in my memory. She then hugged me and looked into my green eyes. Tears filled her eyes as she looked me up and down and saw her son's blood over my clothes and coat. My arms were covered in his blood and so too my hands, I couldn't bear to wash them until he was out of surgery alive and well, as well as he could be under the circumstances.

She kissed both my bloodied cheeks and then put both her hands to my face and held it as if in a picture frame. Then she asked me if I loved him, and she knew we had only met that day, but she expected to know the answer she was hoping for; the answer she had hoped would happen.

"I replied I was and still am head over heels in love with him and I'm sure we are soulmates, and I was told by Death." Damn I thought to myself, she'll think I'm mad, insane and tell me to get out of her son's life here and now and never to contact him again.

Then she hugged me again, much closer now. "I knew you were The One, your beautiful green eyes to match my son's. I know all about Death, Paul has told me several times he has spoken to Him and I have prayed to Him as well, to ask for Paul's life no matter what he expected of me. Paul told me all about you and when you both would meet and that you would be soulmates, I'm so glad you're finally here." She told me and I was flabbergasted that she was almost expecting me.

We talked for an hour then another surgeon came out and said he was pleased with Paul, and he was so far doing well. There was still another surgeon working on his hands. He was in surgery for six hours and as he was brought out, a girl from the shop who also needed heart surgery at the shop, was pushed into the operating theatre and continued to be operated on by Dr, well, Mr Reynolds and Angela, the Nighting Gale scrub nurse was also in attendance scrubbing their hands while the girl was being finally put to sleep. I followed the bed up to Paul's medical suite and Alan was standing guard outside the door. Paul's father was there and looked directly into my green eyes and smiled.

"Welcome to the family, I'm Neil, Paul's father."

I committed his face to memory and looked at the young woman who was almost in tears as she saw Paul being pushed into the room and set up with drips and morphine pumps.

"This is Sarah, Paul's personal dresser and close associate. We are all close, it has to be to work, and we expect a lot of each other not just the staff," Neil was explaining as Brenda stood by his side."

As soon as the nurses had finished sorting out Paul, Sarah walked briskly up the right side of the bed, bent over and kissed Paul on the lips, a long loving kiss. Tears filled her eyes, as some fell on Paul's still face but she didn't remove them and held his arm as if she were in love with him, perhaps she was Paul would tell me in his own time, or I was sure Sarah would very soon have a stern word with me.

She turned to face me with tears still rolling down her face. She ran to me and gave me a huge hug and thanked me for staying there and saving his life. She let me go and walked me up to Paul's head.

"I kissed his temple then his lips, a long, loving kiss. Wake up my love, the love of my life and my saviour," I whispered into his ear. I kissed his lips again, a long loving kiss that was witnessed by everyone in the room, Sarah was holding my hand and willing Paul to wake.

"He opened his eyes and looked straight into my green eyes and both our eyes grew slightly brighter, as if there was a much deeper connection between us, our eyes looking into our souls. I heard a loud sigh from Sarah behind me and she put a hand to her face. Paul looked at me then said, "I saw you holding my heart while I was talking with Death. I was with Him a long time, but it was seconds in this plane of existence. How are you doing my love?"

"I told him I was fine and meeting his family. He grinned and asked me to kiss him again. I didn't know then he would change so much for me, and I would love him and stand by her, and we would have such a happy life and live forever, hand in hand heart in heart. After our kiss I looked up to see Brenda waiting to kiss her son and wish him well, it was written all over her face how happy she was to see him awake and talking, even if it was just to me at the moment.

"I'm sorry Brenda, you are next it seems," I said to her.

"It's mum and dad from now on my girl, she replied and leaned over to kiss Paul.

Everything was happening so fast; it was like I was in a dream. Brenda sat in a seat next to Paul, there was plenty of room, it was a huge room. John brought a very comfy chair for me and sat me at Paul's head, so I could hold onto his arm, both his hands were covered with bandages, and I knew they would be very painful and take a lot of work to get through but no matter what scars he had, what his hands would be like in the end, I would stand by his side and love him unconditionally.

Brenda told Sarah to go out and buy me some new dresses and a complete set of underwear, my bra was also covered in his blood, and I doubted if it would ever come out, not that I really wanted it to. It would be a reminder of what he went through for me.

Sarah looked at me, studying my size. A few seconds later she asked me for my shoe size. She asked me if I had any favourite dress styles or sizes. Any particular designer I liked and to wear their expensive clothes she gave me a hug then kissed me. I told her I would leave it up to her and wear what styles she thought would suit me. She was also getting me something to wear in the hospital at night because she knew I would be staying there day and night. I wouldn't want to leave his side.

"Alan escorted Sarah out of the room without waiting to be told and he said he would take over from John who had left my side and was standing guard when he returned. I had no idea what he meant but John was sat on a chair outside the door. I didn't understand why then, but I would a few days later.

"Later in the morning a Dr came to tell us about Paul's hands then in the afternoon we were told Paul's kidney was failing and he would need a partial kidney transplant. They had searched their database but had no luck in the peculiar match. I offered half of my kidney, after all it was my fault, he was in the state he was, and I liked the idea of him having something of me keeping him alive inside his body.

"I gave my blood, and it was a match, I wondered if Death had something to do with it and guessed He did. The following day we were both prepped for the operation that would secure a bed next to his for at least the next ten days.

"During that time, we got to know each other more and more and I helped Paul get back on his feet and his love for me kept my operation pain low.

"Three weeks later I was signing my books again in a different bookshop, we had tried once in the same bookshop, but the staff didn't like the atmosphere, too many of their colleagues had died there and despite a deep clean by specialist cleaners it was not the same.

The shop was finally demolished with a garden and memorial to those who died left in its place. The owners of the shop paid for all the burials and gave a million pounds each in compensation and paid for any further medical treatment they would need. It would be several years for some of them to recover, mentally and physically. The horrific pain they suffered and what they saw as their colleagues were knifed, some had their throats slit because they were going to cry out in warning. Two girls were skewered by Ian's sword, through the back and out the front of them. They must have been petrified seeing the end of a sword passing through their stomach and out through their dresses. Then they were stabbed, several times and had their breasts slashed, just for the fun of it.

When Paul finally got out of hospital his hands were still in bandages and would be for several months. They had tried everything to get the tissue to grow onto his bones, but the bones kept on rejecting it. Something else would have to be done. While we were in France, in secrete he had both hands of a dead woman transplanted onto his wrists and the transplant took, very well, he had full use of his hands and fingers. That they were more petite and from a woman, he didn't mind, in fact if I didn't know better either he or Death organised it.

Paul took me to the Shard for a meal but after, we were just sat talking with coffee, he started to bleed again, and I had to call John over and I ripped open his shirt and with the help of a decent first aid kit I had most of his staples out so I could get my petite hand in and find the bleed. I pinched the artery with my finger and thumb until the paramedic arrived and it was the same man who helped me that night.

He smiled at me and asked if I couldn't keep my hands from his insides. We discussed while he was getting ready to put his hand into Paul's stomach which artery it was and where the bleed was. I told him to hurry up and seconds, just seconds later it was clamped off and we were getting ready to get him to hospital once again for a three day stay, which he hated, but I did see him in the evenings and as soon as I started to sign books again, Paul made Alan my very own armed bodyguard, licensed to kill.

We cleared my flat and donated all the computers and computer games to the Children's Hospital in London. All my clothes were torn to shreds by Ian and George in rage and the laptop which I made my living from was damaged beyond repair, but I at least had the USB with all my work on it for my next book.

Paul had his hand operation and when we were in France a few weeks later where once again I was signing my books with Alan by my side and my brave Paul not far away, Paul went off with John and had the biggest rock made I had ever seen and before all our friends, he proposed to me and we were married in France a few weeks later, husband and wife but there was still one big secret he was unwilling to share with me for the time being. It was as if he was ashamed of himself, but I had a fair idea myself of what he was and why he was feeling ashamed and unable to tell me his secret.

I was learning French fluently, Paul's way, which was as easy as falling asleep and listening to a tape through the night.

I stepped in for a lady called Gabrielle doing the catwalk showing off his Hats & Bags to his buyers in France. It was strange everyone was asking about Gabrielle, where she was and was she okay and how was Paul getting on with his new hands and the pain he was still in?

"When I looked through his green eyes his soul was telling me something else. Paul was longing for something; he was missing something, it showed at the catwalk, he longed to be up there, after all, Paul was Gabrielle. All his friends knew about her and were just going along about her for me, how considerate his true friends were.

Before he told me his secret, I had a broach made of a butterfly by a special jeweller Alan took me to. It was quite large, 50mm wide and 30mm long. The wings were made up of diamonds, sapphires and emeralds, with a large ruby for each eye.

My own money was coming through to me now with the sale of my books, a film contract and a forward payment for my next book which was hoped to be about the fight and my love for Paul and how the couple would arrive, in the book and a happy ever ending.

The butterfly cost me thirty thousand, with insurance. It had a double solid silver chain to attach to a dress or jacket so it would hopefully not get lost and the box it came in must have cost a hundred pounds, but the money didn't matter, all that mattered was that he understood the meaning of it and of course wear it, as much as Paul could.

I wrote a lovely letter to go with it and had it wrapped professionally in pink and blue paper. The night when everyone was leaving early, I knew something was about to happen, and I knew exactly what it was, and I had made my own plans.

Paul was very generous; he had given me my own personal bank cards to his fortune. Then there were the store cards I could use, and I didn't need a credit card, but one was there if I needed it.

There was no upfront contract, I could have taken him for millions if I wished. He told me I had to pay for nothing and the only time I was allowed to spend my own money was for Christmas and Birthdays. He bought me a laptop, top of the range with Bluetooth which matched up as soon as I entered our large apartment in London with every TV, which was also a computer with speech recognition in most languages. I could now speak four languages, all fluent and on my fifth, Dutch.

Alan was sat with me in the lounge on the large sofa, while Sarah was doing something with Paul downstairs in the red room. I knew by now they had been in love, maybe they were still in love and had the odd lovemaking session now and then. Paul had asked her to marry him, but she said she wanted children and wasn't sure. He had given her a year and she had not committed herself then I came on the scene and she knew instantly I was The One, because it had been foretold by Death.

Now we waited with bated breath for the couple to return to the lounge. Alan knew what was happening but didn't tell me, it would spoil the surprise. Eventually they returned to the lounge and Alan got Sarah's coat and they left smiling wishing us well. I then got up and left Paul alone with his thoughts.

I returned a minute or so later, pausing to really think if I had got it right and if this gift of the butterfly would carry the meaning it was supposed to, to him.

I sat down almost next to him, we kissed, but it wasn't one of our usual kisses, romantic, it was a peck nothing more and it carried nothing more than a warning that he was worried about something big. Something which might change our lives. I looked into his green eyes and could see the concern inside him so I decided to make a start, or this evening would be a complete waist and an expensive one if I got things wrong.

I handed him the box and letter which he read immediately, without opening the box. His hands hurt him, and he still had to rub cream into them to stop his fingers curling into themselves and he was on heavy pain killers and tablets to help stop the rejection of his new hands. I helped him all I could and sorted his medication for him as there was so much.

I soothed his hands morning, noon and night. I soothed them now and rubbed some more cream into them as I could see the pain in his face. He went to pull away, but I stopped him, holding his arms towards my body.

"You're in pain, let me help you or you won't be able to open your present. This is the first gift I have bought for you which I have paid for out of my own money. I hope you like it. I rubbed cream into his hands and made them a little more supple. He sat forward and picked up the box and looked into my eyes, wondering what could be inside.

He read the card, put it on the table and removed the wrapping then opened the red, velvet box. His eyes beheld the butterfly and he removed it from the box and examined it. He knew the workmanship and knew this was not a cheap present.

It's fully insured, if you don't want me, I fully understand I can leave tonight, although I would like to take my laptop, but I'll leave everything else. I understand if you don't want me, I'm damaged and have scars where a woman shouldn't have them. I can check into a hotel anywhere in London and I can afford to buy my own apartment outright with my money. I wouldn't take a penny from you I promise."

"It's not you it's me," he replied quietly. "I need to go and do something; I'd like you to wait here and if you want to leave, I'll understand, it's not what you signed up for. Will you sit here and watch TV while I do what I have to and come back up, then you can make your mind up?"

He looked at the butterfly again and returned it to the box and closed the lid. Thank you, it's beautiful is all he said as he closed the lid. He picked up the box and as he held it in his hand he winced, the cream had not fully started to work on his tender skin yet. He kissed me as if it were the last kiss, he would ever give me and finally gazed into my green eyes, which were a dull green, as his were.

Neither of us was sure what the other would do, but I knew I would have to stand by him no matter what he was going to do or finally say. If he insisted that I leave the apartment and him then I would go to the nearest hotel, get the best I could and go back to see Death and beg him to take my soul and do what He liked with it, I didn't need it any longer.

I ended up watching a little TV as he was so long and if he were doing what I thought he was, it would take him some time. There was a new photo on the shelf, a six by four colour photo of two women on the catwalk, Sarah and Gabrielle, Gabrielle who he said sometimes stayed here when she was doing a Catwalk show for Hats & Bags in London.

Gabrielle looked very glamorous, thin sexy body with long brown straight hair and wearing six-inch high heels. Just the thing to get the men interested in her and buy more hats or bags.

When I questioned Sarah about some of the clothes I was wearing and the underclothes in my bedroom drawers, she said she never chose the clothes, none of them or my jewellery. I was amazed when she told me it was Paul who told her where to buy my clothes, my size, my underclothes, even my shoes. As I was getting dressed, he would tell me whether to wear tights or stockings and the dress which matched the occasion we were going to and the size of heel I should wear so I was almost as tall as him or a little shorter, but I always wore high heels. I loved them and could walk in them all day if I had to.

I was wearing a very pretty silver evening dress. I don't know why I chose it but sometimes I liked to wear some of the beautiful clothes Paul had purchased for me and I knew he liked to see me wearing them. Before we went out to meetings or to visit his shops on business, he always checked my makeup and made sure I was wearing the correct earrings and my hair was implacable.

He knew exactly how he wanted me to look almost as if there was something else behind it. Was he thinking of something else, or was it my intuition kicking in?

Paul always treated me so kind, held my hand everywhere we went. Introduced me to other billionaires as if I had known them all my life and these people, they were just like you or me, normal people. It was just that they had been in the right place at the right time and money made money and money talked you into other investments.

I was wearing fifty mm long drop diamond earrings, with a heart shaped diamond on a solid silver fourteen-inch chain around my neck. I had my engagement ring on as I walked back to the sofa, I put on the dainty silver three-quarter length sleeved jacket that went with the dress. I wanted him to see me looking like a million dollars, something not to be cast aside. I wanted to look like he had always seen me, with love and understanding. That he wanted me, all to himself and would share me with nobody else. I was his and his alone and I would do his bidding, not that he asked me to do anything that he wouldn't do himself. We had a perfect love; I could finish his sentence and he could do the same. We laughed together we made love passionately.

Paul was so good at making me aroused and no matter what the time of night, he would make sure I was satisfied with our love making and I was happy to fall asleep, blissfully in his arms. I prayed silently to Death that I would once again fall asleep in his arms tonight and he would want me as he always had. I could not live without him.

I heard the door of the red room close and once again, standing by the shelf over the open log fire, I wondered if he would understand the meaning of the butterfly but now, I was unsure he did? It was as if he didn't know why I would give him such a feminine gift and how could he wear it at a shop in a suit? I was stupid, he would never get the sentiment it held, he was not a woman.

I glanced at the photo of Gabrielle and thought about her. She would understand the sentiment behind it and proudly wear it all the time if possible. I held the picture in my hand and wished. I wished so hard as I returned it to its prominent position in the centre of the shelf, which had been changed by someone recently and looked towards the door as I heard Paul walk slowly along the short landing.

I closed my eyes and wished again, then said a silent prayer to Death. In my mind's eye I could see him standing there and as I opened my eyes; I was surprised to see a woman wearing a very pale gold long evening dress. She had long brown, straight hair and was wearing long drop diamond earrings. A diamond encrusted rose was on a long chain around her neck, and she looked elegant. She stood at an angle by the door to the lounge. One arm was at an angle, supporting her as she was wearing four-inch-high heels. At the top of her matching lace covered jacket was my butterfly, matching her own choice of jewellery.

"Where is Paul?" I asked.

"Paul is gone, he left the apartment and I live here now. My name is Gabrielle and I do all the catwalks for Paul, but I'm taking over now. I'll be ruling this apartment now, Paul won't appear again, unless he's needed for some pacific job."

She stood upright and stepped into the lounge. She was nervous, that I could see. She had no idea what I would do, and I knew what I would do. I was moving from one type of romance to another. The thing was, did I really want to go along with this strange to me, woman?

I looked at the photo again getting something in my head to say that would not upset her and try and make her understand what I was going to say next.

You look just like you do in this picture, you look happy, relaxed, at ease with yourself, was this taken in France?"

"Yes!" she simply replied. I turned to face her front on, and she stood upright, shaking, petrified as to what I would say, do. Would I walk past her, grab my laptop and fur coat and walk out of the apartment without saying another word or would I say something else that would hurt her so bad? She would return to her bedroom and face Death head on in her own form and demand Him to take her soul, she couldn't live without me. Life would be meaningless, she would leave it, immediately; there would be no second chances. She had been hurt before and she would not be hurt like that again.

She stood still, looking at me, also standing still, looking at each other. A lifetime must have passed between us until I finally took my first petrified step towards Gabrielle. Would she love me like Paul had or would it be different, more different than just a husband and wife?

I took my second step towards her, she was still standing upright, still, rooted to the ground, not being able to move a muscle. Just her emerald, green bright eyes followed my steps towards her. Would I walk past her or approach her, take her hand and kiss her?

I took another step, slowed to a halt and gazed at her. She was magnificent, beautiful, radiant and I fell instantly in love with her, and I would never leave her for the rest of my life, if we had all eternity together.

I couldn't just let her stand there now, I ran the rest of the short way to the door and Gabrielle, the love of my life. I was such a lucky girl.

"I love you Gabrielle, I blurted out. I buried my head into her breasts, small as they were, she was to me a woman and I was sure with all my heart that she was falling in love all over again and this time, despite that were married man and wife, I would have to do something about it.

"I love you too," Gabrielle finally blurted out.

We kissed, long and hard, like lovers do. A meaningful kiss that told each other of the deepest love and feelings for each other. There would be no more secrets between us that way we could be so very deeply in love that it didn't matter. We knew each other's deepest secrets so there was nothing to be frightened about. No lies to tell and they could have an open and honest relationship with no worries, just love and more and more love.

We embraced each other, held each other as if it would be our last hold as the world exploded around us. We kissed again and again, our mouths rotating about each other as our tongues explored each other's mouth and tasted the love coming from inside us.

I went into the top bedroom and coat room off it. I put my fur coat on, it was still cold outside, and I found another fur coat a few days previous. I took it off its hanger and walked into the lounge. "Come on Gabrielle, arms down straight and watch your hands."

I pulled the coat up over her arms and carefully, watched her hands were not hurt and pulled it onto her shoulders. I was around the front of her in an instant, grinning like a Cheshire cat. I buttoned up her coat and checked her makeup again, especially her lipstick which like mine had smudged slightly due to our intensive kissing. I put it right, checked her again and placed the strap of a matching colour bag onto her shoulder and pulled her hand through the strap so it would not fall off.

"Where did this come from?" Gabrielle asked.

"I'll explain later, come on, let's leave here for a while."

"Okay, a short walk around the block," Gabrielle replied.

"Like Hell," I replied grinning. "Come on." I led her to the front door, opened it, set the alarm, closed the door and locked it.

John was already out of the car with the engine running keeping it snug and warm. There was fresh snow on the road and paths. I looked up and through the snow clouds, I could see stars, thousands of them. This night was just meant to be, I thought to myself as John assisted Gabrielle into the back of our shorter limousine.

"You two still deep in love?" John asked. We were open with everyone, they all knew what we were like, young lovers who couldn't leave each other alone.

"John, I fell so deep in love with Gabrielle all over again. I love her to death, I won't leave her side, forever."

"Gabrielle?" he asked. John had seen Gabrielle loads of times, even got her back home when she got drunk and was so low after one of her girlfriends left her trying to take some of his fortune; she was getting drunk a lot then they spent four months in France, expanding her business empire. All her staff knew Gabrielle and

Paul, but they all loved Gabrielle, she was softer, happier, at ease with the staff and herself.

Gabrielle took the staff to long lunches where they ate and drank in the cafes, talking in fluent French, having a good time, getting to know each other and Gabrielle, everyone loved her. Paul on the other hand, was much stricter, a different person altogether, sombre, not at ease with himself, looking at the girls wishing he were them, something he couldn't be.

Café lunches were rare, but no wine, coffee and a meal and back to the shop to work, depending on his mood and how lunch went. The girls always tried to cheer him up, so they had an extra few minutes for lunch and a slow walk back to the shop for two-thirty.

"John, I too fell in love with this ravenous, distrustful, and deceiving woman."

"Did anyone tell her about me?" Gabrielle asked.

"No," I replied, "I knew about you in hospital and of course Death told me that the person who would save me would change just for me. I never wanted a man; I wanted a woman, and I got the best of both worlds. Well for now, I'm sure Paul wants a sex change. Who would spend a fortune on a hospital, especially Kings Cross which is famous for its sex change operations?"

"Would you mind?" Gabrielle asked.

"Hell no, when do you start?"

"I need to get my hands fixed properly first, but I have gone through all the pshyco talk and I've been given the go ahead for the operation. It's been finding the time to get it done, although I am taking female hormone tablets, behind your back I'm afraid."

"Well tonight, get them out and we'll add them to your daily tablet regime, is that fine with you?" I asked Gabrielle.

"Of course, my love, I can't wait to be like this all the time, if you're happy with me like it. I know my psychiatrist will want to speak with you as well."

"Fine with me. We kissed again as we held hands gently."

"Where are you taking me?" Gabrielle asked.

"Well on the day we met you were going to take me to the Shard, so it's only fair that on the night we met, I take you to the Shard. The table is booked and don't worry about your hands, I'll help you with your food if you need it. I know you have taken clients to the Shard before as Gabrielle and the staff there are quite at ease with your change of dress. Just think of me as one of your most expensive clients and you have to get an order from me that will keep your shops going for the entire summer."

"That's easy," Gabrielle replied, we kissed, and we talked a little more about her likes and dislikes until we reached the Shard. When the three of us reached the restaurant floor, I made her walk backwards, not easy in high heels the short distance to our table.

"Close your eyes and turn around; I just want you to see the layout to be a surprise for you."

As she turned around everyone was standing and they applauded her and cheered, shouting her name. Even her mum and dad were there, and I sat beside Gabrielle grinning and talking with everyone, her staff, Alan, John, Jenny, his wife, Sarah was sat next to Alan, I could already see a match being made in Heaven. They were getting closer, and I noticed Alan was never concerned when he had to take Sarah shopping.

I was very, happy for them, but Alan was mine as well; he was my personal bodyguard and Sarah would have to come second if we were out and about together.

We all had a happy and memorable evening. Gabrielle was now out in the open with her wife and her parents were so happy I accepted her and still loved her as I did yesterday, but today I loved her a little bit more.

I cut up all Gabrielle's food and helped her when it was difficult and sorted out her wine glass, so she didn't have to pick it up; she drank her wine through a straw.

Near the end of the evening, I stood and tapped my glass with a knife, just like any man would when he wanted everyone's attention. Everyone went quiet.

I was up and ready to talk, but now I was worried, I hadn't talked this through with Gabrielle, but I hoped she would go along with it.

"I want to thank you all for coming at such short notice, but Gabrielle took her time to tell me what I already knew." There were a few laughs along the long table with thirty of his staff and her family there.

"Things are about to change, Paul will hardly ever be seen in your shops again, it will be myself, when I'm not signing my books, and Gabrielle. I think Gabrielle is a much happier person than Paul, and she's happy with her body and the way she looks. It will be Gabrielle who is in charge now and I hope everyone will get along with her and help her when she needs it.

"She's been a long time coming but now she has arrived. I would like you all to raise your glass and toast my very, beautiful and ravenous wife, Gabrielle."

Everyone raised their glass and shouted, "Gabrielle!" She went to stand to reply but I gently pushed her shoulder down and she was back in her seat looking up at me. We started to break up then, it was just gone eleven thirty and most of us had work tomorrow. It was still snowing outside. and the roads would be slippery.

Mum and dad came over to me and held my hand. Mum was first to hug and kiss me then it was dad's turn and he kissed me on the lips, he knew I didn't mind, I felt honoured that this billionaire had taken me in to be his daughter-in law before we even got married and they both loved me as if I was their own child. "Thank you for accepting Gabrielle as you have. I was worried things would go wrong and Gabrielle would not come along, I knew you knew about her and you didn't let on. I'm so happy for you both," dad said.

"You are staying with us tonight, aren't you? You can't have Mike drive you thirty miles away, and in the snow as well. You can have the red room; Mike and Penny, can sleep in the basement as usual."

"We don't want to intrude, this is your first night together, well, you know, making love can be noisy at times."

"Mum, you're not intruding; anyway, I had our room soundproofed when Paul, Gabrielle, came out of hospital because he was shouting out in the night and crying in pain.

When we finally got to bed, Sarah had left us matching satin short nighties and panties. At the bottom of our bed were two matching pink and rose covered satin negligees and two pairs of pink slippers.

I gave Gabrielle all her tablets then rubbed cream into her hands and massaged them until they were supple. We kissed often and long while I was doing this which made it last longer, but we didn't mind. We were dressed in our nighties and once we were under our duvet, we were playing and they soon came off and we had our first night as Lesbians, it felt so good. I was proud of Gabrielle and always will be.

I suddenly came back to reality. Had I been dreaming or what? How much time had passed? We were still kissing our mouths rotating, I felt Gabrielle's tongue inside my mouth and licked it profusely as we played our kissing game.

I glanced at my watch, three minutes fifty seconds had passed, the time it took Paul to kill two men and save four lives, putting his own life on the line and dying, even if it were for a short time, he was dead; his soul had left his body and was in Death's hands. A chill ran up and down my spine and I was petrified. This had to be a sign from Death. He was going to make Gabrielle fight for my life for three minutes fifty seconds. How much damage could a maniac like George and two of his mates do to her in that short time?

She could be hurt badly, and once again must go through months of operations and hospital stays if Death had His way and brought the whole fight to its different ending in this second timeline.

I had recalled every moment of that timeline, every minute that hurt Paul and me, because I knew he had been fighting for my life, just like he would be fighting for my life once again and once again the fight would be one sided and who knew what Death had planned for that early evening?

I knew for sure that my memory of the event in that first timeline took longer than four minutes. Perhaps Death had taken me out of time again and made me recollect the event from my perspective and that of my cameraman. Listening to him then, he had filled in some of the blanks I was worried about. Here I was now, safe in the arms of my wonderful wife, Gabrielle. How could Death be so cruel as to put us though the first fight all over again?

I had just imagined and lived through it second by second, it all happened so fast. I shut my eyes and cringed as I thought once again about the double-edged sword and Paul's shredded hands. I didn't want him to go through all that pain for me again. I had to think of something, some way to get Death to change His plans. Gabrielle was a woman now, God, surely, He wouldn't strip her of her new shape and sex? Please Death, don't do that, I'll give into George and hand myself over to him and see what happens, how the cards fall.

A voice, a powerful voice entered my head. "No, I will not do that, it would be too cruel Gabrielle is a woman now and she is not as strong as Paul, it will make a more interesting battle. The only gift I will temporary take away from her will be the Jump, I want to see how much she is in love with you. How far she will go to protect you and how far she would be willing to go to save your life.

"She will not be able to die, Fate has seen to that and pointed out some of the rules we set up between us, behind your backs so to speak. There is still the bigger quest and I want to win that's for sure. This will show me how good my chances of winning are, I might just be able to change the end game.

"I am growing tired of this game; I would like to set it up on another planet in another solar system where the game can start afresh. Your people have ruined the planet, Mother Nature is getting more and more annoyed with your species.

"You contaminate the oceans where you have no right to be. Your plastic waste kills my fish and your atomic bombs and futile rockets have contaminated the atmosphere so bad, you have Climate Change and this will in the end change the shape of the land masses and cause me a lot of problems with Mother Nature and She will; have no option but to stop this from happening and reset your planet to an earlier timeline which will instantaneously wipe your species off the planet and into oblivion where I will not be able to rescue your souls and do what I wanted to do with them."

"Does Mother Nature really exist or is this some ploy you are trying to plant into my mind. Because if she does exist there is nothing I or Gabrielle can do to stop her resetting the timeline as you yourself can do. Who is in charge of our game here; as you call it?"

"I am its ultimate Umpire, and it is up to me who dies and who lives. Fate can plan lives, but I can over-rule Him, as I have already done by recreating the first timeline for George and now you, to be the cup, the ultimate prize. Gabrielle must fight him once again, fight him to show Me how much love he has for you."

I realised something then, Death had used the word love a couple of times, who loved me the most? George in his mad mixed-up state of mind or the love of my life Gabrielle? It was not a fight, but a battle and a battle involved more than one person. I just might be able to get Alan to help Gabrielle as the battle continues into its limited time of three minutes fifty seconds. That is all the time Gabrielle would have to do to stay alive without any scars, but would she win the game?

I knew how much Gabrielle loved me, she had showed me more times than once and fought to the death for me in our first timeline together. Death also knew how much she loved me and what George thought of me, all he wanted me for was to be his whore and wants me raped day and night and have my body cut apart by his mates who would think it funny to see me bleed and hurt. To scream out in pain and beg for mercy. Give my body time to recover while I considered the many ways of dying so my body was no use to George and my soul would probably end up in Hell for all eternity, but it couldn't be any worse than what I would be going through if George won the battle.

Death had said Gabrielle would fight George and Gabrielle, now a perfect woman, did not have the strength Paul had or the expertise with the knife throwing. She had been practicing daily in the back garden but no matter how she tried, she could not get the knives up to their hilt in the thick plastic bodies she had asked to be produced to help her build up her muscles.

Her thin arms, to fit her fine clothes could not grow the muscle she would need. She would need to use another tactic but was she really up to it? A fight, no matter if the odds were stacked in your favour was still a fight and the other person would have to be very clever to stay alive long enough to win the fight, even if it were to the death again.

I was back in my own time and our kiss was continuing, I felt her love for me, I hoped I was passing all my love to Gabrielle. We slowed and our romantic session ceased, slowly and serenely, my hand came around to Gabrielle's front and I lowered my hand gently and in a sexy way over her breasts and down to her belly. I held her dress, which ended just above her knees and told her to put the trousers on.

That is what she had been asking me a few hours ago in my time, but a few minutes in her time. She was laughing it would be strange to see her in a suit again, a man's suit anyway.

"You've got hips now my love and a thinner waist, a woman's shape. Put the trousers on and let's have a look, I'll call Sarah in to get her opinion. She knows all about clothes, she'll tell you if you need new trousers and look at this waistcoat. It's for a man, a woman's is cut lower and wider for her breasts."

"I'm supposed to wear a man's suit, oh why did I agree to that? I was so stupid, I could have worn a miniskirt and hoped he would fall in love with my legs and jump off the Empire State Building himself, just for me."

"Gabrielle, you are not going to wear a miniskirt at any time. You are not a silly teenager who is hoping the boys will want to have her for sex, just because they get an erection seeing her legs and probably her ass as well when she bends down on purpose, just to get a boy's attention.

"You will wear this suit and do not get blood all over it, it cost two thousand pounds. You will win this fight with my love behind you and in your heart. Now put the trousers on and I'll get Sarah."

Sarah looked at the trousers and laughed. "Take your dress off and let's see the rest of the suit on you. I think it might be better to buy a woman's business suit for a boardroom meeting.

"Let me take all your measurements and I'll see what can be done for you. The coat is falling off your shoulders the waistcoat is too large for you. At least let me buy you a smaller sized suit so I have something to work with?"

"Okay, I'll leave it all up to you. I will need to be able to move my arms easily and not fall over my own trousers."

"Take the trousers off, they make you look silly. Put your dress back on, no, get a white blouse out and put that on with a skirt of your choice for now. Your shirts will be too big for you as well and the blouse will give you a little more room in the arms and be lighter for you than a shirt. If you are going to fight George and he kills you, then I want you to die in something that looks good on you," she said annoyed, and tears were welling in her eyes.

She didn't want anything to happen to Gabrielle, somewhere deep in her heart she still had some feelings for her; she loved Gabrielle in her own way. She collapsed into her arms and kissed her on her lips.

"I'm sorry Lynda, that was unacceptable of me."

"No, it wasn't, we all love Gabrielle and feel for her. Nobody wants to see her hurt again or have to go through this battle with George," I replied.

"Battle, I thought it was just a fight, for about four minutes, the exact time the first fight took to complete?" she asked.

"George said it was to be a battle and something about the exact time of the first fight."

Sarah slapped her forehead with her open palm. "I didn't realise it was a battle, that changes things. I need time and we might have to put our time of leaving back by an hour or so. I must go. Alan, get the car," she shouted through our bedroom door and into the apartment.

She grabbed her phone with all the measurements on and practically ripped the waistcoat from her body.

"Oh, I need to wear this double knife holder as well." She threw it at her, Sarah caught it as she ran out of the door into the lounge. She put her fur coat on and grabbed her bag pushing her phone into it.

Alan was already in the underground garage getting the car ready to drive out. The garage door was opening as Sarah jumped into the car and told Alan where they needed to go. She explained what she had realised when Lynda once again went through what George had said at the mansion and Alan agreed, in theory anyway, which for Alan was halfway there and Sarah's theory deserved to be thought through a little more.

Sarah used her top of the range iPad to sketch out what she wanted and what the waistcoat would look like. Alan told her to design a knew knife holder for a woman's shape, as the one she had in her hands was for a man and the knives would get caught on Gabrielle's curvaceous bottom. The belt would have to sit higher up her body under the waistcoat so that she could get easy access to the knives once they were inside it and there should be a hold and fast release system, so Gabrielle could retrieve them fast and with ease, not catching on her clothes or her body.

"Gabrielle might need both the knives in a hurry and the third knife would have to go inside her jacket, once again easy to get at and retrieve. The knives would all need to be retrieved ready to use; Gabrielle wouldn't have that much time," Alan told her.

They arrived at the shop where they needed to be five minutes later as the roads were still Icey and snow covered in places. All the traffic lights went in their favour and Alan wondered if some traffic controller was giving them a helping hand. There was even a vacant parking bay outside the shop. They were both out of the car; Alan checked around them and followed Sarah into the shop. She had already phoned the manager and told him what she wanted and to expect them very soon, but even Sarah was amazed at the time it had taken them to drive the eight miles through London traffic.

They were taken through to the back room where Dave, the main clothes designer, printed off the designs from Sarah's iPad. He was already getting the material from out the back again as they didn't have that much call for it for some reason.

The material was already double sided so that both layers would be running in the same direction and when it was cut out and stitched together, both parts of the legs would be the same.

The outside would be on the inside of the leg and the inside of the trouser leg on the outside.

Dave was already sketching out one of the trouser legs on the special material and talking to another man about the knife holders they would need to make this evening. Sarah kept looking at her watch, time was moving on and there were still other things she would need.

"You need to be somewhere else?" Dave asked.

"Yes, a couple of places."

"I have all I need for now, can you bring her in for eight in the morning, we'll work as late as possible and get as much of the suit done, but Gabrielle will need to come in and try the clothes on before we finish them off. I will also want to see each of the knives she is taking. They may difference in thickness and we'll be using a special material that knives are held in inside a suit jacket like you have designed and the double knife holder. I want to make sure it fits properly so she can access the knives easily. I also want her to wear the blouse she is wearing on the day; can you do that?"

"We'll be here at eight on the dot," Sarah replied.

"She might be here for a few hours, but Gabrielle will make the midday tide, or my name isn't Dave Raley."

"Thanks Dave, we'll see you in the morning. I may have another little job for you then, but it shouldn't take long." They left the shop and headed into the centre of the city and the larger shopping Malls. The first shop they went to see was a shoe shop she always used. Sarah knew exactly what she was looking for. She raced around the shop looking for a Cuban heel black boot, thigh high, with a zip on the inside, in a size six.

Rather look she asked the sales, girl who looked at her feet which were a size five.

"They will be expensive," she said. She was a new girl and wanted to look down on this woman who was three inches shorter than herself. Sarah looked around and called out.

"Roselin, can you help me please; this young girl doesn't seem to know who I am? I'm in a terrible hurry and I need to visit a few more shops before they close."

"Of course, Sarah, what do you need?"

Sarah explained again and what she needed them for.

"I know just the thing, is Gabrielle really going to go through with it?"

"You know?"

"We all know about the fight, George's thugs used to get money from us, but the Mafia has put a stop to that and until this is all over, we have Andrea on loan to protect us. She carries a Glock like Alan. Tell her good luck from us. I'll be back in a moment, there is a special pair of boots out the back.

"What do you think of these? They have a fifty mm Cuban heel as you asked for, up to just below her knee and look, they have a special hard leather insert which keeps the boot upright and protects the heel. They are two thousand pounds, but Gabrielle can have them on us."

"Are you sure? She might lose."

"At least she would have tried, nobody else will stand up to George. Our prayers will go out to her."

"Thank you Roselin, you're a star." The shoes were put into their special box, then into a bag and the women kissed cheek to cheek.

"Good luck!" Then Alan took Sarah's hand, and they were gone, hurrying to the next shop further along the Mall.

"Stacey," Roselin said when Sarah had left the shop. Stacey, who had first spoke to Sarah, walked full of young teen spirit to the head floor manager.

"When Sarah comes in again, if you ever speak to her like you're looking down on her, you'll be sacked immediately. Next time she comes in, you will apologise to her."

"I bet she doesn't have enough money to shop here, and those boots cost two grand and that would have been a good sale for me; you gave them away. I knew she had no money. I'll tell Tom the manager of the shop. It will be you who gets the sack for giving them away."

"I'm well aware who Tom is. Go and tell him now, see what he has to say." Roselin pointed to the back door where the stairs led up to his office.

She knocked on the door certain she was going to get her manager into trouble. As she told her tale again, Tom stood up.

"Is Sarah still here?"

"No, she left with the two thousand-pound boots which she didn't pay for, Roselin gave them to her."

"You stupid girl, Sarah works for Gabrielle Grayson, She, could buy this Mall in cash. Sarah buys all Gabrielle's shoes from here and spends at least ten thousand pounds a year here. Next time she comes in, you will apologise and grovel to her. So,

Gabrielle is going to fight George, I'm glad she's wearing our boots. That will make excellent coverage in the press.

"Go and clear up the Stock Room and I want to be able to see it all very clean."

"But the cleaner does that?"

"Stacey, sometimes you have to work from the ground up. For the next two hours, you're the cleaner. Now go!" Tom pointed to his door with an outstretched arm.

As soon as Stacey left his office, he picked up the phone and started to call different shops in the Mall speaking to all the managers. "Gabrielle's going to fight George, she's leaving for the USA tomorrow in her yacht."

Word was spreading through the Mall as fast as lightning. By the time Sarah got to the glove shop, the manager there already knew all about her needs.

"Sarah, welcome to Gray's Glove & Hat store. I think you are looking for strong women's leather gloves in a size seven?"

"Yes, how did you know?"

"We do have phones you know," he laughed. "All your money couldn't buy anything in this Mall this afternoon, so put your Gold President card away."

"Thank you!"

"You tell Gabrielle our prayers go with her. Now you are getting her special suit made at Masons Suits, aren't you?"

"Yes, why?

"I had a quick word with Dave Raley, he will do another job for you in the morning. Just a moment." He paused calling for another assistant. "Joan, can you turn these gloves inside out for me please?"

"Of course, Andrew." She took the gloves and was gone in a flash. "Dave will need a special needle to do the job and this twine. Here is a packet of five needles just in case and a new roll of twine. Drop it into him on the way home and he will know what to do with it. None of his needles will do the job they need to and Gabrielle needs to look the perfect woman, like she always is. May I also suggest a bit of bling on the back of the hands? Here is a special bottle of glue to do the job. Samuels are waiting for you," he said handing her the bag with the gloves inside, inside out ready for Dave.

They went up to Samuels Diamond Rings shop and the door was opened for them by one of the assistants. "Please Sarah, go to the top counter Peter is waiting to serve you."

"Welcome Sarah, I've made some designs for the back hand of the gloves. Andrew has given me the basic idea he has for them. Here is my design. Take these diamond chips, and Dave will glue them onto the gloves. The glue doesn't take long to dry, it will be invisible once it's dry.

"I didn't want to add too many big stones that I would normally suggest to you. These chips will be enough Bling to perhaps give her a few extra seconds when she needs them. They will certainly help protect the back of her hands.

"By my reckoning, it will take about fifty stones per glove to make the design, so I have added a few extra." The diamond chips were in a black, glass tray and he poured them into a small envelope and sealed it shut.

"Give this and this design to Dave and he will sort the gloves out. Tell Gabrielle our prayers go with her and wish her all the luck God can give her."

The two items were put into a small black velvet bag. Sarah put it into her handbag so it wouldn't be lost. Then they were onto the next store, Sonya's Hair bands. Sarah needed a strong hairband to hold Gabrielle's long hair at the back of her head and some to curl around her neck making her look sexy. She also needed some bling for her hair and started to look around. Sonya watched as Sarah and Alan entered the shop.

Sarah, I have what you need I think, come and take a look. I'm Sonya, the manageress."

"Hello Sonya, word is spreading fast."

"Yes, like the other shops, your money is no good here today. You need some bling for Gabrielle's long hair. If you use this or this hair band, it will still drop around her neck making her look sexy and may give her a few extra seconds."

"Seconds will count in this fight. I like the feel of the hairband and oh, I love the bling you've sorted out for her. What do you think Alan?"

He stepped forward and looked at the bling, picking up a couple of pieces and smiled. "That will do simply fine, just what she needs to put George and his mates off her for a good twenty seconds and that's a great deal of time for her. Good bling Sonya."

Sonya put the bling and ten hairbands in a bag and handed it to Sarah. "Please give Gabrielle all our love and our prayers will go with her."

"Of course, I will do just that, everyone is being so kind today."

"George and his thugs have terrorised this Mall and put customers off coming here. It's about time someone stood up to him, I'm just sorry it's Gabrielle."

"Thank you again, I'll tell all my rich girlfriends to come here. Bye for now, I'll be back, a lot." Alan opened the door for her, checked outside then they were gone, off to the next shop, Harold's Tie Bar.

Sarah picked out a sparkling light grey silk tie, wide enough to make a good Full Windsor knot. Alan used the same knot, as too John and Mike, it was what made a man look smart.

"I'll take this tie please," she said getting out her card. "It's free to you today. May I also suggest you add this single diamond tie pin to add a bit of bling, which is what you are looking for. Gabrielle will need every second she can get; this just might give her a few seconds.

"Is she wearing a blouse with long sleeves and double cuffs?"

"Yes, she is," Sarah replied in shock, she had given no real thought to Gabrielle's blouse, but she had one with double cuffs. She had purchased it just a few months ago to help hide the scars on her wrists.

"Then may I suggest these, emerald nine carat gold cufflinks.

The emeralds will match the colour of her eyes. It's a bit more bling, and it may catch George's eyes and make him stop and smile for just a few seconds.

"I do have another suggestion; these emerald encrusted tie pins could replace the last button on her suit jacket. It's just bling really, but they are real emeralds. They are ten millimetres in diameter, set in nine carat gold. There is a small eyelet at the back in case you wish to sew it for security on her jacket sleeve. More bling?" he said grinning.

"Let me put them in the bag and you can make a decision when you see it on her suit jacket."

"Everyone seems to know what is happening," Sarah said smiling.

"I had to pay half of my takings each week to his thugs and they checked my books to make sure they were getting the correct amount of money. They used to take a new tie every week, not that they could tie a decent knot, they looked silly, not worth wearing a tie in the first place.

"Since Gabrielle and Lynda got that Treaty signed, the Mafia have moved in and kicked a lot of George's men out. I've never heard from them again, perhaps they're all dead but good riddance to them. The Mafia guys are good and talk to everyone just like the cops did, but they carry guns which they are not afraid to use, and the Mall is once again full of people."

"Do they take money from you?"

"Hell no, they pay for my ties and extras, in cash, almost every week. They are so friendly; nobody steals anymore, not even the kids and they all behave, or they might get shot in the leg. It's a real safe place to shop. I'll be sorry to lose them when they have to go."

"I'll tell Gabrielle and Lynda, perhaps they can arrange for them to stay if you all agree?"

"Thank you. Tell Gabrielle we're routing for her and sending her our prayers. I hope the bling gives her the extra seconds she needs."

"I'm sure they will. Thank you."

They left the tie bar and Sarah looked at her watch. "We have time for coffee, and I do so fancy a cake right now. I must make sure I have everything, and I need a few calm minutes to think. What do you say?" she asked her husband.

"You my love are in charge and if you want coffee, you shall have it. Tomorrow will be too late to come here again and shop. You'll be with Dave Raley most of the morning and it will be a late evening for you packing."

"Sweetheart, I packed our cases, you'll be wearing that suit tomorrow morning and when we get on the yacht, you can change into something casual. We'll have time to relax and get some sun on our bodies, if it comes out on our way to New York."

They went to the nearest Star Bucks and Alan ordered two cappuccinos and two lemon tarts, just the right cake for his wife. Once again, he was told it was all free, the staff were just, glad to help. Alan sat down at the table Sarah had picked for them and they waited for their drinks to arrive.

They went to one more shop then back to the car and off to see Dave Raley.

By the time they got there, Dave had cut out the trousers and a seamstress was now carefully sewing the material together and adding a grey satin lining to the legs. Their laser cutting machine was cutting out the design of the waistcoat and the lining.

Another man was working on the leather knife sheaths that would be added to the jacket and the double knife holder she would wear around her waist.

By the time Sarah had gone through the glove designs with Dave and made the suggestions for the jacket sleeves, Sarah left everything he would need, it was almost eight pm and their evening meal would be on the table in the dining room.

They arrived at the apartment just as everyone was getting ready to sit down for food. Sarah explained her thoughts for the special day to Lynda and Gabrielle over the meal and they agreed to be up early, like they usually were, and leave the apartment at seven thirty so they had plenty of time to get to Harold's Suits. There would be a lot to get through and Lynda had her own jobs to complete before they left.

Despite having loads to do herself, Gabrielle found herself looking at the tie and getting out her long sleeved double cuffed satin blouse. It had a collar the same as a man's shirt, which was the general idea for when she had boardroom meetings. She also had to try on and walk about the apartment in her new boots, which Lynda said were very sexy and she was getting smiles from the men as she started to break them in, and the Cuban heels made a lot of noise as she walked on the wooden floor.

Chapter 5

The boots had made them both feel sexy and when they retired at midnight, mum had retired at eleven and was now asleep. In bed, they were soon making love, exploring each other's body, playing with their breasts, kissing them, licking them, fondling them in the way two women played with each other.

Gabrielle was so happy; she couldn't get enough of Lynda's body. She licked her all over and was kissing her breasts while her fingers were playing with her clitoris then she inserted them into her vagina and was bringing her vagina walls towards Lynda's first orgasm.

When Gabrielle found Lynda's G Spot, Lynda let out a small scream, which no one in the house heard, only Gabrielle, knowing she had achieved her goal, making Lynda feel so desired by her wife.

Gabrielle didn't stop there, she wanted Lynda to have another orgasm so slowly, kissing her breasts down to her stomach, she kissed her way to her clitoris. She kissed it profusely, licked it, sometimes slipping her tongue into her vagina. Her hands held Lynda's slim body and then her hips as she inserted her tongue into her vagina as far as she could. Licking it, kissing her clitoris again and pushing her tongue in and out of her vagina. Her fingers took over from her tongue; her lips now started kissing Lynda's thighs, legs, making her even more aroused as her fingers worked their magic to her G Spot.

Just before Lynda was about to have her orgasm, Gabrielle moved quickly up her other leg, kissing and licking it, then to her thigh and finally, just as she was having her orgasm, Gabrielle was kissing her clitoris and then inserting her tongue into her vagina as her hands massaged her thighs. Lynda came, her love juices swirling around her vagina walls making them very wet and her juices running over Gabrielle's tongue and into her mouth.

When Lynda calmed back down, her hands were clawing Gabrielle back up her body, slowly, so she felt every kiss and lick Gabrielle made. Finally, their lips met once again, they kissed passionately, their mouths rotating about each other, their tongues in each other's mouth. Their heads were at an angle so their lips could kiss softly and show each other how much they were loved by their partner.

Lynda, grinning and laughing, commenced to lower her head and kissed Gabrielle's breasts. She cupped each one in her soft hand, licking it and kissing it, sucking her nipple, making it hard and large.

It was thrilling for her, there was no urgency, and Gabrielle was so careful and oh . . . so very sexy. Lynda knew she was loved, she felt loved and their love making was all about love, not the urgency to fuck her and come inside her then leave her alone after only a minute had passed, that was most of the time for George and she was glad it was all over so fast.

With Gabrielle, she wanted their love making to last as long, as possible and Gabrielle made it last. She enjoyed her sex organs; she couldn't get enough of them, and her mouth enjoyed them as well. Not like some men who didn't have a clue what a clitoris was let alone play with it to arouse his woman.

Gabrielle was so gentle with her and now it was her turn, which she loved, to bring Gabrielle to her orgasm, then they would relax and kiss, hold each other's naked body. Stroke each other's soft feminine skin, slowly arousing each other so they fingered each other and saw who would climax first.

They would cry with delight as they whispered, "I love you," into each other's ears, kissing and gently biting them in a sexy way, pushing the tip of their tongue into their ear and licking it, then down each other's cheek so their lips met and started to kiss passionately again.

Knowing time was against them they had to be up early again, they slowly fondled each other's body. Gabrielle moved so she was on her back and Lynda slithered over her body and lay on top of her, so their bodies were touching head to foot. While they still kissed their souls passed deep feelings of love to each other, making them feel loved, wanted, needed and partners for life, no matter how long life would be.

They would need no other person to make them happy, because they couldn't get any happier than they were now. Gabrielle's soft arms wrapped themselves around Lynda on top of her. Her hands stroked her back, curving into her slim waist and over to caress her small bum. Her arms were fully stretched now, but it didn't stop her caressing the love of her life's back, slowly, sexy, all the way to her neck. She looked into Lynda's green eyes and both their eyes grew brighter, stronger and lit up the room in their love for each other.

Their green eyes lit the room up and the light slipped effortlessly through the ultra-thin gaps between the doorframe and into the passage. Their light passed through their bedroom window and into the garden then the street. People must have wondered where the light was coming from. As their kisses and feelings of love intensified, so the brighter their eyes became and tonight, they were showing so much love for each other, their green eyes were brighter than they had ever been before.

They wanted to meld into each other's body, be one person but in the same body so they could melt into each other's love which would encase them forever into a spirit that would travel the universe. Together, eyes now paired, souls so close to each other they touched and rotated about each other as if they were kissing in one body.

Lynda was petrified as Sarah made her plans to try and protect the person she once loved, but she was married now and happy with Alan but deep down there was still a fire burning for this woman. A desire that would keep her flame burning for the rest of her life.

All Lynda had to offer was her unconditional love. Her love for Paul had kept him alive and even brought him back to life as she stayed at his head, talking continuously, praying to Death for the man she had so quickly fallen head over heels in love with. Their love so deeply in love even though they had only met a few hours previously. Her love had overcome his injuries and his broken body would heel with her love to keep his spirits high and want to be with her faster and faster. He would want to be out of the hospital as soon as he could so he could hold her naked body and make love.

It would be so very gentle because he had been through Hell and back, had died and spoken with his friend Death, and had his soul returned to his body so he could live to meet the woman who he loved dearly, he had saved her life. He would make her incredibly happy, and they would be together all their lives.

Now the threat was coming closer. The trip to the States made it more real and in her heart of hearts, she knew the love of her life would suffer once again with only her love to keep Gabrielle alive. Why of why did this hideous game have to take place? She was a human being, not a dead soul which was already behind the Black Velvet Curtain of Death.

The first timeline was crushed; it was only a few which had been given access to its existence who could recall it had ever happened. Now they were in a different timeline; the future, their future had changed. Death had given them a Second Chance at life together.

Now Death was playing a game with them, their lives, both their lives were at stake. Death was playing a deadly game with Gabrielle this time. Our timelines were merging with George who was now certain he was in the first timeline. He was confused and deadly furious at Gabrielle, Paul for taking his life so early and he wanted her back, in that timeline not this one.

He wanted Lynda for himself so he could make money from her and he could take her any way he liked. Cut her where he liked. Watch her bleed out if necessary, she would be his to do with as he liked and Paul, Gabrielle, would not be there to give her his protection. Death's reaper could reap in any soul He so desired and Death would and could change their lives and destiny in an instant. Once done, Fate would be no longer able to intervene. The body would be gone, burned to ashes no longer able to protect its soul.

Lynda wondered if her love would be enough to save the woman she loved so dearly. It would have to with the help from Sarah's idea and whatever she had planned for the following morning; the morning they were in now and one day closer to a battle for life; a battle neither woman wanted to be involved with. They had already fought and finally, over time, won the battle they had gone through. There was no need to put their souls through it again.

Lynda came back to her own thoughts, their eyes were still bright green, their mouths were rotating against each other, and she felt Gabrielle's warm arms over her back, holding her in place on top of her and making sure Lynda would be protected by her no matter what she had to go through.

Lynda was petrified of losing Gabrielle by some freak accident. What if George managed to throw her off the Empire State Building, unless Fate or Death intervened, there would be no way she could rebuild her body. It would be smashed, brutally to Death, more than likely flattened and the force of the landing would crush every organ in her body including her brain.

"Why oh, why am I still thinking about something that is a month away, four whole weeks, twenty-eight days?"

She could feel Gabrielle's arms firmly around her. She didn't seem worried or concerned about the days to come However, there was one change in her. They had kissed more frequently outside, in their shops and at a restaurant or coffee shops.

They had gone out more, enjoying each other's company, holding hands, she hardly ever let go and oh . . . the kisses out and about were sexier, sometimes she was nearing an orgasm. Gabrielle left work for the evening when for one hour, she would sit in the office and talk endlessly to Susan, the name of the computer there. She would call our French office speaking fluently in French, asking for information about members of staff. What was she planning, what had she in mind?

Every night now she found herself in Gabrielle's arms when she woke in the morning. They kissed, slowly, tongues sneakily entering each other's dry mouth from their night's sleep. Their saliva entered each other making their mouths wet and ready for more sexier exploration.

She would feel Gabrielle's hands and arms run up and down her back, yet she knew Gabrielle wanted more of her, and she gave Gabrielle everything, every ounce of love she had to give her. Her body ached to have sex with her because Gabrielle made her come so well.

Every morning since the meeting with George, they had made love and she had come every day, not that there was any difference, they usually made some form of love in the morning to start their day right.

They were kissing again now, Gabrielle's hand was gently over her vagina, her fingers fondling her clitoris. She breathed in deeply as Gabrielle's fingers entered her vagina after gently fondling her clitoris. As her head moved, she glanced at their bedside clock. It was only five thirty, they had barely three hours sleep. She was looking forward to their time on the yacht, at least they could have sex and play for as long as they liked without having to get up early.

She relaxed into the bed allowing Gabrielle's fingers to enter her vagina. She grabbed Gabrielle's other arm, holding it close to her side then concentrated on her orgasm. She could feel Gabrielle's fingers get deeper inside her and she had found her G Spot so fast. She was working it fast, and Lynda couldn't stop herself from coming. Gabrielle didn't stop, her fingers and hand saturated with her lovers, hot love juices.

Gabrielle was playing with her saturated vagina walls, moving her fingers in and out of Lynda's body as they kissed profusely, lips rotating, tongues intertwined, their eyes glowing in the early dark morning.

"Relax my love, we're still together and we'll be on the yacht later today. I'm not going to die, Death told us, I'll just have to go through it all over again. I won't let George win you know that.

I'll give my life to save you and I promise you, no matter what happens, you'll never have to go back with him, there is another way out, but I'll tell you later, for now, relax and enjoy our sex play."

Lynda relaxed a little more and felt Gabrielle's fingers playing with her clitoris again and then in and out of her vagina, caressing her G Spot on every movement. Lynda pressed her lips hard against Gabrielle's as she came for a second and quick third time.

Gabrielle was kissing her breasts a minute or two later and working her way slowly and sexually down her body. When she reached Lynda's clitoris, she licked it and kissed it, playing with her, making her feel so sexy and wanted by her. Loved by her and Gabrielle was eager to please her wife.

She moved her lips to kiss the inside of her thighs and then moved up and down them. Gabrielle's hand was caressing Lynda's thigh as she kissed it. Lynda was loving it, her body was twisting and turning as Gabrielle played with her.

Her tongue once again entered her vagina, and it was all too much for her. She was so stimulated she could not hold herself and had her forth orgasm over Gabrielle's tongue and into her mouth.

Gabrielle waited for her to finish having her orgasm before she commenced to lick her clitoris and then vagina walls dry. Gabrielle's breasts were laying on Lynda's thighs as she played and finished licking her vagina and straight after, started on her thighs again.

Lynda pulled her up her body so they could kiss again, mouths together, love to love, soul to soul. Lynda didn't stop kissing her wife, even when the alarm went off. They parted briefly as Lynda hit the clock hard, not that it had done anything to her, but she hit it all the same.

They were kissing again, both their hands playing with each other's breasts, gently massaging them, bringing their nipples to an erection. They rubbed them gently between their fingers as they both felt erotic and once again Gabrielle's fingers were playing with Lynda's clitoris and entering her vagina. They moved in and out, easily locating her G Spot.

It was like being in Heaven for Lynda. She arched her body allowing Gabrielle's three fingers to get deeper within her. Her fingers played with her G Spot and ran over her vagina walls, moving faster in and out, it was so beautiful, so sexy and yes, yes. Lynda couldn't stop herself from having another orgasm.

When Gabrielle finished cleaning her up and gently fondling her clitoris again; she worked her way up to her face and they kissed. They climbed together, out of bed, laughing and giggling and ran into the shower.

They were both putting their makeup on, dressed only in their bra's panties and tights, it would be cold on the yacht later. There was a knock at their bedroom door, a short pause then Sarah entered their bedroom.

"Breakfast in five minutes you two. Gabrielle, put your white blouse on that I put out for you last night and wear," she paused a moment going through Gabrielle's skirts. "Ah this one will do just fine."

It was her long grey skirt, a maxi length for the cold outside. "You can wear this cardigan, you won't be out in the cold for long. Lynda, I would like you to wear this baby yellow dress, jumper for later and you will need the same bag as you used yesterday. I've packed your other ones."

Sarah was out of their room before she called back. "Come on girls, a lot to get through this morning, I've been up since five while I bet you two were," she turned to see their grinning faces.

"Okay, I get it, now finish getting dressed and breakfast."

Before they left to see Dave Raley, Gabrielle went to her bedside table and opened the secret drawer inside the drawer. She removed the Glock gun with two clips. She inserted one into the gun and put the gun in her large handbag with the second clip. She still didn't trust George and his thugs. There was no telling what they might get up to and she also wanted Lynda safe. She gave her some final jobs to do on the computer and asked her if she could get the last of their paperwork together so she could quickly go through it before they left and put it in her briefcase.

Her last job was to pack all their jewellery they would need including their two hearts. There would be at least two Hat & Bag shows in New York before the day nobody wanted to see.

It was seven fifteen when Gabrielle called John into her bedroom. "John, I'll go out with Sarah and Alan, I'll be safe with him. I want you to stay here and protect my wife. She will be going through our jewellery as well and I think you are better off here with Mike to assist you as well as Tina should anything happen.

"I'm hoping we'll be no more than two hours, if we are, I'll call you. I won't be happy until we are on the yacht and off down the English Channel. I don't know why I didn't think about my suit sooner."

"You have a lot on your mind Gabrielle. It's cold outside and I checked the long-range weather forecast. On the day it will be close to zero if not a few degrees below where you need to be. I sure wish this was not happening. I hope you know that I would exchange places with you if I could."

"I know John, I thank you for your help and you know I rely on you a lot to keep us safe. If your fully packed, get the last of the cases into the long limo. Mum will be fine here once we're gone, and Marco is providing extra security for her as well. Once Lynda has sorted out our jewellery, lock it all in our travelling safe and load it into the limo. I want as much packed and ready to go as possible before I return."

"Yes Gabrielle, I won't let you down and I'll take care of Lynda with my life should anything happen I thought you were taking mum with you to have her there on the day as she was with me watching what was happening and I'm sure she would like to be there again." John said.

"Thanks John, you're right, get her sorted as well and get Wendy and her husband, Walter, here with their passports and some clothes. I will give each of them five thousand dollars to get some new clothes when we arrive there. Have I forgot anyone else?"

"Oh, there is Tina, she is desperately in love with Noah, and he might be good to have along. He comes up with some brilliant ideas," John suggested.

"Okay talk to him, yourself, I don't want Tina knowing about him until he is here. I'll tell you what send him straight to the yacht, he can help with the luggage. I don't want him seen by Tina until we are in the English Channel."

"Yes Gabrielle, I like your plan," John added.

"Can you send in Alan now please?"

As soon as Alan entered the room he stood at ease, ready for his orders. He knew things were all on edge and he knew they would be safe on their yacht.

"Alan, just to say you'll be taking Sarah and me this morning. I know you have to do an errand for Sarah, so get on with it as soon as you've dropped us off and we're safe inside the shop. I would like to be back here by ten thirty if possible."

"Yes Gabrielle, I'll let Sarah know. We'll be leaving in ten minutes. I'll get the short limo rolling in five. It's very cold out, we had a heavy frost last night and more snow, but the roads have been salted."

"Thanks, tell Sarah I'm almost ready to go."

"Yes boss," he replied crisply and left the room.

Gabrielle called Lynda to their bedroom where they kissed again, very passionately. Lynda held Gabrielle's hand as they walked to the lounge and Sarah, with her fur coat on, brought

Gabrielle's coat out and helped her put it on.

She had the knives Gabrielle would be using in her bag and hoped at least most of the suit would be ready for its first fitting. They arrived at the shop at seven forty-five. The door was unlocked so they went inside. The shop was warm, people had been working here for some time. The trousers and waistcoat were completed and ready to try on. The jacket needed a few buttons sewed on and it too would be ready.

By eight am., Gabrielle had the suit trousers and, boots on they were checked with one very minor change, trousers and boots off. The trousers had all the cotton ends cut off and with the minor change completed, the trousers were pressed, and Gabrielle was back into the trousers and boots.

Thirty minutes later, the waistcoat was completed, and she was trying the knife belt on. Ron, who had made the belt, checked the knives were ejected fast and ready to throw in an instant. The belt and knives fitted her perfectly, Gabrielle tried it for herself with no trouble at all. She could even put the knives back into their respective sheaths.

Sarah was checking the clothes as Gabrielle put them on and how the knife belt was hidden from view beneath her waistcoat. Sarah got the tie and tie pin from her bag, putting that on her and adding the tie pin. She also put the emerald cufflinks through her double cuffs. When Dave helped her on with her jacket, it really made a difference to her. She looked like a million dollars, a top executive in any company, even her own.

Her trousers did not need a belt because of her hips and narrow waist so there was no need for belt loops, as they fitted snug around her waist with no protrusions and nothing to stop her knives coming out, ready to throw.

Inside each front leaf of her jacket was a hard sheath for a knife. With her jacket buttoned up, you could not even see where the knives were hidden.

The last button on each sleeve had been replaced with the circular emerald tie pins with the chain cut off and secured with strong cotton.

When she stood upright, you could see no knives only an expensive suit with a little bling on it, which any woman executive would like.

Last came the gloves which Gabrielle loved. They were a little stiff when on but supported her cold fingers better and the diamonds on the back of them sparkled in the light of the room and had a heart pattern on the back of her gloves. When she curled her fingers into her palms it was hard at first but then the material moulded into her hands, and it became easier to bend her fingers and even hold a pen as if the gloves were on her hands in her office. Alan was still not back so Sarah did Gabrielle's hair, put it in a ponytail and made it so at times it fell around her neck making her look sexy. There were four bright expensive slides to go into her hair which she hoped would catch George's eyes or his thugs, giving Gabrielle an extra few seconds; she needed to kill the men and try to kill George.

Alan arrived just as Sarah finished completing her hair and agreed with Sarah, Gabrielle's bling could give her another thirty seconds of time, when the men would be looking at her bling, and not at what she was about to do with her knives. It could make all the difference.

"Stay in the clothes Gabrielle, I want Lynda to see you as we walk into the apartment."

Gabrielle was talking to Lynda telepathically, making sure she was doing the jobs that needed to be completed and making sure all their jewellery was what they wanted to take with them.

Sarah could see the unease on Gabrielle's face so let her talk with Alan while she paid the bill.

"How much do we owe you Dave?" Sarah asked.

"Sorry Sarah, your money is no good here today, take Gabrielle home, it looks like she has someone on her mind."

"Thank you so much, we will not forget this."

"We all just hope she beats George. She has made the world of a difference here since she got rid of his thugs."

"I'm glad she could help. Bye for now and thanks again for the suit and everything."

Next, they were on their way home and Alan was not holding back on the throttle. Sarah was talking to Alan and Gabrielle. The journey home would normally take twenty to thirty minutes, but this morning Alan did it in eight minutes. He could see Gabrielle was anxious as he pulled up outside her apartment.

He was out of the car and at the apartment door ringing the bell. Wendy answered the door smiling.

"Hello Alan, I'll get tea going for you all," Wendy said.

"Wendy, can you help Gabrielle with some bags please?"

"Yes Alan," she replied. "I'll get my jacket."

"The bags are on the floor outside the car, it will only take you a minute." Alan was forceful.

"Of course, Sir," she replied.

There was no hierarchy in the apartment but there were codewords and this told him there was a man behind the door, how they had got in he had no idea, but John and Mike were incapacitated.

He already had his silencer on the end of his gun, it was in his left hand now. He looked in the hall mirror which was always at a slight angle so he could see behind the front door. There was a man there in a balaclava. It made them look more frightening to the people inside. As Wendy walked out of the apartment into the cold snow, she held up four fingers to her face. This is what Alan needed to know, there were four men in the apartment.

Wendy got into the back of the car and closed the door. Gabrielle was screwing a silencer to the end of her gun. She placed a hand on Wendy's cold hand and handed her a blanket. "Where is John?"

"They have him tied up in the lounge, he was hit on the head with an iron bar and his head is bleeding. They let me put a bandage on his head, but the cut is quite long and deep. He is still drifting off to sleep and coming around, and Lynda is sat on a chair they got from the dining room with a syringe pointing to her neck, both men have needles ready to inject something into their necks. The fourth man is in your bedroom searching for jewellery, but

John has already locked it in the limo."

There was no need now for other questions, all she needed to know was the locations of the men. She pushed the information into Alan's head.

The man behind the door was now dead and Alan stopped his body falling to the floor. He slowly approached the lounge door as Gabrielle was giving Lynda instructions. As Alan entered the lounge, Lynda jumped to the back seat of the car while Gabrielle disappeared and killed the man who had been holding a needle against her wife's neck. Alan killed the second man from a hip shot, right between the eyes. Gabrielle was gone again, into their bedroom.

The man there was amazed to see Gabrielle pointing a gun at his head.

"Did George send you? Answer me or die now."

"You won't fire that gun, I bet it isn't even loaded. Who would put a loaded gun in a woman's hand?"

"I would!" the barrel of the gun lowered as she shot him in his kneecap.

He cried out in pain, but nobody heard him as their bedroom was soundproofed. He fell to the floor holding his bleeding knee.

"Who sent you?" Gabrielle asked again, pointing her gun at his other leg.

"George, we were to bring you both back to his new base to save him going to the States."

"Is that your cars further along the road?"

"Yes, two of them."

"Any drivers inside?"

"No!"

"Anybody else in the house?"

"Greg, but he went into the bedroom opposite and I think he's dead."

"Right, I'm going to drop you into the driver's seat of the first car, you have the key?"

"Yes!"

"You will drive to your new base and tell George your mates are all dead and we're both alive and safe. He will have to meet me as arranged. One month from today. New time, do you remember?"

"I can't drive like this."

"It's an automatic, you only need one foot. Don't stop until you get there understand?"

"Yes. But how are you . . .?"

He was sat in the driver's seat and the engine was running.

"Now drive, the police will be here in two minutes."

Gabrielle was gone and she felt him drive off, not bothering with his seat belt but his left knee was still bleeding. Tina, Jenny's bodyguard, stopped the four- wheel drive car outside the apartment on seeing Gabrielle's car with its red warning lights flashing. They had been to the yacht, taking more of their luggage and their laptops.

"Jenny, stay in the car lock the doors. I won't be long," Tina ordered.

She had her gun in her hand and was out of the car, she heard the doors lock and she cautiously moved forward to Gabrielle's car.

"Are you two alright?" she asked knocking on the rear window.

"We're fine now, the others are inside," Lynda replied. The sound of police sirens was getting closer, as Tina entered the apartment, her gun pointing forward and held in both hands. She looked at the body slumped behind the front door and guessed it was Alan's handywork.

"Alan?" she called out.

"In here," he replied.

She went into the lounge to see John being untied and two men dead on the floor.

"Can you check on mum and Mike please, in the red room?"

"Of course, anyone else in the house?"

"No, I dealt with him," Gabrielle replied as she appeared in the lounge by Alan.

"I'll check on mum and Mike." Tina said.

She was gone to the red room and called out to Mike before she opened the door to see a gun pointing at her. Mum was on the floor by the side of the bed. Another man was lying dead on the floor, Mike's work.

"All clear Mike, I'm checking the other bedrooms. I'll check the basement."

"Fine. You can get up now mum, where is John?"

"In the lounge with Alan and Gabrielle looks like he was hit on the head. As soon as we have the apartment clear, I'll let Jenny, Lynda and Wendy back in. The police will be in the apartment in any minute."

Tina left the red room as mum got up with Mike's help and sat her on the bed resting, letting her heart rate fall back to normal. Mike quickly checked her over and left the room. Tina opened the basement door and went cautiously down the stairs, her gun forwards, held in both hands. Her knife in her jacket ready to draw. It took her two minutes to check all the rooms and return to the red room.

"We'll go up to the lounge now mum," Mike said and helped her off the bed and escorted her, over the dead body into the lounge. Four armed police officers were in the lounge talking to John and Alan.

An ambulance arrived next, and the paramedic checked Brenda over and declared her fit; but would need a hot cup of tea with a little brandy. He looked at John's head and put some paper stitches over the cut holding it together.

A police forensic vehicle arrived next and two men in white suits entered the hall taking photos of the man behind the door. They frisked him removing two guns, four large knives and a syringe filled with a substance they would examine in their lab. They cleared him for removal and two large police officers put him into a black body bag and put him into the ambulance before the press arrived. The next man they looked at was in the red room as the lounge was crowded and the officer at the front door called out, "the press and TV crews are arriving."

The dead man was again frisked and photographed. He had two guns, four large knives and a syringe, again full of a clear liquid with a plastic cover over the needle. His body now in a black body bag was put into the ambulance just as the TV crew set up their antenna and got their camera rolling.

They filmed two more bodies being put carefully into the back of the ambulance and then it left. The forensic team left ten minutes later, having collected all their evidence. The guns they took as well for fingerprints and four syringes, full of an unknown clear liquid.

Jenny was crying, hugging her husband, asking if the bleeding had stopped. She had a damp cloth in her hand cleaning up the blood and soothing his head. Wendy was in tears in the kitchen as she made tea and coffee for everyone including the police. She was upset as well that John was hurt as it was her who opened the front door allowing the thugs in.

Jenny helped John to sit on the sofa giving him a loving hug and kiss on the lips.

As soon as Lynda met Gabrielle, they hugged each other and kissed. As their mouths were kissing, they were talking to each other explaining what had happened.

They stopped kissing and Lynda walked over to John, soon the lounge was bright green as she healed John's cut on his head.

"There, that's all done," Lynda said as her bright green eyes, checked John's eyes, she also walked around him her eyes looking into his head seeing if there was any internal bleeding. "Your brain isn't hurt John, but I bet your pride is.

"I take full responsibility for the fight so please don't blame yourself, and I would still let you care for me anytime in the future." Lynda said smiling and put her hand on his shoulder then kissed his lips.

"How do you feel now John?" Jenny asked holding him close to her, kissing his face all over and her lips pressed against his lips, letting him see she loved him with all her heart.

"Just a slight headache," he replied rubbing his head smiling at his and holding her hand. "I'm sorry Lynda and you too Gabrielle, I let you both down. I was supposed to look after you Lynda and I didn't check the backdoor before I opened it, I just burst straight in and was hit on the head with an iron bar."

"John, I should have jumped out first and alerted Gabrielle and

Alan, I also put into Wendy's head it was Alan and Gabrielle who had forgotten her keys because of the suit. Let's put it all behind us and take a closer look at Gabrielle's new suit," Lynda said looking at everyone in the room.

"Yes, let's see this suit Gabrielle, I must say from here you look fantastic in it, so do you my love," John added speaking to his wife.

"Lynda stood back looking at her wife. "You look beautiful in that suit, I like the bling and jewellery, makes it a little more feminine."

"Glad you approve, do you like the gloves as well?"

"They are very pretty, lots of bling on the back of them."

"The bling is real diamond chips on the back of the gloves and real emeralds everywhere else you see them." They held each other close and kissed passionately.

"Wendy brought in a tray of drinks for everyone and placed it on the table, then sat on the sofa, with Tina putting her arm around her back, helping her to calm down.

"Everyone in the Mall were so good to us, you have really made a difference getting rid of George's people taking money from them. They gave us everything we needed free of charge and the suit came free as well," Sarah explained.

"The suit is layered in Kevlar every part of it. George is calling this fight a battle, so taking it literally, if we go back a couple of hundred years, all our Knights, and Gabrielle is a Knight and Dame of the realm, went into battle wearing armour. The suit is Gabrielle's armour.

"The bling on it are all real emeralds to match her green eyes. The tie pin is also an emerald and the way the tie is almost slithering like a snake into the inside of her waistcoat. The waistcoat is cut lower for her breasts, so she doesn't feel uncomfortable and had it been a normal waistcoat, it would have put added pressure where she didn't want it and she needs to show her breasts, rather than the shape of them.

"The bling, oh show them your cufflinks, emeralds again, large enough to be seen. Alan and I have agreed the bling on her suit should give her an extra twenty seconds of time while George and his mates get distracted by it.

"I've tied her hair so that at times she can flick her head and the ponytail will wrap itself around her neck so she will look sexy, again to add vital seconds for her. It is the same as they stare at her breasts and wonder why a woman as cute as Gabrielle would be fighting George?

"Gabrielle's gloves have Kevlar covering the back and front of her fingers to protect her if he has a knife and tries to cut her hands. The gloves will also protect her hands if she needs to do the same again with the sword. At least this time, she will have some protection. The pattern of bling on the back of the hands is all one hundred percent, diamond chips. We think she might get four or five seconds of time for this bling and of course, the diamonds will help protect the back of her hands.

"Gabrielle's boots have a five-centimetre heel, and they are square, so the shoe part will give her better balance. The boots go up to just below the knee, not that they will see them, but once zipped up, there is a very, strong; piece of leather inside the leg of the boot which also covers the ankles. Should she fall over, it will be impossible for her to sprain her ankle and should her ankle be hit with a knife or sword, the leather will protect her ankle and leg.

"Undo your jacket, Gabrielle. You can see she has a knife she is used to working with in each leather pocket which is low enough for her to pull the knife out of her coat and throw it straight or use it for close combat.

"Turn around Gabrielle. Rather than explain, just show them." She put both arms around her back and brought them forward less than a second later with an eight-inch knife in each hand ready to use. It took the same time for her to put the knives back into their sheaths. Sarah lifted the back of her jacket showing everyone the double knife holder. Then Gabrielle turned face on again and Sarah showed them where the belt buckled up and was hidden by her waistcoat.

"Finally, the red rose for love in her top lapel buttonhole. This we hope will give her another four seconds as they wonder why she is wearing a flower to her death. Paul was also wearing a red rose on his top left lapel on the day.

"Now, as she is standing, she looks like she is going to a meeting rather than a battle. She looks and is of course, sexy, and that is what she needs to get over to the men, so they treat her as a woman and pull back their punches and threats with knives.

"If someone does bring a gun, which I will remind you, George had one on him, the Kevlar suit will save her life. I have done as much as I can do with her armour, it will be up to Gabrielle how she gets herself out of this mess.

"There is one more present for her. Alan, the bag please. Here you are Gabrielle, open the bag," Sarah said smiling at Gabrielle. Gabrielle did as she was told and pulled out a grey material coloured briefcase. Her name was on the front in gold letters and the material matched her suit.

The briefcase is fully lined with Kevlar. It has a double three-digit lock with an elite tracking system which I have already added to your iPhone. If you misplace it or it is stolen, you can track it to its exact position. You can if you wish and have secret papers or something else inside, add a small explosive device that will destroy the case and everything inside it, except the tracking device, which will also tell you if someone has tried the numbers more than four times and blown it up. The lock is currently set to six zeros.

"Open the briefcase please. As you can see, it has a grey coloured cover to the lid pockets and the inside of the case. At the bottom are two straps, same colour material, to hold your iPad safe and stop it moving around when you're carrying it. The lid has its normal pockets for paperwork, diary, and pens etc.

Sarah took the small box Alan was holding for her and took the case from Gabrielle. then handed her the small, long box. "Open it! It's for you."

Gabrielle opened the red velvet box and inside was a twenty-two-carat gold woman's expensive fountain pen, slim biro, and a drop lead pencil. Each one had her initials engraved into the item with a gold filling for the letters and polished up.

"I know you like your pens, and these are meant for the businesswoman. You can keep them in your jacket pocket or in the briefcase. Alan has already put spare leads for the clutch pencil into the case and spare blue and black ink cartridges.

"One more thing about the suit, you will have noticed there are no pockets on the outside or inside except the one top pocket for pens etc. and there is another slim pocket for your iPhone, which you will not have on you on the day.

"There are no pockets in the trousers either. I did not want anything to be able to snag on them as you are fighting. The suit is slimline and made perfectly to fit you. There is no belt to hold the trousers up, your hips and waist do that and there are no loops to snag your knives when you pull them out.

"I have done as much as I can to protect you, now all you have to do is kill George like you did on the day," Sarah explained.

"Thank you for the briefcase and pen set, I really like it. I also love the idea of an exploding briefcase," Gabrielle said and kissed Sarah on both cheeks.

"I have the two exploding devices in my bag, I'll show you how they fit in and armed on the yacht. Everyone, what do you think of my knight in grey lined armour?"

Everyone applauded her and stepped forward to examine the suit a little closer.

"Sarah, you have certainly thought all this through, and you couldn't have done any better to protect Gabrielle. Not only that, but you have also thought the battle through and given Gabrielle the chance to wear armour. I'm so glad you're on our side," Lynda said holding her wife close and kissing her.

"Thank you, she stands a much better chance against mad George now than she did before the change of dress," Lynda held Sarah, kissing her cheeks and gave her a huge hug.

They drank their tea and coffee. The doorbell rang which John answered and allowed Walter and Penny, Mike's wife into the apartment with their cases and a small bag for their money and passports.

"We will not make the midday tide, but Captain Patel has assured me, we will be fine if we can get abord by one thirty," Gabrielle said.

"Under our current circumstances Gabrielle, I want you to wear the clothes you're wearing to the yacht," John said sternly. Gabrielle agreed and Lynda loved her in them, so it didn't matter. At least she would be as safe as she could be.

Collecting her tablet and papers, Gabrielle soon had her new briefcase full of the items she would need while they were en-route to New York. The last of the bags and small cases were now stacked in the lounge.

With the apartment looking a little better than it did with the bodies on the floor, John and Mike packed the last items in the long limo.

Locking up the apartment, Alan got into the front passenger seat and put his gun on his lap. Everyone had come to the garage to get into the car and everyone except Gabrielle were wearing thick jumpers supplied by Gabrielle to keep them warm as they boarded the yacht and started their journey to New York.

The garage door opened and closed behind them, fifteen minutes later they arrived at the carpark for their yacht, and other people's boats and yachts.

The main crew, all wearing thick sea jumpers, with the name of their new hundred-foot four deck yacht *Gabrielle* were on hand to unload the car and take the last of the luggage to the yacht. It was all put in the lower main mess. They were in a hurry, not to catch the tide, but to get Gabrielle away from London.

With the luggage all aboard, the guests started to get aboard. Gabrielle insisted her mother went first then Lynda, Sarah, Wendy, Penny and Jenny then herself in that order. They were all escorted to the lower main deck out of the snow and into the warm. The bodyguards remained at the rear and by the entrance to *Gabrielle*. The crew got the walkway aboard and stowed on the main bulkhead ready to be used next time they stopped at a port. Two men were ready with the bow and stern ropes.

Getting the go ahead from John, Captain Chris Patel, ordered the bow line let go and with the engines at idle, he ordered the aft line let go and both men jumped back aboard. The engines were brought up to slow ahead and *The Gabrielle* left the dock.

Chapter 6

Alan and Mike remained on watch while John and Tina inspected *Gabrielle.* They put a twenty-five-calibre machine gun with its tripod in the small drop in the bow deck, especially made for the gun. A fifteen-calibre machine gun with its tripod at the underside of the second deck steps to the top deck. Another light machine gun with six rounds of ammunition was placed with it.

Another 25calibre machinegun with two boxes of ammunition was placed in the aft cut out for it. They put another eight machineguns with six clips each and handguns with three clips each around the yacht. With what had happened at their apartment, John was not taking any chances. There were still other guns and weapons they could call on if needed locked away in the bow gun locker,

Everyone was shown to their cabins and Gabrielle joined Tina just as she opened her door. "Gabrielle, she called as she was about to walk up to her stateroom. There is another case in my room. Who does it belong to?"

"I'm sorry Tina I was just told by Captain Patel, that he needed an extra bed for the extra man who would be sharing with you. For one night until he could put him with another of his men, or woman if you wanted to pass on him, apparently, he's good looking," Gabrielle said, hardly able to control herself.

"Gabrielle, I've only brought short thin satin nighties with matching panties. I just wasn't thinking of having to share my bed with a man."

"He won't mind."

"I'm sure he won't. she replied in an upset voice. "How could you do this to me Gabrielle?"

"Quite easy really. Ahhh here is the man coming now."

Noah thanked Gabrielle for holding his room and smiling, entered the bedroom. Tina had her back to the door as tears filled her eyes. He gently placed his hand on her shoulder and Tina pushed it away from her.

"Look I can cope with you and I've only seen a picture of you. Tina is that your name?" Noah asked her.

Tina nodded in silence.

"Well Tina I think we should share this bed properly, which side do you like? I like the right if it's alright with you?"

"I can't sleep with you, I don't know you, and I've only got short thin satin nighties and matching panties with me."

"That sounds very sexy to me, let's give it a try?"

"No!" Tina shouted.

"I'm so glad you said that. Tina Wesley, would you please do me the honour of being my wife?" Noah asked.

He walked in front of her with Gabrielle, Lynda John, Alan, Sarah, and a few others jammed in by her bedroom-door and other people were waiting for the news on the steps leading up to the other decks and bedrooms.

"Tina Wesley, will you be my wife forever?" Noah asked. "I have the ring here as we didn't have one the last time, I asked you."

It then clicked and she opened her eyes to look at the large ring

"Noah, of course I'll marry you," Tina screamed.

"She said YES!" Lynda shouted up the stairs everyone was cheering and clapping their hands.

Noah and Tina were kissing each other as Noah slipped the engagement ring on her right-hand engagement finger. Gabrielle, and Lynda got in first to congratulate them.

"Congratulations you two, you deserve each other," Gabrielle said kissing each of them on the cheek. Lynda kissed them both then others from Gabrielle's staff congratulated them. Gabrielle and Lynda were on their way to their Stateroom, at the very top of their yacht, as big as they could make.

They kissed and lay on their bed, holding each other close, fondling each other and wishing they could be in bed right now, but their guests would need to see them in the lounge.

Lynda was already dressed for the sea, but Gabrielle had to change so Lynda was going to enjoy herself for ten minutes. She helped Gabrielle out of her suit, examining the lining as she put it on a hanger and into a plastic suit bag.

Gabrielle was just wearing her bra, panties, and a pair of twenty-denier tights, so her legs slipped into the boots easier. Her hair draped around her neck and that was enough for Lynda. you look so sexy; I'm going to have to do something about it."

She pushed Gabrielle onto their bed and was on top of her in an instant. Lynda pushed Gabrielle's bra up around her neck then she started to lick and kiss her breasts, sucking her nipples, making them hard and big. Her hands took over caressing and fondling them, making Gabrielle feel extremely erotic.

They kissed profusely, their mouths rotating about each other, their heads turning, their lips kissing their faces all over each other as Lynda still fondled Gabrielle's breasts.

They were both feeling erotic now as Gabrielle pushed her hand under Lynda's thick jumper and tee shirt.

Gabrielle's other hand was now fondling Lynda's breast as her arm wrapped around her back, holding, and pulling her closer to her side. After what they had just gone through, Gabrielle had no idea what would have happened had the man injected the substance into her neck.

She did not and could not lose her now, she wanted to show her just how much she cared for her. Their fondling had a meaning of urgency, to show their love for each other, to show they cared and could not bear to lose their wife.

Their breathing became harder and faster as Lynda slowly lowered her hand over Gabrielle's body, gently massaging it, rubbing circles over her and slipped her hand under her tights and panties. The tips of her fingers, fondled her clitoris, making it and the walls of Gabrielle's damp vagina even wetter. Her legs parted to accommodate Lynda's petite hand into her vagina and started to move her hand in and out.

Gabrielle was feeling so erotic, as her petite hand was rubbing Lynda's breast as she pulled her towards her laughing and giggling then crying with glee as she felt herself having her first orgasm. Lynda's hand was saturated with her love juices as she pushed her hand deeper inside Gabrielle finding her G Spot, rubbing it fast and kissing her mouth, their tongues intertwined making them both feel loved and needed by each other. Then Gabrielle had her second orgasm which was just as good for her as the first.

She was so excited, she rolled on top of Lynda, holding her as close to her as she could. One hand on her naked back holding her close, the other on her breast, fondling it softly, gently, girl to girl as they kissed passionately. Holding her tight, Gabrielle rolled off Lynda and pulled her onto herself, holding her close, they just kissed as their hands remained where they were, resting.

"I love you so much, my heart was aching when I was talking to you this morning while I was in the shop. I thought I was being clever leaving you alone, alone from me that is. I assumed with you at home, John, Mike and Tina would be enough to protect you."

"They must have noticed we were taking luggage to the yacht and waited until Tina and Jenny left, perhaps not realising Mike was still in the apartment. John had just taken our makeup bags and the jewellery safe to the limo. They rang the doorbell and Wendy was by herself, well I was in the lounge getting the final data you wanted onto our iPads I looked at the clock and it was five past ten. I said to Wendy I bet that's Gabrielle coming back and she has left her keys here as she was getting the suit. Wendy went to the front door and didn't check the door screen because I had put the idea into her head that it was you returning home.

"When she opened the door, they were straight in. Luckily mum and Mike were in the red room. Mike heard Wendy cry out and kept mum safe. I did not expect him to help me; he had his priority and it saved her.

"One man came into the lounge with a gun pointing at Wendy's head. He told me, scream, shout or do anything and she's dead. I couldn't warn John three men entered the lounge and one man put a needle against my neck. One of them then left the room looking for John, but he found Mike and I heard the gunshot.

"John heard it as well in the garage and came running in, his gun was on the coffee table behind me. He was carrying the safe and three bags to the car, he said he didn't want to damage his gun and told me not to play with it. I don't know if he thought it was me playing with the gun and it went off accidentally or Mike's gun, but as he came in through the back door, two men were waiting for him.

"They hit him on his head with an iron bar and that knocked him out, with blood pouring from the cut down his face. They then tied him up and brought him to the lounge. Wendy begged them to let her put a bandage on his head, as she said, she didn't want his blood all over the furniture. The men laughed and told her to get the bandage at least it put the three men at ease," Lynda said with tears falling down her face.

My other arm was now around Lynda's waist and my hand was gently rubbing her lower back comforting her as tears were still falling down her face.

"I was worried you would come bursting in through the front door and I tried to tell you, but I couldn't form the correct words in my head. They brought John into the lounge, sat Wendy down and held another syringe against John's neck.

"Memories were coming back of my past in the first timeline which were now frightening me, oh where was my Gabrielle?"

"They said if either of us moved or said a word, we would both be killed at the same instant. Wendy looked at me as if expecting me to jump, but I was frightened and couldn't concentrate enough on a safe place to jump to and I didn't have an image of the shop you were in.

"When I was raped and abused. I had been injected with stuff to put me to sleep while I was raped multiple times and sometimes front and back together with a third man coming into my mouth.

Sometimes a fourth man would be playing with my breasts with a Stanley knife. I was terrified. Tears were streaming down my face.

"They were asking me where you were, but I couldn't speak and as they threatened me, Wendy blurted out that you were shopping with Sarah and Alan. She was right to tell them, I may have been injected with the stuff and Wendy could see I was in no shape to talk.

"They shouted abuse at me for not talking, then said they wanted you as well so they would wait until you returned. They knew what time we were supposed to be leaving on the yacht and guessed you would be back soon.

"John could do nothing, and Mike was doing his job. One of the men went to our bedroom and was looking for our jewellery, opening and closing drawers. He returned to me and demanded to know where the big stones were and I said on the yacht, in the big safe.

"John heard what I said and tried to breathe deeply as he held his head low, making it look like I was telling the truth. The man went back to our bedroom looking for other smaller jewellery. There was no way I could warn you, I tried to tell you but the man holding the needle against my neck was constantly shouting at me calling me a whore and telling me what George had in mind for me and what he was going to do with you. He was planning on slicing your body up like he had done to me.

"The man told me that you would be cut and quartered before me and George would tear your heart out; the same heart I held in my hands and brought you back to life. How he knew that I have no idea. He said George was then going to rape me and so would every man he had working for him one after another for as long as they liked and they could kiss my mouth, breasts, or cut me, beat me, but I would not be allowed to bleed out. He was intending to make a lot of money using me and had already forty rough men lined up and paid upfront, a thousand pounds for an hour with me to do with as they pleased.

"I was a mess and Wendy could see it. She tried to talk to me but was told to be quiet or I would get injected. When Alan rang the doorbell, I knew he had a key, he would never ring the bell. They made Wendy answer the door, saying if she warned anyone, I would die first then John," Lynda told Gabrielle.

"Alan had us behind him, and he was screwing the silencer on his gun, I was doing the same. Wendy gave us a warning by just saying the word 'tea'. We all drank coffee she knew, but there were other words she could use, I guess that was the easiest," Gabrielle said.

"When Alan ordered Wendy sternly to go to the car and help with the bags, she didn't know what to do. The man must have said go because she came out holding four fingers to her face. Alan understood her immediately; four men in the apartment. "Alan said come on Gabrielle, it's cold and we are late getting back. Wendy will get the bags like she is supposed to do. By that time, I had my silencer on the end of my gun. We waited until Wendy was safe in the back of the car and Sarah was sat in the front passenger seat.

"I then noticed the two cars parked up the road, Alan must have seen them instantly and guessed who they were for. Alan used the hall mirror, always at a slight angle so you can see behind the front door from outside.

"He said come on Gabrielle and Alan was looking in the hall mirror as he put his gun to the man's head and killed him. He had to push the door right back to stop his body falling loudly to the floor warning the others that something was wrong.

"He nodded to me and started to walk towards the lounge talking to me about the cold snow. I could hear you now easily and that is when I sent you the picture of the car outside and the position of the back seat."

"When you told me to jump, I jumped in front of the man who was holding you and killed him by shooting him in the head, he died instantly.

"Alan raised his gun from his hip and killed the man who was holding the syringe against John's neck. It was a good shot from the hip to the astonished man's head, right between his eyes. I don't know how he does it. We lowered both men to the ground so the last man would not hear us.

"I left Alan in the lounge and jumped to our bedroom, surprising the man inside. I asked him who sent them, he refused to answer and said I couldn't shoot him, and the gun was probably not even loaded. I shot him in the kneecap without aiming. I got out of him that it was George who sent them, and he has a new base where they were going to take us.

"I told him we would be in New York and if George wanted us, he would have to join us there on top of the Empire State Building, one month from today, so I have got four extra days before the fight.

"I told him the police were almost here and I wanted to know if he had the key to the first car? He said yes and I said he was to drive to the new base without stopping. He tried to argue out of it saying about his damaged knee. I laughed and told him the car was an automatic and he only needed one foot to drive and stop the car.

"I jumped him to the driving seat and started the car before he knew what was happening. I told him to drive as the police were arriving and he was off, not even bothering to put his seatbelt on.

"I then jumped back to you and you know the rest. With the men we killed at his mansion in Liverpool, and the ones we killed today, he is losing a lot of men. I don't think he will bother to recruit any replacements; he'll be too busy getting himself and his men to New York.

"I wonder how many of his men have a passport and will be allowed into the States due to their Status as they all have to get a Visa as well? George is going to have problems with his leg which is gangrene. However, on the day or just before, I have a feeling Death is going to heal it; just to even the odds."

Gabrielle looked into Lynda's green eyes which were growing brighter. They had been dulled since Gabrielle held her when Lynda was finally allowed into the apartment by Tina, but Gabrielle was glad Tina was on hand to help and not in the apartment with Jenny at the same time. They may have killed Jenny and Tina.

Lynda opened their suitcase and found a thick tee shirt and thick jumper for Gabrielle, after pulling her bra back down, placing her breasts inside the bra cups, she pulled the tee shirt over her head and arms, slowly, pulling it down and flattening it over her breasts and body.

Next came the thick and warm jumper. Last of all, the maxi skirt she would wear for the afternoon and evening. There was a loud knock on the door just as Lynda was putting Gabrielle's trainers on. Standard wear for everyone on the yacht. No high heels, they would damage the wooden deck and the women didn't want to fall overboard if the yacht was tossed about in the sea.

Sarah entered their suite without waiting to be asked. She had often seen them both naked making love, so it wasn't embarrassing for any of them. She was pulling another large suitcase and holding their large makeup and deodorants bags.

Alan was behind her with Gabrielle's new briefcase, Lynda's briefcase and two more overnight hard bottom and side cases. They were all put on the deck at the bottom of their bed. Lynda noticed Alan was wearing a thick jumper, he was still carrying his gun,

"Alan, we're on the yacht currently in the English Channel heading to the Atlantic Ocean. Is there really any need for you to be carrying your gun now?"

"I'm concerned for your safety while we're still in the Channel, George could have a fast speed boat catch us up or leave a dock ahead of us. John and Tina have put the heavy machineguns fore and aft. The smaller big machine gun with a few others under the upper deck steps. Other machineguns and handguns are placed at prominent places around the yacht just in case George tries something when we think we are safe. When we enter the Atlantic Ocean, I will leave my gun in our cabin, until then, I would, with your permission, like to keep my gun on me. John Mike and Tina are doing the same."

"Feeble excuse Alan. Yes, you do as you all think best. Can I have a go on the big machine gun?"

"No Boss, it's big, heavy and very noisy, we only carry so many rounds for them. It's not really a gun for such a beautiful woman as yourself. The same goes for you Gabrielle,"

"What about Sarah?" Lynda asked grinning.

"The same goes for her as well. Not even the smaller of the big guns," he replied grinning. Sarah gave him a ghastly look. She too had been hoping to have a go on the big guns.

"Permission to leave your stateroom and start my tour of the yacht with the binoculars?" he asked.

"Permission granted," Lynda replied.

Alan turned and winked at his wife then left the stateroom for his turn at lookout, which would last an hour while they were in the English Channel and close to the shore. Mike would be next to do lookout duties.

"Now my husband has left us, may I unpack your cases and hang up all your clothes for the voyage?"

"Yes of course Sarah, do you need my help?" Lynda asked.

"No Lynda, you two go and rest in the lower lounge and enjoy the views. Christine, your chef for this trip said fresh coffee is always on hand. Dinner will be at 20:00 hours and she will make fresh sandwiches if we get hungry. Lunch tomorrow will between 12:00 and 13:30 hours. Breakfast is between 06:00 to 09:00 hours for a cooked breakfast. You can have cereal or toast whenever you like. I've read her credentials, she's a brilliant chef and has worked in a few five Star restaurants under four top Chefs.

"She makes proper meals like you have at home for the crew and us. Enough food to keep you going all day if you know what I mean. Now, off you both go and let me get on with unpacking your cases."

"Come on love, let's get some coffee and biscuits inside us," Gabrielle said as Lynda lowered her bra putting her breasts back into the bra's cups.

Gabrielle put Lynda's trainers on her feet then took her hand, pulling her off the bed into her arms. They kissed again, before Gabrielle spoke once again to Sarah.

"You can kiss your husband whenever you like aboard the yacht. You are all on a break like us. enjoy your break and have a few beers, larger or whatever your poison is. The trip will be five days, because I need to think about our business and where we should be heading in the US. We will have a meeting at 10:00 hours tomorrow in the lower lounge.

"I'll explain everything in the morning

"Get the unpacking done and be with Alan. Oh, by the way, where are the trunks stored?" Gabrielle asked Sarah.

"They are in the aft hold, and I'll have all our suitcases put in there too."

"That's great, they'll be safe there."

"Your jewellery is still in the safe and secured in the aft hold." Sarah added.

Gabrielle stopped, let go of Lynda's hand and went to her bag she had the gun which she used that morning. She took her gun from the bag and put it in her bedside cabinet drawer with ten clips and a box of spare ammunition. She looked deeper in her bag, found the silencer and put that in the padded drawer as well.

"That's done, ready for me to get to if needed, which I sincerely hope it isn't on this journey."

"Gabrielle, if the journey is taking us five days, where are we going in the Atlantic Ocean?" Sarah asked.

"We're heading north to the Arctic and the Northern Lights. I want some good photos of them for some of the girls in Grayson House. I also thought some photos can be enlarged to a wall sized picture for our new office in New York."

"First, you don't have a camera which has a big lens and a photo card large enough for a wall picture, let alone big A3 pictures for some of the girls. Second, we don't have any offices in New York. The business there is being run from the back office in one of our stores," Sarah replied.

"Ah, I ordered a Nikon camera and a number of lenses and extras on-line and had it all sent to the *Gabrielle.* Captain Patel, has it secured somewhere, I'll get it later and we can get together if you like and put it all together."

"That would be nice, how many lenses did you order?" Sarah asked.

"Ten, four small ones, two big ones and three super- sized ones and 1 supersized for looking at the stars. about six of the largest picture cards they do, a tripod, loads of filters, a big camera case, and a few other things. The Nikon camera body cost five grand and the biggest lens I ordered was eight-grand.

"I want to take hundreds of pictures of you my love and you can take pictures of me and Sarah can take pictures of us together in different poses. I can also take pictures of Jenny wearing our hats and bags and I'll have some blown up and put in our shops, get people more interested in our goods."

"Now that sounds like a good idea. We could take pictures of all the girls we use on the catwalk. We have four shops so far in New York, we can have all the girl's pictures framed and put up in all our shops." Gabrielle suggested.

"Perhaps we could get some of them into the papers," Lynda said getting excited about the work.

"If we are going to do a couple of Hats & Bags shows, we'll need advertising and pictures of the girls wearing our goods will be a damn good way of drawing buyers and people to the show, especially if they will wear the short dresses, like the one Jenny wore last time we were here," Gabrielle added.

"Perhaps we can get that TV company who were interested in us and Jenny to do some advertising for us. Have some of the girls on TV, do a good press release. Tell the people where to find our stores and what we intend to do," Sarah suggested.

"Good idea Sarah, we tell the press we are going to expand into New York and other States as well with our Head Offices in New York," Gabrielle added. "This is the sort of thing I want to discuss tomorrow. There is a great deal to sort out while we are out of reach of secretaries and endless phone calls," Gabrielle explained. The three girls were now extremely excited about Gabrielle's plans for New York and the US. They all started to come up with ideas at once. Gabrielle grabbed her iPad and set it to video and pressed record.

Lynda was coming up with names and faces she had committed to memory and Sarah was expanding on the names, places they had been to. Other stores they were associated with and a way they could push money into them to get more people visit the stores.

Lynda was suggesting outworkers and where to find them like they had in Rome and Italy. Lynda could do a few walks with different clothes, and hats and Bags on and Gabrielle herself, known around the world, would also have to do some walks.

The last thing they wanted was the fight with George getting into the press and getting Gabrielle to give interviews that would take her away from their company.

As they were talking and laughing, Gabrielle felt the yacht alter course sharply. They were now heading further out into the English Channel, and they had increased speed. Gabrielle could hear the wine of the powerful engines as they pushed the yacht through the water.

"Something is wrong, stay here while I see Chris. I promise I won't be long. Start unpacking both of you and get our clothes stored away. Don't put our makeup out yet, we may be making some fast course corrections," Gabrielle said. She put her arm around Lynda's shoulder and kissed her passionately for a minute while Sarah started to unpack the first large suitcase.

Gabrielle was about to leave her wife when there was a knock at the door and Tina came in. "Gabrielle, I need to have a word with you and Chris would like to see you on the bridge."

"Can we all know what is happening?" Lynda asked.

"Let us talk to the Captain and I'm sure Gabrielle will be back shortly to explain the problem if indeed there is one. We are just changing course and increasing speed," Tina said quickly.

Gabrielle let go of Lynda's hand and followed Tina to the bridge. The 2nd Engineer, Ian Day, ran past them heading to the engine room to assist Andrew Parkinson, the Chief Engineer. Christine Forks their Chef closed the galley and moved the glass, of hot, black, coffee jugs, to their secure crates in the galley. The clean mugs by the side were all put into a tray and secured beneath the counter.

The Cook, Sandy Crane, ran into the lower lounge and removed all the half drunken coffee mugs the crew had started. There were a few plates of food left. Everything she put on the counter then ran around to the other side and started to clear the mugs first of dead coffee, putting the mugs in a tray and when it was partly full, she opened the dishwasher and pushed the tray inside.

She cleared the plates of food into the food container that would be emptied into the sea. The fish would eat all the food so it wouldn't go to waste. The four plates also went into the dishwasher. She closed the door ensuring it was locked, then helped Christine with the rest of loose containers.

When the galley was safe, they discarded their whites, and put on their sea jumpers, it would be cold on the decks. They ran into the lounge at the far end and picked up a machinegun each with for now; three extra clips each. The lights in the lounge were then turned out and the two women ran to their stations.

All over the yacht the lights were going out except where they were needed. One under the rear steps, the other in the fore rope locker, where John was collecting more ammunition for the large twenty-five-millimetre heavy machinegun, He closed the fore deck hatch after him and with two heavy duty plastic containers which fed the bullets into the gun. He hurried to the bow.

Mike was on top of the top deck with the fifteen-millimetre machinegun and his own Glock with ten clips in his fur coat. Tina picked up her own slightly smaller ten-millimetre machinegun and escorted Gabrielle to the bridge,

"We are at high alert, I'm afraid there will be no food or drinks until this is over," Tina informed Gabrielle.

"Understood. Do you know if we are outside the three-mile limit yet?"

"We are heading that way now."

They climbed another set of steps and Tina opened the wooden bridge door for Gabrielle to enter her bridge.

"Hi Chris, where are we and what is happening?" Gabrielle asked. She walked up to the radar scope with Chris standing by her side.

Lt. Ben Armstrong was operating the radar on the blacked-out bridge. The green light of the radar scope was the brightest light on the bridge, which had a cap so the light was reflected back into the bridge and couldn't be seen from the outside.

"Gabrielle, Captain, we have four craft approaching us at high speed. This blip here is one point five miles behind us and closing fast. It is a small speedboat, eight feet long powered by two outboard engines. It would hold about six or seven men fully armed.

"Then we have four speedboats, twelve feet in length powered by two outboard engines. They will hold at least fourteen men each, fully armed. That is why they are slowing over the choppy water.

"We are here," he said indicating the position of their yacht and there is the three-mile limit, half a mile away. However, we will need to change course to ensure the speed boats are chasing us, trying to head us off and possibly board us.

"We need to change course to West 132°, it will take us towards the shore, but we will change course again in three minutes out to the three-mile limit."

"Sir, Mam we need to change course now."

Gabrielle nodded her head and Chris spoke swiftly to Steve Norman, the first mate who was operating the wheel.

"Steve, turn West 132°, remain on that course for three minutes then return to our current course," Chris ordered.

"West 132°," Steve repeated, so the Captain and Gabrielle knew he understood the command.

He turned the small steering wheel which was facing him before the compass and clock which was also a timer. Once the yacht was heading in the right direction, he set the clock for three minutes and it started to count down.

This was an ultra-modern bridge with all the latest controls. Gabrielle looked at the scope again. The speedboat three quarters of a mile behind them, altered course to follow them. The speedboats before them also altered course back towards the land. Gabrielle's heart almost broke.

"What is it with George, he knows he'll have to come to New York?" she asked nobody.

"How many men does he have?" Chris asked her.

"About a hundred and we've killed a few of them. He is just throwing their bodies at us. I'm no longer talking to the men, it's a killing ground when they meet us. They are also trying to abduct us by injecting some substance into our necks to knock us out for a couple of days,

"I will not allow Lynda to be captured by these thugs. They'll rape both of us as often as they like and use us as whores. They will even allow men to beat us up and cut up our bodies with a Stanley knife. If they got us, they would get Sarah, Jenny, even Wendy and Tina and inject them so they too could be raped multiple times and beaten up as much as the men liked.

"I will not allow this to happen. If his men try to get us, then they must expect to die," Gabrielle said sternly.

"I totally agree," said Chris. "Steve, what time is left?"

"Thirty seconds Sir, Mam," He replied crisply.

"Return us to our former course. Increase speed to flank and get us past the three-mile limit."

"Returning to previous course, East 265°, Speed set to Flank." There was the sound of a bell. "Flank speed has been accepted. Speed increasing from 20 knots to 22, 24, 28, 32, 35 knots.

Maximum speed."

"Steve, how long until they intercept us?"

"The speedboat behind, approximately five minutes, the ones in front, approximately seven minutes. We will cross the three-mile limit in four minutes on this course. We will then see if they follow us or drop back."

"Let's hope they follow us then we can sink their boats and kill the men." The captain was beginning to get quite angry thinking about what these thugs intended to do with the girls.

Chris picked up the microphone to talk with the crew. "Steve, sound the warning signal for five seconds, I don't want to give the speedboat crews too much advanced warning that we know their intensions."

Steve sounded the warning signal. which was, a high-pitched warble.

"This is your Captain, prepare to be boarded with force, fore, aft and amidships. You may use full force and try to sink their craft. You have permission to kill people when you hear the next signal." He returned the microphone to its receptor and looked at Gabrielle. "I'm popping down to the forward gun locker and get us some Glocks and spare clips."

"I'll join you," Gabrielle said.

"Steve, when we cross the three-mile limit, I want to be sure all the boats follow us at least half a click past the limit. If I'm not back by then sound the alarm."

"Yes Sir, Mam," he replied, referring to Gabrielle because she was on the bridge, and it was her yacht.

"Come with me Gabrielle."

"We were down in the fore locker room in under a minute. Chris was looking at the guns and picked out three Glocks, with fifteen-twenty bullet clips. He slammed a clip in each gun and put the rest in his pocket. He saw a machinegun, put the strap over his shoulder and picked up two spare clips of thirty rounds in each clip. He put a new clip in the gun and the other two in his jacket pocket," Gabrielle explained.

"Help yourself Gabrielle." Chris stood back so Gabrielle could get in and pick out her guns.

She decided on three Glocks. She put a clip in each gun and realised she had no pockets. There was a plastic bag at the bottom of the gun locker. She picked it up, dropped the guns in it and added twenty-five clips. This could she realised be a nasty fight. George's thugs would be armed with machine guns and AK47's they may even be carrying a small rocket launcher with at least five rockets in each boat.

She knew the *Gabrielle* would not be able to stand up to rockets. Then she thought of Jenny, she didn't want her alone or hiding behind John, he would be operating the forward large machinegun and would need all his concentration.

She put another Glock in the bag with six more clips. Picked up a machine gun with six clips. She pushed another into the gun; then she thought to Lynda. "Find Jenny and get her to our suite please. I'll be there shortly," Gabrielle didn't expect a reply and didn't get one.

As Gabrielle and Chris made their way back up the steps towards the bridge, Gabrielle turned right and headed to her Stateroom. She heard the warble and closed her eyes. George's men had followed them over the three-mile limit. Now they could fight and hopefully sink their boats with all the men aboard. They would never swim to shore.

As Gabrielle opened the door to her suite, Lynda jumped into the room with Jenny holding onto her for dear life.

"Here you are girls, a Glock each. You've all fired one and put clips into the handle." Gabrielle inserted a clip into the last gun she picked out. You have five spare clips each, I hope you will not need to use them, but you will be able to defend yourselves in here. Do not go out onto any of the decks to see what is happening. There are approximately sixty men with machine guns and possibly rocket launchers in four speedboats. They intend to board us and take us women back to George and kill all the men. If the yacht is still floating, they will take it to get back to a port and George will have the yacht brought up to his new command post. Stay in this room, please, do you all understand? If the men get aboard and find this Stateroom, shoot to kill. They will abduct you all if they can. Kill them but don't kill me when I knock three times on the door or jump in."

Gabrielle was by her bedside cabinet. She opened the drawer and threw the contents of her handbag onto the bed. She put the Glock into her bag with the spare clips in the drawer and five spare clips from the bed.

"We are at flank, top speed and past the three-mile limit now. *The Gabrielle* may move port or starboard quickly to get out of the way of the speedboats. Just hang on and don't worry. I'll be on the bridge and try to keep in touch with Lynda letting her know what is happening." She walked up to her wife with the machinegun and her bag over her right shoulder.

"I'm only on the bridge, not far away from you my love and if the men get this far in, I'll be in here with you." They kissed and Gabrielle turned to leave the room.

Lynda suddenly realised something and screamed out. "Gabrielle, what about mum, Wendy and Walter?"

"They'll all be together, jump into mum's room first, if they are not there, try Wendy's cabin. Bring them all back here and keep them safe. Let me know when they are here." They kissed again and Gabrielle walked out of the room and up to the bridge. Lynda jumped to her mother's suite, but she was not there. Next, she tried Wendy's cabin. The two women were huddled behind the bed, Walter was nowhere to be seen.

"I'll take you to our Stateroom, whose first?"

"Take Wendy first, I'll wait for you to come back," Brenda said. Before Wendy could argue, she was in Lynda's Stateroom with the other girls. Brenda arrived a few seconds later.

"Where's Walter?" Lynda asked Wendy.

"He went off to see Tina and he is guarding some stairs. He has a machinegun and wants to help and see some action. He wants to be protecting me like Gabrielle and the other men will be protecting you lot," Wendy replied.

"I would let him stay where he is. I doubt if he will fire off one shot," Wendy said offhand; but she was frightened for her husband. She didn't want him to die out here or anywhere else fighting George's thugs. She wanted them to die together, if possible, in their bed or sat on the sofa, hand in hand, in love.

Lynda spoke to Gabrielle using telepathy telling her they were all in their room and Walter was guarding something. Tina knows where he is.

"Thanks love, everything's fine we're about to change course again, we're well past the three-mile limit now, in neutral-waters."

"Alan had a twenty-five-millimetre heavy machine gun aft, and two boxes of ammunition open ready to follow the next bullet into the magazine.

"There were another two boxes of ammunition by his side, and he had his Glock on him with another ten clips," Gabrielle said into her head.

Tina was guarding the entrance to the mid-section of the yacht. She had a fifteen-millimetre heavy machinegun set up on a tall tripod so she could fire down on any speedboat trying to drop off men to the mid-section of the yacht.

Gabrielle started to cry as she explained why George was after them. "It's difficult to explain as you might think some of what I say sounds Science Fiction.

"In timeline one, which ended about ten years ago, Lynda was signing her books in a bookshop I was Paul back then,.I arranged to meet her at six twenty we only met at eleven o'clock and we instantly fell deeply in love with each other. then George and Ian, Lynda's husband at the time entered the bookshop with six throwing knives each in the back of their jeans and a double-edged sword on their backs, I heard two girls scream as they ran to the front of the store. I had no idea what they were screaming at, neither did Lynda.

"George was trying to cut her photographers hand off at the wrist. I had a large book in my hands I heard Ian shouting at her book manager. This was my chance. As I crept around the corner of the book aisle, Ian was shouting at the book manager about money and threatening him with his knife. I put the book I was holding up to my shoulder and when he went to stab him again, I swung the book into the knife's path and the book went right down to the hilt. Ian was shocked as I went to the back of his jeans and stole one of his knives. I threw it at George's hand and the knife went through his hand and pinned it to the wooden floor. This gave the photographer time to run.

"I went back to the back of Ian and stole another knife. This time I held Ian by his throat. I almost got him to stop the fight when a police officer came down and tried to arrest me. He didn't see the sword on Ian's back as my head was in the way. As I moved to the right with the knife still in my hand, Ian grabbed his sword, brought it over his shoulder and cut the copper's leg off at his thigh.

"One moment he was standing upright, the next he was on the floor looking at his leg as it bled out, I took another knife from Ian's jeans, as Ian turned around with the sword and pointed it towards Lynda, He knocked me to the floor as he told George to decapitate the copper. I had no option but try and save his life. I threw the knife at George and it hit him in his heart and killed him. I then stood up and pulled the sword towards me.

"Ian pushed the sword down towards my stomach, I took hold of the sword with my right hand then my left and Ian put more pressure on the sword as it sliced all the skin and bone from my hands. They were both bleeding profusely. and for a while I couldn't control the sword. Ian was pushing the sword into my stomach and twisting it around inside me I pulled it out of my stomach and pushed it away from me.

"I then put my back against the sword rolled along it to Ian's back took the last throwing knife. Tossed it from my left blood-filled hand to my right blood-filled hand. I then turned around and held the knife again at Ian's throat and slit it from left to right. His blood spilling onto the book table. Then in case he somehow survived I stabbed him in the heart twice and slithered down to the floor. I was in a hell of a mess, but Lynda stayed with me, then got help from a paramedic and a doctor who started to stitch my stomach area back together.

A heart surgeon arrived just as my heart stopped and after opening my chest with a bone-saw, he took my heart out of my chest and placed it into Lynda's hands as he looked from where the blood was coming from then stitched my heart back together and Lynda started to pump my heart and got it going on the tenth pump. Mr Muhammed put it back in my chest. I told Lynda that I loved her with all my heart. She kissed me on my lips I was then in excruciating pain as they sat me up and put cling film around my back and front laid me down on a stretcher and with one more kiss from the love of my life I was gone onto the helicopter.

"In timeline two which Death created for our *Second Chance* Ian was killed by John, He suggested George give himself up which he did but after the police shot him in the leg and his head George escaped. Now he has been chasing us through Europe and we are supposed to have an end fight on top of the Empire State Building in four weeks.

"George does not want to do that he wants to take his revenge on me for killing him too early and now thinks Lynda is his wife. and whore which she is not. Lynda is legally my wife as man and wife and woman to woman wife to wife.

"George wants to have Lynda back so he can make money from her, while his men rape her, then beat her up and finally slash her body open with a Stanley Knife then just below her breasts. She has been through Hell for four years and I will not allow her or the rest of the ladies aboard *The Gabrielle* to be taken and abused in this way."

Gabrielle was crying hard now, and Chris Patel put his arm around. her shoulder. "We will do everything in our power to stop these men attacking you or taking you all prisoners."

"Thank you, Chriss," Gabrielle replied.

"Now let's find these boats," Chris said with his arm around Gabrielle's shoulder. "Then we will open fire on them and kill all the men in their boats and sink them." He picked up his microphone and spoke to the crew. "This is very, important. At all costs we cannot allow George's men to get aboard this yacht," he said. "If we do, his men will abduct all the women and make them whores then have them beaten up after being raped and have their body cut open with a Stanley Knife then cut again under their breasts. Are you all with me to kill these men and sink their boats?"

"Yeses," were heard from around the yacht.

They were now in neutral waters. They could not be prosecuted for killing and destroying speedboats out here. Gabrielle wondered if they knew how far out, they were? It was just like waiting for the war or battle to start and they had started the battle for their lives that very afternoon. Now it was evening, and they had to go through it all again, this time with more men and they were all armed with machineguns.

Everyone on the yacht was waiting for the first of the men to open fire, then they could fire back. They might say they were playing with the people on the yacht, so everyone waited, patiently.

Gabrielle was watching the radar scope as her yacht was still moving further out into neutral waters with the speedboats following them.

"Is there a gunboat or any other naval ship close at hand we could ask for help?" Gabrielle asked. "No nothing Mam," Glen replied.

"How cold is the water out here?" Gabrielle asked.

"One or two degrees, cold enough to kill anyone who fell in the water in three minutes." Chris replied.

"Is our radio operator in the radio room?"

"Yes, the rest of the crew are at their stations fully armed. My two engineers are in the engine room."

"Is there any way I can talk to John, and the rest of my crew without letting everyone else know what I'm saying?"

"Yes, here, use this." Chris handed her a small microphone and switched it on.

"Thanks. John, Tina, Mike Alan, Noah when they start firing try and sink their craft. I have an idea they will get as close as they can before opening fire. They will probably tell us to stop and prepare to be boarded. They won't consider we're heavily armed, that you will just have your Glocks with a couple of spare clips each, after all, we're off to another country. Kill everyone you can as well," Gabrielle out.

There was no reply from anyone, she expected them to carry out their orders.

"Where is Edward and Walter?" Gabrielle asked Chris.

"Edward is above us with Mike, he has a nine-millimetre machinegun. Walter is on the bow with John, same size machinegun."

"Excellent!" Gabrielle replied. She was glad her two men were not alone. "How far away are the speedboats?"

"A hundred yards and closing, keeping up with us at an angle." Gabrielle picked up the bridge, night-time binoculars and looked forward. She could see the speedboats bouncing through the choppy water. The men looked cold, and she could see their machineguns. They were shuffling around in their boats, rubbing their gloved hands together.

She left the bridge and stepped outside, looking aft through the binoculars. There was a man trying to stand up in the boat and he had a microphone in his hand. He was holding onto the handrail for dear life and another man was trying to help hold him upright.

"How far away are they?" Gabrielle asked Steve.

"One hundred yards," Steve replied.

"This is orders from George, you are to heave too and prepare to be boarded or we'll open fire. We'll give you ten seconds."

The crew were ready to repel the boarders and sink their boats. Some of the men were wearing night vision goggles. She couldn't understand why they would want them on now. She slowly panned the binoculars, looking in the direction of the men with the goggles on. There was nothing behind them nothing but . . . she looked further back again and there was another speedboat being towed by the first. There was no wash, they were low in the water, about the same size as the boat towing them. George did not want them to get to New York and she guessed they had orders to sink *The Gabrielle.*

She looked a little further back and behind each speedboat there was another speedboat. No engine running, no lights on, just a couple of men smoking, trying to hide the glow of their cigarettes.

"We have a severe problem Chris, look behind the speedboats we can see on radar. About forty yards." Gabrielle handed Chris the binoculars.

He took them from her and cursed as soon as he saw the outline of the second boats. He picked up the small microphone. "This is your Captain to all hands. Foreword of us are six boats not three. Their engines are off and are being towed approximately forty yards behind the first speedboats.

They do not show up on radar so are either made from wood or plastic. Have a go at sinking these first. They are low in the water so must be carrying extra men or heavier gunfire.

"As we can't see it, we'll assume there is a second speedboat directly behind them coming aft of us."

"All the crew can hear me over this system," Chris said proudly.

Gabrielle was thinking quickly.

"Can I have another look at the speedboats please Chris?" she asked.

He handed her the binoculars then went to a cabinet and brought out two more pair of binoculars for the bridge crew. As Gabrielle looked forward, she could see six men with night vision glasses that came down over their eyes. Then she had an idea.

"Chris, some of the men are using night-vision glasses, if we put the spotlight on them, the men will be blinded for a minute or so. Can we sweep the spotlight from the bridge over the boats, or does it have to be done by hand?"

"It's slow by remote control, if someone goes onto the top deck, it can be released and moved by hand, which I assume you want. To move it fast from boat to boat and the ones behind?"

"Where is the lever to change it too manual?" Gabrielle asked.

"Just beneath the righthand side of the spotlight."

"Can I turn it on and off from up there?"

"Yes, there's a switch on its post, right side. It's the only switch there. You can't miss it." He suddenly realised what he was saying. "Surely, you're not thinking of going up there yourself?"

"Yes, you three are needed here." She buttoned up her fur coat and left the bridge, handbag on her left shoulder, machinegun on her right.

She climbed the steps to the upper deck and crept past Mike and Edward to the spotlight. She turned it to manual and got the idea of how fast she could move it and pan it over the boats. Chris pressed the button for the warble alarm. He left it on for five seconds. Everyone in the small speedboats looked in their direction, just as Gabrielle turned the spotlight on the first boat. Most of the men were blinded, then the second, third and fourth speedboats.

She panned the searchlight over the boats behind, seeing them packed with men and extremely low in the water. One of the men raised his machine gun and fired a short burst towards the spotlight but he was blinded by it and the bullets went high.

That was enough to start a battle. John could still see the first boat being towed. He fired a long burst, sweeping it along the top of the boat, cutting the men in half. He then fired just below the waterline and the boat began to sink with all hands, who were not already dead.

"Whoever is on the searchlight, light up the back two speedboats. Come on hurry up." John shouted to the unknown searchlight operator.

The searchlight lit up the back two boats and both craft were sinking three underwater sweeps later. Some of the men were shot in their legs as the bullets broke the wooden craft apart and started to take on water. Gabrielle used her machine gun, raking it over the men who were still in the boats, she just could not let them get close to her Lynda.

The first three speedboats were now lit up and were passing the bow of the yacht. John heard another heavy machinegun taking over killing men and sinking the boats. Mike continued to sink the boats while Tina was killing some of the men.

Some men were using grappling hooks to climb onto the mid deck, only to be shot by the crew. Then ten-inch spikes came out of the lower side of the yacht. Some of the men were led against the side of the yacht as they tried to pull themselves over the gunnel using their ropes and grappling hooks.

They were instantly stabbed in the chest or stomach and were stuck to the side of the yacht. They could do nothing to help get themselves off the spikes and at least fall into the sea. The men stabbed in the stomach were laying backwards as they bled out and with their weight on the spikes, it was tearing their stomach open.

The men stabbed through their heart were now dead, just waiting for one of the hands to push their body off the spike and let it fall into the sea, as they fired multiple times sending bullets into the person to ensure he was dead.

Alan was firing at the boat coming up behind. The bow was sitting out of the water as the speedboat behind was pulling it down as it went through the waves and the men in the second boat were soaked and very cold.

The first boat was having a huge hole shot in the front of its bow. Then Alan hit some of the linkage and the boat fell into the water which flooded the boat and with the weight of the men, began to sink. The two powerful engines at the rear were pushing the speedboat, out of control deeper into the water making it fill faster until its gunnels were lower than the water. The sea flooded into the boat making it sink fast.

The man driving the boat had been shot several times in his legs, stomach and arms. Other men in the boat had died under the onslaught of bullets from the crew of *The Gabrielle*. They were not going to let anyone get aboard their yacht. This was a lot of men to send after two people, especially at night in freezing conditions. George must have either wanted them really bad or did not wish to face Gabrielle for the last fight in the USA.

Amidships, Mike was on the upper deck with Edward. Tina stood across the walkway of the lower deck, ploughing bullets into men and the bottom of the boats. Then one man looked up and seeing Mike and another man, with the more powerful and bigger machineguns. With two bullets in each arm, he rested his machinegun on his right leg that was bleeding badly from bullet wounds.

His machinegun fired and he managed to move it left to right sending bullets up and into the two men's legs. There were two cries of pain as the bullets entered their calves and hips. Then Tina and the men below her fired their guns into the boat, filling it with bullets that sent it straight below the waves. The man who had fired his gun was hit over fifty times. On hearing the cries of pain, Gabrielle turned from her position at the searchlight, looking across the upper deck platform at the two men who were now laying on their backs. She ran over to them looking at their injuries.

"Whoever is on the searchlight, pan it over the last speedboat," John shouted up to the searchlight operator. Gabrielle ran to the searchlight.

"Sorry John, Mike and Edward have been hit in their legs, calves and hips I was just about to speak to Lynda and ask for her help.

"I'm so sorry Gabrielle, I didn't realise it was you up there. Sorry for shouting at you. You should not be up there, you could be shot or killed, John said, getting back to destroying the boats.

"Back on the light now John. She switched it on, and John fired across the mid-section of the boat then just below the water twice and another line of bullets went just above, breaking the side of the boat apart as it started to fill with water.

"Now Gabrielle, get back to Mike and Edward, get them some help." John said to her. He then turned to Walter who had been firing beside him. "Go find Noah, take him to the forward gun locker, give him the twenty-mill gun, take two cases of bullets and help him set it up on the roof to take over from Mike and Edward. Then come back to me."

"On my way back over to them." Gabrielle shouted to John. As she looked down at their injuries, she could see blood gushing from their wounds. "Lynda," she thought to her wife. "Mike and Edward have been shot in their right leg, twice in their calf and twice in their hip. Can you help them?"

"I don't see why not, I need light, so bring them in here, put them onto the bed, one each side."

Gabrielle got by Edward, held him close to her and jumped into their suite. Helping hands got him to the far side of the bed for Lynda to work on him. Then Gabrielle was gone and lay next to Mike, putting her arm over his stomach and pulling him to her side, then she jumped and helping hands got him onto their bed on the other side. The room was already covered in green light and using a clean piece of gauze to cover his wound, Lynda started to work on Edward's Leg.

There was no hospital out here and they were still in the middle of a fight with George's men. She concentrated her eyes into the top hole in his right hip. Using a pair of tweezers. She carefully inserted them into his hip wound, grabbed hold of the bullet, pulled it out, and dropped it into a clean mug. She then cauterized the bleeding artery and cleaned up the inside of the wound with her eyes.

She did the same with the other bullet wounds in his thigh and again on the two bullets in his calf. Finally, she wiped over all the wounds with the gauze. Edward was no longer in any pain and was off the bed walking around the bedroom and saying a huge thank you to Lynda, he walked back up to his position and took over the large fifteen-millimetre gun, firing into the first boat that came his way and sank it, after killing everyone on board. Noah was finishing the boats off, smiling at them as they got to his gun position.

"Mike, I'll soon have you up and about," Lynda said to him, "now for your calf," Lynda said, and her eyes flared bright green again then the bullets came out and the bleeding stopped. Eight minutes later his leg was healed, and he was off the bed walking around in no pain at all "

"This is brilliant, no pain at all, thank you, Lynda, I won't forget this," he said. When he was standing next to Edward, he picked up the slightly smaller machinegun and was firing into the head, torso and legs of the men below who passed him in their boats. Two more men emptied their two clips of bullets into the men below as the boat began to sink, first the engines, ensuring there was no escape for the men.

With the three boats now sinking or sunk, and bodies piled up on the lower deck, they started their search once again of the English Channel. They were looking for anymore of George's boats and hoped he had nothing larger available to him.

Tina and the crew in her section including Noah, Mike and Edward, went to the port side of the yacht and looked out for more small boats. Noah held Tina, tight and turned her into him. Do you like your ring" he asked her and kissed her lips.

"It's beautiful, really beautiful, she replied kissing him. And kissed her ring, smiling at him, holding his hand and pulling him into her. As she looked into his eyes, she could see the love he had for her. It was real, heart-warming and everlasting. She didn't have to worry about him or his deep love for her. She could feel the love pouring out of him, he was hers and she was his, forever. She knew they had little time to talk together, even kiss together, as the battle started, but she knew they would have time when it was over, at least they would get to sleep with each other.

"The shop manager said you could change your ring even if we're away for three months," Noah said to Tina, as he held her tight, then turned her thin body into him and kissed her on her lips.

"That was nice of him, I didn't think jewellery shops would do that. Does the manager know where we are going and the jobs we do?" Tina asked.

"Oh yes, Alan met me and took me to the special Jewellery shop Gabrielle and Lynda use. When Alan said I worked for Gabrielle and Lynda, he bent over backwards for me."

"Really?" she replied and looked again at her ring. It was a Solitaire, a single diamond. She didn't think much about it when Noah placed it on her finger. They had only time for a hug and one quick kiss before they had to go to their assigned places. Now she was looking at her ring, she noticed it had an almost flat top with triangular flat marks cut around the side of the diamond, taking the sides to the bottom of the ring, which stood upright, sparkling at her eyes.

This wasn't a cheap diamond by the looks of it the diamond must be five carats at least. She rubbed her fingers around the top of the ring, feeling its size, feeling the love it was given to her. She knew of the jewellery shops Gabrielle and Lynda went to, the rings they bought each other were not cheap, at least fifty to a hundred thousand each.

This ring couldn't be that expensive surely? She guessed in her head at ten thousand, perhaps five thousand. She didn't think a Government Gunslinger would be paid very much, unless like Alan you worked for the Royal Family security forces,

Noah was twenty-three, the same age as herself, Tina had been lucky, firsts at every exam. Picked up by Cambridge University studying High End Business Studies at Fourteen. At fifteen she took her Masters in High End Business Studies, Geographic world-wide Landmarks, Major Routes in and out of each country, location of Airports and military installations. She passed every exam with honours. At weekends, she took Target Practice and Gymnastics. Getting a degree in each course.

At seventeen she was picked up by a Private Bodyguard company and did two years getting a degree with honours at Target Shooting and caring for rich clients. She also took a year's course in Gun Shot Emergency Trauma in the field. How to remove a bullet, with a bullet picker, a small device used by the army SAS, secret service, and now bodyguards. She had met John at training school for bodyguards and they often challenged each other at shooting matches, she always came third, John was first Alan Second, then herself. She was good, very, good, which is why she was here now, protecting John's wife. She would take several bullets for her.

She could already speak ten languages, now she was learning Chinese and Japanese, as John said they would all need to learn Chinese, as they were going to set up shops in China and Japan.

They kissed each other, a long romantic kiss, their mouths rotating about each other, tongues in each other's mouth, playing with each other, sharing loving emotions together.

As they started their patrol on the port side of the yacht, they held hands and when they looked out to sea, they kissed each other.

"How did you manage to get on the yacht with us?"

"I had a phone call from Gabrielle asking me if I would like to join you on your trip to the states and she would sort out who I would work with, and John would do some gunshot evaluation with me while we're at sea. Then an hour later, Lynda called me and told me to come here first and help with the luggage until you came aboard and keep out of your way and one of the girls would find me and tell me the plan. Is it alright with you sleeping together?" he asked and placed his arm around her back as they looked out to sea.

A man wearing a black wet suit and holding a loaded crossbow came into view, he was hard to see with his body bobbing up and down in the sea. But Noah had spotted him and pulled out his Glock. His right arm held Tina behind him, his whole body guarding her. He waited until his head was above the water and fired twice, the body floated to the surface, the crossbow with it.

"Of course, it is you fool," she replied. "Oh, good shooting by the way, I didn't see him, I wonder if there are any more men like him?" Tina asked her future husband.

Alan ran up the gangway to find out who fired their gun at what or who. As Alan looked out to sea, he could see the dead body in the water, it was now going past their yacht.

"Who is the gunslinger who killed that in the sea," Alan asked.

"It was Noah, Tina replied, two shots to the head which was bobbing up and down in the sea. Hard to locate and kill." Tina added.

"Well done, Noah, we'll have to keep some men on this side of the yacht just in case there are others. Noah, you have good eyesight, do you want the job until we move away from here?"

"Yes, sure he replied, eager to please."

"Excellent, Tina you stay with him, he's your fiancé not too many long kisses, you both are on watch. Grayham, can you get a large blanket from the stores for them please? It will be cold where they will be sitting. Right up there on the fourth deck, there is a comfy seat up there, and no dosing off," he joked. He clapped his hands, "Okay everyone, move on and search the rest of this side of the yacht, we are not out of the woods yet!"

On the starboard side, with the shooting stopped and the last of the dead falling to the deck on top of other dead bodies, two men, one shot in the left arm and a deep graze to his stomach, the other shot twice in the right hip and a bullet through his right arm, gradually stood and made their way to the first cabin on their level.

"Even if we don't survive, George will know we fought to the very end to get both girls off the yacht. Where do you think they are Martin?" Clive asked showing the pain he was in, with his right hip.

"Oh yes and who's going to tell him?" Clive asked.

"We will when we meet him on the other side, he can't last much longer with the state he's in," Martin replied.

"Bite down on the morphine capsule around your neck, it will help get you up and down the steps we will have to negotiate. I have some more here take three, I took them from the dead men outside and the medical bag from Stan. Let's get each other bandaged up then look for the girls." Martin replied.

While under the influence of the morphine, they managed to remove one bullet from each other's arm and get themselves bandaged up in under four minutes. Martin's shot hip was bleeding profusely, very painful to move and put his weight on

They checked their guns and the number of the clips each other had and discarded everything else they didn't need.

"We'll make our way to the Stateroom, I'm sure that's where the little bitches will be," Clive suggested.

"Then let's make a move, I'll be taking some more of that morphine soon," Martin replied.

Clive opened the door and they walked up the Port side staircase to the next level, then across the deck and looked up and down. There was an old man sitting on the bottom steps guarding the way through.

Clive turned, put his finger to his lips and pointed down the steps. Martin nodded, showing he understood what he meant as he bit into another morphine capsule.

They made their way slowly up the next set of steps and then up another set of eight steps to a deck that went forward to the upper deck and pool, and back to the starboard side of the Stateroom. Clive indicated they return the way they had come, there was nobody on guard there anyway. When they reached the door, Clive knocked it twice.

"Ladies; are you okay in there?" he asked quietly.

"Who is it?" Lynda asked also in a quiet voice.

"John, we have four of George's men wandering around the yacht, just wanted to make sure you are not harmed." Gabrielle heard what was being said by this man.

"We're okay thanks John," Lynda replied, her Glock in her shaking hands. She knew it wasn't John.

"Lie again, lie harder this time, think of something sexy to say; you shouldn't have a problem with that," Gabrielle said into her head and sent her a picture of them together making love while they were in Rome.

"Sorry John, stop it now," Gabrielle, let me talk, "Ohhhh that's fantastic don't stop now," she added. "I was getting frightened with all the shooting going on," Lynda said in her sexy voice. The other girls in the room were laughing because they couldn't hear what Gabrielle was saying to her.

"I'm going to come into your room there is no reason to panic now, that will come later." Clive replied quickly.

"What do you mean later?" Lynda asked in a genuine frightened voice.

"George has no intention of going to New York, he will fight Gabrielle to the death at his new mansion. He will then have his way with you and make as much money as he can from you and the price for just an hour with you is starting from a grand. The lucky man or woman can do what they like with you, including cutting you up but not your face. You will be stitched up by the same fully qualified nurse that is treating him, you will be pleased to hear his gangrene leg is healing quickly but not so his memory.

"There are only a few of you, how do you intend to take over this yacht?" Lynda asked, her voice shaking to show them she was frightened.

"I thought you said Gabrielle was in the room with you?" the man asked.

"Gabrielle is here, but her head is between my legs right now and her tongue is licking my clitoris and Oh that was lovely, please don't stop, do that again," Lynda squealed.

"That sounds lovely, I think I'll come in and watch if it's fine with you? You could rub me off, so I come over Gabrielle's face. It will give her some idea of what you will endure under George's care. What do you think, you were under his care before, now you will be so again?"

"I was never under George's care Ian was my husband. Leave us alone so that I can concentrate on my wife and where her tongue is right now."

"That's it my love I'm almost in position to kill them." Gabrielle spoke into Lynda's head. She had managed to work herself onto the deck section before the pool. As she tip-toed towards the starboard side of the yacht.

At the end of the bridge section, she stopped just in time to hear the man calling himself John, give them more orders.

"Okay Lynda, now I want you to order the captain to change course, back to the UK, I will give him our destination. If you do not agree, I will kill all the women in your suite including all your staff and the crew. I can take this beauty back to port and I will beat you into unconsciousness while I have Gabrielle keelhauled, bow to stern."

"Now to start this new command, send out Jenny, I want to kill her so that you know I mean what I say. I killed her husband an hour ago, he died fighting hard. But he was no match against me, knife to knife. His body is currently in the Atlantic Ocean with all my men he killed. His body is being consumed by the large number of sharks we have attracted. Now, send her out to meet her maker or I'll come in and kill her by be-heading her," Clive said.

"Not unless I kill him first a bullet right between his eyes," Jenny laughed.

"Oh no, please let me shoot first, a bullet right between his legs," Lynda laughed.

"Me next a bullet right through the heart he hasn't got?" Sarah added.

John had finally made his way to the bridge spoke to the captain suggesting they move as far away from this battle as fast as the yacht would travel. It would now be safe for the first and second engineer to leave the engine room. As he climbed the steps to the pool deck, he saw Gabrielle and noticed she was smiling to herself.

John had heard what the man had said to the girls and threatened his wife. He tapped Gabrielle on her shoulder, and she turned into his open arms.

"Are you okay?" he asked her.

"Fine!" she replied still smiling.

"What are they saying that has got you smiling at a time like this when that bloke is threatening to kill my wife?"

"They are arguing about who will shoot him first Jenny wants to put a bullet between his eyes, Sarah wants to put a bullet through his heart because he doesn't have one and Lynda wants to shoot him between his legs."

"Well, none of them will get to shoot that man, I'll kill him myself," John replied smiling.

"I was hoping to do that," Gabrielle replied.

"You pay me to look after you," John retorted holding her hand.

"And you pay me to look after Jenny," Tina said standing behind them. She took hold of John's hand and looked into his eyes. "There are two men, let's kill one each?" she suggested.

"Agreed!" John replied.

Together, gun in hand they walked around the corner of the bridge.

"Who are you two?" the man calling himself John demanded to know kicking Martin in the side, so he got to his feet and fumbled around for his gun.

"Well, I'm John, Gabrielle's bodyguard. Jenny is my wife, and this is Tina, her bodyguard."

"Oh shit." John replied.

There were two sounds of thunder as both men fell to the deck a bullet between their eyes.

"I'd know that sound anywhere, it's John and Tina," Jenny cried aloud to everyone. She dropped her gun on the bed and bounded over it towards the door.

By the time she reached it, she noticed Gabrielle had jumped into their suite and was holding Lynda in her arms. As she pulled the door open, she jumped into her husband's arms, holding him tight, kissing his face, lips, neck, and then the same all over again.

"I love you John, lovers forever," She whispered into his ear then kissed it and licked it and turned to his face where their mouths met in unison, kissing, their mouths rotating around each other showing their love for each other, something that would never die.

"I love you too munchkin," John replied kissing his wife hard, their tongues intertwining in each other's mouth. Their hands were moving up and down each other's back, feeling, holding, bonding each other, wanting to make love to each other there and then but it would have to wait, there were jobs to be done, the yacht needed a deep clean of blood, before they ran into another ship.

Nobody had expected this attack so close to home waters. *The Gabrielle* was made to expect trouble and repel boarders. It had happened and a lot of young men had died through promises of riches and power to come. Death had taken his side of a plan He had planted in George's head when He gave him his leg back. It was all part of His plan, to test a couple's never-ending love for each other.

This game would end soon it didn't; matter who won, but this nightmare had to end, and the main players had to fight, a battle to the death. On one side love for eternity the other would know the truth and mourn forevermore in one of Death's ever revolving black rooms

In their suite, Gabrielle was holding Lynda as close as their bodies could get. Their lips touched, rotating around each other, tongues intertwining, hearts raced, as their love for each other flowed, encompassed them as they caressed, hands, arms, breasts, heads, lips showing so much love for each other into a world they were both willing to go, hand in hand into a world filled with excitement and love.

They parted, holding hands "Let's see how much damage they did to our yacht and see how our crew fared. John, do you know of any fatalities?" Gabrielle asked.

"I've not heard of any. We'll have a crew count, dispose of any more bodies into the sea then clean the decks stem to stern. Is Mike and Edward, okay?" he asked Lynda."

"Oh yes, all bullet holes closed and repaired. They both returned to their posts."

"Well done Lynda and well done you Gabrielle for thinking of using the spotlight on the men with night vision glasses on. Oh yes, Chris Patel told me all about it, he didn't think at the time you had intensions of going to the light yourself."

"That sounds good, tell Chris Patel full speed to the Northern Lights. Now, stow away all the heavy artillery and machineguns. For now, each member of the crew to carry a handgun; one clip in the gun three clips on them, just to be safe for now."

Gabrielle looked at her watch, it was now just past eleven thirty at night. There had been no sign of any other ships, this she knew was more than a planned battle and she had no idea what lay ahead of them.

"When our yacht is clean, break out the star cameras and I'll do some Stellar photography for a few hours and during this time, we'll run blacked out, radar only and make sure there are two men at the radar, we've all had a long hard and frightening evening.

"When we're ship shape and Bristol fashion, I'll ensure there is a good hearty meal for everyone."

"Gabrielle, you can't cook," John replied laughing.

"I can it's just that you don't eat the food I make; anyway, I employ people to cook for us. You see Captain Patel I'll get the girls together some of us will clean the canteen on B Deck while the rest clear up the galley and prepare the meal," Jenny said.

"Right Gabrielle I'll get the crew onto cleaning the decks and every part of the yacht with that special blood cleaner. By any chance did you foresee this happening?" John asked.

"No, it was just a hunch," she replied smiling.

During a time of battle John was in charge, allowing the captain to remain with his Bridge officers. At all times Gabrielle was in charge of *The Gabrielle,* it was her yacht or Lynda and hers'. As John walked off to give the captain his orders from Gabrielle; Gabrielle and the other girls gave their suite a quick tidy and made the bed they had all took shelter behind. They put a new duvet cover on the duvet, replacing the one covered in blood,

Tina headed back to Noah and the rest of their watch which was another thirty minutes of kissing, holding each other close and their arms wrapped around each other.

Gabrielle and Lynda headed down to Deck B and the main canteen. During their travels they couldn't see any interior damage to the yacht in some places there were several shell cartridges on the deck which they commenced to pick up and discard over the side into the Ocean.

Gabrielle took Sarah to where they stowed all the cleaning materials and very soon had their buckets filled with scented cleaning water, to mask the smell of gunfire. Once that deck was smelling better, they descended to the lower decks cleaning each one thoroughly. Outside they could hear young men singing together as they cleared the decks of the heavy guns, stowing them in the secret weapons locker. Where Alan had used his heavy gun, there were hundreds of shell cases. Each one was picked up tossed overboard and the search for more went on.

The rear gunnel was scrubbed to clean off the automatic gunfire residue from Alan's large gun. The exterior of the hull was also checked for bullet hits but there were none, they had been incredibly lucky. The entire yacht was now being checked on its exterior for gun shots. The only damage to the hull was a few scratches to the exterior hull where the three speedboats had allowed those men left alive, to scramble aboard the yacht only to be met with light machinegun fire by some of the crew, as their bodies fell back into the cold ocean.

There were many AK47's, with spare clips left laying over the deck, which were all picked up and discarded over the side. The starboard side deck was then scrubbed and washed clean with the special blood cleaning liquid which had been brought aboard before they left. When Gabrielle was given the news that their yacht didn't have one hit, she was sure someone else had a play in their safety.

Ninety minutes after they started the deep clean, they were sitting down to a large meal with their Captain, Gabrielle and Lynda at the head of the table. They ate their meal with their usual rivalry.

Gabrielle stood up and tapped her glass and the room was silent. Her voice could now be heard throughout the yacht.

"Captain, crew of *The Gabrielle*, never before has this yacht come under such an attack by thugs with no concern to who they killed, injured or the damage they caused. You all fought bravely and thankfully there was no loss of life on our side. I must say and I mean this from the bottom of my heart, I would sail the seven seas with you all. You carry out orders from a man you barely know all to protect the ship and two women.

"I would also like to thank John, Alan, Tina, Noah and Mike for operating the heavy guns and Ben Styles who was repelling boarders beneath Tina, keeping her safe while she sank the speed boats bringing more men to this insane attack. Can we have a round of applause for these people please?"

There was a loud applause with cheers and slaps on the back from the crew to John, Alan, Mike and Tina and Noah. When the cheering died down, Gabrielle spoke again.

"Thank you, now, give yourselves a round of applause."

When the applause was over and everyone had settled down, Gabrielle looked around the room, smiling at each person her green eyes met.

"Trever, if you can breakout the star night camera and stand, we'll also need the Deep Star Net camera and stand. If you could set it up on the pool deck, please, Cindy, if you could give him a hand, please. The decking is in place now. When you are all dismissed, I would like two people fore and aft using the night-time binoculars you will be looking for any ship which appears to be following us. I don't think we are quite out of the woods yet, but there will be no more gun battles."

"George, the man who sent those men after us are after Lynda and me. George Rainer is under the impression that Lynda is his wife, whereas he killed his wife and her parents for telling Lynda what was about to happen to her life. This part is difficult, but it is only fair as you have been caught up in this, that you know what's happened, even if it makes no sense.

"In a terrible fight, in what we will call timeline one, when Ian, who was then Lynda's husband, came into a bookstore where Lynda was signing her books; with George, armed with six eight-inch KA Bar knives in the back of their jeans and a very sharp double-edged sword on their back. I was Paul back then. Lynda and I had met each other seven hours previously falling, literary, head over heels in love with each other, we were soulmates.

"I was going to meet Lynda after she finished her book signing and take her to the Shard for a meal. She was then separated from her husband because of the abuse she suffered under his care with George raping her every night of the week with Ian's blessing. I killed both men and was almost killed myself."

"Now George recalls the part where I killed him, and he wants to kill me. He also wants Lynda as his own wife and sell her body to other men for very rough sex which includes cutting her body with a Stanley knife and then under her breasts.

"We agreed to a final fight in New York in four weeks' time, but he does not want to come there, and this is why he has sent some of his men here tonight to stop that future event from happening. I will do anything that is asked of me to protect Lynda. I was a man when I killed George and Ian and if I must fight George as a woman, I will give my all to protect my wife and stop her from being put through the hell she was put through for four years in timeline one.

"Lynda has gone through Hell once she will not go through it again. I love her with all my heart and soul. We are soulmates, forever," she said with tears flowing from her eyes.

From somewhere near the back a man shouted out. "I remember the first timeline you were cut up really bad but all those lives you saved."

"Come to think of it I recall the first timeline as well. I'm with you Gabrielle, you go right ahead and kill George. He's been a right pain in our necks, taking money from small shops, pubs and clubs, then he goes and brings in the Mafia to show his men how it's done. Gabrielle, we're all behind you and Lynda." The crew stood applauding them as Lynda held Gabrielle's hand and they kissed, with Lynda holding Gabrielle close to her side.

The applause went on for some time before it slowed and finally the room was quiet, except for Gabrielle still crying. John handed her a tissue so she could wipe away her tears.

"Thank you, thank you for your understanding," Gabrielle said smiling at everyone.

"We're behind you girls, now let's get away from this warzone and see the Northern Lights. Take some good pictures of the light's girls," Captain Patel said, shaking each girl by the hand.

"Crew, Dismissed! Let's give Gabrielle and Lynda time to recover with a cup of hot chocolate. For those with no night duty carry on. Those on lookout, get your night vision binoculars from Commander John Fletcher, you all know who he is by now, he's the man who's been ordering us around all night. Commander Alan Watts has also been giving orders, so follow them both but John is in charge if we need to get the guns out again. Have a restful evening and for those off watch, a good night's sleep.

"Tina and Noah, you are to go straight to your cabin and try to get some sleep. Try not to make too much noise, enjoy the rest of the night." As the couple stood holding hands, everyone applauded and cheered them as they left the main mess hall.

Christine put two hot mugs of milky hot chocolate on the table behind and tapped them on the shoulder, indicating where it was.

"Enjoy!" she said and left them alone.

They took a seat each, and holding hands, slowly drank their drinks, thinking together of the night ahead. When they finished their hot chocolates, Alan met them and escorted them up to their suite. He stood watch outside while the girl's changed into something warmer and put their fur coats on.

Once outside on the pool cover, they finished setting up the four different cameras and stands. The people with binoculars on lookout duty were at the bow as, *The Gabrielle* was slicing through still ocean heading north, for the Northern Lights. Once seen, they would return south and out into the middle of the Atlantic Ocean, before a right turn towards New York and business.

The Gabrielle was completely blacked out so there was no light damage to the pictures they were taking and sending some of them straight back to their own observatory where the young astronomers could print them off later and put them into a presentation folder. Gabrielle and Lynda would no doubt give the group a talk on the Northern Lights, upon their return.

Gabrielle was taking photos on the deep sky camera when Lynda called her to her side. She had an extra-long telephoto lens on the Nikon camera with a two-inch collection mirror attached to the camera's base. She had been taking photos of Saturn and its moons when something else had caught her eye.

"What have you found my love?" Gabrielle asked and took hold of the camera and looked through its lens, in the direction Lynda was pointing.

"Oh, dear I do believe that is a German warship, possibly a missile destroyer."

"Surely George doesn't have connections with the German navy?"

"Have no fear my love, the ship is running with lights dark as are we. I doubt they have noticed us yet, visually; although they may have picked us up on radar."

"Will they fire on us?" Lynda asked showing concern in her voice.

"No my love, it would cause an international incident. Not only that, but it would also cost them a lot of money to replace *The Gabrielle*. And three years to rebuild her."

"What of us if they did open fire, we could not save everyone?

"Put that out of your mind, did you feel the increase in speed and our new course?"

"No, I wasn't paying attention."

"Somebody else has seen the ship and informed the captain and more than likely John." Gabrielle told Lynda holding her tight in her arms, moulding a shell around her to keep Lynda safe. They kissed, lips rotating, cold nose upon cold nose as Alan joined them.

"Lynda, Gabrielle, everything is fine. I take it you have noticed the German warship following us. You couldn't miss it with a lens like that on your camera. You must have been looking at Mars."

"Saturn actually," Lynda replied in a shaky voice.

"It's alright Lynda, I wouldn't lie to you." Alan gently placed his hand on her shoulder, something very few men were permitted to do.

"John has spoken to them, and they were surprised to be spoken to in fluent German and they thanked him for not having to speak English. They saw us and noticed our running lights were off and thought we were running from someone or trying to creep up on another yacht.

"They are satisfied now and wish you both well with your photography. If you have a picture of the Man in the Moon, they would like to see it," Alan said laughing.

They had been sailing north for several hours and ninety minutes later they could see the Northern Lights. During this time, they had been cuddled together looking at the stars, kissing and not wanting the inevitable fight to happen. Soon they could see the green banners of light hanging in the dark sky, swirling about each other, the green and orange colours mixing high in the sky.

They got their camera out of the box which had kept the Nikon camera warm, ready to use over their cold night's voyage and started to take photos of the Northern Lights. Members of the night watch were also taking photos of the Northern Lights on their expensive cameras and phones. Other people were taking pictures for their friends who were now fast asleep or like the kitchen crew just waking up and getting into the shower.

Two hours later, with the pictures and film taken, Gabrielle gave the order to make a slow turn south and head south for New York.

"Has this trip been worth it? Do you have a better idea of how you can fight George?" Lynda asked as they stood together hand in hand.

"Gabrielle, Lynda you are not going to believe this. Here read this I just got it off the news channel," Ben said aloud cheerfully. Gabrielle started to read the news report "There was a fire in the annex of a mansion belonging to the wanted man George Rainer. Ten of George's men were killed in the fire and the rest of his men were out doing a special job for George.

"Had the rest of the men been sleeping in the annex they would have all been burned to death as the door was locked closed keeping them in the room. Pictures and route maps of New York were found scattered throughout the main complex police have said."

"But Gabrielle, what does this signify?" Lynda asked.

"The men who attacked us tonight and we killed, were meant to die in the fire and Death had their souls so we will not be attacked again tonight or on our way to New York. By what the police have found though, at some time he will be in New York, but with only a few people," Gabrielle explained to Lynda.

"Perhaps once the police investigation is over, we might be able to ask them how many rooms he was looking to book and where and when he might be arriving?" Ben suggested.

"Excellent idea Ben, keep your eyes on the news. When you think the time is right, I have a friend in the London Met Police, who may be able to help us." Gabrielle replied.

"Glad to be of help. Breakfast in half an hour."

"Is it that time already?" Gabrielle asked.

"Yes, and you need to put a little weight on if you want to throw your knives accurately," Lynda added and stroked Gabrielle's thin arms.

"We'll meet you in the Mess Hall," Gabrielle sighed, then took hold of Lynda's hand and led her to their suite.

Once there, they hugged each other close, kissing, each other, hands sliding up and down each other's back taking away the chill of the knight.

"I think we had better change into something more becoming of you and me being the directors of our company. We need to lower our defence grade to zero; nobody else will attack us on our trip," Gabrielle said into Lynda's ear.

"You've been talking to someone haven't you?" Lynda replied. Thoughts of a conversation taken hours ago entered her head, but it was between Gabrielle and another Deity, one she had not met before. Lynda was not frightened, she was petrified. But Gabrielle was not frightened, she was at ease with herself, in control of her emotions. But Gabrielle had always been the stronger of them, she had never been afraid when she had talked with Death, but Gabrielle had talked with Death many more times than Lynda.

Despite all the torture she had gone through, Lynda never had the courage to attempt suicide. She knew Gabrielle wasn't weak, she had shown that when he was Paul, it was a fight to the death for her then husband Ian and his close friend, George. Nobody could have foreseen the intervention of the police officer. It gave Ian a chance to win, an edge that would lead to Ian losing his life and the police officer paying dearly for the few words he spoke to Paul.

As Paul stepped away. The police officer brought upon himself the wrath of Death and very soon, as he fought for Lynda's life to be spared, with no fear for his own soul, committed his body to its final strikes against a man he had never met or knew, for one everlasting kiss. Ian was now dead; Paul had killed George with one knife he had thrown at George to save the police officer's life.

It was far too late for Paul; the double-edged sword had entered Paul's stomach. sliced through other organs and into his heart.

As Paul lay dying on the grimy bookshop floor all Lynda could do was scream for help. Help that would not come until someone with the courage she needed, could let go of the man she loved so dearly, ran the length of the bookshop screaming all the way. She had pushed her way through the police cordon, snatched a paramedics green bag, which she knew she needed, but had no idea what she was going to do with it and ran with the paramedic chasing her back to her soul's partner. She hugged Paul and whatever he may become for dear life.

How could she know, that as she put her arms around the man, she had fallen head over heels in love with, would very soon be somewhere on the other side? Their green eyes matched, a love that could never be broken, was made in Heaven.

In that one loving move, as her bloody arms surrounded his body, holding him close to her, she was not afraid to do exactly what the doctor was now telling her to do. Somewhere else, another Deity was being given orders by a much higher Deity the Omega. At that point in time, it was surrounding Paul's heart, holding it together until a heart surgeon would take over and by order of the Omega, Death, would once again talk with Paul and release his soul.

What Death did not know was that while He talked with Paul, the small Deity was giving herself to Lynda's soul and her hand, which at the right time would bring Paul back to life and into her world where her soul would meld her way into Paul's life. She would get closer to Paul's lifeless body than any girl had ever got before.

They had now been together over ten years; over two lifetimes when Death had given them a second chance. Now here they were again, this time getting ready to face Death head on having no idea of the outcome. As Lynda placed her arms around Gabrielle's body, she pulled her close to her side. Once again, they both felt a white-hot fire deep within them, it was as if their souls were merging, ready to fight for each other, protect each other, keep each other safe and alive.

Lynda recalled the feeling from their first lifeline a moment in time that her mind had decided to hide until it was needed once again, and here was that moment in time.

Holding each other close, the hot light was sewing their bodies together with more love than they ever thought they had, but it was there. As they looked into each other's eyes, they turned bright green, illuminating their suite and the side of the yacht outside their windows.

As the light and unnamed Deity left them, their eyes remined bright green.

"I am no longer afraid Gabrielle, our lives have been planned out for us and now, like you, someone will always be there to protect our joined souls. I know I don't have to say this, but I love you with all my heart and soul," Lynda said softly into Gabrielle's ear.

"I love you too, with all my heart and soul." They kissed each other, passionately, tongues in mouths, facing an unknown future that Gabrielle would have to fight for their lives. "I think it's time we changed and got something to eat breakfast," Gabrielle added, her green eyes shining bight.

They changed and when they looked at their watches, only three minutes and fifty seconds had passed when they had been talking together for what appeared to be ages. They left their suite hand in hand, their shoulders touching, illuminating their way, with the green light coming from their eyes.

Upon entering the mess hall, everyone could see how different Gabrielle and Lynda looked. They looked wide awake, full of life, ready for a day of heavy sex and telling people what to do. Despite the previous evening's battle, the fight for their lives, and the night on what everyone called the Star Deck, then finally to see the Northern Lights, they should have been cold and tired, yet now it was like nothing had happened.

They took their seats near the head of the table as the rest of the night crew took their seats. John took his seat by the side of Gabrielle, Tina took her seat beside Lynda as Jenny was fast asleep in her own suite, which was a deck down from Gabrielle's and next to Alan and Sarah's suite.

"Welcome to this bright and peaceful new morning everyone," Gabrielle said, her bright green eyes looking about the room. She was holding Lynda's hand, feeling her love from deep within her. "Thank you all for the extremely hard work you all did. After breakfast I want you all to get a good night's sleep but pass by Lynda on your way out of here. Now, let's eat!" Gabrielle said and started a full English breakfast, according to Lynda, to keep up her strength.

After breakfast everyone passed Lynda who just touched them for a second on their arm. Each person glanced into her shining bright green eyes and felt a warmth inside them that filled their bodies, making them rested and calm for their short sleep so they would wake totally refreshed in a few hours and not miss the heat of the day and the feeling the yacht gave you as it glided over the ocean.

As the morning crew arrived for their breakfast everyone passed by Lynda who touched each one on their naked arm, so they all felt revived from the battle and ready for the day ahead. Later, on the sloping bow deck Lynda and Gabrielle were sunbathing in the winter sun which was hot for today and in New York they were having a heat wave. On the sundeck, Gabrielle and Lynda were with their mother discussing the type of building they should have for their new headquarters for the US.

They all agreed it should be New York and that would be their base. The one thing they all agreed they didn't want to do was to go public they wanted to keep the company under their close control. Even though they were expanding much faster than they had ever thought, all because of one man, George Reiner,

They suddenly realised they had no office in the UK, like it would be in New York. They had used their home which doubled as a headquarters for their UK Transgender charity which was still going on and working even though they had not been there much for the past four months. Now they were helping another Transgender group in Rome their names and emblem of Hats & Bags on the main building. They had a British couple in charge of the charity there.

As Paul had done in London the charity in Rome was pouring money into the main local hospital; twenty private rooms were being built with two, large up to date operating theatres. Most of all was the aftercare, which could continue for years if the new girls decided to go to university, which they were all encouraged to do. The younger they could get the boys and girls who said they were born into the wrong body, the sooner they could get them onto the right drugs, which would even before their operation, allow them to be girls, go to school with other girls their same age, learn the ways girls acted together in groups, go out with friends. They would not miss out on the younger life they should have had so it was natural for them to dress as girls, walk like girls, and not being afraid of their change of sex long before their operation.

As they lay sunbathing, holding hands, like they were one entity, feeling each other breathe the rise and fall of their chests, the hot sun warming their bodies, as they talked more in depth, they suddenly realised how big their empire was getting.

They now had fifteen shops in the UK. ten in France, six in Russia, four in Holland with two more opening soon. Eight shops in Spain and another four planned for to open within the next three months five shops in Italy all with very, good relationships with other shop owners and free of the Mafia taking their hard-earned money, two shops in Greece and eight shops in Australia and expending fast.

Everyone loved the range of Hats, Bags & Wraps and the shops making huge amounts of money a week. Now they were under demand to open stores in Sydney and Brisbane.

Nobody had seen the type of Hats & Bags before or for the women to enjoy once again the finest material in different shapes and colours with a hat box in the same colour material with a hat brush with Hats, Bags & Wraps engraved on it. Then there were the handbags made in the finest leather, to last a lifetime. With a box made to fit their expensive bag.

Women now wore their hat when they went shopping and had coffee in the many restaurants, meeting others who had a different hat to them, discussing it, talking to each other into buying another hat and bag the following week, and so their business that started with one shop in London was quickly growing and taking on women and a few men to sell Paul's hats to women who loved to wear his hats, even to horse racing and cricket events Where it gave the women time to dress up to the nines and show themselves off as they enjoyed the sports.

Now they had five shops in New York and the bigger store they wanted to open in Manhattan and move out into more States where the air was hot, faces and heads needed shade and women once again needed to look and walk around like women. Proud of who they were, proud of the clothes they wore, proud of their hats and carry their small handbags around the local malls.

Chapter 7

In New York, Clarice and Jack took their guidance from Gabrielle and Lynda, following their ideas of free advertising for their stores.

Each girl employee would be expected to arrive at work wearing one of their hats and carrying one of their bags. It was all part of their uniform which cost them nothing the advertising was free as the girls told women who asked after the hat, they were wearing were sent to one of their stores.

The other job they were asked to help with, was the Hat, Bag & Wrap shows especially on the cat walks. Clarice who was now Managing Director of USA sales while her fiancé Jack was managing Director of USA Finances. Whenever Clarice needed to go out to meet with a new buyer, Jack would accompany her as her bodyguard, so they always travelled to work together, went home together, did everything together and loved to be together.

The catwalk shows always brought a large crowd of buyers and new buyers who wanted to show their Hats & Bags in their stores to bring new customers in and spend lots of money. Clarice didn't have Gabrielle or Sabrina to step in and get the buyers on hold, so she had started to look around her staff. All the time she was escorted into her stores by Jack and the girls always gave him wolf whistles, which he loved then he would show them his gun and one girl would start off saying.

"Oh, Jack please protect me, I'm worth it please Jack look after us," she would say.

Jack replied, "I do protect you all on catwalk night, you all know that." He then noticed somebody crowded by people looking at their new line of Hats, Bags & Wraps. They followed him around the store asking him questions that might better be answered by a woman. It was his manner that caught Jack's eye, the way he pointed to a hat, held it in his thin, long hand, then gently, ensuring the plastic bag to keep the hat sterilised, was put carefully in a proper lady like manner onto the girl's head. He would then position her using his whole hand to emphasise the way she held her hat on her head. Showed her how to get to the floor to pick up a spoon without her hat falling off and stand back up wearing high heels.

Then he showed her how to carry a bag properly, either in her hand to make a statement or wear it from her shoulder. Deric would still be talking to the woman, amazing her with his voice and feminine movements.

"Molly," Jack called, "come here please."

"Hi Jack, what can I do for you?" she asked in a sexy voice.

"First, what is that boy's name who just sold that two-thousand-dollar hat and fifteen-hundred-dollar bag in a matter of three minutes?"

"Oh, Deric as his name appears on the payroll, but he is also known by us as Shantell."

"Could you pop to the office and tell Clarice I need her out here now. Say it's very urgent if she tries to put you off tell her Gabrielle's in front of the store."

Jack watched the group of women around Deric all looking for a new hat and bag. "Heather, can you come here please?" Jack asked.

She knew something was going down, he was usually gone after the first wolf whistle.

"How can I help you, Jack?"

"How many hats does Deric; Shantell sell on average a day?"

"This morning he's sold fifteen hats, fifteen bags, and fifteen wraps, I think it's this heat wave we're having. This is his best morning yet but sometimes he sells more between one and two if a couple of members of staff help get the next hat or bag ready for the customer, then Shantell goes through her routine and it's a sale. I saw you watching him sell that other woman her hat, bag & wrap. That's his routine women and girls love him. Please don't say you're going to sack him or send him to another store?" she begged.

"Have no fear of that," Jack replied smiling.

Clarice hurried out of the back office and ran over to see Jack. "Where is she, why didn't you tell me yourself?" she asked Jack frantically.

"Silence Clarice, just watch there," he said pointing towards Deric.

She stood still and watched Deric. He was modelling a top of the range three-thousand-dollar hat. It was on her head in seconds and Deric was going through his routine. Moving the woman, left then right, they were laughing all the time and he was talking using his best feminine voice with a French accent. Sometimes he would talk to her in fluent French. The bag she had chosen to try cost three-thousand dollars and he was moving it around himself like he owned it. Then he took the wrap he had chosen at two thousand-five-hundred dollars for his client from Christine, another member of staff. The wrap was on her shoulders, being dressed by Shantell to look nice on her then the bag was finally draped over her shoulder. Shantell moved her with ease to the long mirror pointing out how the items looked on her and how the wrap could be moved to make a statement as she held the bag in her hand.

"Now watch this." Jack said to Clarice.

"What if you drop something, this is how you pick it up without losing your hat or bag," He bent down and picked up the pen.

"Easy for you in flat shoes, I'm wearing high heels, the woman replied.

"Just a moment," he replied. He walked over to the door removed his flat shoes and put on his six-inch-high-heels then returned to the woman. He threw the pen down again and went through the motions of picking up the pen, just like Gabrielle would do on the catwalk in her six-inch heels. He then walked her in his high heels to the till and talked to her while the girls did the packing and the sale was completed with a kiss on the cheek to the woman, again showing her how to kiss her close friends when meeting with a hat on.

"He's beautiful, just like Gabrielle, does he have a fem name?" Clarice asked, still looking at Shantell.

"Shantell isn't she just great, she's got to be our Gabrielle," Jack replied.

"She has to be, there's no doubt about it," Clarice sighed and looked at the man who wanted desperately to be a woman, make his nineteenth sale of the day and the next customer was only six feet away. Clarice and Jack couldn't stop themselves watch this young man sell women's hats, bags and wraps as if she were wearing them every day of the week.

They had to wait another ten minutes while she sold another six thousand dollars' worth of hats and bags.

Jack walked over to stop him grabbing his next customer. Instead of a customer, he felt the strong hand of Jack on his thin upper arm.

"Hi Shantell, could you come with me please Our Managing Director of sales would like to speak with you."

"Oh shit, am I being fired or something?"

"No far from it. We watched you selling our hats, bags and wraps to our customers and girl, you are so slick. Here we are, Clarice, meet Deric, AKA Shantell," Jack said smiling, as everyone was looking at him wondering if he would get the sack for being too flamboyant in work.

"Shantell, I've been told you're happy to be called by that name?" Clarice said smiling at him.

"Yes, have I done something wrong?" he asked.

"No, it's us who have done something wrong. Don't worry. I would like to ask you a few questions. Have you heard we do Hat, & Bag catwalk shows?"

"Yes, I've been in a few, I'm the only one who can get down with the buyers wearing six-inch-high-heels. I have a slim body and I can get into a size one dress, so I don't really stand out in the crowd of girls, and we all change together, and it's been fine up to now."

"I go to every show, and I have never noticed you, which to say is good that you help and blend in with the other girls, I hope you enjoy the shows and doing the catwalk?"

"Oh yes, I love it, it's where I like to be," he replied.

"There is another Hat & Bag show in two weeks."

"Yes, I know I've already got my name down for it."

"Excellent but I would rather you don't sign up for the show. Now don't get upset, because if you say yes, things will move really fast. So, this is our idea.

"Do you know of Gabrielle?"

"Yes of course I have that's what brought me to her store."

"Well Gabrielle can't be here for every show, although she is on her way here on her yacht. We would like to have our very own Gabrielle, which I thought impossible until I saw you. So how would you like to be our permanent anchor to all our Hat shows? You will be called, if you have no objections, Shantell and you will be the star of our Hat, Bag & Wrap shows. We will have your picture blown up to ten-foot tall by six-foot wide on the outside of the building and smaller pictures put around the room.

"Do I get to wear some of her dresses?"

"I'm afraid she still wears them when she can do a show, so you'll need a set of all new dresses in your size, making you look like a million dollars. You'll have your own makeup artist do your makeup and help you with your dress. So, what do you say?" Clarice asked.

"Yes of course I do."

"That's great, I'll get onto our top makeup artist to have you in for a face over have you put in at least ten dresses have a professional photographer take all your photos and our display team will do the rest. All you need do is relax and enjoy yourself. We'll have small cards with your signature on and on the back where you can be found, to help you sell more hats and bags, not that you need that."

"Will I still work here?"

"Of course, we don't want to lose a top seller."

He turned around and jumped into the air and shouted to everyone in the store "I'm the new Gabrielle."

Everyone in the store got around Deric and congratulated him on his new venture with the company and it would be great to have her as an anchor for the shows, as that was what was missing as people had been watching old Bags & Hats shows on YouTube, so they were expecting to see Gabrielle in the shows.

The following day Shantell was picked up from her apartment by Max in a black BMW and taken to a makeup and photographic studio where she had her own makeup stripped from her face and given a facial scrub then a face-pack, while she sat in a comfy reclining chair, her fingers and toes were seduced by the most expensive oils and perfumes to soften her skin and cuticles.

"Now let's start my creation. You're going to be the new Gabrielle, well lucky for you, I worked with Gabrielle when she did her first Hats & Bags show here and walked the catwalk," Julie said.

"What was she like?" Shantell asked.

"For the first time in another country, she was so confident in what she had to do and you know the trick you do picking up a pen delicately in six inch high heels well she could do that and at the turning point she would always get down low and showed some breast but her hat never fell off and her bag always remained on her shoulder so she could open it and show the buyers what it was like inside and answer any questions they had."

"She could tilt her hat move it to the side and it still remained on her head as she stood up, did a second turn on the circle and winked at the buyers, nearly always men and a few women, but she knew how to handle them and got the orders she wanted. Look her up on YouTube, one-word Gabrielle.

"I will be doing your makeup as if you were going to do the walk. First let's start on your toes. Clarice wanted bright colours; do you paint your toenails much?"

"Only when I go to clubs I'm known at and then I take it off. I don't want to go too far in work, you never know what my boss might say."

"I think after this you could go in wearing just a pair of panties and a bra, I want you to look amazing for the shows, and stunning, real sexy for the younger girls who come into your store and move some of the lower priced Hats & Bags, you'll still have your shot at the expensive Hats & Bags. How do you like this red?"

"Looks very feminine."

"And that's what I want to get over. I want the women to be you, have the touch, make them feel sexy, ready for an orgasm in the store, '*show and effect'*. I want the boys to love you and only want to screw you. Now does that sound sexy to you?"

"Yes, but the fucking could be difficult."

"That could all be arranged, if you want, you really want it. I'll have a word with Clarice. This company is after all, for the Transgender, just look at Gabrielle. Why is it all the really good-looking boys like you, desires a cunt instead of a prick?"

Shantell laughed and lifted her right foot onto the angled stand so Julie could paint her other toes. "Right your hands, Clarice wants you to wear long false nails on the catwalk and for now, so you are used to handling your hat and bag and selling hats in the store. It's different wearing false nails, you can't always get the proper feel of the material. You'll need to practice a lot in the store, so you are ready for your first night as anchor."

Julie took her time preparing the long nails and gluing them to Shantell's nails before painting a bright colour design on them. Another woman, Heather came in and moved Shantell's chair to the sink then started to wash her hair and cut it in a young woman's style and finally blow-dried it into its final shape.

"Now we'll get on with your make up, you don't need to wear as much face powder, you can get away with this all-in-one light cream face makeup, just put a little on your face and rub it in all over."

"You will not be able to paint your eyes like I can looking at you, but you can still practice putting your eye makeup on looking into a mirror. Julie looked at her ears seeing she had them pierced went to the dressing table and picked out a pair of long drop gold and diamond earrings and put them in her ears.

"We are nearly there, what do you think of these?" She asked holding up a pair of gold-coloured skin-tight jeans with a three-quarter length leg and stretch material for when she had to bend over or gyrate her body to impress the man who was paying for the hat or bag.

"I like them do they have a top to go with them?"

"Yes, do you fancy satin or silk?"

"Satin it's more feminine."

"Right get changed and you'll need these I take it you've worn the new Pantie girdle before, the clothes are so tight your unwanted bits might show and we are looking for a flat look, even if I stroke my hand over it and you can put on these light pink panties and

I'll put your bra on you. I know you don't have tits, but I think that should be taken care of urgently. I'll talk to Clarice about it gosh, look at the time, come on get your clothes on, we're running late."

She soon had her new pink panties on and was getting into her tight jeans when Julie Came into the changing room and fitted her into a small pink satin bra with size A cups, she added a small padding which gave her form and would help when she wore the evening dresses. Julie gently put her top on trying not to mess up her hair. Finally, she was back in her chair. Leaned back and had long false eyelashes put on. While Heather touched her hair up and covered it with a strong hold Gabrielle range new hair spray, then she had lots of Gabrielle perfume around her neck and wrists.

Julie slipped Shantell's feet into a new pair of gold coloured six-inch-high-heels. "You must wear these in and be ready for the night, there will be Hell to pay if you can't walk in them and do your ending, which will become your ending not Gabrielle's.

"Before I put your hat on, look in the mirror."

Shantell was up on her feet, twisted them into the new shoes then walked like a woman around to the mirror. She looked into the bag amazed, her female haircut made her look like a young woman and the small amount of padding gave her small breasts to go with her slim body.

"What have you done to Deric?" she asked.

"Turned the man into a sexy looking girl. Heather replied.

"You look absolutely radiant. Don't worry too much about your hair, I'll look after it from now on and on the big night I'll be there as well to fit you into a wig and do your hair after. From now on you're our Gabrielle and soon people will see you out and about and you'll be selling our wares in the streets. Colin, get your camera ready, we'll go for face only looking in all directions.

Then I'll put her hat on and you shoot her again, finally with her bag."

"I forgot her eye drops," Julie said. She got the bottle of drops, asked Shantell to put her head back and inserted two drops into each eye. "This will make your eyes shine for the camera, open your pupils and make the whites of your eyes sparkle, are they okay?"

"Yes, fine thanks." She replied, blinking her eyes a couple of times.

"Now move to the photo area and be prepared to have your photo taken; a lot." Colin took photos of Shantell with and without her wig for Clarice to look at and decide which way she wanted to go.

For now, the four people in the room including Max their driver, decided she looked better with her long hair, which most of the catwalk girls wore.

When Heather put Shantell's hat on which was a Loreen Green, hat, Shantell was amazed to see the hair cover was removed and it was sitting on her hair with hat pins holing it firmly into her long hair. She raised her hand and despite never having worn false nails before, got the hang of moving her hat so that when she moved her head the hat didn't move, even when she knelt down and managed to pick up a pen between her nails.

Shantell went through the whole routine with the rectangular shaped bag on her shoulder. The opening clasp was twenty-four karat gold with a design of four circles in rubies. Inside the bag was a matching card holder, with a company credit card inside in her name with the code behind the card. There was also a set of keys, which she recognised were to her apartment and locker at work. The small clasp that could be added to a favourite coat or dress kept the bag attached to something solid in case someone tried to steal the bag on the run. It was rolled up and placed in the bottom of the bag.

"These items are no longer saleable with the hat liner gone and the bag, what can I say?" Shantell asked.

"Thankyou. You will be expected to wear the hat on your way to work, out of work when you go to lunch and going home from work and when needed in the store. You are Hats, Bags & Wraps now; enjoy the show. Max, can you get the limo ready please, we're finished here. Oh, could you put the hat and bag boxes in the trunk please? There is also her goody bag."

"I've put a box of all the nail varnish I've used on you with all your new makeup a large bottle of Gabrielle perfume, Gabrielle hairspray; take another bottle of perfume or hairspray from your store when you need it. Make sure you tell Michelle first. It will have to be accounted for and go against your name. Right Shantell let's make a move, we're going to meet Clarice and Jack. We will all be with you, fussing with your hair and makeup and taking your picture."

"What shop are we going to?" Shantell asked.

"Leslie's evening dresses and designer clothes. They have a camera room there we can use to take more pictures of you in the long evening dresses you'll wear on the catwalk. They also have some pretty tight jeans, short skirts and tops I think you would look pretty in. You're in for a long afternoon." Julie replied as she picked up her own bag of makeup and watched as Shantell gracefully walked down the stairs to the open door onto the sidewalk and as Max held the rear door open, she melted into the limo. Heather, Julie and Colin got in through the other doors, took their seats and put on their seatbelts.

"When we stop outside the shop, wait until we are all out and when you get out, I want big smiles looking at Colin and the lens. The camera will flash a few times to get rid of any shadows. When you're out of the car be Shantell, the new face of Hats, Bags & Wraps. Sway your hips when you walk, dip and move your head so people watching you will see your hat and show off your bag like I know you can do," Heather said.

Ten minutes later they stopped outside the multi-story store. There were a group of women waiting outside wondering what all the fuss was about. Colin got out first dropping his heavy camera bag on the floor, getting his camera ready to start the show, Clarice came out of the store she hadn't even seen a snapshot of Shantell so was extremely nervous of what she would see.

Jack stood behind her, holding her hand, in complete control of the situation and hoping he made the right choice. Heather and Julie got out next showing their bags carried the vital things a superstar would need on a camera shoot.

The crowd of women were talking until the back door of the limo was opened by Max. He took Shantell's hand in his and assisted her out of the limo then closed the door behind her. Colin immediately started to take her first public photos, the flash lighting her up like a spotlight.

Shantell looked into the camera lens then moved her head up and down, left and right. She walked slowly towards her boss and kissed her on each cheek without moving her hat. "Shantell, is that really you?" Clarice asked.

"You bet," she replied. "Now get on with it and tell them who I am, we can't just stand here snogging all day, although it would be nice, but I have a job to do and stop shaking, I'll be fine."

"Ladies and gentlemen let me introduce to you the new face of Hats, Bags, & Wraps. Welcome Shantell," Clarice said in a shaky voice.

Everyone was looking at Shantell as she walked around the wide sidewalk with Colin taking her photo, sometimes with a woman, more often with a man, his arm around her back pulling her close to his side so Shantell had to tilt her head, but his wife or girlfriend soon pulled him away as Shantell spoke to him, telling him what shop he could see her at and to bring his credit card giving his wife a new hat, bag or wrap. She moved her body in a sexy way all the time, showing off her six-inch-high-heels and doing her trick when Colin dropped his pen. As she lowered herself to the floor, she made the whole procedure look so easy even in high heels. The women especially were watching her every move, as she stood up, rotated her head slightly so she could see where she was going and popped the pen into her expensive bag.

She got a long round of applause as she turned again to face her photographer. He took more pictures of her and a few of the crowd for the Evening Post together with the wright up Clarice had written.

"Shantell has a photo shoot now and will be trying on some evening dresses, to compliment her hat and bag for our Hats and Bags show and Shantell will be on the catwalk showing her favourite hats and bags. You can see the camera shoot in the client area."

"Next door you can relax with a hot cappuccino and a cake while you look through the catalogue of clothes Shantell will be trying on this afternoon and which ones we decide to buy for the next Hats & Bags show in two weeks at the Treetops Catwalk show Downtown. I hope we can see you there," Clarice said now much calmer seeing her walk around and greet the women and men who were all patting her bum, but you could see she loved it, it was all part of the show.

Four floors up, they were guided to the client room, where Clarice had already picked out ten evening dresses in various colours.

"Well Clarice what do you think of her?" Julie asked.

"She looks fantastic, a real natural model."

"Yes, she is, but I think some small breasts would help her more and if we could give her a vagina, she'd be on top of the world."

"You think so?"

"I do."

"I need to talk with her, and I'll consider it. Now let's get through these dresses. Where has Heather gone?"

"One floor down looking at the short skirts and jeans."

"Let's get on here. Which dress shall we start with?"

"The orange one, I like the design and the way the skirt hangs on it. "Shantell," Julie called, "Come here and put this dress on please."

She changed in double quick time, using her time at the catwalk shows to help her change, used to girls helping her on and off with her clothes.

Another photoshoot then another dress and so, it went on with Clarice, Jack Julie, Heather and Colin making the decisions. Finally, they decided on six dresses which all fitted her perfectly and she looked elegant in them.

Picking out the best one, an apricot colour which went with the colours in her hat, Shantell put it on, turning around in it for the camera.

Going out into the main store and café area, Shantel was shown off to the press, which had heard all about the New Face of Hats, Bags & Wraps so now even more cameras, were pointing at her, the lenses moving back and forth as she was framed in the picture, wearing one of the dresses she would wear on the night and looking like a million dollars. The only thing missing was a man to welcome her to her new job.

"Jack, this is your find, and now it's your time to make her a woman," Clarice said smiling.

"How do I do that, I'm not a surgeon. I could put a hole between her legs with my gun I suppose but then we would lose her."

"How do you make me feel like a woman that is there to be wanted?"

"Kiss you?" he suggested.

"There is a woman wanting to be showed she's wanted and you're the only man here who I know would take it all in the show and think no more of it. Look Shantell is pulling off one hell of a transformation for us, so help her out, with all the press here it would be the picture of the day.

"But whatever you do, how far you go, don't knock her hat off or I'll knock your head off. By the way I want her on double pay and on the Model books, backdated three months, you should have discovered her earlier and oh, I want her in a new apartment, ground floor in two days. You have all evening to find her something, I have a lot of photos to go through."

Jack walked up to Shantell and put his arm around her back. "Ladies and gentlemen, as Managing Director of Finance for Hats,

Bags & Wraps I'm very proud to introduce to you our new face of Hats, Bags & Wraps; Shantell." There were a lot of camera flashes including a few from Colin.

"She will be on the catwalk at Treetops Catwalk Studios Downtown and walking about the shopping malls wearing our hats, bags & wraps, in different outfits so you can see what type of clothes you could wear with a hat and one of our gorgeous bags, while wearing one of our latest wraps from Paris, France."

"Shantell will also be visiting all our stores in New York, so you will be able to see more of her there and she will also be giving the ladies advice on what hat would suit them and how best to wear it.

"It just leaves me to welcome Shantell to our family," With his arm further around her shoulder, holding her close to him, then his lips were on her lips and they were kissing as Shantell rubbed her wide-spread hand up and down his waistcoat, while Jack held onto his girl, his Shantell.

She moved her lips to meet his and as their bodies got closer to each other, it just naturally happened with the smell of her perfume, their tongues met in each other's mouth and the crowd went wild, the men were green with envy and the cameras loved every second of the kiss.

Jack pulled away from the kiss and stood beside her holding her close to him. "Shantell. As Managing Director of H B & W Finance, I welcome you to our family of Hats, Bags & Wraps. May you enjoy a long relationship with us." He couldn't shake her bloody hand, so he leaned forward and kissed her on the lips once again, then held her out to the press for the final photos.

Clarice watched her fiancée carefully; a thought went through her mind, but she dismissed it instantly. It was her idea after all she had told Jack to go for a kiss, to make the girl feel like a real woman. She knew he had done that.

Clarice met with the sales lady, thanked her for the loan of the photo room, ordered another set of dresses then came up with a plan to make a little money, if she managed to send some women to her store to buy one of Shantell's dresses, she would get ten per cent off each sale, for their future buys and they were always at the store.

"Shantell will wear her dress home tonight, so can she have a bag to put it in? I want the other five dresses doubled up and I want another dress like Shantell is wearing. All sent to Michelle's Hats, Bags & Wraps on thirty fourth street." She looked through her bag and found a card for Michelle's store with the full address and phone number.

"There are more clothes for this model behind the counter, who pays for those?" the assistant asked.

She knew Shantell had not been buying clothes, they had been together for the last three hours. Then she remembered Heather went off looking for clothes for her. She trusted her judgment. Add them to my bill but I'll take them now please."

Ten minutes later they were all standing on the sidewalk and Colin was taking the last photos of Shantell as she got into the limo.

"That was a long, exciting day for you, but there is more to come. We'll drop your new clothes and boxes off at your apartment, take you to your store so you can show yourself off to everyone. Then out for an early evening meal as you haven't eaten all day. What type of food do you like?" Heather asked.

"I don't mind, I'll go with the flow, but nothing messy if I have to eat in this dress."

"That is something else you need to get used to, eating in expensive clothes. If you're offered a glass of champagne, one glass only, never, I repeat, never get tipsy and blow all your secrets

"Stay away from alcohol altogether if you want to continue being Shantell.

"Now there are some other things we need to go through. From now on you're, on the model books as Shantell, top model and your salary is doubled to what a top model would be paid.

They are backdating your pay-rise for three months I think that's what Clarice said," Julie said, grinning at Shantell.

"You are being moved to another better ground floor apartment. I don't know where or when, but I would imagine close to one of our stores. They both want to talk with you in the morning and a car will pick you up as today no doubt it will be Max. You don't need to wear the dress you're wearing but hang it up in its cover tonight and put it ready to change into later tomorrow. You can wear one of the short skirts I chose for you, which I put on your bed.

"Here we are at your store. Colin out first then us then you." Once again, they got out of the limo and the back door was held open for Shantell, Colin took more pictures of her as she entered her store and talked to one of the girls.

"Hello madam, can I help you?" Malisa asked politely.

"I would like to see your manageress please as there is a problem with my hat and bag."

"Just a moment please."

Malisa was gone in an instant and back with Michelle. She was smiling from ear to ear.

"Shantell, you look magnificent. Turn around! Everyone, this is our very own Shantell, the new face of Hats, Bags & Wraps. You'll never guess who she was snogging with this afternoon, tongues in mouths as well." Michelle passed around her iPad with the photo, Clarice had passed to all her manageress's.

"Snogging with Jack you lucky girl," Malisa said.

They each had their photo taken with Shantell, then after a few words with Michelle and use of the toilet they were off again. The early evening newspapers were full of pictures of Shantell and the kiss with the write up on the new face of one of the fastest growing store-chains in New York, Hats, Bags & Wraps.

Next, they stopped outside Thornton's Shopping Mall and before they left the limo, Julie touched up Shantell's makeup then with a new card in his camera, a change of lens and a new battery pack for the flash, they all got out of the limo with Max holding the back door open for Shantell as Colin took more photos of her getting out of the limo with her large hat and bag on. Shantell was already getting interest as they walked slowly through the huge mall.

People were stopping then asking who this woman was then they saw the papers, bought one and were asking Shantell to sign it. At first, they were all looking for a pen, before Heather ran into a store and bought a couple of biros and a black felt-tip pen.

"Just sign your name as Shantell HBW," Julie suggested. With the photos came more people with papers to sign and Shantell was now getting used to being a celebrity and loving it. For the first time ever, all their stores in New York had to stay open to allow people to look around and buy one of their hats bags or wraps and sometimes all three. More women were out on the streets dragging their husband or boyfriend behind them wearing their new Hat although their dresses didn't compliment the expensive hats they were wearing. Then it got around where Shantell was that evening and crowds of women in their new hats converged on Thornton's Mall, hoping to see Shantell in person and get some ideas from her on what to wear with their new hat, bag and wrap.

Halfway through the Mall, the group of over a hundred women wearing their new hats carrying their small new bags with a box in another Hats & Bags carrier bag converged on the central stairway as Shantell was slowly edged up to the central stairwell. These women attracted more women from different stores and soon the Mall security were asking questions from Julie, who was already on her phone making a video call to Jack.

When Jack and Clarice arrived at the Mall there were more couples entering the Mall all hoping to see the new face of Hats, Bags & Wraps. Other press photographers had also arrived.

The manager of the Mall was not worried about all the extra people entering his Mall, he knew they would soon disperse after a few words from the young woman he was sure would mess it all up. She, he thought would do a runner even in those gorgeous, sexy high heels. So, he told his security people to leave her alone and have a couple of first aid girls on hand in case she was trampled.

Jack and Clarice hurried along the second landing praying Shantell was still standing and breathing. Then they saw her trapped on the second stair-landing. With only Julie, Max and Heather to protect her while Colin took photos of her and the crowds. Then Colin saw Jack and beckoned him to make his way down the stairs to Shantell, who was talking in a French accent to the crowd.

"Well ladies, you could wear a suit with your hat to work and if you need a second hatbox for work, pop into one of our stores with your hat and they'll fix you up with another for a small fee then your hat will not get damaged in work.

"Another suggestion is three quarter length jeans, the brighter the better, a sparkly top and you and your hat will be seen for miles." Shantell was telling everyone.

"That might be fine for the young woman who has a thin figure, but for the slightly older lady, with a fuller figure what would she wear?" a woman close to Shantell asked, expecting a reply. After all, Shantell was a woman a top model who should know all about dresses and skirts.

"A real woman who deserves to wear something extravagant and walk the streets as if she owns them, I suggest a white tee shirt under a tight-fitting jacket, shorts, or a knee length skirt and some high heels you feel comfortable wearing. I love my six-inch heels, I wear them all day, but I do have a shorter heal for dancing, after all we girls have got to enjoy life, get to the night clubs and shake our best body parts." Shantell replied, as if it were natural to answer questions on female clothes. Everyone laughed, and their phones were out taking pictures of her.

Jack stood behind her, looking at the crowd. Shantell was speaking again to the women.

"I see many of you young women have bought a new hat tonight, thank you for visiting our stores this time of the evening. There is something I must tell you about your hat, no doubt our girls were rushed off their feet to tell you personally and you'll find the full instructions inside your hatbox. So here is the general dos and don'ts.

"After wearing your hat when taking it off, ensure there are no twigs or blades of grass caught up in it and remove them. I know what you ladies are like with your men, keep them close, keep them happy." Everyone was laughing.

"It's true," she said grinning, showing her perfect white teeth.

"Put your hat back in its box and put the cotton straps over it which holds it secure, put the lid on and make sure all the air holes are not covered. Our hats do not like to be stifled or feel dried out. Don't, store it in an exceptionally dry room or next to a radiator or heater. Your hat will like a slightly damp airyated spot, this might be on top of a wardrobe near a small window which is always left open or in a cool room. Look after your hat; it wasn't cheap.

"I heard some girls asking about my dress, we bought this dress and five other designs from Leslie's Gowns, the dresses we bought today are all on show there, fourth floor. As luxurious as it is and girls, it feels, really sexy, but you couldn't eat a curry in it, the special dry-cleaning bill would cost almost as much as this five-thousand-dollar dress. But if you can't afford the real thing, it's well worth it, the material is so soft and makes you feel sexy before you go out in it."

She massaged the front of her dress and felt a hand on her shoulder. There were a lot of wolf whistles and applause as she gently turned her head. She knew it couldn't be a strange man as Colin or Max would have stepped forward and moved him away.

Colin's camera could be replaced and at this moment in time so close to the catwalk show, she couldn't be replaced.

As she turned her head her eyes beheld Jack. She couldn't understand why he would be here then she looked up to see Clarice and the large crowd on the second landing, all listening to her voice, she was glad she recalled what Gabrielle did to hide her male voice, speak using a French accent, so she had learned to speak French fluently. She could also speak Spanish and Italian, so if people asked, she could say she was born in France and loved the French language.

"Oh, look this is my new bodyguard Jack and my boss Clarice is up there waiting to take me to dinner. Do you ladies like Jack? He's adorable, isn't he?" she said in perfect French as if it was her native language. This was something else Clarice didn't know about Shantell, but she saw how she held her audience for the past forty minutes. She knew Jack had found a diamond in the rough but what a diamond she was.

A lot of the women had scanned through their newspaper and seen the kiss and were not going to leave until they had the chance to take their own photo, then they would leave her to her meal and call into Madeline,'s where either tonight or tomorrow they would be able to buy a copy of her dress for half its price.

"Jack," she pronounced in French, "I think they want to see another kiss," she said in French.

"Shantell don't take this too far Clarice is up there watching us," he replied in perfect French.

"Think of the money Jack, that's what this is all about, and I want to use the credit card you gave me. I have an idea." She said in French then it happened, Jack held her tight, and close to him and their lips met, then the room was full of flashlights. They turned together, lips still touching so the women on the second floor could get their photos, but they were not facing Clarice who was on her phone ordering a table for seven further along the Mall.

As their mouths rotated, Shantell was again drawing in the crowds, making them see she was a real woman and not the man he was, for the present time. When they turned back to face the crowd, Jack knew this could end good or bad, but they could not remain here all night.

"Thank you, ladies and gentlemen, you will find me during the next few days on walk abouts, showing myself and our hats, bags & wraps off to New York in different outfits, so you can see what I dress like off the catwalk. If you want any more help with your hat or bag visit any of our stores and the assistants will be pleased to answer any of your questions.

"Now Jack and Clarice are taking me to dinner, I hope to see you all soon at Michelle's Hats, Bags & Wraps store, bring your friends, let's enjoy a hat, bag & wraps day." She kissed her flattened fingers and threw the kiss into the crowd, turned around and did the same to the people on the second floor.

"Thank you," she called aloud still using her French accent. She took hold of Jack's hand and let him escort her through the crowd with Max, Heather, Julie and Colin behind them. The crowd had dispersed, going into other stores; the women looking for new outfits to go with their new hats.

They entered Orento's, the most expensive food outlet five minutes later and were shown to their reserved table and given a menu each.

"Shantell you can have whatever you like to eat, except my Jack but I appreciate what you have done for us today. Holy smoke," she said looking at her tablet. During the last ninety minutes our stores were open tonight we've taken over fifty thousand dollars, and that is all down to you Shantell."

"Glad I could be of service. On the way out, can we look in Sampson's? There is a suit in there which would go well with the hat to show women going to work they can still wear an expensive hat and get away with it?"

A short time later, Shantell had picked out a white silk tight fitting blouse, a beige suite jacket matching short culottes and a knee length skirt for a woman in a top job going to work. Leaving the Mall, the manager was there as usual but tonight he had good reason to be.

"Goodnight Shantell, please come again. the store managers are extremely pleased with their extra business tonight, it made the stores worth staying open for," Martin, the Mall Manager said kissing the back of Shantell's right hand.

"I'll be back very soon, Goodnight Martin," she replied accepting the business card and slipping it into her new bag.

Feeling Jack's arm on her back edging her forward, she moved on and into the limo. Max was carrying Colin's camera bag and Heather the four bags of clothes they had purchased on the way out. Jack held the side door open for Clarice to get in and he got in behind her.

"Where too boss?" Max asked.

"No, I just need to speak with Shantell for a moment. Shantell you're a right little chatterbox, more than most women I know. Girl, you're a natural. I can see you'll need a bodyguard.

"But that can't be me I'm afraid. I have other jobs to do as well. Don't get me wrong, I could have the time of my life listening to you all day long." He saw the look of hurt in her face even though she tried not to show it.

"How did you get on with Heather today?" Jack asked her. "Fine we got on like a house on fire didn't we Heather?" "Yes Shantell," and she meant it.

"Heather, do you have your gun permit on you?"

"Yes Jack," she handed it over for his inspection. He looked at it, then examined the photo of her and her face now.

"Where is your Glock?"

"At home in an underfloor safe with ten clips and a new box of refills."

"How would you like to be Shantell's bodyguard?"

"Yes, if that's okay with you Shantell I'll even take a bullet for you. I carry a real gun just like Jack's, with real bullets too. Nobody's going to hurt you girl and no matter what, you'll always be a girl to me," Heather replied.

"Right job done. Heather tomorrow. Wear a suit with your jacket gun holster. Buy a new suit tomorrow, get Shantell to pay for it on her card, yes shoes as well, no hat, I want you to have full vision around her. For now, when Shantell needs the loo, you go with her," Jack ordered, showing he cared for her safety.

"And Shantell, not that you need me telling you, I'm sure. Ladies sit on a toilet or hover, no standing up like a man I don't want other young women catching you out like that," Clarice said and smiled at her.

"I'll keep an eye on her boss," Heather replied for Shantell.

"Do you want me in long hair or my own short hair?" Shantell asked.

"Good question, for now, let's keep it long, if in a few months if you need a change, I have an idea of how we can change your hairstyle for the public. "Do you want me to do her makeup in the morning?" Julie asked.

"Could she come to your studio?" Clarice asked.

"Yes, of course. Do you want photos taken?" Colin asked.

"Yes, please Colin, I want a young fresh look for her going shopping. Put a pair of shorter earrings in her ears. Gold I still want her to look just like the model she was today. Shantell, I want you to pick out some more earrings and something for your wrist, very feminine. Drop by your store and pick up some business cards for your store so you can hand them out to people, say you'll be working from there in a few days, I want people to see your face and how you wear your hat and what you wear. By the way I did like those tight jeans and top you were wearing this morning. My look at the time nearly nine. Right girls and boys, it's time to head home and get some beauty sleep."

"When we get to Shantell's house, I'll take her makeup off, I don't want those false eyelashes being ruined or have Shantell damaging her own eyelashes," Julie said.

"I'll see to her hat, dress and other clothes," Heather added.

"If you drop Colin off first, can you download some of the pictures you've taken today and send them over to me for later tonight?" Clarice asked Colin.

"Of course, no problem," he replied.

Jack held Shantell's hand, "Really great working with you today," he said smiling.

"Yes, me too, we'll have to do it again sometime, the public loved it and if that is what it takes to bring in massive sales, I'm all for it," Shantell said, thinking of their afternoon sudden kiss. She was feeling more like a woman now than ever before.

Jack opened the door and got out of the limo, then held it open for Clarice. They walked to their car holding hands and when inside, Jack took Clarice in his arms and kissed her profusely. Their mouths rotated about each other, making Clarice feel very wanted and excited to be with her fiancé.

The problem was, Gabrielle wanted them to expand further into the USA, but Gabrielle couldn't be everywhere at the same time and for expansion, she needed a springboard.

Then it came to her, a new larger store inside Thornton's Mall, they had passed a couple of empty stores on their way out and this could be where they open it with Gabrielle and Shantell. They could also sell dresses and jeans to go with their hats and who would be in front of the store selling? Shantell.

All this was going through her mind while she was still kissing and hugging Jack. He had made all the right decisions without asking for her input, Shantell did need a bodyguard and they had one waiting to take the roll when it came, and today was that day.

Jack had seen Heather shoot at the local police shooting range. She was good, accurate on each shot to a kill between the eyes. She was fast as well, sliding the gun from its holster into her hands and pointing at the person who was threatening them. She only gave the person two options, move back and apologise or die, she was licensed to kill, Jack made sure of that, and she had passed all the police medical and mental tests, so they were sure she would not run wild killing everyone in sight.

They mutually stopped the kiss at the same time, but then Jack got another kiss in.

"You know I love you so very much, with all my heart, don't you?" he asked quietly.

"Of course, I do stupid. I love you with all my heart too. I would also love a chicken curry tonight, so let's let our romantic kiss finish in bed, where I can ravish you to my heart's delight and we can hold onto each other until the sands of time run out."

They headed home stopping for a curry on the way after they devoured their curry they went straight to bed, tearing clothes off each other, they were beneath their duvet seconds later, bodies touching each other, lips together, rotating about each other as their tongues intertwined, filling each other with loving thoughts and desires. Soon, they were making love better than before, first Jack was on top of Clarice then Clarice was sitting over Jack's penis, rotating her body around it, consuming it with her vagina, the Shantell kiss long forgotten from both.

Clarice came first, her orgasm seemed to last forever, as her fingernails dug into his back, pulling him deeper inside her until Jack came filling her vagina with his sperm. He lay on top of her for a brief minute, kissing her profusely, then he was on his back pulling his mate onto him, holding her close, then closer still, thinking only of her, the love he had for her and the time he would like to spend with her. If it were permitted, he would love to spend all eternity with her, his love for her would never end, but he knew that was impossible, so they would spend their lives together, deeply in love with each other only and they would die together at an incredibly old age.

They started to make love again, their bodies slowly moving up and down each other. Jack was kissing her breasts, holding them in his hands, gently caressing them, making her nipples large and hard, which his mouth sucked and licked.

His right hand moved up and down her chest then down and further down until they were expertly playing with her clitoris, then into her vagina bringing her to another orgasm, then drawing out and in again right up to her G spot and another orgasm, so she was panting for breath, pulling him close to her then closer still, so they kissed and kissed and with the excitement of the long day, they both fell asleep in each other's arms but rose with the first sound of the alarm.

When they arrived at their office, they could both see Gabrielle's idea of a large office in glass or brick would be a big help for them besides looking like a company that had made it in New York, but where to start looking? They didn't have much time, but they had to find something. From the text she got from Lynda, Gabrielle was much calmer and seemed to have worked out a plan for the last battle.

Clarice was feeling a lot better now, perhaps their wedding would go ahead as planned. At the same time, she wanted to be here for any move to a big office. They had one secretary between them, and Toni had the biggest office because they both dumped all their paperwork and emails on her, now she was going to get some more work.

"Toni, do we have a new employee form for a licensed to kill bodyguard?" Jack asked her,

"Yes Jack, who's the new gunslinger?" Toni asked as she flipped her fingers through a file box and pulled out a two -page form.

"Heather Baker, she's been hanging around for ages to get this type of job."

"Who's she guarding?" Toni asked.

"Shantell, I can't look after her, Clarice and do my job as well.

If you have to rush your job, that's when mistakes are made."

"Does that mean you're giving me a decent pay rise Jack?"

"No, I'm afraid not yet, but you can have a look for high glass office blocks in our district." Clarice replied to her and placed a sheet of A4 paper on her desk.

"Are we moving?" Toni asked clapping her hands and smiling.

"That's what Gabrielle would like. New York is to be the grand office block of Hats, Bags & Wraps as we expand into other states. Keep your head down and work hard you could become Executive Secretary. You are keeping up your Executive-Secretary studies, aren't you?"

"Yes. Clarice my final exams are next week, which reminds me, I'll need Thursday and Friday morning off to take the exams."

"Okay, put it on the calendar."

She looked at the note on her desk. "Hey, I know of a new build glass office block. I don't know if they're letting yet, but I bet they have one office completed for new tenants to look at. It's on 34th Street."

"Sounds good we should take a drive past," Jack added.

"I want to view those empty stores in Thornton's Mall. Jack, we need to have something to show Gabrielle with figures and can we afford it? Oh, I wish I had the name of the manager at the Mall and his personal number," Clarice said.

"Call Shantell, she has it she was chatting him up, he'll have us back anytime, seems the other stores love us giving them extra trade," Jack said laughing.

After speaking to Shantell who was surprised to get a call from her boss so early in the morning, they agreed to meet up at Thornton's Mall for lunch and discuss her change.

"That girl is a goldmine. She has his private and business card I guess he's jealous of you Jack, getting to kiss our latest model." "Did you do tongues Jack?" Toni asked.

"Yes, but don't make it public."

"Good on you Jack, I bet that was just what she needed to prove to all the women and men she's a real woman. You were on TV last night, with the kiss, you made it look so natural and the way you protected her with your arm around her back. You had me convinced."

"You mean to say it was on television as well?"

"Yes, Jack and you looked great. Holding her hand to the end of the mall."

"I was holding Clarice's hand as we left the Mall,"

"Got you there, Jack. But you really made her a real woman and that's what you wanted wasn't it. I mean look at Gabrielle now. Even before Death stepped in and gave her that terrific body, she looked the part. Nobody would have thought she wasn't a real woman."

"I just hope Gabrielle doesn't think we're trying to take the US Hats, Bags & Wraps part of her empire, away from her," Jack said as he filled the gun certificate form in.

"Clarice, I'm sending you the address and phone number for enquiries into those new glass offices, the enquiries are open 10,00 to 4.00pm."

"Thank you, Toni, that's what I call fast work. If you could write the two letters of change of job description for Heather and Shantell, make sure you call her Shantell. I also want you to download a change of name form and I'll take her to our solicitor to have the form stamped later today. Jack will give you their new hourly rate. Now I need to make some calls. Buzz me if there are any problems."

Clarice closed her glass office door so she could see Jack all the time and he could see her.

She sat down opened her phone on her iPad, went to her second phone book and video called the New York Transgender Charity which Brenda helped set up three months ago. She hoped her name and position in the firm would get her to speak with someone who could make decisions. After explaining who she was and what she wanted she was put on hold.

She was on hold for three long minutes. she almost hung up to try again. Then there was a loud click as she was connected to the person who was not in the States at the moment, but quite close. Brenda's face appeared on her screen.

"Hello Clarice, what can I do for you? I saw Jack on TV last night kissing that beautiful girl the new face of Hats, Bags & Wraps for the USA."

"Did Gabrielle see it?" Clarice asked in a panicked voice.

"Gosh no. Heather forewarned us. Shantell is a lively girl and Gabrielle can't be everywhere at the same time, she is thinking of expanding further out in Australia, providing she gets through this stupid fight."

"Yes, we all hope nothing goes wrong for her I hope by the time you dock we'll have some places Gabrielle can look at to take her mind off the forthcoming event. We also have a Hats, Bags & Wraps show for her to watch and take part in if she likes."

"You aren't calling me to discuss my daughter, are you? Oh, that feels so good to call Gabrielle my daughter. Shantell will go far with you and I'm glad she can wear high heels. I used to make Paul and Janet wear six-inch-high-heels all day so Paul could start being a girl and here is the crunch, isn't it?"

"Shantell isn't a girl, and I can see by how she holds herself and controls a crowd of women and a few men, she is very, proud of who she is but would love the change and I think that's what you want for her as well. Taking the fast route with no psychiatric help is not really the way to go and you want it fast for the upcoming catwalk show. I'll tell you now, she can't have the bottom change before the show, she wouldn't be able to walk and do the trick Gabrielle does. It's usually ten days in hospital after the bottom change, there is so much healing to do. However, breasts that's another matter, in and out the same day but she must wear a good support bra until the stitches come out.

"We can supply the support bra and she would have to see our after-care nurse once a week, and it will be the same for the bottom operation until she is discharged. She can then apply for the certificate that will allow her to get a new passport etc in her name as a woman and have her birth certificate changed from male to female.

"Now to help her out, I would suggest she is a C cup, it will help push out the dress, give her some breast to show off to the men at the catwalk. She can go smaller if she wants, but it's a good size to start with.

"Today is Wednesday. I want her to visit Dr Clark Jenkins at the Mandrake Private hospital on 34th Street. Our office and boardroom are next door. I have sent a packet of pills to you for Shanell, she must take two tablets four times a day. Today she can double up. Have her there by two o'clock.

"We will open the office, hospital and hotel where our current fifty young children under fourteen stay and go to school as they like, girl or boys. We also have eight boys aged between sixteen and twenty who want to be girls."

"You did that fast,"

"Money talks and there was a couple of million in the bank from those people who donated money when Gabrielle suggested the TG gender clinic. I will get Gabrielle to open it next week, so it takes her mind off the event."

"That sounds great; there are a few things we are planning as well. "Thank you for the help with Shantell. She'll be over the

Moon," Clarice said smiling. There was a knock at her door, and she beckoned Toni into her office.

"Here is a package for you." Clarice took it from her hand.

"Brenda, it's just arrived."

"Get them to her as fast as you can."

"I'm having lunch with her soon."

"Excellent, and good luck to her. Gabrielle won't mind about her I can assure you. By for now see you soon."

"By Brenda."

Toni went back to her office clapping her hands and grinning like a Cheshire cat. She knew who she had been talking to, and what the call was more likely about.

Jack walked into Toni's office and before he could utter a word, Toni said. "You have to take that to a police station, and have it stamped then they will give you, her ticket. Soon we will have another four gunslingers with us. Make sure all their credentials are up to date," Toni said still smiling.

"Yes, I'll check up on that." Jack walked through to Clarice's office and knocked on her door. She beckoned him in.

"I have to go to the police station to get this paperwork stamped for Heather's ticket to prove who she works for."

"I have to meet Shantell at twelve at the Thornton's Mall for lunch and her surprise. She is going to have her breast operation this Saturday. She'll be home the same day, so I want her new digs sorted out by then. She has her bottom operation the Sunday after our hat and bag show She will be in hospital for about ten days. So, Gabrielle can take over her rolls, and Gabrielle will be opening the new hospital, offices and hotel where all the current kids are sheltered. They must be looking for a Train Station."

Jack knew what she meant, somewhere for the Transgenders to eat and chat safely.

"We'll leave now then," Jack said.

When they were in the car Jack realised, they had some extra time, so he drove to the glass building complex. When they arrived, the front glass was covered in dirt and brown dust. Jack drove them around the other side of the building and there, were offices to view on the ground floor.

"I think it's worth a second look around I bet it's a good view from the top," he said.

"Oh, it overlooks our new hospital and office," Clarice said smiling holding Jack's hand. "That is the hospital where I'll have our first baby."

"Are you pregnant? I would have liked to be married first but if you are, I'm fine with it. We're getting married in a few weeks anyway."

"Oh Jack. I'm not pregnant, we have never discussed children."

"We'll have as many as you like, a football team."

"Not that many, two or three would be fine if we could afford it."

"Yes of course."

As they started off Clarice placed her hand on Jack's leg, rubbing it all the way to the Mall.

When they stopped, he put his arms around Clarice, pulled her close to him and kissed her lips. She started to cry as Jack kissed her tears away. "What's the matter?" Jack asked, as he wiped the tears from her face and gently kissed her eyes.

"I'm worried we'll have to put our wedding further back again if something happens to Gabrielle or Lynda for that matter. I just want to be married to you to call myself Mrs Jack Fleming."

"It won't be long love and I promise you, nothing will happen to Gabrielle or Lynda, our wedding will go ahead as planned."

"But I want to be married to you right now," Tears rolled down her face again, but Jack kissed them away. They got out of the car and holding hands walked slowly up to the place they were meeting Heather and Shantell. As soon as they saw them, they could see Clarice had been crying and Shantell hoped it wasn't over the kisses.

"Please don't say that you're crying over me. the kisses meant nothing it was just a publicity kiss?" Shantell asked.

"It's not over you, she's worried if something goes wrong with Gabrielle's fight, we will need to postpone our wedding again, maybe for months. Last time Paul was in hospital for over a month then he needed home care after and another month for his hand transplants and physio," Jack explained.

"I'm sure she won't be injured, she wouldn't risk it otherwise," Shantell replied.

"You know how deeply they are in love with each other, neither wants to die," Heather added.

"That's right, now sit down and order your meal I'll have a steak sandwich. And give Shantell her good news." He hugged Clarice and gave her a long loving kiss.

"Heather, can I have a word please?" Jack asked.

"Of course."

"I want to see if we can get married tonight, stop her keep getting upset. I was hoping you and Shantell would be our witnesses and Colin take a few photos?"

"That will be lovely of course we will."

"Could you get Clarice to buy a new dress, one for the wedding, get one for yourself, Shantell, and Julie and you had better get one for Toni, there would be hell to pay if I didn't invite her. We will still have the real wedding when all this mess is over, what do you think?"

"I'll get it all sorted. Why not ask Max to pick us all up then you two he'll drive us to the church in style and then drop us all home Max doesn't drink being a driver."

"You had better get Max and Colin two new suits each, three white shirts and a black pair of shoes. Get them to put it on their company card, they must look smart for Shantell, same for you and all the dresses. I'll sort it all out later. Now I'm off to get your firearm ticket and make some phone calls. Say we're all going to a friend's wedding, two gunslingers, man and woman."

He cuddled Clarice and gave her a long loving kiss then he was gone. At the police station he was told the wait would be twenty minutes. He started to make phone calls, vicar first. Because their wedding was all arranged, there was no trouble with the new wedding, and they could still have their main wedding when they were ready. The problem was it would have to be at nine pm after choir practice. Which was fine by him.

Next, he called the jeweller's where they had already purchased their, his and her wedding rings. He also ordered a 24-carat gold cross and sixteen-inch gold chain. They would be ready in fifteen minutes. The flower shop gave the same time for the small order of flowers he had just placed. His number was called, so he picked up Heather's Gun Card to show the public and police who she worked for. This also validated her liability insurance for up to ten million dollars.

He left the police station called in the jewellers then off to the flower shop. Then back to meet the girls, who had miraculously finished their lunch and bought their dresses while Max and Colin bought two new suits, three shirts, and a pair of shoes, so they looked smart for the wedding and Shantell.

They looked at the smaller store first and all agreed it was too small for a main store. Jack took Clarice's hand, and they walked the short distance to the larger store in a more prominent position. Shantell walked out the back and found the toilets and rest room where they could have their coffee breaks. Next on her list was the storeroom it was quite large, air conditioned, with plenty of sockets and internet points.

Her last place to look for was the office, which was much larger than their current store, it already had a large desk, planning table, plenty of sockets and two internet points, one with a router for wireless internet throughout the store.

In the showroom, there was plenty of room to show off their hats, bags and wraps and clothes they were already selling. There was more than enough room to show twenty women their new hats, try them on and let them walk about at a time the area Shantell mentally put aside was enormous for the bags. There were power points for the spotlights, seats the customers could sit on to examine their bag. It was all in her head. It needed a lick of paint, store shelving, spot- lights and a general clean up. But in Shantell's mind it was just what they needed.

"This will be fine for our main store in New York, I have it all planned out in my head," Shantell said sounding very, excited.

"Good put it on paper and show them to Michelle it will be her store. Don't look so disappointed, you're the new face of HB&W and you'll be out bringing customers here and I would like more of how to look after your hat and bag talks, I'll ask Martin if we can use the middle staircase again which is just outside our store."

"How convenient," Shantell replied smiling.

"This store is eighteen hundred dollars a month and we pay for our own gas, electric and water. We can now buy those low emission spotlights and have the lot on a timer, so we don't waist power like we do in some of our stores. Colin, can you take some photos of the store then we can send them to Lynda to see what she thinks. It's still her decision, it's their money not ours?" Clarice asked.

Then Heather recalled all the receipts she had folded up in her bag. As soon as Clarice left the store to talk with Martin; she handed them to Jack. When Clarice returned, she had a big smile on her face.

"Good news everyone. Martin will let us have this store for fifteen hundred dollars a calendar month. He is happy to wait until next week when Gabrielle arrives for her to sign the official lease. He's happy for you Shantell to give your talks to the public on the stairs as long as you can bring some customers into the Mall." He said it would be good business all round."

"That's very nice of him," Jack replied, looking at Shantell, he knew he would have to find another man who could do the job Shantell did and love their hats, bags and wraps, perhaps Shantell. He decided to ask Michelle to start at Transgender House.

"Martin said it would be nice if Gabrielle, Lynda and you Shantell, could open the store."

"That's fine by me," Shantell replied then recalled she might be in hospital then recovering from her operation, this was something you couldn't rush. Most of all, Clarice said she would get some proper plans made up from her thoughts on how the shop should look. She had never before had a store laid out to her designs and plans.

"Did you manage to make an appointment for us to view the office block?" Jack asked Clarice.

"Oh yes, can we get there by three thirty?"

Jack looked at his watch. "Yes, we can just make it."

"When we arrive, I must ring Mike, the salesman and tell him how many of us will be going in and he will bring out the safety hats we have to wear. Sorry Shantell your lovely hat will have to come off. Colin, bring your camera. Pics of Shantell in the safety hat please," Clarice suggested.

"Of course, boss, they should look good," he replied.

They all got into the limo and fifteen minutes later arrived at the showroom side of the building; it was very, clean and the entrance to the building was just being cleaned up. Mike came out with the safety hats and helped Shantell on with hers.

"I know who you all are now, I saw you on TV and in the papers. Shantell. The new face of Hats, Bags & Wraps and Jack the most envied man in New York kissing this beauty here, right before my eyes please Shantell, let me take your hand and I'll steady you as we go in?"

"What about me?" Clarice asked.

"You have Jack, you, lucky girl."

Colin took photos of Shantell wearing her yellow safety hat, primarily for Shantell to keep.

Jack took Clarice's hand, and everyone managed to get into the office.

"Welcome everyone, to our new unnamed office block, are you, junior staff just looking or what?" he asked. "I ask this question to all our provisional customers, so I know who I'm dealing with," Mike continued.

"I'm Clarice Gray I'm Managing Director of Sales for the USA."

"I'm Jack Fleming Manging Director of Finance for the USA "This is Colin our official photographer. Will it be okay to take pictures?" Jack asked.

"Take as many as you like."

"Before we go any further, I'm afraid you don't look like you could afford the holding fee."

"Let's move on and let me worry about the money," Jack replied sternly.

"But you only have five stores here."

"Soon to be six, then we have four stores in Toronto, eight in Texas, one big store which does very well in the shopping district of NASA's Space Port, six stores in Washington, eight stores in Washington DC and nine stores in Vancouver. We are expanding into your country, and this is where we are considering having our head offices or if you like we'll buy the entire building. Have you heard of Gabrielle or Lynda Grayson?"

"Yes, the two lesbians."

"Those are the two people who would be signing the lease."

"Right, well each room is thirty-foot square. Airconditioned when needed, underfloor heating on every floor. The winters can get very cold here usually, but this heatwave is very unnatural. Climate Change no doubt. You can have your layout done as you like, with our in-house designers. No unsightly wires or cables, everything wired into your computers or laptops. Intercom between key rooms all voice operated."

"What's the price like?" Jack asked.

"The higher you go the more expensive it is. We like to discuss this at the time of buying as there are so many factors to take in. It's not easy to change a wiring design when you're six hundred feet up."

"But let's say six hundred feet you lease by the entire floor, at thirty thousand per calendar month," Mike said thinking the price far too much for them.

"Sounds fine to me. I think Gabrielle will like it. What about computers do we supply our own, set to our company layout?" Jack asked.

"Yes, you can do that, or we can arrange a lease contract with insurance cover should anything break down."

"This sounds fine, do you have any pamphlets on it and possible layouts? Gabrielle and Lynda are on their yacht on their way here from the UK, we could send them by email, so they get the chance to discuss them in private so to say while at sea?" Clarice asked.

Two hours later they were sending emails to Lynda with a message to say photos would follow soon. Then they were home, and Jack had the problem of getting Clarice to fall for the friends getting married, to get her dressed and ready to go to her own wedding. When they arrived at the church, they all got out of the limo, the men went in first followed by the girls.

Clarice was amazed and extremely happy to be getting married to the man she loved so very much tonight. In the pub after, they were both surprised to meet staff from all their stores, all carrying gifts and cards.

The landlord put on a nice spread for the party which even had a DJ which Jack couldn't see how they had all managed to accomplish such a task with the time they had.

Halfway through the party, Michelle set up her laptop and called Jack and Clarice over to it. On the screen were Lynda and Gabrielle, holding hands with the others on board the yacht in the background. Some were using another laptop which was playing congratulations very loud.

"Hello Clarice and Jack, yes, we got invited to your wedding night as well. Congratulations on getting married ahead of time and we look forward to being at your second wedding when we arrive," Gabrielle said.

"Yes, this was a real crafty surprise Jack played on me and you as well," Clarice sighed.

"Something you were not expecting, but in your heart wishing for Clarice. Jack, you did a superb job arranging your wedding and for those who assisted in getting the party organised, you had better do another good job, when they have their second wedding.

"We couldn't think what to give you for a present, so we looked back over your work records on what you have achieved since we sent you both to New York. You have managed to expand our business there and we both know how hard it can be and how to split your time in two, looking for stores, staff and making them part of our close knit-family. You two have managed to grow our empire in the USA much faster than we ever dreamed. During your time in the USA, you have expanded our company even more taking on other States to get our stores up and running.

"Take a fortnight off for your honeymoon This will give you both the time you need to see how your presidential office is under construction," Lynda explained. "You chose the two offices, and we think the office in Thornton's Mall will bring in a great deal of money, more than enough to subsidise the cost of the new Head Office of the US Hats, Bags & Wraps. Clarice you already see enough people who deserve to be seen in a prodigious new building as head of Hats, Bags. & Wraps.

"The same goes for you Jack. You both have wise heads on your shoulders, and it looks like you have chosen well. Use the buildings and staff as you see fit. "So, all it leaves is for Michelle, to do the honours on our behalf of presenting your wedding presents. Could we give them both a huge round of applause?" Gabrielle asked as Michelle handed them a box each which contained their own official stamps as Jack Fleming President of Finance for Hats, Bags & Wraps USA and Clarice Fleming President of Sales for Hats, Bags & Wraps USA.

"I don't know how they managed to achieve this, but one of your staff needs a new change in her work title to go with a much bigger pay rise in the new glass offices. You will find all your email templates have your new names and job titles. Of course, you will both get a commanding pay rise for your new jobs," Gabrielle said smiling, looking at them.

"There is something else, being Presidents of Hat & Bags brings with it new decisions of which way to go and what risks to take so we are making you our new Parent Company, which will remain Hats, Bags & Wraps USA under both your command, as a parent company we're giving you half a billion dollars to get you going and give people a few pay rises and may we suggest you start with your secretary and your bundle of laughs, yes I've seen Shantell," Gabrielle said laughing.

"This we were not expecting, it is a gracious gift and trust you bestow upon us. Thank you, Gabrielle, Lynda," Jack replied for them both.

"The money is in your company accounts now I believe our mother has already made some suggestions as where to look next to expand. Enjoy making the right decisions. Congratulations once again from Lynda and myself, we'll see you all soon," Gabrielle said applauding them smiling.

Jack took Clarice's hand and looked straight into the eyes of Shantell. On any other occasion, it would have not mattered. It was just a glancing look. She smiled and waved at them mouthing the word congratulations. He waved back without realising what he was doing, then he turned, still holding her hand, kissed his new wife on the lips, but his mind was throwing a question into his head. Who was he thinking he was kissing, Clarice or Shantell?

Then he kissed Clarice again, their lips pressing hard against each other their tongues intertwining, coiling like snakes in love in each other's mouth. There they remained, frozen in time, for only them to know they existed, kissing, deeply in love, with each other and each other knew they were being loved most deeply by their soulmate. Their arms wrapped around each other, pulling each other close, her breasts pressing hard against his chest, both oblivious to the shouts and applause from their close friends around them, who had come to join in their wedding, their marriage; showing true love between two people and those two people, completely happy to show their everlasting love for each other.

Then they were back in the room, laughing, their hearts on fire with love as they danced together on the small dancefloor, they danced well together, like they would spend their lives, dancing through time, seeing the expansion of Hats, Bags & Wraps, a project they had built together to see its ultimate end. Max suggested to Jack now was the time for their departure. It was twelve thirty and the pub would be closing soon plus some of them had work the following day.

"Ladies and gentlemen, our new married couple are about to leave and would like to say a few words," Max said over the tannoy.

"Yes Max, well, thank you all on behalf of myself and Clarice, whose hand I am holding and will never let it go. Thank you all for making this event, thee, event, I could never have made it happen without our friends here. Thank you all once again, and don't be late for work in the morning," Jack said smiling. Everyone laughed and followed them out to their limo where their wedding presents, and cards were put in the trunk and wished them well as they drove off into the night.

When they arrived at their apartment, there was a large bouquet of flowers and a bottle of Champaign waiting at their front door. The card said, Good luck Congratulations love Gabrielle and Lynda. As Clarice picked up the flowers and Jack picked up the Champaign, Max took in all their presents and cards, putting them in their lounge. Jack picked up Clarice in his arms and carried her over the threshold, kissing her and laughing, as Max took their picture with his phone, sending it to Heather who passed her phone around for all their guests to see.

Saying thank you for his help and goodnight to Max they kissed a long passionate kiss when they were alone. Going to their kitchen Jack made them a hot chocolate each while Clarice put the flowers in a vase, then they went straight to bed. They cuddled together kissed each other passionately, using their lips to show each other how much they loved each other and how far they would go for each other. They made love four times, exploring each other's love and romance.

Tonight, was different than any other night. It was their wedding night and every time they made love, whether it was Jack on top of Clarice or the other way around, they both felt alive for each other. They would not let go of their partner no matter how long their journey through life was to take. They would take it in deep love together, step by step into a future they would help form around them.

Eventually, with Clarice sitting on top of Jack with his penis growing inside her, she started to rotate her body around his penis then, with the alcohol she had consumed at the party and the excitement of their love making she collapsed forward into Jack's open arms which held her tight, not letting her fall from him, slowly caressing her back, kissing her forehead then her lips, despite her being asleep, he didn't stop kissing her body, holding her in his arms. Gently stroking her back then breasts until he too fell into a deep sleep. When they woke, daylight was filling their bedroom and love was filling their hearts. They smiled at each other, and Jack said, "Good morning, Mrs Fleming."

"That sounds so nice," Clarice whispered into his ear then realised what position they were in, and she started to rotate herself around his penis which had managed to remain tucked up inside her vagina and was now coming back to life.

"What are you thinking of doing to me Mrs Fleming?"

"I'm thinking of making love to my new husband and holding his hand forever as we walk slowly through time, taking in all the different sights as we expand our empire. Now my love, come to me fill me with your love."

He knew exactly what she meant and wanted. Clarice wanted him to come inside her, fill her vagina with his love juices and show her he was in love with her and then she too had an orgasm, crying out in hunger for him then they were kissing again, their arms around each other, holding their bodies close and tight together. Jack's hand was gently running up and down the front of her body, caressing her breasts, kissing them, licking her nipples until they were hard and erect so he could gently squeeze them making Clarice cry out for more as she became sexually aroused, wanting more of him to love her, fill her with excitement of making love, consuming it as they enjoyed each other's body.

Jack's hand was now just above her vagina and his fingers explored and played with her clitoris for a while and when her body was moving with his finger movements, he inserted two fingers into her vagina and commenced moving his hand in and out, lubricating her vagina walls with their previous combined orgasms. His fingers were exciting her even more as they rose higher inside her vagina and found her G spot.

He was rubbing his fingers over it, making her body arch as she climaxed again then her body sank into their bed and their lips touched as her arms went around his back, pulling him towards her, his chest pressing against her breasts, arousing them, making her feel sexually excited and wanting more of him.

Then on their first morning as man and wife, he lowered his head, licking her breasts, then her stomach and down, between her legs, his tongue licked her clitoris and then he was kissing it, loving it, making her excited stimulating her before he inserted his tongue deep inside her vagina licking her vagina walls, exciting her, bringing her to another orgasm, which slithered over his tongue and into his mouth. He slowly withdrew his tongue, licking her vagina walls all the time.

All this time, Clarice was holding his penis in her hand, rubbing it up and down, faster and faster, until as she had her orgasm, her new husband had his. It didn't worry her that his seaman was covering her hand, she was now rubbing it back into his penis, making it hard once again, as she felt his tongue lick her clitoris and kiss it before moving up over her body, kissing her all the time, arousing her, making her body arch and shudder with delight.

After their final act of sex play, they got into the shower together and massaged each other with shower creams and washed each other's hair; before getting out and drying each other in thick white towels.

"Well Mrs Fleming what does a new promoted employee wish to do on her day off?"

"How about spending some of our new budget on two buildings and shake a few people's heads?"

"I think that's a brilliant idea, and how much did Madam President think of spending?" Jack asked laughing and kissing her body.

"Around fifty thousand and I want to make a couple of changes in our staff which we can do from here. It will only be a few emails with their job description as an attachment.

They dressed ready for meetings, in their very, best clothes and then Clarice called Mike and asked him if they could pop in and have a look at a lease? When they arrived and talked business for the top seven and eighth floor, they said how many people would be using the offices and then as President, Clarice paid the deposit, added her stamp and left a very confused but happy man for leasing the top two floors subject to seeing the layout plans by their internal designers.

Next to the Mall where their lease for the large store went through as agreed. The store next door was smaller than the first store they had looked at, but Clarice had plans and after talks with the owner of the store which was next to theirs, the store owner would be moving into the first store they looked at and would gain more space, while they had his store for a modern looking office for Michelle and her new secretary.

They agreed to pay for the move from spot 16 to spot 22. They had their main store and next to it, their head office for the present as it would be another five or six months before the glass front offices would be ready for occupation. For now, they would have to work as Gabrielle did when she started Hats & Bags. They would get the two store signs designed and ordered then the interior work would be hopefully started before Gabrielle and Lynda would face George.

They really wanted to have something to show them. Michelle would have the large office next door with a secretary the interior work for the offices would not take long, the store a little longer. Then they would start looking for new stores in Manhattan and expand their stores in another direction before hitting another State.

Chapter 8

As in most works parties, when people have a little too much to drink, the occasional email or text message gets sent to the wrong person and although nobody got drunk, one email from a phone, did get sent to the wrong person after all the speeches were over.

As Gabrielle and Lynda were talking in bed in their suite, Gabrielle had an email. It didn't matter who it was from, it wasn't addressed to her anyway, so she showed it to Lynda.

As soon as Lynda read it, she laughed and got the entire joke as it was meant to be just a joke between colleagues.

"High gorgeous do you think Shantell, our New Face of Hats, Bags & Wraps will get a rise in the forthcoming future or just get it chopped off?"

"I don't get it love, and why would Shantell get a rise?"

"Well first dear they are not talking about money, Clarice and Jack heard that we may be going to Australia to expand our business there and give mum somewhere to settle with Janet, Tom and the grandchildren. It is nothing to do with the fight, they are both and the whole team fully behind you on it.

"The catwalk shows were not pulling as many people as when you were there to pull in the buyers and onlookers who would then go to one of our stores and purchase the Hat and Bag you were wearing on the catwalk, so they needed a new face for Hats, Bags & Wraps, Shantell is that person."

"But Shantell is a man," Gabrielle replied.

"Exactly my love, just like you started off as anchor on the catwalk. The rise is a hard on and he wants to be a real woman, and have it chopped off; get it now?" Lynda asked laughing and holding Gabrielle's hand firmly in hers. They both laughed and kissed passionately, still laughing together, Gabrielle, recalled the moment when Paul had his penis chopped off and she couldn't stop laughing for a while.

"Mum has her TG group and a hospital you have to open next week, Shantell is having breast implants this weekend and the bottom half chopped off just after the catwalk show, but let mum tell you herself and act surprised."

"I will," Gabrielle answered still laughing and holding herself between her legs, which started Lynda laughing again, as they collapsed into each other's arms.

"I've been thinking," Lynda finally said as they stopped laughing. "For the operation to happen, Shantell will need time off, a month at least when she should be opening new stores and showing herself off in different hats and bags and clothes. I think we may well be able to do that job for her using our eyes and thought. I wouldn't do it before her main show, let her have that enjoyment, but perhaps just after the show? What do you think? Then she would be like you after Death changed you."

Gabrielle thought for a moment. "I like your idea, yes great plan we'll try it. Clarice and Jack will need a new face for Hats, Bags & Wraps in the US, I couldn't do all the shows with our work in the UK, Europe and soon Australia, although there will not be so many shops there as in the US, but I want us to be a proper international company, owned by us, not on display like some other shops similar to us.

"The managers and directors have board meetings at least once a month like our charity and accept what the board says if they want to go on. I want us to be in charge of all our shops, not a board of people who don't love our stores like we do," Gabrielle said.

"I totally agree with you, it's hard enough just to get staff for the shops," Lynda added then they turned to face each other and kissed, a long loving kiss, showing their love for each other their arms around each other's back, pulling them towards each other holding themselves close to the other, they kissed.

"There is one other thing I must mention. I have been eavesdropping on Clarice and Jack's thoughts. They are deeply in love with each other, hence why they married tonight, but they both have said they would like to live together in love forever, just like us. Now, as I see it, we were given the opportunity to save two hundred thousand couples, we haven't even asked John, Alan, Tina and Mike if they would like to join us. Say we were to take Hats, Bags & Wraps as far as we could through time, we want people with us who would feel the same as us over our passion.

"I think it would be a good idea to put the idea of living forever into their heads and get their answer when we arrive in New York and change them."

"We need to start thinking about people we would like to spend our time with in the very distant future," Gabrielle agreed.

"Shantell feels the same although she doesn't have a partner yet. Jack is lining Shantell up with someone who she will work with who he thinks she would like when she's a real woman. It will certainly prolong her looks and figure," Lynda explained.

"Yes, it would, if she is up for it, we could give her the gift of long life and change her at the same time, and the person she falls in love with, later," Gabrielle suggested.

"Agreed!"

"I think Tina and Noah would love to live forever," Lynda said with a smile on her face.

"Noah, I watched them talking to each other with a twinkle in their eyes and a fire in their hearts. Noah tried to protect Tina as they walked around the shops with us in Rome, walking close to each other, shoulders touching, sometimes holding hands when the opportunity arose. We could change them, yes."

"An excellent idea, I saw them holding hands as well and looking into each other's eyes, over breakfast as they always sat opposite each other. Now they are engaged, they'll soon be married," Gabrielle added.

They kissed, then held hands firmly, as they looked into each other's green eyes and they started to shine very bright. Gabrielle kissed Lynda on her lips, their mouths slowly rotating, their tongues playing with each other as their eyes shone brighter and they sent their deep love to each other.

As their eyes grew darker their kissing didn't slow or tail off, it got stronger and faster, their sexual feelings for each other being brought to the front. They wanted each other, to show their deep love for each other and for Lynda to help take Gabrielle's mind off the forthcoming fight with George.

"Oh, thinking of George which you were, I'm fine, please don't worry until we are much closer to the actual day we meet. But I will need a tight fitting, but comfy white fitted silk blouse, a well fitted trouser suit and a pair of two-inch high heels. With all this heat that shouldn't be here, but I think I know who is behind it. With a pair of skin-coloured tight gloves.

"I will also need my hair tied back on the day and my makeup made to look like a woman on fire with blood red nail varnish on my fingers and toes, which Sarah gave me. I love the suit Sarah got me, but it was meant for a winter fight not a hot summer's day," Gabrielle said breaking into their romantic kiss.

"Yes my love, I unfortunately agree with you and Sarah will understand. we'll get the clothes you need when we look for dresses for the catwalk event. I'll do your hair, makeup and put the nail varnish on your fingers and toes. Anything I can do to help you I promise," she replied with a tear in her eye.

They held hands, put their arms around each other and lay back on their towels on the sunbathing deck, just holding each other close, gazing into each other's green eyes that started to glow, as they spoke to each other, mind to mind, not holding back the hurt Lynda was feeling that her lover would have to face George again and fight him, possibly to the death. One question she then asked Gabrielle.

"If people are going to get hurt badly and even killed, what are we going to do about their bodies, on top of the Empire State Building? What about all the blood that may be spilled? We can't just throw them off and down onto the street, they might have bullet holes in them, there would be an enquiry of sorts. The men who were killed on our way over, fell into the sea and sank, their dead bodies being eaten by sharks and other fish. On top of the Empire State Building, it's a small square, have you considered that George or one of his men might try to throw you off the top and my love, it's a very long way down?

"Even with your prolonged life, you wouldn't survive hitting the ground at the speed you would be falling." Lynda was crying, tears streaming down her face. She held onto Gabrielle with all her might, frightened once again, now for the second time, she might lose her. Gabrielle was the love of her life; she knew she would not be able to go on without her by her side. Throwing herself off the Empire State Building seemed to be a good idea if Gabrielle was taken from her.

Their mother beckoned them off the sunbathing deck and down to her suite. There she told them what she had been up to.

"I have sold all my businesses and shops, together with some stocks and shares. I have now amassed ten billion pounds with the sale of my large houses which we will not need again. I have my apartment in New York which is large enough for Mike, Penny and myself. I will be staying in New York for quite a few months as I am now a silent partner. In the new Hats, Bags & Wraps USA, with Clarice and Jack. I have put one billion into the company bank so it will help with getting the offices completed and the new store and Manager's office, which I'll let them tell you about.

"I have already spoken with Janet and Tom; even though she has objected, I have transferred two billion UK pounds into their private bank account, and I have done the same for you. You know Emanuel, he will help with any investments you wish to make when you get back to the UK. I'll not let Death take my girl away from me without a fight. I spoke to Him once, I'll do it again, even if I have to die in the process," Brenda said annoyed at Death.

"Mother it won't come to that I'm sure," Gabrielle said, trying to calm her down.

"Now, where was I? Yes, the TG group in New York will need more money put into it and many more staff. Clarice and Jack have just found some buildings that can be demolished not far from the TG hotel and on the way home from schools and University. The hospital also needs some new x-ray machines and extra blood pressure monitors, the usual stuff we people take for granted but nurses must run all over the place looking for equipment. I want it all by each bed and that's what I'm planning. I want it just like yours is in London, and with the right people behind me, it will be. I will be expecting you to open the hospital and hotel next week as your names will also be on some of the buildings.

"Then there are my other charities. The catwalk venue needs upgrading with new lights, seats and carpets. There are also a couple of stores that need upgrading and we will need money to accomplish that. So, my money is being well spent in different areas and you will need more money when you expand into Australia. That will leave enough for my travelling back and forth from the USA to the UK and I want to have a world tour, something your father and I always wanted to do but there was never the time, work got in our way.

"Now; I want us all to have a great time in New York can we do that and let's not try and think about the fight?" she asked.

"It will also leave me enough money to remain in the US billionaires club, which I want you two to join as it will give helpful hints in business, and you get to talk with owners of large multi-storey stores."

"Yes, mother you get us in and introduce us to some people who can let us open a small unit and sell our or your Hats, Bags & Wraps We would still like to help Clarice and Jack with our experience. We may be of some serious help to getting new stores, units and orders, then there is my perfume and new hairspray. Which smells of my perfume, rather than the usual smell of hairspray. I would like it sold in all our shops and I have already made arrangements to sell the perfume and hairspray in the USA new stock is on its way," Gabrielle explained.

"Good, that's a great help, with just your names it will help increase the orders in the catwalk shows and we can have photos with both of you holding your perfume and hairspray. They will be blown-up and put in all our stores by your perfume," Brenda said smiling and stood walking to the door.

"Now I am going to get some more sun on me. while I can my loves." Both girls said thank you again for the money, stood and kissed their mother as Gabrielle opened the door for her. "We had better start working out the bonuses and go through our trunks," Gabrielle said to Lynda, as their mother left her suite.

They walked to the lounge and with a coffee each, sat down and started to go through the crew putting their seven-thousand-dollar bonuses into their bank accounts. They also had a seven-thousand-dollar clothes allowance each as at least half the crew had their clothes covered in gunpowder and blood. Many of their clothes were covered in gun oil and oil used in the heavy rounds of bullets in the large automatic guns.

Chris got them into clear waters as fast as he could and giving them a smooth sail to New York, so he'll have a ten-thousand-dollar bonus with a seven-thousand-dollar clothes allowance. Each bodyguard had a twelve-thousand-dollar bonus and a twelve-thousand-dollar new suit allowance as some of their clothes were damaged in the battle and they need to look smart all the time. One, three-piece suit could cost four thousand-dollars easy. This time in New York, they could be carrying extra clips and two throwing knives each in case we encountered more of George's men.

They decided to give Walter a five-thousand-dollar bonus for guarding the stairs to the upper decks and helping John at the bow gun. He was also given a seven-thousand-dollar clothes allowance as his only suit was smelling of gunpowder and oil as he carried extra ammunition to Alan on the aft twenty-five mm gun,

Life would be different in New York and other States as they toured the stores Clarice and Jack had purchased.

Wendy was also given a five-thousand-dollar-bonus for helping with the clear up work and a seven-thousand-dollar-bonus so she could get herself a new dress for the catwalk show and opening of the new hospital.

They wanted to be able to give them all the advice they could before leaving for the UK again and then down to Australia, providing Gabrielle lived through the fight with George and his men in eight days' time.

With everyone paid, and an expense account on their books, for Penny, Mike's wife, for the work she had done during the battle and clear up after. It was also there for her looking after their mother in New York and their planned trip around the world, she would need a lot of dresses to look pretty as they walked through the multi-story stores in New York, and other multi-story shops in the different countries they would visit on their world trip.

Their mother loved to shop in the large stores and small stores off the wide sidewalks. Penny's credit and personal bank account cards would be in their apartment. both cards had an unlimited sum on them. The cards no matter how high their debt, would be cleared each month by their bank; so, she could buy all the nice pretty dresses to escort their mother around New York and attend the Catwalk events in their new hats and carrying a matching bag.

Every girl was advertising their hats and bags as they travelled to work, going out for lunch and home for free. Gabrielle liked the girls to look pretty. Clarice and Jack would soon learn this was well worth the expense of a new dress and the loan of a hat and bag.as the girls handed out business cards to the women they spoke to, with the name and address of their particular store where they could buy hats, bags and wraps like the ones they were wearing. Lynda then sent a text to each crewman telling them of their bonus, clothes allowance, where to buy good quality clothes to represent Hats, Bags & Wraps as they toured New York and other cities. Finally, was the address of their hotel.

They were asked to take a small bag of clothes etc, with them and as soon as they checked in, had a shower, then they would go to the stores and buy some new clothes and a suit each as the hotel had a clothes expectation.

If they were staying in for an evening meal. Suit and tie for the man, dresses for the women, they all had to look smart; it was the main meal of the day and they had rules that everyone dress appropriately for the evening meal.

They would all be expected to attend the catwalk event to help with numbers and represent Hats, Bags & Wraps.

Gabrielle had a new gold badge made for Hats, Bags & Wraps with their emblem on which each person would be expected to wear whilst in New York. They would get their normal wages for a trip to New York and back to the UK when they returned to the UK with a small bonus.

Before going through their clothes and packing, Lynda was suddenly overcome with emotion, so they returned to the sundeck for her to lay down and get her thoughts organised before packing.

As they lay side by side, Lynda held Gabrielle's hand for dear life as thoughts of their past entered her head.

She recalled their first timeline before Death gave them a Second Chance and turned back time. She had walked by Hats & Bags back then, looking into the shop window. There she saw a man with green eyes putting large expensive hats on a stand. She always tried to do a book signing, which she would be attending in a few hours further along the road, to sign her latest book *"The Wife Beater"* usually in costume, but Ian, her husband, who she was legally separated from, and George, his close friend, had destroyed all her hats and costume dresses a month previous and was still demanding money from her, five hundred pounds a week for beer money, to leave her alone to write and support him as the book was, George and Ian said based on them, telling everyone about their rough relationship.

George had raped her almost every night since he killed his own wife and her parents for attempting to report them to the police, that was four years ago. So, they called in friends who paid them to have sex with her, cut her body open with a Stanley knife or slash her breasts.

On a couple of occasions, she had almost bled out and had to stay in hospital for a few weeks while deep cuts to her stomach, breasts and five broken ribs healed. She had terrible scars all over her body and a long one just below her right ear and down around her neck. She tried to style her hair to cover the scar, but she could not cover the mental scars, they had remained with her to that day.

Gabrielle helped stabilise her and enjoy life, she lavished her with fine dresses and gold. Nothing was too good for her. If she wanted anything, Gabrielle paid for it and let her keep her book money as she still found time to write. Gabrielle made sure of it, buying the latest computers and laptops she could talk to, to write directly onto the page as George and Ian, had broken both her hands and all her fingers a number of times. The nightmares and screaming in the night had stopped, with the help of Gabrielle.

Ian was demanding another £500.00 for his week's beer money which she did not have. Her quarterly book sales did not go into her bank account until the end of the month. and she was hoping the book signing that afternoon would boost her book and download sales. But there was no queue yet. Later that afternoon would change their lives up until now, over ten years over two lifetimes. They had been hunted throughout Europe because of Ian and George. Now Gabrielle would face George all over again.

When they first looked at each other through the glass shop window, covered in snow and frost their green eyes met and started a fire inside each of them. She thought the young man wouldn't be able to buy them a coffee each, let alone take her on a date, if he found her attractive, but under her clothes, she was not attractive. No smooth skin, it was covered in scars where her body had been sewn back together. She knew he wouldn't want her, let alone take her for a coffee. She didn't like alcohol, people got drunk and got carried away with her body and she didn't much like men.

After their eyes met and they smiled. A warm loving smile at each other, she walked on, slowly making her way through the snow-covered pavement. She walked around the corner and up to the bookshop where she would be signing her books. Her books, her words in print and people she hoped would be buying her books and reading the words she had painstakingly at times, with broken fingers put down on her laptop. That was now gone, Ian had destroyed it in a violent rage one evening a month ago, because he had no beer money and Lynda was out of her flat so he couldn't rape her himself or allow George to rape her for fifty quid to get him through the night's boozing session he was planning.

That was behind her now, she had managed to save enough money to buy a second-hand laptop which wouldn't save her work properly.

She visualised herself turning around towards the most dangerous and happiest time of her life. A time she would never forget and was now recalling it again as her body soaked up the vitamin D and helped her body heal, but not her mind, for no matter how long she lived, she would never forget Paul, who she had only known a short seven hours, risked his life for her. Would have died for her and for a time, did die just to save her life, and that of a police officer who lay on the cold, dirty floor, his right leg cut off and lying to his right side as he bled out. His blood pooling around his open stump and leg.

Seeing nobody waiting in the bookshop, she turned around and ambled back to the man she hoped might still be in the shop window. She wasn't sure if he was still there, but Paul had left his shop and gone looking for her. Not seeing her, he returned to his shop put his suit jacket on and going against his own rules, told his secretary he was just popping out for a moment around the corner.

He was running fast when he turned the corner and ploughed right into the woman, he had seen from his shop window, Lynda. They collided, their bodies going into the air then falling to the snow-covered pavement. His arms covered her body instinctively, holding her still and safe from injury on top of him as they fell, slowly back to the pavement.

They remained there, looking into each other's green eyes, thinking of what to say or do next. She could feel his arms around her, as she pushed her arms under his back, pulling him close to her. She breathed over his mouth and only wanted to kiss him on the lips.

No matter if he could afford coffee or not, she would pay for it, if he would join her. Although she didn't like men because of Ian and George, she wanted to discover more about this man, even if he was a poor window dresser. She had kept men in beer money before and paid for their apartment, she could do it again, she thought to herself as she lay on top of him, getting their breath back.

Then he started to move and pushed her to her feet, then got up himself, holding her hand.

"I'm so sorry," he said to her politely, with a nice sounding voice. "Are you okay?" he asked.

"Fine thank you just a little out of breath."

He took hold of her hand then asked her if she would join him for a coffee? There was a coffee shop just up the road before the bookshop.

"Yes," she replied. her heart thumping hard, feeling like she was walking on air as he held her hand and escorted her to the coffee shop and opened the door for her. He asked her what she wanted and went to the counter after he found them a vacant table and held her chair for her as she sat down. She heard him speak to the saleslady, speaking to her in fluent Italian. He returned to their table and took his seat.

The woman arrived with their drinks and a cake each and once again they spoke to each other in Italian as if they were good friends, which they were. He held her hand again as he introduced himself as Paul Grayson, not just the manager of the shop but the owner of Hats & Bags, the shop and others throughout the UK and Europe. He could afford their coffee and take her out for a meal if only he would ask. He was not interested in talking about himself and his shops, he was just interested in hearing about her and talking about her books which he had read, all of them as too his mother. He was in no hurry to return to his shop, he could have stayed talking to her all day, and it might have been better if he had.

They had another cappuccino each which he asked for again in Italian, not showing off that he could speak to her in her language but having respect for her and conversing with her in her native tongue like we should all do and later, she would do and understand the respect she earned being able to speak to Europeans in their native tongue.

They remined holding hands until it was time for her to leave. Before she left, he insisted on taking her to his shop and putting her into a costume period hat that the woman in *the Wifebeater would* wear to hide her scars. She could see different hats going through his mind as they stood together and once again got closer and for a second or two their lips touched, not a proper kiss, but as close as she could expect for now.

Then he asked her out that evening for a special meal and she accepted. There was still so much to get out of him, all she had managed to do was tell him all about herself which he seemed to love. Her talk also included some of the hurt and pain she had gone through and gently stroked her neck.

They walked to his shop where despite other women in the shop he ran around looking for a matching handbag while Stella got the hat he wanted and put it on Lynda's head, holding it on with a hat pin.

Next, he had taken her handbag and put the essentials into the new bag and put it over her shoulder.

She was smiling now as the hot sun tanned her body and feeling happy. Her mind was now back in Paul's shop; women in the shop started to recognise her and asked her to sign their books, then they wanted to take photos of her and then together with Paul, as most of the women shopped there a lot and knew Paul. That was when they first kissed for the camera and he didn't mind, despite seeing the ugly scar on her neck, but he finally styled her hat, so it hid her scar without even talking about it. They held each other close and kissed just as if they had been in love all their lives.

She knew he was the man who Death, when the last time she was sliced open and was beaten so bad with a kick in the head she had died for a while, she didn't know for how long, but it was Death who had brought her back to life, returning her soul to her body. Ian was spaced out on cocaine, too far gone to worry about her safety.

Death had told her she would meet a man who would save her life who had green eyes. The weeks had turned into months before she finally met him and now, she was not going to let him go. He had to take a phone call in the shop and a man wearing an expensive suit came in to talk to him.

When Paul returned, he said he would meet her at the bookshop around six fifteen, just before she was due to finish signing her books, the shop would close, and they would go out for a meal together. He opened the shop door for her and parted the crowd that were cuing to have their new books signed. Their lips kissed and were once again caught on camera. He said goodbye as he had to sort the man out in the shop and let her walk the short distance to the bookshop by herself.

The next time she saw him he was standing in the queue waiting to have two hardbacks signed by her. And have their photos taken a lot by her photographer. He had just moved to her left when George slammed her book down on the table and Ian demanded money. As she looked at them, she could see they were both carrying long double-edged very sharp swords. She thought the man who would save her life had left the shop on seeing the two-armed men. He was too much of a gentleman to get into a fight and Ian or George were not interested in words. They only liked action and decapitating people who would not pay their bills.

Tears had already started to fill her eyes and slide down her face as she thought of the horrendous fight that followed. As Ian demanded money from her and George demanded she sign a form signing her royalties over to them, a fat lot of good it would do them in prison.

As Ian started to threaten her with an eight-inch knife which he had ready to thrust at her while she was standing still petrified as to what would happen to her. Paul stepped forward and slammed a thick hard back book the full length of the knife; Ian was now barely holding the handle up. In seconds Paul had taken another knife from Ian's jean belt.

Her photographer was now on the floor. His hand had been badly sliced open by George's knife and George was about to cut his hand off at his wrist, when Paul threw the knife, he was holding at George's hand and pinned it to the floor, the knife going through his hand into the wooden floor up to its hilt.

Paul had grabbed another knife from Ian's jean belt which was now around his throat and Paul was asking Ian to let Lynda and her book manager go. As Ian was about to give in, for a while at least, which would give Paul time to decide his next move as he knew it would not end like this.

A policeman, thinking he was doing the right thing and despite Lynda's screams that Paul was the good man and Ian was the dangerous man, a very, dangerous man, he forced Paul to move to his right, getting ready to arrest him.

A second later the policeman was on the floor in shock with his right leg by the side of him. Ian had drawn his sword, then brought it down as hard as he could on the officer's thigh. slicing it off. Paul was pushed to the floor as Ian started to threaten her book manager and Lynda with his sword. Lynda heard Ian order George to decapitate the officer.

As Paul lay on the ground for now, he could only save one man, the officer or the book manager. He quickly made his decision and as George drew his sword ready to kill the officer, he watched Paul throw the knife he had in his hand at George, and it hit him in his heart killing him instantly. Now he had to save his life, Lynda's life and that of her book manager.

He stood up and grabbed hold of Ian's sword that was threatening Lynda's stomach. She watched in horror as Paul grabbed the sword with his right hand, wrapped his fingers around the sword's double sharp edge and pulled it towards himself as he shouted for the book manager to run behind him with Lynda, but she fell to the floor and stood up again to see Ian pushing his sword into Paul's stomach.

Paul's left hand grabbed the sword's side as he tried to stop it from entering his stomach. But there was nothing he could do; his bloody hands were sliding along the sword's sharp edges.

Then from somewhere deep inside. Paul pushed the sword out of his stomach.

As Paul released his body from the sword, Ian started to push it back towards Lynda. Paul grabbed the sword again and pulled it away from her, so it gave him time to turn around with his back to the sword, his hand pulled the last knife from Ian's belt. While they were back-to-back, with the sword now facing the wall where Paul had been seconds before, he somehow managed to hold the knife in his left hand and pass it to what was left of his right hand, then he turned around and placed the sharp knife edge against Ian's throat and slit it wide open. Just in case he might somehow survive the cut he held the knife firmly in his shredded, bleeding, hand and thrust the knife into Ian's heart, not once but twice just to be sure he was dead.

Paul then collapsed to the floor before Lynda's eyes. She was crying hard now on the sun deck, as her thoughts returned to what happened that evening.

When Paul was on the floor, he pulled his belt out of its loops and wrapped it around the officer's bleeding stump, creating a tourniquet to stop the bleeding. He spoke to the officer for a few seconds before falling on his back to the cold, dirty, floor, his stomach pumping blood and other liquids from inside him, out of the large hole Ian had made with his sword.

Lynda had no idea if he were dead or alive, whatever he would be in a very-bad shape. She knelt beside him seeing all the blood coming out of his stomach, he was still breathing, and she knew Paul needed help.

Lynda ran the length of the bookshop passing dead or badly-wounded bodies on the floor in the book aisles. She ran screaming for help into the police cordon. The police were stopping the medics getting into the bookshop helping people as the senior officer had lost the plot. He said he called for backup, but the call never went through.

Lynda grabbed a green bag from a paramedic and started running back to Paul. The Paramedic caught her up, took his back from her and followed her to Paul.

Soon there was a Dr stitching up his intestines as she was holding his stomach apart for the Dr to get his hands inside Paul's body. Then a heart surgeon joined them just as Paul's heart stopped through the damage the sword point had done to it. Now it was bleeding. A minute later, Lynda was holding Paul's heart in her hands and being filmed by a TV crew which was sending pictures of Paul's dead heart being sent around the world. As the heart surgeon stitched up Paul's heart, Lynda started to pump it using her hands until it started again, and the surgeon put his heart back into his body. The next day she was giving half her kidney to Paul as his was badly cut apart.

The rest was history as they stayed together in the same private, hospital, suite. They grew closer together as Lynda met all his family and bodyguards. Lynda was given Alan to protect her when they were out and it had also been Alan who had first spoke to her, when Paul was lying on the floor, and got the surgeon to let her stay with Paul, talking to him keeping him calm, as he had no anaesthetic.

On the sunbed, Lynda could not stop crying as she thought about what Paul, now Gabrielle, the love of her life, the woman she was prepared to live with forever would have to go through yet again.

She placed her arm over Gabrielle's body. As their cheeks touched, her tears were being spread over Gabrielle's cheek. Lynda did not want her wife to have to go through that fight all over again. For her to go through all that suffering and pain. She could not lose Gabrielle and face the rest of time by herself. No matter what healing powers she had, a sword she knew in the right hands could destroy the innards of Gabrielle.

She was crying hard as Gabrielle placed her arm around Lynda's body and held her close to her side, kissing her head, eyes, her tears and trying to understand why she was so upset. A quick flash of her green eyes told Gabrielle all she needed to know. Lynda had been reliving their past, thinking it would all happen again, and she might lose her lifelong lover.

"I'm sure things will turn out just, fine. I can still throw a knife, all I need is a tight-fitting three-piece woman's trouser suit, so it matches what I wore on that day," Gabrielle said.

"But you didn't have a woman's suit on, that day, pink panties yes. One of the nurses brought them into the room and told me they would need a good soaking in cold salt water, before washing and could I attend to it as she thought I was your girlfriend after seeing us on TV only hours before. But then I wanted to be your wife so we could spend our lives together living off my book sales. I didn't know then how rich you were and all the money you had didn't matter to me. It just meant you could pay for our special meal on our first proper date, Lynda said surprising Gabrielle that she knew all about her that first night.

"Gabrielle, I can't lose you: if you should die, then I'll throw myself off the top of The Empire State Building."

As they held each other close, with Lynda still crying, her tears over both their faces. She looked through her green eyes and spoke to Gabrielle. again.

"My Love, I cannot live and continue without you, knowing all this mess, this madness of George chasing us, thinking I'm his wife and whore. We have been chased all our lives together and been through Hell together. First the drug Lords sending the rest of George's family after us, chasing us through France then the rest of Europe and when we disposed of them, others thought they would cash in, and attempt to ruin our wedding and we were saved by the Royal Marines.

"Then in this timeline, George has managed to get the Mafia on his side. We were attacked on our way home in our plane by aircraft from another country and almost shot down had it not been for the air force from Malta who shot, down both planes then we were escorted home by two Royal Air Force Jets. As we helped battle George's men who threatened our and other shops took half their income each week. We lost dad in above all, a car bomb which also put Mike in hospital for a while and out of action as a bodyguard until his arms were better and he could handle a gun again.

"Through George's men, the Queen and government made us Envoys for the UK to bring peace between the UK and the Mafia. Had it not been for Draco, and us taking him under our wing in London, the peace treaty would have been much harder to get signed.

"I know we had to spend a lot of money to get the Italian and Roman TG's a home, Train Station and get them settled in but it was well worth it, even though we had to rebuild most of a local hospital, put new wards in, find surgeons who could do sex change operations properly, with the correct operating theatres, MRI scanners and new X-ray machines with all the medical equipment they would need for the operations either way round.

"At least Marco has helped with the costs and protection, of the TG's. Now we are heroes in the UK, Rome and Italy. Many of the Mafia have now left the UK and most of George's men have either been arrested or killed."

"Now you must fight George all over again and he will have a double-edged, sharp, sword with him and all you will have are four knives that you took from Ian's belt.

"And all this chasing and threatening of your life and mine and our bodyguards is all because of me. What happened to me in my past how I was treated it's all because I was damaged goods and Paul didn't listen to me and just drew me into his life."

"You're not that much better, you have drawn me into your life. Well not just drawn, fallen in love with me so deeply you will do anything to protect me am I right?" Lynda asked.

Gabrielle took Lynda's arm in her hand and in just a few seconds, Lynda was laying on Gabrielle's front, just as they first met. They looked into each other's green eyes as Gabrielle started to speak.

"Yes, Lynda the love of my life, you're absolutely right. We have been chased by gunmen, Georges family and other people, but we have enjoyed life together, gone through it all and we are still here, alive together with our friends. I wouldn't have missed a second of what we have gone through. My life was boring, but it's been full of excitement with you by my side, holding hands, kissing each other on the move and oh our glorious nights together making non- stop love and I love being a lesbian with you."

"I would not have had it any other way."

"Now stop thinking about George and the men he has left.

"Alan can be there to help protect me with his gun and John will be standing in the wings. I am not afraid of George. I was not afraid of Ian at the time and George, well he just got in the way, and I was glad I killed him, and I know I'll kill him again. Just have a little faith in me like you did on that night two lifetimes ago."

Gabrielle held Lynda tight on top of her and they kissed, their mouths rotating forgetting those people around them. Gabrielle needed to show Lynda, she loved her, would care for her forever and want this fight she was so frightened about over with.

"We know the unknown is frightening, but I am not frightened, believe it or not I do have a little faith in Death that He will not go back on His word and not only that but just between you and me, there is another prominent player watching us who could help change the course of things if they start to turn nasty," Gabrielle explained, trying to give Lynda hope they would both survive.

"Do you mean Fate?" Lynda asked.

"No, but She might just show Herself, who knows?" "Then who?" she asked.

"A friend to us both," Gabrielle replied.

"If you haven't worked it out by tonight, I'll tell you in bed and I also want us to get some matching lingerie, especially for tonight, you're a little down. Now come here Mrs Grayson, and I haven't called you that in a while.

"I haven't finished with you yet the love of my life, the jewel in my crown."

Gabrielle kissed her face all over licking up her tears, kissing them all better; her hands were running up and down her back, scratching her back in places Lynda loved as it made her feel sexy. Their green eyes lit up for barley a second and everyone knew they had spoken with each other, mind to mind. Lynda had a huge grin on her face their heads parted for a moment, then they were kissing again, very romantically.

"Perhaps you should take it to your suite, it looks like you're going to make love to each other, and mum is watching you," Jenny whispered into Gabrielle's ear. The next moment they were on their feet and gone to their suite.

Their bodies touched each other from head to toe. Their hands exploring each other and their lips kissing each other's breasts, front, clitoris and at the same time their tongues were licking each other's clitoris then exploring their vaginas until they were both very sexually aroused.

Their hands were pressing on each other's bottom, Lynda pulling Gabrielle again closer to her mouth. Their fingers were running up and down each other's bottom, caressing it, making each other feel so sexy they each neared a climax. Gabrielle had her orgasm first, crying into Lynda's vagina as she came then Lynda had a huge orgasm, her love juices flowing over her vagina walls and into Gabrielle's mouth; she swallowed the warm juices then licked her vagina walls until she found her G Spot and brought her to another orgasm, her hands fondling Lynda's bottom. They turned around and played with each other as their faces got closer together so they could kiss each other properly.

Their fingers were now inside each other's vagina, rubbing their vagina walls, playing with each other's clitoris and bringing each other towards another orgasm. As their mouths rotated about each other, and their tongues licked each other, licking the inside of their mouths again.

They were both very sexually aroused as their arms wrapped themselves around each other's back, rubbing it, fondling it, getting each other excited. Then their fingers were back inside each other's vagina and once again Lynda came first and seconds later Gabrielle had her orgasm then they kissed each other on their lips face and neck. before laying side by side, arms over each other's front and quietly talking to each other as they both calmed down.

"Lynda my love this is what I mean when I say I love you; I want you all the time. I don't want another man except John or Alan, to touch your body if it means it will upset you in the slightest way. We'll go anywhere to keep you out of trouble by plane or boat if we're together to hold hands and show our love for each other when we make love. I don't want to lose you and I'm sure I'll get through this fight and live to tell another tale, without being cut to shreds. Will you believe me and let it go for a while?"

"There will be times when it's nearer the fight, that we can all sit down and talk the fight through and input our suggestions. For now, we have clothes to go through and pack our trunks and cases, plus check the safe or what jewellery we will want to wear," Gabrielle said, hoping the job ahead would take Lynda's mind off the fight for a while.

"The gold hearts definitely," Lynda replied quickly.

"I totally agree, Gabrielle added grinning. She got off their bed. Put her negligee on, walked out their door and a minute later, opened their door dragging in one of their trunk's which she left at the bottom of their bed.

Gabrielle brought in the other trunk from outside their suite and they started to go through the clothes they had brought with them just in their negligees. Which meant they kissed a lot, their hands going inside each other's negligee, feeling each other's breasts, fondling, and kissing them, their hands going up and down their bodies as Lynda pulled Gabrielle onto the bed.

She pushed open their negligees, her hand sliding down her wife's and lover's body and started to play with her clitoris, then her fingers went inside her vagina, moving in and out bringing Gabrielle to an orgasm. Their lips touched as Gabrielle came over Lynda's fingers, which she dried on Gabrielle's back, as they got together so they could kiss more and insert their tongues into each other's mouth. They were both laughing, something they hadn't done together since the gun fight.

Gabrielle's mouth was covering Lynda's, their lips pressing hard together, rotating around each other their green eyes looking at each other as they talked quickly to each other, still kissing, their tongue pushing through their lips, into each other's mouth, feeling, exploring the other's mouth, their tongues interacting, licking and tasting the other's tongue which kissed as their tips touched and circled each other before they returned to their own mouth, leaving the lips to rotate and share each other's love.

The following day after the yacht had docked. Gabrielle, Lynda, their bodyguards and Sarah were sent through customs first on their diplomatic passports. Their two trunks and three suitcases with two small makeup cases were put aboard the van first, then their safe was taken aboard with their jewellery inside.

Three crewmen who had been cleared by customs, were allowed to load the rest of the cases and trunks into the van. They brought out Brenda's small trunk, makeup bag and put them into the trunk of her car with three suitcases.

Then the women got into the limo followed by the bodyguards. Gabrielle and Lynda said goodbye to their mother and watched her drive off in the private car with Mike and Penny to their new luxoury apartment they would all be staying in while in New York. They were going to live in a luxoury home from home with anything the couple wanted to make them feel at home and that included big televisions and top of the range laptops already there and installed.

When they left, the others were driven to their hotel with Clarice and Jack telling them what it was like as they had found the hotels for them and the crew. Gabrielle and Lynda's party would be staying in the Elexis hotel on the entire tenth floor.

Gabrielle and Lynda got into the limo and John closed their door. He got in then they drove off to their hotel. When they arrived, their luggage was already on their floor and being put into their rooms as Clarice went to the front desk and sorted out room keys for everyone then they were off to their rooms. An hour later they were back in their limo being driven to Imagines, multi-story store for elegant evening wear.

They parked a short way down from the store and left their limo, clean clothes on, looking smart with their hats on and carrying their small shoulder-bags. They entered the large store and walked up to the saleswoman, Gabrielle and Lynda holding hands.

"Hello," Lynda said, "we would like to look at some of your Dion-le-Jar evening dresses please for all of us." Lynda said prounouncing the French designer's name in French.

"I'm sorry, but those dresses are extremely expensive, I doubt if you could afford one between you all," Madelline said looking down on Lynda and Gabrielle.

"Could I speak to your manager please?" Lynda interrupted annoyed.

"What is it Madelline?" Andrea asked on hearing Lynda's voice.

"These ladies want a Dion-le Jar dress each, but I doubt they could afford it," she retorted.

"Madelline, apologise, don't you know who this is?"

"No," she replied sheepishly.

"This is Gabrielle and Lynda Grayson, they own Hats, Bags & Wraps, now get them what they want. I'm so sorry Gabrielle, Lynda, what is it you would like to see?" Andrea asked.

"We've just arrived in New York, so we need some dresses to go out this evening to see Cats. Then there is tomorrow night, Gabrielle and I will be on the local catwalk so special dresses for that. I would say, three evening dresses each for our friends and us, then two special dresses for tomorrow evening, I'm paying. Do you sell men's suits?" Lynda asked.

"The men are our armed bodyguards, all licenced to kill. This is John, Gabrielle's bodyguard, Alan, my bodyguard, Jack, Clarice's bodyguard and President of Hats, Bags & Wraps USA Finance," Lynda said introducing the men.

"This is Tina, Sabrina's bodyguard."

"The men's suits are on the seventh floor," Andrea finally replied to Lynda's question.

"Boy's upstairs, three suits each, new shoes, "I'm paying," Gabrielle added holding Lynda's hand, pulling her close to her. They kissed each other as the boys sorted themselves out.

"Leave your guns with Tina. She and Jack will protect us for now. As soon as the first of you have your suits, around five to six thousand dollars each, four white shirts, black bow ties for tonight, a special tie for tomorrow and when We open the TG Hospital. Hardware, leave with Tina for now, Sarah, do you have a bag?"

"Yes Gabrielle," she replied getting the small fold up bag from her Hats, Bags & Wraps bag.

"There you are, hardware in the bag, all of it, I don't want any accidents upstairs. It's okay, Tina is here with Jack, they're both packing." Gabrielle held John's hand for two seconds. "I'll be fine," she reassured him.

Gabrielle looked at his face and was sure there was a tear in his eye. Both girls knew John was feeling upset that he was not there to save Paul, at the time, now Gabrielle would have to face George again.

He blamed himself for what Paul had to go through with Ian to save Lynda's life. John often thought about the intense pain Paul must have suffered as both his hands were sliced open by Ian's double-edged sword, trying to stop it entering Lynda's body and then failing to stop it as it entered his stomach. Ian took pleasure in moving it around inside him, damaging other organs until Paul pulled it out of himself, pushed it away from him then leaned against it as he turned around, grabbing the last knife in Ian's Jean belt, holding it in his bleeding right hand then slit Ian's throat and stabbed him in the heart twice in case he survived and tried to decapitate him, then Lynda.

"We have one problem with the evening dresses, Tina, come here please," Gabrielle called as the boys unloaded their guns and deposited them into the bag Sarah was holding, then came their eight-inch throwing knives, two each. Madelline looked in wonder at the amount of hardware they were carrying, but this was not normal times.

George Rainer, Ian's accomplice was back from the dead and sure he was Lynda's husband and wanted her back for his whore and that was not going to happen. Gabrielle was due to fight him at six twenty, the same time he killed George, in London by throwing a knife into his heart and now Gabrielle had to go through it all again, fighting George to the death, this time on top of the Empire State Building, but his men were now in New York and hunting for them.

"You see, Tina is Sabrina's bodyguard, our top model and she carries a Glock and during this time, one eight-inch throwing knife. all our bodyguards are carrying a lot of extra kit in case we get into a fire fight with his men, which we seem to do a lot off, either in France or Rome, so I want her to be able to get to her gun and knife with ease," Gabrielle explained.

"She'll need a couple of extra panels in her dresses, but we have a seamstress who can put those in for you today.

"Thank you," Gabrielle replied. They were there all morning as the women chose their evening and day dresses, three of each then Gabrielle and Lynda picked their dresses for the following evening on the catwalk as did Sabrina and Tina. The boys all needed extra panels put into their jackets for their knives and gun but had two seamstresses working on the suits which with everything else would be delivered to their hotel later that afternoon.

It was the same for the dresses and the extra work for Tina's dresses. Gabrielle would have to return in the morning with John to have her special tight-fitting trouser suit finished with its special alterations. For her four throwing knives and back twin knife ejector.

Gabrielle paid the bill, over sixty thousand dollars and there would be more to pay tomorrow for her trouser suit. They left Imagines' and walked up the road to a jeweller's and watch shop.

Gabrielle wanted to treat her staff and friends, she didn't know if she would be alive in a few days and wanted to lavish them with gifts, so a new top of the range Rolex watches for the men and gold and diamond watches for the girls and a small wrist chain in gold and diamonds for the girls.

They didn't take long making their purchases, but Gabrielle, Lynda and Sabrina needed links taken from their watch straps. She also bought a gold and diamond watch for Shantell with a gold and diamond bracelet. If she is to be the new face of Hats, Bags & Wraps then she would look like a million dollars in every way with a gold fourteen-inch chain and a heart on it with a pair of long drop gold and diamond earrings.

Another hefty bill and they were off, having all the items delivered to their hotel. Next, was a restaurant that Clarice and Jack knew well and had reserved a table for them. They entered the restaurant at one thirty all talking to each other, happy and carefree, looking forward to the evening performance of Cats, at three thirty they left the restaurant.

They looked in a few more stores before returning to their hotel, to change for an evening meal then off to the show. Before Gabrielle and Lynda joined the others for their evening meal and changed, they lay on their bed naked, kissing each other and holding each other close, not knowing how much longer they would have together madly and deeply in love before George possibly killed Gabrielle.

The timing of the fight for her life was at six twenty the exact same time Gabrielle, then Paul entered the bookshop of death, with young, eighteen-year-old boys and girls left dying on the cold, dirty, floor of the bookshop, with severe knife injuries; then Paul had the fight of his life for the new love of his life, the girl he was ordained to save with his life.

He was not afraid as he stepped into the jaws of Death, there was nothing he could do to stop it, it was meant to be, it had to happen to free Lynda from the Hell she had been put through with Ian and George. Save her life and help her repair her body and mind, which was still affected to this day.

Paul would need to change to help her recover with a sex change which he did and now the two girls shared everything, including their bed and sex. Their love for each other was so deep, but Gabrielle knew she would have to face Death once again, it was ordained.

They held each other so close, their green eyes were shining brightly as they spoke together, mind to mind, no secrets, just a passionate love for each other that would last forever, at least that is what they had been promised by Death and Fate a few years ago. But there would be a price to pay, a higher price than they both thought, Death had already taken Gabrielle's soul and was holding it on this side of His black veil.

Paul and Death had many long talks as Paul stood on the narrow shelf Death had made for him when Paul took massive overdoses and was clinically dead for five minutes or longer and his body cold and still as his mother prayed to Death to send his soul back for her son so she could love and help him move onwards to the life he was ordained to live.

Now Gabrielle was vulnerable to the bullets George's men might fire at her and John was still willing to take one or more bullets for her.

Lynda had been crying hard as they kissed and Gabrielle held her in her arms, telling her how much she loved her and she would kill George before she would let him take her back and have her abused and cut up again, even if she had to give her life and soul for her.

Sarah came into their room through the adjoining door to John and Jenny's room.

"Come on girls, into your elegant evening dresses which you paid a fortune for, I'll get your gold hearts ready to put on.

Each gold heart with a sixty-karat diamond in the centre made into a heart, each diamond a slightly different colour. They cost over a million Euros each and Gabrielle bought them to impress Marko Don the leader of the Rome Mafia just because his wife had one similar. For a multi billionaire it was a drop in the ocean and well worth the expense and they had worn them as often as possible because they liked them.

Ten minutes later they were both dressed, with their jewellery on. They helped each other with their makeup as Sarah did their hair.

Five minutes later, Sarah entered John's room and he left through the same door, entering the girl's room. As Sarah entered her room through the other adjoining door Alan was waiting for her. He was also her bodyguard if they were shopping for Gabrielle or Lynda, but Lynda always came first. Alan had taken two bullets for her in the past and protected her with his life.

Tina entered Sabrina's room (AKA) Janet and escorted her to the restaurant. Both girls looked radiant in their long evening dresses, both being over six foot six, their dresses fitted well on their slim bodies.

"Good evening, ladies, you both look very beautiful and sexy tonight, if I didn't know better, I'd take you both for multi billionaires," John said, seeing that Lynda had been crying.

"Looking smart yourself John, I like the bow tie, it makes you look like James Bond, licensed to kill. You are packing, okay?" Gabrielle asked him.

"Thank you for the compliment, the suit is fine although I wish I were wearing my Kevlar suit, I could protect you more. The gun holster is easy to get too, and my two throwing knives come out of the jacket with ease," he explained and drew his gun to show both girls the gun was easy to get to and kill anyone who threatened them.

"You can wear that tomorrow if you prefer, but tonight, I'm sure nothing will happen," Gabrielle said holding Lynda's hand with all her love and affection for her.

Gabrielle touched John's hand briefly as he passed her, she knew he was also hurting inside and being a man trying hard not to show it. He walked down to their door, unlocked it and went outside looking down the landing, he had nods from the other bodyguards.

"Ladies we are ready to go," he said to Gabrielle and Lynda. He stood, with his back to the stairs and elevators and kept his hand holding the door open as the girls passed him. then closed and locked their door. He put their door card in his pocket, they would never need it. John or Alan would always escort them to their room, open the door and check their room for intruders before allowing either of them into their suite. Alan joined John instantly and stood by Lynda, protecting her body from the front and side as Lynda held Gabrielle's hand firmly as John and Alan escorted them with the others to one of the large elevators.

When it arrived two men walked out right into Gabrielle. John's gun was in his hand pointing it at the two men; Alan had his gun out as well as everyone else looked forward. John could see they were not carrying guns and slipped his gun back into its holster.

"Watch where you're going boys and apologise to the lady," he said firmly,

Gabrielle was against his body with his left hand gently guiding her to his side and behind him.

I apologise for not looking where we were going," the taller man said and moved with his friend to the side of the elevator letting John get Gabrielle inside. Alan got Lynda into the elevator next to Gabrielle. Their eyes glowed bright green, illuminating the inside of the elevator as Gabrielle assured her it was a genuine mistake. The others boarded the elevator with eyes watching the two men.

"He's a bit jumpy pulling his gun on us, who does he think he's trying to be, a bodyguard?" the tall man asked Tina.

"He's bodyguard to Gabrielle Grayson and he's licensed to kill. This is our entire floor so get off it please, now!" Tina ordered.

"And who'll make us?" The tall man asked eyeing up Sabrina. He was just about to touch her naked arm when Tina pulled her gun and twisted his arm around his back, making him cry out in pain. Tina was now standing right in front of Sabrina, her gun pushed against the man's head.

"Now leave this floor and don't set foot on it again, there are a number of bodyguards on this floor, and you might get hurt. Her left hand pushed his twisted arm up to his neck making him squirm.

Tina pulled the hammer back on her Glock and pushed it harder into his head.

"If you don't move now, I'll kill you and I'm licensed to kill, the police know who I am and who I protect. Now shift and keep your hands to yourself," Tina ordered.

Both men turned and walked to the stairs, looking back at the tall thin woman who nearly killed him.

"Nice one," John said to Tina, "you alright my love?" he asked his wife.

"Yes fine, Tina looked after me," she replied smiling.

Dinner went without a problem and when they were in the main reception waiting for their car to arrive, the hotel manager walked over to Gabrielle.

"Gabrielle, Lynda, my name is Andrew, the hotel manager. I cannot apologise enough for what happened earlier, I'll have all the lifts locked off for your floor and give John a few keys to pass around to your other bodyguards. Here you are John if you need more just ask. I apologise once again and enjoy your evening." John put the five lift keys in his pocket then handed one to Alan who was stood by Lynda's side, eyes front, then all around.

"Thank you, Andrew, my man sorted it then Tina finished him off," Gabrielle replied smiling. They shook hands and parted with John thanking him for the lift keys.

As the automatic doors opened, John was outside by their limo, looking around and holding the car door open for Gabrielle who was ushered to the car by Alan, then he returned for Lynda, gently putting his hands on her arms and talking calmly to her as she joined her wife in the limo. Alan was in next and sat next to Lynda, his jacket sleeve just touching her naked arm. Soon they were all off to the theatre and inside being shown to their seats.

There were three spare seats at the end of Jack, who was sat next to his wife Clarice. Then their mother arrived with Mike and Penny. Everyone moved up one seat so Brenda could sit between her two daughters as Mike and Penny sat by Jack and Clarice.

They were all excited being in the third row back so they did not need to strain their necks and could easily see the performance of Cats.

The safety curtain went up, the theatre fell silent, and the show started, At the thirty-minute intermission, so people could spend more money in the bar for a quick drink, Brenda took Gabrielle to meet another billionaire who owned a huge multi-story store where he often let some space to other businesses, to help bring in the customers and buy his stock.

Lynda and Sabrina, wanted to take a quick look around the theatre, so Alan and Tina accompanied them. A few minutes later, Brenda was introducing Gabrielle to the store owner.

"Hello Gerald, enjoying the show?" Brenda asked, starting their conversation.

"Hello Brenda, and who do we have here?"

"Gerald, this is my daughter, Gabrielle Grayson she owns Hats, Bags & Wraps. with her wife Lynda Grayson, and they're both multi billionaires."

"It's a pleasure to meet you Gabrielle," he replied shaking her hand. "Your reputation precedes you; you make a killing bringing the customers in with your Hats, Bags & Wraps would you like to open a place in my store? I've seen the crowds you have drawn into Thornton's Mall and your store isn't even open yet."

"That is what we are hoping for helping our fellow store owners bring in the women to buy our wares," Gabrielle replied.

"Here is my card, call my secretary and make an appointment to see me and my floor team and we'll sort you out. Please bring your wife and Clarice and Jack, I know them well."

"Thank you, Gerald, we'll see you very soon," Gabrielle replied as they shook hands again then parted.

Gabrielle smiled at her mother. "Thanks for the introduction mum," she said as they started to return to their seats.

Sabrina and Lynda were enjoying their walk about and decided it was time to return to their seats. As they walked along the wide aisle between levels, a man said good evening to them.

"I'm Robert Chamberlin, I own Chamberlin stores and who are you two beautiful women? Oh, I do like you," he said to Lynda.

"We should be going Lynda," Alan said to her and gently put his hand on her shoulder, he knew this was upsetting her. Robert took no notice of Alan and looked at Lynda.

"How about a drink and you can sit next to me, let your boyfriend go, you'll spend the night with me, and we'll have a great time," he said in an inebriated voice.

"Just step forward Lynda," Alan said quietly into her ear, but she was already back in her past, just with the tone of his voice. Alan knew something was not right, but he had to protect Lynda and he was just getting ready to lift her from the floor and carry her back to her seat when Richard grabbed her naked arm, twisted it and pulled her into the vacant seat next to him. His right hand tried to pat her legs as he mouthed other obnoxious words to her. Alan instantly leaned forward put both his hands through Lynda's shoulders and lifted her out of the seat into his arms, then his gun was out with a silencer on, and he pushed it into Robert's forehead.

"I said leave the lady alone, I'm her bodyguard licensed to kill. So apologise to her."

"I just wanted to have some fun with her, you could watch if you like." He smirked at Lynda then at Alan, Sabrina and Tina. He was arrogant and not listening to a word Alan said to him.

Lynda was returning to her past very quickly and tears were forming in her eyes. Alan was still holding her close to him when there was a bright green flash which filled their side of the theatre then a second flash on the other side and Gabrielle was by Lynda's side taking her into her loving arms, then the theatre was bright green as the girls spoke to each other and Gabrielle started to calm Lynda down with all her love. Alan pistol whipped Richard's head bringing him out of the trance he had been in.

"Owe, what happened?" He asked confused.

Gabrielle, holding her wife close looked at Richard as her eyes turned a very bright green flashing around the theatre. Engineers were thinking there was a short in the cables and Sabrina looked at Tina.

"Hell, she'll roast him alive," she said to Tina who was smiling.

"He deserves it," she replied, and they both laughed.

Gabrielle was looking through his body at his soul, it was ice cold, and Gabrielle knew the only way it could get that cold was if Death was touching it. She concentrated and warmed his soul sending a thought to Death.

"You cannot use other souls against us like this, now he will pay for your actions," she thought then Richard emptied his bladder into his pants and seat, the next moment Gabrielle and Lynda were back in their seats with John and Alan in their seats protecting them. Gabrielle's arm was around her wife's shoulder as Lynda told her what was said and how upset she felt, especially with the fight so close.

As their green eyes darkened, the safety curtain went up with the engineers looking for the major fault in the cables, but they were fine for the moment, and everything was working properly.

At the end of the show, Gabrielle and Lynda kissed their mother goodbye. "Now my love, my daughter, listen carefully to what your wife has to say to you. I'm so sorry this nasty event happened. It was all down to Death, there was nothing you could do to stop it happening," Brenda said calmly to her. They kissed their mother again, then John walked past them and opened the back door of their limo.

Alan escorted Gabrielle to their limo then returned for Lynda as the others opened other doors getting into the limo. Then they were off joining other night-time traffic.

Arriving at their hotel, Alan could see John was angry, the man in the theatre had pushed him closer to the top. He was annoyed another man had managed to get through their protection, even though Alan was doing everything he could to stop him abusing Lynda and touching her. But it was hard to beat Death.

"Right; everyone, silencers on and make sure you have a full twenty clip in your gun. If we see anyone who looks to threaten us or any of the girls kill them," John ordered.

Alan thought, the last time John gave an order like that, they were in Paris. They killed a lot of George's men and had a lot of severe injuries on their side as well.

John was out of the car first, he looked around then Jack got out and went through the automatic doors waving for John to follow him. He then went to the elevators, inserted his key into the control panel and held the lift ready to take them to the tenth floor.

With his gun in his hand, looking everywhere for anyone who might attack them, Jack waved to John, to come to the lift with Gabrielle.

The girl holding the night desk on seeing Jack and John with their guns in their hand, thought their evening did not go well and it seemed true, gun fights did follow them around.

John waved to Alan to bring Lynda to the door. As John escorted Gabrielle into the hotel, he was determined to kill anyone who was against them. He knew he would take every bullet fired against him for Gabrielle while he fired his full twenty round clip into the person or persons shooting at them. He knew he might die, but he was determined that Gabrielle lived.

John called Alan to the elevator and got Gabrielle inside. Then John was outside looking around with his gun ready to fire. Noah was at the front doors, getting everyone else to the doors and straight through to the elevator. Everyone moved as fast as they could. Clarice hoped they were not fired upon now then Jack appeared at her side. At the front doors, they kissed each other before going on to the elevator.

When they were all inside it, Jack turned his key, the doors closed then they were at the tenth floor. Everyone left the elevator and walked quickly to their respective doors and the bodyguards got their charge into the room, after checking it for any intruders.

John opened Gabrielle and Lynda's door then went inside checking their room while Alan stood guard outside with the girls holding each other close behind their door. Soon they were in their room with Sarah following them in. Alan closed the door and locked it from the outside then walked down to his and Sarah's room, checking it out.

Sarah soon had both girls out of their expensive dresses and into their satin short nighties and matching panties. Then they got into bed holding and kissing each other.

When the girls got into bed, Sarah left them alone. Returning to her room she told John to make sure their door was locked and turn off their light. They were talking for a short time, but Lynda was crying, just the feel of his hand on her arm and throwing her into the seat was enough with George in the forefront of her mind, to send her back to the time she was raped every night by him, and she couldn't shift it. The feel of Gabrielle's arms around her back holding her close helped and the feel of her lips kissing hers and the smell of her perfume was really helping; telling her they were girls deeply in love with each other.

John entered their room when they were fast talking mind to mind, and their green eyes were lighting up the room.

"Goodnight girls," is all John said after he had checked their door and turned off their lights. Leaving them alone in the green light of their eyes, he entered his room and got into bed with his wife, and they talked the evening through, and the concerns John was now having about the time Gabrielle would have to face with George. Even John was now thinking what they would do with the bodies, if there was more than one and how to help Gabrielle in the event she was hurt.

"Perhaps we should get or pay for a Paramedic to be there just in case she's hurt," he said to Jenny.

"Yes, that might be a good idea. You love her, don't you?" Jenny asked her husband outright. "It's alright I've known for years. It's hard not to feel something for the person you're protecting. I'm getting used to feeling Tina's hand on my naked arms and sometimes when we've been in a crowd, she will put her arm around my waist and hold me close to her, almost lifting me into the air. You've put up with designers seeing me naked in some of their ridiculous transparent outfits. They and seamstresses have handled my body and I expect that as a top model. You have handled it very well and I don't blame you for loving her.

"You helped Paul struggle through his earlier life, and you got on well together, especially during his change and you've had to deal with his talks with Death and overdoses. Now, with the help of Death Gabrielle is a very-beautiful woman and couldn't be in love with a better woman than Lynda. Their lives were ordained to collide, and they did collide, it's just a shame you were not there or Alan to protect Paul as the fight for her life started.

"Paul could have run off. Walked away from the fight, there would probably be a good chance Lynda would have signed the contract and they may have let her go then Paul could have got Lynda as she walked out of the bookshop and away from him, claiming to have a bad headache after what had happened at the other end. As far as Lynda was concerned Paul would have left her to die, but he didn't and paid the price for it."

"Yes, but had I been there I may have been more forceful than Alan, not that I blame him one bit. There were others in the bookshop dead and dying and he had no idea until the fight was over what was happening at the end of the main aisle. Alan did return order to the police and put himself in charge which was not easy relieving their commanding officer and putting a Sergent in control, getting him to request another senior officer under Alan's authority. Then when he realised the horror inside, Alan organised ambulances. Paramedics, Air support, doctors and nurses with a heart surgeon who could work in the field and fast police cars and motorbikes as many of the boys and girls would need a police escort to the hospital.

"I never blamed Alan, he did what he could and went through Hell with what he saw on the way down to Paul, then got Lynda to stay with Paul, talking to him, keeping him on this side of Death until more help arrived.

"Mike said he was crying all the way to Kings Cross hospital and they sat in his car for half an hour, as Alan went through the dead and injured girls and boys he had seen, when he was with Paul and he blamed himself for not getting to him sooner, but the fight was already over, in the first three minutes and fifty seconds according to Lynda's book manager. Paul had pinned George's hand to the floor, stopping George from cutting the cameraman's hand off.

Paul was about to try and put an end to the fight when the copper interrupted him. Five seconds later the copper was on the floor legless, and five more seconds passed before Paul killed George, a knife through his heart. Two minutes later Paul killed Ian. But had I been there, I would have shot Ian and George and now I would be facing George with a gun in my hand to kill him again."

"My love, that would never have been so, it was ordained for the fight to go ahead as it did. It had to be Paul who would save her life an pay a heavy price for it, so Lynda held his heart in her hands and will never forget it. I bet she loved Paul at that moment for all eternity. Their lives have been planned out by God more than likely, or perhaps before they were born, they planned their lives themselves, just like we did my love."

She held John close to her kissed his lips and the tears falling from his eyes, before she finally calmed him down and kissed away the tears on his face, forgiving him for being in love with Gabrielle. not that it would go anywhere but he wanted to protect her like he would protect Jenny, it was a very platonic relationship.

They made love; still kissing each other, with John knowing their night of romance would not be interrupted.

Gabrielle was still holding Lynda on top of her, as her hands closed around Lynda's back, their lips touching, their tongues touching as Gabrielle whispered to Lynda, she would not let anyone hurt her and she would always protect her with her life, just because she loved Lynda so much.

"I cannot live without you, I love you so very much, my heart and kidney are yours forever," Lynda replied.

They talked for some time before Lynda fell asleep on top of Gabrielle who was also now asleep.

They woke together and were fondling each other in their soft satin nighties then a long passionate kiss before getting into the shower then dressing each other in one of their new everyday dresses. Gabrielle wore a pair of two-inch heels which she felt comfortable in, well enough to fight in, hoping the sight of her would give her an advantage over George's male feelings.

During breakfast Gabrielle spoke with Lynda. "Are you sure you want to join me at Imagines, it may take a couple of hours to redesign my suit and make the alterations. You could join the other girls the time may pass faster. I want an early evening meal as I don't want my stomach too full when I have to do the catwalk and I would like to change Shantell after the show, do you agree?"

"Yes, my love, she replied hardly able to eat her breakfast, but Gabrielle was pushing spoon full's of cereal into her mouth.

"This reminds me of when you used to feed me in hospital and the Shard," Gabrielle said smiling.

"Yes, it does, and I want to be with you no matter how long it takes to get your suit altered. I want to see you in it." They were holding hands and despite the cereal, tears were forming in Lynda's eyes as she understood what the suit was for.

They all got into the stretch limo and were driven to Imagines' store where Gabrielle, Lynda, John and Alan got out and entered the store, as the limo drove off taking everyone else to a different part of New York and a private tour of New York's famous Landmarks.

As soon as they entered the store they were met by Jasmine, the seamstress.

"Good morning, Gabrielle, Lynda, John, Alan, I've picked out a trouser suit as you have suggested in pale pink. It is in Lycra and satin which will bend as your body bends. This is it, what do you think?" she asked holding the trouser suit in the air. The girls looked at it and felt the material.

"This is just what I was looking for, what do you think my love?" Gabrielle asked holding Lynda's hand.

"I love it, will you be able to do the alterations today as John suggests so Gabrielle can get used to wearing it?" Lynda asked.

"Oh yes, my sewing machine is all set up and I have already cut out the strengthening material, I didn't add it in case there are other additions John wanted to add to it. Would you like to try it on?" Jasmine asked.

"Yes of course," Gabrielle replied smiling, holding Lynda's hand.

"I'll make the alterations as we go along," Jasmine replied.

"Let's make a start," Gabrielle said. She took the suit and entered the large changing room with her wife right behind her. Five minutes later they walked out into the bright lights of the showroom where Jasmine worked.

Lynda held Gabrielle's hand and played with the suit getting it to fit properly.

"Just do a couple of turns and bend over for me so I can check the fabric is stretching with you," Jasmine suggested. Gabrielle did as she was told under Jasmine and Lynda's beady eyes.

"That looks fine, do you agree Lynda, John, Alan?"

They agreed and John felt how smooth the material was to Gabrielle's bottom. He took out one of his knives and slipped it up under the bottom of her jacket and let it slip down over her bottom. He tried it a couple of times then looked to Alan.

"Alan I'll have the knife holder and see what it's like on her." Alan handed John the leather knife holder he was taking care off.

John knelt before Gabrielle and fed the black leather belt around her waist and buckled it up. Lynda started to cry, Alan put his arm around her shoulder, holding her as close as she could get to him and started to talk with her to calm her down.

John moved around Gabrielle's back and adjusted the part of the knife holder which would matter the most. He placed a knife into one off the sheaths and pressed the point of the knife, so it slipped out of its sheath, but it stopped as it hit the top of her bottom. Gabrielle was not fat and had a beautiful sexy figure. John tried the knife in the other sheath, and it stopped in the same place. He looked up to Jasmine for help.

"I have just the thing you need Gabrielle. You might have a small bottom, but for this knife thing to happen, you will need to wear a pantie girdle that will hold the top of your bottom in." Jasmine walked to one of the rails of underclothes and picked out a nude colour pantie girdle and handed it to Gabrielle.

"Pop into the changing room and put it on for me please. John you will need to remove the knife belt for her."

"Two minutes later she was in the changing room with Lynda and together, with some laughter, put the garment on. They returned outside, Lynda in a better mood and John put the knife belt around her again and adjusted the height of the knife dispenser. His hand went over her bottom feeling how smooth it was and made sure there were no bumps that would stop the knives. He pulled two knives from his jacket and inserted them into their respective sheaths then watched as they were ejected into his palm ready for throwing. Alan looked at him and nodded with approval.

"Right Gabrielle, can you feel the two knives in their sleeves?" John asked.

"Yes, I can feel them, but I don't want the tips digging into my trousers."

"It's okay, we'll have that sorted. Just touch the tip of the knife and it should slide into your hand ready for throwing. Try your left knife first."

John watched her hand come around the back of her suit jacket and push the tip of the knife up, into its sleeve. The knife then slipped out of its sleeve into her hand.

"Now try with your right hand on the right-side knife for me, I've got the other knife," John said calmly. He had already identified the one problem he discussed with Jasmine the previous day while Gabrielle was buying her dresses. Her right hand came down fast, touched the tip of the knife and it was in her hand ready to throw. John took it from her and stood up.

"Right Jasmine, as I mentioned yesterday, I want a thick panel added to the bottom of the jacket so it will be firm and not flap about. The side panels need to be added with a sleeve in hard enough material to take the weight of the knife but soft material inside so the knife will slide effortlessly out of the pocket. One needs to go here and the other here," he said indicating the places he wanted the sleeves added.

"Can I take a knife with me? just to get its size and weight as I have a few different materials here, don't worry, I'm only over there, I'm not leaving the floor. This will take me about twenty minutes before your next fitting. I'll get Andria to get you all a cappuccino. There are seats and a coffee table behind you.

"Thank you," John, replied for them all and escorted Gabrielle to their seats, as Alan and Lynda followed them. Their drinks arrived a few minutes later as they listened to the sewing machine adding material to Gabrielle's jacket. Gabrielle and Lynda held hands as they drank their cappuccinos, but Lynda was still crying small tears, as the reality of the fight was becoming more real as Gabrielle, the love of her life was having clothes made for her that just might help save her life. Gabrielle finished her drink as did John, but Lynda and Alan were lagging behind. Jasmine came over to them holding the improved jacket in two hands ready for Gabrielle to try on.

"There are still two more very thin and light panels to be sewn on, to cover up this thicker material of the knife sleeves. Now just try it on and we'll see what John thinks of it."

Gabrielle put the jacket on and turned around so John could feel the thickness of the material and see how it looked on her. The first thing he did was insert two knives into their holders and moved the bottom of the jacket about seeing how stiff it was and it did not flap about at his slightest touch.

"That's excellent Gabrielle the left knife first please, then the right, one after the other, I'll catch the knives."

Gabrielle had the knives out and ready to throw in two seconds. Her jacket remined where it was and didn't show the knives being ejected or moved about.

"Excellent Gabrielle," Alan said on seeing her move.

"Well done, Gabrielle, now let's see how fast you can draw the knives from your jacket sides," John insisted and watched how easy she made it look and as also amazingly fast.

"That looks fantastic Gabrielle. Now if I can have your jacket again and John, you said you wanted something added to her waistcoat."

"Yes, this is a piece of Kevlar which I would like sewn in just to cover her chest and bottom of her breasts when the jacket is done up."

"Another quarter of an hour. Would you all like another coffee?"

"Yes please, it will calm our nerves," John said smiling.

"When is this fight supposed to take place?" Jasmine asked as their drinks and biscuits were brought over.

"Next Wednesday around six pm, but don't tell anyone, we don't want the press on hand," John replied.

"Mum's the word," Jasmine said smiling taking Gabrielle's jacket in her hand, was off to her sewing machine.

She returned half an hour later having made she hoped the final alterations in double quick time.

"I had to vandalise another suit jacket to get the matching inside lining of the jacket and it now hides the panel sleeves of the knives. There is also the added thicker and stronger material which will keep the top of her left collar straight and will not bend. Now if you could go through drawing the knives again, we'll see what the jacket looks like. If you re intending to button the jacket up to get to the back knives, button it up now so I can see if the buttons need changing."

Gabrielle buttoned up the jacket and with the knives inserted into their back sleeves, she had them out in seconds, without catching them on her jacket or bottom. It was the same with the side panels.

She removed her jacket, while Jasmine completed the work on her waistcoat. Jasmine brought it over and showed John then put it on Gabrielle, making sure the thicker material fitted properly and protected her where John wanted.

"Are you happy with the suit and does it fit you well? I must say you look terrific in it," Jasmine said.

"Thank you it feels great on," Gabrielle replied.

"I want you to practice drawing those knives."

"I will be assured of that."

"How much do I owe you?" John asked and got his bankcard out to pay Jasmine.

"The suit itself is five thousand dollars, then I had to use another suit jacket, but you do get a spare pair of trousers," she joked. "Then there is the extra material and my time this morning. That will be twelve thousand dollars please." Hands appeared from each person with their bankcard in their hand.

"John, I will not allow you to pay for the suit and alterations," Lynda insisted and pushed her hand forward to pay Jasmine. "Oh Jasmine, you may have helped save my wife's life, take another three thousand for yourself. I'll have a word with your manager on the way out to ensure you get it today," Lynda said.

"Thank you I hope it all goes well for you and I'll be thinking of you on the day. Oh; good luck for tonight, I'll be there watching you."

"We'll see you there," Lynda replied now a little happier seeing her wife in the suit. "Wear it now, it will help you get used to it and everyone else will want to see you in it," Lynda said.

"Here are your dress and spare trousers from the second suit I needed," Jasmine said as Gabrielle took the bag from her and thanked her again as they walked to the main doors. The manageress came over to them as they were about to leave.

"Are you happy with Jasmine's work?" she asked.

"Oh yes. First class and fast thank you, we gave Jasmine a three-thousand-dollar tip on Lynda's bankcard. Could you transfer it to Jasmine's bankcard before she leaves this evening?" Gabrielle asked.

"Of course, she may wish to order something, more like a hat and bag tonight and I'll be joining her, so good luck for tonight, I hope it all goes well for you both."

"Thank you and we'll each be wearing one of your dresses we bought yesterday, we'll be back in again very soon, we have a host of stores to get around and in different States as well," Gabrielle added then the doors opened and there was a cab waiting for them outside, which Alan ordered after the final fitting was tried on.

Soon they joined the others in Welam's Dept store. Gabrielle turned around a few times as the other girls and bodyguards admired her trouser suit and were saying how young and sexy, she looked.

As they were talking, Lynda recalled that on the day, Paul was wearing a tie. She didn't want Gabrielle wearing a tie, but a petite elegant scarf tied around her neck, would give her a little more safety just in case a knife or sword should get close to her throat, the material she had in mind would snag anything, if tied the right way and she had a lot of experience with scarves hiding her neck scars.

"I'm looking for scarfs, anyone any idea on what floor they are on?" Lynda asked aloud.

"That will be the sixth floor, madam, is there anything else I can help you with?" The female assistant asked.

"Oh broaches," Lynda added.

"That will be on the second floor, madam," she informed Lynda.

"Thank you," Lynda replied.

"Good luck for tonight I'll be there watching you both," she added smiling and put her hands together going off to tell her mates she had seen and spoke to Lynda personally.

With Alan, John and Gabrielle in tow, Lynda found exactly what she was looking for and tied the scarf around Gabrielle's neck after paying for it so she could get used to it. Gabrielle was turning in all directions. Testing her trouser suit out. All she would need to do now was add the knives so she could feel the weight of them in her suit and feel the knife holder on her back.

Gabrielle held Lynda's hand wherever they went. Inside she was now getting excited about the evening show and starting to look forward to it.

Clarice took them to a restaurant that she and Jack attended once a month for that extra special meal. As they all looked at what meals were on offer, Clarice looked around at all their close friends.

"Everyone, this meal is on Jack and me, so order whatever you like, Gabrielle, Lynda, keep your bankcard in your purse. It is for us all being friends and for the catwalk this evening. Lynda, I want you advertising one of our Hats and Bags and I have a beautiful wrap to go with your evening dress."

By the time the orders arrived on their large table, it was one pm. They talked through lunch, mainly about the evening show, who the models would be from the local stores, who were all used to being a model now and changing fast to show off a different hat and bag while wearing a different coloured wrap. They all loved the catwalk, and all the boys attended the show, standing close to the catwalk, acting like bouncers in case someone got too close which rarely happened, as some girls were dating the boys, it was a very-close family unit.

They would help clear up after, help pack up all the clothes and hats, which all went into a secure airconditioned van, and would be unpacked the following morning, once again, everyone helping. When everything was put away, they would all go to Gays Bar and restaurant to celebrate the end of a good evening and the orders they had; tonight, they were hoping for a lot of orders.

They talked longer over coffee and got Gabrielle's view of the evening ahead. Clarice wanted to kill more time so ordered cappuccinos for the bodyguards and Irish cream coffees for the girls.

Despite there was only a small amount of alcohol in the coffee's Clarice knew the bodyguards were all alcohol free, except when they were on the yacht or some location where they could relax knowing nobody was after them and they would not be interrupted but then they only had two cans of larger at the most.

Jack was the same, he only had one small glass of champaign at their wedding and he only drank half of that. His job to protect his wife came a long way before a drink, when you had a gun in your hand, you needed to be completely sober without the merest drop of alcohol in your blood, urine or mouth. If you killed someone under the influence of alcohol, it was just not accepted by the police or the bodyguard fraternity. It was three thirty before they left the restaurant and Clarice left them a decent tip. The limo was outside which took them to the venue they would be at that evening allowing Gabrielle, Lynda and Jenny to walk up and down the catwalk and into the dressing room.

On the front wall by the side of the main entrance was a six by ten feet framed photo of Shantell with her name and the New Face of Hats, Bags & Wraps at an angle across the photo which was currently covered with a light-weight canvas and it would be uncovered after Lynda and Gabrielle arrived.

Gabrielle and Lynda walked around the place getting a feel of where the buyers would be and getting used to the smell of perfume and makeup from the previous show, three weeks ago.

There were forty bottles of Gabrielle perfume ready for the boys to give to some of the customers who with the order for hats, bags. and wraps always put in a large order for Gabrielle perfume and now the latest Gabrielle hairspray. There were also four cans of Gabrielle hairspray in the changing area for the girls to use as they positioned their hats and long hair or long hair wigs.

Clarice had brought a list with her, showing the order of the girls who went out first then second and the name of the hat, bag and if applicable, new wrap to show off to their clients. There was a pause before Shantell went out, for Clarice to introduce the New Face of Hats, Bags & Wraps. Then Sabrina would go out followed by another announcement from Clarice to introduce Gabrielle and Lynda. Lynda would start her walk when Gabrielle got to the turning point at the end of the catwalk.

They would show off their hat, bag and wrap. Then Lynda would join Gabrielle at the turning circle. They would hold hands and kiss then return to meet Clarice and do another walk together, kissing again at the end turning circle.

Then all the girls, some in a new dress and wrap, would walk onto the catwalk. They would all curtsey then return to the dressing room and Clarice would close the show, taking any final orders. The girls would then mingle with the buyers including Clarice and hopefully Gabrielle, Lynda and Sabrina, with the very watchful eyes of Tina behind her. Sabrina did not want her legs played with or touched as she walked with the others into the crowd of buyers. It was getting late, or rather close to the time that Clarice hoped would end their afternoon, killing time before the evening event.

They all got into the limo and took a slow drive back to their hotel, where once again Gabrielle went in first followed by Lynda, escorted by John and Alan the other girls and bodyguards, followed them, the bodyguard's eyes constantly scanning the sidewalk and parked cars, looking for anyone suspicious.

Once inside, they all went to the restaurant for a planned light meal for the models, which once consumed with another cappuccino each, they went to their rooms to relax and get ready for the evening and for Gabrielle to get out of her tight-fitting trouser suit, she looked great in it and was walking about as if she was wearing it for a year or more. The extra drinks kept them all hydrated, because under the hot lamps on the catwalk, they could sweat and lose fluids from their body very, fast, the catwalk was a hot place to be, especially when you were constantly moving about showing off your clothes hat and bag in at least four-inch-high heels. It was only a few girls who could walk in six-inch high heels and that included Shantell who managed the high heels with ease.

Sarah walked quickly into their bedroom, catching the girls laying on their bed, arms in arms, kissing each other in their underwear, much happier than they were in the early morning. Their breasts were pressing against each other through their thin bras their panties were also right against each other. But they didn't have time for full sex, that they agreed would come later in the evening after the show.

"Come on you two lovebirds. sex later makeup and dress now," Sarah told them as she walked into their dressing room. By the time Sarah had picked out their long dresses for the event and put them on the bed then got out the dresses they would be wearing to the event and the party after, they had done each other's makeup, concentrating on their eyes, adding more brighter colour just above their eyelids. They brushed each other's hair and put plenty of hairspray on, finally they put their dresses on, new gold and diamond watches and their gold and diamond hearts. The final touch was putting on their perfume and shoes they would wear all evening, Gabrielle would be taking her six-inch heels with her to the event.

With the girls ready to go, Sarah went into Sabrina's room and helped her with her final touches before she put her shoes on and was finally ready to go, Sarah found Sabrina's dress for the show and added it to the girl's dresses on their bed.

Tina needed a little help with her hair and to put on the small hat she was going to wear, and the matching bag clipped over her shoulder and to the side of her dress, just above her waist. Now ready to leave, Sarah helped with her gun belt and small holster then put her gun into her holster and walked out onto the landing, meeting, Brenda, and Penny who were also wearing a small hat so as not to obscure buyers seeing the girls walk up and down the catwalk.

Sarah was an expert at getting herself ready after she had helped everyone else. She had previously picked out the dress she was wearing and quickly put it on, followed by her hat, bag wrap and shoes. Then back into the girl's room, picked up all the evening dresses and out onto the landing leaving John and Alan to ensure all the bedroom doors were shut and locked.

Five minutes later they were all in the limo driving to the theatre where the show would start in forty minutes. It would also be the first time they would meet Shantell, which they were looking forward to.

They first parked at the front doors of the venue for Brenda, Mike, Penny and Alan to get out with Tina, who would be another set of eyes in the gallery. The driver of their limo then reversed around the corner to the side entrance where Gabrielle, Lynda,

Sabrina, John and Sarah got out and walked straight into the dressing room.

Clarice was there to greet them and introduce Shantell, who was looking gorgeous in her long evening dress, large hat and bright eye makeup which looked brilliant on her especially over her eyes.

"Gabrielle, Lynda, Sabrina, this is Shantell, our new face of Hats, Bags & Wraps. I'm sorry about the New Face, but you are not in the US all the time and in another country and soon, you plan to open more shops and expand into Australia. Soon, you'll have to travel all over the world to do catwalk shows," Clarice said as they all shook hands.

"Don't worry about finding a new face. Shantell, you look absolutely gorgeous. You take me back to when I was Paul doing the catwalks under the name of Gabrielle. I was mainly in France at the time, and I liked the name so too did my staff and the buyers who came to see us." Gabrielle said, unable to take her eyes off Shantell.

"I'm so pleased to finally meet you, I must admit, I've been terrified at what you might say about me taking over your job on the catwalk. You have been my inspiration for walking the cat and after I started to get on with three-inch-high heels, I quickly advanced to six-inch-high-heels and wore them all over the weekend, I even walked to work in them and did my sales gimmick for the customers at lunchtime who came in to see me and buy one of the hats I was wearing.

"You my love with your super long legs are utterly fantastic on the catwalk and I have watched you a lot on the way you walk. I watched hours of YouTube seeing both of you Gabrielle and Lynda, I know you're not a model as such, but you are the well-known other half of Gabrielle and buyers love to see you walk up to your wife and that kiss. Are you ready to do the catwalk and hold your wife's hand and your unforgettable kiss tonight? I can't wait to see you both in action," Shantell told them.

"When it's your turn, we're going to watch you if that's alright with you? We can't wait to see you in action," Lynda said. Taking hold of Gabrielle's hand.

"I feel honoured that you want to see me in action, I'll not let you down, I promise," Shantell replied. "Oh, Clarice when are you going to reveal that photo out the front if you want our customers to see it coming in to see us?"

"Oh yes, everyone outside the front for a photo shoot." Everyone followed Clarice through the lower door which took them into the large room where the buyers would be in twenty minutes.

When they were all outside, Collin took photos of Clarice pulling down the paper after she had told the staff officially who Shantell was. Then there were photos of Shantell kissing Gabrielle on her cheek as she officially took over being the New Face of Hat, Bags & Wraps. Lynda kissed Shantell on her cheek to welcome her into their business.

When the girls were back in their changing room, Clarice stood up and talked to everyone. "Right girls, I'll start the show and I want the first four girls ready to enter the catwalk as soon as I come back in, Gabrielle, Lynda, get into your dresses and put your hats on. Jack will make a path for you both so you can see Shantell then escort you both back in here. John, you know what to do in this area, you've been here a hundred times before. Is everybody ready?" she asked smiling and in a cheerful voice. Yeses were heard from the girls and Clarice went out onto the catwalk.

"Welcome ladies and gentlemen to our Hats, Bags and Wraps event tonight. This evening we have a special treat for you all, the new face of Hats, Bags and Wraps Shantell who I'll introduce to you later, you may have seen her photograph on the way in, I couldn't see how you could miss it," Clarice said laughing.

"You all know what our wraps look like which are selling well in our stores and many other stores, by the number of orders we get from you. We will also be opening our new Store in the prime location of Thornton's shopping Mall in two weeks, the actual date will be on our new website and posters will be put up around the Mall.

"We also have a new merchandise office next to our Store. You will be able to pop in and place your order and once the store has opened, we will be starting an on-line service, where independent customers can order one off hats, bags or wraps and they will be sent out in the post so hopefully the customer will get their order the following day. Once again, the opening and start date for on-line orders will be on our website and posters put up around the Mall.

"Last message for you all, you can hand your orders into Teresa down on my right or Nigel by the turning circle. We will endeavour to get your orders completed within the next few days depending on the size of your order. With that said, I think it's time to start the show. May I have the first four models come onto the catwalk please?"

Clarice walked back into the changing room and the first four girls walked onto the catwalk and showed off their hats, bags and wraps they were modelling; they were showing their latest designs of their wrap in four different designs and colours. The next four girls were ready to show their hat in a different colour and a different wrap on each girl with different edges.

The next four girls were ready to do their walk, this time the wraps they were wearing, had shorter sleeves and a coloured fur edge to the front of the wrap, when the first four girls returned, the next four got ready to leave while the first four changed dresses and got ready to walk out again, this time wearing a different hat carrying a different bag and wearing a different wrap. And so, it continued until the girls had shown off three hats, bags and wraps each. As the last girls returned, Shantell was stood by the entrance to the catwalk while Gabrielle and Lynda were escorted by Jack to a place, they would be able to see Shantell on the catwalk do her trick.

Clarice walked onto the front edge of the catwalk with a microphone in her hand. "Ladies and gentlemen, the time has come for me to introduce to you our new face of Hats, Bags & Wraps. So, could I please have a big round of applause for Shantell?"

Clarice stepped back as Shantell walked onto the catwalk to shouts of hurray and applause. then she was off, in a very sexy walk past everyone on her way down to the end of the catwalk in her six-inch high heels getting a lot of the male buyers to get a closer look at her. Some men calling to her to lean over and show her hat off and allow them a better look at her bag.

Shantell bent down to please her audience and slowly stood to more applause, walking off again to the circle where she turned around. Nigel placed a biro just out of the circle, and she slowly knelt, picked up the biro and handed it back to Nigel, then slowly stood without moving her hat or losing her bag.

There was more applause and wolf whistles with shouts of more, more. Shantell walked back down the catwalk to meet Clarice. There was a huge round of applause for her and lots of buyers were placing their orders and handing them into Nigel and Teresa. There were shouts of "More, walk up and down again." Clarice nodded to Shantell, and she was off again, taking a slow sexy walk along the catwalk, turning around and walking back down. She did her walk another two times giving Gabrielle and Lynda time to get back to the changing room and for the buyers to get a better look at her.

"Shantell will be at our new store once it's open and touring all our other stores in New York. Where there is enough interest, she will also be giving ladies tips on how to care for their new hat, bag and wrap.

If there are any problems at all with the wrap, if a popper breaks, simply walk into our new store and one of our girls will repair it while the lady waits and if she needs any alterations done, that can be sorted out as well while she is there all free of charge. We hope to have the store open within the next two weeks."

"Now it gives me great pleasure to introduce a face and pair of legs you haven't seen in a long time, since we first opened our stores in New York, Sabrina who will do two walks on the catwalk today."

Sabrina stepped onto the catwalk and as soon as the men saw her legs there was a huge round of applause. Sabrina took a slow, long legged walk down the catwalk, stopping several times to bend down and show more of her hat, bag and wrap. Some men tried to touch her legs, but Alan, Tina, Mike and Jack calmly stood in their way or moved the buyer's arm away from her with a few polite words. "Please don't handle the merchandise."

She walked to the end, turned around in the circle, knelt and showing off her hat and bag then stood without moving her hat or losing her bag. She returned to Clarice, did a tight turn then walked down the aisle again and back to Clarice with people clapping and cheering her.

More and more orders were placed for the hat, wrap and bag she was showing off to the buyers. As she stepped into the changing room, Gabrielle was standing ready to do her walk and Lynda was standing behind her. Gabrielle would do two walks before Lynda joined her, giving her a little more time to calm her nerves.

Clarice stepped out onto the catwalk and looked around the room. "Sabrina will be showing off more hats, bags and wraps at our next event, while she is still here in the US.

I am now so very, pleased to introduce to you another face you haven't seen in a while. Our first face of Hats, Bags & Wraps, when we first opened here in this great city, I give to you, Gabrielle."

The noise of yeas and yes, and applause was deafening and when she walked out onto the catwalk, looking at everyone and mouthing the words "Thank you" the sound increased as she slowly walked along the catwalk, knelt a few times to show off her hat, bag and wrap, then stood in her six-inch high heels. Everyone loved her. In the circle, she stopped, turned around and watched Nigel place the pen on the catwalk. Gabrielle knelt as if it were just yesterday and had done it before. She picked up the pen, stood, then bent down again and handed it back to Nigel who took it, not believing he was next to Gabrielle. She returned to Clarice, then did another walk, turned, and walked back down the aisle.

Clarice stepped forward again and spoke to the crowd.

"It now gives me great pleasure to introduce the second half off Gabrielle to you, her wife Lynda." There was another huge round of applause and shouts of yes, they wanted to see her with Gabrielle. Hold hands "and we want to see a kiss just like the old days," people shouted.

Lynda, on hearing the words was thrown back to when they put on their first show, and they held hands as they walked to the circle and kissed. It was the ending of the show, and she remembered every second of it which made her heart skip a beat, they had not forgot them.

Gabrielle held out her hand and Lynda took it, stepping out onto the catwalk. Gabrielle, held Lynda's hand all down the aisle, allowing her to kneel twice showing off her new hat, bag and wrap. As soon as she stood, buyers were writing down the numbers of her clothes, hat, bag and wrap and the number of items they wanted to put into their stores, or other stores, they were buying for.

They took a slow leisurely walk down the aisle, held each other close then turned to face the crowd. Finally, their heads moved together and kissed. The shouts of hurray and more were again deafening and as they kissed again, the noise grew louder so they kissed again, as buyers were shouting their names, and filling out more order forms, handing them to Nigel, who they were closer to and those buyers at the far end they handed their orders to Teresa.

The couple walked toward the end of the catwalk holding hands then put their arms around each other and kissed once, twice and a third time. The noise of applause was even louder again, and even more orders were placed. They walked into the dressing room and kissed again, Lynda feeling glad the walk was over with, but very, pleased they were welcomed back with so much enthusiasm.

Sarah helped them change into the dress they arrived in, put their long, elegant dresses into their plastic bags and put it with Sabrina's. John then put them into the trunk of their limo. It took half an hour with everyone helping to clear up after the last of their buyers and customers left, everyone saying they were looking forward to their next show, which was excellent news. With the hats, bags and wraps packed up and in the airconditioned van, Gabrielle and Lynda took Shantell to the back of the changing room.

"We have herd you want a sex change through our charity but how would you like to be a real woman tonight?" Gabrielle asked her.

"That would be brilliant, but how could it be done?" she replied.

"We could change you right here and it will only take seconds, and how would you like to live forever as a woman?" Gabrielle asked her.

"Forever, who lives forever?"

Lynda told her who had been changed and that if she found a partner man or woman, she fell deeply in love with, they would change that person as well.

"Yes, why not?" she replied.

They put their arms around her, thought to each other and their eyes turned bright green lighting up the area they were in. Shantell felt her body change, her breasts growing to a 38C cup and as she smoothed down the front of her dress, her penis was gone, and she could feel her new vagina between her legs. We are now going to remove all your body and face hair except for your head of course. We will also make your arms thinner and your hands petite. As they moved lower over her body, they made her legs thinner and her feet smaller so she would fit into a size 71/2 USA show and high heels. When they looked at her face, they changed it slightly, so it was a more feminine shape.

"Thank you," she said and realised her voice had changed to that of a woman and her hair had grown to halfway down her back.

"This is fantastic," she said trying out her new voice.

"Glad you like it," Lynda replied, and they joined the others who were getting ready to leave and walk down to Gays Bar &

Restaurant. Clarice had put all the orders into her bag, which she gave to Jack for safe keeping.

When they arrived at Gays bar, they ordered soft drinks apart from some of the models who had white or red wine and food. Clarice and Jack sat at their usual quiet table and with a calculator by his side, they went through the orders. Forty minutes later, they told their staff they had done an excellent job this evening and they had orders to the value of four hundred and twenty thousand dollars, the most they had collected at one of their shows.

"Gabrielle, Lynda, Sabrina, please come again, the crowd love you. Shantell, you did an excellent job too and the crowd love you, which Jack and I are very, pleased with what you have done for us," Clarice said.

"Thank you I enjoyed myself I've had a brilliant evening so far and I don' think it could get any better," she replied in her new female voice.

"What's happened to your voice?" Clarice asked.

I've had a sex change; given to me by Gabrielle and Lynda," she replied.

"I see, that's what the bright green lights were for then. I'm really happy for you," Clarice replied smiling at her taking her dainty hand in hers and squeezing it.

"Yes, and I got to live forever like you, Jack and the others," she added.

The next ninety minutes flew by with everyone talking to each other and Shantell telling everyone about her new sex change, new breasts, and long tawny coloured hair. She loved to hear her own voice. Heather moved her chair next to Shantell's and spoke to her.

"Tomorrow, Max will pick you up at eight thirty then you and I are going shopping for some new bras that fit you properly. Some clothes for your day to day use and some dresses in your new size on the company card, for you to walk about in and show off our new hats, bags & wraps. Then I guess you'll start work." She said smiling and put her hand on Shantell's shoulder. "Lucky girl," she added and kissed her cheek.

Jack went over and spoke to her. "Welcome properly to our family Shantell, you look fabulous, I'll have to find a new man to take over from you in the shop. You're far too valuable to be doing that job, we need you out and about telling people where we are and showing off our new hats, bags and wraps you'll be wearing in New York, Manhattan and touring the other States we have stores in, soon I want you to be a household name and we'll have to get you on TV, how about The Ed Sullivan Show? in a TV advert as well?" He asked her, looking into her eyes and her long hair.

"That sounds great," Shantell replied smiling and very happy," Shaking her arms about as she couldn't believe what her future was going to be like.

"It sounds absolutely fantastic Jack, thank you both, very much for putting your faith in me," she replied.

"I'll have your new higher salary and contract ready for you tomorrow. Thank you, Shantell." Jack leaned closer to her and gave her a huge kiss on her lips.

"Just to welcome you as a real woman into our family and make you feel like a real woman, which you are," he kissed her on the lips again and smiled at her. He turned, returning to Clarice and kissed her as well.

"Just welcoming her to our family as a real woman this time. It was the first kiss she had from a man, and I hope made her feel like a real woman. She loves your idea and has agreed to do it, I told her she'll get her new contract tomorrow and the size of pay rise she'll have. Clarice, she'll make us a fortune."

"I'm so glad she has accepted the offer; we'll have to give Heather a new contract and pay rise as well if their travelling a lot together.

"Of course, it will be worth it in the end."

He held Clarice close to him and kissed her passionately, inserting his tongue into her mouth and then playing with her tongue as she put it into Jack's mouth; feeling very much wanted and loved for the rest of their lives. They held hands as they stood up to order food and two more cappuccinos.

The rest of the evening went so fast and by twelve thirty the girls were back at their hotel and in bed together. Lynda seemed much happier than the morning as she kissed Gabrielle, their lips rotating, tongues intertwining, lying next to each other, breasts touching, hands on Gabrielle's back pulling her closer and tighter to Lynda not wanting them to part forever.

It put George out of her mind knowing John had done all he could with Gabrielle's clothes to protect her. Lynda's hands were over Gabrielle's front and moving down her body then two of her fingers were inside her vagina, fondling her clitoris until her vagina walls were wet with pleasure, as their kissing continued with mouths rotating about each other, Gabrielle started to move her hand closer to Lynda's vagina and soon her fingers were playing with Lynda's vagina and clitoris. Then her fingers were inside her vagina, far enough to find her G spot and bring her to an orgasm. They held each other close, whispering to each other how much they loved each other, and they didn't want to be parted after Death had promised them immortality together. They should be seeing how the world progressed together, not losing each other for both knew what George was like.

They fell asleep with Lynda lying on top of Gabrielle, her hands and arms around her back holding her close so she didn't fall off her and felt protected.

When they woke in the morning, they showered together, and Lynda helped Gabrielle dress in her trouser suit with necktie, so she got used to wearing it. And not only that it made her look sexy. Gabrielle helped Lynda into her day dress.

Clarice suggested the previous evening that Gabrielle use the office next to their new store in the Mall to practice her knife throwing with John. For the morning or as long as she needed it. After breakfast, Gabrielle kissed a tearful Lynda goodbye and said they would meet up later.

Gabrielle walked out of the restaurant with John's arm around her back. Brenda burst into tears as the fight was only two days away. Alan tried to comfort Brenda and at the other end of the table, arms were trying to comfort Lynda who was also crying hard.

Gabrielle and John got into a cab and were driven to Thornton's Mall. A short time later they were walking towards the almost completed store and the office next door.

They walked into the office and there in the back room, with the same amount of lighting they had in their previous fight, was a board with a picture of a man made out of black spray paint. Then Gabrielle started, her two drop knives first, the first one hit the heart and drove deep into the wood, a second later the second knife hit the head again going deep into the wood.

"Well at least your throwing arm hasn't changed, and you made the knives go in deeply with ease. Now try your side knives," John ordered. They were ejected just as fast into the hand of an expert thrower. The knife went in deep where the heart would be.

"Hold onto your last knife and let's see how you can protect yourself against this stick which will represent his sword," John said then gently started to prod her chest where she was well protected, and Gabrielle was thrusting her knife to John's body when she could get past the sword. But it proved the sword would once again prove hard to overcome. At one pm they stopped, her arm now aching after a morning's session.

"You did very well and don't forget the actual fight on the day lasted only three minutes, fifty seconds as Alan worked it out, so it may well be the same again," John suggested. "Oh, and if you have to grab hold of his sword, it's not a straight hard sword, it's thin double edged and with all the honing of the sword to get both sides sharp, you might just be able to bend it in half, so keep that in mind," he said as they walked through the main door into the Mall. The men who had been working all morning in the store, were outside clapping their hands together and cheering her.

"Nice throwing Gabrielle, you'll get him. See you tomorrow." They said as Gabrielle and John passed them with his arm around her back. keeping her close to his side, his right hand ready to get hold of his gun and fire it at anyone who looked suspicious or holding a gun at them John knew he would kill, a bullet between the eyes.

They got into their cab and were driven three miles away to where Lynda and the others were having lunch, with Lynda just picking at her food. When she saw Gabrielle, she was on her feet, shouting her name. Then her arms were around her neck, and they were kissing, mouths rotating about each other. John hugged Jenny and Jenny's hands went around his neck, kissing him and holding him close to her with tears in her eyes and tears in John's eyes.

That afternoon they went to a park, walked around for a while then found some seats and started talking about the old days, when Paul first started his business and Brenda filled everyone in on his childhood, a boy trying to grow up as a girl and turn herself into a woman. Then there were the shops and catwalks Paul did as Gabrielle. They ended the afternoon, with a coffee from a local stand before heading back to their hotel.

The same thing happened the following day then Tuesday arrived, the day of the opening of the hospital. Gabrielle arrived for breakfast wearing her suit and carrying her knives, just to get used to them in her suit.

"Gabrielle my love, if you would rather wear your beautiful suit, you don't have to wear a dress to open the hospital," her mother said with tears in her eyes.

"It's alright mother I just want to get the right feel of the suit. There is plenty of time, I'll put my dress on later, it's already laid out on our bed."

Halfway through breakfast a man burst in through the wood and glass panelled door. He had a gun in his hand and many of the women eating their breakfast screamed, this was not something they were expecting and who was the man after?

"Where is the bitch, Gabrielle? stand up so I can see you," the man shouted. Gabrielle stood as too did John, Alan was sat at the far end of their table and already had his gun out. "I have a message for you Bitch. George is on his way He will kill you tomorrow at six twenty and take his wife and whore Lynda with him."

That was enough for Gabrielle. As the man was about to fire his gun Alan fired his, hitting his gun so as he fired at Gabrielle the bullet went high into the air and away from Gabrielle.

As John was about to fire, Gabrielle put her hand in her side pocket. The knife was ejected into her right hand. Then it was in the air, turning end over end and straight through the middle of the man's eyes, standing twenty feet away, he fell to the floor dead, and people were applauding Gabrielle then his body disappeared. Alan retrieved her knife, wiped it in his napkin and walked down to Gabrielle.

"Damn good throwing girl, twenty feet away and straight between his eyes, you're right on Gabrielle, well done," Alan said then hugged her. She put her knife back in her pocket then her mother was in front of her.

"I never knew you could throw so well at a subject so far away. I'm so pleased all the knife throwing and gun practice while you were at university has paid off and you've not forgot it," Brenda said crying.

"Well done my love, another of his men gone," Lynda stood crying, grabbing hold of her neck and their mouths met rotating about each other.

"Thank you for saving my, our lives Gabrielle."

"I told you, I will gladly give my life to protect you," Gabrielle said kissing her lips and tears dry.

"But I don't want you to die or even get injured." She cried and thought back to that day and the state Paul was in before help arrived to sew his body back together. Her hand dropped down to the front of Gabrielle's chest where Mr Muhammed, cut his chest open with a bone saw, then took Paul's heart out of his body and handed it to her, while Paul spoke with Death. She prayed hard, calling out to Death not to take him now, she loved him so deeply.

Mr Muhammed sewed his heart up, stopped the bleeding, and Lynda compressed Paul's heart until it started to beat. Then Mr Muhmmed put his heart back into Paul's chest. Lynda had one more moment with him as two men dressed in green, lifted him onto a stretcher. She kissed his lips and said, "I love you, with all my heart," then he was gone, pushed into a helicopter.

Alan's arms were suddenly around her body lifting her to her feet, then he carried her, running through the death and carnage, past the two dead little girls and onto the pavement by a police car that would take her, his mum, dad and John to Kings Cross Hospital where Paul was being taken to. It all flashed through her mind so fast, then she was looking into Gabrielle's green eyes, and she was back in the restaurant, holding her hand.

"I think it is time for me to change into my dress and put some gold on and you my love are coming with me, John, Alan guns at the ready please."

Each man drew his gun and held it in his right hand as they escorted the girls to their room.

Once inside, Lynda helped Gabrielle out of her suit and hung it up, removing the four knives putting them on their lounge table, with the twin knife holder then helped her into her long cream dress, she was opening the hospital in. finally they put their gold hearts on, diamond watches and returned downstairs to the restaurant where the others were waiting for them. They all got into their stretch limo and drove off to the still unnamed hospital. When they arrived, the front hospital walls were cleaned and there was a name plaque covered over with a ribbon falling to the ground. All they were waiting for now was the photographer and film crew from Channel Six news. The press arrived twenty minutes later, just as the staff and specialist Dr's, came out for the opening. Then all the boys and two girls who wanted a sex change with all their staff, joined the Dr's and staff from the hospital, all wearing their new dresses supplied by Brenda.

"Gabrielle, if you can stand by the ribbon that will open the name of the hospital and stand next to your mother," the TV man shouted, "Lynda, if you would stand next to your wife and hold the bottom of the ribbon.

They got into their positions with the photographer taking plenty of still pictures while the TV crew, filmed the people there.

Brenda put her hand on the ribbon then Gabrielle put hers just above Brenda's with Lynda holding her wife's hand and the bottom of the ribbon, then looked at the TV camera.

"Ladies and Gentlemen, nurses. Doctors. our young boys and girls and everyone else waiting for a sex change. It gives me great pleasure on behalf of my mother, Lynda, my wife and myself to name this hospital; Kings Cross Hospital," Gabrielle said and with her mother and Lynda, pulled hard on the ribbon and the covering over the name plaque fell to the floor.

"We hope with the help of our TG Charity, to change the lives of hundreds of young girls and boys who have been born into the wrong body. Like myself, I too was born into the wrong body and I admit I tried to pay for it with my life several times through my youth and into my teens.

"If it were not for the help of my mother and father, I don't know how I would have got to where I am today," Gabrielle said.

"You are now a lesbian, is that right?" The reporter boldly asked.

"Yes, I am, this is Lynda my wife," Gabrielle replied. "We have been married for ten years, and we have been very happy together. We have helped a lot of people on our way and now we have helped this charity my mother started on my behalf." Gabrielle took Lynda's hand in hers, holding her tight and close to her side.

Seeing the TV man make a kiss with his hand, Gabrielle, gently pulled her wife to her side and they kissed. Everyone applauded them as they joined everyone in the hospital restaurant where a huge cake had been made with dishes of crisps, peanuts then row upon row of sandwiches and other goodies you could eat with your fingers without ruining your clothes.

During the afternoon, they had a full tour of their new hospital and spoke to two surgeons who could do a sex change operation and the nursing staff who would care for them after the operation. There were also two psychiatrists. experienced in sex changes who would help those being changed through the operation and after.

Then they toured their Charity offices, saw Brenda's private office and theirs, when they had the time to pop in. Finally, was the opening and tour of the TG Hotel `They talked with many of the young girls and boys that wanted a sex change and to the four men aged twenty-eight to thirty waiting to be changed. Before Gabrielle and Lynda left the TG Hotel, Gabrielle asked the four older men to join them in a small room for a quick talk. They were in a private room with curtains drawn and John and Alan outside the door ensuring they were not interrupted.

"We would like to offer you all for a voice change, long auburn hair, a female face, and breasts whatever size you want, and we'll give you a sex change here if you're sure that is the way you want to go.

"We would like you then to tell the press of your experience and you would welcome any more slightly older TG's and those in their early twenties to come here and have their operation, before they get to a much older age, and enjoy their lives in the body they want to feel comfortable in, possibly on TV our mother will sort all that out for you. Would you do that for us?" Gabrielle asked.

"Yes, of course Gabrielle, Lynda," they all replied.

"What about the voice change and everything else?" Lynda asked.

"Yes!" they said together.

"Yes, I agree Lynda, Gabrielle replied to Lynda's idea. Lynda and Gabrielle smiling at each other, put their arms around the four of them and thought to each other, their green eyes glowed very bright as the boy's voices were changed to that of a woman, their faces changed shape and their hair was growing fast, down past their shoulders. Then they felt their breasts growing to the size they asked for and their male face, body and leg hair was gone, their legs and arms made thinner with dainty hands.

The boys expected the changes to stop there but they suddenly felt their penis disappear and between their legs was a vagina. Their feet were made dainty and smaller.

"Thank you both thank you so very much they were saying in their new voices and kissed Gabrielle and Lynda on their cheeks as women usually do.

"Now one last thing," Lynda said and put her hand into her bag, pulling out four of her new plastic covered business cards handing them to Gabrielle and thought to her. Then her hand went back into her bag and found the four prepaid store cards, handing them to Gabrielle.

"There is one last thing for you," Gabrielle said handing each woman a business card and store card each. "You can reach us through our new store in the mall for now. The girls there will transfer your call to Lynda's mobile and as you know we are always together so we will both hear you.

"If you find you need anything special or advice, ring us and we'll do everything we can to assist you, day or night, we don't settle down till three or four and we're up at six for those special kisses to start our day off right. The store cards have a three-thousand-dollar limit, already paid to each card," Gabrielle told them.

"Go to Miss Bella's dress and make up store around the corner and she'll help you all she can with clothes suggestions, shoes, and makeup, you'll find we've left a small surprize for you there. Buy yourselves a few outfits each, skirts and tops or dresses. Get some nightwear, silk or satin will keep you warm and it feels sexy on," Lynda said laughing.

"No trousers please, you're a woman now and you have spent too long in male trousers, so please keep to a skirt dresses and blouses, your arms are now thin enough to wear a small size blouse. Please, be the woman you've dreamed of being," Lynda told them.

"Why did you decide to go all the way?" Andrea asked smiling.

"We have something big coming up and we wanted to give you all we could," Lynda replied holding Gabrielle's hand firmly in hers.

"Well, thank you so much, I feel incredible," Andrea replied in her new female voice.

"It's our pleasure," Lynda replied.

"Now, don't forget, it's tights if it's cold out forty or sixty deniers, depending how cold it is," Lynda advised them. "In the store, ask to speak to Gill, she's the manageress and will help you, she will measure you for your bras, dress and blouse sizes. you'll need three or four bras first off and at least fourteen pair of panties. And some bra and pantie sets, we love those on," Lynda said smiling.

"With smaller arms and hands for those thin sleeves come thinner legs and feet so you're more feminine. You are all a size seven US shoe size, I'm sure that's right but Gill will tell you. You can all wear the new clothes you've bought from now on, please don't wear your male clothes, your all women now," Gabrielle said to them.

"I think that's about it I would go to the store tomorrow if I were you. You all need to get a proper fitting bra as soon as possible if you don't want them sagging. We'll arrange for one of the carpenters to buy you each a wardrobe, chest of drawers and a dressing table. There are a couple of very, large rooms on the top floor if you all wanted to share a room. Or have a room each but help each other with your makeup and hair let the carpenter know what rooms you are in and if you'll be needing the larger rooms. That's it." Gabrielle said smiling at them.

"Thank you both so very much," they said together and thank you for the store cards that is very generous of you," Marilyn said for them all. She kissed the girls on their cheeks.

"We had better be going, we have a lot to do tonight and another big day tomorrow," Gabrielle said and taking hold of Lynda's hand they left the room.

When they were in their limo they were taken back to their hotel. Gabrielle didn't really want to eat a cooked meal in case she put a few ounces on where she didn't want them to be. Lynda talked her into having a salad which she helped her eat. Over coffee they remained at their table talking about the old days, the good times when Gabrielle was in Paris walking the streets with Ms Sophia and her staff.

Gabrielle would always be there with John close by as she became wealthier and wealthier. In the first five years of her business opening in the UK and throughout Europe, she became a multimillionaire, and her shops were expanding fast.

With guidance from her parents, she invested wisely with good returns. Her wealth increased without her having to do a thing. Her staff ran the shops, each area had its own accountant. Soon she was known in all the best restaurants, bars and clubs in London, and did a lot of her business at the Shard where Gabrielle took her important European clients for a long lunch hoping they would spend a lot of money even if it were Euros. Gabrielle spoke twelve languages all fluent. She would never expect her clients to speak English, they would talk in their language which gave her more respect than other people trying to break into the French or Spanish shops, with their salespeople only able to speak English.

Gabrielle always dressed the windows of her prime shop in London, which is also where she did a lot of her work collecting young children who had asked for her help through her charity. The boys who had been beaten just because they wanted to wear girl's clothes or had been caught wearing his sister's or mother's clothes and beaten hard for not being a boy. These were the boys and girls Gabrielle wanted to help the most and her legal team had help from Social Services to get the children away from their parents into their care, where they could wear the clothes, they wanted to dress in.

They were got into the nearest girl's or boy's school wearing dresses for the boys and for the girls wanting to be boys' male clothes. Each child saw a child psychiatrist once a fortnight who talked through their love to be the other sex.

There would be a board meeting once a month unless an emergency occurred, and they discussed the case of each child, adult and any new people who needed their help, which could be a talk to their parents to help them understand they were born into the wrong body or a place to stay to go through their transition.

The old times talk went on for three hours, mainly led by Brenda and Jenny who knew what Paul had been through with John.

It helped to pass the time and after more coffee, and more discussions, it was ten thirty and Gabrielle suggested it might be time to turn in, so she was fresh in the morning. Everyone watched Gabrielle and Lynda stand and holding hands left the restaurant with John and Alan by their sides.

John checked their room while Alan waited outside with the girls who when John was happy their room was safe to enter, they walked in.

Lynda helped Gabrielle out of her suit again, placing her knives and knife belt on the coffee table in their lounge. When she was out of her suit and into her satin nightie. Lynda removed Gabrielle's makeup and cleansed her face, checked her nails were okay and her nail varnish blood red, had no chips from it. Then Gabrielle helped Lynda change into her matching nightie removed her makeup and checked her fingernails. Gabrielle wanted them to be as good looking as possible as Lynda stood by her side or close to her.

They got into bed and John turned out their light and said goodnight with a sigh. He was not looking forward to the following day, he did not want to see Gabrielle die, despite all her hard work she had done with her knife throwing. He closed their adjoining door, undressed and got into bed with Jenny.

John and Jenny talked until three then got some sleep. Gabrielle and Lynda held each other close, talking for a while, then kissing each other but no sex, that would be for tomorrow night if Gabrielle lived. They had been kissing for a while when Gabrielle realised something and spoke very quietly to Lynda. She was too frightened to use telepathy in case she was right.

"Lynda, do you remember when Death changed me and gave me this body, Fate and Death made a bet, using us for their test. I think this could well be that test."

"But the test was supposed to be about us taking a man instead of each other in some high-flying restaurant," Lynda replied.

"Think about it, a man is trying to come between us. The man willing to kill one of us to win this bet and will do anything to win no matter what. I don't know which of us will represent Death and which of us Fate, but unless I can kill George who is the man trying to split us up and remember we are also playing for all the souls on Earth.

"By the way, I tried to jump earlier but that power has been taken from me, but Death is holding my soul on this side of his curtain. Let us hope that if I'm killed, my soul will remain on this side of his curtain and be returned to me if you can convince Fate, we need to be together and don't forget there is another entity who will help you. Even if I'm dying before your eyes, listen to her voice from the beyond and do as she tells' you."

They held each other very tight as Lynda realised that two entities from the other side were using them to try and win their bet. Fate would take the Earth and leave them and their chosen ones to live out their lives on Mars while Death would take every soul from Earth to do with as He pleased.

Lynda couldn't stop herself, her hand moved down Gabrielle's front slowly, recalling where all her scars were because Paul decided he loved her and didn't wish to live without her, so he would give his life for her to live. But she brought him back from Death, and the surgeons sewed his body back together.

Now Lynda was recalling all the scars and despite the fight tomorrow. She didn't want Gabrielle to die, without Lynda bringing her to an orgasm. This was something Lynda wanted to do for her wife, as she loved her so much.

To show there was nothing she wouldn't do for her, all she had to do was ask.

Lynda started to kiss Gabrielle as her hand fondled her breasts, making her feel sexually excited. Gabrielle smiled at her, as they continued with Lynda's kiss, their lips rotating about each other and their tongues kissing each other as their emotions shifted into giving their love to each other. Lynda still concentrated on caressing Gabrielle's breasts, then she moved her hand slowly down to Gabrielle's clitoris, rubbing her fingers around the soft sexually stimulating skin.

Lynda then pushed three fingers into Gabrielle's vagina, moving in and out, stimulating her as she moved deeper inside her, still kissing, as Lynda found Gabrielle's G spot. She played with it, feeling Gabrielle's damp walls on the back of her hand. As Lynda pushed her tongue through their soft lips and started to play with Gabrielle's tongue, with her finger's moving in and out of her vagina, Gabrielle breathed deeply and arched her back as she held her wife close to her. Gabrielle was breathing faster and deeper as Lynda's fingers were moving inside her vagina bringing her to an orgasm.

Lynda felt Gabrielle's body arch again and holding her to her body as close as possible. Then Gabrielle had her orgasm, her love juices running like a torrent over Lynda's fingers, which continued to rub her wet fingers into her clitoris; then her hand was around Gabrielle's back holding her close, still in their nighties which was a first for them.

They looked into each other's green eyes which were shining bright as they talked together, mind to mind, telling each other how much they loved the other as their arms increased the power of their hold.

"I love you so much, please don't let him kill you later today. I don't want to lose you. I just couldn't go on by myself. I'd throw myself off the Empire State Building, I can't go under George's care again, I've had my freedom with the woman I love so much, and I have loved our life together, so my love, I'm ordering you not to get hurt or let that man kill you. Don't forget you are protecting me, the love of your life.

"I know you will do your absolute best to stay alive, let's just pray that you do my love. It's late and I hope you enjoyed me making love to you."

"Yes, Lynda I did, and I'll do my absolute best to protect you from George and stay alive, so he doesn't take you away from me. Now, slide over onto me and let me hold you tight." Lynda slithered over Gabrielle's body, and she felt Gabrielle's arms holding her tight and close to her body, as Paul did on the morning, they bumped into each other and Paul hit her off her feet into the air, onto the front of his body, then they fell to the snow-covered icy pavement.

They kissed each other goodnight and Lynda closed her eyes, praying to Death to let Gabrielle live, no matter what happened during their fight, please do not take the love of my life who has helped me get over all the horrendous things that George did to me. Lynda fell asleep, and her body relaxed into Gabrielle's arms which closed around her back, holding her safe.

At breakfast, neither girl wanted to eat but Brenda told them they had to eat something to keep them going throughout the day and they would devour a cake each later in the day at their new shop.

Lynda buttered a piece of toast and covered it in strawberry jam before cutting it up into small pieces. Gabrielle looked at the toast and sighed before taking a piece and putting it onto her plate. She buttered it and spread raspberry jam all over it, looking into Lynda's eyes at the same time they smiled to each other. Gabrielle cut the toast up as Lynda had done then they swapped plates and started to feed each other.

They were laughing at each other as they repeated what they had done before, getting food inside of them to get through the morning with the opening of their latest store in Thornton's Shopping Mall. They talked again over another coffee until nine fifty when everyone stood and walked out to their stretch limo. When they arrived at their store, there was already a large number of women waiting for the store to open. Shantell was outside talking to the women, telling them how to store and take care of their new hat and bag.

Brenda showed Gabrielle and Lynda into their store. Everyone had worked hard getting the store finished and all the hats, bags and wraps on display.

Clarice came out of their office and greeted the girls who had helped them so much. She picked up the new plastic covered introduction cards handing twenty cards to Lynda who slipped them into her bag. Clarice gave Brenda the same number of cards then she gave twenty cards to Gabrielle.

"Do you think you should give them to me now, I might not get through the fight?"

Lynda burst into tears on hearing her words, did she think George would be too powerful for her?

"Gabrielle, I have every faith in you, I'm sure you'll get through the fight and kill George. You love Lynda too much to leave her now, she'll die without you beside her side, holding her close, making love to each other. You hold hands and kiss each other in the stores and sidewalks. Everyone knows you two are deeply in love with each other, surely Death could not split you up?" Clarice asked no one, tears falling down her face.

Clarice grabbed Lynda holding her around her neck, kissing her cheeks and Lynda kissed Clarice's cheeks, comforting each other leaving Gabrielle to look closer at her business cards. Before her name was the word Director, this word should not be there. When Lynda and Clarice parted Gabrielle looked at Clarice then her wife.

"Lynda, take one of your business cards from your bag and look at it," Gabrielle said smiling at her.

Reading through the card, she looked at Gabrielle then Clarice.

"Clarice, we gave you Hats, Bags & Wraps USA as a Parent Company so You and Jack could take it in any direction you liked and expand your USA Company into other States," Lynda said and took hold of Gabrielle's hand after putting the card back into her bag.

"Lynda, Gabrielle, we still need your guidance and help getting into some States. So, ask your mother what is on her mind, it was her idea, we just went along with it."

"Gabrielle, Lynda, Clarice and Jack still need your help and guidance after all, your names go before you, so too the company you represent. Help Jack and Clarice to become like you two.

"We need to take this company into the next century. If you continue to expand your company further down to Nigeria, South Africa, you'll be doing catwalk shows all over the world. The people you put in charge of your business in other countries will also need your help and guidance, so help Clarice and Jack as they expand," Brenda said to them placing her arms around their shoulders, pulling them into her so she could kiss each girl on their cheek.

"Okay mum," Gabrielle finally said, glancing outside. "I think we had better get this store open before Shantell is squashed," Gabrielle said.

Everyone looked through the window at the size of the crowd outside and hurried out through the door to meet Shantell. There was a huge shout of hurray's and clapping on seeing Gabrielle and Lynda.

The TV crew were there recording the size of the crowd and the front of the store and office. Collin was also there with his large Nikon digital camera, taking still pictures that could be put up in all their New York stores, for people to look at and see if they could see themselves on the enlarged still photo. It was another way of getting people into their stores, another idea which her mother had come up with, after seeing Gabrielle and Lynda use it in one of their Italian shops.

Clarice with Jack by her side holding her hand, got the crowd of women to quieten down so they could hear her.

Gabrielle and Lynda stood to the side of Shantell as Benda stood by Clarice and Jack. Mike and Penny were stood at the far end of the shop, Mike looking around for anyone who might have a gun or started to run through the crowd at Brenda.

"Ladies, and a few gentlemen," Shantell said through her microphone so everyone could hear her. "As the New Face of Hats, Bags & Wraps, I have been asked to open our latest store in New York. There will be other shops as we find good places to put them. Besides this new store, we have put our new office for a while, where you can pop in and order any hat, bag or wrap and take it away with you. This is also where we will repair any of our wraps or carry out alterations on them free of charge while the customer takes a comfortable seat with a cappuccino and cake.

"We also have a new on-line ordering system, with the places of all our stores in New York and other cities we have already opened stores in the USA. Yes Ladies, we are expanding deeper into your country. We hope our new offices in the tall glass building on thirty fourth street will be ready for us in the next six months, we have the top two floors, it will have to be an exceptionally long ribbon to remove the covering of our name on a new piece of glass." People were laughing at her, knowing how high the building was.

"Now, the time has come for me to open our latest store in this luxurious shopping Mall," Shantell said taking hold of the ribbon. "I hereby name this store Hats Bags & Wraps I hope you enjoy shopping here." Shantell pulled the red ribbon and the cover over the nameplate of the Store fell to the floor. Everyone applauded as the covering ribbon fell to the floor revealing the red and cream nameplate, the name of the store in gold writing in the centre of the plaque and their motto on the right side of the sign.

The door opened and the closest women to it pushed themselves into the store to see what it was like; their hats wraps and bags on show for people to buy, Colin took a picture of the first woman into the new store and handed her his business card if she wanted a colour picture of herself entering the store. Then he was by the tills, ready to take a picture of the first woman to pay for a new hat, bag or wrap and now on sale, copies of

Shantell's dresses she was wearing on the catwalk and around New York.

Gabrielle and Lynda were talking to people telling them all about the new online service and Hats, Bags & Wraps in general. Posing for pictures on a camera phone and of course, their kiss which inspired others to kiss in public and show their love for their husband or wife. They shook women's hands, and kissed some women on the cheek, posing for a camera photo and finally they kissed together for the camera.

They watched the women enter the shop and they were pleased, it was going so well, Gabrielle and Lynda were also enjoying it, as they popped into the new office to the back and started to kiss each other with passion and all the love they had for each other, letting the two entities know, they loved each other deeply and did not wish to be parted.

Lynda was holding her breath, praying she would be able to lay on her wife's body and sleep there as she usually did that night. They looked around the office and after another kiss, holding hands, slowly walked out of the office into the crowd of women, who seemed to be moving in and out of the store wearing their new hat, bag and their new wrap, moving their head around showing off their new hat to the women waiting outside the store.

"I like the look of your hat and bag, do they still have that design?" a woman was asking.

"Ladies, if I can have your attention for a few moments, I can promise you all, there will still be all the hats, bags & wraps, in the store now as there were this morning, John said borrowing the microphone Shantell used a little earlier.

John called Jack over to him. "Jack our two prime girls look as if they are ready to mingle deeper into the crowd and might walk off on us. Can you get two people to take our place watching the women and younger girls in their early twenties coming in and out of the store, so we do not have too many people in our store at a time?" John asked.

"I think Shantell has her eyes on Andrew, just like you wanted. We can only hope they will fall in love together," Jack replied laughing.

"I'll get Clarice out here and send Shantell over to you. She'll be able to get closer to him and even talk to him at times," Jack said smiling, thinking back to what John asked him to do.

John and Alan finally got up and joined Gabrielle and Lynda, with Shantell taking her seat and looking at Andrew, with

Clarice watching the crowd going in and out of their major new store.

Every soul on Earth. including the love of her life, she would she knew, be paying an extremely high price today Gabrielle thought to herself, taking hold of Lynda's hand.

After their relaxing coffee they went for one last walk about and talked their last half an hour away before they eventually said farewell to Clarice, Jack and Shantell. Everyone was crying as they hugged each other, wishing Gabrielle all the luck in the world.

They left the store and took a relaxing slow walk to the exit before they left the Mall and got into their limo. It was now five thirty as they set off for the Empire State Building. As Gabrielle and Lynda hugged each other and kissed, Gabrielle was glad they had made their close friends and all the bodyguards with their wives and Tina and Noah able to live forever. Gabrielle prayed Death would spare their souls and He would not take them for His pleasure.

They arrived at the Empire State Building at five fifty, the time Paul left his shop on that day. They entered the Empire State Building to see long queues of people wanting to go to the top to see the unusual sunset with the hot weather. The other elevators on their side suddenly stopped working, the doors opened, allowing the people to get out of the elevators, as they were packed in tight, by the people behind, who also wanted to get to the top.

Women at the very back who entered the elevator first were screaming to give them some space so they could breathe, as some men were lifting their wife or daughter in the air and placing them onto their shoulders so they could breathe and give a little more room at the back. The men by the doors were hammering on them and shouting to be let out and could someone call the fire brigade to come and cut open the doors as the elevator started to fill with carbon dioxide. If they couldn't get out within the next fifteen minutes, they would all die.

The people behind the man talking to the men at the front, started to quietly tell the people behind them and those at the very back what was going to happen to them very soon. Everyone looked at the roof, it was not far from them, just how much oxygen would this elevator hold? The people at the back who were being crushed by the people at the front got to hear the latest news about their situation. Everyone was now panicking, the women screaming "Let us out. Help us please!" The men by the doors were hitting them hard with their fists or palms of their hands. The man near the controls was pressing all the buttons and held down the "Elevator help" button.

Eventually a woman answered. "Hello, can you tell me what the problem is please?" She could hear women and men screaming for help in the background so she pressed the button that would bring an experienced engineer to her phone. He was there in a few minutes. The man near the front tried to tell the engineer their problem and how long he guessed they had left before carbon dioxide filled the lift and killed the forty people crushed inside. The engineer said he would get them help and called the fire brigade.

The six women at the very back who were screaming help and to be let out, were breathing quickly, taking in gulps of air and quickly breathing out carbon dioxide, then the air got thinner and when they tried to breathe, there was no oxygen there to take in. They panicked and the panic spread to other women in the elevator. They too started to scream as they realised there was not so much oxygen there for them now.

The women at the back had passed out, their bodies being held up by those behind them, Then the people in the row behind passed out and their bodies slipped to the floor unconscious, suffocating as they slept.

Gabrielle looked at Lynda as they listened to what was happening in the elevator next to the elevator they would soon be using.

"I've had a thought," Gabrielle whispered to Lynda. "The way the people are dying inside the elevator, could represent the young boys and girls who were killed or left dying in the bookstore by George and Ian. I think George has just arrived and is walking about down here as he waits for his time to go to the top."

"Yes my love, I think you're right. I love you with all my heart, I never want you to leave me," Gabrielle said and kissed Lynda's soft lips.

Gabrielle smiled at her wife as she thought of something a silent and frightening thought. *Would this be the last sunset their souls would see and take with it for all eternity?* She held Lynda's hand with all the love in her heart, praying she would survive, but knowing deep inside. Death had other ideas. He wanted to win. They had forgot about the queues for the elevators but at six fifteen, the time Paul was halfway along the bookshop with two hardback books of *The Wife Beater*, he had just paid for, for Lynda, the love of his life to sign for him.

George and Ian had just finished killing the last two girls. They cleaned up their knives and sword, removing the blood from them so nobody would realise what they had done, what horror was behind them. Paul, back then, now Gabrielle, thought how he would take Lynda to the Shard for an A-La Cart meal, holding hands in the back of his car as John drove them to a wonderland of food and luxury.

Paul knew he would kiss her and never stop kissing her. They would be married and tour the world together, hand in hand visiting his shops as their empire expanded. All these thoughts planning their future together as he stood in the queue to have his books signed. Soon he would see Lynda, sat at her table, happy, smiling, her heart already full of love for him and praying hard Paul would turn up and save her life as it was foretold to her by Death.

Lynda was looking down the short queue then their green eyes met and passed all the love they felt for each other between them. Her heart skipped a beat, she held her breath. The man she had literally bumped into just seven hours ago and instantly fell deeply in love with, was here and she knew she would marry him even if he was poor. They would live off her book money in a small cosy flat deeply in love for the rest of their lives as they talked about her books planning the next Blockbuster.

Then the elevator doors opened at the exact moment, Gabrielle looked into Lynda's green eyes, and they passed all the love they felt for each other between them.

As the other lift doors opened, people further down left their elevator, not realising what had happened. As the doors opened on the elevator of death, the people at the front, now dead fell to the floor before everyone.

Gabrielle's group entered their elevator with George entering his elevator taking him to the fight for all humanity which they would never know about until the second it was all over, and the decision had been made who won.

Chapter 9

They stepped into the express elevator going straight to the top of the building, where they felt disorientated for a moment. The doors opened, and everyone set foot on the concourse that would take them to the side of the building overlooking New York. The elevator doors closed behind them with a loud noise, making everyone wonder if they would ever see the ground again.

Gabrielle held Lynda's hand with all her love as. Alan and John escorted them around the side of the building. They heard the elevator doors close as voices approached them.

"It's alright my love, I promise I'll protect you with my life, listen to the voices, do as they say," Gabrielle said to her. They kissed, possibly for the last time.

Gabrielle stood still in the fast-setting sun, looking at the far side of the building holding Lynda's hand tightly. George appeared with one man holding a gun. Alan drew his gun, but as John tried to do the same, he found his gun would not stay in his hand and now he wished he would not have hung around seeing the boy was settled into his room. Tears filled his eyes and ran down his face as they had happened to Alan on the day. Had he not done so, he would have been there to kill George and Ian himself. George and Gabrielle faced each other, George smiling, seeing Lynda by her side holding her hand.

"At last, he bellowed. "I'm afraid you'll have to let go of her hand, although you two lesbians look good enough to fuck all day and all night. Gabrielle, you have so nice lips, good enough to kiss for hours and I bet the inside of your mouth tastes simply great too," George started shouting with a wide grin on his face looking Gabrielle and Lynda over, imagining what he could do with them right now.

"He's playing with you Gabrielle, don't take it in or get upset over what he says. Concentrate on the job you have to do," Lynda whispered to her.

"Gabrielle, you took my wife and I want her back. Even if she's a lesbian now. It makes no difference for the plans I have for her. Once again, she will be my whore and I'll have punters queuing up to see her naked, fuck her, kiss her then as some men like, carve her tits up and her torso. This time my love, I'll not allow anyone to cut your face or neck, it put a lot of men off you last time, so it'll not happen again.

"Come to me now my love and this can be all over. Gabrielle can go off with her tail between her fanny and forget you.

"I'll give you a week to get used to your new accommodation and dirty bed.

"I'm afraid I had to get other girls to take your place while you've been gone, and a few men went too far and some of the girls bled out and died on the bed. I had to get rid of their bodies in the usual quarry, you know the one. The rubbish dump with its water at the bottom. There must be more than twenty bodies down there now, rotting under the water; I'm warning you now Lynda, stop playing up.

"I'll have you tied to the bed so my paying customers can fuck your min for a few hours then beat you up as usual and use their Stanley knife on your breasts, they are not allowed to cut your nipples off, or cut the top of your breasts, just the underside.

"They will not be allowed to kick you in the head as some men did before, but hard punching and using a knuckle duster is allowed. New rules for my new girl; Lynda. You will enjoy every second of your new life, or I'll personally rape you every day of your life, before I'm finished with you it will be you who bleeds out then you'll join the others in the quarry for your body to rot under the water and guess what?

"No, you'll never get it, I might not let you bleed right out, I did it with another girl last year. She almost bled right out and six months earlier I added ten Parana fish into the quarry pool and when I tossed the girl into the water, she screamed like, a good un as the fish bit her to the bone. We all had a bet on how long she would stay alive, three minutes fifty seconds of hell. I think with your kicking and splashing, you might last a few seconds more. How does that sound my dear wife? better than all that punching? Just imagine as the fish nibble at your tits, where you'll also be bleeding from

"Don't forget my love you'll also have to service me every night, a good long blow, job with you swallowing all my come, and if you don't, it'll be my fingers in your mouth pushing it down your throat and don't forget how sharp my fingernails can get as they scratch the inside of your mouth making it bleed. Do you recall it?" he asked Lynda grinning. Lynda fought back the tears and held onto Gabrielle's hand as tight as she could.

"You'll end up swallowing my come and your blood with no water to wash it down with.

"But each night around ten thirty, I'll give you half a bottle of vodka to drink straight, so it helps you forget all the nasty things that have happened to you through the day. When It's gone it's gone but if some bloke brings in a couple of lines of cocaine, you'll have one of those, like it or not it'll blow your mind away and if you don't cooperate, then it'll be crack cocaine as well.

"You'll soon be hooked on it so bad you'll do anything and everything, enjoy being sliced open tits down to your cunt, then the left side of your belly to your right, just as if you were having a baby cut out of you, only the bloke's hands will be dirty with grime from work and when they push their hands into your open stomach and swish around your blood, you'll be infected with some shit and I don't have any penicillin, you'll have to be fucked again and again to earn the money to buy that.

"How is it sounding so far Gabrielle? This is what she went through before you took her from me. She's damaged goods, very damaged, let her go to return to the only life she knows."

Gabrielle squeezed Lynda's hand recalling the talk and shouting which came before the fight and pulled her hand to her side.

"If she decides to come with me now and you walk away from my wife, not your wife, mine is that understood?" George shouted at them.

Behind them Brenda and Jenny who had also been in the car with John, as they wanted a young woman to be with the boy and talk to him from his home in Newcastle down to London, were crying their eyes out, and only managed to shout.

"You're a monster, how can you do that to any woman let alone Lynda who has managed with Gabrielle's help to forget her ugly past? I could hardly believe what she was telling me of her past life, it brought tears to my eyes then and again now. I feel sick in my stomach I hope Gabrielle kills you," Brenda shouted back, but her voice went unheard in the fight ring, only in George's ears.

"Oh there's more to come, because if Lynda comes to me now, she saves Gabrielle's life now but before she leaves, she'll be tagged so I know where she is at all times; she won't be able to get the tag out, it will be deep inside her stomach, don't worry, my man here will hold you down while it's done, then you'll be free to go for a year, then you'll join your lesbian lover and you'll both make love to each other and fuck each other with a dirty dido.

"I have herd Gabrielle used to cut herself, well, my paying guests will pay a lot of good money to see you cut yourself so deep into your arms they burst open with blood. I'll allow your lesbian friend to watch you then she can start helping you while she's under the influence of some mighty strong drugs she would have been fucked hard for.

"How about you Gabrielle, do you like being fucked? Or are you a virgin where men are concerned? You might be silent and holding hands now, for that's how you'll both die holding hands as you walk into my fishpond, bleeding out through your legs.

"Gabrielle, you might think you'll kill me, but you can't, you're a woman and I'm a man, much stronger and heavier than you. Tell Lynda to join me, then my dear, you'll have a year to yourself, before I come and get you and you can join her I promise you both a week together to share your love for each other, but by then she'll not be looking in good shape, especially with two black eyes, that I'll give her myself before you arrive and I'll scratch the inside of her mouth so it hurts her to kiss you, you'll be able to hold her but not her hands as I'll break all her fingers, both hands, before you arrive but you'll be able to comfort her with words and false promises of you'll kill me, because right now all you have are two knives in your back to my six in my back

"Gabrielle didn't need to check her knives she could feel them with the weight in her jacket. She knew she was told she could have them. George had six knives on him and his double-edged sword.

"You'll have to take Lynda's place once your week is over with, you'll not have much time with her as you'll be working all day with my clients and after your Vodka and drug rush, you'll be working until two in the morning, then and only then will you see her as the days march closer to your joint deaths in my fishpond.

"Don't worry, I'll add a few more fish so it's more interesting. I don't think you'll last six months until you start cutting yourself so deep and so fast, you'll almost bleed out, you'll even beg Lynda to join you and you'll do the cutting for her, just because you say she's your wife not mine.

"But I know who I am, and I'm Lynda's husband, Ian was my mate who used to come in and fuck her every night, because he killed his whore wife and her parents because she tried to go to the police. Now their bodies have been consumed by my fish. I know who I am and Lynda, you are my wife," he shouted at her,

"Now bloody well join me and let your lesbian lover have a year to herself before I give her back to you. Once your fingers, mouth eyes and ribs have mended you can do what you like together and I'll record you and put you both on You Tube, hey that's a great idea.

"I'll add some adverts and get paid while you two fuck each other, how about that?" he said laughing.

He tried to step forward so he could grab Lynda's arm and pull her to his side, then he could hold her and threaten to kill her if Gabrielle did not walk away, but as he tried again to move his foot, he found he couldn't move it.

"Hey what's going on here? Have you put glue on the floor?" George demanded to know.

"Well Lynda, I guess all you have to say is I'll come with you, hold out your hand and we'll be free to leave, all of us. What do you say? Tell me why you won't join your husband and live the life I expect of a whore, and Lynda, you are a genuinely nice whore at that.

"Join me, your husband, let your lesbian friend go for a year then you'll love her all the more and make better films for me to earn money from. Please Lynda either tell me why you can't be with your husband who only wants to give you a very well-paid job, but you'll never see any of the money. Come on, let Gabrielle have a life at least for a year, let her go, there is no need for us to fight over her if you'll join me now. What do you say?" he asked Lynda.

She felt Gabrielle squeeze her hand again and hold it to her side. Gabrielle looked at Lynda and moved her eyes a little indicating to stay silent. She realised the more time he asked them questions or begged Lynda to join him, there was more fear in his voice and concern that he may end up having to fight Gabrielle and although she's a woman, he was not looking forward to fighting her himself.

He had hoped all his men would have found them, bringing them back to him where he had command of the situation. Now he brought his last man to try and take his place, but would that be allowed? Gabrielle wasn't sure now who she would be fighting, but it was looking like George was not interested in fighting her so he would go for the kill. fast and hard with his sword.

This had already taken up so much time, more time than he argued for Ian that day, but all this talking and begging had made him nervous. Lynda just looked at him, holding Gabrielle's hand calmly in hers', she knew all this talking had to end soon, she had also picked up that he was getting scared he just might have to fight Gabrielle and her eyes fell on the top of his sword which he would use against her first.

"Please Lynda, I don't want to have to kill Gabrielle, she should live and allow me to earn money from her. Okay, she'll get beaten up a lot, cut a lot, bleed a lot but you'll have each other for four hours a night once you have cleaned her up and she has cleaned you up, perhaps less, but that is life it is what you make of it, and I want to make money from the pair of you so join me knowing, Gabrielle goes free for now, then you can love each other again, if you're still alive and of course, the same goes for Gabrielle, as I put her name on the open market for a long glorious fuck.

"The clients. man or woman will pay for your GPS position and then they will find you. If you move away, they will have to pay me again for your new GPS position. Does that sound fair enough Gabrielle? You have to make money for me during your year of freedom, you'll be my running whore," he said loudly to himself, laughing loudly.

"Come on Gabrielle, take the offer I'm making you. It's a damn-good offer, Lynda comes with me for a year, twelve short months, three hundred and sixty-five days, it's not long, it'll pass in no time. Gabrielle, do you really want to fight me again? After all I have a double-edged sword and you didn't like it last time, it cut your hands to shreds and made a right mess of your stomach, kidneys and it touched your heart I was told.

"Then there were all the young kids we knifed and sometimes put our sword through their back and out their front then we knifed them to make sure they were either dead or left for dead. It was not me who killed those two little girls, that was Ian. had I seen them first I would have tossed them out of the bookshop onto the pavement.

"Okay so their mother was dead, they still had a grieving father who wouldn't be grieving as much, and he would with just his wife dead. He would help us get off with his words of mercy because we didn't kill his girls. He could find another wife, marry her and let her bring up his kids. But we made a mess in there, blood everywhere and in the office, that girl with her nice tits, I had no option, but slice them off her body while she was still alive.

"She screamed but I put my blood covered hand, with her blood mind you, over her mouth. The manager, it was fun cutting off his prick and balls, we made him into a woman, and it was me who gave him a free vagina, then I put the dead girls' tits I cut off onto his chest, so he had a full sex change in less than four minutes.

"The woman manageress, was awesome, I pushed my sword straight through her heart, and did you see the way I cut off that copper's leg? One swish of my sword and he was legless, and fell to the floor looking at the bottom half of his leg as I ordered Ian to decapitate him but you Gabrielle, got in his way and you killed him, leaving me and my wife facing each other and I was so mad she was so close to death before you Gabrielle, jumped in, thinking you loved her more than I hated her and saved her fucking life by killing me, her husband, but now I'm back through your Second Chance and I want my whore of a wife back to do with as I please. Not how you please, but I will be pleased to take you under my wing.

"Do you mind letting her feel your tits, because as your dying, I'll cut them off while you're still breathing if you don't persuade my wife to join me."

"Look I don't want to fight you and I bet you don't want to fight me I would shake your hand on it if I could. Just agree to let her go; walk away from her. She'd be no use to you; you couldn't make the kind of money I can make from her.

"All you two want to do is hold hands like you're joined at the hip; do you think I could get a surgeon to sew the both of you together at the hip to help me? My customers would go wild over you both and I'd make you both stars on You Tube, I'd rake in a fortune and be a self-made millionaire in two weeks and I want to make all this money myself, not given to me on a silver platter.

"So, what do you think Gabrielle, have we got a deal? Just tell her you want to have a year away from her and send her back to me where she belongs. There will be no need to fight each other we can walk out of here free men, well you're now a woman and a good-looking chick as well. Really fuckable in an instant, why I'm getting a fucking hard on just thinking about you. What do you say Gabrielle, have we time for a quick fuck?

"I'm nice and hard now, ready to fill your vagina with my come, then Lynda could lick you out, get you to have an orgasm and she can lick both our juices out and swallow them. Now that would be sexy, our first of many fucks together while Lynda watches us, to make her jealous, well, that's the plan, come on Lynda reach out to me and I'll give you two weeks to get used to our place before you start work.

"Gabrielle, I'll make my deal sweeter, I'll go halves on what I make from Lynda which will buy you your first month's supply of crack cocaine, and at least ten half bottles of vodka to help you through the night. Come on Gabrielle, help me out here, I want Lynda, I also now want you. We don't need to fight, bloody knives and swords.

"It was Ian's idea to wear them all and I felt a right idiot with everyone staring and pointing at us as we walked up the road to the bookshop. Well, that is until we got inside and saw all those young girls and boys, ripe for killing. Then I lost it for a few minutes of my first kills, but all that blood made it all the better and like Ian, I started to use my sword on the boys and girls, I knifed the boys four times, trying for their spleen, that really pumps out the blood. It was easy to get at with their height, they didn't know the knife had entered their body before it was twisted, out again and with me holding them around their neck, I stabbed them in their chest, twice, sometimes missing their heart, other times stabbing it.

"I'll tell you what it took it out of me, killing all those kids. It was hard work, good work and we made names for ourselves; that will stay in people's minds for decades. Now Gabrielle, come on, make Lynda come with me, it's only for a year, then you can be with her every day of the week, for a few hours. It's better than nothing, it's better than lying on the floor dead.

"I'll have both of you, together, you can have one bed together if it will make you happy. Come on Lynda be with me, your husband. I don't like the idea of splitting you two love birds up, I'll kill Gabrielle if I have to, but I don't want to I like the way she looks, stands holding your hand as if there is no tomorrow, perhaps there isn't one for either of you, but which one will live, my wife or the new lesbian who I like the look off Gabrielle?

"Please Lynda, come to me, I know what you can do, how much punishment you can take before you pass out. So please my love, be the whore of my life, just open your mouth and say yes, it's not that hard to do. Gabrielle, by what I have told you now no doubt over exaggerated and no doubt Lynda has lied as well, or over exaggerated as to what happened to her at our house. I will admit, Ian used to come around every night after the idiot killed his own wife and her parents, to screw Lynda for free, I don't know why he didn't pay. Oh, hold on, of course, he was the best drug cutter the big boys had in our area, and he used to get me heroine, or cocaine or crack, or any drug he could get his hands on.

"Look at me, forgetting the names of the drugs he got for me? That was his payment for screwing Lynda. Sometimes he would beat her up or cut her about, making her bleed. But he would bring me extra drugs the following night, which I could sell to my clients before they entered Lynda's room and pulled out their cocks, they always kept their trousers on in case the cops raided the joint. at least that is what I told them. The real reason was so that if they got too violent with her, I could grab hold off the back of their trousers and throw them out of her door, with no trouble at all.

"They knew better next time not to go too far or else their time was cut short. I looked after you Lynda and you had four hours to yourself, or with that nurse stitching your body back together and she would say 'she's not to do anything for ten days,' but I made her bandage you up tight, so you could be fucked and played with by my clients, but not allowed to cut you across your midriff until you healed up again, then someone would come in again and cut you up.

"Won't you please change your mind, Lynda? Gabrielle, help me out here she doesn't really love you she loves me and would want to be with me if you would only tell her to join me, her husband. Remember, Gabrielle, she is not your wife, you might think you want to be together; can you tell me you can honestly love a scared and broken woman like Lynda?

"I bet she howls every night in bed, thinking of her past and how she was treated. She needs to be treated that way again, it's the only life she knows. Now Lynda, come with me. Gabrielle! Tell her, she has to come with me, or I'll have to fight you for her and she's not worth it. Not one bit, you don't really love her, all you can do is hold her bloody hand, as if that will save her life.

"Do you love Gabrielle? Lynda, does she bring you to an orgasm without hurting you? Without, beating the shit out of you? Does she hold you in bed like my clients did, or does she hold you like a woman might hold her child? Does Gabrielle treat you like a broken child, gently rubbing your hair, smoothing your back and arms to make you feel good?"

"Well, I can arrange that by having two clients fuck, you at the same time, one front on and the other back on and if you're really feeling low or run down, I can get one of the younger boys to stick his cock in your mouth and you can suck him off and of course, swallow his come or else it's just not cricket as we say in the good old UK.

"Now Lynda, come on come to me and leave that lesbian Bitch alone. Gabrielle, tell her you no longer love her and want to leave her for me and have the good life you deserve. Come on you two, make your minds up, which one of you wants to be with me?" he demanded to know in a raised angry voice.

Neither said a word, just firmly held hands not speaking to each other except for their finger tapping in the palm of their hands, Morse code, ensuring neither replied to him

"Lynda, see sense woman, you'll be better off than with the lesbian going from one place to another nowhere to really call home where you can at least lay down in the warm and be fucked all day and night, then have some nice drugs to put your mind in another world and take away the mental pain you may have suffered during the day. That's got to be better than going from one slum bedsit to another with your lesbian girlfriend. Gabrielle, I could give you both a permanent home.

"How about this, one big king-size bed, you lay together side by side so you can hold hands and I can have two clients come in and fuck you both at the same time and if by holding hands it gives you some form of bonding, you can both be beaten up at the same time and cut and slashed then you can bleed over each other and cry to your hearts content. You'll soon get used to it. Gabrielle.

"I'm getting to like that name even more than Lynda, I'm sure my clients will fall in love with your name and you. Just look at you, nice tits, tight ass, tight, cunt as well I expect, just as I like it, we could have nights of pure pleasure together. Come on girl, come with me leave Lynda to have a year on her own before I return her to you, a broken woman, scared for the rest of her life. How does that sound to you? Gabrielle, answer me, don't just stand there holding her bloody hand. Lynda, speak to me, come with me now woman I'm your fucking husband you should obey my commands.

"Gabrielle, you're supposed to be her friend, tell her how much better off she'll be with me, rather than with you. I'm sure you want to be fucked by a real man sometime in your female life. For God's sake that must be why you wanted to be a woman or if you wanted to be with a woman why change your sex? I can't understand you two, I'm offering you both a far better standard of life, all you have to do all day is lay on your backs and let a real man fuck the living daylights out of you. Later you could compare notes, which man fucks the best.

"Oh Gabrielle, there is only one rule, you can't get pregnant. I can't send you to the doctors for the pill each month or have the long-term injection and none of my clients will wear a condom, so you may get a couple of VDs in the process. I have a woman who can make you unpregnant in a few minutes. it only hurts for a short time isn't that right Lynda, what is it now, five? No, you've had six abortions and lived to tell the tale.

"You get a day off after and the following day, one of my clients will beat anything left inside you out of you and cut open the front of it, isn't that right Lynda? Yes, my wife has lived through it all. Now Lynda come with me, let Gabrielle walk away and she'll live, or else my trusty sword, which has killed so many girls and young boys at the bookshop and beheaded at least ten people who couldn't pay their debts to us, will have to kill Gabrielle.

"Even if it's just for the fun of it. I'll kill the bitch, because that's what she is a bitch just like you. Now I want one of you right now, I'm determined to split you up, so Lynda as your husband, I demand that you come with me and let Gabrielle go, you know what I'll do to you when I get you home if you continue to disobey me. you'll have two black eyes for a start, then I'll slice the bottom of your tits open so I can watch you bleed out and maybe for added fun I'll cut your stomach open just to hear you scream." he hollered, getting red in the face and angry.

"Now Gabrielle surely you can see sense? If you love her so much, protect her by coming with me now, then I'll let your lesbian lover live by herself for a year before I get her and your lovers again. At least you would have given her a year of freedom apart from those clients who follow her and catch her, they get ten-hours of fucking her, beating and cutting her up before she's on the run again. Come on Gabrielle, it's got to be a better life than you can give her? even if you're wearing an expensive trouser suit, is that to show her that you play the man part in your sex games?

"That's it, I was wondering how you made your money, you film yourselves fucking, each other with toys then put it on You Tube, get the sex adverts and get paid a lot of money. Well, you can both do the same thing with me. It won't stop you servicing my clients, they need and enjoy a good long fuck. Most of them are sadists and they enjoy beating you up and they pay me a lot of money for that enjoyment; you'll soon get the hang of it Gabrielle and you'll soon enjoy it as Lynda has had to endure it for the past four years while she has been my wife.

"Gabrielle, did you ever wonder why her parents stayed away from their home so much and lived in Spain most of the year? I paid them to stay away, so Lynda had nowhere to run too. The locks were changed so her key didn't work.

"I beat her up really good one night, cut her up bad, put her in my car and drove to her house. I called her dad outside his house and made Lynda stand stripped naked before him and watch me cut her tits up so they both bled over his snow-covered drive. Lynda was crying, begging her father to take her in or call the police even give her a coat to keep her warm as the snow was falling. Or call an ambulance.

"I admit I had a gun in my hand and threatened to make him watch as I screwed his wife and their younger daughter then put my gun barrel inside their vaginas and pull the trigger. Then I would kill Lynda and finally him. I loved Lynda and didn't want to kill her, she was getting cold, not that it mattered, she was bleeding into the snow-covered ground. I gave him two thousand pounds in cash and two credit cards worth ten grand each and told him to take his family to Spain and not return for at least six months, at which time I would clear both cards then they would go away again, or else, the family unit died, and I had people watching them in Spain.

"I never did, but he didn't need to know that. He agreed and watched his daughter get boxed ears for begging her father to save her life. I opened the car door and closed it hard catching her hand in the door crushing her fingers and breaking her hand. Boy did she scream, but her father just stood there watching me open the car door again then closed it hard across her fingers that she didn't have time to move due to the pain she was in. I opened the door again and asked him if I should make her put her hand in the doorframe? he said no and I simply closed the door, unfortunately, her hand was still there, so was crushed again.

"Now I don't know if you have parents, oh I forgot, it's just your mother now, I killed your father in the car bomb. That man Mike his bodyguard, with glass in his stomach and back full of glass deafened by the car bomb, collapsed to the floor which was also covered in sharp glass. He took out his gun and killed two of my men and my best cutter who was in the front passenger seat, then another bullet, came in through the back window, sliced open my face as the bullet passed me and hit my driver in the back who died half an hour later. I had to wait an hour for more of my men to arrive, drive me home and put the car through a car compressor with the dead bodies inside. I must say, he's one of the best bodyguards I've encountered, where they have been injured so bad, their boss killed and yet still he opened fire on us and managed to kill four men and wound me."

"Gabrielle was getting mad, but Lynda calmed her down, the last thing they had to do, was retaliate. The exact wording of the test was coming back to her now. Someone or two men would try to split them up all they had to do was not give into his or their demands until they agreed time was up or one of us gave in. Lynda tapped the test out to Gabrielle, who responded that she got it. Hold on.

"Come on Gabrielle, that must have hurt, come with me and try to get your own back on me.

"Come on Gabrielle, join me or tell Lynda to join me so I don't have to kill you I don't want to fight you Gabrielle and I'm sure Lynda doesn't want to see you killed in the fight like before. Let's end this nicely, Lynda comes with me, you walk away for a year then you get to join her again, isn't that great?

"The other option is you Gabrielle, join me now and Lynda join's you in a year's time so you're fucked together as you both lay on a king-sized bed holding hands as if it will stop the pain from the beatings after being fucked for an hour or more. I know, this is the best deal, you both come with me now, I don't want to fight you Gabrielle and Gabrielle, I know you're a woman and all that, but I really don't want to have to fight you and then kill you. For God's sake, one of you make up your bloody mind and come with me, or as God is my witness, I will kill Gabrielle, right now, if only I could get my foot to move off this bloody floor.

"Now come on girls, make up your fucking minds which of you is coming with me now? You can't both refuse me. I'm good looking, rich, have fabulous TV recording equipment. Which you'll both love to see in operation and over a hundred clients to keep you busy and your mins occupied with better stuff than your lesbian play at trying to satisfy each other. There is nothing better believe me, like a bloody good fuck, then a beating for not coming yourself. After a short breather, the blades come out, new and extremely sharp so as they cut through your skin it's not so painful for you and your blood acts like oil to make the cut easier, quicker and deeper. Come on Gabrielle, Lynda you can enjoy this unique experience together, you will really enjoy it I promise. Lynda, join me, please. Gabrielle, tell her to join me and I'll let you go so I don't have to fight you." George glanced at his watch and took two deep breaths.

"Now one of you has to join me, right now," he took another deep breath and tightened his cheeks as if he were getting angry with himself. "For God's sake make up your bloody minds. I'll either take one of you or both of you, I don't give a fuck which. Now Lynda. You're my wife, you should really come with me and leave your lesbian friend behind, she can't love you as much as I love you. A man is supposed to love a woman and a woman love a man and you Lynda being my wife, should love and respect me. Two women can't really love each other it wasn't meant to be it's just infatuation, that's all, you love the smell of each other the taste of their makeup, the smell of their perfume, the softness of each other's skin, the kind ways you touch each other.

"You need the roughness of a man, the feel of a hairy chest or back, the feel of his prick when it penetrates your vagina The fact that when he comes it's love for you, he can turn his back on you, but with me, I can put another client straight in after and the fuck lasts longer and longer and the beatings get stronger and stronger bringing you to a lovely orgasm before you get cut apart.

"Lynda come on wife, join me stand by my side, now, and we can leave this place together and I'll even hold your hand if you want me to, just like Gabrielle is holding your hand now. Gabrielle, please if you don't want to die when I fight you, tell her to join me now, tell her you don't love her and want to leave her. Or if Lynda won't answer me, you join me now, together we'll live. Gabrielle!" he shouted at the top of his voice with anger in his tone.

"Lynda, join me now!" he shouted again at the top of his voice with anger and an urgency.

"Gabrielle, Lynda one or both of you join me now, I'm begging you on my hands and knees if I could get down there; please join me, come with me, enjoy the life I have planned for you. Come on girls, I'm begging you both, join me, come with me, the three of us together; we'll have a wonderful life, I promise. Now girls, both of you, join me. Lynda, come with me. Gabrielle, come with me or I'll end up having to fight you and I don't want to fight you because I want you so dearly, please, don't make me kill you. Lynda my wife, come with me and do as you're told," he shouted with fear in his voice. "Gabrielle come with me, let me take your hand and we'll both walk out of here alive.

"Gabrielle! Lynda! Come with me, you don't need each other like I need you! Lynda! Gabrielle! you just can't feel for each other like I feel for you, I want you by my side, for me to watch you being fucked and beaten, you'll enjoy it as much as I will. Lynda, come with your husband, stand by my side and want to be with me more than her. How can you love Gabrielle more than me, your husband? It's not fair, it's not right, a woman loving another woman more than you should love me. Lynda, I'm begging you on my knees, please, please come with me. Gabrielle, tell her you don't love her anymore; Gabrielle, help me out here, tell Lynda you don't want her, you no longer love her, tell her!" he screamed at the top of his voice.

"Lynda come with me, take my hand love me like you did once before all this mess started. Love me again and I'll love you back. Lynda please, I'm begging you join me forever, Gabrielle, you join me I'll love you like a woman as beautiful as you should be loved and cared for Gabrielle, Lynda, help me out. There has to be a way we can all survive. I'm begging both of you, join me, come with me, take my hands and all of us can walk out free. Come on girls, Lynda, my wife, come with me, Gabrielle, tell her to join me, both of you join me, but let's do this right now," he begged.

Then a grey swirling mist came down over them all.

George felt as if he was being pulled away, his feet and arms moved now as he was slowly lifted from the floor. Gabrielle and Lynda could move again, but for a moment, as they looked at each other and smiled, holding hands together, they kissed, glad that the test was finally over with. There was crying coming from behind them, and angry voices threats of killing George, but it was all for Gabrielle now, all she was thinking about was Lynda, by her side, they were so much in love with each other they had been questioned by George, told all his secrets, things he held in his head trying to separate them, get one or the other to join him, to split them up.

As Gabrielle was thinking this, George was being told the truth, Lynda was not his wife, he had killed his wife with her family, Lynda, was Ian's wife but Ian was dead Paul had killed him, by slitting his throat and stabbing him in his heart twice, to make sure he was dead. George had killed his own wife and her parents when she tried to go to the police, such was his rage at the time.

Ian was good to him, he allowed him to sleep with Lynda most nights and help keep control of Ian's clients not his. Ian's. It was Ian's drug ring Ian was the cutter and an extremely good one. When Ian was killed in the Second Chance, John had tried to help him live, nobody killed him, but he was injured, a bullet sliced open part of his brain, it was like having an enormous stroke. He really didn't need to chase Gabrielle and Lynda around the world, they were legally and possibly incredibly happy as wife and wife. So why had he felt so intensely that Lynda was his wife?

He felt it, knew it to be so. then the test came into his mind. He was supposed to see how deeply they were in love, could Gabrielle and Lynda be separated? He would get a reward if he could make them separate from each other, even if it were just a couple of minutes, but they had remained silent holding hands, he was not happy as the truth was being told to him by some form of entity.

It wasn't human he was sure, he thought he had heard its voice before if you could call it that. It was a long time ago when he and Ian were together on a journey, going to another place, he couldn't remember where, but it was warm and he felt joined with some friends he knew who had died from a drug overdose or shooting, so why did he leave? How did he leave that safe place? Where was he being taken to now? Who was taking him? Moving his body, he could move his legs and arms now. The feelings he had of warmth and safety were disappearing as he saw Gabrielle and Lynda before him.

The test entered his head again, he had failed to separate them. The test was over, another entity was with the first and they were discussing their bet as to who would have the world and who would have all the souls? George realised he had been used, made to think things had happened when they hadn't, he was never married to Lynda, even though she was good looking. All those things he had done to her in the past, how long had she been used by him? To live a life that was not hers to live.

The entities, after talking for what appeared to be days or decades, decided it would be a draw and they would leave the Earth alone and all the souls would be allowed to live their lives out, with the exception to the special ones they had promised for taking the test.

George did not know who they were talking about and at that moment didn't care. He wanted to ask them a question, but they carried on talking over him. Once again, he was being ignored as Lynda and Gabrielle had done earlier.

He still wasn't sure who the entities were but guessed they had the power of life and death and the taking and caring of souls. He had seen them before, but he couldn't remember where exactly, but it was the time he had been here before with Ian.

There were tiny points of light, millions upon millions of them, is that all that is left of them when they died a tiny point of light? Your soul carried the pictures and things you had done through your life, was that it, your soul? Taken when you died and out into another realm where your soul could mingle with others when two souls touched each other, they could talk to each other, he had done this before, now he was here again, well almost. he was still in the Earth Plane as the cloud cleared from him.

There before him were the two people who he should have separated but their love for each other was so deep, they couldn't say yes to his questions or stop holding hands like lovers do. He could see Gabrielle, Lynda, who had been made to be the bane of his life.

He was so angry, incredibly angry as he heard voices tell him,

"Now, the test is over, we have come to a decision, you did well." But it didn't stop his rage and he was still just in the Earth Plane.

Seeing Lynda, alive and smiling he pulled his sword over his back, as Ian had done in the fight before. He directed it towards Lynda's heart. He pulled his arm back and thrust it forward aiming for Lynda's heart, but Gabrielle got there first, and it entered her right side, making it bleed profusely. Gabrielle felt Lynda's hands on her shoulders, they were hot and sending healing power through her body.

George pulled his sword back aiming for Gabrielle's chest. But his sword hit the Kevlar armour in her waistcoat. She felt his sword try to dig into her as she looked at it and grabbing it with both hands, attempted to bend it as John had suggested. It bent to an angle, before George pulled it out of her hands, but this time Gabrielle didn't hang onto it, she let it go.

George pulled it back from her and thrust it once again at her heart. This time, the sword entered her skin. He pushed hard and the sword went in deeper, wiggling around inside her and cut her heart in two places. George thought he pushed the sword right through her heart, but he wasn't sure, whatever, it would be a terribly slow bleed. Already blood was pumping out of the front of her heart and from the large cut in her side. As George pulled his sword from Gabrielle's heart, he ran it across the top of her waistcoat, making small scratches and cuts which were also bleeding into the material of her waistcoat,

Then, glaring at Gabrielle, his sword was in the other side of her body, twisting around and up and down, Gabrielle gripped the sword with both hands and pulled it out of her side. Blood was gushing from the cut and as Lynda looked at her wife, she knew she would have to help her soon, but George had only been three seconds, then Gabrielle took as deep a breath as her lungs would hold with her heart bleeding.

George tried moving his sword up Gabrielle's body, but only just got to her heart. He tried to push the sword into her heart, but he barely had the strength to control his sword. It penetrated her body once again but not going in far. Gabrielle pulled the sword from her heart before George had the chance to make a big hole and cut up her heart too badly.

Gabrielle's hands went down beneath the back vent of her jacket and retrieved both knives ready to throw, her right hand sent her knife to the right side of George's heart slicing the right side of his heart away from its centre. A second later her left hand sent its knife to the left side of his heart, cutting off the left side of his heart, making him bleed profusely inside his body. Some blood was being pumped out of the two holes the knives had made.

Gabrielle saw him take a deep breath as the pain of the two knives went through his body. Gabrielle was not going to let George stab her again. She was now angry with him, extremely angry, she held her last two knives in her hands. Thinking of Lynda and how much she loved her, Gabrielle lunged forward, the knife in her right hand plunging deep into the centre of George's heart. Gabrielle looked him in the eyes and shouted,

"I smite thee with all my might and condemn you to live in Hell's Domain for all eternity."

Then her left hand sent her last knife into his throat and slit it from side to side. Blood gushed out of his neck, just like it had, when he killed Ian the same way.

As Death took his body away with his soul, Gabrielle fell back onto the front of Lynda's satin dress, something she would never wear again. Gabrielle slipped to the floor, hearing screams behind her and as she touched the ground Gabrielle's head twisted and she looked up into the loving green eyes of her wife. which were now crying.

"I love you," is all Gabrielle could say.

Alan put his hand on Lynda's shoulder, crying himself as John pulled Gabrielle straight on the floor. He was just about to start heart compressions when Lynda stopped him and listening to the voice in her head. she knelt down, placed her hot hands over Gabrielle's bleeding heart and her eyes turned very bright green.

She could see into Gabrielle's heart where the sword had severed the parts of her heart, her green eyes heated the cuts up and her hot hands welded them back together. Gabrielle was once again with Death as Lynda willed with all her love for Gabrielle's soul to be returned to her. Gabrielle was talking with Death, asking for her powers and soul back and able to live forever as agreed with the people they chose. As Gabrielle looked down onto her body, she could see the first wound was still bleeding inside her.

"Can you please mend my body and let me have my soul back?" she asked Death.

"Why not let your wife heal you?"

"Because if you, do it, she will know where I am." With a flick of his staff, it was done, and Gabrielle was back in her body breathing, but still in trouble.

Lynda was on her knees, tears in her eyes, she thought with all her love to speak with Death and get Gabrielle back. Then her body collapsed to the floor and she was standing on the same ledge she had done before with Paul, who was now back with Death, Gabrielle still had bad injuries, her kidneys were cut in two, bleeding profusely inside her. Lynda thought back to that day, they were reliving it as it was formerly ordained. "But will you now do the same for her?" Death shouted into Lynda's mind.

"Yes anything, just tell me what you want," Lynda thought to herself.

"She has proved her deep love for her soulmate, now what have you done with Gabrielle's soul?" Fate asked annoyed.

"It is behind my curtain mingling with her past ones." "Retrieve it and heal her. The Omega is getting annoyed with our bet." Fate warned Death.

"If you really love her this will hurt, a lot," Death said to Lynda's soul.

"Do it!" Lynda thought to herself.

Death moved His staff and tore half her kidney from her body far below them. Lynda felt the pain even where she was. It was horrendous, much like the pain Gabrielle had to endure earlier. Death moved His staff again and put her torn kidney into Gabrielle's body and stopped the bleeding, He moved His staff again, healing the cuts on both their bodies, leaving a scar that would last for all eternity, reminding them of this day and how they fought for each other's eternal love.

"Now return their souls for all time, the Omega is on Her way to see what we have done."

Death moved His staff again and their souls were returned to their bodies, now soulmates forever.

Lynda sat up holding her side and felt the scar Death had left on her and Gabrielle. Her hand took Gabrielle's and leaned over to kiss her lips.

Gabrielle opened her eyes and looked into her wife's green eyes which were getting brighter as too Gabrielle's.

"I was dead, again and with dad behind Death's curtain. I saw you on His ledge, how did you get my soul out?" Gabrielle asked.

"With all my love for you. George is gone, he is in Death's lower domain and will remain there for all eternity as Death told me. Now let me help you up, your side will hurt for a while, but it was the final price I had to pay, I'll tell you all about it later, for now we have friends to give our good news to and celebrate. The boys have your knives, you won't need them again my love; they fell to the floor when Death took George."

Lynda held her wife's hand, as she helped her to her feet, then Alan and John hugged them and Alan put his arms under Lynda's arms and lifted her into the air, as he did on the day.

"Paul will be fine, he loves you deeply," he said and kissed her lips as he did on the day. He put her down into Gabrielle's open loving arms.

Everyone cheered as Lynda helped Gabrielle to her feet and their mouths locked together as they kissed then laughed at each other and finally held hands as they walked to the elevators. As they looked over New York, stars were showing in the bright red sky and tiny points of light like fireworks were passing through the air. The souls happy the Earth was saved so they could once again return to it and live their human lives again as it was ordained.

They watched the points of light knowing them to be souls from the beyond. They were celebrating, but the souls on Earth would not know what the couple had done for them, the sacrifices they had made together to save all the souls on Earth for their eternal love until they too returned to the beyond ready to start all over again, on Earth.

The elevator they arrived in was still there, they got in and descended to the ground floor like a falling rock. Upon leaving the elevator, all the elevators started to work again.

As they slowly walked out of the main doors of the Empire State Building, they could see ten ambulances and six Paramedic vans. Further back were fifteen police cars with Forensic Scientists running in and out of their vehicles. Nobody could understand how the elevator doors locked closed and every hole was covered over holding in the carbon dioxide. They still had not got to the back of the elevator, but a thick piece of square metal bar, was jammed between the doors near the floor keeping the elevator doors open. Nobody wanted to be trapped inside if the elevator doors closed again.

Soon Gabrielle and Lynda's party were allowed through the police cordon to get to their limo.

"Crikey, Death has created the past, the people in the elevator representing all the young girls and boys and older staff, that were in the office. The only thing missing is the snow," Lynda said.

No sooner said than done. The red summer sun vanished behind the new white and grey clouds which had suddenly appeared, as the temperature started to fall. The souls had been called back by Death to where they came from. Large white snowflakes were falling from the sky, covering the sidewalks and roads, cars and trucks that were parked up.

Everyone realised they would have to change into their winter clothes. The strange summer was over they would have to put their heating on and turn their air conditioning off, winter was back, probably with a vengeance.

Captain Patel called Lynda's mobile phone, congratulating them on winning the fight.

"Death must be very annoyed with himself on a draw," Chris said.

"A draw it was, Chris, now, how can I help you?" Lynda asked getting into their limo, sitting next to her wife with her arm around her shoulder, holding her close to her side.

"Don't leave yet," she ordered the driver "And put the heating on, this limo does have heating, doesn't it?" Lynda asked.

"Yes mam," the driver replied and switched off the air conditioning and switched on the heating, something the drivers hardly used in the winter as their long vehicles were banned from the slippery roads in case they were stuck in the snow.

"Sorry Chris, what did you want?"

"I need permission to recall the crew and get *The Gabrielle* out of port before the sea freezes over, which is quite common here. If we don't move it and the sea freezes over, it could crush *The Gabrielle* and damage the equipment beneath the waterline and of course the massive carbon fibre sail, which keeps us upright in the water."

"Permission granted, make way as soon as possible, tonight if you can, ring me when you are under way or of any problems, tell the crew to call into a winter clothes store, buy a second, thick jumper or sea jumper and a winter overcoat, I'll get the nearest store to you very soon. Tell them to use their bank cards and they will have the money for the clothes before they get home. Nobody from our top guests or ourselves will be travelling home on our yacht. We will see you back in the UK in a few days."

"Thank you, Lynda." Chris already had one of the crew members who stayed on the yacht with him at times, ringing all the crew mustering them to join the yacht.

Lynda searched the internet for a winter clothes store that was open at this time of night. She found a store close to the yacht barely fifty metres away from it. She rang Chris Patel and told him the name of the store and where it was. She had just spoken to the manager and told him to expect the twenty crew of the *Gabrielle,* they would be needing sea jumpers a thick overcoat and winter gloves. He said he had all of them in different sizes in stock and he would keep his store open until they arrived.

"You may leave now," Lynda said to the driver, still holding Gabrielle at her side. "Do you have a blanket in this limo?" Lynda asked.

"Yes, I have two blankets, they are in the trunk, would you like me to get them for you? The temperature can fall very, fast when the winter arrives," he replied and was out of his door and running to the trunk in the settled white snow.

As they drove off to Thornton's shopping Mall, Lynda, with help from her mother, was putting a blanket over Gabrielle, the second blanket her mother and Jenny shared.

Lynda was kissing Gabrielle, cuddling her up in the blanket, kissing her and letting her lean into her or on her lap as Lynda's hand rubbed her arm and side, keeping her warm in the thirty-minute journey to Thornton's Mall.

When they arrived, everybody got out of the limo first. They were running to their store to give everyone the good news. Her mother and Jenny also got out of the limo. taking a more sedate slow walk to their store

"Lynda, you've been incredibly quiet during our journey here, is Gabrielle, okay? Is she hurt?" her mother asked almost in tears.

"It's okay mum, this is what we were expecting, or rather we were expecting a lot worse. Death sort of operated on her a couple of times, maybe four times and me once. Her kidney was damaged, and she needed half of mine, what with her heart and spleen being put back together, then her soul was returned to her twice and my soul was returned to me.

"Gabrielle is a little tired, like anyone else who has been through an operation. She's in a little pain and I have some pain killers back at the hotel," Lynda replied and gave her mother a hug and kiss on her cheek. "We both love you mum, very much, she'll be fine after a good night's sleep.

"How does it feel to be in charge?" Alan asked Lynda.

"Haven't you noticed I'm always in charge?" Lynda replied smiling. "Can you both please help her out of the limo and keep an eye on her as we walk to our store," Lynda asked John and Alan.

Lynda got out of the limo first and watched as her wife
slipped down to the back of her seat,

"Come on my love it won't be long now," Lynda said getting close to her head. She gave Gabrielle her hand as John got out of the car and Alan moved in close behind her and removed the blanket from her back.

John picked her up and Alan helped push her out of the limo. When they got her onto her feet, Lynda took both her hands in hers and looked into Gabrielle's eyes. The sidewalk turned bright green as Lynda spoke to Gabrielle, and gave her all her love and some power, to be able to stand upright and walk to their store holding Lynda's hand so she could keep giving her all her love, which was another way of helping her through this difficult time.

"Thank you, my love," Gabrielle said looking at her wife. Lynda put her arms around her neck and pulled her towards her, they kissed, tongues in mouths, then parted, Gabrielle took Lynda's hand and they walked off together, Lynda talking to her all the time.

Chapter 10

When they entered their main store, there was pandemonium, as everyone was shouting, clapping and cheering congratulations. Clarice came running from the back of the store and when she saw Gabrielle, she ran forward and jumped into her open arms with tears running down her face. When Jack came out, he gave Gabrielle a huge kiss then kissed her on her lips, he then kissed Lynda as well holding her close to him.

"I'm so very pleased to see you both alive, Gabrielle, you have blood all over the top of your blouse and waistcoat and down both your sides are you okay?" Jack asked.

"I would have been dead had it not been for Lynda," she replied.

"Could we all go to the café further down? Let's get the story over with or you'll get no work from anyone for the rest of the day, and that includes you and Clarice?" Gabrielle asked sounding a little tired.

"Yes, of course? Everyone down to the café for a celebratory drink," Jack shouted.

Clarice wrote a short note and taped it to the glass door. Locking the store door, Clarice joined the others as they walked to the café. Gabrielle held Lynda's hand as they walked slowly towards their destination. John was behind Gabrielle with Alan behind Lynda. John was watching Gabrielle walk and he didn't think she looked okay. Then he noticed a red blood spot on the back of her jacket, which was getting larger. They were just about to sit down when Gabrielle collapsed into her seat.

"Lynda she's bleeding from her back, now where have I seen this scenario before?" John asked Lynda.

"Just lay her on the coffee table on her back I know where the bleed is coming from, we are still in the test and I doubt everyone will remember what happens here, but she will be weak after and we must get her back to the hotel," Lynda said.

"Okay I'll carry her to the limo after, she can lay on the long side seat," John replied, as he lifted Gabrielle in his arms and gently laid her on the coffee table before them so Lynda could hopefully do her work and stop the bleeding.

As soon as Gabrielle was on her back, John removed her Jacket and undid her waistcoat, removing that so Lynda could see what was happening. Lynda looked at her wife and pulled her blouse apart at the back then her front as she turned Gabrielle over with John's help.

"Hey, you can't do that here, wait till you get home, there are women about." A man shouted at them.

They had heard that voice before as John pulled out his gun and pointed it at him. The man put his hands in the air as Lynda looked at Gabrielle, kissed her lips then the area where earlier she had to repair her heart. Once again, her hands were very hot and as she looked at the scar which had already formed over her chest from the sword wound. Her eyes flared bright green, brighter than ever before as she looked into the back of her heart.

Her right hand went around her back and her left hand over the front of her heart. With her green eyes shining she concentrated their glow over Gabrielle's heart, she pushed her left hand through the opening her eyes had made. Her left hand was closing the hole in the back of Gabrielle's heart. Then her right hand once again compressed Gabrielle's heart. John watched her work, hardly believing what he was seeing, but it was really happening before him.

Alan too was watching Lynda's hands and recalled the time she had compressed Paul's heart, now she was compressing Gabrielle's heart again. Then her heart started beating again. Lynda used her eyes to help her withdraw her hand from Gabrielle's heart. When it came out it was covered with her blood.

There was an open part of her chest where Lynda's hand had entered Gabrielle's chest and came out. Keeping her right hand on her back, her left hand covered the gap and with her eyes glaring, she called to Death demanding to know why He had done this to Gabrielle.

"Yes, you have won, but I just wanted to ensure you loved Gabrielle as much as she loves you, after all she gave her life for you."

"I would give my life for her as you well know," she cried.

"Yes, but I wanted to make sure, I'll heal her heart now." He moved His staff and Gabrielle was breathing properly again and the hole in her chest and back were healed, leaving another scar so they would remember this day and how they proved their love for each other.

"Enjoy your lives my children for forever as promised. You both have all your gifts back, but I would not let her jump- until tomorrow, when she feels a little better," Death finally said to Lynda and Gabrielle.

As Gabrielle sat up on the coffee table still holding Lynda's hand, there was more of her blood covering Lynda's clothes. Lynda still had blood covered hands and Gabrielle's blood over the front of her dress, just as it had been in the Shard with Paul in their first two months of their lives together. Paul had collapsed and she had to open his chest and put her hand inside, pressing her fingers between an artery that had burst open, until the paramedic arrived.

John covered Gabrielle's naked front with her jacket as he did to Paul on that day in the Shard in their first timeline.

"I'll escort you to the toilets so you can wash your hands," Alan said.

"No Alan, I'll wipe them in my dress as I did on the day, isn't that right John?"

"Yes, you did," he replied and watched Lynda dry her bloody hands in her dress, as she did on the day.

"I think you two girls have had enough excitement for the moment. Mum, Alan and I will take the girls back to the hotel and put them to bed. They have been through quite a lot and have both been talking with Death who has done an operation on them both," John explained.

"They'll be fine mum you tell everyone what happened, you were closer to the front and heard everything," John told Brenda.

Half an hour later the girls were laying on their bed together with Jenny and Sarah helping them into their nighties. They looked at the blood over Gabrielle's satin white blouse and the two holes the sword made. Then there was another hole, still cold to the touch through Gabrielle's blouse and Lynda's dress. Again, cold to the touch. They put their damaged, bloodstained clothes to one side and let them get some rest. They just fell into each other's arms, kissing each other, telling each other what they had said to Death.

They both slept for an hour' as usual, Lynda on top of Gabrielle, who was holding Lynda in her arms, keeping her safe. At eight, Jenny came in with Sarah, woke them up and made sure they were not bleeding then asked them to join them for dinner. They heard whispers from each girl, got them into the shower washed the blood from their bodies and dried them. Sarah got out their clothes and underwear they would wear that night. They sat on their bed as Sarah did their makeup and put their gold hearts on. Then with John and Alan behind them, they went down to join the others for their evening meal. Everyone on their table clapped to congratulate each girl. Over the meal Lynda and Gabrielle told their friends how they felt about what George was saying to them.

"I thought he was an animal. How could he possibly treat Lynda like he did? He was treating her as if she were his to do with as he pleased. Lynda I am so deeply sorry for what you went through, how you were treated and the punishment you had to endure under that man. I'm just so glad my Paul was there to take you away from it.

"George deserved to die I'm so pleased Paul pulled you out of their hands and I will never forget how humble I felt while you were holding him, helping the doctors to stitch him back together and for you, holding his heart and getting it started again. While I watched you on the car's TV, I could see you were deeply in love with him, and I would very soon have another daughter to call my own. Lynda what you did today, where you went to, to face Death once again for Gabrielle, there are no words to explain my sincere gratitude," Brenda said crying.

"It's alright mum, it's all over now and I Love you," Lynda replied holding Brenda's hand.

"The test was something Lynda and I agreed to, we just didn't expect it to be like this," Gabrielle said. At least now the test is over with and George is now with Death, where he needs to be," Gabrielle said to her mother.

"There will be no more gunfights for us being chased all over the world. We can now relax and take all the time we want in one place. But I have to say, the Empire State Building and so many other places bring back bad feelings, memories, emotions, it was not easy going through what George was saying about us, there were times Lynda wanted to leave, but I held her hand close to me. When I wanted to retaliate, Lynda held my hand keeping me silent and by her side.

"We couldn't reply to any of his questions, or we would have lost the test. Death would then have taken all the souls on Earth and Fate would have destroyed the Earth, burning it to a crisp with the sun's radiation. It would be a lifeless planet for over a million years. Those people we had helped, would have lived on Mars, eventually going into space and living out there on spaceships in the company of the stars.

"I would have been dead, and Lynda would have been George's whore for the rest of her life." Gabrielle explained to everyone, giving them the full picture of what they went through and felt now. Gabrielle was still holding Lynda's hand like she would never let her go. Her other hand went to Lynda's arm, turning her slightly and drawing her closer to her body.

They kissed, smiling at each other and holding hands firmly, not wanting to let go forever. They kissed again as Lynda stood behind Gabrielle, her hot hands gently caressing Gabrielle's shoulders.

"Everyone!" Lynda said getting the group's attention.

"Gabrielle is very worn out with the afternoon fight with George and fighting for her life with Death to return her soul to her body. Then the final operation and encounter with Death in the restaurant.

"Death told me this would happen, and we are still in the test for another few days, but George is gone forever, he will not be back, Death has locked George in one of his special rooms and is now at the bottom of Death's Domain.

"I'm sorry we cannot stay any longer to talk to you about the afternoon's events so I'm relying on mum to tell you all what we had to endure and mum, tell them about the people who died in the elevator next to ours and then what happened as we left the Empire State Building. Snow mum," Lynda said giving her a clue.

"Oh yes, I remember," she replied with tears in her eyes for her daughters.

"Jenny, Sarah could you join us please and bring your medical bag? John, Alan, do you wish to join us and your wife's?"

"Yes Lynda, I'll tell them, and please look after my daughter, your wife. I would like to know if she deteriorates, Please." Brenda said crying. Penny was holding her in her arms and using a pink lace hanky to wipe away her tears.

"Gabrielle will be fine mum, and safe in Lynda's arms," John said trying to reassure Brenda everything would be fine. Gabrielle will be safe with Lynda holding her close. If she deteriorates, I'll let you know and bring you along to their suite.

"Lynda, I'll join you, there could still be some of George's assassins in the area and we don't know what orders he left for them should he die and lose the fight, so I'll check your rooms before you go in."

"Me too, I'll guard you both as John checks your rooms out," Alan added and stood up.

Lynda and John helped Gabrielle to stand, then they excused themselves, helping both girls to their room. Gabrielle was still unsteady on her feet as Jenny and Sarah joined them in the elevator with their husbands. They were talking all the time, until they got to their room.

"Lynda, I'll just get my bag, I won't be long."

"John, can the girls come in now? I need to take Sarah to get her bag."

"Yes, Alan, send them in, it's all clear," John replied as he walked into their bedroom, looking along the lounge, watching the girls and his wife, walk slowly towards the girl's bed. Alan closed the door and holding Sarah's hand, they kissed and walked to their room where Alan checked the room first then called his wife in to get her bag. A few minutes later, Sarah was checking Gabrielle's status, her blood pressure, heart rate, oxygen in her blood and her temperature, which was higher than normal.

As Sarah and Jenny got the girls into their nighties and matching panties the two girls got into bed. Gabrielle felt floppy as she snuggled up to Lynda's side. Sarah checked her pulse and temperature again.

"If she is not better in an hour, I'll call a doctor to come and see her. Give her all your love Lynda and place your hot hands over the scars Death gave her. Are you feeling, okay? No problems breathing or where Death removed half your kidney?" Sarah asked her.

"No, I feel fine, just a little tired after what happened today," Lynda replied.

"Okay, sleep if you want to, try and keep your hands over Gabrielle's scars, I'll be back in an hour, now, snuggle into each other and no sex until Gabrielle's feeling much better." Sarah told her sternly and covered both girls with the duvet that had been put onto their bed due to winter settling in fast and there was a problem with the heating.

"I'll be back in an hour, and behave," Sarah said and left their room with Jenny. John and Alan were in their respective bedrooms.

When their rooms were empty of people, Lynda started to give her wife all her love and healing powers. Her eyes were bright green as she glanced over her body and warmed her heart as it was still cold with Death's influence over her. After ten minutes, she could feel Gabrielle's heart was much warmer and settled down, returning to its normal beating rhythm, her pulse and temperature had returned to normal.

Lynda held Gabrielle in her arms and pulled Gabrielle gently into her, so their breasts touched, and they could kiss each other, remaining in their current position. Most of all, Lynda wished to speak with her wife quietly, and normally. Lynda didn't want to speak mind to mind, it would tax them both, as she was still giving Gabrielle all her love and healing powers.

"Gabrielle, I know we were thinking of staying here for a while, but I think our work here is done and we should leave our business in the hands of Clarice and Jack as we wanted to do.

"We'll remain Directors but leave them alone to enjoy the journey as we did together. There are still a few things we need to do to wrap up our affairs here for now," Lynda said. as they lay together arms wrapped around each other. Smiling and kissing with meaning and all the love they had for each other.

"So what would you like to do, after we have wrapped up our affairs here. Tour the world?" Gabrielle asked.

"Well actually, I was thinking we might go home for a while, to our apartment and our bedroom, we have work to do in London and there will be times we can wear our fine dresses," Lynda replied, kissing her wife.

"When do you want to leave?" Gabrielle asked.

"As soon as possible after we have finished up here which should take no more than three days, perhaps a little longer with the snow here and can aircraft take-off in the snow?" she asked.

"Oh, what about *The Gabrielle* and the crew?" Gabrielle asked.

"Captain Patel called me asking for permission to recall the crew urgently, and put to sea as soon as possible, before the port iced over and destroyed our yacht. It is on its way home as we speak. The crew have new sea jumpers, an overcoat, thick trousers, and gloves. For the women, one hundred denier tights, a thick snow dress and snow gloves. With an overcoat and everyone has a snow hat."

"Why, surely, we are still in the heatwave?" Gabrielle asked, thinking that yesterday, it was boiling hot.

"You've been out of it for a while," Lynda replied laughing, holding her wife close to her and kissing her lips profusely. As soon as we left the Empire State Building, the sun went down very quickly and it started to snow, really big flakes, it was so cold. I asked the driver to get us two blankets from the trunk. One covered you, the other Mum and Jenny. I'll fill you in with everything else that happened after we have made love if you're up to it. I completely understand if you say no, as long as we can still hold each other close."

"I'm pleased you have taken hold of the rains of our company and made all the decisions yourself, but I always have had confidence in you. If I were unwell, I know you could control our company and take control of our charity.

"However, my love my wife, I think I should now make a decision," Gabrielle sighed. She looked into Lynda's eyes, kissed her lips and put her arm around Lynda's back. we said last night that we would make love tonight, but we didn't know what we would have to go through and the fight for my life, so if you don't mind," Gabrielle paused, looking at the disappointment on Lynda's face. Gabrielle kissed her again smiling.

"Of course, we'll make love tonight and much more if you're up to it my love," Gabrielle said and pulled her wife on top of her, kissing Lynda's soft lips and running her hands up and down her back, scratching it in the places she knew her wife liked to be scratched.

Gabrielle turned Lynda onto her side and started to caress her breasts, then she kissed them and kissed her body and her face moved lower and started to kiss her clitoris, moving her tongue into her vagina, followed by three fingers which soon found Lynda's G spot. She was panting, crying out for her wife to lick her vagina again.

Gabrielle inserted her tongue into Lynda's vagina, just as Lynda started her orgasm. Her love juices ran over her vagina walls and into Gabrielle's mouth.

Gabrielle licked Lynda's vagina again then her clitoris, licking and kissing it. Gabrielle kissed Lynda's stomach her breasts and up to her lips, where they grinned at each other and kissed, their tongues entering each other's mouth their tongues played together as their mouths rotated, kissing all the time.

Their tongues receded through the two sets of soft lips to their place of rest. Their arms held them firmly together as Lynda looked into her wife's green eyes.

"That was lovely Gabrielle," Lynda said. "Ohhhh, I do love you so very much. Please don't leave me for someone else for the rest of our long lives," she whispered with tears in her eyes.

"No, my darling, I promise I won't leave your side, you are so special to me, I don't want you to leave me either. I would find some tall building and throw myself from it," Gabrielle replied, and kissed Lynda's eyes, removing the tears there.

They heard their interconnecting door unlock and Sarah was speaking with Jenny. The door opened as they were pulling the duvet over them, hiding their naked bodies.

"Hello girls, how are you both feeling now?" Sarah asked as she entered their bedroom with Jenny in case, she needed help moving them.

"Hello Sarah, Jenny, is the hour up already?" Lynda asked.

"Yes, it's surprising how fast time goes if your happy making..."

"No, we've been lying here together just talking and kissing each other," Gabrielle interrupted and smiled at Sarah.

"Well, you must both be feeling better now," Sarah replied.

"When Death repaired her heart, He touched her heart for longer than I thought. Hence her heart was ice-cold, so I heated it up, with my eyes and hands, as you suggested Sarah, then I heated up her kidneys. They have joined together fine. There is no internal bleeding, and they are working perfectly, like they are supposed to do. Her temperature returned to normal as too did her pulse. Gabrielle is fine now, all she needs is a good night's sleep as do I," Lynda replied, telling Sarah and Jenny what she had done to her wife.

"Right. No sex tonight, call us if anything is wrong during the night, Jenny is next door, and she will call me if there is a problem." "Sarah, I'm sure we will be fine through the night," Lynda said smiling at both girls, standing before them. Lynda didn't realise, they could see their nighties shoulder straps were off their shoulders and they had pulled the nighties off each other.

"Goodnight Lynda, Gabrielle," Sarah and Jenny said together as they turned and walked back through the interconnecting door to Jenny's bedroom.

As soon as they were alone, they kissed and continued to make love until three thirty in the morning when they went to sleep. They didn't need to be up early, but it was hard to change years of tradition so their early morning kissing and love making went on a little longer than normal.

They were thinking of having a shower, when Lynda suggested they go into their lounge and sort out what jobs they could get done and what jobs Lynda could do.

Lynda discovered the manager of Winter Sea Clothes had allowed their crew to board the *Gabrielle* with all their clothes saying he would contact Lynda the following day and give her their total bill.

He knew Gabrielle and Lynda as they often used his store when they were in town for Christmas shopping and to do a winter hat and bag walk, when they changed the style of their hats, bags and wraps which still brought money into their stores and kept their staff in work.

As Lynda paid the bill, Gabrielle was working out who they would be taking with them, how many trunks they had and how many cases they would be taking with them and the size of van they would need to get all their luggage to the airport, ready for their departure. Then there were the jobs they both wanted to wrap up as fast as they could. Talking the time over with Lynda, Gabrielle quietly spoke to her sister asking her if she had one of her aircraft available to take them home.

Janet immediately said yes, and started to dance around their office, she would be seeing her sister again and they could talk about the fight with George, she said yes, she and Tom would fly the plane themselves then she asked Gabrielle if she could get their mother on the plane, and they could all have a chinwag together. Everything was set up and Janet faxed all the paperwork she would need to Gabrielle's fax machine.

When Gabrielle showed Lynda the paperwork from the private leasing company, she was over the moon with excitement. She put her arms around Gabrielle's shoulders and pulled her into her body. Lynda kissed her wife repeating the words thank you, over and over. She knew, Gabrielle would have rather stayed here for two or three months but she had listened to her request and had done it without her knowing all Lynda thought she was doing was looking at the State they would visit next, helping Clarice and Jack get into another State, and open some stores for them.

Instead, they were returning home to the UK and helping the children and young adults in their Charity. They hadn't visited any of their shops in a few months and they needed to visit the shops and talk with their managers and staff giving them a personal update of what happened in the fight.

"Lynda, in your haste looking at the paperwork, you missed something. Look just here."

Lynda's heart skipped a beat, what had she missed? She was so happy, certain they were not off to another State or country first.

Gabrielle was smiling as Lynda again took the paperwork from Gabrielle. She started to read it seeing the word Australia. Did this mean they were going to Australia first, before going home? She read the booking form once again. The private booking form was from Australia Airlines, owned by Janet & Tom Grayson.

"Are Janet and Tom coming here to take us home?" She asked Gabrielle now over the moon again and incredibly happy.

"Yes they are, and we'll be the only ones on the plane, sitting where we like with our friends. Janet also wants us to get mum on the plane as well. Once in London, Janet will take mum to a few shows and take her out a few times for a meal and we'll join them at the Shard. After a week or so in London, they will take her to Australia for a month or so to see her grandchildren. She's been working too hard and long hours in the US for us and deserves a break," Gabrielle said,

"If it's still snowing hard like you said, it will be good to get mum back into a warm climate and leave the slippery sidewalks of New York to the people who live here all the time and are used to heavy snow, ice and freezing conditions," Gabrielle said laughing.

"I think we can do that, but we must complete the jobs we have planned done quickly," Lynda replied. She kissed Gabrielle on the lips, hugging her close to her.

Oh, I'm sorry girls, I didn't think you would be up too early with what you went through yesterday," John said standing in their joint doorway, half dressed.

"Don't worry John. Is it still snowing?" Gabrielle asked.

"Yes, but some of the roads look cleared."

"Do what you like for now, we'll go down for breakfast at eight. Oh John," Lynda called to him," "You still have an hour and a quarter to make love to your wife to get the day started right," Lynda said to him smiling. "At least have a cuddle."

"Yes John, come here, we don't get a lay in very often and the girls seem happy with themselves," Jenny called from her side of their bed.

John closed the adjoining door, slipped off his shoes and trousers and got into bed. Then Jenny pulled him towards her side and after a long morning kiss, they started making love. Jenny hanging onto John with all her heart and love.

The girls looked out of their window; Gabrielle looked at the large snowflakes falling from the white sky. "They truly look adorable don't they and see how they have covered the road and sidewalk. Did it really just start snowing as we walked out of the Empire State Building?" Gabrielle asked Lynda.

"Well, you did not really walk out of the Empire State Building. You were carried out by John and Alan helped get you into the limo, as the other girls and bodyguards, took their seats further down the stretch limo."

"Was I really that bad?" she asked her wife.

"Yes, you were you had me worried about you, but we were still in the game, and I was worried for you on that night. I put a blanket over you, and you collapsed into my lap all the way to Thornton's Shopping Mall, then we had a long job of getting you out of the car, Alan was pushing your backside and John was trying to pull you out of the limo and when he did I helped him stand you up, as Alan ran around the back of the limo to help John get you onto your feet and able to walk with my help, holding you up, with your arm around my shoulder and my arm around your back with John and Alan a couple of steps behind us."

"Well let's make love again, and use a vibrator on us, how about that," Gabrielle, said smiling, and took hold of Lynda's hand and slowly guided her to her side so they were sat on the side of the bed. "I love you with all my heart," Gabrielle said slowly to Lynda. "We have a little time, and we won't take long getting dressed and putting our heart necklaces on. Would you like to make love again, my love?"

Lynda looked at Gabrielle then smelt her mouth. It was not her usual clean smell like after she brushed her teeth and she knew Gabrielle cleaned her teeth, they did it together.

"Gabrielle, would you mind if I looked at your body?"

"Who me?" she thought for a moment then looked at Lynda.

"Why do you want to look at me? Do you think I'm pretty? I would like to be your girlfriend do you have a partner?" she asked in a slurred voice.

Lynda just couldn't stop herself. She screamed "John." He was putting his trousers back on then pushed their interlocking door open. He ran through their lounge and called his wife's name. Get Alan and Sarah, tell her to bring her first aid bag," he shouted on hearing Lynda sobbing her heart out repeating Gabrielle's name.

He entered their bedroom and saw a floppy Gabrielle laying on Lynda's lap with Lynda's arm around Gabrielle holding her close.

"She doesn't know who I am John. She was slurring her words. We made love, and she seemed all over the place, she was rushing about and speaking fast, "What could be wrong with her?" Lynda asked with tears in her eyes.

"What time did her strange behaviour start?" John asked as Alan and Sarah entered their room.

"I just asked Lynda when Gabrielle's strange behaviour started."

"It was about an hour ago. We were making love and she seemed all over the place and was moving really fast, not taking the time with our love making as we usually do," Lynda said for everyone in the room.

"Has she drunk anything?" Sarah asked Lynda.

"No, we've had nothing to drink except coffee last night.

"Let me look at her," Sarah said putting her special first aid bag on the floor. Lynda pulled up the back of her nightie and Sarah looked all over it then ran her hand over her back, there was nothing, no pin holes or anything that could do this to her.

"John, Alan, get Gabrielle on the bed, on her back, before you put her down, I want to lift up the front of her nightie and check her body," Sarah said moving away from her.

When Gabrielle was on her back, her nightie was up covering her breasts. Sarah took out her blood pressure instrument and clamped it onto Gabrielle's arm. In a few seconds it gave the result which Sarah was not happy with, her heart was beating fast with a low blood pressure.

As Sarah ran her hands over her body, Alan was looking at her as well, then he had a thought and picked up her left arm. His hand was running up and down it then he lifted her arm into the air and looked under her armpit.

"Sarah, look here," Alan said keeping her arm in the air. Lynda could now see it, a small piece of plastic stuck under her armpit.

Sarah leaned forward, looked at the small piece of plastic and pulled it out of her armpit. She had a piece of gauze, ready to soak up anything that came out. There was a liquid still inside the small capsule. As Sarah examined the needle, she pulled it out with a pair of small plyers and started to smell the contents of the capsule. Sarah smiled and passed the capsule to Alan. He smelt the remains of the fluid and passed it to John who smelt the almost clear liquid. John breathed a huge sigh of relief and handed it to Jenny, who knew what it was in the first small smell of the liquid.

"What is it?" Lynda asked everyone.

"This," Alan said, "is a mixture of two drugs, Speed and Ketamine."

"How did it get there?" Lynda asked confused.

"If days were minutes and hours seconds, I think we would be in hospital and Paul would be in bed when a nurse came in with a syringe which John flipped into the air, then called the hospital security team and the woman, pretending to be a nurse was arrested by the police and inside the syringe was Speed and Ketamine. Lynda, you said yesterday you were still in the game when we were at the restaurant, and I recalled this incident, and knew what it was," Alan said, thinking he was clever.

"It was me who disarmed her anyway," John added.

"Yes, I remember it now, you were very clever to realise the woman was not a nurse," Lynda added, for John's sake.

"Gabrielle will be fine soon, it's nearly been two hours now, I would say another two hours at the very most and she'll be demanding to know what's happening with her," Alan added.

"So how did it get there?" Lynda asked, then she felt stupid as she answered her own question. "Death!" she said and breathed a sigh of relief, at least she knew He couldn't kill her.

"So how long will it be before she's back to herself?"

"The worst of it will wear off in a couple of hours, the ketamine will take a little longer but by four pm, the effects of the ketamine should be gone," Alan replied.

"Will Gabrielle be alright to go out shall we say at eleven?" Lynda asked.

"She might be a bit wobbly on her feet, but I would say she'll be okay to go out by twelve," Alan replied.

"I agree," John said.

"So, do I," Sarah added. Now, can you think of any other incidents, Paul was involved with?" Alan asked everyone. There was no reply.

"We'll keep our eyes open. I think this would have been the worst," Alan said smiling.

"Right, boys, take breakfast in shifts, you go first John, oh, thank you Sarah for all your help, I'm so glad you came, you too Jenny. John and Jenny will go to breakfast after you two, so make sure the staff know they will be down when you come up."

"Yes Lynda, but it's only just six fifty breakfast is until ten," Alan said smiling.

"Really, is that the time? Lynda asked. "Before you all go there is one other piece of news, perhaps you Alan could give it to the others over breakfast. We are going home, back to the UK. Janet and Tom will be flying us back. You all have to decide if you want to stay here, or join us? We intend to travel around the UK to all our shops there and give the staff an update on the fight, what has happened in New York and what we will be doing with Hats, Bags & Wraps.

"We want to see if the main construction is completed on our apartment, with the upper floor completed and the telescope put back together and working. We need to talk with our TG boys and see how they are doing. John, Jenny, Alan, Sarah, we would like you to join us but if you want to stay here and tour the USA, we understand. Finally, we'll be going to Europe to see all our shops there. We leave in four days as Gabrielle, and I still have few jobs to do."

"That's okay, I think we can pack everything by then, are you getting a van to take all the cases and trunks to the airport?" Sarah asked.

"Yes, I've got a company in mind. John, we will need a four-by-four car to take us out later today to where we have to go, with driver of course. If the car goes into another car or a wall, then it's the driver's fault not ours and we can still leave on time.

"I want the car for about one, we'll give Gabrielle another hour," she sighed, with her arm around Gabrielle's back holding her close while her other hand, held Gabrielle's hand. Lynda kissed her lips, and hoped this was it, the game was finally over.

"Who will be going out today?" John asked.

"Yourself, Alan Gabrielle and myself. We have to go to our new store first and after we've finished in there, we might be an hour or so now, then we have to go to our hospital and the TG Hotel," Lynda explained.

"Oh, by the way, you can't get rid of us that early, I want at least five hundred years notice if you intend to sack us," John said smiling.

"Same for Sarah and myself, there are still dangerous countries you want to visit, and you'll need bodyguards to protect you, but at least it won't be George," Alan added.

"I'm so pleased your both staying, I just hope the rest of our happy group think the same."

"I'm sure they will," John replied smiling.

"John if you can order that car for one-fifteen please, and Sarah, when you come back up, I don't know where all our cases and trunks are, but if you can locate them and get a porter to bring them to our rooms, then you can start packing all the fine dresses and our shoes.

"And anything else you can put into the trunks. Take out our necklaces with a heart at the end of the chain and put our jewellery box in there somewhere near the bottom," Lynda asked Sarah to do.

Lynda kissed Gabrielle on her lips again, hoping for some response. "John why isn't she responding to my kiss?" she cried.

John walked to Gabrielle and opened her eyelids with his thumbs. "She is just unconscious. He got her a glass of water and handed it to Lynda. "Try to get her to drink this, don't worry if she coughs, it will start waking her up."

Lynda felt a heat wave travel through her body and cover her heart. She knew it was Love she was trying to help her. While John got another glass of water, Lynda held Gabrielle's hand tight, sending her all her love as the heat wave circled Gabrielle's body giving her lots of love, helping to heal her body and remove the drugs inside her. Gabrielle drank the water this time and looked up into the green eyes of her wife.

Lynda's green eyes lit up as she sent more of her love to her wife, then Gabrielle's eyes turned bright green and they started to speak fast together.

"Can you say my name?" Lynda asked.

"Lynda you're my wife," she replied.

They kissed each other and Lynda was laughing.

"You're back," she cried holding her close.

"Stand her up and walk her around the bed," John suggested. Half an hour later they joined the others in the restaurant and ordered breakfast. After Gabrielle had downed another two coffees, she flopped her hands in her lap and looked with glassy eyes at Lynda.

"What's the matter Gabrielle?" Lynda asked panicking.

"I think I need to go to the toilet," she replied.

"Then I'll come with you," Lynda said boldly. They both stood and Lynda helped her across the room. Tina stood and helped Lynda with Gabrielle to the toilet.

Back at their table Gabrielle took her seat and a sip of a new cup of coffee. "I know I have to keep drinking, to get the drugs out of me," Gabrielle sighed and grabbed her wife's hand, holding it tight. She was shivering, and Tina could feel how cold she was.

"I'll see if I can get her a blanket," Tina said and was gone in a flash. Sarah had left to sort out their luggage, and John was in his room looking for car hire companies with a driver.

"Here you are Gabrielle," Tina said and threw the blanket over Gabrielle then a second blanket went around her back and Lynda's back, as Lynda held her wife close to her, putting her arm around her shoulder holding her into her side. Lynda kissed her lips getting very, little response. Her hand was holding Gabrielle's hand as tight as she could. Then Gabrielle fell asleep. Lynda panicked and looked at Tina who was taking her pulse and lifting her eyelids," She's alright Lynda, pulse is a little fast, she's just asleep. It's a good thing, the ketamine is going through her body, so hopefully all the speed is gone. Let her sleep for a while."

As Lynda took a sip of her cappuccino, she heard a voice in her head. "Another two hours," it said. It was an Entity; Love, she smiled to herself.

"Alan, take Noah with you and visit the department store, just up the road. Get yourselves an overcoat and gloves each and anything else you need. I also need an overcoat for Gabrielle and myself both English size ten another for Tina and a winter skirt and some warm tights and gloves. Tina, Jenny, would you like to join them, then we may get something to our tastes?" she asked smiling.

"Yes, that will be fine. Oh, one other thing, Noah and I would love to join you and fly back to the UK. Will we be staying in your new apartment?"

"Yes Tina, it's all finished now, here take a look," Lynda replied, and opened her phone to pictures, which their builder had sent her. The outside looked fantastic, with double electric doors to enter the front of their apartment. Upstairs, where they would be staying, a large bedroom with an en-suit toilet and shower, big enough for two people. An eighty-five-inch TV on the wall facing their bed, a two-seater sofa and coffee table and a large lounge office. The other rooms were the same size, she couldn't wait to see them properly.

"The rooms look so nice, and the outside is fantastic," she said handing back Lynda's phone.

Noah arrived with Tina's small jacket so she could get to the shops. Noah had his suit jacket on with his gun inside.

"We'll be off then, call me if you need my help. Alan, take good care of her," Tina ordered.

"Put everything on your company card," Lynda added.

Tina looked at Gabrielle still asleep leaning against Lynda, warming her up with the blanket around her, Lynda kissed her. and gently stroked her face. An hour later Tina and the boys returned in their new coats and gloves. Tina was also wearing a ladies' red shoe that would grip the ground in the snow and ice. She also had a pair each for Gabrielle and Lynda, as well as their new winter overcoats and all their other clothes they would need for the cold outside and it was very cold at minus eight degrees C.

"There are signs everywhere advising people only to travel if they need to. It's on the TV as well, if you were looking at it, which you're not," Tina said.

"If that's the case, I guess we'll have a snow day and start packing what we can. There are a few jobs I can still do, but I'll stay here with Gabrielle for now, when she comes around and feels strong enough, we'll go to our room. Tina, are you still packing?"

"Yes Lynda."

"Then you stay down here with me and Alan, tell John we're having a snow day, and take him up to the store you went to. I don't know why I didn't send you all at the same time. Noah, I need to put what job you're doing into our pay books. I can't just say you're a bodyguard to nobody, so how would you like to be Sarah's bodyguard?"

"Yes, of course," he replied looking at Alan.

"It's all fine by me, she'll be over the moon to have her own bodyguard to look after her. You tell her," Alan said smiling.

"Boys, go with John, show him where things are and take as many photos as possible with your phones that we can use in the stores and our TG house in the UK. Try not to fall down."

Another hour passed and Gabrielle started to stir, Lynda felt her grab for her hand, and hold it as tight as she could. Lynda kissed her lips and had a little response as she felt Gabrielle return her kiss. Lynda put the glass of water to her mouth and got Gabrielle to swallow it. They were kissing again as Lynda held her tight in her blanket. They kissed once more, and Gabrielle returned her kiss, so they were kissing together.

"Do you know who I am? do you know your name?"

"You're Lynda I'm Gabrielle, we own Hats, Bags & Wraps, were married together, lesbians."

"Oh yes," Lynda replied crying and kissed her wife on her lovely soft lips, again and again. Her arm was still around her neck and her other arm was now around her chest, just below her breasts, holding her close to her, kissing her again. "Let's see if you can drink a cappuccino before we go anywhere."

Tina arrived with three cappuccinos and placed one before Lynda, one before Gabrielle, the last she put by her seat and put the tray on the next table.

"How do you feel?" Tina asked Gabrielle.

"Fine I think, what happened to me and where are we?"

Lynda and Tina told her what had happened to her and what they had been going through with her. Thirty minutes later, Tina and Lynda were standing between Gabrielle who was still wrapped up in her blanket. They got her to the elevator door then Tina remembered her elevator key, in the early morning, Noah had used his key, while hers was in her other jacket up in her room.

A young man came over to them and inserted his key into the lift floor control panel. "Floor ten, I do believe. How is Gabrielle now?" he asked.

"She's awake now and most of her memory has returned thank you for asking," Lynda replied.

"Glad to hear it, I'll get Housekeeping to get you a large blanket for her, it looks like she might sleep the afternoon through, good job it's a Snow Day," he said, "Oh, my name's Paul by the way."

"I'm Lynda, this woman almost asleep in our arms, is Gabrielle and the woman on the other side, Tina, one of our bodyguards," Lynda replied.

Paul turned to look at Lynda, seeing Gabrielle between her and Tina. He slowly lifted his hands and put them on each of Lynda's shoulders and allowed them to slip slowly and gently down to her elbows as if she were made of glass.

"Gabrielle will be fine I'm sure, she just needs to talk a little longer with your friend Death. She'll see again by this evening, I'm sure. We're at your floor now." His hands, gentle, soft, slipped off her arms and she looked into Paul's light green eyes as he smiled at her.

"Thank you." Lynda uttered, pulling Gabrielle as close to her as she could.

As the three of them walked out of the elevator, Paul stood holding the doors open for them. Once outside, Lynda turned back to take a last glance at Paul, his green eyes glared softly, like they had when they first met. She didn't know what this could mean or even if Tina had heard him speak or saw him touch her arms.

The elevator doors started to close shutting Paul, or her Paul into the cold light of the elevator. Then Paul's hands slipped quickly through the centre of the elevator doors which opened once again.

"Lynda," he said grabbing her attention.

"Yes?" she queried.

"I'll have three cappuccino and the lemon tarts sent up to you, it will help pass the time."

"Yes, thank you she replied talking in a soft voice she hadn't heard in many a year. "Thank you," she said.

"My pleasure," he replied, Paul's eyes glared bright green as he allowed the elevator doors to close again then he was gone.

They got Gabrielle into bed and Housekeeping sent up two large blankets that the woman opened up and threw over the bed, making a shivering Gabrielle a little warmer. No sooner had the woman left the door call was heard once again.

Tina opened the door, a woman stood before her with a tray of drinks and cakes in her right hand.

The porter entered the room with Tina watching her every move, she didn't recall ordering drinks or cakes. She placed the tray on the small table beneath the large bay window.

Lynda looked at her, recalling Paul's last words to her.

"The drinks and cakes are a compliment from Paul, another of our porters." She said in perfect Italian.

"Thank you, and thank Paul for me please," Lynda replied in perfect Italian.

"Enjoy, think of the good times, the first time," she replied in Italian.

Lynda felt her entire body shudder with warmth and love from her husband and wife.

The woman left them closing the door behind her. The room was instantly filled with the aroma of pure Italian cappuccino coffee, just like Lynda recalled, she had with Paul on their first meeting and there on three small plates with a knife by its side were three identical lemon tarts like they had on that day.

Tina and Lynda sat at the small table in their large comfy chairs, as Lynda reminisced their first meeting while Gabrielle's drink and cake remained as hot and fresh as it was when it was made.

Lynda got into bed beside her wife, getting her close to her body and kept an eye on the time, hoping Gabrielle would be back to normal soon.

As she lay with her arm around Gabrielle's shoulder, holding her hand and gently pulling her to her side, to keep her warm, she took hold of her hand, and felt Gabrielle squeeze it tight. Lynda kissed Gabrielle and felt Gabrielle kiss her back, this time, her lips held their kiss.

"Gabrielle?" she asked quietly. There was no reply, but she did turn into her body and sighed. As Lynda lay on her back looking at the ceiling holding her wife close to her, she had a thought. If they were still in the game what was her part in it?

She thought back to the time of the incident, after John had the woman arrested, she had held Paul as close as she could get to him in his hospital bed when he was out of hospital they were living together. She was doing everything she could for him, setting out his tablets and giving them to him, helping him dress and undress. Helping him eat and drink, even when they were out. Loving him and telling him she loved him.

She looked over to her wife now in her nightie. She leaned over and pushed her face into her breasts, telling her she loved her with all her heart.

"I love you with all my heart, I couldn't live without you by my side, please my love, the love of my life, come back to me and talk to me. Talk to me, please, my love, my wife, talk to me."

"What is it you want my love; I love you with all my heart?" Gabrielle whispered.

Lynda leaned over and kissed Gabrielle on her lips and soon they were back kissing together, holding each other close, Gabrielle fondling Lynda's breasts, she moved her head and started to kiss them. She looked up into the green eyes of her wife. I've been waiting for you to figure it out, I was on a ledge talking with Death about our future it's going to be fabulous, and we'll enjoy every moment of it. I'm so glad you worked out the time and what you did and had to do for me to come back to you."

"So, you're back now?" Lynda asked.

"Yes, my love, what day is it? What time is it?" she asked.

"Today is Tuesday, the same as it's been all day long and the time is, six thirty at night. Your Italian cappuccino and lemon tart are over there and still as hot and fresh as it was brought in several hours ago."

"He has no clocks up there, we were talking for ages. What is that gorgeous smell?"

"Sit up, I'll bring it over to you, what would you like drink first or lemon tart?"

"Cappuccino, we'll share the tart, being like our first meet all those years ago. Do you know, while I was upstairs; I looked down on us and we haven't aged at all since our first meeting. I looked about twenty-five, same as you, except I'm female now," Gabrielle said as she sipped her drink and ate the piece of lemon tart that Lynda had shoved into her mouth.

"Gabrielle you've been gone, properly, from about six this morning. I was worried sick, and I was telling you that I love you with all my heart, and I do of course."

"He said you wouldn't work out the clues. I said you would, but you have taken all day and you worked a lot of it out by yourself, well done my love."

"Is that it now, has the game completely finished?"

"Yes, Dear all over with."

"Death isn't going to take your soul anymore when He's lonely?"

"No my love, well I hope not. What have I missed? did you get any jobs done?"

"You've missed nothing we've had a Snow Day and you've been led on me and in my arms all day, oh and I've been kissing you a lot as well. Are your legs alright, can you stand?"

"Let's see."

Gabrielle worked her way to Lynda's side of the bed, so they were next to each other. They sat together arms around each other holding each other close and kissing, their mouths rotating. They looked at each other and slowly stood together. Lynda held Gabrielle as she got to her feet and steadied herself.

"Let's walk over to the balcony window," Lynda suggested. It was a slow walk, but they were soon there. "See my love, snow everywhere."

"It looks deep, is it cold out?"

"The snow is four inches deep well it was when the boys went out to play in it. They bought some winter clothes and Tina got clothes for us. It looks lovely, everyone is coming back with us to the UK, packing has started. There are no hire cars until tomorrow. The boys have been taking photos of the snow, and then playing in it taking pictures of them playing in the snow. The people watching them think they are mad Englishmen.

"Who's been looking after us, or you?"

"Tina, she's in the lounge, sorting out the new camera, getting it ready for tomorrow. She's removed the card that was in the camera, put it into its holder and marked it for you. Lots of people at breakfast and after wished you well and hope you'll get better soon."

"That was nice of them."

"Yes, it was, I put Noah on our staff books under bodyguard to Sarah, Tina looks after Jenny, so it won't hurt to have him take care of Sarah, especially where we might be going," she said smiling.

"Let's walk into the lounge and see if she's picked the right lens for tomorrow and unpacked everything."

"I certainly hope so, she did a camera course at uni as well. I looked her up and she's a well-known photographer. You didn't know that did you?"

"No, she's better than me then. We'll get her to take the photos of who we want here and the places we can get to." They entered the lounge in their nighties and negligees. "Hello Tina, are you getting used to the new camera?" Gabrielle asked, making Tina turn to look at her.

"Gabrielle, you're awake at last, how do you feel? Can you walk over to the lifts and down to the restaurant for our evening meal?" Tina asked.

"Yes, I think so, but not dressed like this," She replied laughing.

"I'd go out with you no matter how you're dressed or undressed for that matter. I'm just glad to have you back," Lynda said and kissed her lips.

Tina took pictures of them standing by the window then standing at the far end of the room. She checked the pictures then noticed something.

"Girls, look at each other's hair, there is a white streak in through the side of your beautiful long hair," Tina said surprised and took more photos of them kissing each other with the snow and hotel thermometer showing minus eight degrees.

"A present from Death?" Lynda asked.

"I think so, looks good on you."

"You too," Lynda replied as she stroked her wife's hair, feeling more love flow through her as she felt Gabrielle's petite hand flow through her hair.

"It's still cold downstairs, there is a problem with the radiators, but they should have it working by tomorrow morning. Sarah put your underclothes and tights at the bottom of your bed here are the dresses she picked for you both to wear, and you're both to wear these cardigans down for the evening meal. Especially you Gabrielle."

"What no jacket?" she asked.

"Gabrielle, it's no longer summer, we're in the thick of winter and it's what temperature is it outside." Lynda asked. Tina looked through the window to the building opposite.

"It's minus eight degrees C at the moment," Tina replied.

"Where's the thermometer?" Lynda, asked.

She turned around seeing the large thermometer, lit up.

The next morning, with Gabrielle feeling a lot better, Lynda made some phone calls, first to Jack.

"Hello Jack, can you open our main store this morning for about eleven? Are the roads clear by you? I want to see if you can get Shantell and William to come in we need to change him before we leave and all being well; we'll be leaving in two days. They live that close? They can walk then. Tell William to bring a bra for the size she wants her breasts. Yes, fine thank you," Lynda said.

She next rang their TG House and asked if the roads were cleared by them and could they keep the younger boys and girls, who are at least ready to speak to their psychiatrist in a few months inside the Hotel until they arrive in a few more hours.

John was ordering a four-by-four car, they could have one with a driver for a few hours that day, but the car would have the new plastic chains on its wheels.

By ten thirty their car arrived. John and Alan wished they could drive it, but they couldn't it was the company driver only. They had been standing outside the hotel for a while, having their pictures taken by Tina. Then they had a few pictures taken of John and Alan throwing snowballs at the girls, they didn't like it very much the snow was cold it was now minus 6°C.

When they got to Thornton's Shopping Mall, the main doors were open with managers of the stores inside, walking around their store making sure there were no leaks in their water pipes, and putting their heating on, the Mall would open the following day once its heating had warmed the main building up.

Inside their main store, Alan, John and their driver, Simon, were drinking a hot cup of coffee while Gabrielle and Lynda changed William into Christine with a D cup, long brown hair, a woman's face and body and a woman's voice. She had no male hair over her body, thin legs and arms, small hands and feet. Nothing she had would fit her now so after all Shantell's pictures were taken by Tina, Shantell took Christine to a woman's clothes shop further down on the ground floor.

Shantell introduced herself and Christine to Gerald the manager who she knew well, as she did most of her talks opposite his store. She asked him if she could buy or put by wear today some clothes to fit Christine, who only arrived this morning dressed in summer clothes, and she fell down in the snow and needs some new clothes. Gerald was only too pleased to help. So, they walked around the store picking out three different outfits and bras, they also picked out a winter coat and shoes. George totalled all the items up and wrote it down, Shantell signed it then Gerald looked at her and tore up her bill laughing.

The two girls had their, photos taken together with Tina promising to print their pictures and leave them at the reception and also, send them to their phones. Then with all the pictures of the new store and office taken, they returned to their car and drove off to the TG Hotel.

The group of ten boys twelve and over, were changed to girls with their doctor's permission, and given young girl's breasts which would naturally grow with the girl growing. The ten boys fifteen to eighteen, they changed to girls like they had the younger boys. The four girls who wanted to be boys, were also changed and they felt good walking around as a boy with a boy's voice and have hair growing over their body. with thicker arms and legs and bigger feet to hold their frame and bigger hands than when they were a girl.

They talked with the doctors and nurses for a while and discovered one of the doctors and nurses were seeing each other and had been in love with each other for six years and wanted to live forever, Gabrielle and Lynda looked at each other and took Peter and Rose to one side, then changed them in a side room. They would now live forever with the others and trying to be quick as their time was running out with the driver and car. They told them who else they had changed and if they knew of other couples who were deeply in love and wanted to live forever, they were not to tell them they had been changed but to keep their names ready for when they returned to the States to change them all.

Saying goodbye, they returned to their hotel as the night started to get colder and darker.

The following day they dressed in their best clothes, and everyone wore their Knight's medals and John managed to get a four wheeled drive car for the six of them, and they visited their friends and staff at Thornton's Mall. They all shared a last cappuccino together, had a last look around, shaking hands with people, being led by Shantell around the Mall. They said goodbye and returned to their hotel to finish packing.

During the afternoon their mother, Mike and Penny arrived at their hotel and took another two of their rooms on the tenth floor. A driver arrived in the late afternoon with a van to take all their luggage to the airport the following morning.

The porters started to bring their chests down first and put them into the van, then they loaded their other cases. Their gun cases would go down first thing in the morning. They were all dressed in their best clothes again for the evening meal.

When they entered the restaurant, Gabrielle had the feeling everyone was looking at them. She held Lynda's hand firmly in hers and John was seen to place his hand on his Glock. Tina was also dressed in her suit, still packing her gun as too, her fiancée Noah, had the time to go to an expensive jeweller's and buy Tina an eternity ring at twenty thousand dollars. He also bought his and hers matching wedding rings. They were all a family, they lived together and went out together they also took care of each other, especially in a gunfight.

As they ordered their meal, another table was drawn up close to theirs and Gabrielle was getting worried. She asked the waiter what was happening. He said they had to move some tables around as more royalty people had booked a meal here. Gabrielle still thought it strange as the table was laid out for an evening meal with settings for four people.

The main doors opened and the head waiter, bowed slightly as he showed the four people into the dining room. They were all wearing a Captains Pilot uniform, the first two, with their Knight and Dame badges on. Gabrielle jumped to her feet as much younger looking, Janet and Tom walked slowly across the room. Lynda was now standing up, smiling and holding her hands together before her as if in prayer. Gabrielle could not stop herself and with Lynda a few paces behind her ran across the room and hugged her sister, kissing her face and lips, saying her name over and over.

Lynda was hugging Tom, they were kissing each other, hugging each other close then Gabrielle and Lynda swapped partners. Tears were streaming down all their faces as they showed them to their table, the other two pilots following them.

As they got close to their table their mother stood embracing her daughter and son in law. She too was crying as she welcomed them to the USA.

"I'm so pleased to see you again, it seems ages since I've been to Australia., did you bring my grandchildren?"

"Not this time mum, but you'll see them soon, and my sisters have said they will visit us before you come back here to finish your work," Janet replied.

"Let's all sit down so you can order your meals, its Greg and Malisa, isn't it?" Lynda asked the other two pilots.

"Yes, it sure is Lynda," Greg replied in a strong Australian accent. They hugged each other close and kissed each other Gabrielle was hugging and kissing Malisa, and then they swapped over and finally they were all seated with a round of applause from everyone in the room and Tim their Head Waiter asked Gabrielle and Lynda to stand and accept the applause, as it was for their time in the fight, which everyone had heard about. They stood and acknowledged the applause trying to say thank you to everyone. As they took their seats again their starters came out then a short time later their main meals arrived.

When it was time for dessert, the main doors opened again and two men in chefs' whites and their white hat walked in pushing a huge trolly with a cake the same size as the table. Everyone in the restaurant stood as the Head waiter motioned Gabrielle and Lynda join him. They walked up to the cake, the two girls still not understanding what this was all about.

The rest of the people at their table stood and watched Gabrielle and Lynda holding hands walk up to the cake. When they looked at it, it said:

Gabrielle & Lynda, Congratulations on winning the fight and for saving our souls.

"Thank you," they said together, holding hands. The applause was deafening as the photographer took pictures of them by their cake, a knife in both their hands, smiling together and making the first cut in the cake. The Head Waiter escorted them back to their table where they took their seats. A moment later, everyone on their two tables were eating a slice of their cake, while people continued to take pictures of them on their phones and sharing with their friends all over the USA and further out to the world.

The group talked over cappuccinos, still trying to work out what the words on the cake meant.

"Has nobody told you yet sis?" Janet asked and looked at her mother who was shaking her head telling her No!

At midnight they went up to their rooms as usual, John checking their room first, although he didn't think there were any more assassins after them, but you could never tell with George what his instructions were to his men if he died. The girls were escorted by Alan, with Sarah following them helping them out of their suits and into their nighties. Each girl took the other's makeup off after saying goodnight to John and Alan.

Once in bed, Gabrielle held Lynda in her arms, caressing her back as she held her tight, closer to her body tears falling from her eyes, down her face onto her wife's cheek. Lynda felt the tear on her face, turned, put her arm around Gabrielle's back, holding her tight.

"What's the matter my love?" she asked.

"I don't really know why I'm crying, so much has happened to us in New York, running, preparing myself for a fight where I didn't know what or who I would be fighting, and if I would survive, would I be able to save your life, like I had in our first timeline? I didn't even know if Death would return my soul to me, and we both had to fight Death for that to happen."

"Gabrielle, everyone applauded us, or rather you, as you were the person who would have to fight George, who caused so many problems in so many countries. His men doing everything he asked of them. Many more people would have been killed had it not been for us taking on his men and look at what you did with the TG house and the hospital in Rome. We set up a Peace Treaty with the Mafia and UK.

"You got the Mafia to help our police looking for George and arresting a lot of his accomplices. We've done a lot, and mostly it was all about you Gabrielle and everyone seems to know it, I have no idea how, but it's all for you my love, and no matter what anyone says, you fought George well and protected my life and showed your love for me while George shouted those horrible words to me, hoping you would retaliate and split us up, try and grab his neck, choking him to death.

"Instead, you stood still, holding my hand, saving my life and when the time came when he used his sword against me, you Gabrielle. My Gabrielle jumped into the sword's path, and it entered your heart instead of mine. Then you did fight for me using your four knives against his six knives and his sword.

"It was you who killed him, again, with a knife as you did the first time you killed him. Then came my time to fight for your life, by giving you all the love I had for you, then pleading with Death to give your soul back to you and heal you, which He didn't really complete as he tore half my kidney from my body and somehow grafted it to yours, which happened before, then we went through every fight and problem you had to overcome like the first time."

Chapter 11

We have overcome it all, including the last one when I thought I lost you forever and the answer to getting you back was showing my unconditional love for you, which you know I always have for you, I wouldn't swap you, leave you, hurt you. I would and will only love and cherish you for all the days of our lives," Lynda said quietly to her wife.

Lynda moved forward and their lips touched, kissing each other, cherishing each other as their love for each other flowed into their bodies, filling them with love, warmth and desire for each other. Lynda's hand started to slowly caress Gabrielle's breasts, then slowly moved her fingers down her body, to her clitoris.

"This is what I love the most about you, the way we make love, the way you let me take you into my arms and heart. Gabrielle, I am so deeply in love with you, allow me to bring you to an orgasm, then I think we had better get some sleep. It's two thirty and we have to be up at five thirty for a very, early breakfast, the very last bit of packing and then board Janet's plane and go home," Lynda said.

"I love you so very much too, yes, I suppose you're right, I would like you to bring me to an orgasm my love. Lynda smiled, and kissed Gabrielle's soft lips, then putting her tongue into her mouth, she started to play with Gabrielle's tongue, as her fingers gently caressed her clitoris, making Gabrielle feel very sexy as she felt Lynda's fingers inside her, playing with her vagina, then finding her G spot, she was rubbing it bringing Gabrielle to an orgasm she could not stop happening.

As they turned over to get ready to go to sleep, Lynda felt Gabrielle's hand move down her body and play with her clitoris, then inserting three of her fingers into Lynda's vagina, pushing them in and out of her vagina bringing Lynda towards her orgasm. As Gabrielle played with her G spot, she felt Lynda's body arch as Gabrielle's fingers pushed deeper into her vagina and brought Lynda to an orgasm. Gabrielle moved her fingers over her vagina walls and took some of her orgasm out to her clitoris, making her wet as Gabrielle's fingers, caressed Lynda's Clitoris.

"You didn't think I would let you go to sleep without me playing with you and bringing you to an orgasm, on the last night of our stay in New York, did you? Now come here and lay on top of me, as always, I still want to protect you from all those horrible days and nights you had to go through," Gabrielle said quietly to her wife, hugging her body next to hers, their lips kissing each other goodnight, then Lynda fell asleep, glad to be safe in her wife's arms, protecting her through the night.

At five thirty they were both awake and having a shower when Sarah came into their bedroom fully dressed, make up on, the girls came out of the shower as Sarah was looking for their nighties and panties, putting out their underwear and dresses on a hanger in their bedroom.

Their coats, they would put on when they were ready to go to breakfast.

"Come on girls, time you were both dressed, is there any other clothes in here?" Sarah asked.

"No," Gabrielle replied holding Lynda close to her as their towel dropped to the floor, Sarah had put all their night clothes and an odd bra she found, into her bag. "Oh, I just thought there will be our makeup cases and our ring and necklace cases to add to your bag in a bit."

"I'll be back for those last items in ten minutes, Now come on and get yourselves dried off and dressed, it's cold out there." Then Sarah walked into John and Jenny's room, shaking them out of bed and into the shower.

At six thirty, they were all dressed, Gabrielle and Lynda had their most expensive engagement rings on, their diamond eternity rings, and their gold wedding rings. Around their neck were the heart shaped diamond necklaces. All the empty jewellery boxes, now inside one of the bags which were inside the last suitcase. All the gun safes were also packed into their suitcase, which was triple locked and heavy, they were packing their guns as John didn't know what would happen in London, so he ordered everyone to pack their gun, they were well hidden in their suit jackets, including Tina's jacket.

They looked at each other as if waking from a dream, they held their breath and then kissed each other, not stopping for several minutes.

"Are you properly awake now my love?" Gabrielle asked her wife.

"Oh yes, I'm fully awake now and I recall everything like you," Lynda replied, laughing and kissing her wife again. "Something must have happened and it's getting close to our time to leave."

"I do believe you're right, come on, let's get dressed, we need to get back to our Train Station to see what is happening," Gabrielle said smiling, pulling her wife closer to her so their breasts touched, and their lips rotated about each other.

John came running into their room smiling, Janet close behind him. Alan and Sarah followed Jenny into the girl's room also laughing.

"Are you two fully awake Mam?" John asked. The other three were asking the same question to each other.

"Yes, everyone we are fully awake now," Lynda replied holding onto her wife's hand. John stood still and called everyone to orders. Silence immediately filled the room as John and Alan stood before their respective Captains and saluted them. Gabrielle and Lynda returned their salute and they all congratulated each other.

"It seems we are all back in the land of the living, let's hope the others have woken as well. Right, everyone, to Orders, finish getting dressed and let's get down to breakfast, we will all have a talk on the plane as we fly home," Lynda ordered.

"Yes Mam," John and Alan said together.

Ten minutes later, everyone was dressed and ready to leave. A Porter arrived at Sarah's room. She was dressed, with her jacket on with her Dame's badge from the Queen when she made her a Knight of the realm. The porter saluted her and stood to attention, as Sarah opened their door.

Good morning, Mam, I'm here to collect the last of your cases, overnight cases and your secure gun case. Don't worry, the van driver knows what he's carrying, and your gun case will be locked in another safe on the van which is also triple locked, and the bottom of the case is welded to the chassis," Desmond said to Sarah and Noah.

"Great, thank you all we have left is our overcoats which we'll take with us to breakfast," Noah replied, getting used to the way a big bodyguard group with their charges were moved in and out of a large hotel and soon he would see how they boarded their plane and went through customs with all their luggage.

When the porter left with the last of their luggage, Sarah turned to Noah and kissed him on his lips. As she took a step back, his eyes opened wide, like he had been suddenly woken from a long dream, but what a dream.

"Are we back Mam?" he asked amazed.

"Yes we are, come on things to do and places to go. Let's meet up with the others," Sarah replied.

"Yes Mam!" he crisply said, stood to attention and saluted her then added "Mam!"

Sarah returned his salute and Noah picked up their overcoats opened the door and looked outside. As normal, John looked along the landing making sure everyone was ready to go. Then they all walked over to the lift and for the last time, put his lift key into its slot, turned it and soon they were in the dining room. John handed the lift keys into reception and thanked them.

"Do they know yet?" the woman receptionist asked John.

"Not a clue, John replied laughing. He walked off to the restaurant joining the others at their enlarged table.

All the morning staff were either saluting them or speaking to them adding Mam or Sir before they left their side. As they ordered their breakfast, it appeared once again everyone was looking at them.

"Why is everyone down in the restaurant at six forty-five?" Gabrielle asked her wife.

"I have no idea, but something is going on, perhaps it's because were all wearing our medals and they have never seen so many Knights and Dames in the room at one time, Lynda replied, her eyes looking around her. Gabrielle was told the van had left the hotel and was on its way to the airport, where it would pass through customs under a new diplomatic pass which covered everyone's luggage.

Gabrielle looked at her watch, soon it would be time for Janet and Tom to inspect their plane, kick the tyres, shake the ailerons see if they have enough of the right fuel and the engines had enough oil, she was certain like a car, water for the engine had to come in somewhere.

"Highya sis, thanks' for getting mum here, 1 can't wait to get her home, you see her more than I do and get to have her stay at your place for a while, it will be good for the kids to see their grandmother, she has been working hard for you on your new TG Charity and what about this fight and you dying again?

"I'm so glad Lynda could save your life and you both seem to be very close with Death, you're talking to Him and Fate all the time, I heard from mum that Lynda actually asked to speak with

Death, and she was lying across your body, apparently, dead, having a right old chinwag with Death as if He were her friend and they were just having a row with each other. Lynda certainly has some guts, I wouldn't like to talk with Death, but you have both been talking with Him for years, I'm surprised He hasn't given you a pass so you can talk to Him whenever you like without having to die to speak to Him," Janet said putting her arm around Gabrielle's shoulder and kissing her lips, as they took their seats at their table.

As soon as their lips touched, Jenny's eyes opened wide and looked at her sister. She turned and kissed her husband, waking him from his long dream.

Nobody seemed concerned about both Australians talking loud as they too were wearing their Knight's and Dame badges.

"Is that what mum said?" Gabrielle asked her sister to an earlier conversation they had about the fight before her husband took over the conversation as they sat at their table waiting for their food to arrive.

"Yep, that's right," Tom replied for Janet.

"Well, what mum says, must be right. She knows more about the fight than Lynda and I do, we were not allowed to hear what mother and the others were shouting at George. Lynda didn't tell me that she managed to speak with Death on her own terms. In fact, we haven't discussed the other side very much since the day when I spent the entire day with Death talking for ages. Oh, I met Dad when Death put me on His side of the black veil. We were talking our rather our souls were talking to each other. Dad said it didn't hurt dying and he sends his love to you all and will meet you again when it's time."

"Thanks for telling us that sis, I'm just glad his soul is okay."

Their breakfast arrived so they stopped talking and ate their meal. After breakfast, the manager of the hotel Alexander Grayham walked up to a small podium where a microphone was situated.

"Ladies and gentlemen, the time has come to tell them what has happened. The Lord Mayor of New York, will tell them what they do not know and thankyou to their friends and colleagues for keeping this secret, here is the Lord Mayor David Jenkins."

The Lord Mayor swapped places with the manager as people in the restaurant applauded him.

"Dame Gabrielle, Dame Lynda, if you would stand please," two photographers were taking their pictures as they stood and

Channel six news was once again filming them live for the whole world to see as their telescopic satellite dish had rose to its correct height and was now locked onto the satellite that would give the worlds press and TV channels, a view of what was happening here in real time.

Gabrielle and Lynda stood having no idea why. They held hands and looked at those people on their table who were smiling at them for some reason, whatever the secret was, they were in on it, so too their mother, sister and Tom.

"Thank you, now I have been told you have no idea of what has happened to everyone, they picked me to tell you. Everybody knows you had to fight George who has been taking money from our store owners to ensure their store is not burned down or people killed inside it sometimes for a great deal of money. This has been happening in the UK and all over Europe right down to the Mediterranean Sea. The UK Government sent a task force with HMS Queen Elizabeth, the latest British Aircraft Carrier in command to help the Mafia arrest and sometimes kill many of George's men with their helicopter gunships, so you can guess what our two ladies, knights of the realm had to deal with and for Dame Gabrielle taking a bullet in her right shoulder and three of their bodyguards two of whom are also Knights of the Realm and highly decorated, getting shot in an ambush outside their hotel in Rome.

"But they still carried on and got the Peace Treaty signed between the Mafia leader, Marco Don, and his wife Sereniti, with Gabrielle and Lynda who represented the UK Government.

"They also brought together the UK Charity for all TG's and have updated Kings Cross Hospital with a new wing which has a new operating theatre for TG's to be changed sex and twenty private rooms for their aftercare and loads of other things the hospital was in need off. Then they got the Don to help pay half with them paying the other half out of their own money for a new TG Charity and housing buildings for those TGs in Southern Italy and Rome to stay in while they go through the first stages of being a Transgender person.

"Then they had to update the run-down hospital in Rome, adding more rooms and an up-to-date operating theatre, which is now completed, and the first, ten Transgender people have had their sex change.

"Then they come here, to the USA and New York, where they have updated another run-down hospital, built the Charity office and refurbished an old hotel for all their TGs to stay in while they go through the first stages, then they found four houses which were knocked down, and in their place, they have built what they call a Train Station, which the other two buildings have in London and Rome. It is where the young and older boys and girls go for their evening meal as they come home knowing they are all the same and nobody else is allowed in unless they have a Universal TG Card, showing they too are Transgender.

"They have gone through a great deal to rid the world of George's Drug Empire. This is for starters, the last thing is, Gabrielle, you were not just fighting George to save Lynda's life and soul. Lynda, you had to show your unconditional love for Gabrielle to bring her back to life after George thrust his sword into Gabrielle as she moved in front of you and had the sword enter her heart, instead of yours and saved your life.

"You argued with Death to get Gabrielle's soul returned to her then Death ripped half your kidney from your body and put it into Gabrielle's body joining the two kidneys together as Gabrielle's was damaged when George thrust his sword into her body a second time.

"Once this bet was over, and you had left the Empire State Building there were hundreds if not thousands of tiny lights in our sky. Nobody knew what they were or represented until a few hours later, then our souls spoke to us and everyone knew what you had done for them.

"You both saved every soul in the world, by you killing George and Lynda showing her unconditional love for you, challenged Death and brought you back to life with your soul, back in your body where it belongs. It seems now you both must face me.

"So, we all know about your fight with George and what you were fighting for. It seems everyone in the world has heard about you, so there is no getting away from it. You will both be stared at wherever you go. Apparently, in a month, we will forget this ever happened and our souls will settle down, doing the job they were intended to do, and we'll all think this was just a nice dream and our lives will go on. We will recall both your names and that you saved everyone's soul from oblivion.

"The good people of this world have set up a collection for you both where all the money goes straight into a special bank account which your mother set up with your bank, so nobody knows how much you have. We have also been told you will live forever, but again that will fade from our memories in a month's time. That is when you officially take control of your bank account and you must use this money for yourselves, after all, you have done a lot for us, even though some people tried to kill you both. To finish if you will both come up here, please."

They started to walk up to the Mayor smiling at each other, the cheers and applause was deafening.

"Thank you." the Lord Mayor said as the applause died down. "Gabrielle and Lynda, wife and wife, it gives me a great honour to give to you a solid nine carat gold key for you to wear around your necks. It is a Key to our city, allowing you to travel anywhere you wish for free. When you see the emblem of the key on a store's window, anything you buy there will be free, don't worry I also have two keys here to wear on your jackets and please do use them, after all what is a few pounds compared to losing your life knowing your loved ones will die too if you both had not stepped forward and took on George and his thugs."

As each girl leaned forward, the Mayor put the large key on a gold chain over their necks and handed them a small gold key each.

"I Believe now you are about to leave our fine city and country to return to the UK where you have your Charity to look after and the children there to give your help and advice to. So, the people of New York wish you both well on your journey and please return to us with your staff very soon."

Thank you," Gabrielle and Lynda said together.

"No it is us who want to thank you," he replied shaking each girl by her hand. As he jumped down from the podium, he called Gabrielle and Lynda over to him.

"I just wanted to say thank you and good luck in your long future, enjoy it." He held both their hands loosely and carefully kissed Gabrielle on her cheek then looking at Lynda who nodded her head, kissed Lynda on her cheek.

They returned to their seats with more applause for them.

"You should have told us," Lynda said to everyone, you know we did it for ourselves, for Gabrielle to save my life and I would save hers as I did in the first timeline," Lynda said. "But the keys are cute," she added grinning.

"Well, now is the time to be leaving here sis," Janet said. Everyone stood and picking up their overcoats, they left the restaurant with more cheers and applause for them. Gabrielle and Lynda went over to the reception to pay their bill.

"Hello, how much do we owe you?" Gabrielle asked.

"Hold on I'll just get the manager who is dealing with your account," The receptionist said and went off to call her manager. Alexander Grayham, who had spoken to them on the podium came around the front of the desk and smiled at Gabrielle and Lynda.

"It seems you have friends in very high places," he said smiling. "Someone called HRHTQ has cleared your bill on behalf of everyone in the UK for saving their souls. There is also an invitation here for you to see the Queen at your earliest opportunity," he added handing Gabrielle the fax letter from the Queen. He shook both girl's hands and looked at the red carpet they had unrolled from the main doors to the road which had been cleared of snow.

He walked them and their party down the red carpet to their stretch limo, which would hold all of them. The Lord Mayor was standing by the open back door. They had their overcoats on as it was still minus seven degree C, and they were not even sure if the airport would be open, and their plane could fly in this weather.

Lynda got in first then Gabrielle then Alan and John sat next to them while everyone else got in through the other side doors. Saying goodbye to everyone again and waving to them, they were off to the airport. Lynda snuggled into Gabrielle's side, their heads touching, holding each other tight as they kissed, saying "I love you," to each other.

"I've just spoken with the airport controller, he said to come, our plane is dry as too the runways and they are trying to get everyone in the airport away as fast as they can, so there is a lot of traffic about, but we will be able to take off," Janet said to everyone.

Arriving at the airport there were more handshakes and red carpets to go through before the manager of the airport met them at the bottom of their red carpet over the walkway to the aircrafts open passenger door where Annabel, their stewardess, welcomed them into their aircraft.

"I am so pleased to meet you and thank you for saving our souls and for this morning. When we arrived all the runways were dry and so to all the aircraft parked here. I suppose we have your friend in high places to thank for that?" she said then they were on their plane, with Janet and Tom at the controls taking off and flying the plane for a while.

PART TWO

DEPARTURE

Chapter 12

After landing in the UK, and visiting the Queen, who gave them another three houses, to be altered free of charge and furnished, free of charge, next to the houses they have already changed for the children and young TG adults to stay in. They gave Gabrielle and Lynda a Victoria Cross for saving all their souls before they left.

They went to the Shard, and everyone had whatever they wanted. They remained in the Shard talking about their new lives, again. Nobody had any idea why they were woken this early; it was far too soon.

They left the Shard and went to their Prime shop on the Strand where Gabrielle and Lynda first met. They were going to have a look at two of their other shops.

"We'll let you all get on talking with your staff, and Walter and I could go back to our apartment, it is completed now isn't it," Wendy asked.

"Oh yes it's completed, the new second floor is completed and furnished as well." Lynda replied smiling holding Gabrielle's hand tightly.

"That's good, you had me worried there as you haven't said much about it, with the problems with Gabrielle," Wendy said, holding her husband's hand.

"Okay, you two go home, take the limo and send it back to us here. I think, with what happened with George and us all being woken so early, you had better take Tina and Noah with you. Just in case an assassin is still on the loose. Tina Noah, check the apartment out first," Lynda ordered.

"Yes Mam," they both replied.

An hour later after a phone call from Tina, who was crying down her phone, so that Noah had to take over for a while, they hurried home in their limo.

When they entered their apartment, everyone headed for the lounge, but Gabrielle could see the look of concern on Wendy's face, she too had been crying.

"What is it, Wendy?" Gabrielle asked making her sit and explain her concern to her.

"Someone has been in the Board Room."

"How do you know? You can't open the door."

Wendy handed her an open envelope, which had not been sealed. Gabrielle opened the envelope and quickly read the note. She got up and with a face like thunder and walked off down the hall.

Lynda was also reading personal letters to Gabrielle, from all sorts of people including one from Margarette, their head of the House.

"Surely nobody can get through all the security of the House and down to the Train without knowing all the passwords and face prints?" Lynda asked Brenda as she handed the letter to her to read.

Lynda was crying as she handed other handwritten letters addressed to Gabrielle and a few to Lynda. Gabrielle was out of the Board Room now, walking slowly to her office. Wendy was waiting at the door with a cup of coffee, and a miniature bottle of whiskey.

"How many?" she asked Wendy

"Eighteen hundred, then the machine ran out of space, the idiots didn't set the second answering machine up," Wendy said annoyed.

"Can you open the special single drinks, cabinet please and tell everyone, including the gunslingers, they can have one bottle this evening. Even yourself, and Walter. Tell everyone to take a seat I'll be in shortly and turn the TV on please."

Gabrielle drank her cappuccino and opened the miniature bottle of whiskey, poured it in her cup then downed it in one. When Gabrielle had managed to compose herself, she set up the answerphone so it could be heard on the big TV in the lounge. Picking up the small remote control she slowly entered the lounge.

Lynda had a seat in the middle of the big sofa and had reserved a seat for her. Gabrielle sat next to her wife, put her arm around her shoulder, pulled her close to her and they kissed.

"You may be wondering why I have opened the single drinks cabinet and have not allowed you to inspect our apartment yet. It seems while we have been away in the States and Lynda and I fought George, it seems Death has not finished his bet with us yet. The House has been taken over by a woman called Teresa, she has managed to get the builders to open the Board Room Door a few inches so she could squeeze in. Luckily only a few files have been taken, but the rest I assure you all are still secure.

"I had over eighteen hundred phone messages, had the man who set it up added the second drive, there would have been a lot more, I'm sure. There were the usual first messages for work and a few congratulations, the rest are all like this:" Gabrielle explained and pressed the play button on the answerphone remote control.

"Muma Gabrielle, we are all going to be fed to some big fish up north. Come home quickly and save us please. Miss you all and mummy Lynda.

"Mummy Lynda, help us please, I'm being sold tomorrow to a fileman, whoever that is. We need your help, love you, Ivy. "Uncle John come home and shoot, this bitch Teresa; she's making our lives hell. Ariane, love you and your gun.

"Mum, Lynda, help us, I hurt my foot and cut my leg but Teresa, didn't even put a plaster on it. Elizabeth and Kathleen are now trying to help us. Nima and Ayia, Love you.

"Gabrielle, Lynda the bitch is selling us all to a bloke called Ken Mattingly. He's got a base up north. He tells Teresa he works for George, but I thought you killed him in the States. If you're still alive come home quick before they sell us all, Kathleen.

"Lynda, a further update. The bitch is selling us all and sending some of us back to our parents with a letter signed by Gabrielle. The TG House is also up for sale. I have to go love you all. Come home quick. Kathleen and Elizabeth.

"Love you all.

"Some men came through the House last night, a hundred of the girls of all ages have been sold now, this is her second week in power. What happened to Margarette?

"Update, about ten men came through the House last night, they were smashing TV's, most of the equipment in the Games Room, they took all the game platforms and shot holes in all the games throwing them into the air and then shooting holes in them in the basement. They had a gunfight over one of the latest game platforms and there are two dead bodies in the basement.

"It's a mess down there. The hospital is all shot up, all the small instruments shot up. They couldn't get to the main X-ray machines, we boarded it all up. Sorry for the mess we have made in there, but we didn't have much to work with.

"We took all the small meds for cuts excreta upstairs and split them up between Kathleen and Elizabeth, they really are doing a fantastic job, and they're in love, good for them, enjoy life while we got it, we could well be dead tomorrow.

"Continuing, the bitch has left to take Ariane home by car, but she lives in Devon, so she will be a few hours. It has given Skye and I, Rose, sorry should have said earlier. The basement is a right off, bullets in the walls and some of the woodwork. The kitchen has been shot up, and all the fridges, washing machines and dryers sold earlier today.

"She turned all the water off to the upper floors, so we have no showers, but one, on the ground floor. The heating was turned off, two days ago, but it is still warm in some of the bedrooms we occupy, and we seem to have lost a floor or two, we're sure.

"There is a new floor in the basement. It just appeared as we were looking down there. Is the House alive? All the food in the kitchen is gone, the men took it all and had fun shooting the milk bottles wide open. Milk is everywhere, but on our food or in our coffee, oh, that's all gone too.

"Bitch has made the Train Station a proper restaurant, with Nancy, Bethany and Beatrice waitresses. They are dressed in nice clothes and wear black stockings and high heels. They look very pretty in their black dress and white apron. High heels, black stockings and their hair up. All their makeup on and nail varnish, colours changed daily. They get to shower in the Train Station. We all have our cold breakfast there and one warm drink of the day. We take it in turns to see as many of the younger boys that are left to get over the top gate to get to the Train Station after midnight, when the restaurant is closed, and our waitresses get to come back and tell us what is happening. Simon feeds the ones who come to the Train Station after midnight.

"It's Rose, Teresa is telling us Gabrielle and Lynda were killed by George, we know it's a lie, because our souls have spoken to us, but we don't know why Teresa and some of the men, don't know the truth.

"Bitch has cancelled most of the sex change operations and changed the female hormone pills to male hormone pills. Megan, Skye, Ruth and I are to have our sex change operations tomorrow, which will be watched over by the bitch, and Ken Mattingly. Please God, protect us during our time of great need.

"Hopefully will see you all on the Dark Side in a week or two. Isabell and Sofia have agreed to take over our jobs when we go to hospital later tonight.

"They are shipping out another forty of us after the operations are over, I hope they let us stay in hospital because we won't survive without their care. Our love to you all and we pray you are alright. Rose and Skye.

"Update, sorry for crying, I can't help it. Sofia, you tell them." A long pause, both girls crying. Phone hung up.

"Sorry about that, it's Isabell … crying again. It's Sofia,

"Skye, Rose, Megan and Ruth went for their operations two days ago. Ken Mattingly and Teresa were in the operating theatre with the girls as they had their operation. Rose was in first and Mr Ferguson started the operation, with a gun at his head, as Ken watched closely what he was doing. Two hours into the operation when he was forming the vagina, he needed more light, and told Ken to move away because he couldn't see properly. Ken shot him twice once in each eye then laughed. Now he can see much better, he laughed. Ken tried to complete the operation, and just cut off the rest of his male bits what were left and told a nurse to stop the bleeding, while he had Skye, Megan and Ruth brought in together.

"Ken said he would make the operation much faster and said he would change the three boys into girls in less than an hour. Luckily, they were asleep for the operation, you carry on. It's Isabell again, sounds of Sofia crying loud behind Isabell.

"Ken took a bone saw and cut the three boys testicle bits off and some bits left hanging. He told two nurses to stop the bleeding. They said they would need to introduce a drip to them to help stop the bleeding. Brian and Thomas, the anaesthetists gave them blood clotting agents and as much morphine as their bodies would take to ease the pain they would be in after the operation, but Ken had not finished yet, He had Rose brought back into the operating room, by which time, she had a catheter of some sort put into her stomach so she could empty her bladder.

"Two surgeons were trying to repair the damage Ken had done and at least complete the vagina as fast as they could but ran out of time as she was taken away back into the operating theatre.

"Ken took a scalpel, had their legs spread wide apart and made a deep incision where he thought the opening for the vagina should be. He opened it up and pushed his hand through the hole he had made and pulled some tubes which made the penis jerk about and pulled it out of the hole and cut it just outside the hole for the vagina he had made. He threw a few bits of discarded tissue over his shoulders. Pause, more crying phone hung up.

"Sorry about that, it's Sofia again, come here Isabell, I won't let that happen to you I promise. We'll all have to run away dressed as best we can and find our shoes. That was Isabell, he did the same to Skye and even pushed his hand into the new vagina Mr Ferguson had formed and cut it inside with the scalpel. There was a lot of blood and urine over the floor, and he allowed one surgeon to come in and insert the catheter through their stomach as they had nothing else to pee through. Not that they could have stood if they tried just then.

"It took the surgeon and nurses an hour to stop all the bleeding and make them as comfortable as possible before they would have major surgery later that day to repair the damage Ken had caused.

"Ken took command of four ambulances and had one person put into each ambulance once they were woken up. He took forty of the thirteen and fourteen-year-old girls in a coach and they all set off for his new base and new fishpond.

"There it is said. We are all crying for them and hope beyond all hope that you will all return soon. As soon as you get this message, please try to help us, the bitch is still in control.

"Update, this is Alia, three days later, we discovered the bitch has been to your apartment and pretending to be Lynda, has somehow got the builders to force open your Board Room Door, the bitch had to squeeze through the opening, but she was only inside a few minutes, long enough to break open one of your file cabinets and remove a couple of files, but we now have two of them in hiding.

"Isabelle and Sofia who have coats and good shoes, left early yesterday morning and walked to your apartment. They gained entry through a new side door being made and got warm in your kitchen. They put the gas cooker on. When the boss arrived at nine, it's dark now till eight thirty in the morning.

"They told him what the bitch had been up to. They looked in the Board Room and managed to get inside. It's not been damaged. The builders are in the middle of rebuilding the right safe wall in special brick. That's the only way they could get in.

"They told us Gabrielle is still ill after the fight with George. We hope you get well soon, and everyone sends their love, even those who have been sold or sent home. The boss said the men who installed the safe, are going to fix it, that was yesterday, so we hope it's done by now. The boss said they would finish in three days; the scaffolding is coming down today and they are getting proper cleaners in to start on the top floor and basement. He took them out and bought them breakfast, then lunch and an evening meal before dropping them here just after midnight with a load of chocolate bars.

"He's going to try and come into the House a few times to see what is happening with us. Oh, guess what, while Isabell and Sofia were waiting for the boss to arrive, they looked around your apartment and found all your pictures pushed into one of the cupboards in the downstairs loo. They put them all up on the walls all through downstairs, so they would know who Gabrielle and Lynda were and what they looked like.

"When the Boss, Zack I think they said his name is, saw your pictures, he couldn't believe it, swore a lot, at himself. When his men came in, he shouted at them all and showed them your pictures and told them who you were. Some of his men were also angry they had been taken in by the bitch.

"Gabrielle, it's Sofia, she whispers, the bitch has sold me to six pervs about six miles from the House. Isabell, Jessica and Clara are with me for now, but we will be sold off again soon, to some bloke in France. Help us, wherever you are. Love to you all bye.

"Gabrielle, Lynda, it's Cloe, the bitch brought me back home today, she had a letter signed by you to give to my parents. Dad beat me on and off all afternoon, it's now one in the morning, I've come downstairs to use the house phone, dad took my mobile off me and threw it against my bedroom wall in anger.

"Lynda, Gabrielle, it's Heather, the bitch brought me home this afternoon. My dad's a copper and he went ballistic beating me and mum. Mum is in a bad way, a broken arm and leg I think, she didn't stop crying for hours. I've got a broken arm and two black eyes, I can only see a bit from my left eye, my right eye is completely closed. Help us Lynda, Gabrielle, where are you? Love you all Heather.

"Update its Darcy we've heard that Skye, Rose, Megan, and Ruth

are still alive but in bad shape. They are being given paracetamol,

four a day for pain to stop them screaming, but they are still alive, just.

"Update, it's Ursula is the House alive? We have somehow lost floors two and three the basement has a new end wall and has put a wall up between the kitchen and the games room, not that there are any left. Last night we heard a voice it said This is Louise, where are my gunslingers. I'm going into Protection mode in three days. Putting in a call to ship for extra gunslingers. When we woke up, the rooms we occupied had working hot showers and toilets, and the room is lovely and warm. The room next door to ours is empty and has no running water and is cold.

"The House shrunk last night, we now only have forty rooms on each floor and all the floorboards on the top floor are repaired. It smells nice up there. I was on the ground floor when some men came into the office. A door opened in the wall behind me where there is no door. I was pulled backward into a small room and the door slammed shut.

"Continue, it's weird, a light came on, nice seat, pleasant music and Louise spoke to me. Ursula I'm in defence mode and looking after all the boy girls left here. If you think you're going to be sold, stay in your rooms and I'll lock them, nobody will be able to get in I promise. I've sent for new gunslingers. It was nice and warm in the room and I heard a lot of shouting and cussing from the men, apparently the stairs turned into a slide and the men slid down the wooden stairs on their bums because there are no carpets on them. I couldn't stop laughing as all the stairs, turned into slides. Louise kept me warm and company for two hours. It sounds utterly fantastic out there in space, come home fast love Ursula, Louise, and everyone else, can you take us there?

"Machine is running out of space, no second source to record more calls. .... Machine is running out of memory I think......Bye."

Everyone was in tears, the women hugging their husbands, a few of the men getting out their guns, checking the bullets in the clips.

"We need to rescue the girls as soon as possible," Alan said.

"We could all go now to the House and bring the girls there here," Isaac suggested.

"We need to discover where the bitch sent the girls too and those, she has sold off to pervs as one of the girl's called them," Brenda said tears rolling down her face.

Tom put his arm around her shoulder and gave her a cuddle like Neil would have done.

"What if, tomorrow morning early, Gabrielle and I go to the House, we look around at the other houses first then just wander into the House as if we were interested in buying the place, the new houses and Train Station. John and Alan will need to be in the defence training room opposite the main entrance to the office. There is separate heating in there, I'll speak to Louise about getting it hot while Gabrielle starts to look around, pointing to rooms and telling me what to write down on my iPad while it's set to record.

"We get all the girls into the defence room, get rid of the bitch after we get all the information, we can out of her. We then concentrate on a proper rescue of the girls as soon as we know where they are. Oh, Louise is going to need two gunslingers, at least for a while, volunteers' step forward, please." Lynda asked.

"We'll be her gunslingers, it will be good to speak to Louise again before we go away," Isaac said, holding his wife Geraldine's hand. They kissed each other, checked their guns and number of clips they each had.

"We'll need some spare clips Gabrielle," Isaac said.

"Double basement down, you know the way," Gabrielle said.

"Are you sure it's not been got into?" Isaac said laughing.

"Let's hope not, or Big Mamma will move orbit tomorrow."

"You're not kidding, are you?"

"No, we'll get all the TG's and leave," Gabrielle said looking at her wife. "Do you agree?" She asked her.

Lynda paused thinking the situation through, "Yes, I'll call Christine and let her know what is happening." Lynda got up and followed Isaac to the double basement, talking all the time with Gabrielle, sending each other all their love.

As Gabrielle and Lynda were walking around their first set of buildings, the new three large houses were being converted to their designs, with a walkway, that would join all their buildings together which would hopefully be completed in four months. This would give them fourteen single rooms on the top two floors all en-suite, two classrooms, on the second floor. The ground floor would have a Photography room and an Astronomy room, for extra lessons. The rest would be offices and a waiting room.

Gabrielle and Lynda entered the House. They both touched the front office door and heard a distinct sigh from Louise. They walked upstairs, with the House getting warmer. Lynda was talking to Louise constantly using telepathy. They checked each bedroom they passed and opened a door to a vacant room. No beds, wardrobes or chest of drawers and no carpets. They heard talking not far away. They listened for a short time to two fifteen-year-old boys, dressed in girl's clothes and wearing makeup as they talked quietly on the bed.

"Alright, I'll ask Teresa if we can sleep together, and we want to be lesbians and live forever. Perhaps when Gabrielle and Lynda get here, they could change us," Elizabeth said to her girlfriend Kathleen.

"I love you so much," Elizabeth said,

"And I love you with all my heart, I wish we were girls. I had a terrible life before I came here, I was beaten daily by my dad for wanting to be a girl. From eight years old, I was beaten every day until I was eleven then I was looking on the Internet and found this Charity, I sent them an email, but I didn't think I would get a reply. Just a week later I got a reply from Lynda. She wanted to meet my mother and myself in London. I gave her my address and received a train card two weeks later, to get us here and a bus pass for each of us. We came here and I've never looked back.

"When mum got home, dad gave her a beating for taking me to London. When he asked where I was, she didn't tell him, so he beat her again and again. It was all my fault. My mum packed a case and went to her sister's, she is divorced from him now. I never want to be a man; all they do is fight and beat up their wife and kids. But I'll tell you what I'd be a wife to you, that's if you wanted me?"

"You bet your life I do, with learning all these languages, we could go anywhere in the world together and we'll live forever, in love with each other. Kathleen said.

"Come here," Elizabeth whispered, and their young lips touched, hands caressing each other. They kissed putting their tongue into each other's mouth.

"I wish we were girls," Kathleen said kissing her girlfriend.

"So, do I," Elizabeth replied.

"I think we've heard enough," Teresa said, making them jump.

Teresa the house manager who was now showing Lynda and Gabrielle around after she found them walking around the House, thinking they were new possible buyers, pushed between the two women. Lynda was just about to speak to her when Gabrielle put her hand up to stop her moving forward, then whispered to her, "let's see what happens."

"Kathleen and Elizabeth, you're old enough to know better, have you two been kissing each other again? You are not going to share a bed or sleep together. I don't know what you would get up to. You should both be thinking about kissing a man, getting married to a man not another girl, and this place is turning out girls by the dozen, but not so many now.

"Those getting near to their time she should be changed, I put their ages back and got them a place at university as a man, so then they will meet other girls and marry one and have children like it should be, not lesbians, who cannot have kids. I'll change your female hormone tablets to male hormone tablets which will stop you both wanting to be Lesbians," Teresa shouted at them.

Lynda could see them from her position Kathleen was about to start crying. She smiled at her and put her finger to her mouth, wanting her to remain silent

"Excuse me, we need to get on, are there many more empty rooms on this floor?" Lynda asked holding her iPad in her hand pretending to write on it, but all the time it was recording.

"Yes, there are ninety rooms in total on this floor, well, I'm sure there were, the girls must be playing tricks on me again. There are only six rooms taken, no five, Olivia is being returned to her parents today. In the letter she has on her I have said we cannot keep him as a boy, he wants to be a girl, and he is not helping us or himself. He will never have the change operation, like I've told many of the other parents. Of course, I sign my name Gabrielle Grayson."

"Teresa what about the two lower ground floors? We were told there is a lot of room there, but aren't there at least eighty kids there in single rooms? We would need one of the floors to start work on," Gabrielle asked.

"There are currently twenty-two children under thirteen here. I've sent most of the young un's home or if they say no, I send them to a place up north, the home for the kids is run by a bloke called George Rainar, he pays me handsomely for the boys, if you wanted the bottom two floors empty, I could get rid of all the young un's within the next three days. The older boy, girls, I call them may take a bit longer, but it all depends on when you would want the floors empty.

The houses next door will all be changed within four months, and I could have the plans changed to whatever you wanted it to look like and it would all be done free of charge."

"How can you get that done?" Lynda asked.

"I'll call myself Gabrielle Grayson. I got a friend to open their apartment, well it's had a load of building work going on and I've called myself Lynda Grayson to the workers. I just removed all their photos after they left. The builders have never met Lynda. I wanted to see where their board room was and do you know, it's in a steel safe bigger than this room," Teresa replied laughing.

"It took the builders a day to get the door open just a few inches. Although they were not happy about doing it. They said they wanted confirmation from Gabrielle before they started work. After a week I rang one of the other builders there pretending to be Gabrielle and gave them permission to open the door just a bit to allow Lynda into the room to get the documents she needed.

"The boss there, I got him to come here and fix a leaking pipe under the floor. Once he was here, I gave him some other jobs to do so he was here all day, which gave his men the entire day to get the door open enough for me to get in there and see what I could find. At four pm I went to their apartment and some of the men were still working on the door.

"I heard a loud bang as they managed to get the door open a few inches. I managed to squeeze myself into their very, nice board room. Lots of computers big TV screens and files. I borrowed a long thick screwdriver and a hammer from a bloke and took ten minutes trying to open the doors, then I heard shouting outside and it was their boss. He was giving his men a right telling off, he even threatened to sack the chap I spoke to pretending to be Gabrielle. I managed to get my hand in the cabinet but only had time to take out two files. There are over a hundred in there.

"Just think of the money in those filing cabinets. I have three months to get into the safe properly. The chap in charge called the people who installed it to come and put it back together and then he had the wall rebuilt with special bricks."

"Oh, is there another building called a Train Station? What sort of name is that? We would be interested in buying that if the price is right?" Gabrielle asked.

"That is where the kids go and have their tea for free. I use it now as a paying concern. It's a restaurant and is licensed to sell hot food so that is what I do. The food comes out of their charity account and the chef and waitresses are paid by their charity account so am I, so I've given myself a pay rise. I deserve it, having to care for all these queers. I thought of killing them all, but where would I put their bodies? Apparently, George knows what to do with them if they don't behave. George says he has a fishpond, and he has put a load of I don't know what they're called but the big fish eat people in small bites," Teresa said grinning.

Gabrielle was almost in tears she had killed George in NY, now here he is again. Lynda coughed, I'm just interested, if you can access their Charity Bank Account, how much a rise did you give yourself?" Lynda asked.

"Fifteen thousand a week, I tried for twenty, but it refused to accept it for that amount. I'm content with fifteen thousand a week, at least for the next four months. I also make at least eight thousand a day from the restaurant, food is going in there three times a day and I always have them order a really nice curry for me the last thing at night."

"You've found yourself a cushy job, I was thinking, two things, first because I really want to know, who is the man in charge where you send the kids to, the ones you want to lose?"

"That's Ken Mattingly."

"Has he put any of the kids into the fishpond yet?" Lynda asked.

"No, but he takes all the kids there every day and ties a long rope around them under their arms and pushes each kid over the side with their feet just above the water. He then gets a wild dog and throws it into the water and the fish eat it to the bone in three minutes and fifty seconds. Some of the fish jump out of the water and nip their legs or feet, before they are pulled up and allowed to get dressed again." Teresa said with a smile.

"Do you mean he sends them down there naked?" Lynda asked without trying to show her hurt.

"Oh yes, it's fun apparently," Teresa laughed.

"If they are due back in four months, have you got some money put away and an have escape plan ready?"

"Yes, I'm not stupid. I skimmed a hundred grand from their charity and another hundred-grand from their own bank accounts. It's all mine now in my Lloyds savers account."

"That's brilliant." Lynda said.

"Tell me, how did you get rid of the woman who used to work here? 'cause you can't have been here very long, we've had our eyes on this place for months."

"I came in and told the manager who was over, what's her name? Doesn't matter. I said I had a lot of experience with TGs as my son is a Transgender and I watched your manager talking to the young children wrong and a number of boys had walked out of her class about thirty minutes ago. He went off looking for them and when he returned, we walked to the room where they had last been in. He counted the kids and they had returned, well they never left. He took the woman outside the room and sacked her on the spot. She left the building, I had her job, easy as that," she said and started to laugh.

Gabrielle laughed with her then said she needed the loo. Teresa sent her to the loo furthest away from us.

"Gabrielle went to where the two girls were first."

"Kathleen, Elizabeth," she said getting their attention. "How many more girls are on this floor?"

"Four, all of us next to each other. That woman is horrible to us and especially the younger boys."

"That will have to wait, I want you both to go to your rooms, get your clothes and shoes, any makeup you have and put it all in a carrier bag. Tell the other girls to dress as girls and do the same as yourselves. As quiet as you can, go downstairs, how many of the younger ones are left here?"

"Around twenty-four. Six more of the younger boys will be shipped out tomorrow to that man up north," Kathleen replied.

"That won't happen, Lynda and I are so sorry we have been gone so long and left you in the hands of this woman. We will have you all out of here by tonight. We have a lot to do.

"Take the younger boys, as quietly as you can to the ground level, you know the room where John and Alan give you talks on self-defence? Get everyone in the room. John, Alan and Sarah are there. We need to interrogate Teresa a little longer," Gabrielle told them.

"Gabrielle, can we sleep together?" Elizabeth asked holding Kathleen's hand.

"Can we talk to you both when we get you all out of here? It isn't a no, it isn't a yes, you need to move now, I have to get back to the office. Tell you what, keep holding hands and with your lipstick on you can kiss each other and put your arms around each other like you'll never let go. Now move and get everyone else on this floor moving."

"Thank you, Gabrielle, I'm so glad you're both back," Kathleen said holding Elizabeth's hand.

Gabrielle left the room heading back to the office. On the way down, she met eight of the younger children, about to leave the building.

"What are you lot doing out of your rooms?" Gabrielle asked them.

"We are going to be shipped out tomorrow, so were leaving here tonight," Olivia told Gabrielle quietly with tears in her eyes,

"We're back now, and you're not being shipped out tomorrow. Now, stop crying, we're here to help and make amends." Gabrielle took Olivia's hands into hers, then put her arms out and the eight boy girls huddled into her open arms. "You know the room where Alan and John teach you how to defend yourselves?"

"Yes, it's just across from that door there," Alison replied pointing to the door.

"Go to that room and stay there with the others. Tell Uncle John, I need him in the office in about fifteen minutes. The others will meet you there."

"That's great mummy Gabrielle, thanks for saving our lives," Jenifer said. They ran off and joined the other girls, walking out of the house into safety just eight feet from the main house.

John and Alan had no idea what was going on and where was Gabrielle.

"Gabrielle needs you in the office in fifteen minutes. Are you packing your guns?" Rebecca asked John.

"Of course, we are, why?" John asked.

"You'll need it when you get into the office, now move out of the way, there are more of us coming," Rebecca said smiling. She was much happier now, so were the other girls.

"Rebecca, you seem to know what's happening, tell us what you know until the others arrive," Alan whispered in her ear.

"Okay, Teresa the bitch was going to sell us tomorrow to Ken Mattingly, who owns the big fishpond where they eat people. He works for George Rainer. He has a hundred men working for him and they have taken all the girls up there and drop them naked, so their feet and legs are just above the fishpond then he throws in a dead dog or other animal, so the fish take bites out of the girl's feet and legs before they are pulled back to the top when they get dressed. Everyone must behave, and do as they say or the next day, they'll drop them into the fishpond. They say it takes three minutes and fifty seconds to devour a girl my age."

"My God, I thought we had finished with his gangs, and the fishpond, what can we do?" Alan asked John.

John opened the door to see another small twelve-year old girl walking slowly along the path, she was shaking as four more twelve-year old girls followed her.

"Come on girls, Amy, Hannah, Imagen, Jessica, hurry up in the room with the others, Alan is in there," John said ushering the girls into the room.

Emma had taken charge just outside the door, smiling, with her finger to her mouth, was waving the other girls into the room. Alan was holding Leah and Nima who were sobbing, very frightened on each knee.

Kathleen and Elizabeth were bringing the last of the girls and two bags of shoes and girl's clothes. Holding hands, they were slowly urging the last of the girls forward.

John watched them walk by him, tears in his eyes. He opened his phone and fast dialled his wife.

"Jenny love, it's a right mess here, most of the kids have been sold to a man called George Rainer," John was sobbing, as too Jenny on the other end of the phone. "Bring everyone here in all the transport we've got."

"Alright my love, back up is on its way," Jenny replied.

"Oh blankets, as many as we have," he added.

"Elizabeth, Kathleen, let me have those carrier bags, help is on the way."

"Is that really you Uncle John?" Kathleen asked.

"Yes, it is Kathleen." He opened his Jacket to show them his gun.

"It really is him," Kathleen said. She turned with tears in her eyes still holding hands and kissed Elizabeth's lips.

"You two still in love? Sleeping together yet?" John asked.

"No, the bitch won't let us, she says she hates lesbians," Elizabeth said looking at John.

"She has picked the wrong lesbians to upset, Gabrielle and Lynda won't like that at all."

"I know they came into the room we were snogging in and didn't look pleased as the Bitch told her what she thought of us and all Lesbians. Gabrielle had tears running down her face and Lynda had to take over," Kathleen added and ushered Grace along the path in her bare feet. John looked at her then picked her up in his arms.

"Did you lose your shoes Grace?" John asked her.

"Yes, but Elizabeth came into our room and found them, they are with a load of others in her bag."

"That's good then." He smiled at the two fifteen-year-old girls still holding hands. He thought of Paul when he was fifteen and struggling to be a girl. He had talked with Death again that year.

He walked into the room and put Grace down. "Look through these bags and find your shoes, then you can help me by giving all the other girls their shoes. I know you are all dirty and hungry. Who is the Chef now in the Train Station?"

"Simon, he helps us all he can, but the bitch uses it for real paying customers it's open till twelve at night. We sometimes sneak out because we are hungry. Simon cooks us a meal then and Samantha still helps him." Elizabeth told him.

"Is there anyone else helping in there?"

"They usually dress three of the eighteen-year-old girls nicely and have them wait the tables. They get paid by a small meal at the end of their shift which is usually ten in the morning till twelve midnight. There are two other women who help with the tables and they are very, strict if they see us in there. They leave around nine in the evening but get paid till midnight," Kathleen added.

"Wow, you know a lot," Alan replied.

"We find out all we can to try and rescue the others, they have sold, we found them with this as well and a few other things as the Bitch was going to sell most of us soon. She's been trying to sell our House for two months, since she took over, but we always put the people off."

"Are the eighteen-year-old real girls now?" Alan asked.

"No, the Bitch swapped their meds from girls to boys and cancelled their operations saying they had changed their minds." Katherine told him.

"Get as much of your clothes on now help is on its way, we're going to get you all fed for a start," John said.

John heard cars coming to a skidding stop and people slamming car doors. The people were running and sliding up the steps, then along the flat path to the building's main doors. Nicole who had taken over door duty with John's overcoat wrapped around her heard the cars arrive as well and told everyone the others were here then she went outside and along to the end of the building they were in and directed the adults into the room.

Jenny was in first, hugging her husband and kissing him. Iris took the blanket from under her arm and covered herself and her friend in it. John was starting to explain what happened and what he had planned to do.

"Why not let us explain it all Uncle John, while you go in with Uncle Alan and kill the bitch. Don't worry we are all used to gunfire now," Kathleen said still holding Elizabeth's hand tightly.

"You're right come on Alan, people to kill," he said laughing. Next in was Sarah. She smiled and kissed her husband, with two girls inside his overcoat covering them up. "Come on girls, let your Uncle Alan go now, he has work to do."

As John and Alan left the room, other gunslingers and their wives were following the others into the room. In the office there were three people two standing and one sitting. Alan nodded to John and removed his gun from its holster. They walked silently a few more feet, then John put his hand on the door handle and opened the door. He pushed his head and shoulders into the room followed by his gun. Alan stood behind him, his gun in his hand pointing it at the woman sat at the table.

"Who are you?" Teresa asked.

"Move in John," Alan said behind him.

"I'm John, this is Alan, I'm Gabrielle's bodyguard.

"I'm Alan, Lynda's bodyguard. Surely you have heard of us?" Alan asked Teresa.

"No, well I am that lady's bodyguard, Alan is that lady's bodyguard, does that help you?"

"No not really," Teresa replied.

"Then allow me to introduce Gabrielle Grayson and Lynda Grayson, the owners of this establishment and the Train Station," Alan said smiling. Teresa went to stand but two arms pushed her firmly into her seat.

"Boss we have 30 girls in our room who need a shower, change of clothes and most of all a meal, and two want to be married to each other, Kathleen and Elizabeth."

"Stupid boys, they want a sex change, then get married as girls, Lesbians what next?"

"Will you give us the codes to your bank accounts?" Gabrielle asked.

"No bloody way who do you think you are Gabrielle?"

"Yes," she replied then was at Lynda's side holding her close and they kissed passionately.

"John, Alan, Lynda, do we do this further interrogation, internally or externally, where the fishpond is or let the police have her? The courts would take ages giving us our money back and we have over two hundred of our girls to find and sort out those who have had their grants stopped," Gabrielle asked.

"I say do it internally, then I get the chance to put a bullet through her eyes," John said, pointing his gun at Teresa.

"Not if I do it first," Alan said.

"I agree, do it Internally, we'll see justice done that way and we can drop her into the fishpond if she doesn't cooperate," Lynda said smiling.

Gabrielle pulled Teresa's head back, so she was looking at the wall opposite her. There was a large glass covered picture of Gabrielle and Lynda being handed the keys of the property.

"Shit." is all she said.

"Alan pop outside and tell the Girls to get the younger girls into the cars, we'll leave in five minutes," Lynda said.

"Yes Boss," Alan replied and left the room.

A minute later came the sound of young boys, who desperately wanted to be girls shout "Hooray, the bitch will die tonight not us." Then it was quiet.

"One more time, I want the passwords to your bank account, or you can put the money back into our two accounts now," Gabrielle ordered.

"No, that's the only thing keeping me alive," Teresa replied. Gabrielle looked at her gold and diamond watch, it was twelve forty-five, there was a lot to do and mouths to feed. And where were they all going to sleep tonight? They couldn't stay here there was nobody to look after them?"

"One last time the girls are hungry they need to be fed Codes, Fishpond or prison?"

"I would close your eyes if I were you, a very bright light will fill the room in a moment," Gabrielle said, "I need to speak to my wife to decide your fate."

Their green eyes shone brightly as they spoke to each other. Teresa watched in horror as she saw their eyes shine. She was shaking now, if she went to prison, she would be there for a long time and the courts would give them their money back. The lights went out and Lynda left the room. "Prison it is then."

"No wait.!" She pulled a note out of the desk drawer then wrote down her savings account number and password. She sent the money to Gabrielle's bank account. "Now I want to leave," She demanded.

"Give me your phone!" Gabrielle ordered. She took the phone from Teresa and deleted all their bank accounts from it then she removed the Sim Card and snapped it in half. Her eyes shone bright green, and the Sim Card melted.

"I said I would like to leave now. You have your money back I want to go.

"Where is your handbag?" Gabrielle asked.

Teresa picked it up from the floor. She had a warm coat on because the House was cold. Gabrielle thought to her wife then she smiled. She walked around to where Teresa was sat, touched her body then they were gone. Gabrielle dropped Teresa into the six-foot-deep snow by the side of Loch Ness in Scotland. It was cold there, just like her boy girls were cold where they were. Gabrielle was gone, sitting in the front seat of their long limo.

"Hello girls, are you hungry?" Gabrielle asked.

"Yesss," they all shouted.

"My love, why were you so long? I thought she had hurt you or something."

"No sweetheart I checked the office for books or anything else she had then I did as you suggested."

"Suggested? What was that?" Lynda asked.

"You suggested to drop her off in Scotland. She is now in six feet of snow, freezing cold on the side of Loch Ness. Let's hope Nessie is hungry tonight, dinner is waiting for him."

"You never did?"

"Yes, I did," Gabrielle replied.

"Girl's, mummy Gabrielle has just dropped the bitch into six feet of cold snow by the side of Loch Ness, where it's dark and freezing cold," Lynda told the girls in the back of the limo.

All the girls were cheering and clapping their hands together. "I also got all our money back. It's in our bank account."

"Well done my love, were you looking for these?" Lynda asked and held up two of their files and a thick ledger with the names and addresses of where Teresa sent the girls back home. The names of girls she sold to George and the address of his place plus a load of other stuff, including bank accounts.

"Did you order us food as well?" Lynda asked, putting the four books, two files, from their apartment and six files from the office into a carrier bag."

"Of course, my love." Gabrielle put her arm around her wife's shoulder and kissed her.

The car was nice and warm now but some of the girls were still shivering.

"We're here but let Aunty Lynda and me, go in and throw out all the paying customers. John, Alan, you'll come with us. Noah, can you stay in the driving seat so you can keep the engine running and the heater on, full power please?" Gabrielle asked. Lynda was already out of the car with Alan close behind her. Gabrielle got out of the car slipping on the fresh snow into her wife's arms. Alan helped hold her up as John came around the front of the car looking into the Train Station.

The four people entered the Train Station and looked at the twenty couples sat at tables eating.

"I'm afraid this establishment is closed to the public from now on. If you would all leave this establishment now, please," Gabrielle shouted into the large room.

"And who's going to make, us, not you pretty girls," a man started to argue.

"That would be me then," John said and pulled out his gun.

"And that would be me as well," Alan said withdrawing his gun.

"That's her there," Lynda shouted at the only adult waitress she didn't recognise. She's the one who spat into my food, then she spat into a bowl, opened a fresh roll and rubbed it into her spit and then squeezed it all over my food. God knows what else she may have done with it," Lynda said.

Everyone had cleared the tables by now. The last two men who were sitting at the table near the far side of the room, were looking at John and Alan.

"Put your silencer on Alan I think we've struck lucky," John said smiling, screwing his own silencer onto the end of the barrel.

"Excuse me for asking, by any chance are you the two men who are taking the twelve-year-old boy girls to the fishpond?" John asked them.

"Yes, we are, can we pick them up now?"

"Yes, we have them outside in five of our cars."

"We'll load them now then."

"Who is in charge up there now?" John asked.

"Ken Mattingly. Look we're in a hurry," the man argued.

"So are we, turn around you can see the kids in the cars."

"Oh yea, well come on then let's have them."

"I gotta be sure with the kids, I need to make sure I have the right address," John replied.

John turned around and took the notepad and pencil from the waitresses' waist. "Scribble his address on there or you don't have the kids," John said.

The man did as he was told. John picked up the notepad and looked at it."

John went over to Gabrielle and quickly spoke to her. While Alan continued to interrogate the men. Gabrielle and Lynda ushered the girls into the restaurant with the other adults. Some girls without shoes were carried into the restaurant and sat on a chair. Suddenly they were met by the three older girls who worked in the restaurant. Simon and Samantha welcomed the girls in and started to hand out the younger ones their favourite meal, sausage and chips while the fifteen-year-olds had fish and chips with hot raspberry tart and custard for desert and for anyone still hungry. There was any flavour ice cream they wanted with thick or clotted cream.

"One last question how many kids does he have up there?" Alan asked the man.

"With these there'll be two hundred and thirty."

"Have any of them been changed yet?" Alan asked.

"This group is just north of Macclesfield where the radio telescope is."

"Has he built a new Fishpond?" John asked him.

"Yes, when we left the other place, we have to keep moving around. He made us dig out a new one, with a proper digger of course and it's got a thick liner so every now and then he can have it emptied and any old bones burned. We were almost caught out on the last one, he didn't realise you could get DNA from bones when the police discovered it.

"Yes, three or four of the older ones have been sort of half changed, but Ken helped one of the surgeons do it. They all have to pee into a with a pipe coming out of their belly, it' grows and they bleed all over the place. It's sickening, he chopped the boy's bits off all of them. The surgeon tried to continue for twenty minutes then Ken shot him.

"And you stood by and did nothing?" Alan asked him.

"It's Ken, nobody goes against Ken."

"Is Ken still there now?"

"Ken is now in control. All our wages have been doubled to feed the kids and look after them. We take them to the fishpond and drop them close to the edge, a couple get bitten by the Parana fish, they're bloody big now. I think Ken is thinking of pushing all the kids in; the older ones who are bleeding a lot from between their legs, they'll go first, I suppose they'll be glad they're out of pain."

"Would you agree to that?" Alan asked.

"No option if we leave, Ken will kill our families unless we're killed in a gunfight. Then our wives get two hundred and fifty thousand to see them through and sometimes he will find a house which he'll buy for them to keep them quiet.

"Look I can see you're going to kill us, but we could help you, moving all these kids is not going to be easy, and if you're thinking of rescuing the kids up at the new digs, how do you intend to move almost two hundred kids in one go, a stream of cars? I have a mate with another double decker bus, he could meet us there if you can get them out."

"What tonight?" Alan asked surprised at the man's thinking. "How many men does Mac have there?" Alan asked.

"There are a hundred and twenty of us, next week we start blowing up all Gabrielle and Lynda's shops. Ken told us it was orders from George, he won the fight between himself and Gabrielle."

"John, come here please," Alan called. "There is Gabrielle and Lynda, George lost the fight and Death has him now in one of His special rooms at the bottom of his Domain," Alan said putting the men right.

"John, Gabrielle, Lynda, here please," Alan called again.

"This is Gabrielle and Lynda, no speaking from anyone except the men or me.

Gabrielle and Lynda looked at Alan, not believing what he was saying, but it appeared to be important. John just kept quiet, he had been listening to their conversation and was getting worried himself.

"Really?" Both men asked at the same time. "Glad to meet you both in person and in the flesh so to speak. Unlike George I hear," the first man said.

"Then you had better decide, rescue them tonight, or there will be less kids there tomorrow. The younger ones will go into the fishpond first. He'll push a few in at a time, making the other boys watch their friends being eaten alive. We timed it, man or boy, it takes three minutes and fifty seconds for a fish to devour one of the kids, or a man. It's the same time, every time, weird, don't you think? He will keep the oldest boys to service his clients."

"But they are still boys at the moment, they haven't had a sex change yet," Alan told the two men.

"Ken doesn't care, most of the clients are Sadists or Paedophiles, none of them care, especially the Paedophiles."

"Yes, but where are we going to put all these kids tonight let alone the ones we can rescue?" Alan asked the two men.

"I'm Gerald, that's Patrick. You're John and Alan we all know you two. If I may suggest, this looks big enough to hold all the kids. You could put a few black out curtains up a few tellies,

Games Console. The place is warm, has toilets, I bet it even has showers. It has food, a good chef, I can vouch for, and the pretty eighteen-year-old girls are brilliant waitresses. You also have a twenty-four-hour large Food and Clothes shop down the road, you could buy the kids of all age's clothes shoes and welly boots down there."

"Any other ideas?" Alan asked.

"Blankets or duvets for everyone and a thick coat. I bet there will be a few snow days next week. See what the weather is like, and the long-range forecast is, and if it's still snowing, a few sledges for the kids to play on, so they'll get wet. Have you got washing machines or tumble dryers?" Gerald asked.

"We did but Teresa sold everything including all the kids University notes, although Eleanor, a fourteen-year- old girl, told me all their computers are hidden somewhere in the building and their iPads," Alan replied.

"Have you got to redecorate the place?" Gerald asked.

"Yes, we have."

"Well rather than blow your shops up, there are at least eighty men who can paint, hang wallpaper and put flat pack furniture together. I also know the numbers to the main safe's there is close to ten million in one and the smaller safes, at least five million. We could be paid out of that, and it would give you money to buy all the paint paper and tools we'll need. The rest you could have for your charity."

"Gabrielle, Lynda, the ball is in your court," Alan said, turning to look at the girls who had tears in their eyes, as well as all the women in the Train Station.

"They may look as if they are helping us but for now, keep your gun on them and shoot them if they try to run off," John said to Alan.

"Our TG House is in a hell of a state, no carpets and all the beds sold on the first three floors. Gerald has a good plan and bringing eighty men down with us, it will make the house painting go much faster," Gabrielle said, holding her wife's hand.

"We'll put all the girls in here, get them new clothes, blankets and bedding. The Train Station will hold them all for a week at least," Lynda added, using Gerald's words.

"It sounds great," Lynda said thinking back to when she didn't have a proper bed, clothes or a blanket to cover her.

Gabrielle could see the tears swelling in her eyes and held her hand firmly in hers.

"It's okay love, we'll get there in the end," Gabrielle told her wife.

"Like Lynda said, it sounds great, but we need the TG House now. The paint job alone will take a couple of firms a month to complete the bedrooms, it would be another month for all the carpets to be laid and the beds and furniture put together. They can't stay here with no beds and where are we going to get all their clothes?" Janet added making everyone think.

It took twenty minutes for John to pass on Gerald's ideas. Everyone agreed it was the only way out.

Chapter 13

At seven pm, after getting the girls some clothes from the local shops, Gabrielle, Lynda, John, Alan, Noah, Geraldine, Janet's bodyguard Patrick and Gerald finally boarded the bus and set off to Kens new fifty-bedroom mansion, with three reception rooms that could all be opened to make one long room. Ken's most religious men to him, men he could rely on to kill his own lower men, if necessary, slept on the top floor.

The four boy girls, who were now in a bad shape, were on the second floor and all they were given was paracetamol for their pain, not that they would need it much longer, Ken had decided to throw one of them into the pond each morning followed by ten of the younger boy girls and two seventeen-year-old boy girls. None of them would become girls now, they would all be fed to the fish. He had to start thinking of himself and why he had accepted the last thirty odd boy girls he had no idea. They would all die, just a different way if he could sell them to a paedophile group.

On the way up Geraldene was picking up a District Nurse to help decide if the eighteen-year-old TGs were fit to travel and to see to their suprapubic catheters. She had brought a couple of different sizes with her and leg bags to collect the urine. She also brought a medical bag full, with all sorts of items tablets and creams she might need.

They were now travelling up the M1, catching up to the bus that was ten miles ahead. Geraldine was driving the four wheeled drive Nison Armada.

Patrick was on his phone to Frank, who had another bus. "Hi Frank, like I said before I left, I need your help. Get your bus to the mansion and pick up the youngest kids first, all seats, some on the floor and drive off asap. Meet up at the Train Station like we did before." the last thing he gave him was the Postal Address.

"Trevor, this is Patrick. They are going to plan a rescue tonight, I'm still on the way up with a few gunslingers on board, yes, their packing, John and Alan yes that Alan will be in command. They are in bad shape down there it's completely wrecked and needs redecorating from top to bottom. New carpets, then loads of flat packed bedroom furniture and beds. They'll pay us, rather George will but he's dead. Yes, I've got Gabrielle, she's about five feet behind me with her wife Lynda. Listen it's better than being shot or blown up. I don't trust Ken's top twenty either.

"Okay, Frank is on his way to you with Robert. Will you help get the youngest girls onto the bus? You will also need some help, get Trevor, Phil, Craig, Eric, Zack and Philip, they are good with the kids. The ones nearest the door I guess at least seventy, as many as you can get on the bus, be as quiet as you can, they will be expecting a bus and kids walking about.

"Get Trevor and Craig on the bus to look after the kids, they'll be told of their jobs when they get there. Yes, work for us all. Does he? I got his number I forgot all about him, good idea.

"Thanks. Well Gabrielle, it seems like we'll have our eighty men. Larry has another sixty-seater coach, which will take most of our men, he's going to ring his mate who has a small thirty-seater coach for school runs, the four drivers will need paying before they return, cash only please, you'll need about five-grand for them to keep their mouths closed, cash only. I'll grab as much as I can from the safes."

"I thought you said there are only two safes?" Lynda said.

"I told you about the smallest and next size up then there are two more safes, one about four-foot-high two feet across, which is where they kept all their second copy cook-books. Then there is another safe, eight foot tall, six foot wide and eight foot deep, full of money. We'll see how much when we get there." "

"Children first," Gabrielle said.

"Of course," Patrick replied. "There's a four by four following us, been behind for the past five miles."

"It's okay, that will be Geraldine and Alice," Gabrielle told him. Lynda went to the back of the bus to check.

"It's them," she said into Gabrielle's head.

"It's them, Gabrielle told everyone glad that it was them.

"How many more miles?" Gabrielle asked.

"About eight miles, I dare not put my foot down we could go off the road."

"I understand," Gabrielle said. There was a ping on Patrick's phone.

"A text from Frank. Loading with a lot of help from the men."

Six minutes later, he had another text. "Bus overflowing, eighty-nine aboard, ninety, ninety-five, one hundred on board, 15, 15 to16 year olds,73 12-to-15-year old's.20 men sat on the floor with kids sitting on their laps and legs. All the under 12's aboard, sitting on the floor I'm afraid it's the best I could do sorry. A plan has been formed.

"That leaves a lot of girls and your men." Lynda said trying to work out the exact number.

"Then there are the men, you'll need them to help get the House painted and all the other jobs done if you want it done in a week."

"Yes, you're right," Gerald replied.

A short time later there was the sound of a bus horn and they watched the bus as it took their girl's home.

"Hello mum, we are almost there, the other bus just passed us on the way to you. we will mum, see you soon, love you, bye," Lynda said.

Lynda's phone rang, "speaking, hi Margarette, that's great news, what time are they starting? Excellent, start on the top floor, can you wipe all the paint a with a cloth to get it ready for painting, yes, you name your rate, we'll pay it from our money. The others will be paid by the charity. Yes, thank you very much." She looked at her watch it was now one a.m., and they were just pulling up in front of the other coach.

Everyone got off the bus, they had put blankets over the seats ready for the girls to sit on and get warm. The bodyguards started to look around then saw the state of the boy girls. John started to take control.

Twenty-six boy girls who had shoes on their feet and dressed only in a small nightdress, he took pictures of them all standing ready to leave.

"We don't need shoes; we've been walking around like this for the past four weeks," Hannah said quietly.

"I'm so sorry, Alan said standing behind John.

"Hannah, take out the next twenty girls," John said.

"Emma, get the next twenty in a line as soon as the others have left the building, you take your group to the bus. Chloe, as soon as Hannah's group have left you get out the next twenty girls. Jessica, you take fifteen twelve to fifteen-year-olds, Sophia, you bring up your group. With the last ten of the sixteen-year-olds. when you get onto the bus, it will be very cramped, the last group if needed will board the coach behind. You will have to sit on the floor for the trip down. But Lynda is hoping to speak to you all at some stage. Everyone be quiet and we'll get you home," John said.

Emily was taking the nurse and Geraldene upstairs to where the first half girl was. Both women gasped when they saw the state, she was in. Opening her bag, Alice took out her thermometer and took her temperature. It was 104 F. Next was her blood-pressure then she drew some blood for testing later. She looked down at what was left of her male bits then examined her internally, making her squirm and move her body about. You told me what Gabrielle and Lynda can do, but I think this is a lot more, than they can fix," Alice said.

"She's in a real mess, George wanted to operate on her, give her a sex change, he did that alright, but he had no idea what he was doing. Another surgeon stepped in and inserted the suprapubic, thing but that Teresa sent all four half girls up with no meds or proper bags, so we've done our best and tomorrow, she will be thrown into the fishpond unless you can take her tonight with the others further along.

The crying and sobs were too much for the men on the top floor. Grayham another man who decided to leave the main group and become a worker for a couple of weeks, was on the second floor, checking the girls who were in trouble and was now in with Alice, looking at the poor girl on the raised bed.

"And what's going on here?" a deep voice said bringing them all back to reality.

"Oliver," Grayham said shocked. I had to get a district nurse to see to her, she's burning up, so are the others."

"Let us take them to a hospital, please," Alice asked him. He pulled out his gun, not seeing Geraldene behind Alice, she had her gun already pointing at him, a hip shot. Oliver was waving his gun around pointing it at Alice then levelling it at Ruth, the girl on the bed.

"The answer is no." Then blood was dripping down his face with a hole right between his eyes. He was now falling to the floor dead. Alice gasped and turned to look at Geraldine. There was no sound from her gun, its silencer took care of all the exploding gases.

"He was going to pull his trigger killing Ruth, then the rest of us and more than likely, kill the other girls too. Now if you can clean her up, do you have any penicillin?"

"Yes, I'll give her an injection, get a large dose into her which should bring her temperature down as well. Emily, can you find Gabrielle and Lynda for me please and bring them here?"

"On my way," she replied, running off in her bare feet. Patrick was opening the smallest safe, where they found two hundred-grand. It went into the large plastic bag they had then they moved on to the next safe which Patrick quickly opened. There was a lot more money in there, plus four sets of books for the mansion.

They started to load the money at least three-hundred-grand then Emily found them.

"Geraldine wants to see you both, she just killed a man a bullet right between his eyes, from a hip shot," she said grinning.

"Do you know his name?" Patrick asked.

"Oliver, or something like that," she replied.

"Do you know him?" Gabrielle, asked.

"Oliver is second in command, if he was still alive, then he would have killed them all. Good one to lose."

"Noah, help Patrick load the money into this third bag, I didn't realise money was so big and heavy," Lynda said smiling.

"As soon as you start your next look around see if you can see a suitcase or a large bag for the money, give them to Patrick. Look after him, he's recouping money George took from us. We'll be back soon," Lynda said, smiling at her wife.

They held hands giving all their love to each other as they knew what the task would be upstairs.

"Here they are, you killed the second in command," Emily said to Geraldine.

"Shhh!" Gabrielle whispered on hearing movement upstairs.

Everyone held their breath as footsteps came down the stairs. Gabrielle looked at Geraldine and nodded. Geraldine took out her gun and put another bullet up the spout.

"What are you doing here? Who let you in?" The man asked.

"We're trying to save the life of this girl, and who are you?" Lynda boldly asked.

"Daniel, I wouldn't bother, he looked at his watch. "It's still early, two fifteen. I need some sleep, well at nine a.m. He's got a date with some fish outside," he replied and got out his gun.

There was a quiet hiss and he fell into Lynda's arms then they were both gone, and Lynda came back alone.

"May I?" Lynda asked her wife.

"If you like, be careful I don't want to lose you." Gabrielle replied then her wife touched Oliver's, arm and both disappeared. Lynda was back, alone again a second later.

"Let's get on with this, we need her stood up." Lynda said. Alice and Geraldine started to move Ruth and got her to her feet. She moaned, then Gabrielle spoke to him.

"Tell me Ruth, what colour would you like your hair?"

"Black."

"What size breast cup do you want?"

"Size D."

"What length of your hair?"

"Longer than it is, halfway down my back."

"What about you Emily?"

"Same as Ruth if I can."

"How old are you?" Lynda asked smiling.

"Fifteen next month," he replied.

"We can go to a C cup you'll grow into a D cup as you get older."

"Why ask them the questions?" Alice asked.

"Look and see," Geraldine answered Alice's enquiry as Gabrielle and Lynda put their arms around Ruth, holding her upright. Emily stood on a pile of books and put her arms behind her back.

"Now try and think of your length of hair, Lynda said holding Gabrielle's hands.

Geraldine closed the door. "This part is fantastic," she said standing next to Alice.

The room turned bright green as Gabrielle and Lynda spoke to each other, concentrating on the change in sex, and other problems for Ruth.

Both their hair turned black and started to grow longer, then their heads changed shape, to a girl's face. Their voice changed next and then their breasts started to grow with Ruth's false breasts falling out of her breast tissue and her D cup breasts started to grow as did Emily's C cup size breasts.

They had to go slower now as they were also healing two broken chest bones and the cuts to her skin. Then they moved down to their vaginas, Emily's was changed faster than Ruth, but she still stood there, the girls weren't finished yet by a long way.

They removed all Ruth's mail bits and healed the holes which Ken had left. Then her vagina was made and healed. The suprapubic catheter was left as it was a form of plastic and inside her body. They could have removed it but were not sure about the hole in her belly and bladder.

With her body now healed, they concentrated on both girl's bone structure. They started with slimmer arms and smaller hands so they could wear fine blouses. Then they changed their breastbone structure their hips legs and feet, at the same time removing all the hair from their body except on their heads. Their eyes grew darker as Emily got off the books, feeling her body, her breasts and between her legs.

"Wow, she said in a young girl's voice. This is fantastic, thank you so much Gabrielle and you too Lynda," she said in her new female voice.

Alice was amazed and looked at Ruth, she had thin arms, hands, legs and feet. Her breasts had grown to a size D cup, with her Black hair now halfway down her back, but no other hair on her body. Her breast bones had changed giving her the shape of a woman and she now had hips. She was starting to come around and they helped her sit on her bed.

Alice examined her where her mail bits had been hacked off with a bone saw. Alice put on her sterile gloves and gave her an internal examination.

"Ruth is a woman, and she's fine now. I don't believe what I've seen," she said, "Can you give me thinner arms hands, legs and feet?" she asked.

"We'll see what we can do for you back home. Can you remove the catheter now?" Gabrielle, asked.

"Yes. Let's see what happens, how is the time going?"

"Against us. It's two twenty-five, we should be away from here by now," Gabrielle said.

"I just need to put a normal catheter into her urethral, so her bladder drains into the bag." Alice said, and in two minutes her expert hands completed the job.

"Ruth are you awake properly? Can you stand up and walk?" Lynda asked her.

"I'm a real woman, I feel so different," she said in her new female voice and put her slender hands on her breasts, feeling them, then down her front feeling the area where the remains of her male parts were gone and now, she had a pipe coming out of her urethral orifice.

"Don't worry, I'll remove it when we get back, yes, you're a real woman now, and you look absolutely, radiant, according to Lynda, you have the full female anatomy, which means, you could have children if you wanted," Alice explained to her. Ruth got off the bed and stood up, holding the white plastic bag in her right petite hand.

"I'll go next door and see how our next patient is, Alice said, packing up her bag. She quickly left the room while Lynda and Gabrielle finished sorting out Ruth.

"I'm standing okay, and I'm walking okay, I feel okay too."

"Right let's get you downstairs and onto the bus pronto, there are three more to of you to change and they are all in a bad way," Lynda, said. She held Ruth's hand and they were just outside the bus.

"Now get on and move any girls off the long seat at the back and lay down until we get home." Lynda ordered with Ruth by her side to quietly move the girls away and prepare the front long seat, for the next girl.

"Okay Lynda will do." Ruth was gone, walking onto the bus. Lynda heard a few bad words, but a single word from Ruth calmed everyone down and they were quiet again.

"Is everything alright?" Lynda asked Gabrielle, mind to mind.

"Don't be long Sky doesn't have long to live." Gabrielle said then Lynda was by her side.

"Where is Alice?" Lynda asked her wife.

"She gave Skye an injection of penicillin then went next door with her bag.

"What's wrong with Skye, can she stand, talk?" Lynda asked.

"Yes, to both," Gabrielle replied.

"Let's get her on her feet and changed, then we'll send the bus home, we don't have long, the advanced team of twelve gunslingers might arrive before five, but it's still dark out." Skye was on her feet, standing upright. "Think about the length of your hair, and the colour you want. What size breasts you want, you shouldn't go larger than a D cup?" Lynda was saying to her then their eyes turned bright green. Holding hands over her, they soon had her changed to a woman with an all-new body shape, thin arms, hands, legs and feet, a hairless body, except for her long blond hair down to her bottom.

"You go find Patrick, leave the other money get him onto the coach. As soon as you have had the catheter removed, and a different one put in, I want you to get on the bus. Call out Patrick's name, and Alan's get them on the bus, then leave here," Gabrielle said to Skye.

"Where's Alice?" She's been a long time Geraldine have your gun ready shoot to kill as soon as you see anyone from upstairs," Lynda said to Geraldine.

Lynda and Geraldine left the room and carefully entered the room next door. Geraldine started to cry, not that it would change her aim, but it might help them now if there was a man from upstairs in the room.

Alice was cleaning up the boy girl with a man watching her.

"What's the matter Ruth?" she asked.

"Both girls are dead, they didn't make it. She was sobbing now, real tears running down her face. The man looked at her.

"Better they're dead now than being chucked into the fishpond still alive, with an injection of something to paralyze you, so you don't hurt the fish as they are eating you alive, it only takes, three minutes and fifty seconds."

As Geraldine stood, her gun went to her hip and she quickly fired, a bullet between the man's eyes. She went to move, and Alice just barely shook her head and with her hand on her stomach, pointed behind her and gave her the V sign.

"Can you go next door?" Sarah just stabbed herself with a needle of some kind and she's feeling sick now?" she asked Alice, to try and get her out of the room.

Geraldine stepped across the room bumping into a table.

"Look at me I can't stand on my own two feet I'll keep an eye on this one."

"It's not worth it, she's only got a few minutes to live." The man sat opposite her waved his gun, Alice picked up her bag and walked past Geraldine crying herself.

It left Lynda in a tricky situation, her gunslinger was in front of her and could only get one clear shot off. She would have to put herself into the hands of the gunslinger and do exactly as she told her to do.

Gabrielle spoke to Lynda, mind to mind. "Alice has swapped catheters and Skye is now getting herself onto the bus. The rest of the men are aboard the second coach and Patrick has found the other big safe. He left a mark on the floor, the sign for a female. He couldn't open the door and has no, idea if anything is in there. I'll see if I can open the door if not, I'll jump into the safe, have a quick look then jump out," Gabrielle said into Lynda's head.

"Take care my love please, the money isn't worth it. It takes three minutes and fifty seconds for the fish to consume a person."

"What's happening here, why have we got another George time in the UK?" Gabrielle asked Lynda.

"Gabrielle is dead, she died in the States, Ken is running the show now and he wants some money to be able to pay his guys," the man with the gun said.

Lynda heard two puffs of gas from Geraldine's gun. She turned her head to see both men falling to the floor. They were both dead. She got up and checked on Rose, she was alive and smiling at her.

"Can you stand?" Geraldine asked Rose.

"Yes, I can do that, if you're thinking of changing us and running out of time, why not see if you can change Megan and myself at the same time?" Rose asked.

"Let me see if she's still alive and she doesn't have any guests," Geraldine said and insisted she should go in first, she was the one with the gun. She went next door and still crying looked around. A puff of gas sent the other man with a gun down to the floor dead. Seconds later another puff of gas sent the second man to the floor. Then she heard the door open and the voice of a man about to ask a question."

"Rod is this kid.... who are you?" he asked Geraldine.

"I'm the gunslinger," she replied. Another puff from her gun sent a bullet right between his eyes.

Geraldine shook the girl to try and wake her up. Megan turned her head slightly putting three fingers up and pointing behind her.

"Oh shit," she said and turned around to see a man with a gun pointing at her.

Lynda appeared for one second, touched the man and they both disappeared. There was a commotion outside in the fishpond with a few shouts of "No! No! No! as the fish started to have him for their breakfast. Lynda touched Megan and they both showed up in Ruth's bedroom.

Both girls stood as their gunslinger checked the corridors and stairs while both girls were changed at the same time.

Both girls left the room while Alice removed the suprapubic catheters and inserted another, between their legs complete with a bag they had to carry to get to the front door.

Gabrielle found the spot for the large safe. On trying the handle, it didn't open, the light switch on the left side put the interior light on. They both jumped into the safe. To their surprise it was packed with a number of books and journals, filled with names and addresses. Gabrielle picked up the books, put her hand on a package of money and jumped home. She deposited the money and books in the front room then she was back inside the safe, and Lynda was gone and while Gabrielle got some packets of money as it was now all wrapped up in thick paper.

Both girls were going back and forth for four minutes practically emptying the safe. Then they realised that the other men were coming to get their money, the money they were moving out of the safe. They would not be happy to see an empty safe, so they did another four jumps each before Gabrielle jumped back into Skye's bedroom to see the three girls standing up, no shoes on their feet and only a thin nightdress on. Lynda took the last two packets of money and dropped them off in their apartment.

Lynda jumped back upstairs and helped Gabrielle taking the last of the girls to the front door.

They got the last two girls onto the coach, laying them across two men's knees for as long as they could take it, but they did have a thick blanket wrapped around them.

The men first thought they were going to have an eighteen-year-old boy, girl on their laps, but they didn't mind when they saw the two eighteen-year-old girls, with beautiful long healthy hair. They started to talk with the girls who replied in a young female voice, they wouldn't mind at all.

John and Alan got onto the bus, Geraldine got in the driving seat of the four-by-four with Alice and her bag next to her and in the back, four men huddled together for the drive down to London.

It was hoped at three thirty in the morning they could still get away without being seen. It was still dark as Geraldine started the four by four. They had said goodbye to Gabrielle and Lynda just before they got into the car and they jumped to the Train Station and started their work.

Geraldine was driving the four by four out of the first gates, when she saw six luxury cars coming towards them. It was the first wave of the drug cartel, that was operating in this area. These men were to wake everyone up, get the coffee on ready for the bosses and top cutters to arrive in two and a half hours.

They would also want to inspect all the boy girls they had bought, ready for the heads of the Paedophile rings to come and hopefully buy them. They too had two buses ready to take them away, those they didn't want would have their throats cut and fed to the fish. by nightfall all the girls would be sorted. The four by four went onto the grass verge but it handled well as Geraldine drove past the final car and headed out of the last gates, with Geraldine holding her gun on her lap. A short time later they caught up to the coach on the M1 heading south-east to London.

Chapter 14

As soon as Gabrielle and Lynda arrived in the Train Station, with two boy girls each everyone cheered. now they had a big job to do, and it would last most of the day. The two waitresses Samantha and Esma went with Jenny, Penny and Sarah to the twenty-four-hour supermarket, HAYS. They went inside and looked around. The first thing they were looking for were blankets and towels. They stripped shelf after shelf filling the first trolly up, then they found the girls shoe and wellington boot aisle. They took all they had of the twelve, to fourteen and fifteen-year-old boots. Esma, knowing more about shopping in a supermarket than Jenny and Penny asked a saleswoman if they had any more boots out the back,

Five minutes later, she brought out twenty pair of twelve to fifteen-year-old boots, nine pair of sixteen-year-old boots and the last two pair of seventeen-year-old boots. In another trolly behind were the last of the towels and single blankets they had. Going to the clothes aisle, Sarah started looking for expensive panties and only found a few. She cleared out all the packets, then started on twelve to fifteen-year-old bras, sixteen-year-old bras with a C cup and what she hoped would be eighteen-year-bras, with a D cup. Asking another woman for help, a ten-minute wait later, she had another twenty pair of twelve to fifteen-year-old bras, all their skirts for thin waists, ten sixteen-year-old skirts and all the overcoats they had.

Jenny was getting all the hair shampoo and conditioner they would need, showergell toothpaste and toothbrushes washing scrub balls. She then went to the makeup counter and emptied it of all the lip sticks, face-powder, eye shadow mascara, eye liner pens, makeup creams, nail varnish, nail varnish remover, all the packets of cotton wool they had, again, wiping out the shelfs it was on, then hairspray and deodorant they would all be new girls and want to smell like one as well.

Jenny had just cleared a shelf of deodorant when a man came up behind her and tapped her on her shoulder.

"Can I help you?" he asked.

He felt someone gently tap his shoulder and thought it might be one of the other security men who were walking around watching the women emptying shelves of blankets and towels.

"Can I help you?" A man asked in an Australian accent.

"Who are you?" Mr Samuel Hopkin asked as he slowly turned around to see a Glock pointing at his head. He swallowed the lump in his throat and looked at the man facing him.

"Do you have a license for that monster?" he asked shaking.

"Yes, and I'm licensed to kill in any country and the local police know I am here. Now why were you touching my client?" Isaac asked the man.

"I am Samuel Hopkin the night manager for this supermarket, I wanted to know why this woman and two others are emptying our shelves of goods, possibly to walk out of the supermarket without paying as they don't have enough money to pay for everything and leaving my night staff to put it all back on the shelves," he replied.

"Great to meet you Samuel, I'm Isaac, bodyguard to Jenny, Dame Sarah and Penny," he said putting his gun back in its holster, then shaking him by the hand with a firm grip.

"Penny and Jenny are rich, and I don't know how supermarkets operate, they have their food delivered to them or Wendy will get it for them," Isaac explained.

Sarah came running down the aisle, followed by Tina, with her gun in her hand.

"What's happening? Are you alright Jenny?" Tina asked her gun pointing at the man.

"It's okay Tina, this guy is the night manager of this shack."

"It's a big supermarket, Isaac," Tina told him.

"This is the size of a normal shop in Australia, girl, our supermarkets are three times bigger than this place and we sell food, and animal food by the hundredweight," he boasted, grinning.

"This is the UK, we mainly do a big shop for a month, not like you getting through all that food in a week," Tina replied smiling. "You Australians eat so much food it's unbelievable."

"You gotta keep your belly full, if you get lost in the bush, you could be there a couple of weeks before you're found," he laughed in his loud Australian voice.

"I'm sorry Mr Hopkin, I'm Dame Sarah Watts, I come in here now and then if I have to get clothes or shoes for our younger girls," she said shaking his hand.

"I see, but do you have the money to pay for all of this?"

"Crikey, this is just the start of it, I have another two hundred girls about to drop in on me and eighty odd men to start working on the TG House," Sarah told him,

"The TG House, the Train Station, now it makes sense. We've had a couple of twelve and thirteen-year-old boy girls sneaking in here looking for bars of chocolate and boxes of cakes. They had no shoes on their feet or proper clothes on their backs and no coats, even in the snow, I don't know how they survived."

"Well, that won't happen any longer, Teresa, the woman who took charge of our TG House without our knowledge kicked out Margarette, our real House manager and all her staff who looked after our TG's, and she sold them to a man calling himself, George Rainer, before Gabrielle killed him in New York, but there are a group of a hundred men run by Ken Mattingly in Macclesfield. That's where most of us have been tonight, rescuing two hundred and twelve TG's, on two double decker buses and they are all in the same condition as the TG's who came to your store," Sarah explained.

"Don't worry we have enough money to pay for all this and we'll be needing more clothes."

"If you have a list of what you need, I'll get it by this afternoon," Samuel replied.

"Really, that will be a big help."

"Is Gabrielle and Lynda here in London?"

"They were this morning, they went with the other Bodyguards in a bus up to Macclesfield, to take charge of the rescue themselves, they like to be in the thick of it," Sarah informed him.

"Well let's not keep you waiting, it looks like your all cold as well."

"Yes, our overcoats and thick jumpers are on a trolly."

"Why don't you Sarah come into my office, and we'll go through your list? You'll never get all the items you have in your trolly's into your car."

"We came in the stretch limo," Sarah replied smiling.

"Nonsense, I'll have one of our van drivers deliver it all for you as soon as his van is loaded. Lea, come with us to my office, we have work to do." He looked around seeing another girl, "Amelia, could you find Oscar and get him to bring his van to the back door, there should be some boxes near the door, load everything from these ladies, trollies into the van. Use all the boxes you need. Do we have any more single blankets out the back and all the single bed sheets? They will also need single duvets. Put them from the back into the van and take anymore, you need from the floor."

"Sam, can I have a quick word with you?" Amelia asked.

"What is it?" he asked when they moved along the aisle.

"Sam are you being coerced into this and why on earth do they want all this washing stuff, towels, some clothes and now another woman has taken a new trolly to the IT area and is looking at large TV's and Game consoles.

"She keeps glancing at the games and is talking on the phone to somebody. She keeps asking a girl to give the phoned to another girl and starts looking through games as well. I can fast dial the police if you like, I saw a woman with a gun," Amelia said, showing concern for her manager.

"It's okay Amelia, I know who they are now."

"Do they have enough money to pay for this lot?" she asked continuing her questioning, this was not like her manager.

"Amelia, these women are from the TG House. The last thirty of the TGs from the House are currently in the Train Station, with nothing on their feet and hardly anything on their backs with no coats, having to run around in their bare feet.

"Gabrielle and Lynda are back and have gone up to Macclesfield to bring back another two hundred TG's who were sold to a man taking over from George Rainer who Gabrielle killed in New York. Now all these children are arriving at the

Train Station soon on two buses, let's help get all they need, please. Sarah has her H&B company card, I've seen it," Sam told her.

"Do you have something against TG's?" he asked.

"I suppose they are okay I just don't understand them and you're giving them free stuff that has to be well over a grand."

"I'm surprised at you, don't forget it was Gabrielle and Lynda that saved all our souls we could all be dead by now, in a place we don't want to be."

"I know what the soul said to everyone, I just don't believe in that stuff, I believe when we die, we are dead, the body no longer works for us. There can't be Death who Gabrielle and Lynda supposedly talk to. You would, need to be dead to talk to Him if He exists, and I'll find out when I die, not now. When I see Gabrielle and Lynda in the flesh, I might believe them. But I would like to question them first."

"Excuse me, I'm sending Penny on to fill her list, don't worry I'd rather pay for everything, if you can lend us a van, Isaac will drive it back and as soon as it's unloaded, and with all the TG's we have here, he won't be long bringing the van back. If not, we'll take what we can in our limo. The first bus has arrived with the first hundred TG's getting off it now. Patrick will come here, and we'll load his bus. Oh, and Amelia, I would go careful what you say about Death, Lynda has a direct line with Him now," Sarah warned her.

"I'll believe Him when I see Him," Amelia retorted.

"Thanks for the offer, Sam, if you could get as much as possible from the list, we'll call in this afternoon about two, would that be, okay?" Sarah asked.

"Sam, I bet the guns aren't real and they don't have a stretch limo."

"I wouldn't test their guns; they are real and have killed people. The limo is out the front, why don't you have a look? You can't miss it, it has Hats, Bags & Wraps UK on the side, but you might have to brush the snow off the doors," Sarah told Amelia.

Amelia walked off to look for the limo, proving they didn't have one, then she would get to the tills, to ensure they paid for everything, including all the electrical equipment.

When she got outside it was still snowing hard, as she walked along the carpark and slipped on the fresh snow with her trousers wet, shoes scuffed from the collected snow under the car. Right in front of her eyes were five words in bright yellow Hats, Bags & Wraps UK.

As she started to return to the store, a double decker bus was coming into the car park and parked just behind the Limo. She looked at the side of the bus, it was on Private Hire and on the side of the bus was a picture of a large radio Telescope, with See it in Macclesfield.

Amelia walked to the side of the bus shouting at the driver to move his bus and park it at the far end of the car park. Frank returned the shout saying,

"I'm here for five people from the TG House and I have to pick up a load of stuff, because a member of staff doesn't believe her own soul, she doesn't deserve one. Why did Gabrielle and Linda fight for souls like yours, when it's owner still don't believe they have one."

She returned to the store and decided to keep out of Sam's way until knocking off time when hopefully they would be gone.

"I'm so sorry Sarah, she's after my job and is sleeping with one of the directors who can get the other directors to choose her instead of me," Sam said to Sarah.

"I don't want you to lose your job but if you can fill the order for me for two pm. that will be fine?"

"I'll stay here myself and make sure the clothes and everything else gets here and is made ready for you," he replied.

"Thanks."

Sarah walked down to the IT area and saw what Penny had in her basket. Sarah had another trolly with her and looked around. Penny had four game systems in her basket, with forty games.

Sarah put three forty-inch TVs in her basket, two more different game systems and more games. Then she added three CD players and started on the films. With all the films for the different age TG's, she walked back to the Games area and put spare controllers card batteries and anything else they would need. It was getting time to leave, the bus was outside, which meant a hundred TGs were being fed.

With everything they needed from the IT area, they walked back up through the Supermarket and cleared another area of tights. Sarah thought for a moment, then picked up all the single duvets they had, the single sheets on the shelves, then pillows, again all they had Sarah had another idea. She asked Penny and Jenny to get three more trolleys and fill them with frozen turkeys, all they had, they had over two hundred TGs to feet and it was just three weeks from Christmas. With their trolleys full of frozen turkeys and other frozen meats, they took two trollies each then Tina went back and brought the three trolleys to the checkout.

"Do we have everything now?" Tina asked Sarah.

"As much as they have, we'll have to come back later to get more clothes and anything else the TG's need." The woman on the till Mary, looked in amazement at all the trolleys and sighed.

"Are you from the TG House," she asked Sarah.

"Yes, we are," Sarah replied.

"That woman Amelia, doesn't believe you, she thinks you don't have enough money to pay for all this and is ready to ring the police," She replied.

"Let's hope the card works then, she whispered," and smiled.

"Let me have the card," Mary said, taking the card and taking a pound from it, declared the card was fine.

Mary started to go through the first trolly load of blankets and towels. Isaac was at the end with Tina putting them into bags so it wouldn't get dirty on the bus. All the filled bags went back into the trolley, Sarah made a phone call halfway through the till topping up their bill. They were now on the wellington boots and black shoes. Skirts, tops, thick and thin jumpers, they all went through the till. After the phone call Sarah made her excuses and walked briskly back down to the clothes aisle.

She made another phone call as she checked the aisle, she was in. then Gabrielle and Lynda appeared before her. They all hugged and kissed each other, sharing their love for each other around.

"I'm so glad to see you again, I was worried about you especially when Lynda called to tell me what shape the four eighteen-year-olds would be like when they arrived here. Thank goodness Lynda had taken their clothes and shoe sizes after they had been changed and rang me," she said to Gabrielle.

"I also needed to know the sizes of our seventeen-year-old, but I have all the sizes I need for now, so shall we take a look for their clothes?" Sarah asked them.

"Yes, why not, that woman is looking at us?" Lynda said. "I feel like I should jump behind her and drop her into the snow outside a mile away from here."

"It might be a good idea at that," Sarah said laughing with her. If she causes any more trouble let's do it," Gabrielle said laughing.

Fifteen minutes later, they had twenty-four dresses for the older girls, picked out with bra and pantie sets. Three bras, three nighties each, with thick and thin jumpers, long overcoats and shorter coats for college.

Sam was walking around the store and noticed Amelie looking at three women. He looked at them as well.

"Haven't you got something better to do? Did they have a stretch-Limo? Be careful what you say, because I am going out to help them load up what they have now," Sam said making her jump.

"Sam, I didn't see you there."

"I know you didn't, you've been watching those slender women by the dresses."

"I'm certain they are planning to steal all the dresses they have. I bet they go to the toilets soon, that's when I'll pounce on them and put them under store arrest."

"Don't forget they have not stolen anything until they walk out the main doors. They can change their mind any time up until then. You didn't answer my question, do they own a Hats & Bags Limo?"

"Yes, they do, but that means nothing they could have stollen it or borrowed it for the night, to show off to their friends," Amelia said trying to get out of trouble.

"Do you have any idea who those two ladies are?"

"The shorter lady is Sarah; we saw her earlier this morning. The other two are about to steal our goods and you are doing nothing about it. I'll see you lose your job tomorrow." Sam said nothing but walked over to meet Gabrielle and Lynda.

"While I'm still the manager here, can you please get me a trolley, then they won't have to hold the clothes. Actually, bring two," Sam said to Amelia.

"He met the two women and shook their hands. "Hello Gabrielle, Lynda, I'm Sam the night manager of this establishment for now. Everything Sarah ordered earlier this morning is being packed right now and loaded onto a lorry. Thank you so very much for saving our souls." He shook their hands again. "When you return this afternoon, I'll ensure everything is free. Is all this for the boy girls in the TG House?"

"Yes, Teresa, the woman who pushed Margarette out of her job, has been sacked," Gabrielle said with a smile.

"I know her, she used to come in here every day saying she was the new Manageress there and bought cakes and pies for the men who were working there. She bought a load of tools and power tools, especially those power-screwdrivers. There was also a couple of Tv's and a Game Station with ten top of the chart games and what else was it, oh yes, three DVD players and about thirty-top of the chart films. Whatever they needed I got for them and she paid with the same Hats, Bags & Wraps bank card. She always had to put her pin in the machine, and it worked all the time," Sam said then realised what he had done "It was a valid debit card, Teresa told me."

"Look, just what I need an empty trolley."

"Gabrielle no, my love, please don't do it," Lynda said holding her hand then her arm. "Oh, please my love," Lynda begged.

"What is the problem, Gabrielle? can I help you?" Sam asked.

"It's the smell, mince pies, she loves them and has come in here before and bought every-one you had with cream. She shares them with the girls, but that's her excuse, but look at her body, it was a lot of hard work to get her to look like that, she'll put on weight if she eats them," Lynda replied.

"The girls have had a rough time of it over there and there are still some missing, let me donate all our mince pies and a few cakes they might enjoy. With double thick and spray cream," Sam said looking at Lynda with her head at an angle looking at him.

"Okay, go on then, Gabrielle, I'll be watching you," Lynda replied laughing.

"Spoilsport, this is because I wouldn't let you buy a gun in New York and start up another company, 'Have Guns Will Travel,' if I recall."

"Not really, but it makes sense," Lynda said laughing, then kissed her wife on her lips. not once but twice.

"I'll get that all sorted for you," Sam said smiling and excused himself saying he would meet them at the till. "It seems that you owe us a great deal of money Teresa," Lynda said.

"She must have taken the card from Margarette's desk drawer, that's where she leaves it during the day in the locked steel case. I don't recall how she might have got the pin number, but if she needed cash to pay the builders and Margarette was tied up she just might have given her the pin intending to change it the next day. At least now we know how she got into our accounts.

"But the card should have been cancelled," Lynda said.

"Margarette would have done that from her phone, but you took no notice of the command to stop it being used. Do it now then it's automatically cancelled, again," Sarah told Gabrielle.

"Do you know your people are stealing from us right now at the till?" Amelia said, butting into Sarah and Gabrielle's conversation.

"Are you working for George Rainer or Ken Mattingly?" Gabrielle asked.

"I've never heard of either of them. Oh, George yes, some people are saying you fought him to save all our souls," Amelia retorted.

"Yes, that's right but above all I was fighting for Lynda's soul and for Death to give me my soul back, which he took from me a week before the fight with George, He held my soul on this side of his black veil, where I've stood for over ten times when I tried to kill myself. I always died, but Death put my soul back in my body and brought me back to life."

"Well, I don't think we have a soul, when we die that's it nothing else," Amelia confirmed.

"Do you mind if I check on your soul?" Gabrielle asked her.

"I suppose not, what are you going to do, shout at it to try and get it out?" Amelia laughed.

"No, I'll do this," Gabrielle said smiling at her and kissing Lynda's lips, three times.

Her green eyes started to shine very bright as she looked through Amelia's body. She found her soul and spoke to it, then her soul talked to Amelia's mind.

"I can't believe that happened, how did you do that?" Amelia asked.

"You were drunk and asleep at the moment it was to speak to you, so now you know, you do have a soul," Gabrielle said.

"Excuse me a moment please, I have to put something right." Amelia pushed Gabrielle's trolley to the checkout and spoke quickly to Mary sat at her till.

"Mary, I've made a big mistake so I'm very sorry, cancel this bill it's all free, I've got a soul and it just spoke to me, Gabrielle started it going again now I know what happened." She ran to the back door and spoke to Alister the van driver.

"Alister, there are forty single duvets over there, load them into your van and take them to the Train Station. Get Ten of our biggest tins of matt white emulsion and two of every colour we have, plus a lot of good paint brushes. Oh, they'll need wallpaper scrapers as well, at least twenty. And as much white gloss paint as we have, with smaller paint brushes, rollers and things, everything they'll need to paint a hundred or more bedrooms and some long rollers for the ceilings."

"I won't do all that in one journey. Amelia, those duvet's take up a lot of room," he replied.

"Put those right at the back of your van. It doesn't matter how long it takes you, just be safe in the snow and ice," Amelia replied smiling and singing to herself. I've got a soul and I know what happened."

As she walked through the store, she saw Sam putting large boxes of tarts into his trolly. She found another empty trolly and pushed it past him, putting different cakes and buns, rolls and a few loaves of bread into her basket.

"Hello Sam, what are you doing now?" she asked.

"Amelia, I'm giving Gabrielle all our mince tarts and cream for the TG's. so, you can add that to your list," he replied.

"Do you think they will like all this as well?" She asked. "I've got a soul and it spoke to me. We must help them all we can. I've told Mary to cancel the bill and I have another two members of staff helping to pack everything then go out and help get it all on the bus. Alister is going to deliver all the single duvets and all the paint we have that they will need. I'll put some fresh bacon, sausages, eggs and tomatoes in here to get the workmen off to a good start. Don't be long packing the cakes, Sam, they'll want to be leaving soon," She added and went to the till area, singing to herself, "I have a soul."

Sam looked at her, "Crikey what's happened to her?" he said to himself.

"Your job is safe now Sam, thank you for the cakes and everything else," Amelia said, humming to herself and smiling at everyone.

"Amelia will be fine soon, she was drunk and sound asleep when her soul tried to tell her what happened the first time, I just asked it to repeat what it had to say," Gabrielle said to Sam, holding Lynda's hand.

"You can do that?" he asked her.

"We can do all sorts and Gabrielle speaks to people's soul a number of times," Lynda said standing beside her wife holding her hand, they kissed each other, and their eyes turned bright green for a minute as the couple kissed and sent all their love to each other.

"Wow," Sam said, and got on loading his trolley with mince pies and cream.

An hour later everything from the morning list, was unpacked and the girls, using the two showers, were getting washed, and washing their long hair now the first hundred and forty girls were changed to real girls and getting into clean fresh clothes. All the girls were helping spread out the clothes, so they had two skirts, tops, thick and thin jumpers, underclothes and a bra what fitted them.

At six forty-five Alister arrived with the van. He opened the back doors and saw two fifteen-year-old girls sat at a table drinking coffee, wondering what they were going to do for the rest of their long day, some of their friends were still naked apart from panties and a bra and a blanket around them, all the clothes they had were now used up.

"Excuse me girls, can you give me a hand please?" Alister asked, not expecting any help let alone a verbal reply.

"Of course, sir, what have you got onboard?" Kathleen asked.

"Twenty single duvets for now, some make up mirrors forty hair dryers for now, hairbrushes and combs, then I have sixty skirts, tops, jumpers and twenty dressing gowns, that we hope will fit you, if not ring us, I'll bring out what we have of the next size up and take the others back. The bus is still being packed and the limo is currently having the boxes of cakes loaded," Alister said and handed the girls the first lot of skirts.

"I'm Kathleen, this is Elizabeth, we're real girls now. Gabrielle and Lynda changed us," she said laughing and they took the first piles of skirts and a few tops into the far end of the Train Station and put the clothes on the table.

"Gabrielle," Kathleen called, "We have skirts tops and more, she said aloud. Come on Liz, let's get the rest of the clothes." They returned to the van and picked up more of the clothes while Allister started to bring in the duvets in their boxes.

"Where did all this come from?" Gabrielle asked.

"I only brought a few bottles of shampoo conditioner and shower-gel and Lynda brought all the clothes we had, well, the skirts and tops that is the coats are still on the bus."

"There's a man outside giving us these clothes and has a load more stuff in his van," Elizabeth said putting down, more tops and jumpers.

"The girls who have showered come up and find one skirt that fits you and a top, don't forget the other girls are all your sisters here and another hundred on the coach that will be here in thirty minutes." Gabrielle said and followed Elizabeth out to the van.

Lynda got the girls organised, the girls were having a shower and washing their hair as fast as they could, drying it with towels they had used before. Lynda jumped back to the supermarket and finding Sarah asked her if she knew where the towels were. Soon she had three bags of towels in her hands and two bags of skirts and tights. Sarah found some more towels two hair dryers and four bags of shoes.

"Lynda, drop off what you have, then come back to me and take these bags." Sarah said.

Lynda was back picking up more bags of tights, shoes and wellington boots. She dropped them off at a table, where the girls who were now dressed, looked through the shoes and wellington boots. They all took a pair of thick tights and put them on, keeping their legs warm. With shoes on their feet, they were able to help the other girls unloading the eighty or more tins of paint. Lynda was back again with the bags she had taken from Sarah. She jumped back to the bus, got the last of the towels, two bags of washing soaps and the last of the toothbrushes and toothpaste which they would all have to share for now, they would get their individual tubes of toothpaste, when they had enough to go around.

Lynda started to organise all the washing bottles and the nice clean and fluffy towels. With the van unloaded, Alister drove it back and filled it with more items Amelia had somehow managed to find from her hidden stores, ready to take home, now she knew these people needed them more, so she brought them out of their hiding places and put them by the door where Alister would park his van.

Two girls were helping to load it, as Amelia brought out more of her private stores. Four more girls had just showered washing each other and their hair to free up the two showers for the next girls. and were now drying their long hair with a new hairdryer. As soon as the last two left the shower room. They were all used to washing together, in a big hotel like the TG House. They had no option but wash together as Teresa had turned off the water to the showers and leaving only one shower working, as she was sending girl boys home or selling them to Ken.

At seven fifteen, just as it was getting light, Gabrielle had a phone call from Frank the other bus driver. "Hello Gabrielle?"

"Yes, Frank is everything okay with your bus?"

"No, A break light blew on the way down, were just twenty-two miles from the Train Station and a copper has stopped me and doesn't like the number of kids on my bus."

"Put him on the phone please."

"Hello, who is this?" Gabrielle asked.

"I'm police officer David Hawthorn of the motorway police. This bus driver has overcrowded his bus and has a break light out. He's trying to give me some sob story about all these boy girls which I do not believe for one minute were sold to a bloke called Ken Mattingly and they have been rescued during the night."

"You at least know who I am and my wife Lynda?"

"I've heard of you, not that I like lesbians or gay men.

"Well, you live in a different world now, we all exist and live on this planet, then she had a thought.

"Well, if you are going to live here, find another country to live in where they accept people like you. I just don't like any of you it costs our government and NHS too much with your whining I was born into the wrong body. My son used to say that, but I've managed to beat it out of him now," he said getting angry.

Gabrielle nodded to Lynda who now had a fix from all the girl boys on the bus. Lynda was off materialising on the top deck of the bus.

"First four of you, quickly hold onto me."

They did as they were told as the next four girl boys got ready. As soon as Lynda returned, she grabbed the other boy girls and returned to the Train Station. She returned to the bus and picked up another four girls. In two minutes, she had dropped them off and now held another four girls, leaving one seat free. She dropped them off and returned to the top of the bus, getting four girls who were scrunched up on the back seat. She could hear what Gabrielle was saying then returned to the bus, downstairs and picked up four girls who were sat on the floor. Two minutes later she was back again. The police officer was still going on about how he didn't like the Transgenders, either way around. He was starting to get very mad.

Lynda was back on the bus taking off more children who were sat on the floor. Then she returned and was about to leave the bus when she heard him again threaten his Transgender son again.

"Excuse me for asking was he returned to you a short time ago?" Lynda asked him, holding onto the four girls ready to jump and sending the conversation to Gabrielle at the same time. In her head, she heard,

"Be careful my love, he's very angry and angry men do crazy things, like trying to kill you."

"I'll be careful my love. I love you with all my heart," she replied in thought.

"Love you too," Gabrielle replied.

"Yes, a woman turned up with him saying they couldn't help him any longer, he refused the take the tablets he was given. He just said he wanted to be a girl, so I slapped him like girls get slapped. You just can't trust girls or women.

"My wife, Heather, she went behind my back and took him to your place instead of the psychiatrist like she was supposed to do. I won't be giving her more money to come to London to see him and I'll be kicking him out of the house naked if I must. He will not go around in a dress," he shouted to Lynda near the back of the bus. when Lynda appeared again, she dropped off the girls and returned to the bus. She grabbed another four girls and they all disappeared.

"I thought you lived in Devon," Gabrielle said, taking Lynda's place on the bus and getting another four girls ready to jump.

"Yes, I'm up here for the weekend, most of our roads are snowed in so I was transferred up here for the weekend, I go home tomorrow," David said giving her all the information she needed.

Gabrielle asked him more questions about his boy girl and his wife. He said yes, nobody was going anywhere until the bus was fixed, even then he may make the over number of girls walk home, wherever that was.

Lynda was talking to Patrick about their problem.

"If I was there, I could replace the bulb in a few minutes."

"Where do I get a bulb from?" Lynda asked him.

"You won't know which one to get in the dark it's got to be twenty-four-volt lamps.

"Where are you?"

"Just by the fish and chip shop. You would have passed it on your way to the supermarket.

"Stay there and park up," Lynda told him.

Before he had a chance to park up Lynda was with him telling him where to go. Ten minutes later he had replaced the light bulb and removed all the sleet and snow off the light exterior. Lynda deposited him back in his bus and left. She went to her apartment picked up a five-thousand-pound wad of money, then disappeared again to Heather's house, hoping she wasn't too bad.

She arrived in Heather's bedroom making Helen jump. Lynda looked at Heather the boy girl expecting to see a clean boy figure at least, but it was far from it. He had two black eyes and a broken arm. David, her father, had punched her in her stomach a few times and beat her on her back with a stick of some sort. Helen had also been hit on her back and side with a stick, probably the same one that he used on Heather.

Within five minutes Lynda's green eyes had repaired Heather's broken arm, healed all the areas on her body where she had been hit and healed her aching face and black eyes. Her bright green eyes, almost filled with tears, had healed Helen's face and black eyes. She had removed her top and allowed Lynda to heal her body and vagina, that he had cut with a knife. It reminded her of her earlier years before Paul, who had saved her life and now, she loved Gabrielle with all her heart and always would.

"Helen I'm going to take Heather back to the Train Station with me, Teresa who had managed to get Margarette sacked is now sacked herself and Margarette is back in command. It's alright Heather, you'll be changed sooner than you think, by tonight, I hope. The TG house is in a mess and needs redecorating, new beds and everything else that has been damaged or sold. She will be safe with us. Take this five-grand and do something with it," Lynda said handing her the money.

"Do you have any girl's clothes at all Heather?" Lynda asked.

Heather nodded her head and lifted her mattress getting out the skirt and top.

"I'm going to leave him, this will help me for a time, I'll go to London. I have an aunt there who may take me in," Helen said.

"I can offer you a job if you don't mind helping at the TG House and help the girls who will all be living at the Train Station for a few weeks," Lynda said.

"Yes, I'll help you for bed and breakfast for now, she replied.

"That's all you'll get for now. But if you get upset or want to leave and try your aunts house, we'll take you there. It will be alright.

"Heather, do you mind your mum working there?"

"Not at all, and she's a very good chef, she works at the big restaurant down the road."

"Really, you might not be scrubbing floors then," Lynda said laughing. "Get some clothes for the next few days, Sarah will take you shopping in the week. Don't be worried, we'll pay."

Fifteen minutes later, they were back in the Train Station. Sarah was listening to David on the phone. Gabrielle had called her letting her know what was happening, as David continued abusing Gabrielle by shouting at her.

Lynda said to Gabrielle to come back to the Train Station for a few minutes to change some of the girls, then she would take her place at the back of the bus. A few minutes later, Gabrielle and four girls appeared before Lynda. Heather and three of the clean girl boys got together and between Gabrielle and Lynda, they changed them with long different coloured hair and being a little older at fourteen, they were given a C size cup.

"Next, Heather and Stacey, go and have a shower, wash each other's backs and wash each other's hair. While the others finish having a shower. Kati and Niahm will go in after you two. Then I'll have Lexie. Alexandra, Jessica and Clara; come on girls I hope you know what you want, you'll all have a C cup." Lynda said.

The four girls formed a square while Gabrielle and Lynda put their arms around them and changed them to girls, two with short hair, two with long hair. They went through all the TG's that Lynda had brought in with Heather and Annabelle having their hair dried by other girls as they talked and laughed together. Older girls, were watching them, giving them advice on how to style their long hair.

Heather was getting dressed from the bottom up as other girls sorted all the pretty C cup bras, so the girls had something to look at.

Gabrielle left her phone with Geraldine, who wasn't talking, just listening to David bellowing at them all. Gabrielle listened to Sarah's phone, she looked at the time, and saw the call had been going for one hour twenty minutes. Now she was listening to him shouting again.

"I'm calling for back up and two police vans with a cage in the back. You'll all be banged up in prison soon and at least held overnight, bloody freaks."

"Gabrielle, did you hear what he had to say?" Isaac asked, from his position, four feet away from Sarah's phone. As Gabrielle was listening to Isaac, she walked to a table and picked up four single blankets and handed them to Isaac, she picked up another four blankets and held them tight under her arm.

Isaac was not frightened of the police cells, but the twenty-six girls left on the bus, were too close to David for Lynda to grab them. All the girls were now freezing. David shouted at them to stop moaning about the cold, they were girls, and girls always wore skimpy clothes, showing all their long legs, their arms and as much midriff as they could. The two-new girls, who had been operated on by Ken, Ruth was laying on the long back seat, Rose was laying on the long seat just behind the driver, with four twelve and fourteen-year-old girls holding her in place, and it was the same for Ruth. It helped hide eight girls.

When David got on the bus, he opened all the windows, especially on the top deck as he said there was a bad smell upstairs. Now he was complaining of the same bad smell again downstairs. The girls couldn't help it, it was the conditions they had to sleep in.

"Gabrielle while you are on the coach, consider bringing back Geraldine, Isaac can then take her place. I'm looking through Sarah's eyes, Geraldine looks like she's about to punch David between his eyes and David keeps eyeing up Geraldine. and she keeps putting her hand on her Glock."

"Next two girls in the shower please," Lynda said.

"Lynda are we clear to go? Let's not get close to him. David is returning to his car to call for back up."

"Let me know when he's on his way back."

"Will do," Lynda said, then Gabrielle and Isaac were gone.

They arrived on the lower deck, near the back of the bus. Isaac started to hand out the blankets, ensuing Ruth got one wrapped around her body; the four girls on the floor had a blanket they could sit on. Sarah checked outside the bus; David was still in his police car on his radio. Gabrielle went to the back of the bus, took hold of Geraldine's arm. She had two girls hold her other arm and they were gone, arriving in the Train Station. Gabrielle was back on the bus, arriving just behind Sarah.

"Where is he?"

"Still in his car," Sarah replied.

"Help me get Rose into my arms and I'll take her back,

"We need two tables made ready for Rose and Ruth. I'll get her next. Rose would be difficult to get if David gets back on the bus," Gabrielle said, to Lynda as she started to move two tables together then another two together a little further down the room for Ruth.

Ten seconds later, Gabrielle arrived right next to Lynda's shoulder, she looked terrible, her face was grey, and she looked exhausted. Three women ran up to Gabrielle and took Ruth from her arms and put her on the tables.

"Gabrielle, what's happened to you?" Lynda asked her.

"I don't know what happened to me, I feel exhausted that's all my love," Gabrielle replied.

Gabrielle was falling into the three women's arms as they walked her over to the leather armchair by the doors.

"Ayia, will you please get to Sarah's phone and tell her to get to the back of the bus now and be ready to jump with me plus two girls for me please," Lynda asked holding her wife's arm sending her all her love.

Lynda kissed Gabrielle on her lips then jumped to the back of the bus. Luckily, David was still in his car as Sarah came running down the bus wondering what was happening.

"We have to go now, it's Gabrielle, she's collapsed."

"I'll get my bag," She was back within a minute, then they heard John's voice."

"Jump now or stay, he's coming back," John said.

Lynda grabbed hold of Sarah's hand, and two girls from under the back seat. Martha, who was fourteen, held onto the back of

Lynda's arm. She was cold and David had hit her across her face with the back of his hand. She needed to get off the bus, even if she got a telling off after. She was free from that nutter. A moment later, they were at the Train Station.

"When Ruth was taken, two girls from the floor below her empty seat jumped onto the long seat and lay down, feet against feet, both their heads out of the end of the blanket they had dragged over them to make it appear Ruth was still there. with a blanket over them. The two girls on the floor, were half sitting on a blanket. Amber passed the last two blankets across the bus aisle into the hands of Samantha who kept one and passed the other behind her, which was taken by one of the men.

They arrived back at the Train Station and helping hands took the three girls from Lynda and wrapped them in warm blankets as they took a seat next to each other as Sarah ran down to look at Gabrielle.

"He's back." John whispered over the phone.

"Okay, give me a ring when he's gone if he goes, I'll join you. Gabrielle has just collapsed, and her face is grey, Sarah's looking at her now," Lynda said.

"Stay with Gabrielle, we'll be on our way soon I'm sure," John replied, "Take good care of her Lynda," he added.

"I will, see you soon," she replied, then went down to be with her wife.

John sat on a long seat on the door side of the bus while Noah took the single seat opposite John.

Gabrielle was almost asleep, and her face was a deep grey. Sarah gave her a thorough examination and looked at her phone inputting data to one of her war doctors she knew.

"Oh yes I didn't think of that, yes I have some. I will. Thanks Janet.

"Lynda, can you go to the kitchen and get me a quarter pint of water please?" Sarah asked.

"Of course," Lynda said, she kissed her wife, with tears in her eyes, as Gabrielle fell back into the chair, her body very weak.

Sarah opened her bag and looked inside, picking out different packets of medicine. She found the packet Janet suggested and looked again in her bag, thinking all the time what different packets of medication would do. This was for soldiers in battle who had been shot lost a lot of blood or their heart was slowing down. The extra packet she now had in her hand, should keep her awake for the next twenty hours. She looked at the other packet, she could blame Janet.

Lynda came back with the glass of water and Sarah poured the contents of the packets into the water and let it dissolve. Two minutes later Gabrielle was drinking the medication. As Gabrielle was sat in the chair, the colour was coming back to her face, which was no longer grey. They kissed each other giving them all the love they had for each other. Lynda knew she would be needed on the bus, but they would have to play it out for the moment.

Suddenly, Gabrielle was on her feet, looking down on Lynda.

"Come on my love we must surely be needed on the bus by now," Gabrielle said to Lynda.

Lynda glanced at Sarah who nodded and smiled back at Lynda.

"This is just what it's meant to do, attack anything in the body that is making her tired and wake her up and stay awake for twenty hours," Sarah explained to Lynda.

"Are you alright Gabrielle?" Sarah asked.

"Yes fine, what have you given me?"

"Something to wake you up for the rest of the day," Sarah replied.

"Thank you, Sarah," Gabrielle replied.

They all kissed and hugged each other, then moved further down the room and sat at a table with three cappuccinos. Half an hour later, Lynda was getting the girls organised and everyone was now happier that Gabrielle was up on her feet. Gabrielle tried jumping from one end of the room to the other with no problem then back to their apartment and back with twenty thousand pounds, which she handed to Simon to put in their safe.

"I think I'm alright now my love, thank you Sarah, come on, children to save," Gabrielle said feeling much better.

Getting through the girls, the next four new girls got into the two showers. Although, they had been using the showers since six o'clock that morning the only water from the showers was on two small towels put on the floor for them to wipe their feet as they left the shower into a new fresh towel.

They used all the towels they had and were now having to use them again, but they were just damp. The smaller hand towels dried their hair until they entered the restaurant to have their hair dried and styled. Their underclothes were right beside them and they were all laughing. When all the girls were changed, Helen spoke to Heather.

"Would you like to see your father before you leave him? Stay here now, we'll be together for a while, and I know you'll be safe here with over two hundred likeminded children.

"That sounds fine mum, but will it be safe? Dad sounds very mad on the bus he might kill me. How would we get there?" Heather asked her mother.

"I'll ask Lynda to take us like she brought us here. It might also calm him down," Helen replied.

"Ask her then, but I don't want to die now I'm a girl."

Helen walked off to find Lynda and ask for some help.

"You want me to take Heather and you onto that bus? Your husband is practically insane, seeing you might topple him over the precipice he's on. Let's talk this through with Gabrielle and John," Lynda suggested.

Five minutes later, with some of the men moving about at the far end of the bus and standing up, as David moved forward, still shouting and cussing the Transgenders John got up off the seat he was on in the pretence of stretching his legs and standing behind David, who stepped forward and turned watching his back. So, he didn't see Lynda arrive with Helen and Heather at the far end of the bus. The men moved slightly so the three women could get to a vacant seat.

Two seconds later, looking through Lynda's eyes, Gabrielle arrived right behind John, so David couldn't see her. He was still shouting at everyone on the bus how they should be all exterminated with the rest of their kind.

David had a sudden thought, despite the bus doors being open, there was no moving air on the bus. He glared at Noah sat in his seat, then ran upstairs checking it for the smelly boy girls he had seen upstairs, to him, just a few minutes ago, he had not seen them get off the bus.

Most of them had very, little clothes on and none of them had shoes on their feet, so they wouldn't have got far. He ran down the stairs, looking right and left along the lower deck. There were far less boy girls there than he thought, but the two boy girls who were in a bad condition were still there on their long seats, with the other kids holding them in place and talking quietly to them, although they had a blanket over them, which in his frame of mind he dismissed.

He got off the bus, lay down on his stomach and looked under the bus, nobody was there. He still had the bus driver for no stop light and on the way back to his car he thought he would smash the entire light assembly with his baton.

"David," Helen called as soon as he was back on the bus. At least come and say goodbye to our daughter, doesn't she look lovely? she's beautiful," Helen said, bringing him back to reality.

"That's not her, he had a broken arm and two black eyes, to match your black eyes… which? Did you put makeup on her and yourself and how on earth did you both get here?" He asked raising his voice.

"Keep your voice down, I have a headache and we have all been up since midnight. Rescuing the TGs from Ken Mattingly," one of the men said.

"So where are the kids too?"

"They are all girls now and at the Train Station.

"What train are they catching?" David demanded to know.

"Don't worry about it, you'll only make a snide remark." David looked at John, then marched up the bus. Helen, you haven't answered my question yet, how did you two get up here? I didn't leave any money lying about the house and who is this supposed to be?" he asked shouting again at his wife, pointing at Heather. "Answer me," he bellowed.

With him further down the bus, shouting again, it gave Gabrielle the time to get another eight girls off the front of the bus.

"We brought them up," Gabrielle said from behind him. Trying to get him away from his wife and new daughter, especially her wife, she wouldn't be able to control herself if he hit Lynda.

"The lesbian speaks, does she? You call me Sir when you speak to me, do you understand?" he seethed.

"No, I'm a Knight of the Realm a Dame, and John's a Knight of the realm, you call him Sir, me Mam," Gabrielle told him. John got behind Gabrielle, putting his hands on her arms, trying to draw her back along the bus. Alan was now standing by the side of Lynda, ready to protect her and go for his gun.

"Gabrielle, this is getting serious, someone is about to die, and it wouldn't be you or Lynda," John whispered into Gabrielle's ear.

"David, look at your daughter she's no longer a boy girl and won't show you up to your friends anymore. Please David, speak to her. Tell her how beautiful she looks," Helen said, desperately trying to calm him down. She could see for herself he could kill someone, and it might be her as he carried a gun as well. David took some deep breaths and calmed down, he put his large hand on Heather's shoulder and laughed for a moment. Lynda hoped it was now all over and he would acknowledge her as his daughter and get on with his job.

"No!" he suddenly bellowed and pushed Heather to the floor.

"That's not him, it's a girl you've dressed up and you are trying to convince me this is our new daughter. No, I will not accept it. If you bring her home, I'll fuck her twice a day, so she knows how to treat a real man."

Gabrielle sighed and thought to Lynda. "This will not work, he's insane with hate for our people. Neither could live with him ever again. Do you agree?"

"Yes, my love, unfortunately, I do. Let's hope help arrives soon and another officer can get him off the bus and let us get moving again," Lynda replied.

"David, for the last time, look at your beautiful daughter, she is leaving you like me. I'm leaving you David. We just cannot go on like this, with you beating us up all the time, controlling our lives. Heather needs an education; she can't go to school with black eyes all the time."

David walked up to Helen and grabbed her arm, twisting it and pushing it up around her back.

Back up was arriving in the shape of Adam. He stopped his police car behind David's and put his blue and red lights on. Two police vans were arriving with their lights on. He would arrest both men who thought they were hard nuts, he had his baton, and it was hard. He would have them both on the floor with broken arms and legs before they knew what had happened. They would also be charged with resisting arrest, that would keep the jailors happy.

Adam was walking on the snow on the side off the road and the bus before him, which looked like all the rear lights were fine. Then he heard a man shouting from the open windows on the lower deck of the bus. He paused for a moment, listening to what was being said.

"I don't know how you could have contacted her, I pulled the phone socket off the wall, then threw the house phone in the bin, making sure it was broken to pieces. I took his mobile phone off him and I've smashed it up with a hammer. Oh Gabrielle, why did you send my freak son home?"

"My wife thinks it's okay for him to wear a bloody dress, well it isn't. I don't like it I don't agree with it and you should have let him walk the streets instead of sending him back. It was that Bitch Reresa or something. She dropped him off, I gave her a real piece of my mind. I don't like Transgender freaks calling at my house, so stay away."

"We won't need to come back now David, Heather is staying at the TG house with the other girls."

"I have a job and somewhere to stay," Helen replied, taking his anger away from Gabrielle, it wasn't her fault.

"What is it a man on the side? You'll be going nowhere, you'll both come back with me so I can beat the living daylights out of you and if he really is a girl as he wants to be, I'll fuck her, then she'll know what it's like to be a woman, then I'll kick her out myself and you Bitch will not be able to help her because I'll break your arms as well, both of them," he said grinning.

"This was not a good idea, I thought you would like to see what your daughter looks like and say goodbye to her for the last time," Gabrielle said to him.

"Please David, at least look at your daughter, this is what she wants to be," Helen pleaded.

"Stop saying he's a girl he's not a girl, look," he pushed by his wife grabbing her arm and twisting it again, until she was crying,

"Dave, you can't do that to your wife or girl," Adam said from the open bus door.

"Shut it Adam, this is personal, arrest that bloke there and this bloke here, put them in the lockup vans."

"I can't arrest him, or Alan, I would be arrested as well and don't even think of asking me to arrest Gabrielle or Lynda, I won't. Your wife has grounds to complain to your superior officer about how she and her daughter have been treated and I'm their witness."

"You, fucking lesbian and Transgender lover," David shouted back.

"I'm afraid you won't get a job here in London, we tend to help Gabrielle and Lynda rather than make trouble for them and we even patrol the Train Station so no other people can try and get in.

"Ladies I think you should all leave, it's obvious he doesn't like his daughter, your very beautiful my dear, don't listen to your dad, just be the person you want to be and let him go," Adam said to Heather. David walked down the bus and started to speak to Adam.

"Adam, I don't like queers, and all these people are queers, there should be a law against them and have them all put to sleep, and their bodies burned, bloody bastards."

"Dave you can't say things like, Aggghhh." Adam was on the floor, his arm broken from the force of David's baton, his small eye camera, recording everything and sending pictures and sound back to their HQ.

David brought his baton down on Adam's other arm, breaking it in two then he stomped on both his hands and punched him hard in his stomach. He hit his face with his fist, giving him a black eye. His eye was already swelling, so too both his arms. Adam was in agony and then David brought his baton down on John's arms, so fast, he wasn't expecting it to happen. John was thinking of Gabrielle. He had moved her out of David's way just as he was being hit on both arms.

David hit John on the head as hard as he could with his baton and although John fought it, he was on to the floor unconscious.

"One, no, two down, one man to go. Four queers to go," Dave shouted and pounced on Helen's body, punching her in the back and was about to bring his baton down on her head. Alan stood just in time to stop him killing his wife. He held his arm tight and twisted it around and managed to get him onto his back, he removed David's handcuffs and slapped them over his wrists.

"Here you go," Alan said pushing his body up and under the two bus seats he had been sitting on. "Stay there and cool down David."

Alan went to Helen and held her gently, guiding her to the seat opposite his, as she sat down, Alan asked Lynda if she was alright, as she was starting to cry. He knew she was slipping back in time again.

Gabrielle knelt beside John's silent body; he was hardly breathing. She pushed all her love into his body, then he started to breathe normally. He opened his blurry eyes. Both his arms were aching as he was just lying on the floor.

"Is John alright?" Alan asked.

"He's a strong man, I think he might be," Gabrielle replied,

"Dave does weight training every day, and is the boxing champion in his police force, he never loses a match and it's usually over after the first punch. He drinks all sorts of expensive drinks and has a ten-inch steak every night while we go without," Helen told Alan.

"Crikey, how long has he been in that regime?" Alan asked her.

"About two years," she answered.

"That must cost a lot of money," Alan replied.

"We live in a police house, so no rent, that's how he can afford the expensive food."

"Heather did he hurt you?" Lynda asked her.

"No, he didn't touch me."

"What is hurting on your body Helen?" Lynda asked.

"He's broken my arm and my face hurts."

"Your eye is swelling; you'll have a black eye soon. move over there, Heather and sit down behind the seats Alan was taking up. I'll help your mum.

"Let me see your arm," Lynda said and thought she should really help John first, but this was easy work and once done, Gabrielle could take both women home.

Lynda concentrated on Helen's arm her green eyes shone bright as she looked at her arm. She repaired two cut blood vessels, made the bones in her arm match up and her green eyes, repaired the break. She then looked at her face and healed all the swelling. The broken small blood vessels around her eye were also put back together and with a hot hand on her face, all the swelling went down.

"Feel better now?" Lynda asked her.

"A lot better thanks."

"I'll go down and help the others."

"John is coming around now," Gabrielle said breathing a long sigh of relief.

Adam was in a lot of pain and bleeding from his broken arm where one of the bones was protruding from his body. Lynda walked over to Heather and put her hand on her shoulder, giving some of her love making her feel a little better. She then turned stepped back then forward to go down to John. She suddenly felt a hand grab her ankle; she allowed her leg to turn as David tried to pull her to the floor. David was out from under the seats in a flash, it was all happening so fast. He stood and went to his daughter about to punch her in her face, but Alan stopped him and went to help Lynda.

"Sit with your mother I thought I had him cuffed up securely?" Alan said aloud, annoyed with himself.

"I forgot to tell you his body is totally double jointed," Helen said then shouted, "Lookout!"

David was out with his baton and swung it towards Lynda, it just touched Alan's arm, but he didn't break any bones. John was now fidgeting, and rubbing is eyes as they were still blurry. He was watching Alan, Lynda and David who now had his baton out again. As the two police officers watched from the window, he swung the baton hard across his daughter's back then as he turned around, it hit Lynda's thigh. Lynda's eyes were flashing bright green as David started to stand.

The officers outside could only look and witness what was happening as David, standing upright, threw his Baton with all his might at Adam who was trying to stand to tell David to calm down.

It was too late, the baton hit him right between his eyes. Then there was the sound of thunder and a single bullet hit David right between his eyes. He fell to the floor dead. Gabrielle was already with Lynda, trying to calm her as the sound of gunfire faded away. Gabrielle was cuddling Lynda and kissing her, giving her all her love as she slowly calmed Lynda down and she stopped sobbing. Gabrielle looked through the window seeing the two police officers amazed at what had happened.

When they were by John and Adam, Lynda knelt beside John and looked into his eyes. A few blood vessels had broken behind his eyes and in his brain. She couldn't stop now. Her hands were over his head, moving from side to side with her green eyes healing the blood vessels just beneath his skull.

Gabrielle put both her hands, on Lynda's shoulders and Gabrielle's eyes lit up bright green, sending all her love into Lynda's body, reinforcing her power to her eyes, as they picked up yet more damaged blood vessels, there was also a lot of swelling in his head. Lynda was working as fast as she could to stop him from dying and she knew she would have to operate on Adam's head as well. John's head was healing fast as her hands moved four ways over his head. The swelling was going down and with another push from Gabrielle, Lynda finished healing his head. It would do for now, he would have a bad headache, but she could cure that when she finished on Adam's head.

"Hold him in your arms and massage his head, Alan. Gabrielle, I'll

need your help to repair Adam's head," Lynda said.

Lynda felt John's hand on her arm.

"Thank you, Lynda for saving my life, I should have shot him earlier."

"It's over with now, you killed him," Lynda replied with a smile on her face. "Thank you, John, for saving my life," she said and started to laugh.

John slipped his gun back into its holster and got out his gun license and license to kill in any country. Alan got his ID cards out as well. Alan was now sat down with John lying on his lap. He was gently rubbing his head, but John's arm was still broken. Lynda was sitting on the floor with Adams' head on her lap. Her green eyes were looking into his brain as Gabrielle was giving her lots of love and support from her shoulders.

An ambulance turned up and parked behind the two police vans. The paramedic came running down the side of the road with his green bag.

"You won't need that I think the copper on the floor is dead. The copper at the other end is definitely dead. Shot right between the eyes, from a half laying position with eyes that could barely see," Trevor said to Oscar the paramedic.

"Don't go in there yet, Lynda is operating."

"With what, there is no incision? She has no instruments to work on his head."

"Stand here and watch her. Put your bag down," Trever, one of the men from Manchester said with a smile.

They all watched as Lynda continued to look inside his head. Gabrielle gave her some extra power and more love as her healing hands went over his head and just above his eyes, which were now open.

"Thank you," Adam said quietly, will the rest of my broken bones hurt?" he asked Lynda.

"Shhhhhhh, now try and sleep for half an hour can you do that?" Lynda asked.

"Yes, fine, no blurred vision at all."

"Try and sleep. Lay on your back and I'll set your arms and heal the bruising to your sides and back.

"Lynda helped him get on his back, the paramedic was amazed at what he had just observed, he could see both his arms were broken.

Lynda, with Gabrielle's green eyes helping her, his broken bones moved back together, and she healed, them and any broken blood vessels. Twenty minutes later both broken arms were healed and the bruising inside was gone, so too the bruising on his back.

"Do you hurt anywhere else?" Lynda asked.

"No, I'm fine now, thanks, I can move my arms. Twist them, go back and forth. My head seems fine as well. I can think and talk even though that bloody baton hit me, right in the centre of my head. If you or Alan need someone to vouch for you, I'll do it."

When Adam stood, they all gasped and just stared at him. "I'm sure he was dead before she started to operate on him," one man said.

John turned onto his left side, laying over Alan's lap as Lynda made all the black swelling go away, and repaired six big blood vessels and eight smaller ones. She then turned him onto his front with Alan's help. She mended his broken arm, resetting the bones and healing a few broken blood vessels. Once his arm was healed, she took another look at his head, giving it a deeper examination of his brain and checked his eyes again. With brighter light from both girls, John was fine, with everything working as it should be.

John spoke to Gabrielle quietly then with her green eyes flickering, Gabrielle walked to the back of the bus talking to Helen and Heather, who had now stopped crying and tried to stop thinking of David. He couldn't hurt them any longer. Gabrielle touched mother and daughter and all three silently left the bus, leaving Gabrielle to return to the bus while Heather and Helen told everyone what had happened back at the Train Station.

The other bus passed theirs, and the driver tooted his horn and the driver of the four-by-four car behind did the same.

"I'm afraid that as a shooting is involved, even though you saved people's lives, we'll have to call it in. Here comes our boss, he'll sort you out."

John stood up, with Gabrielle's help. As the Police chief Constable for their area boarded the bus, he looked at John first with Gabrielle beside him, holding him upright.

"Good morning, Gabrielle, Lynda are you alright?" he asked.

"Yes, thank you Luie. What are you doing here?"

"I heard there was a shooting, and bright green lights involved, I take it that was you two. And which of you killed the police officer down there?"

"That was me I'm afraid, he just threw his baton and hit officer Adam Cook right between his eyes. He also gave him two broken arms, bad bruising and internal head injuries, but he's okay now. Lynda saw to all of his problems and managed to repair his broken arms," John explained.

"He gave John no option but to fire," Gabrielle said.

"He had already hit my ward and was about to try and strangle her," John continued.

"I have it all on film," the officer outside the window shouted. Luie waved him down. As he stood to attention and saluted John and Mike. He took their licenses to kill time and handed them back.

"I've heard you've had a little trouble at the TG House and the Train Station, but you are back in control now," Luie said to Gabrielle.

"Yes, and we would like to get back as soon as possible can you sign off John's gun just to say you've seen it," Lynda asked him.

"Of course, then you can be on your way."

John removed his gun from its holster and handed it to Luie. After removing the bullet up the spout and the clip.

Luie, smelt the barrel, the gun had been fired. He handed it back to John and emptied the clip of eighteen bullets into his hand.

"All checked and above board, only one shot fired, right between the eyes no doubt?"

"Yes," John replied.

He put all the bullets back into the clip and handed it to John. He then signed John's shooting paper then shook all their hands and said good luck to everyone.

"Call in the station within the next few days to give your statement, then we'll close the case."

"Sure-thing Luie." John replied, feeling much better now.

"Both officers left the bus and a forensic team arrived with a doctor to ensure David was dead. The two police vans left, returning to their station. Lynda stood by Alan, held his arm and two girls held her other arm and they left the bus returning to the Train Station.

Five minutes later Gabrielle, John, with another two cold girls, returned to the Train Station. Frank would bring the bus the rest of the way when David's body was removed. His own handcuffs that were on the floor beneath the two bus seats, picked up and returned to his uniform. His car was being collected by a police breakdown truck in case there was any evidence in there that could explain his wild actions.

When Alice the District Nurse, finished removing the girl's catheters and bags, Gabrielle and Lynda changed her body slightly giving her thinner legs and arms and long brown hair, they also made her hands and feet smaller.

"Thank you both so much for changing my body for me, I look and feel fantastic now," she said to Lynda.

"Glad we could help and thank you for helping our four girls, and the risks you took. That takes guts."

"And you two have lots of guts, I admire you both. Any time you need a District Nurse give me a call." She handed Lynda her phone number written from a notebook in the car.

Gabrielle said goodbye to Alice then both girls finished sorting out the girls and changing the last twenty-eight girls into real girls. They all had a shower but there were no clothes for them to put on except panties and bra, which they all went through before having a shower.

Over half of the shower wash, hair shampoo and conditioner were used up and the empty bottles put outside in the plastic recycle bin.

There were still twenty-two girls missing, sent home and two more to a private buyer, a paedophile. They decided to get these two girls next before they got abused too much and were killed.

"Where is her diary?" Gabrielle asked Lynda holding her hand.

"Here is one of them, she has four books on where she sent the girls off to," Lynda said, placing the four books on the table. They had a pen and notepad each as they went through the books. Lynda was the first to find one girl who had been sold off.

"It looks like they may have been separated," Lynda said.

"Who is it?"

"Mia, Lynda replied."

"Shall we try and get her now?" Gabrielle asked her wife.

"Yes," she agreed. Both girls looked at the address and jumped into the road outside the house, then they were inside, in one of the four bedrooms.

They found Mia, and looked in the other three bedrooms, there were six more real girls in the rooms with a line going into their arms with a drug in as well. They couldn't just leave them there they took them all back to their base and called Alice back in who had not left yet. She had stopped to help bring in more dresses, skirts, tops, cardigans, thick jumpers, coats, shoes and tights, the first of the new supplies were being delivered to the supermarket despite it being only seven forty-five in the morning.

Alice removed all the paraphernalia from their bodies and put it to one side. John and Alan had been searching for rope and had found two long lengths that were going to be used for a swing.

Gabrielle held John's arm while Lynda held Alan's, as they returned to the house. They checked all the bedrooms again then went downstairs, in the large front room three men were asleep on the sofa and another man in a chair. They all had a young girl about ten sat on their laps with their hands laying over the girl's vagina's.

John had his gun ready as Gabrielle removed the man's hand from the girl and dropped her back to the Train Station. Lynda and Alan had done the same twice as Gabrielle dropped the next girl off. They quickly checked the rest of the house finding one other girl in the downstairs toilet, she had been sick and crying, blood was seeping out of her vagina down her legs.

Gabrielle returned the girl to the Train Station then they woke each man as quietly as they could, as John and Alan tied them up. They were all left with their arms tied behind their backs. Then they took John and Alan home.

They were surprised to see two female police officers and a police doctor there.

"John, Gabrielle, Lynda Alan, I had to ring the police, these girls are missing, except Mia, and they will need help," Jenny said holding her husband's hand and kissing him.

"You did the right thing Jenny; would you like to take over these girls for now?" Lynda asked her, we still have another girl to locate who was sold to another group. Alan spoke to a senior police officer giving them the address they left the four men at.

A man and woman who didn't live far away from the Train Station, had heard about the rescued missing girls, and the damage done to their TG House. Neither were worried about the boy, girls, they were still children to them. They burst through the double doors into the room where the police surgeon was.

"Phoebe, where are you love? The police officer called and said you were here." She looked around at all the girls some still dirty others showered and were having their hair dried and styled by their friends.

At first the woman thought it was a paedophile home, then she remembered where she was and the number of girls that were staying there and there was Gabrielle and Lynda, John and Alan. She called her daughter's name again and saw a hand go into the air.... She ran over to the hand beating her husband. They held a hand each as they looked at the bruising and needle marks on her arms and the black bruises to her body.

"Phoebe, what have they done to you?" her mother cried.

"The bruises and needle marks will go down in a few days, there is a large tear in her vagina, and she will be better off in hospital where she can get the proper care," the police doctor told the worried parents.

"I can sort all the bruising and tear in her vagina," Lynda said to the police doctor.

"I'm sure you can't, she needs time and care in a hospital," he replied.

"Please, let her have a go, I've heard her green eyes can do a lot of things," her mother, Felicity said crying.

"Okay, arms first then," he agreed.

Lynda's eyes lit up and her hot hands went up and down each arm in turn four times. Then her green eyes checked her brain was not damaged and anywhere else on her upper body.

"Is that it then, your little party trick over with?" the doctor asked Lynda, then he looked at her arms and the bruises that were all over her stomach a few minutes ago, were now gone.

"Okay if you can do it, heal her vagina."

Lynda's eyes lit up again and concentrated on her vagina then she went down her legs and finally examined her feet. "There is a needle in the underside of her foot, it's a long way in and must have been used to push drugs into her."

"Where is it?" the doctor asked and examined Phoebe's right foot. There was the needle, it had broken in two, possibly when she stood on her feet. He started to push the tweezers into her foot to get the needle out, but she was waking and crying with the pain.

Lynda's bright-green-eyes shone over where the needle was, he tried again and the tweezers slipped effortlessly in beside the needle and as he pulled it out, there was a little blood, but Lynda closed the blood vessel and healed the hole he made with Phoebe returning to sleep.

"Thank You Lynda, I mean it from the bottom of my heart," Henry said to her. He was about to hold her by her arms and kiss her face, as his wife shouted at him.

"Henry don't touch her or kiss her," Fellicity shouted at her husband, waking Phoebe at the same time.

"I was only going to thank her for what she did."

"A simple thank you will suffice, Lynda was beaten hard and raped every night, Gabrielle has helped her a lot, but she still remembers it and Gabrielle's eyes can defend Lynda far better than you could and they both talk to Death," Falicity said to her husband as a warning.

"Sorry Lynda I didn't know. But thank you anyway for healing Phoebe, they may want you to heal the other girls after they have been examined by the doctor and photographed. No sense in making them suffer in pain when they don't need to."

"Yes Lynda, would you do that?" the doctor asked.

"Go on love I've just found the other address, it's Zara, now we'll know the names of the other girls we have to rescue, and they will all be here by lunchtime," Gabrielle said. "I'll take John with me."

"Alright then I'll repair their arms and any internal cuts and bruising. Be careful my love," Lynda said and held her wife close kissing her profusely.

Gabrielle took hold of John's arm, and they were gone. They arrived outside the house where Zara was being held. They jumped to the bedroom Zara was in and found her on a bed with a line in her arm. Gabrielle pulled it out and was gone, back to the Train Station, then returned to the bedroom.

"Let's look around," Gabrielle said to John.

"Here's my gun, shoot them if they try and run or go to attack me. Your Licensed to kill, it will be fine," John said, removing the plastic ties from his jacket pocket and commenced to strap the six men's hands up behind their Backs.

"Take four girls with you and bring that copper back, tell him first to send some officers here I'll stay here and guard the men, take Orla with you she's in the first three rooms for now."

"I will, I'll be back soon, I'll have to move the girls first, if I can't get them to stand up, I'll make more jumps. Orla should be awake by now."

Gabrielle jumped upstairs and tried to wake the girls, but it was no good. She thought to Lynda and called Orla to the room she was in. A tired, doped Orla entered the room as Lynda was pulling the second bed with another seven-year-old on towards the other bed, so she could reach both girls.

"You alright John?" Gabrielle shouted.

"Yes fine," he replied toying with his gun, often pointing it at one of the men.

"I'm having problems up here, I can't wake any of the girls including Orla," she shouted back. She didn't want the men to know John would soon be on his own and try between them to jump on him. Gabrielle held each sleeping girl's arm with Orla holding her with her arms around her neck.

Then they were gone, Orla, dropped herself to the floor, while helping hands held each girl and placed them on a table. The police officer had already called the situation in and more police cars, were racing towards them to photograph everything there and arrest the paedophiles.

Gabrielle was back upstairs leaving the police officer to take control of the situation. She moved two beds together and took the eight-year-old girl's home. Again, helping hands put the girls on tables.

"There are still four girls there, all in a bad way on beds," Gabrielle said.

"We'll be ready for them," Jenny said.

Gabrielle was gone. Arriving on the upstairs landing. Looking into the bedroom the beds were close together. She quickly entered the room touched the two girls and took them home. Then she was back again, calling out to John. There was no reply, so she silently walked downstairs, into the lounge. The men were gone, and the police officer was talking to John.

"There is no need for me to return to your place, I'll get picked up by a police car in the area."

"John," Gabrielle said entering the room, at the same time she was showing Lynda what her eyes were seeing.

"Be very careful my love, I can't lose you now."

"There are two girls left upstairs, you could get them, I might be a few minutes with John."

"Alright my love I'll get them," Lynda said and was gone, starting to push the two beds together.

"What has happened to my John?" Gabrielle screamed at Mathew, the police officer in charge off Paedophile investigations.

"I went upstairs and pulled the beds together in each room for you. While I was gone, one of the men I released, came back in. He had an old needle from one of the girl's arms, knocked John on the head and pushed the needle into the back of his hand.

"The needle probably had some drug on it, and he just fell asleep, he'll come around in a minute or two. You just have to let time move on. Take the other girls then you can take John back.

"So where are the men?"

"As I told John, before he went to sleep, because you removed the girls which is all the evidence, there is nothing to connect those men to this building except to get in from the cold.

"It wouldn't be worth doing the paperwork, now take the other girl's home, they didn't look too good when I moved their beds. I have all their names and addresses, so we can keep an eye on them and that's all we can do," Mathew said smiling. John started to moan and open his eyes.

"You're one of them, aren't you?" Gabrielle asked him.

"What a thing to say after all the help I have given you. I cancelled the call to bring other police officers here."

"You bastard," Gabrielle shouted. She leaned over John kissing his lips. "Come on my love, wake up, she said her right hand shaking his body. She kissed him again as her hand entered his jacket and carefully removed his gun from its holster. John felt her hand and he knew what she was thinking of doing but he couldn't let her do it. He saw what appeared to be a remote red button in Mathew's hand.

"Take me upstairs now," he whispered to Gabrielle. Two seconds later they were both in the bedroom where the last of the girls were. Lynda was holding their arms wishing she had some clothes to cover them then Lynda heard John and Gabrielle behind her.

"Jump now," John shouted.

There was a loud explosion beneath them, and the rooms upstairs started to collapse into the fire below them, both girls jumped together arriving in the Train Station with the explosion still rumbling in their ears.

"What's that sound," Jenny asked seeing her husband appearing in the room.

"That was PC Mathew something blowing himself up and the house, destroying all their fingerprints and evidence that had been there. He was a paedophile as well, I confronted him about it after he let the men go and put John to sleep. The entire house is on fire," Lynda added.

Gabrielle helped John to a vacant chair and sat him down with Jenny's help.

Lynda walked back to Gabrielle, holding her tight and kissing her as Jenny was kissing John. I thought I lost you there, Lynda said with tears in her eyes.

"I thought I had lost me as well. John was slipping down my side just as I was about to jump. I love you so very much, with all the fibre of my body," Gabrielle said, crying.

"Come on my love its barely nine thirty, let's get these two girls changed, so they can shower and see what if any clothes are left. We'll have more later this morning and paint. Alistair will deliver all that straight to the TG House.

More parents were arriving at the Train Station to see if any of the girls were theirs. The women looked at them with their hearts thumping and crying as they saw the six who were brought in. One woman screamed, then called her husband to her side. They had found their daughter she was a bit beaten up and bleeding in different places of her body.

Another girl Ruby was now crossed off their lists.

Esma was the police GP who replaced the police surgeon because the male Police doctor couldn't get any of the girls to let him touch them. Already the fear of men was setting in. Esma hadn't seen anything Lynda could do let alone the two of them together.

"Lynda, could you come and do your magic over the last five girls please?" Esma asked.

"We are about to change these two boys into girls, you might like to see this, then I'll come and do healing on them," Lynda replied.

There was nothing Esma could do she could do no more for the children, then four couples came in from a large police van. Another couple would be joining the others very soon.

The last two boy girls were standing up, concentrated on the size of their new breasts and the colour of their hair they both wanted long hair halfway down their back and both aged fourteen, they wanted a D cup.

"By next year you will be that bit older and naturally grow into a D cup," Gabrielle told them.

"But Gabrielle, we both want bigger tits," Mia, and Scarlette said together.

"Are you two going to request sharing a bed?" Gabrielle asked them.

"Yes, we would if you'll both let us. We are sure we are deeply in love with each other to last for all time. We know it sounds stupid but that's how we both feel," the girls said together holding hands. Then turned into each other and kissed. A good long loving kiss.

Gabrielle spoke to Lynda mind to mind about the girls request for a double bed.

"There are plenty of nice, good-looking boys out there you know," Gabrielle said.

"But we've both been beaten by our father's and boys alike since the age of seven. My dad used to hit me with a wooden rolling pin, if he caught me in a dress, I would get two black eyes. Mum was kicked and beaten given two black eyes, and often, a broken jaw," Mia told the three women.

"I'm the same, only I got a good kicking as well. My dad cut my beautiful long hair with a pair of scissors, snipping it this way and that, then he cut off the tops of both my ears. He slapped my face tore up my clothes and burned them all.

"The next day mum took me out to buy some more dresses, skirts and tops with panties and a little bra. I had to keep them under my mattress and mum let me use her makeup. Mum brought me to you, and you took me in when I was just ten, but I'm so glad you did.

"Mum went home and got the beating of her life. So why should I trust men or boys. Boys grow into men and some like to abuse women, and some men abuse girls because that's what turns them on. I don't know why they don't use a condom all the time then they wouldn't have kids. I bet they hate them as soon as they are born," Scarlette said crying. Mia put her arm around her, and they kissed, the second time before an adult.

"Right girls, one long black hair, one blond, long hair and two size D cups. Get between us and think of what you want," Lynda said and smiled at her wife. Their eyes glowed bright green as they thought about the shape of their heads, their hair was growing longer, their voices were changed, and they started to grow their breasts to a D cup.

They concentrated on changing their male bits to female bits, a vagina and clitoris then they started to change their body structure, their hips and breast areas. Their arms grew thinner so too their hands. Then they worked lower, changing their legs and feet so they became thinner and had smaller feet. The last thing they did was remove all their body hair except on the top of their head. When it was done, they looked and talked like a girl aged fourteen and a half.

"Mia, Scarlet, we've discussed your request. When the House is finished you can have a double room," Lynda told them and Lynda held Scarlet's hand and Gabrielle, Mia's hand, giving them all their love for each other to start them off in their loving relationship.

"That is truly amazing, unbelievable," Esma said.

"We've been doing four at a time all night and first thing this morning," Gabrielle said, holding her wife's hand.

"We changed all these boys to girls earlier."

"Yes Esma they were boys to start with. We rescued them from Ken Mattingly who works for George Rainar.

"Where did you rescue them from?" Esma asked.

"It was a huge mansion in Macclesfield. We only discovered where they were last night at seven o'clock.

"There was a huge explosion in Macclesfield earlier this morning. Prospect Mansion. Most of the men had run off but thirty were burned alive, Ed Lever and ten of his bodyguards, were also killed, they think trying to open a large safe. It blew up as soon as the door opened, fire spread instantly through the building as more explosions started in the basement.

"There was a lot of dynamite in the building the police up there told the press, there must have been a ton of it they think to cause so much damage to the house, cars and busses outside," Esma said recalling the news on the radio earlier.

"We got our girls out just in time then, when did you hear that news?" Lynda asked.

"On my way into work about six thirty."

"Really, we were very lucky to get away, did anyone survive?"

"Ken Mattingly and two of his men, that's it the building is still on fire," Esma answered.

"Wow," Gabrielle said. Her mind instantly recalled where Lynda had been a few minutes before they got the seventeen-year-old girls out. She could have been killed consumed by the fire, she thought to herself.

"Right, you two girls, get your panties and bra ready to put on after your shower.

"Ask Bethany to find you a dress each and at least a cardigan, thin jumper or thick jumper. Do you need me for five minutes Love? I just have to speak to Esme."

Esme took Lynda up to the first girl they wanted to get healed, she was still in a great deal of pain.

"This is Violet, Violet this is Lynda she is going to heal you, she won't touch your body, I'll be here all the time so will your parents.

"You might want to cover your eyes or look away," Lynda told them.

"Why are you going to switch on a very bright light?" Royston, Violet's father asked laughing.

Georgina, violet's mother elbowed him in the side, to stop being naughty.

Lynda flashed her eyes as bright as she could. She looked at Violet's right arm first. It was broken it was obvious.

"Hey, her arm is broken, it should be in a cast," her father shouted.

Lynda took no notice and thought to her wife, a second later she was by her side, holding her, talking to her and giving her all the love, she had for her and her green eyes, grew brighter as her hands passed her love into Lynda's body.

Lynda's eyes, shone on the arm, her hot hands moving up and down her arm. The bone was mending, and the blood vessels were healing as too her eyes, brighter and hotter with Gabrielle's power being pushed into her body.

Then Lynda started on her left arm, with her eyes going up and down her arm twice all the needle holes were healed, the bruising healed and all the blood vessels that were damaged by the hitting were also healed. Her left hand had a broken middle finger and thumb. She aligned the bones with her hands as the light from her eyes took away the pain. With the fingers mended, Lynda ran her hands over Violet's left hand.

Next, she lifted her vest and examined her chest and stomach with her eyes. She moved lower and removed her panties. Her eyes shone over her vagina and her hips. "It's alright, the men pushed something into you and tore open your vagina wall. I expect it is stinging now?"

"Yes," Violet replied crying.

"I'll take away the pain now then repair the damage, okay?" Lynda's eyes concentrated on her vagina. "Does it hurt now?" Lynda asked her.

"No," Violet instantly replied.

Lynda's eyes increased in brightness and her hands, now boiling hot, moved up and down over her vagina.

"There does that feel better?" Lynda asked her.

"Yes," she replied laughing.

"Do your legs or feet hurt?" Lynda asked as her eyes rested on her thighs. She moved her green eyes up and down her thighs.

"Yes?" Lynda asked Violet.

"My legs hurt here and at the bottom and both feet hurt."

"I'll take a look at them, do your thighs hurt too?"

"Not now, you've repaired them.

"Yes, I have, now let's look at your lower legs. Her green eyes, growing brighter with her wife's help looked into her legs, seeing two broken legs and baton hits across the bottom of her feet.

"It's okay the pain will go away soon," Lynda said. "What's the diagnosis Lynda?" Dr Esma asked.

"Her right leg is broken here and here her left leg is broken here. Can you turn over for me please Violet?" She turned over easily. Lynda picked up both legs in her hand, her right leg, now on her father's side fell-down, as if it weren't joined to anything.

"See her feet, here and here, here and here?" she asked indicating the areas which had been hit repeatedly and broke two bones in each foot and damaged a lot of blood vessels. "I don't know how they will fix that in hospital, it will be a three month stay at least," Dr Esme said to her parents.

"We'll see." Lynda's green eyes ran over her feet and her hot hands followed. Lynda repeated it again and again, then a final time to repair the last of the damaged blood vessels. "Can you turn over to me please Violet?"

Her green eyes shone over her legs then Gabrielle's eyes grew very bright and shone over violet's lower legs while Lynda's eyes did the same, with Lynda using her hands to heal her bones.

"Right, it's done, Lynda said, shall we move to the next girl?" Lynda asked.

"Thank you, Lynda you too Gabrielle, thank you so very much." Esma was shaking her head to both parents so they could touch either of them.

Violet jumped down from the table, moving her arms and hands about and stood upright on her naked feet with no pain at all.

"I'm sorry we don't have any spare clothes for her size, we can wrap her up in a blanket," Gabrielle said.

"It's okay, I have some clothes in the car."

"We can offer you a shower if you want to clean her up. Don't worry, she'll be fine now."

"I'll get her clothes, then use your shower if it's okay?"

"Of course, it's fine."

"Did you bring any spare clothes? She asked Freya, who is Anna's mum.

"No, I didn't bring anything with me, Anna has been missing for three years. My husband loved her so much, he couldn't take the continuous pain and suffering. 'We are still looking for her,' he was out looking for her every night up to midnight. He was knocking on people's doors at midnight, asked if they had seen our daughter. Then last year he committed suicide, he hung himself."

"I'm so sorry," Gabrielle replied and was crying herself.

"How old is she now?" Georgina asked.

"Six but she hasn't grown as much as she should have, it's a miracle they found her, I'm so pleased they got her out before the explosion in the house."

"I'm pleased for you as well."

Freya turned to watch Georgina walk to her car. She opened the door picked up two carrier bags and walked back in. She sorted out some clothes for her daughter and passed both bags to Freya.

"Take what you need for Anna, and pass it on, I don't think the other mums have any clothes either," Georgina said.

It didn't take long to have the children showered and into clean clothes. Amber had been abducted a year ago and she was now five, Eliza was abducted two years ago and was now eight, Bella was only abducted six months ago, but had been passed around the group of friends and badly abused.

Lynda was able to repair the scars on her nine-year-old body, repair her broken arm, hand and fingers, her vagina was badly scratched by metal objects, her bottom was split and was bleeding a lot. Her feet had been repeatedly hit with a police baton while another man sat on her back so she couldn't move forward, which showed how hard she was beaten.

Her mouth was cut badly and as Lynda talked very quietly to her, she knew she been forced to suck some of the men off and swallow, whatever was ejaculated into her mouth. Her mother and father were now abroad and would not be returning to the UK for at least a year. Lynda could repair the visible scars, but not the mental scars.

They would be with her for the rest of her life. Lynda saw herself in this girl and cried for her. Gabrielle appeared next to her hugging and kissing her as Lynda spoke to her mind to mind. Lynda finished repairing the bottom of her feet. With Lynda telling the doctor a police baton was used on her feet, she wondered what officer it would have been then PC Mathew came into her head and she was glad he was dead. Both girls were agreed upon Lynda's idea.

"Bella your parents won't be back for a year. Gabrielle and I were wondering if you would like to stay with us for that year rather than go into foster care. You would mainly be staying here for a while then you could move to our apartment. You could also spend time here, with just over two hundred sisters to play with. You would be the youngest, oh when is your birthday can you remember?" Lynda asked her.

"The twentieth of November 2010."

"That means you'll be ten in a few weeks, Lynda replied. We might have to go to court to get a protection order for you, but we'll do everything we can for you.

"You'll have to rough it, like us for a while, but we must get the TG House finished as soon as possible and we'll have to review it tomorrow, when we have discussed it tonight. We are also doing a tour of the UK to speak to all our staff and check on the condition of our shops, then we are going to Europe to inspect our shops there, you could accompany us if you like."

"We will have to ask the police doctor and the lady there from social services. We are not saying we'll heal all your pain and suffering, that won't happen until you're older and you meet your partner whether it be man or woman," Lynda said holding Gabrielle's hand. They kissed, showing their love for each other.

"Oh, one other thing neither of us know how to bring up a real young girl, we have brought up boy girls from the age of ten to twenty and some a bit older than that, now we are doing it all again in France, Rome and the USA. Soon in Australia." Bella laughed and the doctor looked at her so too did the woman from social services.

"They are getting her to come out of herself, she'll be in a deep state of depression for years and nobody will want her like that taking her to hospital all the time and having her wake up screaming in the night, running away from the house.

"Summer, come here please," Gabrielle called out. Summer walked over to Gabrielle. looking at the girl who had been crying.

"This is Bella, we saved her from the last house where we found Orla.

"This is Summer, she will help you with a shower, then get you something to wear."

There was the sound of a horn outside. "It's alright Lynda, I'll go, you're busy with the new girl," Bethany said.

"It's Alister with more clothes I hope."

Lynda looked at her diamond encrusted watch, seeing it was nine forty-five, they had done well, she thought to herself.

"Yes, it's clothes," she shouted with glee. She had dresses, tops, skirts, nighties and dressing gowns in her arms. She hurried through to the bottom area where it was warmer, stopping by Gabrielle.

"It's more clothes for the ten-to-fifteen-year-old girls. There should be something in here you like Ania, and for the new girl," she said.

"This is Summer," Lynda said. "Ania is going to help her shower then you can find some clothes for her.

"I have another two trips to make, they have given us a lot of clothes. It's from other shops. He's also got more paint onboard and another twenty duvet and pillows.

"Wow," that's excellent Gabrielle said.

"Bella, would you like to go with Ania and have a shower, then Bethany will find you something to wear. Jessica," Gabrielle called to the girl ten feet from her,

"Can you help, Bethany to get the rest of the clothes in please? I'll get John to bring in the duvets."

"Of course, Gabrielle," Jessica replied.

"John," Gabrielle called.

"Yes boss?" he replied standing next to her.

"Can you and Jenny unpack the duvets and anything else he has for us, He'll take all the paint over to the TG House.

"Okay Boss. You, okay now?" he asked showing concern for her even before his wife.

"A lot better now, we still have another seven girls to locate and rescue this morning."

"Yes, and I will be with you this time." John replied.

"Yes, Gabrielle no going off on your own, John is here to protect you, he can't do that if you leave him behind," Jenny said.

"I agree with you," Lynda said smiling.

"And you're not leaving without me," Alan said to Lynda.

"Yes, and I want you both back safe and sound," Sarah added, holding Alan's arm, kissing his lips. John and Jenney left them to do their job.

"Sarah, I want you to take Helen to the expensive shops when they open and take Noah with you until we know what's happening with Ken," Gabrielle said.

"That will be at ten, this morning," she replied.

"Well give her a heads up and find Noah, I bet he's with Tina somewhere.

"You are probably right, she replied, then they were off to do their individual tasks.

Charlotte watched everyone go off helping each other, especially the girls. "How do you manage to remember all their names?" Charlotte asked Gabrielle.

"They are all our children, and older sons, who have come to join our family to live the life they want to lead, until they would have their sex changed, this has not been a normal day by far, and it is not over for us yet. They will do as they are told because they have come to us and their sisters. We have no squabbling or arguments, if they need or want something, then if it is within our power, they'll get it. Nobody is treated any different except perhaps one child, but we'll see what happens with her," Gabrielle replied.

Charlotte went to speak to Bella, but she was gone, holding Anya's hand being led to the showers.

"I wish my girl would act like yours do, and I only have one," Eliza said, looking at all the girls.

"You have Clara back now, love her, treat her, enjoy each other every day, sit with her now and read to her and help her with her homework," Lynda said calmly, looking at Clara who was talking to Sophia.

"Yes, but I'm a single mum, and anyway, you don't know what has happened to her. How she was treated. It must have been horrendous for her to have to endure," Eliza retorted. Lynda looked at Gabrielle, their bodies touching, Gabrielle's arm went around Lynda's back, even now she was crying for herself, her past for Clara and all the other girls in the room.

Gabrielle kissed Lynda's lips, and their green eyes flashed a few times as they spoke to each other. John and Alan left their wife's and ran down to their girl's.

"Are you alright Gabrielle," John asked urgently, holding her hand.

"Are you alright Lynda, you've been crying, what's happened?" Alan asked and very gently took hold of Lynda's hand. Lynda went to pull away.

"It's alright Lynda, it's Alan, try and remember me," he said softly, Sarah was by their side.

"Lynda, it's Sarah. Alan is just holding your hand and your wife has her arm around your back, I'll put my hands gently on your shoulders," she said in a soft and loving voice.

"We are all going to give you all our love just for you. Please Lynda, come back to us," Sarah continued.

"What happened Gabrielle?" Sarah asked.

"Lynda was recalling her past and was going to answer the question Eliza asked," Gabrielle whispered to her. "It's not her fault she didn't know, how could she?"

"Right, let's all try it," Gabrielle said crying herself.

"Gabrielle's eyes shone very bright, flickering all the time, while the others, eyes closed, gave all their love to Lynda, willing her to come back to them and leave the memories of her past where they should stay.

A few minutes later, Lynda started to cry and open her eyes. Gabrielle kissed her and Lynda kissed her back.

"I'm okay now, thank you all," she said, leaving her past behind her.

"Was that little display done for us, to make us feel sorry for her and us think she had been through what my daughter has?" Charlotte said in a harsh deep voice.

"No, it was not. All the girls here, everyone, of them has been abused, beaten by their father's and their friends have laughed at them, when their father dressed them in girl's clothes and forced them out onto the streets. Many of the girls were nice to them, but the boys all tantalised them, making fun of them, catching them and throwing stones at them. They have begged to come here to live their lives as they would like until they could have a sex change at Kings Cross Hospital.

"Lynda met Ian and they got married, then he changed her into his own whore, making money for him. He was a drug cutter, the best in their area and he got men on drugs to come and rape his wife all hours of the night and day, she had no reprieve from it.

"After sex, she was beaten and then had the underside of her breasts cut with a Stanley Knife, or her belly slashed from one side to the other, making her bleed a lot then in the beginning, a woman came to stitch her body back together.

"George killed his wife, her mother, father and two sisters because he thought his wife had told the police about them when he put her in hospital for a month. Ian allowed George to come and rape her every night and paid Ian with drugs. Then she escaped, let her hands and fingers heal, then started to write again, if she gave Ian five hundred pounds a week for beer money.

"Then we ran into each other flew into the air and landed on the ice and snow-covered pavement just past my Hats & Bags shop on the Strand. I took her to a coffee shop, and we were already deeply in love with each other, that was at eleven in the morning, we talked until twelve thirty then ran to my shop where I put her into one of my period hats at thirteen hundred pounds and a shoulder bag at eight hundred pounds.

"We kissed a few times had our pictures taken then at one she ran to the bookshop further along the road, and I said I would see her at six fifteen and take her for a meal at the Shard. That was just seven hours before our next meeting.

"When I got there, I smiled at her told her I loved her then all hell let loose as her husband and George threatened and tried to kill her with their knives and swords, I wanted to save her life, I was in love with her. In the next three minutes and fifty seconds I killed Ian and George. George had an eight-inch K9 knife in his hand because he was trying to cut off her photographer's hand. The other knife went into his heart. I saved a coppers life.

"Then I had both my hands sliced open as they ran down the sharp doubled edged sword. The sword from Ian went into my stomach and was moved about, making the hole and damage worse, as I cut his throat ear to ear, I was losing a lot of blood, I fell to the floor and Lynda stayed with me, got help from a paramedic then a doctor came and started to stich my stomach back together and as my heart gave out, Lynda started to kiss me all over my face until a heart surgeon turned up then I died and talked with Death again.

"Lynda held my heart in her hands and when told started to give me heart compressions. My soul was returned to my body, and I was alive again. I was in hospital for two months. She hardly left my side. She has never left my side nor I hers.

"Everything we do, we do together, our minds connected. Lynda has suffered like Cloe; it took me years to help her through her emotional fright. She was at one time too frightened to go out. In the beginning, she woke every night screaming, frightened Ian was going to cut her open again.

"This is what Cloe and Bella will go through, frightened of the dark and the memories that live there."

"We have spent enough time telling you all this when we should be looking for our other eight children." Gabrielle said.

"I don't believe any of it, you put on a show to make me worry," Charlotte shouted, looking at her daughter who was mixing with the other girls.

"Don't do it Lynda, you'll hurt her more than her daughter. Please don't," Gabrielle said.

It was no good. Lynda was annoyed that the social worker would not believe her, neither would she believe her daughter when she screamed each night, she would tell her to get back to bed and go back to sleep, she was tired of her whining, but Lynda knew it would not be just one night, but every night until Cloe found her partner or committed suicide.

Lynda's eyes lit up. "You wouldn't believe Gabrielle, the love of my life, my wife. So perhaps you will believe this.

"No," was the last words Charlotte heard as Lynda's green eyes, looked into Charlotte's, their eyes met, so too did their minds, they were at least six feet apart.

Lynda made the proper connection and Charlotte, fell into a light sleep. Lynda started showing her past being raped, cut open, beaten, having six abortions, the pain she felt, the fear she had, night after night, being kicked in the head, talking with Death, the things He told her what would happen soon. Being cut by her breasts in front of her father and the decision he made to save the rest of his family rather than help his daughter, it was all happening inside Charlotte's head, she tried to wake herself up, but the nightmare continued, night after night, just like her nightmares would be.

Tears were in her eyes as Lynda woke her up. It took a few minutes for her to understand what she had seen.

"It really did happen to her. It had happened to my daughter. I'm so sorry for not believing you all, it was not a show just for us, you really did get abused badly, what a horrid start to your married life. What Paul had put himself through just for you, to save your life, as it was ordained," Charlotte said in a calm voice.

"If you will allow me to help you, I will just get something from my car," she said.

"We'll be on the next two tables down, looking for our other children who were sent back to their parents who beat them all the time, breaking their bones and upsetting them, every day of their lives," Gabrielle said to Charlotte as she stood and walked to her car.

"This has taken too long; we should have been here an hour ago," Gabrielle said to her wife.

Lynda looked at her watch, it only took three minutes and fifty seconds she said, it's nine twenty now."

"Really?" Gabrielle asked her wife, they moved together nuzzled their noses then kissed, showing all their love for each other.

They took a seat each and started to look through Teresa's diaries. Lynda was the first to find a girl Valerie, she lived in Liverpool, her mother had brought her to them after Valerie had found their charity website on the internet, that her father was right against, according to him, Bryan, AKA Valerie, was showing him up in work, and with his friends, so as soon as he came home from school he locked her in her room, sometimes her mother with her, then he would come home drunk and fuck them both for up to an hour.

"Look at this, why didn't we see it before? It's Tanya and Teresa, they live on the same street, almost opposite each other. It's no wonder they wanted to be together all the time, both regularly beaten by father helped by their mothers, brought here worried for the boys' lives and they said they needed our help," Gabrielle said.

"Here's another, Pauline, lives in Manchester. Lucky she wasn't sold to that group or allowed to be abducted to get her out of the way," Lynda suggested.

"We'll get her first just in case someone has their eye on her now. What is she, fourteen?"

"Yes Gabrielle, they are all older girls now." Lynda told her. Looking at the book before her. "Here's another, Nayome," she marked it with a red highlighter.

"And another," Gabrielle said. She too marked it with a red felt tip pen. "Nina," She suddenly realised there was a pattern to the girls she sent home.

"Here's another Tracey. Look sixteen people down the page," Gabrielle said.

Lynda was counting sixteen names down. "Got her Stella," Lynda said as Charlotte came back into the room.

"This is another urgent one, Stella is being beaten then forced to wear a dress and makeup then give these men a blowjob. They lock her away in her room."

"That's terrible, Charlotte said to the girls overhearing Lynda fill in the diary.

"I've got some paperwork for both of you to read through and sign. It's important that you rescue these girls first, do you mind if we stay? Cloe is just coming out of the shower, so she'll be a while, it's nine fifteen now, that's strange, I thought it was much later than that," she said, looking at her watch.

"It's strange how time goes when you're busy," Lynda said.

"But these forms take an hour to complete," she replied.

"Oh well, we'll get onto them as soon as we return."

"Do you mind if I wait in here?" she asked.

"That's fine sit where you like, have coffee and a cake if there are any left, it's all free here."

Lynda gave Gabrielle the position of Stella's house. As John and Alan came up beside them, taking hold of their hands. Charlotte could see how tender Alan was with Lynda, it was like he knew all she went through and felt her pain as well, even though he was married.

The two girls kissed each other and concentrated on the address. They all appeared in Stella's bedroom as a man was about to put his penis into Stella's mouth.

"Suck on this, Alan said as John made the other five men sit on the long sofa opposite her double bed. Nobody needed to know what was happening here. Gabrielle got Stella out of the way of the man who now had Alan's gun in his mouth not moving a muscle.

"You will let Barry fuck you or he'll fuck Stella as she likes to be called. Now do as your bloody well told." Everyone heard a loud slap across the face, as Cristopher dragged her to the top of the stairs where he slapped her face again. She screamed making Stella shake. Lynda had finished cleaning Stella up and spoke to her quietly. Lynda jumped home with Stella.

"Give her something good to drink, not just water, she just had a man come in her mouth. I got most of it out, get Isabell, to give her a shower and take her makeup off. I won't be long," she said to Jenny and disappeared.

Evelyn the mother was in the bedroom, wearing a very sexy nightie, black panties and black stockings. Her makeup was immaculate.

"Where did you lot come from?" Christopher shouted looking at everyone and where is my money-making daughter?"

"Your daughter is with us, as to the paperwork you signed with our solicitor and social worker. Now Evalyn has something she wants to say to you." Gabrielle said in return to his unaddressed questions.

Evalyn turned to look at her husband. "I'm leaving you Christopher this wasn't how our marriage was meant to be. Treating your boy girl as you have since Teresa brought him back is not right either."

"What are you going to wear? All your clothes are next door and I have the key, you wear that around the house now," Christopher bellowed.

John walked past him and kicked the door open. "Evalyn, come in here, wipe the blood off your face and get some clothes on.You have to go out later, dress for the cold," John said.

She quickly changed wondering where Stella was. She had a dress, thick jumper and overcoat on. She picked up her special handbag with both their passports in and the other cards and papers they might need. There was also two hundred in her purse, but she knew it wouldn't go far. She would have to get a job.

She shoved some other clothes into a bag to go on her back and was out of the bedroom. She knew John had not watched her change, he just stood guard outside the broken door. In the other bedroom, she looked at her husband. "My solicitor will be in touch with you and no doubt the police too."

Gabrielle held Evalyn's hand the other John's. Lynda held Alan's hand and they were gone. Back in the Train Station, Stella was talking with her friends as Jenny came over to greet her.

They both concentrated on the next address, Tracey's house.

They arrived seconds after they left. They could hear a man shouting in the bedroom. "He was wearing this and it's yours," He shouted at her. Another whack with a long stick.

"Why do you do it?" he bellowed and hit his son who cried out in pain.

John walked into the room first and looked at the long stick in his hand. There was a bright red mark across Valerie's face. He pulled Valerie away from her father and handed her to Alan, who handed her to Lynda, who touched him and disappeared. She was back in a heartbeat leaving Valerie to speak to her group of friends, as Penny got a cold cloth and held it against her face, telling her what was happening and what would be happening to her.

At the house John escorted the man downstairs, forcing him to sit in a seat while Gabrielle talked with his wife Iris.

"What would you like to do stay here or leave?"

"The thing is Gabrielle, I have no job now he has started beating me as well, but Valerie wants to be a woman and wear a dress. He wants to go back to you, but he said the house is in a right state because of that Teresa and they didn't get fed and other girls were being sold. Is that right?"

"Yes, but we rescued all of them early this morning, now we have only six boy girls to rescue. Valerie is already back at the Train Station.

"We could offer you a job for a month, helping clean up the mess the workmen are making or something else if you can help."

"I was a teacher at secondary school, years seven and eight."

"Now that is a help. Would you like a job with us until you can sort yourself out? You would have to sleep rough like all of us."

"Yes, I could do that if I can be of help."

"Does it cost a lot to live in London?"

"It depends, where you live and the type of property. are you going to leave your husband?" Lynda enquired.

"Yes, I will."

"Say it now while John is with him."

A few minutes later, they were at the Train Station. Evalyn came over introducing herself and took her to an empty table.

"Next Tanya and Jessica, husbands don't agree mothers okay with it they understand they were born into the wrong body. The thing is, we're rescuing the children and bringing some mothers back as well, we just don't have all the room we need at the moment," Gabrielle said to Lynda.

"Yes, but they can help the girls out while were in this mess," Lynda replied.

`They jumped to Jessica's house who was being beaten by her father as John entered her bedroom and threw him against the wall while Gabrielle took Jessica back to the Train Station. Lynda was talking to Robyn her mother as she came back upstairs and looked at Gabrielle.

"Can I have a few minutes to get all my patterns and a few bits I'm used to working with?"

"What do you do?"

"I'm a dress maker by trade. I work from home," Robyn explained.

"That's good can you teach?" Lynda asked.

"Teach what?" she asked.

"Dressmaking," Lynda replied.

"Yes, I suppose so," Robyn replied.

"Would you like to stay and work for us, for at least three months, you would be a big help."

"Yes Okay," Robyn replied.

"John, up here please. We're jumping to Tanya's house. Mum Tabitha," she called out after Lynda took Robyn back to the Train Station, leaving her husband and her house. It was the same situation in Tanya's house, except the beatings were harder on both women. Tanya had a black eye when they all jumped into her bedroom.

"Hi Tanya, sorry we were so long, we had that fight in the USA to sort out," Gabrielle explained.

"Gabrielle did you win?" she asked.

"Of course, she did Lynda had to do her part as well," Alan added, smiling.

"Where is your mother?" Lynda asked.

"She's downstairs crying because I had her dress and makeup on." Mum helps me all she can we thought he was at work, but he came home early."

"What does your mother do for work?" Gabrielle asked out of curiosity. Would this woman have skills as well?

"She is a secretary in a bank, or at least used to be. I think she got the sack because of her black eyes."

"Lynda, take Alan and Tanya home, I'll get the mother, if I need back up, I'll call you."

John went downstairs first with Gabrielle right behind.

"I won't have it any longer, my mates are talking about us and Tanya is always asking after Jessica, he would like to play with Jessica. I know their other names. Robyn is like you, will help the boys instead of stopping it from happening and why did that Teresa bring him back?"

"That's a long story you wouldn't want to hear." There was a loud slap as he hit her across her face with his hand.

"Let's go in, John said, holding Gabrielle's hand and putting her behind him.

John opened the lounge door and walked in with Gabrielle behind him.

"John." Tabitha exclaimed, "Gabrielle!" she added.

"What are you doing in my house?" Andrew demanded to know.

"This is Gabrielle and John, her bodyguard, licensed to kill."

"Who does he think he is, James Bond?" He shouted getting angry.

"No, but I do have a license to carry a gun in the streets and I am licensed to kill, anyone he added, then pulled out his gun.

"Tanya is back at the Train Station and we're back in control after we rescued two hundred and ten girls early this morning from Ken Mattingly, who's taken over from George. She's safe with us now," Gabrielle told them.

"Can you keep her there for a few more years, maybe five, she said, thinking of where she would live, her ribs and fingers would have to heal first, that could take months and then she would have to learn her touch typing again.

"Can you give me a lift to the Train Station please?" "Yes, we can do that," Gabrielle replied.

"Just a minute can you wait for me?" Tabitha asked.

"Yes, of course," Gabrielle replied.

She ran upstairs to the back bedroom and came back down the stairs. She dropped her case outside the lounge door, hoping John would hold it as her hands wouldn't and her fingers on both hands hurt.

"Andrew, with Teresa safe with Gabrielle, even if she has to sleep rough for a few weeks, it's better than being here getting a black eye for being born into the wrong body."

"Tabitha, is it right you're a secretary, touch typist?" Gabrielle asked.

"She used to be until I kept giving her black eyes and I broke both her hands and all her fingers," Andrew interrupted laughing. Tabitha held up both hands, showing how they were broken, and all her broken fingers.

"Yes, did Teresa tell you?"

"Yes, can you teach touch typing?" Gabrielle asked.

"I used to teach touch typing before I became a secretary for Mica Bank. They have branches near me and another not too far away."

"Would you like a job for a time, teaching touch typing again?"

"No, she wouldn't and if you say yes, I'll break your arms to go with your hands," Andrew shouted.

"Andrew, I want a divorce."

"And who's going to put up with your crying all night?"

"John is, we've been seeing each other for over a year now."

"So, you've been seeing my wife behind my back, have you? I'll give you what for, he said then sat back down in his chair, holding his chest trying hard to breathe.

"Get up again, you'll get worse," John said loud to Andrew.

"John, I'm ready to go if you'll still have me like this," she asked holding her hands in the air.

"Yes of course I will, I live in London mind you," John replied.

"That's fine," she said and felt Gabrielle's hand push him forward.

"Kiss her," she whispered.

John stepped forward, took her in his arms with care and kissed her lips passionately. "Shall we go?"

"I want the bloody house, "Andrew shouted. As John escorted her from the room into the hall and picked up her suitcase.

Gabrielle walked by his side and in the hall, Gabrielle took hold of Tabitha's arm and held John's free hand then they were gone and back at the Train Station. Jenny was waiting for them. She kissed him and realised he had lipstick on his lips.

"Snogging behind my back to get your other girlfriend out of another situation?" Jenny asked him.

"How did you know what was happening?" he asked, then looked at Lynda who was smiling at him.

"You told her?" he asked.

"Every word, and kiss. I know all about your year-long affair," Jenny said, raising her voice.

"I'm so sorry Jenny it was all my fault I just needed an excuse, and it was he who kissed me, with a shove from Gabrielle, I saw you push him," she said smiling.

"I know what happened, but we like to play our little jokes on each other now and again. Welcome to our new home for a couple of weeks," Jenny said. "That looks nasty," she continued looking at her hands.

"Can we please have Jessica, Tanya, Stella and Valerie here please?" Gabrielle called so they would hear their names being called.

The four boy girls stood together and thought of what they wanted, they were nearly fifteen and wanted a C size cup and long hair, two, tawny coloured, two black. Everyone stopped talking as the four girls were changed.

First their hair then their voice and shape of their face. Next their shape, given breasts, vagina, thinner legs and arms, petite hands and feet with a girl's voice and face shape. All their body hair disappeared, and they all looked beautiful.

"Now girl's, real girls, go to the showers and wash each other and your hair, Bethany will find you all something to wear and the other girls will dry your hair and style it." Gabrielle informed them.

"Those hands need looking at," Jenny said to Lynda.

"You look up the next address, I'll be about ten minutes, her eyes are bad too and she wears glasses, so I might need a hand," Lynda said holding her wife close to her.

"Sit here, Lynda said, and gently holding her right hand, her green eyes lit up, examining the hand making all the bones like putty. She moved them gently into their formation then the cooling of her hand made the bones in her hand set as did the bones in her fingers. Her green eyes went up her arm, putting another bone in its right place and looked at her other hand.

"I didn't know you could do that," Tabitha said.

"I can do all sorts of things now," Lynda replied, smiling. Her other hand was back to, normal in a few minutes. Now she was working on her head. She checked her head and brain, healing two bleeds that would have ended up as strokes. Then she looked at her eyes, placing her hands on them heating them and repairing all the damaged blood vessels in her face and putting her eyes back to twenty, twenty, vision.

"Has he hurt any other part of your body, it's alright, tell me now and I can fix it if you're going to sleep with John."

"I'm not doing that Jenny."

"I know you won't Gabrielle wouldn't stand for it," Jenny replied laughing.

"He did something to my vagina and bottom, Tabitha replied sheepishly.

"It's okay we're all girls here except for the gunslingers," Lynda replied laughing and started repairing her vagina.

It was twenty minutes before she finished working on Tabitha then the much better woman was back on her feet drinking coffee with the other new wives.

They went to Tracey's house first. Tracey was in her room dressed as a boy. His father was out but he had tied him to the bed, so he couldn't change his clothes. His mother was also tied to her bed, so she couldn't get up and help her boy, girl, son. Lynda was in Tracey's room releasing her from her bonds.

"Could I come with you? I can't live with all this fear now. I'm petrified what he will do when he comes back."

"What do you do for a job?" Gabrielle asked.

"I'm a specialist painter, I paint murals."

"Can you teach that?"

"Yes, I can."

"Then your hired, here is your husband." They heard him coming up the stairs. Lynda took Alan and Tracy back home.

John got Connie's case and two files from the wardrobe, and from deep down in the back, her handbag with their passports and all the paperwork they would need with a thousand pounds, not that it would go far.

"Right were ready to go," Gabrielle said as Trevor her husband came in with a long stick.

"Who are you, where is that boy girl thing?" He demanded to know and raised the stick bringing it down into John's hand. He snatched it from him and brought the stick down on his backside. He cried out in pain.

"Now you know what it feels like on your daughter and wife," John said hitting his bottom once again.

"I'm leaving you," Connie said looking at him.

Connie threw a letter on the bed. "My solicitors name and address, you can get me through them, I expect I'll hear from your solicitor soon," she said.

"I'm keeping the house, car, everything," he retorted.

"Fine with me," she replied. "I'm ready to go Gabrielle."

John picked up her suitcase and handbag, which was heavier than he thought, allowed Gabrielle to get between them. Gabrielle held John's left hand and held Connie's right hand and they left, appearing in the Train Station. Penny met them and took Connie off to sit with the other mothers.

Gabrielle and Lynda went to Nina's home next. Nina was in her bedroom, crying and in a hell of a mess. Both her arms and four ribs were broken, both her hands and all her fingers. She had extensive bruising in her tummy area so she couldn't sit up both her thighs had cut marks on them which had been bleeding excessively. Both her lower legs were broken with a bone coming through her right and left lower leg. Both feet had been beaten by a police baton and then they were both broken.

Her mobile phone was on the floor broken, not that she could have picked it up and rang anyone, her hands hurt to move. Her testacles were burst, and her penis swollen so much he couldn't pee if he wanted to but was now in a lot of pain from his bladder as it was so big it was getting ready to burst.

Gabrielle went into the other room to see his mother, Vanesa. She too was laying on her bed. Both her legs were broken, as too both her hands and arm. All her fingers were broken.

"Who did this to you?" Gabrielle asked.

"My husband she struggled to say, yesterday morning. He refuses to call for help."

"How long has Nina been in that mess?"

"I don't know, he came in and saw me talking to her in a dress. He went wild. He broke my jaw and pushed me in here then returned to Nina's room and started to beat her. I heard terrible screaming and then he put his hand over her mouth as he beat her hard with his baton.

"Is he a police officer?"

"Yes, here he is."

Mark bounded up the stairs two at a time on hearing voices. He looked in his son's room, he was still on his bed. Mark opened his truncheon and threatened his daughter with it. He went into the bedroom he shared with his wife and looked at her then he saw Gabrielle and John.

"Who are you two?" he asked, shouting at them.

"I'm Gabrielle from the TG charity, this is John, my colleague.

"What am I going to do with you two, you can't leave for now, not with my wife like this. He heard a cry and then some more crying from his son's room.

"Have you come to take that queer son back?"

"Yes, that's what we had in mind, but he's in a bad way and needs medical help," Gabrielle replied.

"Well for now he ain't going to no hospital, But I see a plan forming in my head. Daniel is in the car outside, I'll call him in, and you are the two perfect intruders, who did this to my wife and my lovely son."

"But your wife will tell him the truth."

"Oh no, she'll be dead." He pushed Gabrielle away from him and John pulled his gun.

"Just sit on the floor with your hands on your head you'll kill nobody," John almost shouted in anger.

He started to sit down, then with his truncheon fully extended, he thrust it towards Gabrielle. John shot him in the arm. He dropped the truncheon crying out in pain."

"Carrying and using a gun without a licence is a crime with time in prison.

"So is beating your wife and son like you have," John retorted.

"Drop the gun thickhead," another police officer said holding a gun in his hand.

"Don't worry Mark, we all have to keep together, we'll get rid of these bodies and sort it all out. We'll say Evalyn moved in with this bloke John, but we don't know where he lives, and Stella is back with the TG people that's all you know and I will miss her soft skin as she sits on my lap and I fondle her all over. Crikey I'm getting a hard on just thinking about her." Mark said.

"That's disgusting," Gabrielle objected.

"Well, you won't matter much longer you'll be dead in a minute or two," Daniel explained.

"Will you? Put the gun down Daniel, before Sir John Fletcher blows your brains out or Sir Alan Watts who with Dame Lynda Grayson heard everything you said."

"Sarge that bloke John shot me in the arm, look, I want to arrest him on several charges."

"And what are they Mark?"

"First he has beat up my wife and son, second he has a gun without a licence then he shot me in the arm while I a police officer made me drop my baton to help me make an arrest," he said in reply, thinking he had now got away with it.

"Sir John shot you in your arm, did he?"

"Yes, he did, he needs to be punished."

"He never misses a shot he must have only wanted to wound you. Lynda, you carry on. Let me tell you Sir John and Sir Alan, are both licensed to kill in any country including the UK.

Daniel turned fast holding his finger on his trigger. There was a thud from Alan's Glock and Daniel dropped his gun. Another officer ran up the stairs, followed by another as green light was coming from Stella's bedroom.

"Arrest them both, Mark for beating up his wife and son, and attempting to involve Dame Gabrielle and Dame Lynda Grayson in a cover up with Sir John Fletcher and Sir Alan Watts. Add Mark is also a paedophile. Daniel is to be charged with aiding and abetting Mark and being a paedophile other charges may follow. To both of them. Take them in and have a police doctor dress their wounds in their cells," Sergeant Bob Hopkins said calmly.

Gabrielle was not happy with the way things were going, the arrest was all wrong, they gave enough reasons for the Sergeant being there and the other two officers who came up the stairs.

Then she got to his future thoughts. and quickly passed the information to her wife.

"John, why don't you cut Evalyn free, even with two broken legs, she will feel better, and we'll move her soon, further up the bed she added, getting more information from Bob's head.

"Alan, why don't you cut Stella free?" Lynda suggested. Alan got the idea something was not right and cut the bonds holding Stella to the bed. Lynda had managed to repair all the damage to her male testicles and penis and emptied her bladder into a bottle which Alan emptied out of the window. She was now repairing the bones in his abdomen and giving her breasts and a female look. She then started on her legs, repairing the left one first as it was the easiest and would be the quickest to heal. While Alan was cutting the ropes by the top of the bed, his head went towards Stella's head.

"He's one of them as well and the last two Jacob and Oscar," Stella said.

"Her eyes look bad; the punches must have knocked her pupils about and damaged them Alan said to Lynda.

"Okay I'll look at them in a minute," she replied.

They watched the four men walking down the stairs and Lynda walked up to Stella's head, seeing the damage done to her eyes when she knew she didn't have long. Her, green eyes spent a little time on her head as she repaired her eyes and gave her twenty, twenty, vision and finally a female face and voice. Her glasses which she would not need now were on the floor smashed.

Gabrielle jumped downstairs into the hall and heard the police officers talking together in the lounge. She thought to all the men to sit on the floor when they returned to the station, they would get the other men in the ring to stand with them and they would give themselves up with Bob doing all the talking. They all fell into a light sleep as Gabrielle jumped back to the bedroom took hold of Evelyn's hand and John's hand and they all jumped back to the Train Station.

"We need help here, two tables together please. Then another two tables together," Gabrielle said giving orders. Everyone wanted to help her, four women gently took hold of Evalyn and put her on the tables.

At the house, Bob fighting the sleep, took a hand grenade from his pocket and sat on it.

"They won't take me alive they'll slaughter me in the nick and prison if I get there alive. I would rather die here and now, taking you all with me, there is no way out for you," he said as he pulled the ring from the grenade.

Lynda touched Stella and Alan and they were back in the Train Station.

"I need help here," Lynda shouted, and four girls put Stella gently onto the table.

There was a loud explosion which followed them into the room.

"What was that and what happed to Stella and her mum?" Isabell asked Lynda.

"The explosion was a police paedophile sitting on a hand grenade blowing himself up as we jumped. As for Stella and Evalyn, her father Mark, beat them up with his fists and baton, but he used a homemade baton out of steel, to break their arms and legs and beet their feet, so they could not run or stand up to get to a phone, not that they could do that, they were both tied to their beds, Stella for over a week, Evalyn for two days. Gabrielle, I'll repair Stella's broken right leg and get her bone which is protruding through her skin, back together, then we'll have to finish changing her asap. I'll then help her mother."

"Can I offer her a glass of water?" Hannah asked.

"That would be fine," Lynda replied.

She started to work on Stella's right leg, pushing the bone back in and matching it up with its broken ends, as it was split in two sections. It took her five minutes to repair her leg and heal both her feet, then she had her hands, and all her fingers repaired before moving up to her arms.

All this time Gabrielle was looking through the book getting the name of the girl, she prayed she wouldn't be like this.

"Right Gabrielle, I'm ready for you. As we change you, we'll also repair any other internal damage. Now, think of the things you need and stand still," Lynda calmly informed her. Lucie and Isabell held her mother's head up so she could see Stella being changed from a boy to a girl, what she always wanted.

Her hair grew long, halfway down her back and was dark brown, to match her eyes. She had a D size cup because she was fifteen. Her arms grew thinner as too her legs, then she was given petite hands and feet, all her male body hair and male bits removed as they gave her a vagina. She was also given a smaller breastbone and girl's face.

"There you are," Gabrielle said smiling.

Stella felt her face then her breasts and finally her vagina. Tears were swelling in her eyes as she felt so happy, she was a girl at last.

"Who wants to help Stella in the shower?"

Hannah had her hand in the air first they had been close friends until Teresa split them up.

"Off you go dear, Bethany would you sort her out some clothes please? We have plenty to look through now," Lynda said.

"Are you ready for me?" Lynda asked Evalyn.

"Yes," she sighed, still in pain, happy her daughter was changed.

Lynda repaired her arms legs and feet, then looked at Gabrielle. "She has a lot of internal damage, some internal bleeding her fingers have all been broken several times before and they are not strait, despite my attempt to repair them, they are now back to how they were. I think the best thing to do is for both of us to almost do a body change."

"I agree," Gabrielle said. They had been talking mind to mind.

"Can you stand up please?" Gabrielle said to Evalyn.

"I'll have a go," she replied, sat up and slithered off the tables.

"That seems fine," she said smiling.

"Lynda, you tell her you're the doctor," Gabrielle said.

"We, rather I found a lot of internal injuries in your body and one behind your eyes. You've had a lot of bad headaches, haven't you?"

"Yes," she quietly replied, tears falling from her eyes as she thought of all the beatings she had to her side, back, breasts, belly and the damage he had done to her vagina. She started to sob and Adele one of the adult waitresses, came over and put a hand on her shoulder.

"Welcome to the temporary TG House, this is the Train Station, where we'll have to sleep for now, I'm Adele, one of the waitresses," she said introducing herself.

"Hello, I'm Evalyn, Stella's mother," she replied.

"Whatever they got planned for you won't hurt and it's all Hell here now. When they've finished, I'll get you a cup of coffee or tea, and something to eat, we have a bit of a selection now. Something is going wrong with the time.

"I'm sure they know what's happening and who's behind it, but don't ask them, you would be frightened by their reply," she said as Gabrielle and Lynda talked about her.

"Right Evalyn, we now know what we are going to do with you. How do you feel about a slightly smaller body, get rid of that belly and the fat on your sides, arms and legs?" Lynda asked.

"Yes, that would be fine, do I have to take my clothes off?" she asked.

"No, we can see you naked quite well," Gabrielle said. They put their arms around Evalyn, and their eyes grew very bright, repairing the damage to her eyes and all the internal damage to her brain. They remained looking into her head, their eyes, getting brighter then darker, then brighter again as they repaired more damage. They moved down her body then Gabrielle picked up a thought from her and shared it with Lynda. Her hair changed colour to a dark blond and grew halfway down her back. Her breasts were made a size larger and made firmer. Her tummy was smaller as too her waist and hips.

They made her arms and legs thinner then gave her petite hands and feet, finally they came back up and repaired her vagina and bottom, where it had been repeatedly hit hard with a wooden baton and metal bar, which had also been used on her daughter. She had also been hit hard with a man's wide belt with a metal buckle at the end. As they talked to each other, they moved back up and repaired her heart which had been damaged by being punched hard in her chest, repeatedly.

Parting their hands, they moved around her and kissed each other, holding each other in a loving embrace, their bodies touching, sending all their love to each other, rejuvenating their bodies. They would need all this new energy on the next rescues.

"You are now much better and should be feeling fine, on top of the world. We repaired your vagina and bottom where you were beaten so hard. Your heart was also not beating correctly, sometimes it was missing a beat, this was because you were punched hard in your chest just over your heart.

"We or rather Lynda repaired it, I just gave her the extra energy she needed to accomplish the delicate job. Now if you Adele wouldn't mind taking her to the shower you can wash yourself and Adele will help you wash and condition your hair and Bethany will help you find something to wear.

"Bethany will get your bra sorted but we don't have many in size 32E, but you'll be able to choose some more later when the shops open, she said looking at her watch. It was now five to nine, but it should have been much later than that. Have a look around, meet the other mothers, oh, what do you do for a job?"

"I'm a Dental Hygienist and I play the guitar and violin and I teach both instruments to people in, my spare time, I think I suggested I could come up and teach some of the girls. Oh no, that was to Teresa."

"That's why she sent Stella home; she would be missed more if she sold her onto George's people.

"Would you like a job with us?" Gabrielle asked.

"For now, you would be helping in the kitchen, can you cook?" Gabrielle asked.

"I'm the best pastry cook in the country, Stella says, and loves my flaky mince pies."

"Oh yesss," Gabrielle replied her eyes lighting up with pleasure.

"Can you make about six hundred today?" Gabrielle asked.

"I could if you have the ovens free. You have a lot of children and men, to feed here. I can at least make a hundred in about an hour if you have large ovens."

"We have six, they are behind us, have a look when you've had a shower, if we make a room for you somewhere, would you like to join us as a Dental Hygienist first, then a pastry chef, then teach the guitar and the violin, not both together of course,"

"Yes, that would be fine, where would I sleep?"

"In here with everyone else for now. But you'll have your own room in the main TG House. There is a second hotel type house being built next door. So, you may sleep in there. Now off you go, as we have more rescues to make," Gabrielle said. "Oh, wages we'll sort out later."

Then both girls with Alan and John, disappeared and reappeared in Nayome's bedroom. She was by herself, crying in a dress. Her hands were red, and her left hand looked broken.

"I'll have a look around with John, while you heal her hands," Gabrielle suggested.

"Fine with me my love, be careful."

"I will, she replied then they kissed before they parted. The room turned bright green as she started to repair her hands and fingers.

Gabrielle and John went to the next bedroom and opened the door looking into the room. It was empty and tidy. They looked in the third smaller room. A woman was crying and her mouth bleeding, her glasses were smashed on the floor and her fingers on her right hand were broken. Worst it seemed to me she was stabbed in her right breast with a pair of hair cutting scissors.

Gabrielle sent all these problems to Lynda who replied that had repaired both her hands and all her fingers. She was now ready to go.

"Nayome, your hands are all repaired now, yet you're still crying what is the matter can you stand up for me please. Alan, help him stand up.

Her green eyes lit up checking her legs, which were fine. As he started to stand, there was a squelching sound on the bed and she thought she might have soiled herself but as she slowly stood, fighting back the hold of Alan's hands on her. She was bleeding from her bottom and further up her back.

Lifting her so Lynda could examine her back. The back of her bra had been stapled to her back. She turned her around slowly and examined her bottom and lower back. There it was, her father possibly had pushed a piece of wood up her bottom, snapped it of then pushed it further in so the only way to get it out was by an operation, which he would not give his consent for.

"It was still quiet in the house as Alan stripped the bloody bedding off the bed and threw it in the corner. Then took a clean sheet from his cupboard and threw it onto the bed for Nayome to lay on. He laid her back on the bed. Lynda thought to her wife.

"I'm going to remove the piece of wood first and repair all the damage in her rectum."

"Okay it looks bad, what an idiot to staple her bra to her back as well. Look at this," she said casting her eyes over the scissors sticking out of her mother's right breast.

"He may be a sadist, jump if you have to, let me know and I'll jump with you. Hopefully, I'll get the wood out first or she will be in a lot of pain. I'll be with you as soon as possible. Take care my love."

"I will. Love you."

"Love you too." They kissed each other inside their heads and felt each other's love flow through them.

Alan now had Nayome on the bed and closed the bedroom door.

"I'm going to remove the piece of wood now; you will feel nothing. I promise."

Her eyes shone bright green which subdued all her pain nerves. Then her eyes opened her bottom up and she used Nayome's muscles to push the wood out of her. It was natural allowing her to pull the wood out of her bottom. Her eyes then started to repair broken skin and six major blood vessels further up her bottom. Lynda checked her lower back and repaired two small blood vessels. She took a step further up the bed and looked without touching the back of her now blood red bra. Her eyes were very bright as some of his back was now numb, she gently put her finger on her back and heard nothing from Nayome. She concentrated her eyes where the bra straps met and were joined together. She gently eased the straps away from her back giving her enough room to get her finger behind it and undo the bra. Alan got his knife out and sliced through the straps relieving the tension on the bra.

"Thanks," Lynda said. then took his knife from him and eased the staples out of her back. There was a little bleeding but not much. When she got to one end Alan took the knife and sliced the bra apart so the strap section with all the staples in could be thrown away. The other side was a little quicker as all the work had been done separating the straps. A few seconds later Alan threw the last piece of strap on the floor.

"When are you going to start?" Nayome asked.

"It's all done now can you sit up?" Lynda asked.

Nayome sat up as if nothing had happened to her. She even stood.

"Do you hurt anywhere else?"

"No." She quickly replied.

"Nayome, would you take your top off for me please?"

She did as she was told, knowing she had been asked to do it for a good reason, even if she didn't see it. As she removed her top, blood was slowly dripping down her front.

"Cut it off her as fast as you can," she said to Alan. He cut both shoulder straps in half then gently pulled the bra away from her small breasts she had grown herself through tablets and creams for the past four years. He eased the staples out of her skin as her father reached the top of the stairs, he managed to pull the front of her bra from her body.

As Lynda started to examine her breasts and top of her body, she saw a piece of wood which had been hammered into her chest. using her eyes, she opened the cut it had made, and Alan pulled it out. Her eyes were now repairing all the minor blood vessels around Nayome's breasts and pulled the flesh and skin of the hole together.

"Can you feel this," Lynda asked putting her finger on her right breast.

"Yes, you're touching my right breast."

"And now?"

"You're touching my left breast."

"Great, do you hurt anywhere else?" she asked.

"No absolutely not. Although why are my eyes blurred now, they were fine at TG House, with my glasses. Is it because I'm not wearing them?"

"Do you hurt anywhere else" she calmly asked. Alan was getting worried, her father or someone had been stood at the top of the stairs for a long time. He looked at his watch it had only been three minutes fifty seconds since they entered the room. He knew it had to be longer than that.

Lynda had her bright green eyes looking into her eyes. There were a few problems with the back of her eyes which she repaired and made the muscles which corrected her eyesight stronger giving her twenty, twenty, vision. Then she examined the rest of her brain, repairing blood vessels which had hurt due to hard slaps on the back of her head.

Soon she finished repairing all the damaged blood vessels in her head and behind her eyes.

"That feels and looks so much better now," Nayome said.

"No problems anywhere else on your body?"

She thought for a moment, moving her head from side to side, looking through her new eyes without glasses for ten years. She stood up and walked around her bed then sat down and stood up again walking back to Lynda.

"I'm now okay, everything seems to work."

"If it doesn't come and see me." She nodded silently and pointed to the door, Alan, silently backed away from the door giving it room to open with a hard kick.

"Take her away," Alan whispered, and they disappeared.

Alan stood where the door would open and hit the wall, so it would miss him just as the door burst open.

"Ben, Nayome, where are you?" he bellowed. He kicked the door to his bedroom open and went inside.

"Who are you two?" he bellowed.

"I'm Gabrielle Grayson, Head of the TG Charity in London. I've come to collect your daughter, but she doesn't seem to be here in the house.

"Take Alan now," she thought to her wife.

Lynda jumped into the bedroom then out with Alan at her side and deposited him in the Train Station. All she could do now, was hope Gabrielle could get both of them away.

Selena was now sat up on her bed with the scissors out of her breast. She was going through her handbag. Gabrielle had taken her suitcase with some of her clothes and the six pair of hairdresser's scissors, combes and hairbrushes inside the suitcase. There was also a folder of women's and men's haircuts, now at The Train Station. Selena pulled out a piece of paper then zipped up her handbag and nodded to Gabrielle.

She had a broken leg how were they going to get to their car? Thomas returned to their bedroom still not having found Nayome.

"When I find her, I'll break her bloody neck," he bellowed.

"Thomas, I want a divorce. You can have the house, your parents left it to you when they died in that horrendous car crash. I drove their car the day before their crash and the brakes were fine, there was no need for them to go over the cliff, but you wouldn't let me testify. You suggested vandals got into the garage the night before they set off on holiday.

"You said there were tools and grass cutting machines gone. They don't or didn't have a great deal of grass, just a small patch out the front which dad kept short with a battery-operated strimmer which is now in our garage. You were lying to me and if you come after me or Nayome I'll go to the police. You can contact me through my solicitor, she said putting the letter on her bedside table.

"You'll hear from my solicitor soon. If you don't give me a divorce, then I'll go to the police," She added.

"And how are you getting out of here with two broken legs and all your fingers broke, plus that wound in your breast?" He bellowed,

John moved to Gabrielle's side and she held Jude's hand lightly. They disappeared just as Thomas was about to start again.

They arrived at the Train Station a second later and helping hands were already there. Lynda started immediately working on her left breast, then moved to her hands and repaired the broken bones in both hands. With the top of her body in order, she started working on both broken legs, joining the bones back together and healing her damaged blood vessels.

"Right stand up and walk around." Lynda asked Selena.

She slipped effortlessly off the tables and stood on her feet then picked up a chair with her hands and walked a short way with it.

"Yes, I'm fine now and it didn't hurt at all," she replied smiling and put the chair down. Gabrielle had already asked her what she did for a living, and she replied she was a hairdresser, someone they would need now the girls had long hair. The men also needed a haircut from time to time, so she would be kept busy. She could play and teach the piano, cello and a guitar. She could teach all three musical instruments.

Iris, Valerie's mother, came over introduced herself and took her to join the others, for now, she would be helping to clear up and take food over to the Girls sat at the tables.

They had one girl to collect left Pauline, her parent's name's Alexandra and Janson.

Let's go then, it must be getting on now, I wasn't expecting so much work to do on them," Lynda said holding her wife close to her.

"I love you so much Gabrielle, I love you," Lynda said.

"I love you too Lynda with all my heart. I'll love you forever. No matter what faces us in the future. I'll love and cherish you," Gabrielle replied.

"We had better go," Lynda said. "Alan, John, we're about to leave."

"Not without me," they said together and held their girl's hand and they all disappeared, arriving in Pauline's bedroom. She was fine, wearing a pretty blue satin dress. She was sat on her bed, listening to her parent's arguing again.

"Hello Pauline, are you hurt anywhere?" Lynda asked.

"No, my mum took me out and bought me this dress shoes and underwear. I thought they were understanding my problem, my mum's fine with me, it's just my dad who can't get his head around it."

"What if I went in and talked to them?" Gabrielle asked, she had a thought.

"You could try," Pauline replied.

"Does anyone, even your dad, hurt or beat you?" Lynda asked.

"He used to beat me every day, but I've been at the TG House for three years and he's calmed down a bit. When Teresa brought me back and said I was not coping and causing trouble, she slapped me across my head and my father had to physically stop her hurting me and threw her out. He put his arm around me, even though I was wearing one of my dresses at the time. He kissed me on the cheek and told me to go in the lounge and tell my mum what had happened.

"Mum took me out later and bought me this dress and everything."

"This is a turn around. Let me try talking to them," Gabrielle said and with John behind her, she left the comfort of Pauline's room and knocked at her parent's bedroom door.

"Come in," Alexandra replied to the knock at the door. The door opened and Gabrielle entered their bedroom, leaving John outside the door.

"It's Gabrielle, isn't it?" Janson asked.

"That's right Janson, hello Alexandra. Lynda and Alan are in with Pauline. I like her dress and that you Janson, have come to understand her a bit."

"Yes, Gabrielle I understand her point of view that she says she was born into the wrong body. I've even looked it up on the internet and read two of the stories you told me to read. I understand she feels she has to wear women's clothes, which I allow her to do in the house, but she wants to go out wearing a dress. I'm just against that. I don't hit her now, or my wife."

"Are you embarrassed when she's out, by herself, with your wife or you?"

"Let me tell you, the only person looking at her is you, and perhaps a few young boys at how pretty she looks. We've come to take her back to TG House, can we do that without any problems? Like shouting or hitting me when John will have to intervene."

"Yes, I suppose she could, how many others are like her?"

"Two hundred and ten then we have eight eighteen-year-olds who take our girls out shopping with them from time to time to get them used to going out as a woman. The eighteen-year-old girls have all been changed or had the operation done by surgeons at Kings Cross Hospital. But they don't mind taking the girls out, they usually go out in groups of four and meet up somewhere for coffee."

"That sounds fine, could we come up to see her?" Alex asked.

"Of course, you can, we have nothing to hide, well the TG House is in a bit of a mess, but today we have rescued all the girls sent home, and the two hundred, we saved during the night with three busses, well, two buses and a sixty-seater coach. We also have eighty men with us who are painters and decorators, sparks, plumber and flat pack fitters. The painting at least on the top three floors will be completed in a fortnight. A lot of girls including Pauline, will be sleeping in the TG House, then going to school for their lessons. Allowing the men to get in, lay the carpets and put all the furniture up together. I am hoping within a month it will all be finished, and all the girls will be sleeping in the house. How does that sound?" she asked.

"Okay I guess, she's going to have the operation, soon, isn't she? That's what we signed the papers for, and it will all be done free?" Alex asked.

"I suppose it's different if you have all those girls in the place. They are bound to feel more like girls I expect. Yes, take her back. Give her the operation. We would want to see her then," Janson said.

"We want to take her home, she has a lot to learn about being a real girl, as she didn't grow up in the first years of life as a girl."

"I understand," Alex said.

"Yes, I can see she has to learn all of that stuff," Janson agreed.

"I want to see her before you take her back," Janson said. Lynda brought Pauline in.

"Hello mum dad, can I go with them, back to the TG House and the Train Station?" She asked.

"Yes," her mother replied.

"Yes," her father added.

"Ohhhh thanks mum thanks dad," Pauline said jumping up and down with joy. She gave her mum a big hug then her dad had the same.

They both kissed her goodbye. "We'll see you in two months, we'll come up to see you. We may even stay a few days in a hotel somewhere close to you and take you out in a dress," Janson told his daughter.

"That would be great dad, she said grinning at her father then kissed him goodbye.

"By love, behave but enjoy yourself learning to be a real girl," he replied.

"By love, see you in two months," her mother said then kissed her goodbye.

"Goodbye," Gabrielle said.

"Look after her," Janson said.

"Bye," Lynda said as she left the bedroom.

"Bye," they replied.

"We'll jump in the hall," Gabrielle said to John, Alan and Lynda. Five seconds later, they were all in the Train Station.

"Well, that's all the girls rescued," Gabrielle said, now to finish our job. Pauline, Naomie come here please. Think of how long you want your hair its colour the size of your breast cup.

Your both fifteen, so you go to a C or D cup. Stand still between us please," Gabrielle said.

Lynda put their hands together, their face changed to the shape of a girls face and Pauline's contact lenses popped out of her eyes, as they were changed to twenty, twenty, vision. Their hair was grown three quarters of the way down their backs. They changed their male bits for female bits without either of them feeling a thing. Then they started thinning their arms so they could wear the petite blouses. They changed their legs making them thinner as too their petit hands and feet They removed all the male hair from their bodies so it would never grow again. Finally, they changed their voices to a girl's voice. The girls parted while the two new girls examined themselves, feeling their new bodies.

"Right, you two, wash each other get to know each other and wash your hair and condition it. Bethany, could you get some dresses and underclothes for the girls and sixty denier tights please, they both have a size five shoe, at least an inch heel, try for two and if not make a note to get that size later in the afternoon.

"Am I going shopping today? Can I take someone with me?" Nayome asked sounding extremely happy.

"Four of you can out in two groups. Pick eight girls and you'll be going to the local shopping mall. How many languages do you speak fluently?" Gabrielle asked.

"Let me see, six I'm learning Russian next, then it will be Mandalynn as you said we might be going to China."

"What all two hundred of you on one plane?" Sarah asked.

"Yes, we could double up in some seats and have the seats in the back of the plane, changed to a long bench seat. We would get seven or eight of the eleven to twelve, year olds on one seat, and there are ten rows of middle seats we can have made.

"We have to get the TG House decorated and made better," Gabrielle replied.

"Good thinking though."

Gabrielle called Lynda to her side and held her hand.

"I'm going to pop home, I've called Imagine in to open the file on Pauline, I can't put my hand on it, but I thought something was not quite right with the parents, It was a huge turn around for Janson, if I remember right, he beat Pauline a lot, every day, now he's suddenly allowing her to wear a dress in the house all the time and is now letting her mother take her out and buy female clothes. So why was Pauline crying? She had no idea we would arrive like we did, and she didn't seem too excited to see us." Gabrielle said to her wife holding her hand.

"I know, after what we have been through this morning it was a surprise to me. Do you want to come with me? then we can get John and Alan to move all the money into the conference room out of the way to prying eyes, then we know it's safe.

"I'll come with you, I'll help sort out the money we need today for the men and any tools they want to buy," Lynda suggested.

"Good idea my love, I'll quietly get the boys, I called Imagine as soon as we got back, that was." She looked at her watch, it was now ten past nine. "Three minutes fifty seconds ago," she said amazed. "I'll get the boys and we'll go home and let everyone sort themselves out and get some of the duvets covered. Alister is bringing another fifty later this morning I think that makes it a hundred and five duvets with duvet covers. We are still short on pillows, and the men will need to sort themselves out with a bed and bedding. We could get the girls to sort out extra duvets for them."

"We must above all, keep them happy," Lynda said with a smile on her face.

"Yes," Gabrielle replied and kissed her wife, holding her close to her in a loving embrace.

"Is that all you two girls do kiss each other?" Patrick asked in a cheerful voice.

"No Patrick, we've also been rescuing our girls. Oh Patrick, while you're here, how much will the drivers expect today?" Gabrielle asked.

"With me and the fuel for my bus, eight thousand pounds. The lads with the other buses and coach, but they have decided to stay here for a couple of days to help you out. Can't let over two hundred kids stay in here all day, it will drive them and you mad. They could take them for bus rides, to a mall or superstore if they have money to spend," Patrick said, smiling at both girls.

"Okay thanks, we'll see you in a bit; more rescuing to do."

"That social worker was looking for you,"

"Oh yes, Bella."

"Don't let her leave, come on Lynda." They found John and Alan and jumped home.

"This is unexpected," Alan said. "The apartment is looking good, especially with all that money in the middle of the lounge," Alan added, looking at the bundles of cash.

There was a code ring of the doorbell. "I'll get it," said John. He was gone in an instant and back with Imagine.

"Wow. what did you do, rob a bank?" Imagine asked laughing.

"You could say something like that. I'll take you to the conference room and let you in," Gabrielle said.

Lynda sat down counting out a bundle of bank notes, so she had a hundred-thousand pounds in two piles.

"As Gabrielle is not back yet, you might as well make a start."

"With what? All that money is mine and Alan's," John said laughing.

"It would be nice though," John added.

"And what would you do with it?"

"Buy my wife a fifty-thousand-pound engagement ring some diamonds set in gold in a necklace form and an eternity ring with diamonds around it at about twenty to thirty-grand. And I would like to take her out in a thirty thousand pound or more dress and have a meal at the Shard, just the two of us."

"What about you Alan?"

"More or less the same, she said to me the other night that she would like to lose a little weight can you help her with that?"

"Yes definitely, as soon as we get back."

"She'll need new clothes, if you can do that," he said laughing.

"Anything else?" Lynda asked.

"A beautiful Diamond necklace around a hundred grand if the money was ours to have."

Lynda put another hundred thousand in a third pile and the same in a fourth pile.

"Well, I'm sorry the money isn't yours' it will go to getting the TG House redecorated and everything and pay the workers and the bus men, they need paying. If you could make a start, please, we want all the money put into the conference room and count how much money you are taking in, we need to know how much there is. Oh, by the way, did you get a text from me about your bonuses for the work you did in the USA?"

"No," they both replied.

Lynda took out her phone and found the text messages. "Look, here are your text messages about your bonuses. With all the excitement and problems with Gabrielle, which is when I sorted out your bonuses, I didn't press the send button. Here, look for yourselves." She handed her phone to Alan who carefully took it from her hand, read it and passed the phone to John.

"Don't you two have an app with your bank accounts on to let you know when money is paid into and goes out of your account?"

"No, but I'll set one up soon," John replied.

"Same here," said Alan smiling." They both opened their bank accounts to see an extra one hundred thousand in each of their bank accounts, with their salaries, which also had another ten-thousand-pound bonus. There was also another bonus of fifty-thousand-pounds for all the work they did after the fight and caring for Lynda and Gabrielle. They had only been back one day.

Then they went to see the TG's and discovered what had happened to their beautiful TG House and the changes to the plans at their apartment and the second TG House, next door to the first one.

They hadn't had the time to check bank accounts, but they were now. A hundred grand each was deposited from the Grayson Company bank account into their bank accounts. Two weeks ago, a further fifty thousand had been added to their accounts. This morning a further hundred grand had been deposited to their bank accounts.

"Thank you very much Lynda," they said together.

"We had a sticky situation there and then there was the fight on the boat and fight with George here and what happened after the fight to Gabrielle. and what happened here early this morning. All the other gunslingers got the same fifty-grand for today."

"We had better get started John," Alan said.

"You did lock the front door, didn't you?" Alan asked.

"Yes of course. Now I'll go and check it again, it's locked," he called out talking back to them.

He picked up the first big packet of money wrapped up in bank paper. "I don't believe it, a hundred thousand in this packet alone," John said, amazed at the room it took to hold all this money together. He picked up a second parcel with the same amount in. Alan did the same and they walked to the lower section, where the Conference room was situated.

"Put the packets which are the same on the table for now," Gabrielle said.

She was looking at the large screen above her on the wall. A second screen was on with Edward looking at her, then the table as the packets got higher with the boys quickly moving the money from one room to another.

Imagine was working at the computer, "bring up the files and pictures of Pauline and her parents, with all their notes about their son, daughter with the pictures. There were also Lynda and Gabrielle's notes below. Right now, she had Pauline's picture on her computer screen and the bigger screen to her right. Nobody was speaking when the boys came in.

"John, how much is on the table?"

"One million, six hundred thousand," he replied.

"Is there much more?"

"At least another million I should think." "Thank you both, carry on."

"There, Edward, what do you think?"

"We managed to get back, the million from your Joint account, and the million from the Charity account. My advice would be to split it up, half to your joint account, half to the Charity account and pay as many people as you can in cash." Edward suggested.

"I have to get Ryan to build us three rooms next to the Train

Station and we'll have a path laid around the outside of the Train Station, to where the three new buildings will be. We are also having an extension built onto the kitchen."

"That's sounds great Gabrielle, pay him in cash, he won't have any trouble putting that much into his Company account. Do you know how much the builds will cost?" he asked.

"Around seventy thousand, there will also be the special equipment to put in, we can pay for that in cash."

John, Alan and Lynda entered the room with six more packets the same size as the first ones. The boys left and Lynda walked up to her wife.

"Hello Edward, how did Gabrielle get you up so early on a Sunday morning?"

"It's only." Lynda looked at her watch, "nine o'clock, would you believe it?" Lynda said as Gabrielle and Edward checked their watches. Edward stood and went to another room in his house looking at a clock there.

"You're right Lynda, what's happening with the time this morning?"

"Someone is playing with us, possibly altering all the time throughout the world," Lynda replied holding Gabrielle's hand tightly in hers.

"You must be right Lynda; it can't be anyone else." Lynda turned and held her wife close to her and they kissed each other passionately.

"Is it the person or entity that controlled your fight with George?" Edward asked.

"Yes, it is," Lynda replied.

"Then may God help us all," he replied, with a tear in his eye. The boys entered the room with four packets each the same size as the others. They were gone and back in seconds now, moving faster and faster, carrying four parcels each. They were in and out another four times before they brought the last eight of the biggest parcels in, making it fifteen million pounds.

"How many parcels are left now?" Edward asked as they were about to leave the room.

"That was the last of the big packets, which makes it fifteen million," Alan replied.

"Next are the thirty-thousand-pound bags and there are forty of them," John replied.

They could now carry five bags each with ease. They entered the room and put the first of the smaller bags at the far end of the table. Gabrielle and Lynda were talking to each other mind, to mind. and didn't realise they were there. Edward had gone upstairs to get his wife. They had a drink each kissed each other, with love passing between them and held each other's hand. Edward was finally sitting down when they brought the last of the thirty-thousand-pound bags in.

Before anyone could speak, they were off again, bringing the next ten bags in and another two trips to complete all the thirty-thousand-pound packets totalling one million two hundred thousand pounds. Now they started on the fifteen thousand-pound packs of which there were thirty, totalling four hundred and fifty thousand pounds.

With all those bags in, they started again on the ten thousand-pound packs of which there were forty. There was money scattered all over the floor, twenty and fifty-pound notes, John picked up the loose money totalling one hundred and sixty thousand pounds, which he put in a stack next to the one's Lynda had made.

"It must be getting on now," Alan said looking at his watch.

It was just three minutes and fifty seconds past nine. They walked down the landing towards the Charity room when John thought he heard something behind them.

"Alan, I think someone's in the apartment behind us." John had his gun out and with all the time problems Alan took out his Glock and followed John quietly back down the landing to the main lounge. There was nobody there, but another load of fifty-pound notes, strapped together making one hundred thousand in each bundle and there were fifty bundles. There were also ten piles of twenty-pound notes five thousand in each packet. Then there were ten packets of ten-pound notes, a thousand pounds in each bundle. There was not a lot of money in ten-pound notes and Lynda would need quite a few ten-pound notes to pay people so with Alan's approval, John stacked them on the floor next to the other money.

As they started their way back again, John heard something drop behind him. He stopped looked around and returned to the lounge. On the floor were twenty parcels of more ten-pound and twenty packets of five-pound notes. He packed them up and placed them with the other money then he turned and thought he saw the image of a fourteen-year-old girl. She disappeared after he thought was a few minutes but looking at his watch, it was just five past nine.

He left again and caught Alan up just where he left him. There were no more sounds of money dropping to the floor, so he walked around Alan and called his name. He walked forward apparently unaware that he had been asleep. It was the same for the others, just waking from a dream.

"How much do we have there, John?" Edward asked.

"According to our calculations, thirteen million six hundred and ninety thousand pounds. Alan and I think we should split it all five ways including you Edward," John said joking.

"I think that is a definite no," Lynda said looking at him.

"Didn't I say she would say that?" Alan asked John.

"Yes, you did," John replied laughing and looked at the time, it was nine ten.

"I'll have the money put into two, five-million-pound bundles, the rest we'll use on the house and for new clothes for the TG's." Lynda said to Edward.

"They will want to know how you got this money and where it came from. If you can answer that question, we can put the entire amount in your account," Edward suggested.

"I'll ring you in the morning after I've made the arrangement with your bank. Best to use your bank as you have transferred a lot of money and paid out a lot of money while you were in the

USA," Edward said kissing his wife in between talking. He looked at his watch, it was now six minutes past nine.

"When do you think the time will sort itself out?"

"I have no idea, right now it should be late in the day. If it's any help, we are sure it's Death doing this for some reason."

"With what our souls told us do you think he's coming to our plane to take away all our souls?"

"No Edward, we won their game, Death said he would start another game like ours on another planet somewhere else in our galaxy.

"Thank you, it is a help, we have decided like you two, to show our emotions to each other even when we are out and about and hold hands wherever we go."

"Would you like a bonus right now of about a million?"

"No, thank you. Oh yes, we can put five hundred thousand in my bank account, that would get rid of more of that money."

"Okay, we'll sort you out tomorrow," Gabrielle said.

"We could have half a million in our accounts," Alan suggested.

"Let me sleep on it, if night ever comes."

"Oh, that reminds me, While I was in the lounge, I saw an image of Bella, it was quite clear, I think she needs you."

"Yes, we've been here a long time," Gabrielle said looking at the big screen which now had Pauline and her parents on it.

"That isn't who you talked to today, Pauline is the same, but her parents are different," Alan said, certain he was right. "I agree with Alan," John said.

"I'm sure they are. Let's go back and see how she is now," Lynda suggested then we can also sort out all that paperwork.

"Can you print off a couple of pictures for us please Imagen?" Gabrielle asked.

"Of course, Gabrielle," she replied.

She walked around to where the printer was situated and removed them from the printer, put them into the guillotine cut to size and slipped them into a plastic pocket so they would stay clean and could be shown around. She handed them to Gabrielle who handed one to Lynda.

"Let's go to the lounge," Gabrielle said looking at the pictures. Imagine pressed send on the computer's keyboard, then finally she shut everything down.

"You should now get a ping on your phones. I've sent the pictures to your phone's photo collection," Imagine said and followed everyone out of the conference room. Lynda was last out, so she closed and locked the door.

In the lounge, Gabrielle picked up ten fifty-pound notes and thirty twenty-pound notes. twenty ten-pound notes.

Here you are thanks for coming in so early this morning," she said and handed Imagine, the money.

"Thanks," she replied, not thinking she would get anything but her emergency call-out two hundred pounds, which she paid her five times more Gabrielle had given already. Two thousand pounds straight into her bank account. "Do you want a lift home?" Lynda asked her.

"No, I'm fine thank you, I brought my car, but I think in this weather, I need a four by four," she said laughing.

"Yes, I suppose you do, let me guess, in pink," Lynda said.

"That would be just right, who would want to steal a pink car?" she replied laughing. Lynda closed the front door and Gabrielle was now handing two packets of fifty grand each to the boys.

Four packets each to the boys of twenty-pound notes and four packets of ten-pound notes.

"We'll return to the kitchen; Simon has a small safe there we can stash this which some or most of it will go today to pay the drivers and the men for their first day at work. Are we all ready?" Gabrielle asked.

"Yesses came from everyone. Gabrielle held John's arm, while Lynda held Alan's arm and they all disappeared. Simon was surprised to see them but knew what they wanted. He went to his safe, which held the day's takings if anyone had to pay for their meal and the books for the Train Station. Simon put all the money in the safe. Going outside, Charlotte came running over to Gabrielle and Lynda with Bella looking sad right behind her.

"Gabrielle, Lynda, I've been looking for you all over. I had a phone call from my office, they want me to pick up another boy who has been beaten bad by his father and walking the streets in a dress with a girl's overcoat on for now. He or she will go into a shelter home like Bella if you don't hurry and sign those damn papers."

"How far away is it?" Lynda asked.

"About thirty miles."

"What time do you have to be there? Do you know the person's name?" Gabrielle asked.

"Something like Areop."

"You mean Ariane? Have you got the address?" Lynda asked.

"She's run off seeing the police arrive, but this is the last place she was."

"Lynda, she's our girl, would you like to get her take Alan with you?" Gabrielle asked. She took the pile of papers in her hand and walked into the kitchen. "Simon, could I have two cappuccinos and a can of coke please?"

"Of course, Gabrielle." she only ever asked him for cappuccinos when there was a problem.

She returned to the table she was sat at and beckoned Bella to sit next to her. Gabrielle commenced to read the notes about Bella, which people had written about her. Gabrielle looked at her watch.

"What time did you want to get away?" Gabrielle asked as Simon brought out the two cappuccinos and a can of coke, which he put in front of Bella.

"What? Time yes, ten O'clock, it must be that now? I'm sorry, I'll have to take her with me," Charlotte said in a hurry.

"Hold on, drink your cappuccino, it's only six minutes past nine."

"It can't be," she cried.

"Calm down, everything will be fine."

Those forms must be signed by you and Lynda. Where has she gone?"

"To pick up Ariane. If she can't find her in ten minutes, she'll come back to sign the papers. Pen please?" Gabrielle asked.

"What are these forms for?"

"You will both become temporary foster parents which means, you look after her and care for her until we want to move her on which often never happens unless you want to send her back because you can't look after her or can control her tantrums. Like all ten of her temporary foster carers have done. Some of our full-time carers have looked at the file and said a definite No. she was with two couples for only a day."

"Really, she's not that bad?"

"She's been with me since yesterday afternoon at six. She had a terrible tantrum when I tried to get her to have a shower and then get into bed."

"Have your drink while I read these."

Gabrielle sipped her drink and after checking her watch for the tenth time, Charlotte convinced herself to stay.

"She was on the last page now and had so far signed four times. There was another, cream page at the end of the file and she was just turning it over to read.

"You both have to read it together and sign it before me," Charlotte insisted and turned around to see a boy standing before her.

"This is Andrew, AKA Ariane and here are the adoption papers, which go with him. Signed by a judge and yours truly signed the adoption papers as well. Now where do I sign my love," Lynda asked, took the Pen from Gabrielle and signed beneath her. Your turn, she said to Charlotte.

"Come here you, Ariane what have you been up to?"

Gabrielle asked then kissed her face and forehead.

"That Teresas sent me onto the streets, to some people who she thought were my parents who didn't like me, so I ran away and came back here got some of my clothes and a coat and went walking around all the expensive shops, with a picture of you and Lynda together and another with the three of us on. You and Lynda signed both pictures I was telling all the doormen you are my mum, and you gave me a day off to go shopping. Without any money and see if by being your daughter; I could get something without having any cash or card on me

"At first three doormen didn't want to let me in but then I spoke to them in fluent, French Spanish, Italian, Russian German, Croatian, Dutch and a bit of Chinese, Mandarin. I told them my age and they said, the only girls they knew who could speak a lot of fluent languages, were the TG's owned by Gabrielle and Lynda's charity at the TG House. They sent me to the accounts dept looked up your file handed me one of their store cards and loaded it with what I asked for, mainly it was meals, but I did buy a six-hundred-pound dress and they said, I had been in so many days, it didn't matter, they could put it on your account. I also saw a couple of other girls who had been kicked out for a few days, so I bought all of them dinner and cakes in their A-la – Cart restaurant."

"That was good thinking and you also looked after your sisters as well," Lynda said.

"I bought them an overcoat each, but then they were sold to a man who was working for George, but I knew he was lying because you killed George in New York two weeks before," Ariane added.

"Good, I'm glad they were warm, if only for a few days. That was very clever of you. We'll make sure you all have photos of us and the three of us, for each of you when all this mess is over with."

"Do you want to talk with some of your sisters?" Gabrielle asked. "Oh, Ariane we are going to change you when we've got all this sorted out. So, stay close," Gabrielle said.

"How can you both just sit there and listen to what she's done and talk to her as if nothing has happened?"

"How old are you?"

"Thirty-eight,"

"How many languages do you speak fluently?"

"Just English, I did learn some French at school, but it wasn't very good."

"Well, there you are then, all of these two hundred and thirty odd girls can speak nine languages each fluently and someone has made another language disc and sent it out to everyone's learning system while we were away in New York and that Teresa put herself in charge and sacked our own people.

"Ariane was intelligent, I'm glad she did it, she used her head possibly saving her life in this cold. Right are we done for now?"

"Gabrielle, Lynda, I have to get on."

"So, do we, we have so much to do today," Lynda said.

"Any problems with her, send her back and with all these girls you have to look after, I bet I'll be back tomorrow to pick her up," Charlotte said grinning.

"We'll see," Lynda replied.

"Bella, you know that TG who was here a few minutes ago Leah, would you bring her over here please," Lynda asked holding her hand.

Gabrielle walked off going through all the books and diaries they had recovered from the TG House. She looked before Teresa arrived to when Margaret was in control and she filled in all the names correctly.

She didn't take long to get the information she was looking for. She returned to the table and took her seat next to Lynda holding her hand.

Gabrielle beckoned the two girls over to her.

"Take a seat both of you, you'll be having a shower in a few minutes, I'll get the girls to wash your backs," Bella started to wriggle on her seat and looked around for help, trying to recall faces but they had all changed as they had been turned to real girls.

"Bella, sit still, Leah, hold her hand, like you would any other TG in here."

They watched as Leah took hold of her hand and calmed her down. I'm sorry Bella, we haven't been properly introduced. I'm, Gabrielle this is my wife, Lynda, we are married, wife and wife. You are Bella, AKA Andrew. You arrived here with your mother, after we answered your email a couple of months ago when we were in Rome getting the Peace Treaty signed. Edward was here to welcome you on our behalf, he's, our accountant. You were put with Nicole. Nicole," Gabrielle called.

A moment or two later Nicole joined them at their table.

"Nicole, do you remember this girl?"

"Yes Gabrielle, I tried my very best to stop Teresa from sending her to the wrong so-called parents, but she was paying people to take her even for just a few weeks."

"That horrible woman needs shooting," Lynda said and looked at Alan, thinking of using his gun if she clapped eyes on her again.

"Normally the girls have been with us at least a year so they know what they are letting themselves in for and they can make a proper decision of which way they want to go. So, Bella are you sure you want to be a woman?" Gabrielle asked her.

"Yes, that's what I've wanted to be since the age of seven. My dad didn't like me wearing dresses which my mum bought me then dad started to beat me and mum if he caught me in a dress."

"Does he still beat her now?" Lynda asked.

"I'm not sure, she could be dead and buried in the back garden."

"Was it really that bad?" Nicole asked.

"Yes, dad was beating mum every day and the day we were leaving for London, he beat her before we left to get so called advice from a top psychiatrist who said he could help us. It was of course a lie, but a good one because dad gave mum enough money for four drinks, two on the way there two on the way back," she said, giving them more information about her.

"Does she have a phone?" Lynda, asked.

"She used to but I'm not sure now. I haven't seen her during the last four weeks," Bella replied with tears in her eyes.

"So is your mum a dress maker, or seamstress," Lynda asked.

"She does both jobs and used to work for Marshals who made copies of top dresses, mum was one of the top women who examined a dress to see how they were cut and sewn together and sometimes she designed clothes for them which always sold well. But dad kept hitting her in her sides, tummy and back."

"We'll ring her, and I will speak to her," Lynda said, informing Gabrielle of her idea, which Gabrielle agreed with.

"What do you think Gabrielle? Shall we change her or not?" Lynda asked.

"I think she knows what she wants to be," she replied, holding Bella's hand tightly in hers so she didn't try to run off.

"Lynda, do you agree?" Gabrielle asked. She did not speak but agreed to her change as they spoke more about her.

"We'll change her with you Leah, but we would like you to live with us in our apartment for a year so we can instruct you which the girls like Nicole, have gone through. You will also have to learn eight languages in a year which is not as bad as it seems, the nineth Manganese, will be the hardest, but you must be able to speak it. Do you think the other girls will mind us giving Bella preferential treatment?" Gabrielle asked Leah.

"No, they will understand but may need a sweetener."

"Sweetener?" Gabrielle asked.

"Something to look forward to, a present so to speak," Leah explained.

"I get it and have it," Lynda said smiling. "I'll tell you when you've been changed, had your shower and got some new clothes on. Gabrielle, shall we do it now?" Lynda asked.

The two boys stood between Lynda and Gabrielle and were changed into real girls, with C cup breasts and long light blond hair. When they were halfway down their bodies, they stopped for a moment while Lynda examined Bella's bottom more closely. That looks bad Lynda said to Gabrielle mind to mind. Let's swap places or turn her around so I can help her," Lynda told Gabrielle.

"We don't want either of you to move while Lynda and I swap positions. Bella, we have discovered why you can't sit still on a seat. Don't worry, Lynda can help you and take away all your pain. You should have told us you were hurt. How long has it been a problem to sit down and stay still on a chair?" Gabrielle asked as the room turned bright green and Lynda was examining Bella's bottom.

Lynda gently put her hands, on Bella's bottom and with her eyes shining bright, she slowly, removed the piece of broken wood inside her Colon. She was easing the piece of wood two inches long down her Colon using Bella's own muscles in her Colon to get it out, but Bella didn't feel a anything and there was no pain.

As the piece of wood started to emerge from her bottom, Lynda managed to grab it and gently pulled it out of her. She immediately looked up her Colon with her green eyes. In some places Bella was now bleeding as the wood scraped the walls of her Colon and cut through some minor and major blood vessels. Lynda repaired them all as she went up and down her Colon. The small amount of blood which came out with the wood, would come off in the shower.

"How does that feel now Bella?" Lynda asked.

"Loads better thanks, are you still giving us a vagina?" Bella asked.

"Stand still and we'll be off again," Lynda replied. In five, minutes they were both real girls with proper breasts thin arms, legs, petite hands and feet with lovely toenails they could paint. They had a girl's face, voice and a hairless body except for their head of long tawny hair.

They went to the showers, washed themselves and washed and conditioned each other's hair and were dried by two other girls. Bethany sorted out their clothes and shoes then they had their long hair blow dried and styled.

Skye did both their makeup for them as all the girls now had makeup on and nail varnish on their fingers. They were given something to eat and a hot drink next, and everything was carried out in a slow, feminine way, like Gabrielle and Lynda liked to think it would be carried out. There was no reason to rush.

Lynda made the phone call to Pauline's real parents but there was no reply on either of their phones. They called Pauline over to them.

"Pauline, is there something you would like to tell us? Why were you crying when we jumped into your room, you didn't know we were coming, so you must have been crying for some reason. Would you like to tell us about your parents, you haven't gone and killed them both and buried them in your back garden, have you?" Gabrielle asked. Smiling at her.

"No, of course not."

"Those two people were not your parents, these are your parents," Lynda said showing her the picture Imagine had printed for them. "This was taken from your file this morning. Imagine printed it off for us. So, what has happened to them? The people at your house were nice people and seemed at home with you; but they were nervous, and it looked like they had their lines rehearsed and wanted us out of there taking you with us. I bet if I jumped back in now, they would be gone," Lynda said.

"No, don't do that, please don't do that, you'll be killed."

"Why will I be killed and who is going to kill me?" Lynda asked.

"One of George's men. My mum and dad are now multimillionaires, they won eighty million on the Euro Lottery then a week later won another ten million on our Lotto. Teresa found out and sent me home, while George's men abducted my parents. They put in those two people; as bad as dad was, I didn't want him to go through that, and mum was good to me she looked after me. The woman did take me out in a dress, she was okay, but the man didn't really like me.

"They said if I tell you, they will kill my parents in a road crash and the fake aunt and uncle would be my guardians and all my parent's money would come to me and they would take it from me. They may be dead already I don't know where they are."

"Would you like us to try and find them?" Gabrielle asked.

"As much as dad doesn't like me, yes I would, but I don't want you to get killed, either of you or John and Alan."

"We understand, however, the place where Ken Mattingly made his base blew up early this morning after we rescued the two hundred and twenty girls who Teresa had sold to him.

"This means we'll have to look somewhere else for your parents, but they won't be far from his base. We'll start our investigations later today. We already have people trying to find out who survived the explosion and where they would have gone to.

"For now, get to know your friends again and take Bella with you."

"Yes Gabrielle, thanks for helping me get away from those two nutters, they wanted to do all sorts of things with me during the night.

"Then I'm glad we got you out."

"Next Bella, do we have her file with us?" Lynda asked her wife.

"I found what we have on her, do you want to ring her mother?"

"Yes, how far should I go?"

"Go as far as we planned earlier."

The phone rang and Lynda made sure it was Eleanor.

"Hello Eleanor, can you tell me the name of you son?"

"It was Adam, he likes to be called Bella, he is a TG."

"Well, Adan is definitely Bella now, I can promise you."

"Who is this?"

"My name is Lynda Grayson, my wife's name is Gabrielle Grayson, Gabrielle is the founder and head of the charity for TG boys and girls over ten years old. We were in Rome when you came to London to try and get her into our charity.

"You saw a young lady Imagine and one of our psychiatrists Lewis and after you talked to them, they took him in, and you went home. Now we are back we have had to sort out our TG House as it had been ransacked by a lady called Teresa, who was also in attendance when you were seen.

"To get to the point, Bella is slightly concerned about your welfare. She thinks you might have been killed by your husband. Is he still beating you?"

"Yes, I understand, I would like to offer you a job as a seamstress and making dresses for our girls. and can you teach that? Good. No, you wouldn't need to if that's what you wanted. Yes, we could. Are you sure though, it's a big thing to do, but will you please consider this, for a week, I want you to be as sure as if you were asking your surgeon to amputate your leg, because when it's done it's done? Yes, anytime you like, of course, she would like that. Okay, I will."

"Well, nothing is going to happen for a week. We have to meet with Edward tomorrow morning then go to the TG House and see if they have settled in and when they will start the job.

"Margarette and her team have started going around picking up any rubbish or clothes. I suppose they will need new floor brushes a vacuum cleaner, rubber gloves and new cloths and detergent to clean the floors, and wash down the walls, clean the windows. We'll have to get a window cleaner in to clean all the outside windows when the job is completed. Oh, and kneeling mats," Gabrielle said, getting hyperventilated.

"Sweetheart are you okay, your pulse is going a hundred miles an hour. Sarah, can you have a look at Gabrielle for me please? She' seems to be hyperventilating," Lynda sighed.

Sarah took her pulse then her blood pressure and temperature.

"Lynda, get yourselves a cappuccino each, then sit with her have you got you iPad with you?"

"Yes."

"Quietly over your drinks, and make sure she drinks it all, make a list of the jobs you want done today, the shops you need to visit, anyone to take with you and what you need to get, if the time starts moving again it's been nine ten for ages, she looked again at her watch. Well, it's been three minutes and fifty seconds since you disappeared with John and Alan and rescued Leah, and you've done loads since then," Sarah said, giving Gabrielle a tablet to take to calm her down.

Five minutes later, Simon brought out their cappuccinos and a plate of freshly made flaky mince tarts. "These look magnificent and smell delicious, is this what our new Pastry chef made? My compliments to the chef," Gabrielle said picking up a mince tart and taking a large bite from it. "Oh, yes, they're delicious." Gabrielle sighed. "Try one Lynda or I'll eat the lot."

"We can't have that, now, can we?" she replied picking up a tart starting to eat it."

Half an hour later with Gabrielle feeling much better, they thought; the time was now nine fifteen. They called Bella over to them and told her what her mother had said over the phone.

"It sounds like she's continuing with her life and leaving your dad," Lynda said to her holding her hand.

"Yes, it does,"

"Oh, I just thought, there's another job to be done."

"What's that?"

"The laptops for the University girls were hidden away. With everything we've done and changing the girls I've forgotten who it was. Do you think there is anything wrong with me my love?" Gabrielle asked.

"You went through a lot in New York, it's no wonder you're still feeling rough. I'm going to take you home tonight with John and Alan, Jenny and Sarah. I know it will look bad but I'm sure everyone will understand. We'll make love for a short time, then I'll hold you in my arms and tomorrow we'll see our doctor," Lynda said calmly.

"Will you come in with me?"

"You know I will, you shouldn't need to ask." Lynda took Gabrielle's hands in hers and held it tight, kissing them then, kissing her lips. She put her arm around Gabrielle's back and held her close. Kissing her lips, face, head and back to her lips. Then she just held her close to her giving her all the love she had to help her through this bad time.

"Sarah, Lynda called," when they parted. "Can you check her over again, I'll take her to see her doctor tomorrow, you'll be coming too with Alan and John."

"That's a good idea, she should have gone to hospital after the fight to get checked out, but no, you had to carry on, see our friends at the mall, then you collapsed, and another part of the test happened. Then a few days later all that time you were with Death, you were dead, not that many people can do that and recover like you did. Pull your sleeve up, so I can get to your arm." Sarah took her blood pressure, oxygen in her blood and her pulse all on the same instrument. She then took her temperature and looked into her eyes. She got out her stethoscope and listened to her lungs and her chest, getting her to breathe in and out.

"She can't die," Lynda said with tears rolling down her face. Sarah kissed her and put her arm around her, "I think she can still get ill, you should have read the terms and conditions, when Death made you both immortal, not that our species can really die."

"Yes Sarah, but it's five long years. Five lonely years," Lynda cried."

"She's not dead yet, there is still a lot we can do for her. As a last resort if all else fails, there is the ship, Christine isn't that far off and her ship is now fully upgraded, Gabrielle can be taken there, just a couple of hours in our slow hospital craft if the need be," Sarah said, holding Lynda close to her.

Lynda and Gabrielle laughed. "Your temperature is up one degree, your heart is okay, so are your lungs, your pulse is still racing so you can relax for another half an hour. Have you made your plans for the day yet?"

"Not really, we were talking about tonight, I know it seems bad with everyone having to sleep in here and it will be worse for the men in the TG House, but I'm determined to take her home tonight and sleep there, after we've made love, it might cheer her up a bit."

"Nobody will mind with the way Gabrielle is. Now try and relax for half an hour. I'll get a large blanket for you." Sarah was gone and returned a moment later with a large blanket and put it around them

"I'll keep an eye on her today, and yes, take her to see her doctor in the morning. Now Gabrielle, if you start to feel cold or anything else, tell me, you might need to go to hospital for an X-ray."

"Didn't we pay for an X-ray room to be built at our doctor's surgery with the latest Xray machine put in with an experienced radiologist to teach the nurses and doctors how to read the X-rays properly? The X-rays, can be sent to the local hospital or any hospital specialist to see them and give advice to the GP over the phone?"

"Yes, Gabrielle we did, and it's been used a lot and saved a couple of lives, from people who were about to have a heart attack," Lynda told her wife.

"We'll make sure you have a couple of X-rays tomorrow," Sarah said.

"Is there something wrong then?" Gabrielle asked.

"No, I would just like your heart checked further, I can't understand why your pulse is so high," Sarah replied.

"I'll get Simon to bring you two more cappuccinos and a couple of Mince tarts, if there are any left, I saw a bunch of girls, enter the kitchen a while ago," Sarah replied laughing and left them alone going to the kitchen.

"Oh, the laptops, before the men find them and destroy the work the girls have done on them," Gabrielle said about to stand up.

"Let me sort it out," Lynda replied, taking control of her. "Girls." She called standing up. There was silence in the room. Who was clever enough to hide the university girl's computers?"

"That was me," Cloe said.

"How many laptops were there?"

"Twenty-three."

"Well done, Cloe, Skye, Ruth, Rose, Isabell, go with Cloe, Tina, Geraldine, you've had some shooting practice this morning, will you accompany them please and get the laptops.

Don't hurry, have you all got coats? Has anyone not got an overcoat?" Lynda asked. Nobody replied.

"Put your coats on and leave when you're ready. Any problems, Tina, Geraldine, call for help, don't kill a group of Ken's men by yourselves, give the others a chance to kill them as well." There was a lot of laughing from the other bodyguards. "No running I don't want any broken arms or legs to deal with," Lynda told everyone, sitting next to her wife as Simon brought out their cappuccinos and cakes.

"Is she okay?" Simon asked concerned.

"She's a little exhausted and her pulse is up a bit, Sarah is going to keep an eye on her today, I think she wants to go out and spend some money," Lynda replied.

"I hope she's okay, we don't want her in bed at a time like this."

"I'm sure that won't happen," Lynda replied, but her eyes showed she was more concerned with her wife than what might happen later in the day.

"Enjoy your drinks and cakes. That's the last for now, we need a bigger kitchen really."

"We hope Ryan will be able to get here this afternoon, so make a sketch of your thoughts for an extension and a list of the equipment you need put in by his men. Make it as large as you like with all the ovens you need for making a lot of cakes. Give Selina as much room as you can, you'll need more cupboards for all her tools and electric mixers she'll need a long worktop for making the tarts in their thousands so somewhere to put all her jars of Jam butter milk so another big fridge and where would we keep the cakes, that's for you to work out. You could triple the size of the kitchen if you like. The bigger it is, the more room you'll have. If you want a new cooker, pick one out and we'll have Ryan's team put it in for you."

"I suppose I could have a bigger cooker with six hobs and a double oven."

"Simon, if you look up what you want, we'll get it, if there are any other machines on the market you would like, make a list and we'll get it. Have yourself a long worktop as well," Lynda said explaining what she wanted him to do.

"That's Simon sorted, he'll give us a size of the kitchen soon and Ryan could start tomorrow if he likes in the kitchen extension. I'll sort out Ryan for you when he comes over this afternoon.

"Well done, now let's try these cakes again," Gabrielle said picking a mince tart up and eating it.

"They sat still for an hour, with Lynda making notes on her iPad, during which time the girls and bodyguards returned with the laptops. Jessica had met them outside the door and quickly explained Gabrielle was unwell so ordered them to be quiet and go to the far end of the room and be quiet as they sorted out whose laptop was whose.

Sarah came over to check on Gabrielle, it was now nine thirty and time was starting to move forward again. She checked her blood pressure and everything else as before.

"Your temperature is back to normal, and thankfully your pulse has finally returned to normal, just take it easy today. No jumping all over the place."

"Sarah, is it right that you would like to lose some weight and have thinner arms and legs so you can get into the nice slimline dresses the girls and some of the women are now getting into, but your job won't allow you to go on a proper diet?" Lynda asked.

"Yes, it would be nice to lose some weight, but I don't want to lose my job over it. Alan married me for who I am, I know at the time I was a bit slimmer than now, but with all those fine restaurants in the States we were going to, I put on some weight."

"Put your stethoscope down and come here."

Lynda helped Gabrielle to her feet and the blanket slipped off their backs onto the seat. "Stand between us please." She did as she was told rather than say no and get Gabrielle worked up again.

The girls held hands and thought to each other. The end of the room turned bright green as their eyes shone brighter and brighter, Sarah's hair grew longer and changed colour to light blond. They gave her a smaller face and improved her eyesight to twenty-twenty vision. As they came lower down her body, they made her breasts large to a twenty-six D cup. Then down her arms and legs, dainty hands and feet, a twenty-four-inch waist and twenty-six-inch hips. Her dress was now slipping off her shoulders which meant she would need a new wardrobe of clothes and smaller size overcoat, today, that would cost her a lot of money she thought to herself as she always bought designer clothes and oh, what underwear she could get herself into and the nighties she could get, they would be fantastic.

All she needed now was the time to go shopping and the money to buy all her clothes. They had no bills, and their credit cards were cleared every month, not that they ever bought trinkets to take home, but they both had an expensive Nikon camera with plenty of lenses and filters.

Clothes were all they bought, now she could by a different dress for every day of the week with her new body.

"How do you feel now?" Lynda asked.

"Much better thanks. Look at my hair, it's a beautiful colour and I love the length of it. Look at my legs and arms, my shoes feel sloppy on my feet."

"That's because we made your feet smaller by two shoe sizes. Instead of you being a size seven, you're now a size five, is that okay, we can change you back if you want us to," Lynda said grinning. "You really do look fantastic now, except for your clothes."

"Don't you dare change me back, I'll have to get some new clothes later today if I can have the time," Sarah replied laughing.

"At ten, if it ever comes, we want you to take all the university girls out to get new clothes with the new mothers we have here. We want you to buy at least ten outfits nightwear underwear your clothes, could be donated to our new clothes box. Don't worry, we're paying for all their clothes and your clothes in cash do you believe? You can go on the coach we have at our disposal. Tina, Jenny, Noah, Geraldine can take the forty, sixteen-year-olds on Patrick's bus. I'll get you your money, Lynda said. "Oh, how much do you think your clothes will be?"

"Go to the designer shops you know."

"If it's the usual three items, then."

Lynda put her hand in the air, "Get as much as you like day wear nightwear, shoes, underclothes and nighties. I'll give you thirty-grand will that be enough?"

"I'm sure, it will."

"How much do you think three dresses and shoes each will cost plus nighties and at least three packets of ten denier tights will be and yourself don't forget."

"I would say six grand each and there are forty of them so that will be two-hundred and forty-grand."

"That's a lot to take in cash, use your company card, I'll sort it out tomorrow. Get yourselves ready to go, you do look fabulous," Gabrielle said smiling.

"Thank you."

"I'll see Patrick."

A man from the TG House walked in through the main door kicking the snow from his shoes and shivering from the cold outside.

"Where's your coat?" Lynda asked him.

"I didn't have time to get mine, or a thick jumper, we all had to move so fast."

"Okay we'll have to sort you out. How much is the work coat you wear?"

"Roughly, fifty quid a coat and twenty pounds for the jumper."

"Where are you going to get that around here?"

"There is more than likely a tool shop around here somewhere I'll look it up on the Internet."

"What did you want when you came in from the cold?"

"The DIY and tool shops will be open by now, we need a few tools so does the sparks guy, carpenter, plumber and I'm the head painter, Trever, pleased to meet you, Lynda, Gabrielle." He shook Gabrielle's hand and looked at Lynda, she offered her hand to him, but he only touched her fingers and nodded to her.

"Thank you," Lynda said. "I have a list here of what we think you might need would you look at it?"

"Sure," he replied, sure there would be nothing much on it, paintbrushes and a screwdriver set he thought to himself. He took the piece of paper, reading the tools they had put down."

"Are you serious about this? it will cost six to eight hundred quid or more." He knew they brought no money from the place as there was nothing on the coach or the buses.

"We keep quite a lot of money in the safe, just a minute," she walked into the kitchen and opened the safe. She took out a five-thousand-pound bundle of money and another five thousand bundle of money. She put a bundle of tens and twenties on the countertop there was another bundle of twenties, she put on the counter-top and turned to glance at Simon, who was looking at all the money. "We have to pay for paint materials and tools and now he tells me they have no donkey jackets or thick jumpers, they also want white painter's overalls, but these bills have to be paid if we want the work done and we do need it done, do you agree Simon?"

"Yes, yes of course. There is so much to do, so many clothes to buy and overcoats."

"Do you need an overcoat? I never see you leave or get into work."

"Yes, if you're buying."

She counted out a hundred and twenty pounds and took another five-thousand-pound bundle of money from the safe. She looked at the money left in the safe and thought she would have to top it up, she would get by today, even paying the drivers, two grand each. She put a five-thousand-pound packet on the counter-top, then she closed the safe.

"All this money will be gone soon," she stood and picked up five hundred pounds and gave it to Simon.

"This is for your coat and this is an undeclared bonus for hanging around and helping us. And don't forget to draw that extension for the kitchen. Don't worry about the size as big as you like, it's all on our land." She handed him a five-thousand-pound bundle of money.

"Thank you so much," he said taking the money. He went to kiss her, but he remembered just in time about men and her past.

"That's alright, depending on how long this job takes, there might be a few more bonuses. Now I'll get Trever sorted out with money. She took two five thousand, pound bundles of money then thought again and doubled it.

"Here we are Trever, there are several cars around here with our emblem H, B & Wraps. They all have the keys under the driver's window shield. Don't worry, if they are stollen, we have a remote phone number to cut the fuel off and lock the brakes on. Then we give the police its location to the nearest three feet. If the car thinks it's going to go downhill or into water, it lets out a high-pitched whistle that doesn't stop until the police get there. "Pick a five-seater hatchback, one of the largest cars, as you'll get more in. Here is five thousand to buy the tools and we forgot to add electric sanders and a lot of packs of sandpaper. Here is another five-grand for all your clothes, that's a jacket, jumper and painter's white overalls if the sparks want blue get them and whatever colour the plumber's wear. Look after the tools, because when you leave and the job is completed, the tools are yours to keep, and any others that get spread about or used by specific trades, John will explain it all later. I would get ten sanders if you want more then get them.

"Here is another ten-grand, if you can go to, we think Ikea and purchase what is on the short list, give me a call when you have it all outside the store and I'll come and get it. Get as much as you can of it today if they don't have it, ask if there is another store near you, where you can get the rest. Are there any double wardrobes left over in the house?"

"About a hundred I think."

"Do you mind if we take fifty of them?"

"Not at all, they are all yours anyway."

"We'll pop over later and get them."

"No, we'll do it," Trever said.

"We'll help where we can. If you take Craig, Phil and Eric with you, they can get their clothes and tools and help you with what you have to get, only one rule, I want the receipts, VAT and tax," she replied smiling.

"Here's a bag for all that cash, I would hand some it out to your mates instead of carrying it around in a bag, they may think you've robbed a bank. Here is a couple of my business address cards, if they want to know who you're working for."

"Thanks." He walked off a lot happier than he walked in.

"Sarah, Lynda called out, get your group together get on Patrick's bus and take the four by four if you want with some of the adults in. We'll let you get aboard first then I'll get our group organised on Frank's bus and we'll see you all later. We'll do another trip each this afternoon, may as well get as many girls sorted out as we can."

By four in the afternoon, all the girls had three sets of clothes and underwear, tights and shoes. Trever had also done well, he got all the jumpers and donkey jackets for all his men and also, all the overalls they would need. Between all his men with him, they got all the tools on the list and a lot more for the electrician, plumber and carpenter.

At Ikea, they took every double wardrobe they had, some had mirrors, others didn't. They also took all the five-tier chest of drawers. They had four extra cupboards for the kitchen for Selina to store all her cake making food, and tools she would need.

They had met Ryan in the early afternoon just before they went out for a second time. Simon had made a half decent drawing of the back of the Train Station as to where he would want the extension. It was to be fifty feet wide, with sinks at the bottom and opposite end of the extension. He had also planned for another fridge freezer, a large rotating oven to cook her tarts and small cakes, then there was another cooker at the far end for special large cakes that needed a low heat.

Ryan promised to get the plans drawn up that evening so he could see his friend tell him of the problems they were facing and get the plans passed at the planning committee this coming Wednesday.

He also looked at the side of the building where the three buildings would go for the hairdresser and tooth hygienist and a large sewing room with three top of the range sewing machines so some of the girls could do practical sewing, while they were taught in one of the classrooms in the House. Again, the plans would be drawn up that night and put before the planning committee on Wednesday.

Sarah, John Alan and Noah had to go out again, this time to an Outdoor shop. Lynda had spoken to the manager earlier and told him what they wanted. twenty double sleeping bags, and two hundred and ten single sleeping bags. Lynda explained who it was for and they could pay cash, he said he would see what he could get and ring her back.

He called her back as they were finishing getting the twelve, and thirteen, year olds sorted. Geraldine, Isaac, Tina and Noah took out the largest group of fifteen-year-old girls. At first, the attendants were overwhelmed with the girls, but as they broke up into groups of four or six and went to the expensive clothes area, some of the adults went with them.

"Don't forget girls, you can have for now three of the most expensive dresses here each. You are to also get three sets of underclothes each, if you need help with bra sizes, I'll find an assistant to help you," Isaac said, not embarrassed at all handling the girls and sorting out their underwear.

"Can we have bra and pantie sets Uncle Isaac?" Felicity asked.

"Yes, of course, Felicity, any style you want, Geraldine is looking for your school skirts and tops for you all."

"Thank you, Uncle Isaac, do you like this dress on me?" Bethany asked as she turned around for him to see her in the dress.

"It looks beautiful on you how much is it?"

"Nine hundred and fifty pounds."

"Bethany, while you have the chance today, why not have a look at the more expensive dresses and take Martha with you?"

"Nina, Nancy."

The two girls stopped what they were doing and looked at Isaac. "Why don't you join Bethany and Martha, they are going to look at the two to three-thousand-pound dresses, help each other out, they are your sisters."

"Yes Uncle Isaac we will," Nina said.

They waited patiently while Bethany took her dress off and put her top and skirt on, they were given that morning. Bethany hung the dress up where she got it from and walked to the lift, talking quietly about the dresses they had seen so far and thought about the school ball that would be held just after Christmas.

They were closely followed by a security guard who was certain they were all shop lifting and being in such a large number, they wouldn't miss the few girls going out with extra clothes on them.

He was getting closer to the group of girls who had found what they were looking for and they all disappeared into the dressing rooms. Tina was also on the same floor with eight of her girls who were looking at similar dresses.

As the store detective moved to another set of rails, he put his hand in his jacket pocket and pulled out a camera, taking photos of the girls and Tina. As he turned around about to confront the shoplifters. He felt something touch his head in two places.

"Camera please, a man asked from behind him."

"Look, I don't know who you are but I'm after those shoplifters over there. I'm a store detective."

"Likely story," Isaac said.

"I agree," Tina added. Their girls were all now looking at their two bodyguards making an arrest or were about to execute the man.

"Look who are you and what are you poking into my head?" he asked.

"It's one of these, a Glock supressed gun for bodyguards. And you have managed to walk into a nest of us."

"I'm Tina, the big man standing behind you is Isaac, and the others are around us."

"I'm James Hammond, I work here."

"Show me your credentials," Isaac demanded and pushed his gun barrel further into his head, as he pulled out his store pass.

"He's right," Tina said smiling at him.

"Can I see your credentials please," James asked.

"Look at mine," Tina replied, taking out her gun certificate and letting him see it, as his eyes lowered to read licensed to kill in any country, he gulped hard and knew they might kill him.

"What's going on here?" Michelle the floor manager asked. "I've called the police James, you can let him go now, he works for us."

"And who are you?" Tina asked.

"Michelle, the floor manager for this store. What was it shop lifters, a girl ring yes? And who are you two? And put those fake guns away, the police will want to see them when they get up here," she demanded to know.

"Michelle, I wouldn't go there," James said as a warning.

"Ah here they are, over here officer, James has caught a ring of shop lifters after the three-thousand-pound dresses. I bet they don't have a penny between them. Arrest them," Michelle said sternly. "Oh, and they have fake guns inside their jackets." She continued in an angry tone.

"Go on girls, we're falling behind schedule," Tina said.

"Go on arrest them," Michelle shouted at the officer.

"I'm afraid I can't do that mam, this is Dame Tina Watts," he said standing to attention, saluting Tina then Isaac.

Another woman came onto the floor and walked up to the armed police officer and the two bodyguards.

"What is happening here?" she asked calmly "I'm Nora Hayes, the store manageress.

"I'm officer Luke Palmer. This man is Sir Isaac Anderson and the woman Dame Tina Watts, Isaac is bodyguard to Sir Tom Grayson from Australia, and Dame Tina Watts is the bodyguard to Dame Jenny Fletcher UK. All the girls are from Dame Gabrielle and Dame Lynda Greyson. Their TG House was shall we say, mainly destroyed in the firefight between our police and at the time George Rainer's men, were here when we killed thirty of his men and we have two men in custody awaiting trial. The boy girls have all been rescued now some by Gabrielle and Lynda Greyson but they both went north with all their bodyguards to rescue two hundred and twenty-four of them, as soon as they were informed about their TG House.

"I have been informed there are currently eighty of his men working at TG House painting and doing up all the rooms."

"That's right, they didn't want to stay and be killed or blown up as Ken Mattingly was going to start blowing their shops up next week," Tina added.

"We are still making our own investigations as to who survived from the fire and where they went to," Tina replied.

"I'll keep the two men we have in custody," Luke told Tina.

"Thank you, if you have anything give me a ring later," Tina said and smiled, handing him her card.

"Tina, can we have this dress please?" Phoebe asked.

"How much is it Phoebe?" Tina asked.

"Three thousand two hundred, we know they will be a bit over budget, but they are for the Christmas Ball and Gabrielle said we were all to look beautiful."

"Yes, she did, how many girls are in your group?"

"Six, girls in my group and we all have the same dress off the rails.

"Is that the first, second or third dress?"

"It's our second dress, we left the other dress with a lady downstairs.

"Officer Palmer. I am so sorry that you have been troubled, thank you, very much for responding to our call so quick. If you would excuse me, please, Ladies Gentlemen, I sincerely apologise for the embarrassment you have been put through and Michelle, they carry real guns and are licensed to kill for real. Remember it, for the next time and they are all married, even Tina," Nora said and left the group hurrying down the stairs as fast as she could. She reached the ground floor and looked around, for one of the staff putting dresses back on the rails.

"Victoria, by any chance did a few girls leave some dresses with you before they went upstairs?"

"Yes, they did the little rascals, they were far beyond their parent's reach."

"Are we talking about the same girls, who were with another number of girls,"

"Yes, they did the same, that was thirteen dresses at two thousand nine hundred a dress, that's twenty-one thousand. Where are their parents, look two more have joined them?"

"Good spotting on that part, now put all their dresses back where they were left and be fast, they'll be on their way down soon. They are Gabrielle and Lynda's girls from the TG House."

"Hell, I'm so sorry, I'll get them all back off the rails now," she replied and started to get the dresses off the rails two at a time.

Nora was now hurrying across the floor to where the two girls were with a man and woman.

Sargent Luke Palmer saw Norah running across the room. He got on is radio and called another of his men.

"Andy if a man and woman come through the centre doors with two girls hold them, I'll be right behind them." He walked quickly up behind Nora who was about to talk to the girls.

"Excuse me, are these your children?" Nora asked the woman.

"Of course, they are," the woman replied.

"Summer, Orla what are you doing here you should be with Eliza and Amber if you want those expensive dresses," Nora said.

The girls were stuck, they didn't know any of the adults or the man in a police uniform. They looked around the room hoping to see someone they knew.

"Girl's do you know the first and last names of these people who say they are your parents?" Luke asked. Again, he put his hand to his radio as the two adults looked at each other and decided to try and stay free, the kids were about to ruin their plan.

Geraldine was just crossing the floor when she saw two girls, a police officer and the manageress of the shop. She had spoken to earlier announcing their arrival. She wondered who the other two people were, as they were nothing to do with their groups of girls. She marched up boldly to the group with her gun in her hand.

"Excuse me, these two are mine I do believe, Orla, Summer, where have you been?" Geraldine asked, her gun in her hand. The lift doors opened, and thirteen girls walked out, with two bodyguards at the back.

"Stay with Tina girls, something is not right," Isaac said and then called out to his wife. "Geraldine." He had caught her attention and beckoned her over to him. At that moment, the two people pretending to be the parents turned and ran off. Isaac was quite close to her now as she was getting the man in her gunsight. Geraldine don't shoot, he shouted."

Luke looked at her and realised what she was about to do.

"Noooo, please stop." But there were two quiet puffs of smoke and both people, screamed in pain for a moment and dropped to the floor.

Geraldine got out her gun license and license to kill.

"It's alright, I know you're licensed to kill," Luke said. "They would have made two good squealers with our intelligence officers," Luke said wondering what to do now.

"They're not dead. I shot both in the back of the ankle, you know, that little bit of bone that's down here," she said picking up Orla's leg pointing to the bone she shot. "They'll be fine in a day or two," she said.

"I thought you killed them," Luke sighed.

"Heck no if I wanted them dead. I would have shot them between the eyes before they had a chance to run. and if I would have missed, Janet and Tom would have had me stretched out in the desert for a couple of days to make me remember how to shoot properly," she replied.

"You should have seen her this morning when she killed seven men who had abducted us and were about to sell us to a load of porno men. She was sat down in the corner of the room, with the nurse and Lynda on one side, and the gunman on the right side of the room and he was pointing his gun at Lynda, and she didn't stop working on Skye, trying to save her life. Geraldine shot him between his eyes from a hip shot," Orla said proudly.

"She's a first-class bodyguard, not afraid to shoot somebody who threatens us, or touches Gabrielle or Lynda, especially Lynda.

"That's what bodyguards are for, not to pussyfoot around," Summer added proudly. There was a roar of applause from behind them and whistles to Geraldine from some of the girls and several parents shopping in the store.

"That's why they have guns, to use not stay in their holsters," one man shouted.

"Let's get your girls out of here or I will be having to get my gun out and use it," Luke said, tapping Geraldine on her shoulder.

Two officers had come through the glass doors and went through the two prisoner's pockets. "Crikey, two guns one a small Smith and Western the other some Polish handgun which I have never seen before and a Polish machine gun with a clip of twenty bullets in it. Then look at these, four bloody hand grenades. They were determined to make a mess or kill someone. Maybe Gabrielle and Lynda?"

"Go careful with the machine gun, they sometimes jam then all of a sudden fire," Isaac was saying in a loud voice so the officer could hear him. Isaac was watching the officer all the time; he was having trouble releasing the clip. Then the gun went off. The bullet was heading straight for the police officer by their side. Isaac withdrew his Glock pointed it at the bullet and fired his gun, there was a loud clunk of metal hitting metal at high speed. Then both bullets fell to the floor.

Luke turned around holding his breath, I've never seen shooting like that before," he sighed.

"That's nothing you should see us bend bullets around people and kill the person behind between the eyes, just like Alan did on TV a while back."

"Thanks for saving my life, do you know how to disarm the machine gun?" Luke asked.

"Do you want the handgun and grenades disarmed? The pins don't always stay in and they have lost a lot of men with the pins falling out. They go off with a big boom and bits of body fly everywhere?" Isaac said.

Within two minutes Isaac had disarmed the machine gun, emptied the clip of ammunician and did the same with the handguns. He then started on the twelve hand grenades. He unscrewed the bottom, poured out all the explosive and metal balls into a police plastic bag. He did the same to them all as Chief Superintendent Carl Taylor arrived. An ambulance was following the police car through the mid-afternoon traffic. Carl was about to push his way into the store when special officer Kori stopped him.

"Sir! Sir Isaac is about to disarm three more hand grenades, with loose pins," Officer Kori, said informing his Chief Superintendent.

"That should be a job for our bomb squad."

"There were twelve of them, this is the last two now," Kori said as Isaac poured the contents of the grenade into another bag. When he finished his job, everyone gave him a big round of applause.

"He also saved Luke's life. As I was trying to disarm a Polish machine gun, it fired, I don't know how, but Isaac removed his gun and shot the bullet in flight stopping it and both bullets fell to the floor."

"You're pulling my leg," Carl replied smiling.

"There they are on the floor."

He walked over to where the two bullets had locked into each other.

"You did this?" he asked Isaac.

"Sure did, I think old Luke has aged a few years though. The bullet was going to hit his heart."

"Well thank you Sir Isaac, I've heard a lot about the way you bodyguards shoot and protect their people."

"I was the girl's bodyguard, Gabrielle and Lynda's girls from the TG house. We rescued over two hundred of them this morning or last night," Isaac explained.

"You had better get on and look after your girls. I bet they all want to spend Gabrielle and Lynda's money," Carl replied laughing.

"They'll do that alright," Isaac agreed.

"Girl's show over, get your last dresses, three underwear and three pair of shoes. Is anyone struggling with their bra size or too embarrassed to talk to one of the ladies about it?"

"Amber is," Erin said.

"Violet," Isaac called. "Oh, good there you are. Will you take Amber to the assistant who is measuring bust sizes please?"

"Of course, Uncle Isaac."

"Anyone else?" Violet asked calmly.

Two girls put their hand in the air.

"You'll have a much better bra fit, and you won't be struggling with it. Zara, Ariane, join Violet please," Isaac said.

"Come on then girls, we'll get the job done and pick out some lovely bra and pantie sets," Violet told them smiling.

They all walked off following Violet who was seventeen, but joined them on this trip as she hadn't been in this store before, and she said she would look after some of the girls who got into trouble with clothes sizes.

Geraldine kissed her husband and was glad she was not arrested.

"I'll just finish sorting out their school clothes, light brown skirts and tops."

Geraldine walked off leaving her husband to round up his group of girls.

"You know, those two Aussies are damn good shots, I couldn't have hit the bullet smack on the front even if it was standing still and he didn't really aim and his wife, is a damn good shot right smack in the centre of their ankle bone, they were both moving when she took her shot and with those Polish guns, Isaac knew all about them and warned us of the loose pull rings, then deactivates all the hand grenades. I wouldn't mind having them both on my squad," Officer Ben Howard said to Carl, his Superintendent.

"Yes, they were, damn good shots, it must take a lot of practice," Carl replied, looking at the two Australians as they walked off looking for their girls.

"Excuse me miss," Geraldine said to a young woman working on the same floor.

"Can I help you? OMG you're the lady who shot the lady and man in the back of their ankle. Damn good shooting. That's what we need more off, people who are about to steal get shot in the ankle, we wouldn't have anyone stealing again," Lisa said smiling.

"That's right."

"I'm sorry, how can I help you?"

"I'm looking for more of these and these," she said holding up a skirt and top."

The woman looked at the clothes ticket and spoke into her microphone that put her straight through to the stores. In a few minutes, she had fifty skirts and tops for Lawsons Private Academy for the fourteen-year-olds. Then she was off again making sure all the girls now had all their clothes underclothes shoes and tights. They were all having the same brown bag and purse for school with their names on and TG House, so they wouldn't get stolen, and all the girls were proud to have the name on their bag and purse, it had been their lifeline.

It took an hour to have all their clothes scanned folded up and put into a large bag. Each girl carried their bags of dresses underwear and shoes onto the bus.

Then they were off back to The Train Station. The two buses arrived almost together while Gabrielle's coach was heading for the Outdoor store.

Gabrielle was about to get out of her seat when Lynda stopped her.

"It's alright my love, I'll deal with this, you stay here in the warm and take it easy. I'm so worried about you," Lynda said, putting her arm around her shoulder kissing her lips. Then she let her lips stay on Gabrielle's lips for another minute. "I won't be long, I hope. John, make sure she stays in her seat and let me know of any problems instantly. Can you put a blanket around her please, there are two in the back?" Lynda asked him,

"Don't worry Lynda, I'll get them both and put them around her and I'll sit next to her. She'll not move a muscle, perhaps when we get back you should ring her doctor," John suggested.

"Yes, it might be a good idea what do you think my love?"

"Yes alright, if you really think so," Gabrielle replied.

Lynda left the bus with Alan just behind her. Alan held the door for her and they both entered the shop. The man came out asking if he could help them then thought of all the sleeping bags that had arrived from four different shops earlier in the afternoon. Alan was looking around at the other items they had in the shop. There were some nice binoculars and small telescopes on a tripod.

"What are these like for night vision?" he asked the man serving them.

"Extremely good, obviously the binoculars are the best because they all have stronger lenses. I'm Eliot," he said looking at both people before him.

"I'm Alan, who ones are the best you have?" Alan asked.

"I see you are looking at the Pulsar Accolade 2 LRF XP thermal binoculars 50Hz, a little pricey at £4649, we actually sell a few of these," Eliot said smiling thinking he would not go to that expense.

"Have you got four of them?" Alan asked.

Eliot went to his till and typed in some numbers. "Yes, we have four pairs of those binoculars."

"Do you have all our sleeping bags?" Alan asked.

"Oh yes, they are ready for you," he replied, glad they had got back to the sleeping bags.

"Do you have four of those binoculars?" Alan asked again.

"Sorry, I thought you were just enquiring about them. Just a moment," he walked to his till again and typed in some numbers as Alan looked at all the sleeping bags, "yes, we do actually, do you want them all?"

"Please, add them to our bill if you would please, do you know where the gun shop is which sells good quality rifles?"

"Two shops up, we work together, you'll need a gun licence and some proof of where you live."

"Will a driving license do?"

"Fine, are you going up there?"

"Yes, we are, are you going to call him?"

"Yes. Just to give him a heads up, then he'll let you in straight away.

"Tell him I want four of the very, best live rifles with a damn good night scope. And we'll have sixteen boxes of ammunition with gun cases,"

"Name please?"

"Sir Alan Watts."

"They also sell good handguns if you would prefer?"

"No, I have my own Glock," he replied opening his jacket.

"Have you got your gun license on you Alan?"

"Here he said taking it out of his inner jacket pocket." He handed it back and spoke to the person on the other end of the phone.

"Yes, I've seen it, he's carrying a Glock, licensed to kill any country. Yes."

"Out of curiosity, who are you a bodyguard to?"

"This little beautiful lady here, Dame Lynda Grayson. All their bodyguards live at Grayson Manor. Can we start loading the sleeping bags now, while you get the binoculars sorted and Lynda here will pay your bill."

"Yes of course Sir Alan," he replied.

Alan picked up four bags, with two sleeping bags in each bag.

"This is going to take forever," Alan said.

"Get the girls to help," Lynda suggested.

"Right."

"I'll just go to the coach," he said to Lynda.

"And see how Gabrielle is," she asked.

He was gone and a moment later, John was sorting out the girls to help on the bus, four girls on the far side of the pavement working as a team.

A short time later all the sleeping bags were on the bus, Alan and Lynda went to the gun shop and were let in immediately. Elliot unlocked and opened the door. Please come in Dame Lynda, Sir Alan, I know you're in a hurry, so let's get this done, my son Victor, knows everything there is to know about guns, he has got his PhD in guns, and he plays for the local gun club and is County Champion. He'll play in the next Olympic Games if we can find someone to sponsor him," Eliot said.

"Why are you having difficulties," Lynda asked.

"Please don't spread this around. He says he wants to be a woman. As soon as we tell the sponsors they say they reluctantly decline to be his sponsor."

"What sort of money are you looking for?" Lynda asked while Alan looked at the rifles and night scopes.

"I know you're rich, but I expect twenty to forty-grand is far too much and you have to have a company." Eliot replied.

"Does he work all week here?"

"Yes, he does."

"Will he be in on Wednesday morning?"

"Yes, should be, he's a bit depressed now as he's the only contender who doesn't have a sponsor. Being a TG as he calls himself has huge problems."

"I would imagine it would, don't worry we won't tell anyone."

She turned around and looked at Alan. "Alan come on I want to get going, we have a lot to do this afternoon and evening." Lynda paid the bill and carried the four bags with the night scopes in a bag and all the ammunician in a box inside a bag."

"Oh. do you repair Glocks?"

"No problem there, we carry most spares for that gun, Victor can repair it for you and line up the gun's sights after." Eliot said thinking of more work for his son to do.

"Right, I'll bring a friend with me, it's his gun that is broken and he has a license for his gun."

"That's what we like to see," He replied and opened the door for them and locked it securely when they left.

"Any luck dad?" Victor asked him.

"I thought she might sponsor you or give you a part payment, but as soon as I said you're a TG, she wanted to get out of here. Sorry son I tried hard. I'll try again on Wednesday. What if you were to be what's her name?"

"Victoria, dad. It's Victoria."

"Yes, yes, of course it is, it's just that your mother and I hardly see you changed. So, what is it you want to be on Wednesday?"

"Victoria? Then she could see I'm serious about wanting a sex change, which is also very, expensive if I went private."

"You have nothing to lose," his father replied.

"She would run a mile," Victor replied and turned the Open card in the window to Closed, double locked the door and pulled down the steel curtain which stopped anyone breaking into their shop.

As soon as they got into the coach, Alan handed John one of the boxes which held the rifle. He removed it from the box just as the coach started off. Lynda sat wither her wife. John had put a thick blanket around her and wrapped her up in it and now Lynda was kissing her, giving her all her love, she could for her. Ten minutes later they were turning into their drive and parked outside the double doors.

"All of you carry your own bags. and try to carry at least one of the sleeping bags put one of them by your clothes, hand the others out then after you all have tea," Lynda said. She looked at her watch it was only four pm.

"Isaac, can you help John now with some bags and boxes please?"

Alan put one box on the vacant table with a strong carrier bad.

"Put them over there Isaac and get all the gunslingers up together."

"Yes Alan."

The electric double doors closed behind her as she walked across the snow to the coach. She looked over at Gabrielle, she was cuddling in her blanket, making herself feel warm.

Alan returned to the coach picking up the two bags of binoculars and two bags of sleeping bags. Returning inside, he called four girls to get on the coach and get them off the coach and through the double doors into the building. The girls inside would help get the sleeping bags distributed. A short time later, everyone had a sleeping bag, and the doubles were put on two tables.

"Does everyone have a single sleeping bag?" Lynda asked after putting Gabrielle in a nice relaxing chair she had brought from home. She thought about their house, disappeared, then reappeared with another lounge chair by her side. A few girls put their hands in the air. Lynda quickly counted them then realised what they had done. Girls, I'm so sorry, with everything going on today rescuing everyone and sorting out social services, I've forgotten all the girls we stopped from going up to Ken's place, I think that was twenty-six of you. Ariane, can you run around and check everyone with their hand in the air?"

"Next, can the following girls come here please? Kathleen, Elizabeth, there should be ten couples, will you all come up here please?"

Within a short time, the pairs of girls all had a double sleeping bag and went off to their friends telling them Lynda and Gabrielle had accepted them as a couple and were now sleeping together.

"There are twenty-six girls without a single sleeping bag and four of them are an item, that's Grace and Sophia and Kimberly and Sarah," Ariane told Lynda.

"That's great let me get back on the phone. "Hello Eliot, it's Lynda again, we messed up the numbers, is there any chance you can get us another twenty-six single duvet's and two double duvets?" Lynda asked Eliot.

"I have two doubles and six, no eleven singles in the store and there are fifteen in my son's store," Eliot replied.

"If you could get them up together for me, Eliot, are you alright? Eliot, what's happening there?"

"I told you to put the bloody phone down. Have you pressed a silent alarm?" a man asked shouting at Eliot.

"Listen, if you have and the cops arrive, the first person to die is your son."

"I didn't call anyone," Eliot shouted over the phone which was now on his desk.

"Well, you better not have, we don't want any bloodshed in here, but believe me, I'll kill your son if the police arrive. He says he doesn't care if he dies anyway, so it's a good one to start with." The man continued to shout.

"Hey Dan, look what I've found," another man shouted."

"What have I said about using our names?"

"Yea, sorry, this is his wife and there's a load of female clothes out there so another girl must live here too."

"Where is she?" the man bellowed at Eliot.

"It's Victoria, our daughter, a messy girl, gone out to buy new clothes with her friend, she won't be back till later, I hope," Eliot said quietly above the phone.

"You better hope so or she dies with the kid," the man shouted.

"Do you have any handguns?" the man asked.

"Tell him dear, I don't want Victor killed, please tell him," his wife shouted with tears in her eyes.

"Okay yes, we have handguns, but they are in another safe, with a different set of keys. Get behind me love," Eliot was saying.

"But Eliot, that's our son there, Victoria will be ages. You know what she's like when she's shopping for clothes."

"Alright Kirsty, just get behind me and stand over there out of the bullets way, if they start shooting."

"It won't take many bullets to kill Victor here, I might change my mind and kill you next," the man shouted.

Lynda turned off her phone and a light went off, telling Eliot whoever was on the line was no longer listening to their conversation.

They were alone now, and Kirsty, who was suffering from a bad back, could not stand up to the men with guns.

Lynda looked at her watch. "It's still four PM who wants to walk into the valley of Death?" Lynda asked.

"Me, me, me, me," came the replies.

"Isaac, Geraldine, Alan and Tina, you can be their Victoria," Lynda said. "Take the coach and pretend to be going camping and on a winter sports week school trip," Gabrielle said not looking very well.

"Good idea," Alan replied.

"Give me those clothes," Tina said and grabbed a brown skirt and top and within a couple of minutes, she had both on and looked like a young Victoria, with plenty of leg to show and a bit of midriff made her look like a young university student. They got into the coach and were off. As soon as they were gone, Lynda looked at her wife, she was okay, but feeling cold.

Although they didn't wear too many clothes and what they did wear was always thin and short.

"Jenny, would you sit with Gabrielle pleased while I get us fifty of those wardrobes which are left in the House? Here sit in this chair I brought from home," Lynda said to Jenny.

Once Jenny was settled with Gabrielle, Lynda kissed her wife goodbye, and with the girls creating room at the far end of the room. She jumped to the TG House and found Trever. He was on the top landing overseeing the painting which had been done there.

"Hello Lynda, I'm pleased you have arrived right now, come and see," he said in an excited voice, John was escorting Lynda, leaving Noah and Mike to guard the Train Station. They were now using the new binoculars to keep watch and had a new rifle each, with the night scope attached, Noah was one end and Mike the other.

"I've come for some of the wardrobes," Lynda said.

"Oh yes, but please, let me show you both this first." They entered the first room on the top landing. As she did, she noticed the top landing ceiling and walls both sides were painted an off-white shade.

"Oh, watch the doors, they may still be wet," Trever warned them.

The smell of fresh paint hit them as soon as they entered the room. The ceiling was painted an off white-pink colour while two walls were a very pale pink, and the other two a very, light grey. The toilet was a dark pink. There was no slap dash painting, it was all first class and cut in well to the ceiling and other walls. The toilet door was sliding, open and closed. The door worked perfect, like it was brand new. She recalled, Vanessa had complained about this door sticking and they had someone come to repair it twice with no luck.

"The door works," Lynda said.

"We had to take it out, when it was installed, some idiot, failed to remove all the plastic covering on the end of the door, we removed it and it works fine now," Trever said smiling. The skirting has been painted, as too the door, both sides and the piece of wood for the curtain rail is also Painted."

"Wow, I didn't think you would have got much done today," Lynda said quietly.

"Oh no, we all work very hard and fast. We know you have problems with the girls' sleeping arrangements. The sooner we get them into the House, the better, it's much easier to protect."

"Yes, it is." She looked at John, neither had thought of it, but it made sense.

"Do you want to show me where the wardrobes are now?" Lynda asked, thinking one room and a landing would be enough for today.

"Oh no, please, sign off on these rooms then we go to wardrobes, it will give my men the extra time they need."

Thirty minutes later, they had been shown all ninety rooms on the top floor both sides, the four storerooms for bedclothes and one clothes chute to the ground floor laundry room.

Lynda and John were flabbergasted at the work which had been done. As they walked down the stairs going careful not to touch the walls or handrails, they walked along the fifth-floor landing seeing it too had been painted end to end. Of the ninety rooms on this level, sixty had been painted, and four storerooms had been painted they were now starting to paint the bedrooms on the opposite side to the other bedrooms.

A man stood before them wearing dark blue overalls and a pair of shorts on his head. "And who are you? And what are you doing?" Lynda asked with a smile on her face,

"Hello Lynda, I'm Eric the sparks, I'm painting all the ceilings with Clive, further along. I'll hopefully go out tomorrow and get some florescent lights for the corridors and a bright lightbulb for the bedrooms. We'll soon have this done for you," he said.

"So, it seems," Lynda replied now amazed at how far they had got.

"It's not too bad, if you think of it there are eighty of us, that is just over two rooms each up until now," Trever said, glad she was pleased at the painting job. Now I'll take you to the wardrobes," he said with laughter in his voice and on his face. A man came running up the stairs from the ground floor.

"Trever come and see we have broken through."

They hurried down the stairs and along to the far end of the ground floor where a bright light was shining through what appeared to be a hole in the wall. When they got there, David one of the carpenters had a bright torch in his hand, then a light went on behind him.

"What is it?" Lynda asked, looking at the hole in the wall.

"Come and look, it's a lift. It goes all the way to the top floor."

"Does it work?" John asked.

"We'll find out soon. The internal lights have come on if you want to look. You can see the bottom of the lift on the third floor."

John looked, into the hole and up to the bottom of the lift. He took a deep breath. "He's right, I wonder what this place was before?" Lynda asked no one.

"It was a hospital overflow wing, for the hospital up the road. It was also used for rehabilitation for servicemen in the second world war and the Falklands war. When a lot of men from the navy were badly, burned on HMS Sheffield, in 1982," a lady informed them from behind. "I'm Stephany, pleased to meet you Lynda, you too John. I was a nurse here back then. The lift was always in use. Sandra, Martha, and Inez, we were all nurses, working with men who had bad burns and a few of the army that had been shot in the legs or arms and needed prosthetic appliances to get around and work."

"Are there any men still alive?" Lynda asked.

"Yes, a few, they live down south now, where it's nice by the sea in retirement homes supplied by the Navy."

"Does it work though?" Lynda asked.

"Let me see," Stephany said. David pulled away a small piece of wood from the side wall and they could see a lift call button with three white lights by the side. She pressed the button and from the top floor there was the sound of a motor turning and they could see the lift come down. It stopped at their floor and the lift door opened.

Stephany got into the lift and stopped at every floor on the way up and back down. "It still works perfectly. It definitely needs an overall and inspection, some new lift call buttons and you'll need to cut out all the wood, which is covering the doorways, otherwise, it's good to go, at least now you can take in disabled boys for a sex change."

"Yes, we'll need a ramp put in," Lynda said.

"There is a ramp outside, but the door is boarded up over there," Martha said and taking a pencil from David's ear, she marked on the wood where it was.

"We can sort that out tomorrow. For now, David, Daniel, clear all the wood from the lift doors except where we have been painting, those doors will have to be done when the paint is dry.

And put the wood out the front and I'll order a couple of skips tomorrow, with your permission Lynda," Trever asked.

"Of course, get whatever you need to get this job done, but I am very, impressed by what you have done so far today. Who is the best person the get a lift engineer out here?"

"That would be me," Eric said.

Emily and Olive said together. "Do you have a computer we can use to find the phone numbers?" they asked.

"Yes, give me half an hour to get these beautiful new looking and so well polished double wardrobes over to the Train Station. I see you have put a card on them for their name."

"That was us, Emily and Olive said together. "We'll clean all the new furniture as well."

"Zack and Samuel are on their way over to the Train Station, they put the screws into the back of the wardrobes to hold them against the wall, then they'll start on making up the flatpack stuff you have there. We are all going to stop for a meal this evening at eight o clock."

"Speak to Simon and he'll cook something for you all."

"No that's fine, we found a nice restaurant along the road, we'll all eat there," Trever said. "We can all eat together."

"You could all eat together here," Lynda replied.

"Okay we'll eat here tomorrow night. We have a lot to discuss tonight, whose doing what, materials we still need, colours of paint. Curtains, carpets, you name it, we need to sort it," Trever explained, then we'll come back and start again for a couple of hours. There is a lot more to do with opening the lift up, a lot more painting as well," Trever said.

"Are you the man in charge now?" Lynda asked.

"Yes, anything you want done, see me and I'll get it organised. You would have seen we have already been working in the Train Station. We've had to put wood over the glass to stop the wardrobes from falling over we'll take it off when the job is finished."

"Right, I'll get these over then," Lynda said.

John pulled them apart, Lynda touched them, one at a time and was jumping back and forth taking one wardrobe at a time and dropping them off at the far end of the Train Station. Ten minutes later the job was completed so she split the large pile of wardrobes apart and left them on the floor at the other end of the room.

She sat on the side of the chair with her arm around her wife. kissing her. Then Luie, came into the Train Station with some bad news.

Chapter 15

When the coach arrived outside the Outdoor shop, Alan looked at everyone. "This won't be easy as it's a small shop and Lynda said the wife was being held in the gun store, I suggest you Geraldine, find a place where you can get a good shot off, you'll only have one go at defusing the situation," Alan said quietly.

"I suppose as the police are still ten minutes away, we either kill or wound them as soon as possible so it's all over by the time they get here," Geraldine said.

"Tina, I'm sorry but you go in first, chat away to your mum and dad as if you haven't seen the two men holding guns against them, we'll follow right behind you, I'll go first, Geraldine, you second. Isaac, you last."

They all stopped outside the door to the Outside shop. Tina put her hand on the doorknob hoping the door was unlocked. She tried the door and it opened slightly, she turned, smiling at everyone, then she was through the door into the Outdoor shop. She had no idea what it looked like or where exactly the shooters were.

"Mum, Dad, I'm back, she threw the small bag of clothes onto the table with the till on. I got some really smart clothes for uni. Mum, Dad, are you in here? Victor it's your sister Victoria." She hoped that would at least let them know someone was here to help.

"Muuahhh, dad, where in the hell are you? You left the shop door open, anybody could have got in, she shouted, hoping they had not already been killed, they had been a long time sorting themselves out after the phone was turned off. Then a man with a gun to Victor's head walked out into the passage, she looked over and saw Victor sitting on the floor, he was bleeding from his head. He looked at the man who was eyeing up Tina, which is what they hoped they would do.

"Hi Victor, what have you done to your head? Been bumping into cupboard doors again? You really do need a better pair of glasses."

"Yes, sis where are your glasses you're as blind as a bat without, them stupid girl. He knew she wouldn't have come alone and was more than likely packing. The problem was his dad was in front of the gunman.

"Victoria, dad is standing up asleep again, he's right in front of you. Did I just see Alan walk in behind you? Dads told you about him before. He's older than you."

"Victor let me tell him when I can see him. Can you go upstairs and get my spare pair of glasses please? They're in the same drawer as my panties?"

"Come on babe, we ought to be getting back now. Evening Mr Grayham, it's Alan Becket, I'm in the same class as Victoria," he said and moved further into the shop with his gun at his side, now all he needed was a clear shot. He walked to the end of the counter, looking up at Tina, he knew she must have a plan lurking in her sexy head.

"Dad, you remember Alan, don't you?"

"Yes, I remember him, isn't he a little too old for you, my love?" he asked as Tina put her dainty hands over his face, feeling it like a normal blind person would.

"Please dad," she said as she put her arms around his neck.

"Please dad, come and meet Alan again, I want you to get to know each other. I want to be able to bring him back here and sit with us or have a meal together. I've been to his house and had tea there, his mum and dad are fine, and they like me, despite not being able to see a thing without my glasses." She was now walking slowly backwards, one step at a time pulling Eliot with her.

She was halfway back when she fell backwards onto the floor. Her hand was on her gun now as she shouted at her dad. "Daddy, help me please, where am I?" She asked almost crying. Alan stepped forward as if to help Victoria.

"I'll help you get to your feet," Alan said as he drew his gun with its silencer on and fired once, the bullet went around Eliot and hit the man with a gun in his stomach. At the same time, the gunman was about to shout, he'd been hit. Tina started again.

"Dad help me, I think my arm is broken, Dad, help me." She waved her gun to the left and Eric took a step that way. As soon as he was out of the way he heard two puffs of air from her gun. She hit him in the leg one bullet each leg.

"Quickly go to the bottom of the store and sit on the floor," Tina said to Eliot.

Tina was now on her feet as Alan and Isaac ran past her and pulled the man towards the door of the shop. Just then another man brought the mother into the hall and Tina was halfway along the room. It had worked once she hoped it would work again.

"Mum, are you okay?" Victor asked, hoping it would help Victoria.

"Yes Victor, where's your father?"

"The man took dad out of the door, threatening to blow his head off if he shouted a warning to the police further up the road. He said he wanted to get out of here alive then pushed Victoria over.

"She's blind without her glasses. The girl at the bottom of the room, is her girlfriend Samantha. She helps Victoria about, when her eyes are bad like today."

"Mum, I think I broke my arm, can you look at it for me please? Mum, I can't see anything, where are you?"

"I'm here my love, right in front of you." As she looked at the floor, she could see some blood so not knowing who it belonged to, she stopped and stepped over it, trying to wipe it into the floor.

"Mum please help me, I'm sure my arm is broken. Mum please," she repeated and took a step forward, closer to Kirsty, her mother. Two paces from her mother, she took two small footsteps and put her left arm around Lillian's shoulder.

"Samantha, come and see my arm," she shouted, giving Geraldine a chance to get into the room and walk down the passage a bit to get a good shot off. Time was now against them and the man outside on the pavement wouldn't stay quiet forever. Alan could hear sirens in the distance and looked at his watch, the police would soon come and take over. He would somehow have to get Tina and Eliot out of the store, leaving Lillian and Victor to face the man with a gun alone, as the police tried talking him out of the shop. It would be now or never, he hoped both girls heard the police car and knew it would be the end of their rescue.

"Samantha, come up here and help me, tell mum what I've done and what we have decided. Mum, she cried again, as she pushed her left arm further around her shoulder, she said. "Mum I love you, but it hurts so much. If I move it to my right, no, your, right, at the same time she pushed her hand into the back of her neck if I move it to your right, it hurts even more." She couldn't make it clearer than that.

She held her tight and took a small step backward. "With me," she whispered. Tina took another step back and pulled her mother with her so there was a gap between the man and Lillian. One more step back and Tina pulled her into her as tight as she could and stood perfectly still.

Geraldine got the idea and pulled her gun from her side holster looked at the man then levelled it at her side and fired the gun. Tina felt the air move as the bullet turned around them both and entered the man's lower chest. Tina had her gun out and fired two rounds into his legs. He fell to the ground moaning in pain. Tina stepped around Lillian who was dumfounded at what the woman did taking the shot. Tina walked up to the man then kicked his gun out of his way.

"Excuse me Kirsty, can we now have our order of sleeping bags please? I think it was four doubles and thirty-two singles?" Tina asked.

"You've got nerves of steel girl," Eliot said to Tina from behind her. Eliot continued to walk up to his wife. "Thank you, thank you so much, especially for you putting the plan into action."

"No plan, I made it all up as I went along, getting you both to do what I wanted so my colleagues at the end of the room could get the first silent shot off, then the second and third, we wanted them alive this time to try and find out what Ken Mattingly is now up to," Alan said coming up behind them.

"If we could have our order, I would appreciate it, this has taken a little longer than I thought." It had been six fifteen when they left and now it was six fifteen, they had lost no time at all.

"Victor, Kirsty could you help with the order please?" Eliot asked. "Alan, could you come with me please?" They walked further along the passage and down a flight of stairs.

"The last man," Lillian, said, "he was going to attack you all at TG House when Ken has his men in his control and from his new base. He said eighty men had absconded, because they were frightened, they would be killed or blown up. So, can you please sign all these forms please?"

"What are they for?" Alan asked.

"Ten more rifles for you and six Glocks, there are four hundred rounds for the rifles, and a hundred rounds for the Glocks. There are four telescopic sights, six telescopic night sights four pair of binoculars, gun bags and straps for the rifles. I heard there are some good men you got with you, I should try and keep a few of them on, wherever they are working.

"If you don't kill anyone and want to hand all this equipment back, bring it over and we'll sell it off second hand. For now, you use it, I think you're going to have a small war somewhere near here and if you want another two guns, we'll help you out."

"Thank you so much, I think we have enough men for now. If things change, I'll give you a ring," Alan said smiling.

"Now we had better get these rifles in your car or bus, without the police seeing all this leave our store. They might start asking questions."

They walked through an underground passage to the Outside shop and put all the loose items in strong carrier bags.

Kirsty met them just before the door with Victor. He had run up the ramp asking the driver to drop the coach further down the road to collect the rest of the sleeping bags. Everyone looked at each other, Kirsty had just given them all the sleeping bags and a large box of water drinking bottles.

"Do what he said, Alan isn't on the coach, let's hope he's in the next shop down," Isaac said quietly.

Victor stood on the first step of the coach and was holding on to a ceiling strap. The driver stopped the coach just where Victor said.

"Could two of you please stand by this door and I'll be handing the last of the sleeping bags to you?" he asked two girls at the back of the coach, smiling.

Isaac and Tina stood by the shop door. Kirsty, Eliot and Alan came out of the shop, standing next to each other so they covered the open door of the coach.

They were all hugging each other talking loudly as Victor ran back and forth from the shop to the front of the bus handing the girls who had made a line to the back of the bus to hide the ten rifles still in their boxes. Then there were four bags of ammunician, two bags of telescopic scopes and two bags of other equipment. Victor quickly picked up four bags, with two Glocks in each bag. He ran back for the last two Glocks and a bag of hip gun holsters.

"Let them go mum, you've said thank you a hundred times. Think of the people who are going to use these sleeping bags," Victor said as loud as he could, pointing behind them. Alan turned to see the police walking towards them.

Alan's phone beeped and he listened to the message from Lynda, then handed the phone to Victor.

"Yes, thank you, I understand. It'll take me just a few minutes. Thank you, thank you so much." He handed the phone back to Alan, who listened to Lynda's short orders.

"Yes Boss, I understand we'll get a few things together, you won't have much time. Gabrielle and Lynda will buy you new clothes within the next couple of days."

"Thanks Alan." Victor ran off as fast as he could and even changed into the female clothes he had and stuffed the rest in a satchel, then ran off to meet Alan, kissing his parents' goodbye.

"Don't worry, we'll take good care of her," Alan said to Victoria's parents. Then they all got onto the coach and were off back to their temporary home.

As soon as they arrived, they had help unloading the coach. The first to go were the ten rifles, which were hidden in the fifty wardrobes at the back of the room, which Lynda had brought over and were now screwed to the wall.

That meant one hundred and twenty-four girls had hung up all their new clothes Although they didn't have much room, they filled it with their high heeled shoes at the bottom, boxes discarded, they hid the guns well.

The girls had been watching a programme on TV, so they hadn't bothered to pick out the other wardrobes, but the first fifty had their names on and were full of clothes. As soon as the first girls came in with the rifles, they were quickly passed to the girls nearest the double doors and moved to the far end of the Train Station. The guns, ammunician and other bags were put into the wardrobes, where other girls helped to hide them behind their clothes.

One of the older girls carried more bags of guns in then another girl was bringing in two heavier bags of ammunician.

It was all safely hidden as they saw the blue and red lights of a police car coming slowly down their private road. As it turned onto their drive Alan got off the coach carrying four bags of ammunition and two black bags, containing, four sleeping bags in each black bag. He deposited them on the nearest table to the entrance doors and took his phone from his pocket.

He made a phone call to the PM's Private Secretary as the police officer got out of his car and looked into the coach. Two girls carrying two bags each passed by the police officer.

"What's in there? Are there any guns on this coach?"

"Yes, three," the girls replied.

"Where are they now?" the officer asked grinning, thinking he had caught them red handed.

"I'm not sure, it shouldn't concern you anyway, they are doing their job," Katherine retorted.

"Why do you need all the sleeping bags?" he demanded to know.

"You should know, why didn't you protect us? Why didn't you arrest Teresa and put her in jail so our right head lady could get back into the House and reinstate her ladies to look after us? You stood by and did nothing while Gabrielle and Lynda were in the States to fight George, to stop all this fighting in the streets and bring the shop and pub protection money being taken from people?

"All pub and businesses don't have to pay Ken's men any money now, do they?" Katherine demanded to know.

"No, they don't," he replied in a quiet voice.

"You watched us all get sold to different people," Katherine shouted as tears flooded down her face.

"It's alright Kath, you're back with us now, try not to get upset," Zara said to her and put her arms around her shoulders and gently kissed her on her cheek.

"Get Tina," Zara said to Felicity, outside the coach, waiting to get in and collect more sleeping bags.

Felicity turned and ran into the Train Station, right into the arms of Jenny.

"Felicity, what on Earth's the matter?" Jenny asked her.

"That copper out the front by the coach is interrogating Katherine like she's a criminal."

"Geraldine, can you come with me please and help sort out this police officer?" Jenny asked.

She ran down the room, and stood by Jenny's side,

"It's alright Felicity, go and get yourself a hot drink."

"Yes Jenny."

Jenny slipped her fur coat on as did Geraldine, Isaac followed her down the room and put his fur coat on, waiting by the electric doors.

Jenny and Geraldine walked over to the coach. They could see the constable with his hand on the coach looking like he meant business. Katherine was sobbing and Zara had joined her, as the officer shouted at her.

"Come on girls speak up or I'll arrest you for being an accomplice for illegal gun handling and possible injuring two men who were innocent of any charges," he shouted, not knowing what happened in the gun shop. He had drove by seeing the coach leave the scene where armed police officers were and a police senior officer. He thought he would get promoted for using his head.

Jenny pushed by the police officer taking Katherine's hand in hers, guiding her off the coach. She took two steps down still sobbing and fell into Jenny's open arms.

"It's alright Katherine, nobody will arrest you or shout at you again," Jenny said.

"I'll shout at who I like in the course of my duty, don't move I'm also arresting this bitch." He shouted and grabbed Zara's hand tight, squeezing it closed. Zara screamed and the police officer felt his hand removed from the girl and pushed up around his back.

"You can't do that I'm a police officer, I'm arresting you as well you bitch, just like these two kids, who should be kept indoors out of harm's way," he shouted.

"And you should have protected them while we were away. but you all failed in your job. You just stood back and let it all happen before you," Jenny shouted back, holding Katherine in one arm. Isaac came out into the cold and lifted Katherine into his arms and without listening to the police officer, took her inside, allowing Jenny to help get Zara off the coach.

"You're hurting my arm I'll need hospital attention for this," he bellowed.

"No, you won't but you'll need hospital attention for this," Geraldine said. Jenny quickly guided Zara from the bus in case she was splattered in blood if Geraldine did blow his head off. The argument had been going on far too long.

"Come to me Zara," Jenny said, holding Zara's hand in hers. As she was halfway down the coach steps, Geraldine had enough of the officer's bellowing. Her right hand took her gun in her hand and hit him with the side of the gun across his face and head as hard as she could.

Blood went everywhere including four of his teeth. Zara got blood on her face, and Jenny got blood over her arm.

"It's okay Zara, you aren't hurt, just a bit of blood over you, yes we'll have you tested in case he has aids or any other sexual disease," Jenny said grinning and helped Zara jump off the coach.

Isaac took her inside laughing with Zara as they passed through the electronic doors. The police officer put his hand to his head, feeling how hot his face was and the blood dripping down the side of his neck. He reached out and grabbed Jenny's hand having held it once was amazed how quickly she turned his grasp away from him. Now as he held her arm again, he started to dig his fingernails, into her skin.

"Owe, that hurt," Jenny shouted, as her natural reactions took over, her foot came off the snow with great speed and force then connected with his testicles and penis. making his eyes smart. He couldn't speak as his hands were holding his pride and joy between his legs.

"He touched his microphone which was on all the time. This is officer Carter Mills. I need immediate backup right now and an armed police officer."

"Help is on its way, where exactly are you?" a woman's voice asked.

"I'm in a large courtyard, and two women have tried to assault me. One hit me across my face with her gun. There are more armed men inside a big building with a lot of girls inside. I expect they will be selling them to paedophiles. Send in social services as well. Arrrrgggggg," he said as he held his testicles tighter trying to get rid of the pain. He could hear giggling over the handset.

"Are you hearing me? Send immediate backup."

"We still don't have the right signal from your car."

"I'm by a big building with people and gunmen inside. I'm outside guarding the door."

"Are you armed?"

"Only with my baton. It's now in my hand."

"Be careful Carter, especially if there are gunmen in there," Safire said at the other end of his handset, then she had to cut him off as she burst into laughter.

"Where is he?" another woman asked as she too was laughing. She could hear every word he said and had a fair idea where he was.

"Sorry Carter, our entire system just went down then. We need to find out where you have managed to get yourself to," Safire, the woman who took his call explained.

"I was coming down South Road when I saw a coach leaving the scene of a gun crime so doing my duty, I followed it. Two girls who were in the coach told me there were three people in the coach with guns, when I interrogated them. They burst into tears and two women have come outside, one kicked me between my legs when I tried to arrest her, and the other bitch whiplashed my head and face with her gun."

"Hello, Carter, don't cause any more problems for them, and don't call them a bitch, it's not allowed, let them carry on doing what they are doing. Help is on its way to you, but we know the exact location of your car, but not of you. Is there a big building near you, a lot of glass?"

"Yes, I'm stood outside the main doors by the looks of it," he replied in a high voice, as he had still not recovered from the woman's kick.

"Is there any wording on the building, you'll have to look up."

"Yes, there is. It says T G Train Station, but I haven't seen any trains go by and I don't see any train tracks… Hello, Hell? Has your system gone down again?"

The women on the other end of his line were now almost wetting themselves as they laughed. A senior officer came in asking what all the laughing was about. Safire touched the replay button then ran into the toilets. When she came out, she was trying hard not to laugh, but Barry her supervisor, had heard the entire tape and was himself laughing.

"Hello Carter, can you hear me?"

"Yes, I can. I need immediate help."

"We think we know exactly where you are now, help is on its way. Can you please read the name of the building again for me please?"

"Yes, it's T then G Train Station. Like I said, I've seen no trains pass me by, and looking around, I can't see any train lines either."

"Yes, we know where you are now, a car is turning into the road you are in." He turned his head seeing a police car with its flashing blue and red lights.

The officer pulled up behind his car then slowly got out of his car. He took a deep breath and swallowed the water he had just drunk. As he walked up to the glass double doors, he saw officer Mills with his baton in his hand. The door opened and a woman came out holding a gun in her hand with four girls aged eighteen behind her in short skirts and tops with a black overcoat on. Four seventeen-year-old-girls followed behind. The eighteen-year-old girls walked onto the coach moving all the remaining sleeping bags to the coach door. The girls took one bag in each hand then returned into the building. Mike was, standing by the coach door.

"You girls, you are under arrest for assisting the gunmen inside this building. If you are being coerced into this, Social

Services will help you. Now, give me your arms please so I may apply the restraining straps," Carter ordered.

"In girls please, put the sleeping bags on that table and can you bring in the rest please?"

"Yes, Uncle Mike," Isabell replied as the doors opened and they slowly walked out into the cold.

"Stop girls, you are all under arrest," Carter said urgently hoping the other officer would help him, but he wasn't told the whole story.

The girls continued walking to the coach, they chucked the bags of sleeping bags back and forth to the older girls on the coach, to take up more time.

"How many bags have we got left Skye?" Tina asked.

"Looks like fifteen single, and six doubles, for some reason.

"That means five trips, and oh what in the hell's that?" Tina asked looking at another strong carrier bag.

"It's got two boxes of ammunician in it," Nancy replied,

"I'll carry that," Tina said, "has anyone checked the boot, they might have put some stuff in there. Bethany, would you have a look please?"

Bethany got off the coach showing all her leg she could and slowly walked around to the boot. As she opened the boot, she saw it was filled with more single sleeping bags. She got four bags ready to hand to the girls as they were making their way up the side of the coach.

"Hannah, tell Tina there are another ten sleeping bags here," Bethany said.

Hannah called the rest of the seventeen-year old's up to the boot, passing them on the way back down talking to Tina for a moment and then walked back to the doors which opened as she approached them.

"Hey, you are under arrest, you cannot enter that building," PC Mills bellowed. He went to put his hand on her arm as three more seventeen-year-olds joined her at the open door. They walked in, dropped off their bags and walked past the officer on their right who was shouting to the officer on the left.

"Marlon, you have to back me up, help me, arrest these people, they've got guns on them, and they don't mind getting them out, one woman, actually pistol whipped me. There should be a hundred police officers down here with guns, ready to shoot `to kill," he said seriously.

Marlon took a deep breath and looked at the man behind the door and the woman standing outside the coach. The four, seventeen-year-old girls were taking the next load of bags,

"Take some more from the bottom door as these are tied up and

I'll have to untie them, but my fingers are cold," she said to Lexi. On their way back to the door, he tried once more to arrest one of the girls but all they got from him was a whack on the back of their left arm. Because his hand was on Skye's arm which was holding her tight in the straight-out position, Mike stepped outside, looked at Skye, smiled, then he hit Carter's arm so hard with his Glock, he broke it.

Carter screamed which the women at the end of the phone heard.

"What's happened now Carter?"

"One of the men with a gun broke my arm when I tried to arrest another of the girls.

"Look Carter, you obviously haven't been reading any of your daily reports, now get out of there now," Safire warned him.

"But they are villains, and I must try and uphold the law."

"Marlon, are you there?" Safire asked.

"Yes, mam," he replied.

"Get that idiot out of there before he starts an international situation and they do something worse to him, and you. You shouldn't really be there. A senior officer from the Met is on his way to you with blues and twos."

"I'll do my best Mam."

"I'm sorry girls, get inside," Marlone said.

"I'm hurt Marlone, they can't get away with that," Carter shouted.

"What's your name? you're under arrest," Mike told Carter.

Mike opened the glass doors and stepped outside. "At last, you broke my arm you idiot, look what you've done to me."

Mike withdrew his gun and held up his ID card. "I am a Knight of the Realm, under these emergency conditions. You are Dismissed Constable Mills. I also give you an immediate five-year sentence for not listening to a Knight of the realm and trying to stop him doing his duty. You PC Stevens, arrest this man, take him to his police station and explain Knight Mike Evans has dismissed this man and sentenced him to five years with no parole."

"Yes Sir, I sincerely apologise for being here Sir."

"Mike returned inside then he heard Tina shouting.

"Hannah don't touch the bags it's a bomb. Everyone off the coach Now, Hannah come here Now," Tina shouted.

Hannah looked at the plastic bags then saw a Polish Machine gun and guessed the rest. She ran for her life to the doors. She thought to herself as she ran for safety. Why now? After all this time of waiting, going through all that psychiatric talk, when I was made female today, why now have I got to die?" she was in tears as Carter blocked her way.

"There's a bomb on the bus you idiot," she shouted.

"Another offence against a police officer."

"Enough!" Tina shouted so she was certain he could hear her.

"I'm a Knight of the Realm, let her pass," Tina shouted.

"No way," he retorted then put his hand on Hannah's arm.

"You've been warned," Tina drew her gun and fired, the bullet hitting him in his lower leg. He fell to the floor crying out in pain."

"Carter, Carter what's happened to you now?" Safire asked.

"She shot me she's bloody well shot me with her gun. I need medical help now."

"It can't be that bad, you're still talking, where did she shoot you?"

"My lower leg," he retorted.

"Just be glad she didn't shoot you in the head. Get it? Leg, Head?" she said laughing. Carter put his hand out to try and stop Tina getting into the building. Shooting him in the leg at least moved him away from the doors.

As Tina approached the doors, Hannah was inside the building. Carter was in a lot of pain with his broken arm and a bullet in his lower left leg. But he wouldn't give in. As Tina approached the doors, they opened but Carter put his left hand out to block her way.

"Carter, you idiot, don't try it," Marlon shouted. Marlon stood at attention and saluted the woman passing before him. She turned and returned his salute. "I'm sorry," he mouthed.

"Not to worry," Tina replied.

Carter's left hand wrapped itself around Tina's ankle. Tina still had her gun in her hand and shot him without warning in the shoulder so he couldn't use his arm.

"Bitch, bitch, you bloody bitch you shot me in the shoulder," he bellowed.

"Carter; don't upset her anymore," Safire said urgently.

"The bloody bitch shot me again," he shouted.

"Carter No!" Safire shouted at him, but there was the sound of thunder as the Glock was fired at his other shoulder. He screamed and with the amount of pain, passed out on the ice-cold floor.

"I suggest you drag him inside before he freezes to death. You had better call an ambulance for him," Tina suggested, "And I don't want his blood over the floor, I'd tell him to clean it himself, but he seems to be shot several times and had his arm broken, do you know who did that?"

"No Mam, I didn't see a thing," Marlon replied.

"When you have parked him up, get yourself a cup of coffee. I'm Tina by the way, Knight of the British Empire. We are all Knights or Dames of the British Empire, and all of us are licensed to carry a gun and shoot to kill, he was lucky I was in a good mood. Very, lucky indeed"

"A senior officer from the met is on his way here now."

"Marlon are you there?" Safire asked. "What's happening to him?"

"Dame Tina shot him in his other shoulder, and he's passed out. I'm just dragging him into the Train Station."

"Well, that's something."

"I tried to warn him, but he wouldn't listen to me then he bad mouthed Tina and that was enough for her."

"It's alright we have his entire discussion on the computer and another senior officer has been listening to what he was saying as well. There will be no enquiry, he's under Knight arrest and been sentenced to five years, we heard it all."

Marlon dragged him by his coat jacket which he would no longer need, into the Train Station, leaning his body against the bottom wall near a radiator. Marlon then walked off to where he could smell coffee and freshly baked cakes.

His mouth was watering as he eyed up the mince pies and Victoria Sandwich cakes, Jam tarts and other cakes. He walked away from the food display and sat at a table. A couple of girls walked over and sat with him.

"Are you with the idiot who Dame Tina shot up?" Cloe asked.

"I'm sorry to say I am. But I told him to stop so did one of our controllers. He was already upsetting people when I got here."

"This is a restricted area, how he got in I don't know. There won't be an enquiry, he was dismissed by one of the Knights, then Dame Tina warned him, told him who she was then decided to shoot him in different parts of his body as he retaliated and finally swore at her. I bet all the laughing, will be cut out of the tapes they recorded him on."

"We heard them all laughing," Cloe said. "I bet they were wetting themselves with all the laughing they were doing."

"Yes, I bet they were," Marlon said biting off another large piece of cake. His lips licked his mouth as some of the jam and cream middle burst out of the middle of the cake.

"How long have you girls been living here or rather in the TG House?"

"About four years we both started within a month of each other, that's Jessica by the way I'm Cloe." They held hands and talked for a while until; their senior officer arrived. He was certainly taking his time.

Isaac walked out of the room with John's brand, new bullet proof jacket on done up to the neck.in his pockets were a few tools he would need to defuse the bomb and inside Johns left hand pocket, his Glock. his hands were dry and warm now, and he hoped they would stay that way. He had a small torch light over his head just over his temple. It was now switched on as it was six fifteen and dark. He approached the boot with his heart thumping hard in his chest. It was so loud he could hear it beating.

As he looked in the boot it was just as Hannah had drawn it in great detail. He gently moved one of the sleeping bags and cut the string with his eight-inch knife. He lifted the bag out of the boot and threw it on the floor. Now he could see a little deeper into the boot.

His hand went in deeper feeling around for any wires between the top and bottom bags. Taking a deep breath, he cut the string and removed the bag, checking that no wires were attached to it. He lifted the bag out of the car and dropped it onto the floor. It was harder now. His hand felt below the third bag, nothing. He started to lift it then felt a very slight pull on the bag. He lifted one side of the bag and looked beneath it. A little higher, then he could see a wire it was secured to the bottom of the bag with tape. As he looked at the other bag that too had tape secured to the bag. He took out the small pair of scissors from his pocket and breathing deeply, he cut around the cable on both bags then lifted both bags out of the boot and dropped them onto the floor.

He looked at the wires and followed them into the boot. The left cable went under the eight hand grenades and as he gave it a slight tug, it stopped him pulling again. He tried the right, side wire and it was just like the other, now he was thinking hard.

It took him fifteen minutes to disarm the left side which was connected to a small relay, which when pulled simply closed the circuit and the explosive charge would go off.

Five minutes later the right side was disconnected. Now he could remove the charges and disarm them. He opened the bottom of each charge and threw away the explosive charge, then discarded the metal cases. Nothing happened when they landed forty feet away.

Now he was looking at the grenades, each one was tied to another through the pins. He carefully cut each string and finally removed the string. He had brought a dish out with him, so it collected the explosive and ball bearings. The first two went easy, the third it seemed the thread at the bottom of the grenade was stuck.

He put that grenade down and started on another which went a lot easier as did the rest. He tried the grenade once again using a spot of oil to try and help ease the bottom off it. He gave the grenade more oil around the part of the grenade that split it into two. He held it in his hands for a minute, hoping the oil would get into the screw section.

He put the grenade down and wiped his hands dry of the oil with the tea towel he had brought out with him and placed in the front edge of the boot.

He very gently picked up the grenade checking the pin was still in its hole. He started to unscrew the bottom of the grenade, as he gently tapped the explosive out of the grenade, it fell in one lump, meaning it was damp and had got wet. The ball bearings fell into the bowl with no trouble.

He moved his hand and heard something metal hit the metal of the boot. Not worrying what was left in the grenade, he turned and threw it as far as he could then it blew up. There was a loud bang as the explosive activator set off the remainder of explosive and eight ball bearings were sent flying into the air. Isaac was now on the floor with his head covered by his hands. He heard two bearings hit the boot. Everyone inside the building looked out of the windows and Mike, being used to being hit by glass and bullets opened the door.

"Isaac, you, still alive?" he asked jovially.

"Yes, would you believe it, the last bit of the grenade managed to survive. Then he remembered the machine gun. "Get inside quick there's a machine gun in there.

"Leave it," Mike replied, but Isaac was off the floor with his head inside the boot. Mike closed the door behind him. and looked up to see Geraldine halfway down the room. Penny had her arms around her holding her close to her and talking quietly and reassuringly together.

Isaac was feeling beneath the gun, looking for anything that could trigger the gun to fire. It had a twenty-bullet clip in the gun, which was not good, if it blew up, the bullets would go all over the place. If it started to fire the entire clip would explode sending its bullets everywhere. There was no choice the clip would have to come out plus the bullet already in the firing chamber.

He gently turned the gun over and slowly, lifted it off the bottom of the boot. He could handle it better now, although he still had to go careful. Ten minutes passed before he had managed to remove the clip of bullets and the bullet in the firing chamber. There was nothing else on the gun that could hurt anyone. He ran his hands slowly down both sides of the machinegun then threw it out of the boot.

There were two what looked like rifle boxes, but he treated them as explosives. His knife ran down the side of each box cutting any tape that held the boxes together. He opened each box seeing a bright new live two, two, rifle. He slowly, pulled each one from its box, examining the rifle and blank bullet clip.

They were both fine and the boxes checked out okay too. He placed the boxes on the side of the boot and placed one rifle inside its box. Then he saw the bag of ammunician and gently examined the boxes the bullets were in. It would be his head that would roll if anything happened when he had cleared it as clear, good to go.

He put the bag of ammunician on the floor and leaned both rifle boxes against the boot. He then carefully pulled up the remainder of the boot carpet. When it was off the metal, he looked beneath the carpet seeing nothing. He was still not satisfied and slowly turned the blanket over and threw it away from the boot. The boot was now clear and there were no more wires or bombs. Isaac returned inside to a rapturous applause and the last of the extra wardrobes were secured to the wall.

When Alan finally switched his phone off from the PM's Private Secretary, he finally got them an appointment to see him the following day at midday. For a moment he wondered what all the applause was for then saw all the wardrobes against the wall and girls gradually filling them with their clothes they had bought that day, the couples sharing one wardrobe each while the other girls shared with their close friends. Their underclothes tights and make up left in the smaller bags they had for now, by their shoes at the bottom of their side of the wardrobe.

Looking around, he saw all the girls laughing and joking. A couple of girls were crying which was to be expected after what had happened to them and what they had gone through that day. Two girls were walking back into the room Carrying four sleeping bags each. Two more girls passed them on the way out to the coach. Isaac was returning with the last four bags from the boot. The ones which were tied to the grenades he left on the floor and would inspect them further in the morning as he wasn't sure how far these people would go to add further grenades to the inside of the bags.

Alan heard banging behind him and saw two men who had been working on the main house, putting drawers up together for the chest of drawers. Two more were constructing the outer carcasses and screwing them to the wall. Girls were carrying the completed drawers that had been glued together for extra strengthening, further down the Train Station so the glue could set.

A woman entered the Train Station carrying a bag of wooden name tags and a pin gun, to hold the name plates to the drawers. It was a hive of industry. At the far end of the room, the fifteen, sixteen, and seventeen, year-old girls were putting duvet covers onto the new duvets and finally the pillowcase onto the pillows. Despite only having a hundred pillows, they put the duvet covers onto the hundred and eighty duvets they had, they would have to collect the other seventy-six duvets and pillows tomorrow. But there was still so very much to do tomorrow. Everyone knew the men had been working hard, but it was only Lynda who had seen the work done.

There are three hundred and ten bedrooms in the TG House, four huge recreational halls with eight TVs in each room, not that they were put on very often, they had too much homework to do and extra classes for music, art and astronomy. Some of which was carried out at Grayson Mansion, in the long room behind the bedrooms on the top floor. There was the laundry room, first aid and wardroom.

The kitchen, and breakfast room, doubled as a games room with fourteen computer game platforms down one side of the room and the same down the other side.

All these places were destroyed in front of the boy girls before they were abducted sixty boy girls at a time with two busses, so it looked like a school outing. Many of them were abducted with barely anything on, a silk or satin nightie with matching panties, some managed to grab a negligee and put some slippers on, others didn't get anything on their feet and were forced to walk across the snow to the bus a hundred feet away. But they were all safe and warm now.

Alan's phone wrang and as he answered it, he saw what appeared to be a police officer sat on the floor with a broken arm and gun shots to various parts of his body. He started to wonder what had happened while he was on the phone, surely it couldn't have been that long, all they had to do was get fifty odd sleeping bags out of the coach. And where was his wife, John and the two girls?

"Hello?" he asked after the fourth ring.

"Alan, at last, I've been trying to get through to you for two hours at least." Alan looked at his watch it was six twenty, they left the shop at six ten, where had he been?

"Hello Alan, did everything go as planned at the Outdoor store?"

"More or less; I think."

"Gabrielle got worse, and we had some bad news about her. We had to bring her to her doctor's surgery."

"It looks like we need a doctor here."

"Why do you need a doctor, who's ill?"

"I'll tell you when I see you," Alan replied wondering what in the hell had happened?

"We'll be back in about ten minutes they are just finishing off. I'll fill you in when I get back," John said, wondering what had happened back home.

Thinking he could relax for a minute and ask a few questions his phone rang again.

"Hello," Alan asked.

"This is Police Commissioner Denis Miles from the MET. I have no real idea why I am here, but one of our younger police officers has got into some trouble."

"You could say that." Then he saw another police officer sitting at a table with his mouth full of cake and talking to Jessica and Cloe, both sixteen, as he took another bite of the cake in his hand.

"Did you say one or two of your officers?"

"I believe two officers are there, one is a little confused."

"He looks dead to me." Alan replied.

"He's not dead," Layla, one of the younger girls aged twelve said and kicked him in his bad leg.

"Uuuuugghhhh," the officer uttered obviously in a great deal of pain.

"What happened to him Layla?" Alan asked her.

"He was very naughty, he tried to arrest some of the girls who were outside getting the sleeping bags in, every time one of the older girls tried to get past him to get in here, he would molest them, then he really upset Cloe, she was crying a lot as he molested her, the officer was gripping her arm and despite being asked by Mike to release her, he didn't. Mike pulled Cloe away from him, only a short way so she made his arm stretch and stay firm outright, still gripping her arm.

"Mike hit his arm hard with his gun and broke it. He was still running his hand around her body trying to arrest her, to me I think he was going to snog her. Then Mike arrested him under Knight's rules and gave him five years with no parole.

"Tina told him to let her go but he didn't, so she shot him in the leg while she was by the coach. Then Tina suggested they look in the boot. There were about twelve bags with sleeping bags in so they started to bring them in then Jessica said there some bags tied up and Tina shouted at her not to touch them it may be a bomb.

"Tina ordered everyone inside and off the coach, the copper tried to stop all the girls getting in here, then Tina tried to get in but the officer said he wanted to have sex with her, or arrest her, but I think it was the first because his hand held her leg and felt it a lot so Tina shot him in the left shoulder, he still said he wanted to have sex with her, so she shot him in his right shoulder and finally kicked his body out of her way.

"It was a little while before Isaac put on John's new bullet proof jacket, did it up all the way and went outside to the boot of the coach. We heard him shout two bags were free then there was a long time before he threw two more bags out of the boot then a very, long time before he shouted there's one which he threw into the air behind him and there was a loud boom as the bomb went off. A little later after he checked the boot had no more bombs in it, he picked up the two rifles and a bag of bullets and came in, to everyone cheering him. At some time, Tina told the other officer to drag the shot officer into the room and not to get blood all over the clean floor and here he is fast asleep if you ask me."

"Well thank you Layla, that was a very, good explanation of what happened to him. I think he's lucky to be alive, Tina could have shot him between his eyes," Alan said partly kneeling, so his face was at the same height as Layla's face.

"That would have been good. Bam then Splat, his brain all over the wall and blood everywhere."

"Just remind me when you get older, not to make you a bodyguard,"

"Why?" Layla asked smiling.

"You might shoot first between the eyes, then ask questions later."

"That's what you do and Uncle John."

"Sometimes it seems like we do," Alan replied.

"Hello Denis, I'm sorry I got a little distracted there, how can I help you?"

"I was just being polite really can I have permission to come on your drive?"

"Of course, you can, come on down, park behind the other two police cars."

"Thanks, I'll be with you soon."

Alan was about to turn around and talk to the other police officer when Lynda and Sarah jumped into the room, a moment later, Gabrielle and John joined them.

Chapter 16

John helped Gabrielle to her seat and put the blanket around her. Lynda walked over to her and sat on the side of her chair.

"How do you feel now my love?" Lynda asked Gabrielle.

"A lot better now thanks, it looks like they've done extremely well here, men are good for some things," she joked.

"Gabrielle and Lynda are back, are you better now?" Lexie asked for everyone.

"Yes, I'm a lot better now thank you. I just need some rest and a good night's sleep and I'll be back full of life tomorrow." Lynda and Gabrielle kissed then Lynda saw the officer sat on the floor.

"What on Earth's gone on here? We were only gone," she paused and looked at her watch, it was quarter past six. "Well, it seems we've only been gone fifteen minutes, I could have sworn it was much longer than that, about three hours ago," Gabrielle said.

Then Dennis Miles entered the room.

"Alan what's the Police Commissioner doing here? Gabrielle asked.

"I think that police officer on the floor called him."

"What on earth is he doing here anyway, doesn't he know this is a no-go zone for anyone?"

"Apparently not and there's another down there stuffing his mouth with cake and mince tarts."

"What!" she exclaimed. "Not my mince tarts?" She looked around and called Amy to her.

"What can I do for you Gabrielle?"

"Could you go down and see if there are any mince tarts left, please? If there are, can you get me two please?"

"I'll have two as well," Lynda said, "Put four on a plate if there are any left," she said smiling at her, now glad her wife was much better.

"I think I had better see to that poor man, do you by any chance know what happened to him, the short answer please Layla."

"Well, he arrived, molested our girls so Uncle Mike broke his arm and arrested him under Knight's Law, then Aunty Tina shot him three times, but he's still alive, then a bomb went off. Uncle

Isaac saw to that, Uncle Alan was on his phone all the time speaking to the PM's Private Secretary and you have a meeting to see her tomorrow and we now have another Prime Minister," Layla added.

"Thank you, Layla, you seem to know everything that has happened here," Gabrielle said as Amy came back with six mince tarts on a plate. "Thank you," she said taking the plate from her.

"Simon said there are plenty left and another three large cakes, all ten inches in diameter."

"That sounds very nice, I'll try and get down there later."

"No, you won't, you should be home in bed, not here trying to run things. Now sit and rest. I'll get us a coffee each when I've finished with the police officer. Sarah, do you have that bullet remover?" Lynda asked.

"Yes, I do." She searched through her bag a finally found it at the bottom of her bag. Lynda already had a tart in her hand. She kissed her wife goodbye, took the tool from Sarah and walked over to the officer on the floor.

Green light filled the room as Lynda started to work on his broken arm, with a bullet lodged in his broken bone. She called to Gabrielle to give her some of her love.

The room was now a very bright green as Gabrielle's eyes lit up and she sent all her love to her wife. Lynda then looked deep into his leg, saw the bullet and using the tool, she pulled the bullet out of his leg, then stopped the bleeding and set his leg straight again. She fused the bones back together and finally closed the hole the bullet had made. She did the same to both shoulders and finally repaired his broken arm, which she had taken the bullet out of earlier.

She slapped his face hard with her hand. His eyes remained closed, so she slapped his face a lot harder this time and he woke up holding his face with both hands.

"Now, stand up and walk around in a circle. You have no right being here, you could have been killed," Lynda told him.

"I thought I was going to die, a woman shot me in the leg, then in both my shoulders and a man broke my arm."

"Well, it's not broken now, and your shoulders are fine, so is your leg. Get your friend and leave while you can," Lynda said sternly to him.

"Yes, but I must still arrest that man there, the woman who shot me, the lady down there for having guns without a licence and on show to everyone. Carrying at least eight rifles in that coach and transporting at least ten girls to be sold to paedophiles."

"Please try and listen to me, I am Dame Lynda Grayson, that lady there is Dame Gabrielle Grayson, there are another six Knights of the Realm in here with us, that makes eight Knights and we all over rank you and the Police Commissioner. When we are training, bullets fly past the front gate, that is why there is a notice there, no entry to unauthorised vehicles. You have an unauthorised vehicle."

"I still need to arrest them and I'm not leaving until I do."

"Is he still trying to arrest people?" Tina asked looking at the man before her.

"He's trying." Lynda replied.

"Mike dismissed him and gave him a prison sentence of five years," Tina replied giggling.

"Let me see your Police Card." Lynda ordered.

"Here." he replied, taking the card from his pocket.

Lynda tried and tried to rip it in half. "Tina, take out your knife and cut this in half for me please."

When she pulled out her knife, the man sighed. "That's another offence, carrying a knife especially that long is a crime by a prison sentence."

"Shut it, or I'll drop you in the river Thames. Dennis, could you see to this man please, apparently, he's been dismissed and given a five-year Knight prison sentence and he isn't listening to a word I say."

"Certainly, Dame Lynda, who dismissed him?"

"Sir Mike," Tina replied for Lynda.

"Alright I'll deal with him and his mate," Dennis said.

"He walked off unaware of what had happened. He looked at Carter Mills and the mess his uniform was in, both his sleeves had been cut apart where Lynda operated on him, and his left trouser leg was also split open. He was now standing up and moving both arms as he was about to tell Dennis Miles that he had a broken arm and was shot, then he realised he was perfectly okay.

"PC Marlon, come here please," Dennis called.

"Yes Sir," he replied standing at attention before him.

"Take this man back to your station, have his senior officer there waiting for me. Take him in your car, he's a disgrace to the force."

"Yes Sir," he replied. "Come on Carter, time to go."

"But I need to arrest them, they've broken the law on numerous charges," he continued to object as PC Mills was dragged from the building, past his car, Marlon opened the back door of his car and threw Carter into the car, then drove off back to the station, sorry to leave the young girls and cake behind.

"Thank you for the cakes I'll see you in the morning when you see the PM, I'll be there to explain what the MET will be doing for you, but don't keep your hopes up, there has been a lot of opposition to my plan." He stood to attention, saluted Alan, then John, then walked over to where Gabrielle and Lynda were seated, holding hands.

"I will see you both at noon tomorrow, I hope you're feeling a lot better now Gabrielle." He stood to attention again and saluted them, Lynda stood and returned the salute, Gabrielle struggled to get to her feet and finally standing upright, returned his salute.

"We'll see you tomorrow, Dennis," Lynda said, and Gabrielle shook his hand.

"What happened and where did you go?" Alan asked taking a seat next to the girls."

"I'll tell him Gabrielle, you rest," she said, leaning into her wife, held her head and kissed her lips. As John walked over to be with his wife. As they met, they held each other tight and kissed profusely. No longer afraid if anyone were watching them, now they knew any time, could be the last time they saw each other alive. So, they decided to make the most of it and show their love for each other, tomorrow, they could be crying for each other.

Sitting comfortable with her arm around her wife's shoulder, hands touching hands, smiling at each other as Ava brought them both a cup of cappuccino, a proper cup on a saucer with a piece of cake each on a plate.

"Thank you, Ava, I hope you've had some of this cake."

"Oh yes Gabrielle, it's lush," she replied smiling. "It's so nice to see you back and looking well again," she said and ran off to her friends further down the room.

"That was nice of her to say that," Gabrielle said.

"They all think the same my love and so do I." Lynda's head turned into her wife's and with tears in her eyes, they kissed, holding it for a while.

"Mmmmmm, I love you so very much my wife," Lynda said.

"I love you too, with all my heart," Gabrielle replied, wishing she could crawl into her wife's body and share it with her.

"Sorry Alan, so yes, just as you left in the coach, Louie came in from the House. He was painting walls in the House; it's a great system Trever has made over there."

"It's their first day, not even a full day, I expect it has taken a lot of sorting out and cleaning first. I wouldn't expect them to get much further than cleaning the top floor," Gabrielle said.

"We'll go over soon and see how they have managed to get on," Lynda replied with a huge grin on her face.

"Louie came in here and found us where we are now. He got John, who was kissing his wife, do you know, they kiss a lot more now, showing their love for each other. I like it. Something you and Sarah should be doing."

"John brought Louie over to us and he looked frightened to speak and tears were in his eyes. He told us, during the night of our raid on the Mansion to rescue our girls, the men who were behind Ken and being paid a great deal of money each day in cash, were using bows and arrows as well to fight you, many of the arrows hit the ceiling and fell to the floor. They were almost out of arrows and dipping them in some sort of poison they said it was. Four of them were firing the last four arrows at the same time, three hit the ceiling but I saw one arrow go low and the man who fired it, was cursing himself for being so stupid and not being able to shoot straight.

"But this arrow hit Gabrielle near her heart, it only just went into her body, because the second it entered her body, she pulled it out and threw it on the floor. The man on the second landing was waving his arms in the air.

"Ten minutes later, Louie picked the arrow up from the floor, there was a small piece of arrow from the tip missing. He put the tip in his pocket, not thinking he would be joining us down here and painting his way to freedom.

"He showed me the broken arrow and the top five millimetres at least was missing. I looked at Gabrielle's chest and right on the scar line, was a red line and a red rash of sorts surrounding a small hole. When I looked inside her body, I could see it was all inflamed, this was not something I could easily repair, I didn't know what the poison was or how far it had got into her body.

"I rang our doctor and she said she was at the surgery and Gabrielle would need an x-ray, get there as soon as we could. We turned up a few seconds later in her surgery. I took Gabrielle first and sat her down, so Dr Jessica King could start her examination.

"A few seconds later, with tears streaming down my face, I arrived back in the room with John and Sarah with her bag in case there was something inside she might be able to use. She still has over fifty in war sedation, tablets twenty mills, fast acting morphine capsules in her bag, which Sarah told me Gabrielle could take in the event of a normal operation.

"We quickly moved to the X-ray room only to be kicked out, only the doctor and Gabrielle were allowed in. After a click of the X-ray machine, Gabrielle was moved in a different position and X-rayed again, moved and X-rayed again, then let out of the room. We returned to her room and Gabrielle sat Down.

"We all, except Gabrielle looked at the large X-ray screen, which we also supplied, one for each of the five doctors. The tip of the arrow was noticeably clear, and it had done little damage to her skin. Had it not been for the substance it was dipped in she would have been fine.

"She said she would have to go to hospital. and have it carefully taken out, so nothing remained inside her. She was amazed when I told Gabrielle to lay on her bed.

"No not here she shouted," as she went to get her coat. I told her to sit back in her chair and watch. I asked Sarah what she thought, and she pulled out of her bag a pair of blunt clamping tweezers. I looked at Gabrielle's chest and told Jessica to come over and see what was going to happen.

"This won't hurt my love, you know I wouldn't hurt you, I said to her then my eyes turned bright green. Jessica took a frightening step back. Sorry I told her, my eyes will go darker and brighter as I operate and I may ask Gabrielle for some more love, but we'll talk telepathically. If I need more love, Gabrielle's eyes will turn very bright green.

"I heard Sarah warn her the next part looked bad, but it was normal and wouldn't hurt Gabrielle. My eyes were bright green as I looked at the tip of the arrow then across to her heart. Jessica was amazed to see it beating in place pumping the blood around her body. She was looking hard at your heart so I increased the brightness of my eyes so she could see her heart pumping better.

"She asked me if I could see what she was seeing, it was a black line going down the side of your heart. I asked her which I should go for first the black line or arrowhead. She replied she had no idea how I would operate on your heart without killing you or grab the arrow tip with the strange looking tweezers.

"Sarah told her to answer the question and just watch. She eventually found the arrowhead, but it had to be in one piece and done in a hospital in surgery, they would make a long incision first then another top and bottom so the incision could be widened, and the tip taken flat off the subcutaneous tissue, in English I replied and laughed. Flesh, she told me. I nodded then brightened my eyes and placed my fingers slightly away from the arrow tip and with my eyes growing brighter, I pushed my hand into your chest up to my knuckles.

"Jessica was breathing hard at the time taking small gulps of air as a little blood came out of the hole I was making. My fingers turned up to hold the metal tip. I pushed my other hand right into your chest and helped push the arrow tip out of your body. Sarah got the tweezers and took hold of the very end of the tip at the broken end and with my left hand I pushed it out of your body so Sarah could lift it off the flesh and place it on the glass slide of Jessica's microscope. She went to move it away to her table, but I pointed to the line of black stuff.

"Jessica went to her cupboard and took out a thin suction pipe."

"See if this will do it? She said and placed it in my bloody left hand. I placed it next to the black stuff and Jessica started the pump which sucked up the black stuff as I moved it closer to your heart under your skin.

"Eventually, I had to remove both my hands and repair the hole and the little damage I did to two small veins getting the tip out. I healed your skin and ensured there were no marks left, by placing my hot palm over the operation lines and bonded the skin back together as if it were never opened.

"Sarah gave me some damp gauze and I cleaned the blood off you. When I and Jessica were happy with the skin bonding, I started again next to your heart. It was then I asked for more love and the room, was instantly a very bright green.

"My eyes shone inside your skin and over your heart. I could see the black line now so I inserted my left hand into your chest and took hold of the plastic pipe, pushing it with my right hand beneath your skin so I could hoover up the black stuff. I went right into the wall of your heart and looking inside your heart, I pushed the tip of the pipe down the inside of your left heart muscle and sucked up more of the black stuff.

"Jessica asked me if I could make it so she could look inside my heart like before. Between us, we made my eyes as bright as I thought they would go and concentrated on your heart. Jessica could see right inside the right chamber of your heart, we then looked at your superior vena cava, which brings oxygen-poor blood from the body into the right atrium. The black stuff was about to try and enter the right atrium. Which would have been disastrous for you Gabrielle.

"I made the hole in your chest bigger, I had no option, I had to get inside your heart. My little suction tool was still working as it continued to suck the black stuff off your heart muscle and further back to the exterior of your heart and sucked all over the exterior heart muscle and into the free area near the heart.

"We double checked everywhere around the heart all the blood vessels that were wrapped around the heart and inside the right and left heart chambers. There was no more black stuff, so I repaired the one damaged blood vessel, checked everywhere once again then put your insides back together, removing a small clot of blood which was the remains of another heart operation.

"My eyes healed the holes where I had inserted my hands into your body and Sarah wiped all the blood away and cleaned it before I put my left hand over the small breaks in the skin and bonded it together with my hot hands. There was nothing there to say Gabrielle had an operation.

"My green eyes slowly swept back and forth over her body and we could see nothing else that looked dangerous to you. All we had to do now was discover what the black stuff was. It looked to be alive to travel as it was over her body, up and down arteries and veins over smaller blood vessels and worst of all trying to enter the heart itself.

"We put some of the black stuff on another glass slide looked at it and left it alone for five minutes while we checked the arrow tip to make sure it matched up with the other part of the arrow that I brought with us. It lined up perfectly but Jessica kept it in the slide so she could take it to hospital tomorrow and examine it under the hospital's electron microscope with another doctor who has expertise in these things.

"When we got back to the black stuff. It had moved, all by itself about six millimetres. We were shocked so much so that I went back to Gabrielle and examined her once again under my green eyes. I couldn't see any more of it inside her, but I'll check her again later. The rest has been put into one of Jessica's special

Jars and screwed the lid on tight. She will look at it with another doctor under the electron microscope. If it's still alive, they will hopefully be able to identify it and give Gabrielle whatever medication she needs to kill the rest of it. Hopefully, I got it all out of her. How do you feel now my love?"

"A lot better than earlier, I can't feel anything moving about inside me. There you've made me nervous now, I'm thinking of some monster blood organism crawling about inside my body."

"Let me look again." She loosened her grip of her wife and stood up, Gabrielle undid the buttons on her cardigan and lay back on the sofa as still as she could. Lynda unbuttoned her blouse and pulled it apart so she could see her skin. Her eyes turned bright green.

"Sarah, can you come here and check Gabrielle again please?"

When they were both in place, Lynda's eyes flared and turned a very bright green as she slowly moved her eyes back and forth over her body four times just to be sure.

"I can't see anything, and my eyesight is twenty, twenty which you made for me when you made me slimmer and made my hair grow long, which I love by the way. It's all clear by me."

"I can't see anything either, but we'll check you as often as you like," Lynda said, hoping to put her wife's mind at ease.

"Thank you, my love, you too Sarah," Gabrielle replied.

"You just need to rest and have a restful night in bed. I've already called Wendy, she has turned the heating up full as the house will be very cold, despite having the heating on low earlier. She will make a lovely hot chocolate before we go to bed. I think we'll bring another two hundred-grand here tomorrow and split it for the boys over there. We have a spare twenty single sleeping bags they can have. There are quite a few single beds left there which they'll use tonight and tomorrow, we'll need to get them all a sleeping bag each. The heating is on full, but that's to help dry the building out, as Teresa left all the doors and most of the windows open except in the rooms the last girls were sleeping in Lynda explained.

"This is a stupid question, but I need to ask it," Alan said.

"What is it?" Lynda asked.

"Exactly how long did this operation take?"

"About two hours, then Gabrielle was laying on the bed for another hour, while we looked at the things under the microscope. John was trying to get through to you for a good two and a half hours, but you were continually engaged. I checked Gabrielle once more before she got off the bed, and Jessica told us what she will do in the morning and what Gabrielle has to do tonight which includes getting a good night's sleep in our bed."

"I would say we were gone a good four hours, why? Your job shouldn't have taken very long, two hours at the most."

"Have you looked at the time?"

"It's about nine thirty I expect."

"Look at your watch?" Alan told them.

"It's, six fifteen, everyone thinks so and look at the boys over there, with the girl's help they have put together and screwed fifty-four carcases to the wall. The other men have only ten more drawers to make. Now they are making the last two chests of drawers for the last two units to be put on next to the kitchen. Some of the men in the house have taken the two mirrored doors off their hinges and are carrying them over with another four men, in case someone slips down in the snow, and they are bringing a double wardrobe carcass over which will also go on the wall next to the kitchen. The girls have put all the drawers into the units, but they want the glue to set overnight.

Joshua came in and spoke to Lynda. "Could you help us get some more units over here, they are for the kitchen, so we have put a couple of long lengths of wood to bring over as well and the guys that just left are coming back with their tools and some other bits they'll need for the job."

Lynda kissed her wife and put her hand on Joshua's arm, then they were gone. She was back again at the bottom of the room with two boxes of double wall cupboards. She dropped them off and was back again with another two double wall cupboards. Then she was gone again and was back with two long lengths of wood. She dropped these off at the same place. She popped back and returned with an eight-inch chop saw Finally she returned with a single wall cupboard which was already constructed and painted green, with a square stick-on notice, First Aid Cabinet.

"We'll have to get some first aid bits and pieces tomorrow if we can," Lynda said.

"Look at your watch," Alan said.

"It must be at least six thirty," Lynda replied but when she looked at her watch it was still six fifteen.

"Someone wants this day and evening to last longer than normal, but nobody seems to notice the time, or the amount of work being done," Alan said looking at Lynda and Gabrielle.

"How are you feeling now? Would you like to have a look at the house, see how they have got on?" Lynda asked Gabrielle.

"They can't have got that much done, they've been concentrating on building the wardrobes in here and look, they've even got all the chest of drawers in place and all the drawers made up. Even if they've cleaned a couple of rooms on the top floor it will be something, after all, they had come to a building they haven't seen before, unless it was them who ransacked it?" Gabrielle replied.

"Are you up to taking a walk over there with John and Alan, it will give them an idea to see it as a piece of property we can use it to hold off the enemy, when they arrive properly," Lynda suggested.

"Yes, let's go take a look around, see what damage has been done then when we come back, we sit with the girls for a bit then jump home and after a hot chocolate we go to bed," Gabrielle replied smiling.

"You are the one who needs extra rest, after I've put you to bed, I'm going out."

"Not without me you're not, we either go out together or go to bed together. If you check me and I'm fine, I could put my best dress on and join you."

"No, no, my love, we'll have time to go out together, let's get you well first and work out what Death has in store for us and why?"

"I agree," Gabrielle replied, thinking their situation through. "Let's go and take a look around the house."

"I'll get our coats, it's cold out there and it might be freezing inside the House, if they have smashed windows to contend with. John, Alan, are you going to join us?"

"Yes Lynda," they replied together.

"Then get your overcoats on."

Soon they were walking over the crisp ice-cold grass and path to the House. Lynda knew they had got on well, even when they lost two men, then four men to make up the wardrobes.

They were halfway across the path to the house when Lynda took out her phone and called the last number on her phone. "Hello Hailey, is that thing you found working yet?"

"Yes Lynda, it's in full working order and we've thoroughly cleaned and polished the inside, and the door opens properly now. All the wood on the outside has been polished with beeswax."

"Right, we'll come in through the main door in about five minutes," Lynda said then put her phone away and got close to her wife.

"I love walking like this in the snow, it's more romantic don't you think Gabrielle?"

"It is my love. Especially with you holding me close and taking care of me," Gabrielle replied.

Lynda stopped and looked at her wife. They kissed then Lynda kissed her once again. "I never realised you thought of me as caring for you, but I like it."

"Yes, my love you do, kiss me again please." Lynda moved her face closer to Gabrielle's and they kissed. They were holding hands as two-gun shots went off and hit the ground a good thirty metres in front of them. They were both instantly on the ground, the cold snow reminded them of a time gone by, when they first fell head over heels in love with each other. This time John was covering Gabrielle and Alan was covering Lynda and both had their guns out.

Before they could move their bodies there were two more gunshots, this time much louder. John's phone rang.

"We got them both John, the rifles are spot on, so too the night sites. I think we'll leave it till the morning in case they are carrying grenades or booby trapped their bodies. Don't worry, we'll take care of them first light," Mike said waving his gun in the air.

A moment later they were on their feet. Lynda helped her wife up and then looked at the back of her coat and brushed the snow off. "I love you with all my heart, will you marry me?" Gabrielle asked.

"Only if you will marry me." They kissed each other laughing.

Taking hold of John and Alan, they held hands and jumped together to the corridor outside the front office. Hailey was there to meet them.

"Hello Lynda, Gabrielle, John, Alan. We've managed to get a lot of work done, so we'll start here on your tour and ask you a few questions as we go around if that's okay with you Lynda?"

"Of course, Hailey," Lynda replied.

"We'll make a start here, if you look right, you'll see we've made a start clearing up the ground floor and the room off of it," Hailey explained.

"Good idea to start from the ground up I suppose, but we really need the bedrooms cleaned up first," Alan said wondering why they didn't start from the top down, but there were so many rooms on the top floor, it would be hard to know where to start and anywhere was better than nowhere, and this was more work than he had expected.

"If you turn left, we'll start your tour here, at the old lift we discovered earlier this afternoon. It is now in full working order and apart from a couple of light bulbs needing to be replaced, it's a lovely lift. Eric, our sparks has been up the inside of the lift with Zack our plumber who has checked all the pipes are still holding pressure, I think that's what he said. Anyway, while they were checking everything underneath the lift, a group of us started to finish ripping the cladding from the front doors of the lift and cleaned the inside of the lift and behind the landing doors as they got to each floor. They checked everything underneath and swept away all the cobwebs."

"So where has this come from?" Gabrielle asked.

"It was here all the time, hidden by wood cladding. The NHS, who had this House before you did, covered it up, we have no idea why they did it, but you now have a lift for disabled children and adults who want a sex change," Hailey said laughing, "Oh and we uncovered another door just there which leads to a gentle ramp for the wheelchairs or other wheeled objects." She pushed the call button and the front lift doors opened with the chime of a bell.

"Shall we go in?"

"Will it take our weight?" Alan asked.

"Oh yes, it will hold ten adults and a wheelchair or hospital bed," Hailey replied and moved aside for Lynda to make the first move, pulling Gabrielle with her. John and Alan reluctantly followed them, and Hailey came in last and pressed the sixth-floor button which was the top floor and the lift also descended to the basement. The lift started its assent without jerking and quickly passed the other floors to the top floor. The lift stopped and the doors opened, and they all stepped outside.

"Eric has the telephone number of the lift company which originally installed the lift. He will ring them tomorrow to get them to give the lift a full examination but it's working fine, for now. It will not have the continuous use like it did when it was a hospital. Madeline has told us, as she was an NHS Nurse here at the time."

"Will she be staying on here?" Gabrielle asked, thinking of the girls if they got ill.

"She can with a couple of others if you want. Most of us women were Margarette's staff, and she called us back in," Hailey explained.

"Right, I think we'll have it as before, with all of you back in. Margarette had it all working fine let's hope it can stay that way," Gabrielle said holding Lynda's hand.

"We'll start in the first room. As you can see, the landing has been cleaned, the ceiling and walls painted, and all the wood has been painted a soft pink. Eric will be fitting the fluorescent fittings tomorrow on all the landings and larger rooms which need brighter light. He will need a few grand, for the light fittings," Hailey said looking at Lynda.

"That will be fine, tell him to make a list of everything he needs and get it all at once. I think it would be nice if we could have some of those lights which come on when people approach the building. Get him to look around the outside and work out what he needs. We also need one of those doorbells that when it's rung, you can see who is there and talk to them from your phone or a monitor in the office. Perhaps as well, some outside cameras that will set off an alarm on your phone and you can see who is there and talk to them," Lynda suggested.

Hailey was writing everything down on her iPad and sending it to Eric's iPad.

"Right, the first bedroom," Hailey said and held her arm out showing them in. The room was painted pale lemon on all the walls, the ceiling was pale yellow, and all the wood was pale yellow gloss to match the ceiling. The door to the shower and toilet worked properly now. Lynda was telling Gabrielle what was wrong with it by telepathy. When they investigated the room, it was pink. As they were about to leave, they noticed the main door was painted bright pink on both sides, with a room number ready to screw back onto the door when the paint had properly dried.

"Just watch the gloss paint on the doors and architrave it may still be wet in places. The heating is on full now, we'll leave it on full for the next few days to help with drying the paint and keeping us warm." Hailey laughed.

"Of course," Lynda replied smiling.

"On to the next bedroom," Hailey said leading the way.

"This door is painted a light blond and inside, different hair colours, there are six in total the ceiling is light blond and all the woodwork a darker shade of gold. The toilet and shower room. a light brown, with light blond ceiling and again a folding door that works properly."

"You've done very well to get two rooms painted and the landing painted as well," John said.

"Oh no, there is more, much more. Lynda what we want now is carpets laid in each of the rooms first. Then the carpet fitters can lay the carpet on the stairs and top three landings and the second-floor landing. Could Margarette organise this as we want someone here tomorrow if possible, measuring the rooms, landings and stairs. It would be good if they could start laying the carpets in the rooms Tuesday."

"That soon? I suppose a couple of rooms will be good to see what they will finally look like," John said, then regretted opening his mouth as Gabrielle nudged him in his side.

They were shown room after room on the top floor, all ninety rooms on the top floor including two storerooms, double the size of a bedroom, for replacement bedding, light bulbs, and other items which could break and need to be replaced. There was also room for the one thousand toilet rolls the girls would get through each month.

When they got to the end of the landing, they looked at the large window, which overlooked the ground to the side of the House and front of the Train Station.

"I think two men here with rifles would be a good place to start protecting us," John said to Alan.

"If you don't mind me saying, there are twenty-five of us who would like to help you with this fight. I'm Trever, in charge of this mob of painters, decorators, carpenters, sparks, plumbers and various other trades."

"Can any of you shoot straight?"

"Oh yes, we were all in a gun club. Sometimes we fired handguns, other times, rifles, machine guns and other sorts of guns. That is why George picked us. We had all been in the gun club for over five years, and we are first class shots. It hurts me to say, we've killed several innocent people from roof tops with telescopic sights. There were also police officers and a lot of Marco Don's men when they first arrived. We were also trained to make and deploy the bombs that would have blown up your shops and other people's shops in the name of George. Thankfully, that will not happen now."

"Why is that?" Gabrielle asked.

"Because all the men involved in that operation are here. Before we left the house, I went to the basement and set up one of the bombs that would have went into your shops. We had all the explosive and two thousand grenades, forty boxes of ammo for our rifles and handguns, all Polish I may add and as I knew what was to happen. I put a thirty-minute delay timer on it, when Benny rang my phone, I knew everyone who was going with you were out and all the girls were on the buses.

"I had previously left four explosive charges next to the biggest safe which held twenty million pounds. Most of that was for his top men and Ken Mattingly. George left orders that we had had to continue with his plan and blow up all your shops in the UK. Then four shops in France, killing all your staff.

"When we returned to the UK and our base, we were to be rounded up and killed by his top men who supported Ken. This would be done by machine guns and hand grenades, with the first ten of us fed to the fish, two at a time. We had to get away if we wanted to live, then you came along, our perfect way out. The top men would think we were all killed in the explosion. That is why we have worked so hard for you."

"Trever would you and some of your men defend the House? It would be nice if we could get ninety of our girls in here out of the way?" Gabrielle asked.

"Yes, I'm sure my men would love the chance to kill a few of his top men," Trever replied.

"Let me know how many rifles and handguns you need, and I'll have them for you by Wednesday. We hope the police can hold the army of Ken's men for a few extra days."

"How many men do the police think he has?" Trever asked.

"A hundred, which shouldn't be too bad to conquer," John sighed, thinking of what they were now up against. "Where are they now?" Gabrielle asked.

"Eighty miles north of Macclesfield."

"Ahh, he has another top-secret base there with around a hundred men who will be paid five thousand pounds a day to fight you in London. As they get lower, there are another two groups of eighty men each who will join the main army, making it nearly five hundred men by the time the men who have been training to join the army."

"Five hundred men, with no police back up," Gabrielle sighed. "I had no idea he still had a lot of money ready for men to be paid," Alan added.

"They won't have that twenty million which was in the big safe. Those bombs I put around bottom of the safe, I set off by remote control when I knew the buyers were there and inside the house as their cars were arriving as we left. The bomb I threw into the other explosives and grenades had a twenty-minute delay so they could get into the house. That twenty million burned, but there was no way to get it out.

"There will still be about eight million in the Macclesfield safe to pay the men. Without it they will not work for him. If they are killed in the battle, the money will go to their wife.

"How much are we paying you and your men?" Gabrielle asked.

"We haven't discussed a payment yet, to still be alive is worth more than a million pounds."

"What if we say?"

"Let's see what they have done first," Lynda butted in.

"Okay, I can't believe you could have done any more," Gabrielle said.

"Let's go down the stairs and be careful of the paint Hailey said as Trever walked quickly down the stairs onto the fifth floor.

"We turn right here. There are again ninety rooms on this floor with two Janitor rooms. We'll start here, as you can see the entire landing has been painted and all the doors both sides. Shall we go in here?" Hailey asked.

They looked inside the first bedroom, finally the last and Hailey called the lift. Soon they entered the fourth floor. It was devoid of workmen as they made their way through all rooms to the next set of stairs and down to the third floor and last of the ninety bedrooms. When they got to the third floor, they were met with five rooms, a hundred feet long, by forty feet wide and ten feet high. These were used for learning to dance, astronomy lectures, and a lot of other after school activities. But all their equipment, table's chairs, CD players had been destroyed with everything else. The back wall was painted matt off white, with a light-yellow tinge to it. The other three walls were painted a light gold. It was the same in the other four rooms, all with a matt off wite and light pink, in matt. With the other walls, a light pink, light yellow in the fifth room, it was pale green, opposite the back wall and the two end walls, a very pale blue.

In the first room Olive, one of the younger women who helped look after the girls while they were in the House taught a few girls to paint small pictures, usually a face, or a man or woman inside an oval or circle with a dark brown outer edge. She also taught them how to prepare a mural and paint one.

She was now painting a mural on the back wall of room five. In room four, Lauren was also painting a mural on the back wall, which both women hoped they would finish tonight, there were still another four hours, even taking an hour out for their evening meal. Margarette had got hold of what was on the menu that evening and getting everyone's order, had phoned the orders across to the restaurant which they would eat in at eight pm. Now it was only six twenty.

On floor one, were three rooms fifty feet long forty foot wide, there used to be a proper cinema, film projector with sloping, rising seats just like a proper cinema. There were three cinemas showing different films. The last of the forty-feet-wide rooms could be used for anything the girls wanted to learn in groups. The two closest rooms were now painted bright red on all the woodwork, pale pink on all the walls and ceiling with spotlights which would light up film photos and what was showing in each cinema. They could also get hot dogs, popcorn, in small medium and large, drinks, cold and hot, with other items to choose from, just like a real cinema. Here the girls could be controlled and looked after, and it was all free.

That's what it was like before the other men came in and trashed it all. Now it was all painted again with dangling spotlights, now disconnected and thrown away, ready for the replacement spotlights that would go up Monday or Tuesday.

Everyone including Lynda were now astonished at what the men had done in this extended day. They didn't think it could get any better but as they took the lift to the ground floor, every room and the entire landing, was cleared of rubbish and the landing was washed and now dry. The ceiling had been painted a pale pink. The walls, pail gold above the wooden handrail that went along both sides of the landing and dark gold below the handrail, which was painted dark brown. Four men were still painting the handrail at the far end of the landing.

The first room they entered, coming out of the lift, was fifteen feet wide and forty foot deep, eight feet tall. This would eventually become the nurses and doctor's room for the hospital, which was next door. The entire room was painted white with white gloss on all the woodwork. The room next door was the main hospital and treatment room. It was a hundred feet long, forty feet deep eight feet high, all painted in white. Most of the light fittings had been smashed, and all the special lights for looking into people's injuries were also smashed to pieces, destroyed, because Ken wanted it done.

The room next door was seventy feet long, forty feet deep eight feet high. At the time of the invasion of George's men, the room had been locked on the outside and inside, thick iron bars stopped the two doors being opened or moved just a small bit.

Margarette had found the keys to the outside locks and the locks to the interconnecting door which gave them access to the room. Then there were locks on the inside of the double doors.

Trever had to remove all the bars holding the doors in place. When they were finally opened, and they found the light switch, there were two other doors which had to be unlocked. Inside the room closest to the outside held one X-ray machine and in the next room, another different type of X-ray machine.

Behind the two X-ray rooms was another room holding a CT scanner. There was plenty of room for a doctor and two nurses to observe the patient and see the results of the CT scan on a large screen. All the results could also be sent to the nearest hospital so a doctor could look at them and see if they would need to operate on the patient.

With the front doors being locked and unmovable, George's men left it alone. They had already had enough fun breaking up the hospital beds and putting all the drugs worth taking into a large bag with all the needles and syringes there were available to them, then they moved on, some men already taking the Ritalin drugs and mixing them with Morphine tablets, then three double shots of whisky getting as high as a kite. It was lucky these expensive items were not damaged.

The rooms opposite were all painted for rest rooms and bedrooms for the staff working all night, or if they wanted to stay there rather than go home.

The only place left to decorate and look at was the basement and kitchen. Walking down the stairs, they entered the basement.

"Surely not here as well?" Gabrielle asked Hailey.

"I'm afraid so, there are still some men working in the kitchen, would you like me to ask them to move?"

"No, we'll just pop our heads in and look around," Lynda said.

"This was and still is the girl's restaurant for breakfast and late-night drinks if the girls want any. I'm afraid all the tables and chairs were smashed to pieces by the men. They also destroyed forty computer stations, and game consoles with a TV to watch the game on. They could have left the games which were on discs, but no, they had to shoot holes in them inside this room with machine guns. As you can see, Oscar their plasterer, has with a little help, skimmed the end wall, which was used for target practice, and filled a couple of holes on the side wall, so the end wall will be ready to paint tomorrow. The ceiling has been painted off pink.

"The far wall to your left, matt light brown, the far end wall, is a slate grey, the wall to your right, a light red outline six inches wide all the way around and a mix of orange and cream, to fill in the rest of the wall. The small holes which were plastered over were dry by the time our men started the job.

"Let's walk down to the kitchen. We were lucky, the main cooker and hob, were too heavy to move and the men couldn't be bothered with it when some of the boy girls started to play up just at the right time. The decorators, ten of them, are in the room getting it all painted and painting all the wood to match the room here. When they've finished painting it, we'll send in ten or more of girls and deep clean the cooker, and all the cupboards on the floor, and attached to the wall at a higher level. We'll clear out any old food cartons and clean out the fridge.

"There is one room left to paint and that's being taken care off as we speak. The room is now empty and has been cleaned. It's the main office which you go to when you enter the building. All the large rooms need the wooden floors polished, by a heavy-duty polisher. We'll find a company that hires them out in the morning then collect two of them if we can and quite a few tins of polish so we can get the big rooms finished tomorrow apart from furniture," Hailey said.

"The sooner the carpets are laid in the bedrooms and landings, the sooner we can build the new furniture which goes in their bedrooms and with their beds made up, we'll be able to have the girls move in here where we can protect them much better," Trever explained.

"Earlier, we were talking about money, for today, would five thousand be, okay? And do you want it in cash or put into your bank accounts?" Gabrielle asked.

"Don't be a cheap-skate my love, double it." Lynda suggested.

"Alright how about ten thousand? In cash or bank accounts?" Gabrielle asked.

"That's better my love, are we paying them daily or what?" Lynda asked, trying to get the wages for the men and women sorted out. Then they could bring that amount of cash with them in the morning. She thought to herself and sent her idea to her wife.

"What do you think Trever? How long will the job take to finish?"

"To know that, will depend on a couple more trades coming in like the carpet fitters, a television service that can give us TV channels and Internet, and the lift engineers. We should also check, the other men didn't get into the two boiler houses and damage anything, especially gas pipes. If I ring them first, they may come out tomorrow and check the gas pipes and boilers. "If you want to pay us daily, we'll discuss it tomorrow night after we have sorted what we can. We'll also need two cars to get around and buy some of the supplies we need."

"Right, I'll pay you all in the morning, so that's ten grand each, for the men, the same for the women and we'll give you and Margarette an extra five grand each for having to sort things out. So that's a hundred and twenty thousand for your wages in the morning. We'll see what you've managed to do by tomorrow night and pay you again the following morning. When we must fight, those with a gun in their hand, will have twelve thousand a day and if we win, there will be a large bonus in cash at least forty thousand each or more. How does that sound?" Gabrielle asked.

"Absolutely brilliant," Trever said. "Lynda, Gabrielle, can you help us bring some of the items we need here?"

"Yes of course, but not between eleven thirty and say two pm.

Ring us if you're unsure," Lynda replied.

"How much will you need?"

"Cash speaks louder than a credit card, they lose a lot of money when we're talking about thousands."

Hailey's phone wrang which she answered. "Hello? Yes, thank you for letting me know. Where are you off to now?" she asked the person on the other end of the phone. "Okay we'll be up soon," Hailey replied.

"There are eight classrooms above us and one outside, opposite the entrance to the main office. Margarette wants to know if you wanted them painted in any special colours?"

"No, what are the classrooms like, there was a lot of expensive equipment in there and in the locked cupboards?" Lynda, replied. "Are you alright my love?" Lynda asked her wife her arm was around Gabrielle's back holding her close to her. She was hoping there was no more of the black stuff inside her.

"Hailey, is there a chair around here Gabrielle can sit on so I can examine her?"

"Not here, but let's take the lift to the ground floor, we'll go to the hospital, we've managed to get hold of twenty chairs and David, our carpenter is building two chairs especially for you, no beds I'm afraid. Oh, Margarette is looking for the keys to the classroom cupboards and she thinks as they are still locked the equipment inside might have survived the attack," Hailey replied as they made their way to the lift.

Soon Lynda's eyes were blazing bright green as they looked into Gabrielle's heart, where the arrow entered her body and across her chest, moving very, slow, she knew how difficult it would be to see the black liquid, even in her green light.

"You're clear, you might just be a little, weak after the operation you had, normally after an operation like that in hospital, you would be, lying in bed for at least a week," Lynda sighed, glad her life was no longer in any danger.

"If you're happy to let Margarette pick out the colours, like she has for all the rooms and landings. I think you should return to the Train Station, give her a hot drink and let her rest for a while, then take her home to bed. It must be getting on now?" Hailey said and looked at her watch. She shook her arm thinking something must be wrong with her watch.

"What is it?" Lynda asked.

"I don't recall the time we started this tour, but it's only six-forty." They all checked their watches and agreed with the time. Hailey's phone rang again. With Margarette giving them good news for a change.

"All the classroom cupboards have been opened and all the equipment in them has survived, it's just a few posters which were on the wall and all the special seats attached to the surround desks, would now have to be ordered."

The kitchen was now finished, so too the large pantry, all the fridges had been cleaned and were now ready for use. Eric had changed the four light bulbs that had been hit with a broom. Sienna had taken the coach with six other girls back to the twenty-four-hour store, which had remained open just for them. They had managed to hand in the long list of items they needed to complete the bedrooms and the morning cereals they would need in the kitchen, along with six eight-piece toasters.

The store had managed to get all the remaining duvets they needed, and another three hundred duvet sets with a thousand white sheets and towel sets.

They had come away with the rest of the duvets while Alister their van driver would load up with everything else they had in stock and on the store floor. He would drop everything off in the lower road which went past the basement double doors which gave access to the kitchen pantry, and further along to another set of doors at the far end of the large room next to the kitchen. Here he would drop off all the other items that were for the bedrooms.

Trever had borrowed a computer from one of the older girls and was now looking for different stores that could help them, which also had an emergency number. He was amazed to discover they were still open this time of night, for emergencies. Well, this was an emergency to get the House ready for the girls before the war started.

Gabrielle and Lynda jumped John and Alan back to the Train Station. As soon as John was there, he got the other bodyguards who were not on watch, to gather all the rifles and load four, twenty clips for each rifle and gun, they also had to attach all the night scopes to the rifles and get them ready for operation.

"Are we expecting trouble?" Gabrielle asked John.

"I've been thinking about what Trever was saying and the urgency to get the house finished. I would have thought the girls would be safe in here, but now I have changed my mind.

"There is one main door in and out. I know there is the door behind the kitchen, but if Ken's men blocked it off, there would be no other escape route. At least in the House, there are a few escape routes and if they can get into the basement, there are places to hide in the room across from the House which has a fireproof and bulletproof door. It will hold at least three hundred girls and a few adults. Once the door is closed and locked, there is no other way in. They would be safe there in the event of an attack on the House."

"Did you get a text message earlier?" Alan asked John. "Something like this?" John replied, then showed the two girls his phone. "Exactly like that," John replied.

"This text message changes things if we are going to be tested tonight. Ken is ready to throw his men away like George did. How many extra rifles did you manage to get Alan?" Gabrielle asked him.

"Eighteen rifles and twenty handguns, we have boxes of ammunition for the rifles and handguns. I think it would be a good idea to take Trever up on his offer of men who can fire a gun or rifle," Alan suggested.

"I agree," said Gabrielle and Lynda together.

"I also agree," John added. "We get all the guns loaded with extra clips as well. Do we have anymore binoculars?"

"Four sets, that's the last of them, but we did have four sets on our first trip to the gun shop and we had ten rifles at the time, with those, top of the range day and night scopes, which Mike and Isaac used earlier," Alan replied.

"Alan, John, we could help if you can spare a handgun each. You have trained us to fire a gun on target, we could at least, cover the back door and if they get inside, kill a few of them at least. But let's hope it doesn't get that far," Simon said.

"Right Simon, get your five handguns from Jenny, when she has finished loading the guns and all the spare clips, you'll have."

"Alan did you get any throwing knives, like the ones you carry?" Megan asked. "There is someone I would like to protect, like Gabrielle likes to protect Lynda. Anyway, I doubt if anyone will get in here, but it would feel good to have a couple of knives in my hands."

"I can throw a knife too," Isabell said.

"For anyone special?" Gabrielle asked. Isabell turned and looked at Gabrielle, ready to answer, but she was already peering into her head, seeing a deep love for the girl of her dreams Sofia. They were both seventeen and she knew how to throw a knife right between the eyes, every time.

"Yes," she said replying to her question,

"It's Sofia," she said aloud, frightened at first, she would be reprimanded for their love for each other.

"Okay," Lynda said aloud gaining everyone's attention. She held Gabrielle's hand so everyone could see they were deeply in love. She couldn't remember the last time they had all been together like this in one room. They were boy girls at that time, learning all about a woman's vagina and the sexual glands around it that help her have an orgasm when the man's penis enters her vagina. Then there was her G Spot, which when played with by a man or their lover, could excite the woman so much, she would have an orgasm.

As they wanted to be a woman, even after they had a sex change, they would not be able to get pregnant, although that may change now. So, they were taught how a woman got pregnant, the first stages and what she would feel when she was first pregnant. There was a lot to go through, and every day, they learned a little more about being a woman.

Now they were all women and living together in one House, so with their hormones all over the place, if they had an infatuation for the boy, or now the woman, they were bound to fall in love, so Gabrielle and Lynda both thought they may as well explore the feelings of being in love with another girl.

"We have seven couples in the fifteen and sixteen age groups, who have come to me today, asking if they could sleep together in the same room. Gabrielle and I have talked about their questions for most of the day by telepathy, I'm afraid, neither of us know how you two girls could sleep together in different rooms. Yes, you can sleep together in one bed in one room, but not two beds in different rooms at the same time. So yes, all those girls who have asked if they could sleep together in one room, the answer is yes.

"Now we have Megan eighteen and Lexi sixteen, but a very, intelligent girl who is also going to university to study pure maths, and astronomy, normal through a refractor telescope through a camera onto a screen and using a Radio Telescope, learning what all the maps mean and the sounds being captured by the radio telescope in our galaxy.

"Luckily for Lexi, Megan is taking the same courses and they both have top scores in all their subjects. So yes, to them, they can sleep together and dream of the planets together.

"Next, we have Isabell and Sofia, both seventeen. Yes, to them too, and good luck and lots of our love to all of you couples.

"Before we start ordering beds and bedroom furniture for you all, are there any other pairs of girls who would like to be acknowledged as a couple and sleep together, in the same bed?" Two sets of hands went up.

"Thank you for telling us Cloe and Jessica, that's fine, you may sleep together, Katie and Zoe, that's okay. Just because we are saying okay to couples now, we do not want anyone under the age of sixteen sleeping together.

"It might seem like a good idea, but the authorities I'm afraid would object to it. Sure, maybe hold hands, even kiss each other, but no sleeping together and remember we have staff now that check on you during the night, so please, we beg you, if you think you're in love with each other, leave sleeping with each other until you are both sixteen. Jessica, Clara, you have both been abused as boys, and raped, see us after this is over, neither of you are sixteen yet," Lynda said and blew them a kiss.

"If anyone or a couple are unsure of what to do, come and talk to us and we'll try to answer your questions.

"Is there anyone else who would like to throw a knife? More than likely, they will never get in here and you have all us Bodyguards, their wife's or husband, in the case of our sister Janet and husband Tom, plus the staff here who will be holding a handgun, to fire ahead of you. But if you would like to have a go with a knife, put your hand in the air. We only have ten knives so that is for five girls. There are three girls left if anyone wants a knife, put your hand in the air now.

Clara put her hand up, a minute later, Summer put her hand up then Violet joined her. "Thank you, girls, come down here and John will give you your knives. Please be careful who you throw them at, some of our people might run in because they are injured, more than likely shot," Lynda said and watched as the girls made their way through the crowd of girls to get their knives.

"We were going to sleep at our apartment tonight, but that has now had to change. The reason we were going to sleep at home, is because Gabrielle was shot in the chest with an arrow this morning when we came to rescue most of you at Ken's house. Gabrielle pulled it straight out at an angle and snapped the arrowhead off so it remained inside her.

"What we didn't know, the arrow tip, was dipped in poison and we still don't know what type of poison it is. That is what was making her so weak and tired this afternoon.

"At our doctor's surgery, she had a couple of X-rays taken so we could see the arrowhead. Then there was this strange black line inside her, and it was going towards her heart. I looked at her insides with my green eyes. I had to make a large incision, to get my hand into her chest to remove the metal tip off the arrow. Then our doctor wanted me to get into Gabrielle's heart to remove the last of the black stuff.

"She rested for a while, but we won't know what the black stuff is until tomorrow.

"Gabrielle has had a major operation, which in normal circumstances, in a hospital, the person would be in bed resting for a week and may not even see and capture the black stuff. We are sure it's all out, but I'm keeping a close eye on her. Our doctor wanted Gabrielle to get a good night's sleep and try to stay calm and motionless throughout the night."

"Excuse me miss," Ivy, the fourteen-year-old girl said.

"Yes Ivy?" Gabrielle asked.

"Does that mean no sex for you both tonight?" Ivy asked smiling.

"Does everyone know about our sex lives and what we do in bed?" Lynda replied.

"Yes Lynda, we all love you both for it and you are not ashamed to show your love for each other. You hold hands all the time, kiss each other a lot and ohhhh those kisses, they are truly magnificent, the way you both move and continue to walk at times.

"I think we should all know how to kiss and make your partner want to kiss you back. You should both take the lesson in the main hall on level two," Ivy suggested.

"That sounds like an excellent lesson, we'll try and discuss it when we have time later tonight," Lynda replied after talking mind to mind with Gabrielle.

"I agree with my wife, how to kiss your partner is an excellent idea for you all, because if you were growing up as normal girls, you would naturally experience that more than likely with boys your own age so when you come to sixteen, seventeen, you know what is expected from you as a response to a kiss from a boy or girl your own age, more than likely in the cinema, in the back seats," Gabrielle said making everyone in the room laugh.

"Gabrielle, you really should get a good night's sleep if that is what your doctor suggested. You should have gone straight home," Samantha said.

"Yes, I would have done so, but John and Alan had a text message while we were looking around the House. Apparently, Ken is going to send a force of fifty to a hundred men here tonight to test us. See how we react and how many men we kill later this evening. How close they will get to us in the Train Station, and try to get into the House again,"

Gabrielle told everyone. She had to sit down, it was getting hard to stand for long intervals, she was now worried if there was some of the black stuff inside her.

"It's alright my love, I'll examine you again, your doctor is still on call if we need her tonight. Can I have a blanket and pillow please?" Lynda asked.

Hands holding pillows and blankets came from everywhere. Sarah took a blanket from Nancy and a pillow from Esme. She put the blanket over two tables and the pillow at the head of it.

"John, could you lift Gabrielle onto the table please without ruffling the blanket?" Lynda asked.

A moment later Gabrielle was laying on her back on the two tables with her blouse undone and open over her chest. Lynda had moved her bra up over her breasts so she could see her heart. Sarah was at the top opposite Lynda and Jenny was at Gabrielle's legs in case she started to move or fall off the tables.

"John, Alan, get all the rifles, guns and ammunician together which is going to the House. I'll drop it all over when I've finished with Gabrielle. Simon, Samantha and girls who have helped you here, could you get the girls and our bodyguards a sandwich, piece of cake and a hot drink please, we may not have the time to eat or drink later."

People started to move about helping Simon in the kitchen and putting out tables so the girls could form a line and take a plate from the tables, then go to sit at another table with their friends or lovers.

Lynda's eyes turned bright green and moved over Gabrielle's chest. They couldn't see anything wrong further down her body and there was no reason for her to need to either sit or lay down. As she moved her eyes slowly up her body, she got to the entry place of the arrowhead. She placed her hot left hand over the entry point of the arrow. There was nothing, then she had a thought and quickly moved to the right side of Gabrielle's chest.

Sarah didn't know what she was looking for, then Lynda started to speak very, fast in a strange language. Lynda's eyes grew bright green. Most of the girls had never seen either of the girls make their green eyes glow this bright.

The light was now inside Gabrielle's body, searching for it, while Lynda was calling to it, asking her soul to show itself to her so she could examine it. Then Gabrielle's soul came out from its hiding place behind Gabrielle's right chest bones and the gallbladder, liver and part of the pancreas. Sarah could see it now, pink in colour, slowly moving up through the organs that lived in its path.

It was oval in shape about two inches long, holding everything she had seen and pain she had felt throughout her life. It was normally quite warm but as she called it close to the surface just below her right breast. Gabrielle was not dead, just as cold as her soul. Death had been playing his games with her again.

When her soul was closer to her, she called Death, who answered her instantly. "Hello Lynda, would you like to speak to Me for a few minutes of your time?"

"Do I have a choice?"

"No, I'm afraid not."

"Sarah, Gabrielle, I have to go and speak to Death for a couple of minutes our time," Lynda informed them as fast as she could. Her motionless body fell forwards on top of Gabrielle's naked chest.

"Jenny, get another chair and push it into her body, so if she falls or slips from Gabrielle's body, she will just sit in the chair," Sarah ordered.

Jenny did as she was told, then returned to her place, holding Gabrielle's legs in case she tried to move and fall off the two tables.

John could wait no longer, he found some rope, bundled the rifles up together and looked at Alan. "You take all the handguns and two bags of spare bullets. Tina, you take the two bags of binoculars, Isaac, you take the last of the bullets. Simon, do we have any cash here?"

"Yes, about a million." "How many bags to put it all in?"

"How it's bound up, and in high denominations, I would say six bags minimum.

"Let's be safe and say eight bags."

"Right, get it into the bags."

"Grace, Anabelle, can you help Simon with the money please, make sure you can carry at least two bags each so don't overload them. Put it all into eight bags let's see what that goes like. Lexie, Isabell, go in and help with the money please."

Twenty minutes later they had safely made it across the snow-covered path to the House. Trever was downstairs to meet them.

"Trever here are the gun clips and spare bullets for your men. Your forward payments are in the bags, so are your wages for today. Ken's men are going to try and test us to see what we are fighting like. He is sending between fifty and a hundred men against us tonight. You also have binoculars; as soon as you see his men, open fire and if your men can do it, kill them, I'm afraid we have no option. Has anyone gone out yet?" John asked Trever.

"Yes, Margarette left with Sylvia to get the carpets sorted they have all the sizes they need, and they are hoping to get Lynda or Gabrielle to help them later in the evening."

"Right now, Lynda is talking with Death and Gabrielle is on her back with Lynda leaning over her, Dead, for the duration she is talking with Death, I just hope she knows what she's doing. Anyone else leaving?"

"Eric is just waiting for some cash then he will go and get all the lights and cable he needs with Luke and Scarlett to help decide about some of the lighting.

"David is ready to leave with Daniel to buy all the furniture and order all the beds," Trever said.

"The number of double beds has changed we will need another five double beds. We want all the rooms ready for occupation. Is anyone else going out?"

"Samuel is ready to leave with Leo to see if they can hire an industrial floor polisher with the polish for the floors in the large rooms. They just need the money then they can go."

"For now, give everyone who needs it, money from these sacks and I'll replace it tomorrow."

"If they need help, they will have to ring me, if we are under attack, could you warn them before they come into the premises, we will get no help from the police. There again they won't interfere with the battle, this is still under our agreement with the Queen and Prime Minister to remove and kill, if needed, the rest of Ken's army so London and the rest of the UK can live normally again."

"I didn't realise it had got this bad."

"Oh, it's a lot worse than that, all the special gifts to Queen and all their old vases which are very valuable all the gold in the bank of England has all been packed up and taken by aircraft to Australia. The next in line to the Throne with all his family are now in Australia on a tour that will last as long as this war we are fighting.

"Every other Royal and their families are out of the country visiting other countries affiliated to our country. Buckingham Palace is surrounded by the army with tanks and rocket launchers. There are three helicopter gunships in the back garden ready to evacuate the Queen and the rest of her staff, of which there are only four women. Should there be an all-out war here we cannot win or control, the army are already surrounding London with tanks, missile launchers and all the army personnel are issued with machine guns with more clips than we have. They have orders to kill anyone who may try and get out of London.

When there is no hope, and we confirm it to the police. They will start to move all their officers out of London, their families have now been transported down south. All stores have been ordered to remain open and help us with whatever we need. Right now, another hundred rifles, bullets, a hundred handguns with bullets and extra clips, are on their way. The van will drop off forty rifles and eighty handguns to you, and the rest of the rifles and handguns come to us."

"Wow I didn't know so much depended on us," Trever sighed.

"Is there any more bad news? It might help my men and the women here fight."

"Right now, there are two nuclear submarines and eight Royal Navy fast attack ships about twenty miles off our coast in the North Sea. Upon our word, that we cannot stop the invasion of Ken's men because he has so many. The submarine Captain's will arm four of their nuclear rockets to wipe London from the face of the Earth.

"They will not stop firing their nuclear rockets. The Air Force will fire their rockets at it and fire on anyone they see running from the destruction. Each base they know for sure has been used by Ken's men or are still using it will be destroyed by two nuclear bombs. Any ships no matter how small will be hit with gunfire and rockets from our fighter aircraft and heavy bombers from France will demolish any port they see being used to get people on ships.

"This is the only way they can see to save the country from

Ken's men and women, if we can't do our job, the Queen and our Government are willing to sacrifice our country. They will obliterate it with our own missiles."

Trevor could see John was getting upset as he told Trever what would happen to the country if they failed. John, Alan, Gabrielle and Lynda would stay almost to the end, retreating to the House. For any final showdown, in a last hope something or someone would help them, the very fact now that Lynda was talking with Death, was a hope she might be able to talk a higher Entity into helping us, not destroying this beautiful country for the want of drugs and reprisals."

"If we are going to destroy this country, why is it so important to get this House back to as it was, even better now as we have opened the lift shaft and new lighting will be put up over most of the house, with new beds, bedding, and bedroom furniture. Gabrielle and Lynda have made all the boy girls, real girls and young women. The houses behind us are being worked on just as hard as we have done here. Children aged fourteen to eighteen are coming here and waiting in the coaches by the houses next door."

"The reason we want the House refurbished so fast, is because it is getting close to the time we have to leave. New Caretaker's will live here and at Gabrielle and Lynda's apartment.

"The last fallback option we have lies below us, one mile directly beneath this House, is a Train which is waiting for all the girls, women and men working here and everyone in the Train Station."

There was a slight tap on the floor behind them. John and Alan turned around seeing Gabrielle, looking much better in herself and

Lynda, without the worried look on her face that she had before.

"Hello boys," Gabrielle said. smiling at them holding Lynda's hand with all the love in her body. John turned, hugging Gabrielle and Alan did the same with Lynda only more careful.

"Are you alright? Are you healed now?" John asked Gabrielle.

"It seems so, Lynda will explain it all later. For now, let's complete this story so Trever and the others standing here, can fully understand what we are fighting for what they will get out of it if they so wish.

"Nobody will be forcing anyone to fight, some people just can't when the time comes, to kill people who may have been their friends," Gabrielle said.

"Everything John has said is right up to now, we'll just finish it off. There are four lifts in the basement under this House. The lifts hold five hundred people each. All the new girls will be taken to the basement and put into the first lift, then you Trever and all your men and women who have also worked extremely hard on this House and any of your crew who want to join us will enter the next lift. Those Boy Girls who are outside waiting on two buses, with their caring women, will come in and get into the third lift with anyone else who has changed their mind and want to join us.

"Once the lifts reach their ground floor. We will get out of the lifts and onto the train. It has two engines, one at the front one at the back. Four very bright red lights on the top of this House, the house next door and on top of our Train Station, will come on as the last coach passes our Train Station. We will then travel to the Channel Tunnel and head down to Paris where there is another Train Station like ours. We will stop there for a while, giving Gabrielle and myself a chance to talk with Sophia and Elisha.

During this time, everyone coming with us and the TG's will board the train. When we board the Train, we will be off.

"We will travel to Train Station Three in Rome and pause there while the TG's, their carer's and four surgeon's board our train. Then we will be off again to New York.

"When we get to New York, we will pick up the other TG's and their Carers. Then we'll travel on to Cape Canaveral Texas, pick up more TG's and their Carer's, then onto our final stop, Australia.

"By now, there will be nothing left of England, Wales and Scotland. Once a cancer takes over a body you must cut it all out. That is what we are doing, cutting off the head of the organisation, burning all its money.

"You will be citizens without a country, and you'll need a new Passport which the Australian government, now under the Queen, will make for us.

"We will arrive at Train Station Six. Janet and Tom's sheep farm, one thousand square miles of land to the East of what was once a little town but now is a large Metropolitan City, Alice Springs. There we will start our new lives, until it is time to leave permanently," Gabrielle explained.

"All this destruction and killing we can stop, if we can stop Ken's men getting a foot inside London.

"Gabrielle and I think Ken will send a hundred men at us tonight, just as we are getting tired and want to get to bed, around eleven o'clock. The police are already putting up roadblocks and putting a ring of cars around the outside of our premises, keeping us in and the public out.

"They have given us ten of their blue flashing police lights. They just stick to your car roof," Lynda added.

"Lynda does that mean I can get a laptop and iPad for making notes of how it's working here, jobs they have completed etc?" Trever asked.

"Yes, when were you thinking of going out?" Gabrielle asked. "Tomorrow morning, very early, maybe six am."

"I'll have Alice, seventeen who wants to be a secretary, find the phone number of the shops you'll be visiting around six to tell them to expect you. Take two people with you and I'll send one of our eighteen-year-old girls over to take with you, she will be looking for things we need, and she'll have a list with her."

"I had better get these guns sorted for now, before the van comes with the extra guns and I need to get my men organised to defend this place. We'll do our damndest to not let anyone get in the House or Train Station. Train Station, I get it now, what a brilliant idea," he said laughing then looked out of the door.

"The red lights are on, on top of the Train Station, no doubt on the top of this House too. It's a brilliant idea, whoever thought that up?" Trever said smiling.

"Actually; I did when we first thought of the idea, and I'll tell you all about that another time. Oh look, here comes the van with the extra guns. You take all the binoculars as well I would get a few of the woman behind your men refilling their clips. Most of them know how to do that. We'll let you get on."

The girls and bodyguards turned and left with Gabrielle and Lynda close behind them. As the two men started to unload the rifles handguns and bullets.

"It looks like you are preparing for a war," One of the men said as he carried ten boxes with rifles inside with their telescopic laser sights already fitted and lined up for shooting accurately.

"I suppose you could say that," Trever replied taking the first batch of guns and handing them to Karl, to start handing out to those men who had volunteered to help in the fight. Trever looked at the man returning with another ten boxes of rifles.

"Excuse me for asking, do you have a wife or are you living with your parents still?"

"I'm married with my own house and a heavy mortgage, hence my working long hours. We have just had another baby, we already have a boy aged three, now we have a girl aged two months."

"Wow, a nice little family you have there," Trever replied, thinking a little harder at what was at stake. If they failed, he and his family would be wiped off the face of the Earth in a few seconds. There will be thousands of families like his in London alone, innocent and unaware of what is going on what they were fighting for.

Trever realised then what Gabrielle must have felt like when she faced George with her wife by her side, then having to fight his sword once more and stand before Death, while her wife tried desperately to return her soul to her body. She too had faced Death and Fate to save her wife and every soul on Earth. They were not fighting for souls now, but real people, their families and children, especially the children.

"Before you leave, do you mind jotting your name and address on the iPad please?" Trever asked him.

"Sure, you need it for something? It's Gary, by the way."

"It's a pleasure to meet you, Garry. I'm Trever, once you've finished your deliveries, you should go home pack a bag and get out of London tonight."

"Fine, I'll do that," he replied.

"Hang on a moment," Trever put his hand into one of the sacks of money. He pulled out a bundle of cash and handed it to Garry, who put the loose money into his Jacket inner pockets and realised he would have to split it. He took some of the loose cash out of his pocket and put it into his back-jean pocket.

"Elinor, could you get me a plastic bag please, the ones we have been getting from the shop." They both waited in silence as men came down the stairs, took a box with a rifle in and one handgun each which was placed inside of the back of their jeans. Looking at the open boxes of ammunician they took ten clips for each gun, then shoved as many spare bullets into their front painter's pocket as they could.

"We'll both take the top window looking out at the Train Station," Craig said for Josh.

"That's fine take a pair of binoculars as well," Trever suggested. Craig took the box, and they were both gone with another pair of men ready to take their place.

"Here you are Trever, do you want me to hold it for you?"

"Yes Elinor, go on then. Men help yourselves to a rifle and handgun each take the clips you were told about and put as many spare bullets as you can into your front pocket. Sorry about that." Trever turned and took two wrapped packets of fifty-pound notes out of one of the sacks and placed them into the bag Elinor was holding open. She shook the bag expecting more money.

"Don't be a skinflint Trever, what good will it do for us if we don't make it?" Elinor said in a loud voice. She looked out at the bright lights on top of the Train Station. Hurry up, time is running on she said looking at her watch. It had only been one minute since she last looked at her watch. It was six thirty then, it was six thirty-one now. She thought time was going backwards again, waiting for certain jobs to be done or started and completed.

Elinor brought a second large bag out of her pocket. "Fill it so he can leave here," Elinor ordered.

Trever started to put wrapped bundles of fifty-pound notes into the bag. It was almost full when Elinor shook it and the money went further down into the bag, allowing another twenty-five thousand to get in the second bag.

"Gary take these two bags with our pleasure."

"But there must be over thirty-grand here," he replied.

"Gary, you and your family, even your babies, must wear these badges at all times, here is your TG Pass something like a credit card. Put it into any cash machine, it will tell you what to do next.

If you press two, that is for emergency cash. It will give you two thousand pounds. Don't forget your card, your pin is three zero's one. Ours is Train Station number one. Now off you go don't let anyone else see your money, get out of London as fast as you can, tonight. Don't pass this information on."

"Thank you," he replied took the plastic cards and shoved them into the front of his black trousers put the bags of money into the car and was gone, driving to the other side of the road.

Eric had already left with Luke and Scarlett in a four-by-four truck which had been parked outside the main doors.

Oscar and Zack had taken another four by four with a police light on the roof, to get the floor polishers. While Isabell, Sofia and Theodore, went to the main camera store in another four-by-four van. Lily, Eva, Gladys their tutor, and Christopher their driver and bodyguard had a four-by-four estate car as snow was now falling very, hard. They had to go to the school's art shop to replace everything that was damaged. They would then travel to the school's Deaf shop and pick up more posters and films for learning sign language.

When Gabrielle and Lynda returned to the Train Station, they looked up and there were four tall bright red lights which hadn't been switched on like this since the time they were installed. The tall green lights were raised to the same height as the red lights. Both girls prayed to Death the Green lights would not be switched on. Right now, at every Train Station, both sets of lights were showing above the four corners of each building with the red lights switched on.

At Train Station Five. The red and green lights were raised on top of the Train Station and the House close to it. The last few TGs were now being changed into real girls by Sophia and Amelia Kendrick, another wife and wife, both healers and could also carry out the change of sex.

Upon entering their own Train Station five girls were on their phones giving orders to women in the shops they had sent their people to.

Gary was now parking his van next to the doors of the Train Station. He didn't ask what the lights meant as he carried more rifles into the Train Station, As he carried the last of the rifles into the room, he could see concern on all the girls faces and there were already two men with binoculars, rifles and handguns at either end of the long windows of the left-hand side.

Gary would usually stop for a chat, but here and now, these people were not ready for light talking, they were getting ready to fight something they didn't really wish to fight. He dropped off the last of the bullets then got into his van. John approached the front passenger door. He opened it and a confused Gary looked at him as he pushed two sealed black Bags into the front of his van. Alan handed him two more sealed black bags with baby, new nappies wrote on a white label. Then he noticed two more white labels with three-month old nappies on it.

"It's just in case anyone checks your bags. Do you have far to go?" John asked.

"About ten miles. The Lord Mayor doesn't like the thought of too many guns of different makes inside the capital and we have over a ton of gunpowder for making the bullets."

"Quite so. Here is a special pass that will get you through any roadblocks the police put up. You can use the pass in your private car as well. Now, get this van back as fast as you can, get your car filled with these bags asap. Fill your car with petrol on the way home and get out of London within the next hour. It is important you fill your car with petrol, all petrol stations are closing at eight pm," John explained.

"Thanks for everything. I hope we see each other again and good luck here with the battle," Gary said, closed the van doors and drove out of their complex returning to his base, then going home to his wife and children.

They had an aunt and uncle who lived in Dorset. On his way home he phoned them asking if they could stay for a week or two, they just needed to get away from London for a couple of weeks, just until things settled down in London. With an affirmative answer, he called his wife telling her to start packing the cases and bags.

He saw a garage still open, stopped and filled his car to the brim with petrol. He took a fifty-pound note from his back pocket to pay for the petrol. The man looked at it suspiciously. Garry took another fifty-pound note from his back pocket. Again, he looked at Garry and the money.

"Come on all garages are closing at eight tonight."

"How do you know that it's Top Secret?"

"I know a lot of other things which are Top Secret. Here look at this." Garry said and pulled out the TG card from his front pocket. He felt foolish as he showed it to the man standing before him. He looked at it and gasped.

"Why didn't you show me this before? You're working with the Knights of the Realm. This is your ID card, show it first wherever you shop, it's all free to you people."

"Thanks, I'll be off then."

"What about your money?"

"Keep it."

When he got home his wife had already packed her suitcase and the baby's bags. His case was still on the bed.

"Why haven't you packed my case and where are the babies?"

"Still asleep in bed. What is all this get ready to leave now, business about? What if I don't want to go?"

"Jackey, I love you with all my heart, I would never hurt you or the children. This is for our safety. I'm working for other people now," he had no idea what was written on the ID card, which he handed to his wife.

"Oh Gary, why didn't you say you're working for the Knights of the Realm. That changes everything. I'll get the cases packed, I'll get your case packed first, then the kids."

"Great!" He started to pack the car and put the nappy bags into the boot with the smaller bags of money which Trever had given him, he put under the back seats.

Jackey came to the front door with the two babies. Gary took one and put her into her car seat, then the other going to the other side of the car, putting their son into his car seat. He wondered where his case was and walked to the front door.

"Have you done my case?"

"Yes, it's upstairs, but look at who was standing behind you."
"Okay. Get my case, put it behind your seat and get in the car. Shut your door and we'll be off as soon as we can."

She ran upstairs, to get the case. The back door was locked and bolted. As she returned outside, she double locked their front door and activated the burglar alarm.

"Tom, can I help you at all?"

"As I'm your street warden, I noticed you came home early, and I would like to know why?"

Gary pulled the ID card out of his trouser pocket and showed it to him.

"Crikey Gary, why didn't you say you're working with the Knights of the Realm."

"Because we don't have the time, we need to get out of here."

"Where are you going at this time of night in the snow? It's snowing harder now everywhere and who's this chap coming up her in a brand new four by four? I'll stop him and ask him what he's doing in our road?"

The man driving the vehicle stopped alongside Gary's car. Isaac got out of the vehicle and walked over to Gary smiling. Jackey was looking worried as the man opened his jacket, she saw he had a gun.

"Gary, I'm Isaac from the Train Station, we were discussing your case just as you left," he said with a strong Australian accent.

"Hello Isaac," Gary replied.

"Gabrielle and Lynda just wanted to make sure everything is alright with you. Can we test it?" He asked in French, then they discussed the weather in Spanish and Italian. They were talking fast in nine different languages.

"That's great, I can tell the girls it worked fine. Now, get the children into your new car. It's all insured in your name and Jackey's. Get your children into the back of the four by four, I'll load your cases and bags of very, expensive nappies. Before we do that, I need a word with you. Let's go around to the other side of the car.

"Repeat these words after me," Isaac said in Latin and started to speak in Latin again. Gary was following him word for word. When Isaac stopped talking, he pinned a gold badge on his top jacket pocket. "You are now officially a Knight of the Realm of the British Empire."

They stood to attention and saluted each other. Jackey will get her badge later tomorrow if we are still here."

Soon the babies were back in their car seats fast asleep. The bags had been changed to the four by four as too all the money. Jackey was getting the last bits and her handbag from the car as Gary was again talking to Isaac across the inside of the car putting a belt around his waist with a hip gun holster attached to it. Isaac finally handed him his Glock, which Gary put straight into his holster with his gun and firearms certificate, so he was licenced to kill.

"You'll need this leather bag your Glock has a full clip in it and there are twenty more full clips in the bag with two hundred spare bullets. If you need any more bullets, put your card into any bank machine and press triple zero one, you will then have a number of options, press the number for spare bullets and it will tell you where to get them. They will all be free to you, show them your TG card first.

"I'll say goodbye to Jackey then you can leave, I'll take care of that idiot. Now, where is she? Jackey, there you are," Isaac said and walked slowly up to her and held her head gently in his hands and kissed her on her forehead. He held his kiss and her head still in his hands for a full minute as he passed different languages into her mind and finally sine language which could get her out of trouble at times. He moved from her head, said goodbye in French, which she automatically replied to in French shook his hand and got into their new four by four.

"Sir Isaac, you'll need these," Gary shouted and threw his car keys to him. He caught them with no trouble, got into Gary's old car, started it up, then drove off not bothering to speak to Tom who was shouting at him to stop in the name of the law."

Before Tom could do anything else both cars were gone and a big snowball hit him on the back of his head, then two more hit his back. He went indoors, cursing himself for not knowing what was in the black bags.

As soon as Isaac returned to the Train Station, he unpacked the last rifle handed Amy ten clips so she could fill them. Tables were now being positioned by every window so the bodyguards could shoot above those who were at the bottom small window, which was usually opened in the summer.

Lynda's phone rang then Gabrielle's. They spoke to the person at the other end and disappeared after kissing each other first.

Lynda was at the carpet shop with Margarette who told her where to drop the rolled-up carpets to. She was back and forth several times, dropping slightly over sized carpets to every other ten rooms on the top floor then the same again on the fifth, fourth, third, second and ground floor. The small pieces of bathroom flooring were taken next, two bundles of forty-five each for the top three floors. The ground floor for the odd rooms and hospital toilets. The main office had its piece of carpet dropped off. Next was the long piece of landing and stair carpets. Once all the carpets were dropped off, she dropped everything else the carpet layers would need to fit the carpets on the fourth floor.

At one point, Gabrielle met Lynda on the fourth floor as Gabrielle dropped off the number of fluorescent fittings, they would need on each of the six floors and basement. They managed to stop for a long kiss, then they were off again, dropping items off to the bedrooms.

When Lynda finished delivering the carpet and associated equipment, she jumped back to the Train Station, where her phone rang again. This time she was off to the flat pack store. Lynda delivered one hundred and fifty-five double wardrobes to the House. They were taken to the top three floors and put where they were needed. The other double wardrobes would come from the Train Station, already made up. When that would be nobody knew. She next delivered the two hundred and thirty-six chest of draws, the remainder coming from the Train Station to each end of the landings. Next were two hundred and ninety dressing tables, three hundred high backed chairs, stored in the basement for now. Finally, for the bedrooms, five hundred and eighty bedside tables, the flat packs stored in the basement. All the tables and benches for morning breakfasts were also stored in the basement. A large oak desk, three tables a comfy chair for the desk and two leather reclining chairs for the other side, two high-backed chairs for secretaries to sit at the tables around the wall, were placed outside the main office.

Outside the House Kitchen were four double, wall cupboards in flat pack and five floor cupboards. On every floor two green First Aid cabinets, yet to be filled. In the Basement two more First Aid Cabinets.

Andy had already fitted the curtain rails wherever they had to go. He then started on the First Aid boxes. Next, he was in the Nurses room, at the far end of the hospital ward. He secured all the equipment they would need on the walls and unwrapped the special tables and chairs.

Then he was on the move again, he would be back once the carpet fitters had laid the special nonslip flooring for the ward and nurse's room. They would have to move the tables and chairs for now. He was doing all the little jobs that needed doing on every floor.

The carpet fitters had finished in the first two bedrooms, which meant the carpenters could start on the wardrobes for the top floor. When the men looked at their watches, it was twenty to six, time was moving slowly again. Their Stanley knives were cutting open the cardboard boxes. Removing the pieces of wood and building the two door wardrobes. Some wardrobes had two mirrored doors, so they had to swap with other wardrobes that had no mirrored doors. Audrey and Michelle helped dispose of the rubbish, and as the next two rooms became available. They put a box in each room on top of the carpets which looked adorable. They unpacked the wardrobe pieces and once again disposed of the rubbish.

Four more Electricians arrived and were put to work on the outside automatic lights, to show up people getting close to the House. On either end of the House. They also had to fix the doorbell camera and other cameras that were now ready to put at each end of the House, so the person in the office could speak to people on her phone or from the office outside large monitor.

A team of fire alarm specialists were already getting cables through walls, upstairs and along the landing to the alarm bells and fire alarm pushes. At the same time, they were putting in cables for the warning alarms, a high-pitched warble, that told everyone there were intruders in the House.

Andy was on watch on the top floor with the end window open, a thick coat on, and a pair of gloves that wouldn't hinder him firing his rifle. At his side was a powerful pair of night vision binoculars, but now he was scouring the area beside the TG House and The Train Station with his rifle's night-time telescopic sight. In the bottom of the rifle was a twenty-round clip of ammunician, with another ten clips in his righthand jacket pocket.

When the electricians who were working outside completed their work, they switched the lights on which lit up the entire area of the land to the left of the TG House. At the same time with the bright lights on, nobody could see in very well.

The electricians then went to the basement to complete the work there. John took a pair of night-time binoculars and looked around the outside perimeter. Seeing it was all clear, he handed the binoculars back to Tina who was on watch by the main doors to the Train Station.

He walked up to Gabrielle and Lynda who were talking to Simon. "I think we could take a quick tour of the TG House. There seems to be nobody near us now. Andy is on watch at the top window overlooking us, he should see them first and hopefully open fire."

"John what do you mean by we could take a quick tour?" Gabrielle asked holding Lynda's hand firmly in hers.

"Jenny come here please, oh and bring my other jacket, there is something in the pocket I need."

"Sarah, can you do the same please?" Alan asked his wife. When both women reached their men, they were not sure what it meant. Both men held their wife and gave them a very loving hug. Both men removed their bulletproof jacket's and put them onto their wife then put on their other jackets, that would keep them warm in the air outside.

John smiled at Jenny and gave her a kiss as his hands secured the bulletproof jacket up to her neck. Alan was doing the same to Sarah, but Sarah knew what this was for.

Sarah had been with the family since she had been picked, it seemed as if it were over a thousand years ago, but time flies and can be different in different dimensions and places, everyone seemed to accept that now, enough books had been written on the subject. She would not neglect her duties now.

She fell into her husband's open arms and kissed his lips, as if it were for the last time but she prayed to Death He would not take either of the girls, especially Gabrielle who she still loved now. How could a thousand years of love stop just because she was not The One? The One who would help Gabrielle into the future and save The One's life, not once but three times. Now she would save her for the fourth time as it had been foretold by the old ones who had followed them throughout time.

John looked into his wife's eyes, "We have just got to take a quick jump and look over the House and see how close it is to completion. You won't understand why, but perhaps Sarah can fill in a few blanks while we're gone. We'll only be over there in the House and all being well, we'll be back, but we must see over the House. I don't think the next battle will start just yet, the men must get here first, and they are still a long way off. But I don't wish you to get hurt. If the firing starts before we get back, stand with your back against the window."

They kissed, long and hard, then he looked into her eyes as if he were a stranger to her, but in her mind, she knew she had loved him through two lifelines, and came through Hell and high water together. She cried as they parted, her hands clinging to his normal jacket, then looked down to his Glock, which appeared to be different for some reason, but she couldn't put her finger on it.

Sarah stepped forward to Gabrielle. Tears were streaming down her face as she looked at the woman she had loved for an eternity. Her heart was aching as she put her hands onto Gabrielle's shoulders. She pulled her closer to her and their faces touched. Sarah kissed her lips, still crying, while Gabrielle and Lynda spoke to each other and held hands. Their single kiss has turned into a romantic kiss, with love and trust between each other.

"I should come with you," she said crying, and hugged her neck as lovers do before a battle.

"Not this time my love, there are the girls to care for and you know what to do if this goes wrong. Get the girls to the House, it will protect them better than they are protected here. We must get things ready for an evacuation. John is a good shot so too Alan, and John has been protecting me for eons, okay, once he was in the wrong place at the wrong time and I paid the price to protect The One. We will be back soon, but it will take the both of us to get everything set up."

They kissed once again then Sarah held Lynda to her chest, their breasts touched and pressed together, both girls were crying, they had shared the love of one woman. To the ultimate possible end, which would once again depend on their bodyguards. Lynda and Sarah kissed, lips rotating about each other, tears streaming down both their faces then they parted, Lynda had to do her duty with her wife.

Gabrielle took John's hand and Lynda took Alan's hand in hers. Gabrielle looked at her watch and turned the hands on its face. "It's now six thirty, so we have a little extra time. We should be finished and back here before seven, as time is here." Gabrielle looked at her wife and they spoke mind to mind then with John and Alan, disappeared from the Train Station.

They appeared half a second later, on the top floor of the House.

"John, Alan, we will start on this floor and work our way down. Lynda, do you remember what we have to do?"

"Yes my love, how could I forget? It's been inside my head for a hundred lifetimes, while you have waited for little old me," Lynda replied and kissed her wife, who she had known much longer than age would tell.

They turned with John entering the first room while Alan stood guard outside. Gabrielle placed her hand on the right side of the doorframe and Lynda placed her left hand onto the left doorframe as Alan waited outside the room.

The doorframe illuminated bright red and stayed alight as they moved, room after room along the top corridor. At the same time, they were inspecting the inside of the bedrooms, seeing how far the men had got to finishing the rooms, ready to put the beds in. Trever ran up the stairs on hearing Gabrielle and Lynda were in the House. He ran up over the stair carpet that had just been fitted before they arrived and ran along the top floor landing carpet in time to see Gabrielle and Lynda place both their hands on the wall either side of the window that Andy was stood guard at, looking out of the window through his night site scope of the rifle he was holding. As they removed their hands, a woman's voice filled the House.

"All top rooms are now activated and await their recipients. The top floor is now secure. Thankyou Gabrielle thank you Lynda."

"Did I just hear a female voice talk as if it's inside the House?" Trever asked.

"Yes, Louise is the House. Now, we have a few problems, none of the rooms up here are ready for the beds. I need this House ready to protect our girls and all the rooms must be finished to accomplish this," Lynda said holding Gabrielle's hand.

"It's six fifty, I thought we had done exceptionally well. But it's the time it takes to build these things. He looked at his watch, it must be somewhere near seven," he said and looked at his watch again.

"It was seven pm a minute ago,"

"Well now it's six thirty, which will give you a little more time. So, can you please get the top rooms ready for their beds?"

"Where is that Bitch Gabrielle, where is she?" a voice bellowed from the bottom of the stairs. The carpet layer was unaware of the commotion that was about to happen and continued with his job.

"Come out Gabrielle we know you're here, where are you?" the man shouted again.

Two more men shouted up the stairs, "Where's that slut Lynda, she's worth a lot of money as well. Come out Lynda, don't be shy, you must be used to men screwing you by now," one of the men shouted and laughed.

"Move out of the way," Lynda shouted at Trever then stepped closer to her wife. "Alan, John, shoot to kill," Gabrielle ordered. Gabrielle stood behind John, and Lynda stood behind Alan.

"Fire as soon as your ready boys," Gabrielle ordered softly into

John's ear.

There was no sound of thunder now, but electric blue light flashed, lit up the stairway for five seconds as both guns fired and hit the four men who had been coming up the stairs. After they holstered their guns, Lynda looked over to Trever who was wondering what in the Hell just happened.

"Trever, please get your men moving and get the top landing ready for the beds which are on their way," Gabrielle said and forced her words I nto his head.

"I understand, I'll get four teams onto it immediately," he replied then walked past them looking for bodies on the stair. There was nothing, not even a stain of blood and the carpet fitter had just finished at the bottom of the stairs. He had moved onto the hospital area and started putting the vinyl flooring down. Another carpet fitter had started in the nurse's station with another man.

Gabrielle and Lynda had started securing the bedrooms on the fifth floor. At the end of the landing, they placed both their hands on the last doorframe on that floor, it lit up in mauve light and they heard the next interlock click into place.

"This is the House, the fifth floor has now been activated, I am just awaiting the girls. My sensors have detected ten men in the House, who should not be here, they are on the ground and second floor, alert the gunslingers," Louise shouted throughout the House.

"We are on the fifth floor and all these doors have been activated. Shut yourselves in, stay here and do not move from here, if more intruders come, activate the door and Louise will protect you both."

He put his hands onto Gabrielle's shoulders and reversed her into the bedroom which was completed but for a bed. Alan was doing the same with Lynda as neither girl wanted to leave their gunslinger's side.

"For luck," Gabrielle and Lynda said together and kissed their gunslinger on his lips. The girls moved back into the room and closed the door.

John and Alan looked at each other and smiling drew their guns and pressed the button on the side of the gun to activate it. They descended the stairs by the lift to the second floor where there was a lot of shouting and calling of names. Five men fired their guns as workmen peeked out of the room, they were working in to see what was happening and who was shooting.

John took the lead position by the corner of the first floor of the second landing. Alan was at his side and about to run across the landing and down to the ground floor. Shots were being fired along the corridor towards John and Alan. As soon as the next shot was fired, John pushed his right arm along the side of the wall and with his head now looking along the sight of his lance, he pulled the trigger five times giving Alan cover to get across the landing. John pulled his trigger another five times, this time, hitting four of the men. Then he fired again killing the last man, and vapourising what was left of the other four men.

Another man crept round the far end of the landing and held out his gun ready to try and kill John, but he was too late, John had already seen him move and his lance fired, and the entire landing turned electric blue.

Upon seeing this the men returned to the protection of the room might give them, not that their rooms were activated. Alan was firing his lance making the ground floor room electric blue for a few seconds for each fire.

Intruders on first floor and inside Cinema's one and two Gunslingers urgently needed on first floor by cinemas. In two minutes, The House will enter self-protection mode. Gunslingers to first floor immediately," Louise warned everyone in the House.

"Do you think the two minutes are in her time or ours?" Alan asked John.

"Let's hope it's not her time or Louise will not be happy if we are late at the cinema's. Come on Alan, Ken's men to fight, you take cinema one, I'll take cinema two, any men on the landing are up for grabs," John said laughing and they both ran to the end of the ground floor and up the stairs to the first floor.

Alan was first to look along the first-floor landing. There were at least six intruders, Alan turned his head to let John know the problem.

"Now, where have I seen this before?" John asked laughing.

"Two of us, six of them, no problem," Alan said and taking his life in his hands, took one wide step across the landing. Before John could get next to Alan, his lance was firing, cutting the men down as he saw them. John was also firing at the men behind the first line, which Alan was making short work off.

Together they walked slowly along the landing, their lance's firing nonstop at the intruders.

At the Train Station, Alexandra, sixteen, was looking at the House, hearing the guns being fired.

"Uncle Mike, do you think Gabrielle and Lynda will be alright with all the gunfire," she asked.

"John would have locked them into a bedroom by now. You see that electric blue light?" Mike asked her.

"Yes."

"That's the gunslingers, they have different guns to us. They fire a lance, not a Glock like this," he replied showing her his own Glock.

"What are the gunslingers like?" she asked.

"They are very courageous men and will fight to their death to save the lives of Gabrielle and Lynda. The other thing is, the House or Louise as She is known, does not like bullets hitting her walls and furniture, so that loud shout you heard just now was Louise calling for the Gunslingers to protect her rooms.

"Why don't you tell her who the gunslingers really are?" Sarah asked from behind them.

Mike looked at Sarah, knowing that right now she was hurting inside, wanting to be with someone she loved and had loved all her waking life.

"Please tell me who they are?" Alexandra asked, not realising the hurt she was going to put Sarah through.

Mike looked at Sarah and she nodded her head agreeing he go on. It would take her mind off the gun fight going on in the House, some of the electric blue flashes were coming from her husband's lance.

"On this occasion, it's John and Alan, mainly because Gabrielle and Lynda are inside. I was a Gunslinger in the House for a number of years before I cared for Brenda."

"You said the House is called Louise, is it like a computer?" Mike laughed as too Sarah, looking at each other Sarah nodded her head, then put her hand up to stop him from continuing.

"Alexandra, why don't you go down and join the other girls? We'll join you and tell you more about the House, not that there is much to tell," Sarah told her.

Alexandra walked elegantly along the wooden floor to join the other girls in her new two-inch high heels. The other girls had been straining to hear what was being said. It was Alexandra who drew the short straw in her age group to try and find out what the blue lights were coming from in the House.

"Okay, girls, gather around in a circle and no talking. Mike will stay at his guard position for now," Sarah said when she had joined the girls at the far end of the room, where they were protected more by the wardrobes which blocked off most of the windows.

"Actually Brenda, perhaps you would like to tell them about the House and us, get it over and done with?"

"Well, if you're sure dear," Brenda replied.

She slipped between the girls, her agile body moving in and out of the rows of girls until she got to Sarah. When the girls looked at her, they could see she had lost a lot of weight, but her face had also changed. There were no more lines, her hair was longer and had a sheen to it, as if she were a young girl again. Her breasts were plumper and no longer drooped even a little. Her body had curves again, her legs and arms younger, she looked as if she was twenty-six at the most. Her eyes sparkled with a new look of life. Everyone thought Gabrielle and Lynda had given her a make-over.

Brenda turned around upon getting to Sarah, putting both her younger looking hands on the table behind her, she used them to jump up and sat on the edge of the table. She crossed her legs making herself look like a young female executive. Sarah smiled at her and jumped up onto the table next to her crossing her slim young legs as well.

Sarah continued to glance at the House windows, still seeing the electric blue flashes getting less frequent, as John and Alan started checking the House, floor by floor.

When Sarah turned her head back to face the girls, they could all see there were tears in her eyes, worried for her husband who was in danger, like they all were, until this mess was all over and done with. George Two, or Mac the night was dead, and no longer any threat to them.

Of course, they would have to find all their bases and ensure there was no more money available, for any last assassins to start it running all over again. If there was no money the assassins and the other people they would employ would not be paid upfront, like George always did. The contracts that were once enforced to find and kill Gabrielle and Lynda and all their children abducted and sold to make more money would be forgotten.

The threats to blow up shops and other businesses, would also be forgotten and the men employed as debt collectors to the shops and pubs, would be killed or run off. Then the girls would be able to go to school, pass their exams with honours and get a job where they would be swallowed up by the population of London or other places they may go to, abroad for a start. But they would have to get through tonight and the following few days before any of that could even start to happen.

Brenda held Sarah's hand, seeing the concern on her face. Even now, the colour of her hair was slowly changing from a dark brown to a light blond with red streaks in it. Brenda and Sarah continued without saying a word about it.

"Right attention please girls," Brenda said then paused, looking at the girls around them, all in their various age groups.

"Well, the House has been here a very, long time and served a number of different people. In the seventeen and eighteen hundred's it was a large home to a wealthy family, The Grayson's.

"They had a large family with forty staff to care for them. The staff had a room each on the top floor and were always given excellent food and plenty of holidays. They had two uniforms each so one was in the wash and the other they would wear.

The uniforms were made from the finest linens and their blouses made of silk or satin. They had two pair of shoes for cleaning and a pair of wellington boots for the cold winters which could last several months. They always went to the different events that were open on The Frozen Thames.

"All the staff had appropriate footwear for the ice-covered river, warm dresses and stockings for the ladies and girls, with a fur lined winter coat and hat. The men had a winter suit, shoes or boots and an overcoat, again with a fur lined collar. Every coat had the name GRAYSON's sewn into the top left shoulder of their coats in gold thread, so people would know who they worked for and recall their clothes and hat shops in the city.

"When they travelled to Europe and America, on large ships, they always stayed there for at least four months at a time and took at least ten of their staff with them. On each trip, they would change the men and girls around, so in the end, they all got a trip abroad with them and their work was always light.

"The staff were the highest paid in London and every girl wanted to work for them as one of their maids. Men too wanted to work there, and as soon as a place became vacant, they would have hundreds of men applying for the job.

"Sir Neil and Lady Brenda Grayson were always helping people in distress. In the very cold winters, hundreds of children with no shoes on their feet and very, little on their backs, were picked up by Sir Paul and Lady Janet Grayson who road in a Gig and behind them, a covered two horse drawn wagon by one of the butlers and a boy or girl around twelve years old.

"Sir Paul and Lady Janet scoured the poorer streets of London for young boys and girls who were sleeping in the streets, in a shop doorway or any other place they could find to sleep to get out of the cold or die trying. As soon as Paul or Janet saw a child or group of children huddled together to try and keep warm, they would tell their coachman to stop and they would jump from their coach and run to the child or children and the driver and boy or girl, would join them and put the children in the back of the carriage whether they liked it or not, but as soon as they were in the carriage, the boy or girl would get them to the far end and cover them in a thick blanket.

"Paul and Janet would look around for other children, often finding the odd one or two almost dead on the floor covered in snow. Every other night they went out when they were here in residence. They would pick one poor street where the people had no money, very, little to eat.

"When they arrived at the street, the boy or girl who was now sat in the back of the wagon with the cold children wrapped up in blankets would make their way to the other end of the wagon, jump down and from the side, take as many food parcels as he or she could hold, walk alongside the wagon until it stopped, then ran to the front door put the parcel on the floor then knocked the door and hurried to the next house not looking back. They handed out parcels to every house then left the street returning to the House. Inside each parcel was basic foods, flour and eggs to make bread, fresh fruit for everyone in the house with strict instructions saying one piece of fruit each.

"There were also fifty pence in various coins to help get them through the winter periods when there was very, little work. The last item was a note from Paul and Janet to say it was their charity that had supplied everything as fifty pence was a great deal of money for a poor family to have and provided it was used correctly, usually by the woman of the house to make it last a whole month, maybe two.

"On arriving at the House, the children were carried into the House and taken down to the basement, where they a had a bath then were put into warm nightclothes and put to bed for the night.

"This was all overseen by Lady Janet and her girls, who scrubbed the children before putting them to bed. The following morning, they were given a hot breakfast and drink had their names taken and then dressed in a very warm one- piece tunic all the same colour. They stayed in the basement for ten days before being allocated beds in the under basement.

"There they had lessons on how to read and write and speak French, as this was a common language, spoken throughout Europe and Canada.

"Basically, everything you have here, they had back in their time and many times before that" Brenda explained.

Lucinda put her hand in the air. "Yes Lucinda?" Brenda asked, in a slightly younger voice.

"Lady Brenda, you look absolutely gorgeous. We all love your hair it really suits you."

"Well thank you Lucinda." Everyone around her applauded Brenda.

"What was your question dear?" Brenda asked.

"Are you all.... Like from Earth or another planet?" she brazenly asked.

Brenda looked at Sarah, wondering what to say.

"You may as well tell them, they'll figure it out sooner or later," Sarah said smiling.

"You really think so?"

"I know so," Sarah replied.

"We originate from the Lyra star system. Our star is called Vega Intense, which is a very bright star and outshines most of the stars in our area of space. We have six habitable planets and four Gas Giants. We originate from the fourth planet from our sun called Dyzanne Bright. We are a friendly race and help the Majors, make up our star charts and list all the inhabited planets including Earth, or Utopia Prime. All our stars and planets have names they have picked, to celebrate the way they feel.

"We are called Lythanairs, which in our language means Great Travellers. It took us four hundred years to get here, as we were travelling slow, carrying out star mapping and investigating other planets. But we had been studying Utopia Prime for thousands of years and finally the time in your Earth period, became more interesting.

"We built our ship, a sphere, the easiest ship for us and many other species to build. It took us two years to build our ship then another to finish the inside furnishings. Can anyone guess where we have parked our ship?"

Skye put her hand in the air. "In orbit around the Earth and your ship is called in our language, The Moon."

"Correct Skye, The Moon it is. Our people have travelled out further than this solar system over the years." "How Long have your people been on Earth?"

"Not that long, about a hundred and ten thousand of your years. But we parked up over four point five billion years ago and our people have spent much of that time working around this and other Stellar Systems mapping everything we discovered."

"So how old are you?" Skye asked for everyone.

"Not the sixty odd billion years people here assume. When our ship arrived here, there was another Moonship in orbit. The Gibbons had been watching your planet for at least ten billion of your years and there was another species before them and another over the time. We took over about a hundred and ten thousand years ago and we are due to move on to another star system, a long way from here in a few more years, but this battle must be fought first.

"Alright, my family, including Gabrielle and Lynda and everyone else here, are one hundred and fifty thousand years old. We keep on, regenerating our bodies, especially if we are getting old on your planet and expected to die. We can fake our deaths and return five years later in a lot younger looking body and meet up with our partner, who has gone away, then rejuvenated his or her body and we go on. We all have immediate access to a huge fortune, not billions, but mega Zillions.

"Our ship is currently holding over fifty thousand times the entire world's money. We have trillions of diamonds and other precious stones, gold, platinum, silver and other precious metals and of course, trillions of Universal Credits."

"Will your husband return to us here?" Skye asked.

`"Yes, he will in a few more days possibly. People will assume I have gone to join my daughter Janet and her family in Australia. When I come here with my husband, I will take over the full management of the House and Gabrielle and Lynda will be working hard with new children who are mixed up and thought they were born into the wrong body."

"Wow," everyone said and sighed at the same time.

"Could we go aboard your ship?" Skye asked.

"You would have to ask Gabrielle and Lynda, they are Captain and Captain of the ship, which has two captains one for the interior the other for the exterior of the ship and all the shuttles and small ships. We only have women in the command seat, men are so inferior, aren't they Isaac?"

"Oh yes, we men know our place, but we get to fly all the fighters and research ships, they are really fast, believe me. We also get to fire these beautiful weapons," he said holding his Glock in his hand which wasn't really a Glock, it just resembled it. "We protect our women when we're on a planet or visiting another species and the rewards are well worth it," he said smiling at his wife.

"But Gabrielle was Paul before, a man," Skye said making a point.

"Yes, he was, but he had always wanted a sex change, he just didn't like being a man. He was never happy with himself, always on edge until he dressed as a woman, then Lynda and Gabrielle would get together spending days, weeks at times in bed together, loving each other, making love, kissing, holding each other close, tight. You would think they only had a day left to live, but they have forever. We have the time to get into love, understand it, we all do it, but Gabrielle and Lynda seem to do it more often," Brenda said as her body was still slowly changing to a much younger version of herself.

"Look at them now, holding hands in the face of our enemy, jumping with the beds into your rooms. Let's hope they can get that job accomplished before Ken's men arrive."

"Why?" Skye asked.

"That is one of the biggest moving jobs that has to be completed, it will get your rooms closer to being finished," Brenda replied.

"I think we have trouble coming," Isaac said to Mike and the other gunslingers.

Guns poked out of partially open windows and night-time vision gunsights commenced looking in the direction of the expected army. Sure enough, there was one, then, three and four men and the others just fell in behind.

As Mike, Isaac and the others commenced firing their rifles, ten rifles opened fire from windows in the House. Everyone had at least three hits. The men were tightly packed together, trying to keep each other warm as snow started to fall again. Another volley followed from everyone, and more men were falling into the cold snow-covered grass and rock hard, soil beneath.

Some of the men started to return fire, their shots going to one side of The Train Station or hitting the stone wall of the House. Not one of the men hit one of the people they were supposed to annihilate.

By the end of the fourth round of firing from the House and Train Station, there were not many men left. Ten to be precise. They were now laying on top of their dead mates trying to take aim through their rifle's telescopic sights. When they fired, more gunshots followed from the gunslingers and the workers who had agreed to take up arms in the House.

Gabrielle and Lynda were now back inside the safety of the House, taking items from the basement to the different floors that needed them. There was still so much to do in the House to get it ready for their girls.

As Mike fired the last shot from the Train Station, the last man died in the ranks from Ken.

"Tina, I'm going to take a look at the men, make sure they are dead and take care of the bodies, we don't want the press getting on top of those buildings behind us with their telephoto lenses taking pictures of the dead bodies and we don't want the police poking around either," he said.

"I'll join you, no arguing, get your coat on and we'll leave," Tina said smiling. Tina already had her thick fur coat on as she had looked outside earlier.

Mike returned with his coat on and removed his Glock from its holster and put his little finger on the almost invisible receptor which would activate the Lance. Tina already had her slightly shorter Lance out and held it in her right hand.

They walked together through the glass doors and onto the fresh snow. They walked shoulder to shoulder up towards the bodies. It was earie, the silence was thick around them, not even their footsteps made a sound in the snow. It was like there was a huge blanket around the area. When they were within ten feet of the bodies, they could also see the blood-stained rifles in their hands.

They stood shoulder to shoulder and pointed their Lances at the bodies and pulled the trigger. Electric blue light emitted from the end of each Lance, the bodies disintegrated to dust as too their rifles and handguns. For the next ten minutes, the London skies were lit up in the electric blue light. Sometimes it would stay on for a minute or so, the next it was intermittent.

Children were looking at the strange light from their bedroom windows, asking their parents what it was. All they would say in reply, "It is not of this Earth and pull them back from the window, closed their curtains again and put them into bed.

One girl in her bedroom, not too far from the House asked her mother if the blue light was bad, because she was not allowed to see it.

The mother replied, "No my love, it's good, the people making the light are trying to save us from a very evil man." She tucked her daughter into bed and kissed her goodnight. She took one more look through the curtains, just moving them apart then closing them again.

Even with the curtains closed, you could still see the reflection of electric blue light, which was now flickering from a few seconds to a minute at a time.

The two gunslingers vapourised every dead body and gun but kept walking with intermittent fire sometimes hitting a fox or badger. They would be better off out of this world and into the next, rather than be here when the rest of the army arrived. It was twenty minutes before they returned to the warmth of the Train Station. Penny and Noah were waiting for them and held them in their respective partners open arms. They kissed, holding each other close, they hoped that this would soon be over, but they wouldn't hold their breath.

When John and Alan found the girls, they were in the sixth bedroom on the top floor. They had the bottom of the bed put up together with the casters, removed all the polythene from the base and mattress, bundled it in the corner, put the headboard into its receptors and hand tightened them, or rather Gabrielle did. Then they lay together on the bed, it had been a very, long day and at times Lynda thought she might lose her wife and she didn't want to wait five years to get her back.

They were holding each other for dear life, or that is the way it seemed when John knocked the door and opened it, not expecting to see his ward in a compromising situation with her wife on one of the student's double bed.

"Sorry Gabrielle, Lynda, the fighting is now over for the first attack. Between the men here and the gunslingers, everyone was killed. When Mike examined one of their rifles, he noticed the telescopic, cheap, site was not calibrated so they were firing wide, if the other rifles are the same, we'll be okay.

"Mike and Tina went outside and used their Lance to reduce the bodies and weapons to dust. Their Lances lit up the London night sky for twenty minutes."

"I wouldn't worry about it; the police know what we were up against. I suppose they'll come in later expecting to see their dead bodies," Gabrielle replied.

"How many people did you kill Alan?" Lynda asked.

"About the same as John, thirty, the House is now secure, we have men with rifles on all four entrances. All doors are locked, there is a lorry due to drop off the last of the beds in about an hour, another van will be dropping off all the bedding, even for the stores, all the towels will be arriving by van later in the morning. The rest of the items to get the showers and toilets completed will arrive after towel delivery, late in the day the food for the House kitchen and Train Station will arrive so if we're busy, perhaps some of the girls could help unload the lorry and put it all away?"

"Do you think that's wise with Simon?" Gabrielle asked.

"They have to learn where foods are put in a kitchen at some time. I know, keep Simon out of the kitchen and put Samantha in there to help the girls put the food away."

"A great idea Alan, we'll do that even if we're not busy, as you say, they have to learn where food is stored at some time," Lynda replied and laughed as Gabrielle was rubbing her back in her hot spot.

"Anything else you need doing for now?" John asked.

"Just check everything is getting finished, what can be and get a few teams of women up here to start unwrapping the beds, then four men to assemble them and put the headboard on. As soon as the bedding arrives, ask the women to make the beds, start at the top and work down. We'll have ten girls here bringing the bedding up the stairs, then they can put it in the rooms on top of the bed. When that's done, they can bring the rest up to the storerooms.

We'll need one of the women who normally changes the beds to show the girls where it all goes. Get yourselves a drink and something to eat, the men should be going to the restaurant in," Gabrielle paused and looked at her watch.

"It's seven thirty, tell the men and women to get cleaned up put their coats on and head over to the restaurant while there's a lull in the fighting at least. Tell Trever we'll pay the bill so have whatever they like to eat. We'll pop over just before nine and pay the bill. We'll see if we can open an account, or at least put some money behind the counter so to speak so we don't need to be there and back all the time. I think the men and women will be using that restaurant all the time they're here," Gabrielle said laughing as Lynda was doing the same thing to Gabrielle as she did to Lynda.

"Can you give us five minutes, on second thoughts make it… fifteen?" Gabrielle asked and turned into her wife, their eyes turning bright green as John and Alan smiled at each other and closed the door.

"I love you with all my heart," Gabrielle sighed.

"I love you with all my heart too," Lynda replied as they held each other close, arms in arms and started to kiss each other on their lips, which were rotating as their tongues inserted themselves into each other's mouth. Their hands were running up and down each other's back as they continued with their loving kiss. Their legs entwined, rubbing their partners shin, then Lynda was on top of Gabrielle as she pushed her tongue deeper into Gabrielle's mouth. Tears were running down Lynda's face, falling onto Gabrielle's face.

They paused their passionate kiss as Gabrielle kissed her tears dry. She kissed her cheeks mouth and eyes, holding her tight in her arms. They were like they were when they slept, except now they were facing each other.

"What is it my love? Why are you crying, please tell me?" Gabrielle asked Lynda mind to mind. Gabrielle sent Lynda pictures of them holding each other in Rome, making love in the States, having a meal with friends in Paris picking out clothes to wear in their bedroom at home. Mind to mind, they kissed and held each other tight, close, breasts touching, hands running up and down their bodies. Both sets of eyes were glowing bright green as their sexual thoughts ran through their bodies.

They both felt so sexy, wanting to play with each other in a sexual manner. Their lips were touching now in the real world, their emotions were starting to boil over as Gabrielle held Lynda with all her might.

She no longer had the strength Paul had, or his weight for that matter, she had lost four stone plus and with her thin arms and legs, curvaceous body, super soft feminine skin, petite hands and feet.

Her brain had also been rewired so she had a woman's thought process, slightly different to a man's, but a woman's body and interior organs were different than a man's, she was able to carry a baby, a man was not. She could also feed the baby with her own milk from both breasts.

Gabrielle held onto Lynda with all her might. One second, they were in an illuminated small bedroom on an unmade bed, next they were under the covers of a King size bed in a very, large warm room. Gabrielle was pushing a message into John's head letting him know where they were, and they needed half an hour. They would meet him and Alan in the hospital rooms on the ground floor.

Before Lynda could ask too many questions, they were both naked, bodies pressing against each other, hands going everywhere at once.

"Are you going to tell me what you were crying about?" Gabrielle asked her wife in a soft voice.

"Only if you tell me where we are," she replied.

"That's easy, we are in our large suite, there is a toilet shower, hand basins and a double bath." She indicated the door with her hand. The door to your left is an interconnecting door to John and Jenny's suite, then there is another suite after John's which is Alan and Sarah's suite. Behind us are two more large rooms, an office, with computers, laptops. Secure Internet, which is on a different line to the girls' rooms. There is a second large room next to it, our lounge, with soft sofas, relaxing chairs, coffee table and on the right side of the room. There was a small, or at least it was, kitchen stocked with coffee etc. I'll give you a tour after, we have sorted out why you were crying."

They held each other close, and Lynda looked deep into her lover's eyes. Both sets of eyes grew bright green, illuminating the room they were in.

"Earlier today, before you played with time, I thought I had lost you forever, I love you so much. I didn't want to lose you again those five years were the longest five years of my life. You shouldn't have agreed to be a Knight for the King's army; mind you, I loved being your Lady. We had a lovely castle until you were killed with an arrow, yet again." "It wasn't just one arrow, it was three."

"I think those archers had it in for me, as I turned around, I had two more arrows go into my back. You were well looked after in the King's Court. I bet you had one or two Knights after you," Gabrielle laughed.

"No, I kept well out of their way, anyway, the Knights were being killed every few days, and more wives and children were joining the King's Court daily. At least I had a maid, and those dresses, so heavy, but nice to wear in that timeline. As soon as your five years were up, I came straight here and we met in what was then the hospital, we had a lovely big suite there. So, are you telling me this suite was here all the time?"

"No, my love, back then, it was all blocked off as the House was used by a rich family, but they were not rich enough to have access to this suite. Not only that, their six children may have tried to dig the floor up and see the lifts."

"Oh yes, I didn't think about those. We lived here for twenty years, and you paid your time as a Knight off, so you didn't have to fight in a war, with gold and diamonds. How much did it cost us?"

"I paid him fifty thousand in gold and ten thousand in diamonds, ten thousand in pearls and rubies, we said we got from the Caribbean, that's why we were so rich. I took you with me when I went jousting, even over to France, where you surprised everyone when you spoke French fluently, well me too."

"Oh yes, I forgot about that," Lynda replied in French.

"I love it when you speak French," Gabrielle said and they started kissing, their naked bodies touching, breasts pressing against each other as their tongues intertwined in each other's mouth, as their lips rotated about each other.

Gabriel started to play with Lynda's breasts, then Lynda reciprocated. Gabrielle started to kiss her wife's chin, then neck. She considered giving her wife, a love bite, but they were past that now, better to continue down her body. Gabrielle started kissing Lynda's breasts, and sucking her nipples.

Her right hand was already working itself down the front of Lynda's body, rubbing her belly in circular motions, gently, getting lower, there was no rush, they were together now, with all the time in the world. Her long slender fingers, with a fluorescent blue nail varnish on, not available in the UK or world come to that, gently, touched the exterior of her clitoris, rubbing it in circles as her tongue licked her breasts, kissing them, their minds linked, sending all their love to each other, filling their hearts with love, tenderness and romance.

Gabrielle's middle finger entered her vagina, gently stroking the sides, then getting deeper into it, as her palm gently caressed her clitoris. Gabrielle's head was slowly moving down her body, kissing it with love, not rushing, there was no hurry, all she wished to do was to please her wife after her frightful afternoon. She was humming a love song from the seventeenth century, one they loved to share between them, it was their favourite for that century, she felt Lynda's hand on her naked back, as she too started to hum the song again.

As Gabrielle's lips moved lower down her stomach, she continued to hum, then kiss her body until she reached her clitoris. Lynda was now starting to pant loudly, she could have screamed, nobody would hear her as their room was soundproof.

She continued to pant as Gabrielle's lips kissed her clitoris, then she removed her finger from her vagina and her tongue entered her vagina instead. Lynda arched her back so Gabrielle could push her tongue in a little further, licking the sides of her vagina walls, gradually bringing her to an orgasm. As her tongue was inside her vagina, her fingers were gently caressing her clitoris.

Lynda was rubbing the nape of Gabrielle's neck, gently helping her to get her tongue deeper inside her. As Gabrielle continued licking her Vagina walls, Lynda had her orgasm. She sighed deeply, then stroked Gabrielle's back as she continued to lick the inside of her vagina and swallow her orgasm.

Gabrielle removed her tongue from Lynda's vagina and once again kissed her clitoris, kissing and licking it at the same time until Lynda arched her back again and started to pant quickly, then she cried out and her orgasm was running over her vagina walls and onto Gabrielle's tongue and into her mouth. Once she had consumed it, she licked her vagina once more as Lynda stroked her back.

"Come up here sweetheart," Lynda said quietly to Gabrielle, almost singing the words.

Gabrielle slowly turned around and kissed her way back up to Lynda's breasts, up her neck, to her chin, finally her lips. They kissed each other very passionately, it was like they were in space, floating with no gravity. In an effortless move, Gabrielle gently manoeuvred her wife so as they kissed, she was on top of her still kissing each other.

Lynda smiled and her fingers caressed Gabrielle's sides, then her tongue started to rise from the pit it was in just like a snake, its tip exploring. It slowly lifted itself, feeling the inside of its mouth with its tip, like the tongue of a snake, exploring, feeling the air around it, then feeling the sides of the mouth, moving back and forth as they continued to rotate their mouths about each other, still wearing their expensive lipsticks.

Lynda's snake like tongue, tested the back of its lips, it was as if the snake could detect the temperature and makeup both girls were wearing. It paused by the inside of the lips, feeling them from three millimetres away, waiting silently to move forward. Then the snake struck, pushing itself through two layers of lips into the mouth opposite. It felt around the other dark, damp place, tasting the sides of the walls then it felt something else in the darkness. It started to rise from the damp floor of the mouth, then the two black snakes felt each other, then they were wrapping themselves around each other, licking, touching, moving, playing with each other as their lips continued to rotate about each other.

The two snakes, kissed each other with the tips of their body, loving each other just like their masters were. Their kissing continued as they rubbed up and down each other, bringing more moisture to the inside of the dark area they both now occupied. Many kisses later, the tongues, and lips parted, the snakes (tongues) withdrew and parted from each other returning to the warm pits they had both rose from.

"That was incredible, lovely, filled so much with love and romance, I love you so much, you're a much better woman than you were a man, I love you, I wouldn't change you for the world, saying that Earth isn't worth that much on the Colony Exchange, I checked the other day in case we have to move our ship earlier than we thought.

"According to the Colony Exchange, they are looking for a new buyer for it as the humans have messed up the planet and its atmosphere. It says it will need a great deal of work done to it and the entire atmosphere replenished."

"What will happen to the humans if they find a new buyer?" Gabrielle asked.

"I have no idea; they may be eliminated, when the atmosphere is changed. It is being sold with sitting tenants."

"Is there nothing we can do about their atmosphere?" Lynda asked.

"The equipment we need to clean the atmosphere we do not have aboard, but the Moonship Agraffe Keeper will have it, as I ordered the equipment to be sent to Christine and Katherine's ship. They will be here soon to relieve us of being Carer's for this planet."

"I forgot our time was nearly up, but we must sort out Ken, we cannot leave with him still threatening people and businesses. As soon as the Agraffe Keeper is in orbit, Katherine will obliterate London and any other cities Ken tries to run to until she kills him and his men herself.

"We have enjoyed ourselves here, it would be a disaster if it were all destroyed because of Ken. I loved the eighteenth century, all those lovely walks we took in the hot summers and long autumns. We walked everywhere but I loved it arm in arm, sitting on the park benches and kissing each other, holding hands and holding each other.

"When we were out together during the day, we either walked arm in arm, or held hands, it was a beautiful climate and we had all of this, this House."

"Yes Gabrielle, those were the days, log fires, friends around for drinks tiffin for late afternoon tea and cucumber sandwiches, with the crusts cut off and cut into dainty triangles. All the women when drinking a cup of tea, or glass of wine, always held our little pinkie out. I think it was to counterbalance the tea in the teacup." They both laughed.

"I promise my love, my dearest wife, who I wouldn't swap for the planet Enigma in the Starlight Solar System. And I know you love that planet because you've taken me there over a hundred times."

"Have you been counting the times we've been there? Gabrielle asked.

"Yes, I have, and you took me there in our very own space yacht, you named Lynda. It's the most beautiful part of space, alight with thousands of stars and hundreds of planetary systems. What happened to our space yacht?" Lynda asked her wife.

"Onboard the ship, Elangaline is giving the engine an upgrade. It will take us less time to get there now, so when we leave here, we'll have a trip to Enigma, what do you think?"

"Oh yes, most definitely my love and I promise you, from now on, no more sidestepping, I love us like this, it is much better than when you were a man."

"I'm so pleased, because I love being a woman and in love with you, I wouldn't change us now even for Enigma," Gabrielle replied and they both laughed.

"This timeline has been so exciting. I really love seeing how these generations have advanced so fast."

"Really?"

Lynda looked at her wife. "You didn't, did you?" she asked.

"Not me, or Paul for that matter, but it was someone from the ship, one of the electrical engineers I think, he built something, so simple and dropped it off somewhere in the USA."

"What was it?" Lynda asked, kissing her wife passionately in the hope she would tell her the answer. When they finished their kiss, Lynda started to gently stroke her between her breasts.

"Well, to make a computer, you need a keyboard to start with, then you need a microprocessor and somewhere to store the programmes you write, oh and a TV to see what you are typing."

"One of the early computers by Charles Babbage, who was one of our men from the ship, started the computer race off with help from Eloise, the electrical engineer. They needed a computer to get them into space."

"Yes, my love, I suppose they did," Lynda replied.

"Would you like to have another orgasm?" Gabrielle asked kissing Lynda's lips again, their mouths rotating as Gabrielle repeated her previous kissing session, gradually exciting her wife, just like a good wife should at times.

Half an hour later, much later than they told John and Alan, they returned to the ground floor and walked, hand in hand, along the landing to the hospital, the floor cover was now laid and eight hospital beds, with monitors by each bed, with chairs for others to sit on filled the room. Gabrielle and Lynda held hands, and looked around it, then turned and entered the nurse's station and first response room.

There was a desk, computer, hospital bed monitors and another nurse's examination table, with all the equipment they would need to examine a person and get their vital statistics before they went into the ward or further down for an operation. Lynda was a healer as too, Brenda, Sarah and Jenny. Penny was a hands-on healer, giving long term heat treatment, to a person's body after an operation by the other healers.

If the Healers couldn't help, then the person was too far gone and more than likely dead. That didn't happen very often. John and Alan were in the room, drinking coffee and eating a sandwich. The House was quiet, their helpers having their evening meal.

"We may as well take a look around the House, coming?" Gabrielle asked,

By the time they had completed their inspection of the House, the men were back and once again, enthusiastic about getting the bedrooms completed as near as they could with the items they had at their disposal, there was still a great deal of packaging to dispose of and there was still some of the finer points to complete. They had somehow managed to get all the televisions they required, and teams were now hanging them on the bedroom walls, while the TV and Internet engineers were completing their jobs. All their cables entering the House had quick release connectors fitted although they didn't know why. The House did not draw power from the mains supply, it had its own internal power, it was just the gas and water supplies, the House took from outside.

By the time Gabrielle and Lynda had talked to the women who normally worked for them, they had agreed they would now return to their former positions and care for the girls and the new TG's that were even now waiting in the wings,

There was an emergency floor between the second and third floor that the House could create. The bedrooms were not as pretty as the ones the men had brought back to life, but they were warm, had a bed, small TV and new laptop for their lessons, which once the battle was over, they would start in earnest.

In the darkness, the House was slowly moving floors and increasing the height of the House to accommodate the new seven-foot-high floor. Gabrielle and Lynda, were on the new floor, slowly walking along the landing, opening doors that had not been opened for over a thousand years when the crew of their Moon ship, deployed to Earth, helping to move the people forward, getting them ready for a time, when their Moon would leave their solar system, and another ship, with a new crew would take its place. The people would need to be ready for a change of leadership, not all Captains and Commanders, with their High Council ruled the planet from behind the scenes.

By the time they had finished talking with the House, it was now midnight, the time they were concerned Ken would send in more men to attack them, but for now, the main force of eight hundred men, were being held from getting any further down the country by the police and emergency roadworks, as a hole opened in the M6 motorway and went down twenty feet, as the repair crews commenced to fill in the hole with stone and concrete, all the other routes south were now jammed by cars, buses and trucks.

It gave them extra time and hopefully, they would now arrive in small groups that could be taken easily. Four of the women who usually cared for the boy girls now all girls, had been taken by Lynda and Gabrielle to the Train Station, where they helped settle the girls down in their sleeping bags, and would keep an eye on them through the night.

All the duvets they made were now in all the bedrooms, ready to put on their beds. the pillows would be sent over when they were ready for the girls to take command of their new bedrooms.

Chapter 17

Twelve hours later, the House was almost completely ready for the girls to live in it. Most of the packed roads to the south from Manchester, were getting unblocked and the motorway was getting ready to open one lane south to help remove the congestion that was backing up to the M6.

Ken's six busses of men were getting closer to their objective even at 40mph. As the men talked together on the buses, there were two men there from the main base, which had suddenly exploded from all the explosive that was stored in the basement, there was nothing left of the building as they burned with more and more explosions ripping the building apart, the heat was so intense, it had melted some of the smaller safes and the large safe had expanded, allowing the door to open slightly, enough to allow the flames and heat to incinerate everything inside.

Everyone knew that was where the main bulk of George's money was stored, there were a few million in three other much smaller bases and most of the men, had been promised two hundred and fifty thousand a day to either catch Gabrielle and Lynda Grayson, or kill them. If they were captured alive, they would be taken back to Ken at his last base in Manchester. There he would treat the girls as his and start another empire, selling sex with the two women and drugs of every form.

For the man or men who captured the two girls, they were promised ten million pounds for each man who accomplished this dangerous job, due to their bodyguards being so close to them and good with a gun.

The men were now asking questions of the two men who had escaped the complex with nothing but their lives.

"Tyler, what happened to all the money in the safes?" Zack, one of the men from the Liverpool base asked.

"Tell them Tyler, they have a right to know, we were there in the middle of it all," Royston told him. He had scars from burns to his face, arms and hands. Two of his fingers were joined together by their skin, which could not be separated at the time. His hands would have to heal for a while before operations on his face and hands could take place.

Tyler had similar burns to his face, arms, hands and two of his fingers on his left hand had been amputated, because they sustained really bad burns as he tried to pick up his special gun that was red hot. He held it in his hands only two seconds, then it was stuck to his hand, burning it with the guns' heat. Tyler had managed to get the gun off his hand, but as he did so, he tore the top three layers of skin from his palm and the third and fourth fingers, were burned to the bone.

They were both sent to a private hospital and all their treatment paid for by Ken. When they came out of hospital, he gave them a million pounds each for their burns and promised them more money if they could join him in the last fight to either kill or capture Gabrielle and Lynda.

The offer of money was too great for them to at least, train to hold and fire a machine gun again. Tyler wore a hat to cover his bald head and the burns he had sustained there after his hair caught fire and was finally put out by Royston.

"Well," Tyler started. "There were five safes throughout the base and each one held cash, cram packed as tight as Ken could get it and close the door. None of the safe's were fireproof except the biggest safe which again was packed from the back to the front, floor to ceiling with bundles of money that George had managed to gain through prostitution, kidnapping young boys and girls and selling them to paedophiles for a great deal of money, always cash. Then there were the drugs he sold, anything he could get his hands on, or get chemists to make for him.

"There must have been close to fifteen million in the safe, which was all burned to ashes."

"How do you know that?" Zack demanded to know.

"Because the police, firemen and hursts were there for four days. When we made our way back into the remains of the building, the first place we went to investigate was the big safe.

"The door was opened by some firemen but there was nothing inside, just a wet floor and with ashes drying out on the still hot floors. Then we heard the roof fall into the top floor and got out before we were buried alive," Royston replied.

"All the money is gone, is that right?" Zack asked almost shouting his question to the two men.

"Yes, well there was some in other bases, but not much and all the money disappeared from the Liverpool and Rochester bases. Whether the men there took it and ran off we'll never know. When we opened the safe, all the money was gone,"

Royston explained. By now everyone on the top deck were trying to look over the stairs and some of them had come down them to hear better what was being said. The words were being relayed by those who could hear upstairs, to the back of the crowd.

Neither man could speak very well, they still had severe burns on their lips, the inside of their mouths, were burned and their lungs had ingested a great deal of hot burning air, scorching their lungs. Therefore, their voices could not be heard very well but the important information Pier, spoke on their behalf.

Pier came from base two in Rochester, it was a derelict building now, the forty men left, joined Kens group of followers, with promised millions which were no longer there for them, but with their arms twisted, threats on their family lives, they seemed to have no option as the men were building in numbers. There would be enough men left if they died or ran off, to kill their families. Now things were changing, there was no big money, they didn't even know if Ken could pay everyone on the coaches he had hired. This was also unheard off, Ken usually hijacked buses to move a lot of people around, so how come he had paid good money for the buses? Was he frightened of being caught with so many buses in one line? It would be time for a good shoot out with the armed police and they would kill them all.

"There is money, but not the millions we were promised. I reckon by the size of the largest safe, four by five feet, there is no more than half a million in cash. Is that right Denzel?" who was from the same base.

"Yes, Pier is right, although Ken probably has two or three bank accounts with a few million in each account. He was always driving to four banks and two building societies, depositing money which he took from the very, large safe with him. The four men who accompanied him, were each given a hundred grand a trip, which they could pay directly into their bank accounts while they were out with him.

"Apparently in one building society, we were told he deposited fifteen million three times. It's not unusual to have large deposits into a building society account as some buildings in London, were twenty or thirty million and much more," Denzel explained.

"So, he could pay from his bank accounts?" Zack asked. "Are you kidding me, that is his private stash of money he only carries one bank card on him, which he never uses. The other accounts he has hidden the bank cards or memorized all the account numbers. All the money left is in the Manchester base, we think, but we are not sure how much," Denzel added.

"If there is not much money left, we are not going to get a squint of it. Why in the hell are we putting our lives on the line for Ken, when our families or us if we make it through the fight, will not get the funds we were promised a week ago? I suggest we ditch Ken right now and all of us, get the driver to exit at the next motorway exit as soon as possible and head home. Do you all agree?" Zack shouted throughout the bus.

"Yes," they all replied.

"What about the others in the other coaches?" Lez asked from upstairs.

"We get the driver to stop the bus then five of us will run back to the coaches and tell everyone there is no money and we are leaving Ken's outfit. We are not going to die, for nothing," Zack shouted to the men.

"Good idea Zack," Jason shouted from the back of the bus. He had already lost his left arm when an explosive he was setting to destroy a shop went off in his hand. "I'll go to the next bus, I need five more people, who's with me?" Jason asked.

"I'll go, I'll take the last bus but one. If Ken comes out, I'll just say the engine on the bus has overheated and we're letting it cool down to put some water in it," Zack said.

Within a few minutes they had eight men who would tell the people on the buses behind. They stopped on the Hard Shoulder, all six buses in one line. Their driver, Thomas, went to the rear of the bus and opened the engine cover door.

The men who were going from bus to bus were out and running along the hard shoulder, jumping onto the buses and telling everyone about the missing money and what the men on the first bus had all agreed to do.

Everyone on the second bus, decided to turn around, they were not going to fight for nothing and die for nothing,

The men on bus 3 would not open the doors to the two men, no matter how many times they knocked on the door, with their fists. When the men reached bus four, the two men were allowed onto the bus, but nobody wanted to leave, then four men did put their hands into the air. Other men on the bus pulled their hands down and the two men from bus one, were thrown off the bus.

Tyler and Royston, who they knew had made it out of the fire alive and went through a lot of pain with their burns, while they waited for the inside of the building to cool down enough, so they could sneak inside and look at the large safe.

They told the four men again what they had seen, the safe door was open and there was nothing inside and outside the safe, was millions of ashes, that had been swept out the safe by the firemen with their powerful fire hoses.

Five minutes later, the four men from inside Bus 3 had walked down to Bus 1 and got onboard. The men who were trying to get the others to join them returned to their bus 1.

As the men who spoke to the people on the buses behind bus two, returned to their bus, saying it was no good even trying to talk to them. They wouldn't even be allowed on the bus.

Zack was already at bus five and when he asked to be let on, there was a lot of confusion as to who he was and what bus he was from. Zack knew there was something not right, he knew Ken and his twenty closest men were on the last bus.

The driver opened the folding doors just a little so Zack could not force his way onto the bus.

"My name is Zack, I'm from bus 1, the engine has over heated, and the driver is letting it cool down so he can refill the coolant tank. We'll be stopped for about thirty minutes. Do you mind if I come aboard for minute?" Zack cautiously asked.

"Why?" a man asked not giving his name.

"Hey, I thought we were all in this together, I just want to ask one question, when I get on your coach."

The man looked back along the bus, which like bus six was a single decker. He got a few nods from people, then turned to the driver telling him to open the doors.

Zack stepped onto the bus and instinctively knew he shouldn't be there. Every man behind the driver, had a handgun which was pointing at him.

"Glad to be aboard, it's bloody cold out there. Do you by any chance have any hot coffee going?"

"Chen, get him a cup of coffee, black, we have no milk."

"That's just the way I like it."

Chan brought the hot cup of black coffee over to Zack and handed it to him. It was in a proper mug, no paper or plastic cups here.

"Now what is it you want to know?"

"As we are now out of that heavy congestion, we were just wanting to know when we would be given our assault rifles and would the battle start in daylight, or darkness?" Zack asked, taking large gulps of his coffee, which was quite strong.

"Reassure your men that they will get their guns soon. It is just with all the police around, we don't want anyone showing off their guns to the police, we are not looking to start a gunfight here in the open, we would use up a great deal of our ammunition, and we will need it all to fight Gabrielle's bodyguards. Don't forget, we want to capture Gabrielle and Lynda alive, if possible, wounded will be okay too. There will be a million pounds each to those men who take them both alive. They never leave each other's side, so when you find one, you'll find the other close by." Does that answer your question?"

"Will it be day or night we start fighting and where have you stashed all the weapons?" Zack asked bravely, holding onto his mug still taking sips of the hot coffee.

"Ken decided it will be a night attack, he thinks it's our best chance of killing the bodyguards and getting the girls, plus, the police will hear all the gunfire and walk away until the fight is over, but we'll all be gone by then.

"Ken has some powerful recording equipment which he will record all the shooting and play it through the four large speakers on is bus, which will give us cover while we will all get on our buses. As soon as one bus is full, it will drive off out of the area, heading north. The rest of the busses will follow on behind as the men return to their busses, so tell your men, they will be fighting in groups of ten, so you are all together and if anyone is wounded, they can be helped or carried back to their bus. Each crew of ten men will make their way across to the House wall. Stay in your groups, just space out a little.

"The first group will lay explosives along the side of the House and after the gunfire has started, your man in charge of the explosives, will set them off and blow a huge opening into the House, Zack, you have experience with explosives, haven't you?"

"Yes, I was going to be on the groups blowing up Gabrielle's shops and other large department stores in London and Manchester. But we were sent out after the first time, when one of our men lost his arm. I told him exactly what to do, how to set the timer and switch it on," Zack replied, lowering his head.

"It wasn't your fault it happened Zack, it was just bad luck he didn't listen properly to the man who was teaching you all about explosives, how to handle them, set the charge and not, get your hand or arm blown off. You repeated what you were taught, it was up to him, he should have said if he didn't understand it properly. No Zack it wasn't your fault, so don't dwell on it. I'm Robin by the way, I'm in charge of the six explosive teams who will be going into London. Mitch there," Mitch raised his hand.

"He's in charge of the men who will be attacking Gabrielle's forces. Tim at the back," Tim raised his hand.

"Will oversee handing out your weapons. He will bring two bags full of guns and assault rifles to each bus. When he is on the bus, he will designate one senior man who will hand out the weapons and ammunition. When we all have our guns and have loaded them, Mark, who is not here but in the four, by four black Range Rover, with Bus Mechanics on its side, is following on behind with all the explosives, timers, detonators and firing caps.

"Harold will give your people the explosives in, I think six or seven large holdalls, and another bag full of the firing equipment. He will then go to bus four, where Carl is. You know Carl, don't you?"

"Yes, of course, he was the other senior explosive man in charge of his group of twenty men who were going to blow up the department stores, when it was filled with people shopping, for Christmas great deals on toys for boys and girls, bikes, makeup, women's jewellery and men's watches which were two thousand pounds reduced to twenty pounds. At least that is what our posters say, on the outside of the store to draw people inside and die through their greed," Zack said and sighed deeply.

"It didn't happen, so now he will be taking his team into London and blowing up as many department-stores as he can. Mitch will give him time to set up all the explosives, then drop his crew off at each department store and glue our special signs onto the glass windows of the store and its walls.

"This will also give the police ambulances and firemen something else to concentrate on while you have your fight. How does that sound?"

"Like a good plan," Zack replied, thinking it was really an insane plan. Why kill innocent women, men and children who have nothing to do with their cause just because Ken want's it done?

Ken liked to see large buildings blow up. They were there to do a job, now he realised why he needed so many men. It would take a lot of explosives to even make a small dent in a department store, you just could not set a few packs of explosive and hope to bring down the entire building. They might break all the windows on the first two floors but that would be about it.

"Come deeper into the bus. Amber, Kath, Susan, Stella, Tracey, move off your seats please." The women moved from their seats to sit on their husband's lap. Arms were going around the women, holding them in place as Robin led Zack to the back of the bus.

Robin lifted the false seat covers from the back seat and four double seats in front of it.

"There, have a look. That is half of the assault guns and handguns. There are also four boxes of ammunition at the front of the bus, hid like this, under false double seats. You will want to see them, so you can tell the men in busses 1 and 2, you've seen the guns and the ammunition.

"Shirley, Anthia, get off your seats please." Robin said. Leaving their seats, they were off to get to their partners, Robin put his arm around Shirley, pulled her close to him and kissed her lips passionately. He held her hand as they walked along the bus to the front seat the two women were sat on.

Robin pulled the false seat cover off the seat bottom and there inside were four large boxes of ammunition which were all sealed. Zack lifted one box it was heavy.

"Yes, so where is the rest of the ammunition and guns?"

"Same sort of layout on bus 6, Ken's bus," Robin replied.

"How come some of the wives are on your bus, your wife as well? It's not the sort of situation where our wives should join us," Zack asked.

"You're right, but they are here for a different reason, there are six cars following us a mile behind, with thirty-five of our wives in. We will be the couples, hiding the men planting the explosives and we'll be taking some explosives into the store. The explosives will be in our wives' large handbags. Some wives will go into the female changing rooms, to try a dress on, while the husband remains outside wondering how long she will be. The wife will come out to her husband with no bag, showing him her dress. He says yes, she returns inside, gets changed, opens her bag and removes another, the same colour and size. Two bags from other shops will be on top of the explosives in the bag. If she cannot find a hiding place for it, she will leave it pushed right back to the wall under the seat for her to sit on while getting changed. She puts the empty bag over her shoulder, picks up the dress, walks out of the changing room and buys it, so should the dress survive the explosions, there will be no DNA on the dress.

"They go to a till pay for it, so they are seen paying for the dress, then leave the store and walk away to the next store we plan to blow apart. Other men from this coach with their wives, will also enter the six stores we are going to blow up and will go to different floors, leaving the explosives inside so when they have finished there are two bags of explosives on each floor in a vulnerable place where they will either kill more people or do the most damage.

"When they leave the shops, they will not look back or at any men left setting explosives outside the shop or putting posters of huge reductions on the walls and windows. These men will be from Bus six, who are all wearing a suit.

"When we get to London, you will all have time to look around the shops and do a little shopping. If I, were you, I would call your wife telling her to come to London on the next train, and bring your passports, they will help you when you book into the hotel you will be staying in.

"For those of you who have told their wife to join them, once the fighting is over or you have all not arrived at the Train Station and House, you join your wife shopping and stay in the hotel overnight and get out of the country tomorrow," Robin told Zack.

"How will you all get back onto your buses and the women behind into their cars? The police will more than likely shut inner London down to allow the emergency services get to the fires, you'll leave behind."

"More than likely. When our two buses drop us off, everything we need will be in bags we will be carrying. The two buses will drive off to another destination and stop for five minutes.

"Why?" Zack asked.

"We have sent thirty women on a train to London which arrived at eight o'clock this morning. They have been given their one-way train tickets and a credit card each and pin with £10,000.00 on it. They also have a thousand pounds in cash on them in their bag and purse.

"They will shop all day, buying whatever they like, clothes, jewellery, whatever they like. We will arrive in London around three o'clock and the coach will park in a Bus and Coach Park. We will all get off the coach, walk away and meet our wives who have parked somewhere else, but close to our hotel. I saw the cars drive past us fifteen minutes ago.

"At seven thirty our coach will leave the coach Park and drive to a coach pickup point. The ladies will board our coach and if stopped by the police all they will have is a party of women going home from a shopping trip to London.

Any money left on the card they can spend over the next two days. The women will be told their card will expire after three days, so they must use all the money on the card over the three days, as on the fourth day, the card would become useless. They will then burn their credit card. We don't want anything left that can be linked to us by some woman shouting her mouth off and telling their neighbours what happened and what they have bought."

"Very well planned, so we engage Gabrielle, Lynda and their bodyguards tonight?"

"That's right, those of you who are going to leave Ken, you need to be out of the country, watching a play or hiding in your hotel when the fighting and explosions start. Ken wants the battle to commence around eight thirty, that will be when the first store will explode. I will send you a text message when the last store is going down. That is when you should blow up the side of the House, then ransack it."

"Not that we will be doing that, but the House has already been ransacked once, it's a complete mess, there is nothing left in there."

"I've been told by Ken, when they took the girls, we were hoping to sell, they were hoping to start work getting the House up together."

"Start cleaning it maybe. That alone would take a couple of weeks and if they were just going to slap paint on the walls, it would take over a month to paint, remember, there are over three hundred rooms on the top three floors. The bottom three floors have about the same number of rooms, laid out differently. There is no lift, so everything has to be carried up and down by people.

"Can you imagine one of those boy girls, trying to carry a five-litre drum of white paint up the hundred steps to the top floor? They would never make it. If they took up colour paint, it would take them all day walking up and down the stairs. It couldn't be painted from top to bottom if they had two months, believe me."

"You know what Ken is like, he said he wants an explosion against the House. By what you say, he ain't going to want just one explosion," Robin replied smiling.

"Alright, but we ain't no-way, going back into that bloody House, it's creepy. Like it's alive and watching everything we do. We lost six men in that House. We found their guns, but no bodies, dead or alive. If Ken wants us to go into that House, he can bloody well lead us."

"If I tell him what you've just said he'll laugh his head off, come to your position, blow a hole in the House and lead you all in himself and when you get out, he'll put a bullet or two into your head," Robin replied, a moment later they both burst into laughter.

"Anything else happening I should know about?" Zack asked.

"What say ye all?" Robin asked the men and women on his bus. Everyone said yes, at the same time.

"Okay. Keep this to yourself, I don't want it getting back to Ken. Forty of our wives or girlfriends have packed a bag for each of us. There are two hotels close together, where we have booked twenty women into each hotel for two days. They each have new credit cards they can use that we have already preloaded with fifty-grand; they also have a fifty grand card limit.

"Everybody in busses, four and five have brand new bank accounts with a million pounds in each account. Our wives have a bank card as do we. We all also have a bank credit card and a Mastercard, each has a hundred grand limit.

"Later today I will be adding another two million into our new bank accounts. I will also transfer fifty million to a Swiss Bank account that my wife and I own, nobody else."

"What about the money we should be getting? What we have been promised? With bonuses, we should at least be getting three million each at the end of the fight. If any of us are killed, the money is to be paid to our wives with a death bonus of a new house to live in wherever she likes."

"So, that is why you are really here, okay, let me finish explaining what is happening, then I'll answer your question," Robin said.

"Fair enough," Zack replied, and was getting angry with the whole notion of this stupid job.

"For a start, we know all the cash is gone. The whole lot over twenty million. When we have done our jobs, we will meet up with all our wives, then get on a train and leave London, heading to the Southwest. We get off at Bristol, go to our hotel stay there two nights, going into Bristol for a look around and maybe do a little shopping for clothes and another two or three suits, get bigger suitcases, then three days later, we board the train to take us from Bristol to the Euro Train station. We board our train, get off in Paris. Stay in another hotel for two nights, then board our luxury Boing 747 and fly direct to Australia where we intend to live for the rest of our lives. Buy some houses close to each other, then that's it, we never return, and Ken will never find us."

"Why go to all that trouble, why not just fly to Spain the following day then pick up your flight to Australia?"

"The police will be checking every person getting on a plain, especially if you have booked your flight in the last two days, people going on a holiday, usually book at least a month in advance if not six months. This way, we'll be travelling by train which we hope will not be so heavily searched by the police," Robin replied.

"You don't believe in Ken?"

"Hell no, this is one of his worst plans ever, especially with the notes we will leave pasted to the store windows."

"Saying what?" Zack asked.

"These stores we're destroyed by George's paid assassins, who have been ordered by Ken to continue fighting in London, until all our funds from George have been used. The new leader of the group is Ken Mattingly. Manchester."

"Sounds good, the police will be looking for trains, coaches, cars travelling from London to Manchester over the next week.

"They will want him alive to pay for all his crimes so they can also get their hands on all his funds to repair the damaged stores. You will have hopefully killed Gabrielle and Lynda, with all their bodyguards so that will be more people off his back."

"Where are you getting money from then?" Zack asked.

"I discovered one of his bank accounts and I have been paying money into a foreign account, then sharing it out. He has another six accounts, and I have copies of his bank cards. There is two hundred and fifty million in total in these accounts. I have just emptied and closed one of his accounts," Robin explained.

"So, how are we being paid?"

"Ken is not intending to pay any of you, you will all die when the Bodyguards come out shooting at you."

"That's rubbish some of us are very good marksmen even with dodgy sights, we all know how to get the guns firing straight and true," Zack retorted.

"That's good to hear." They were still standing by the boxes of ammunition as Robin leaned over, and picked up a box of ammunition, not the one Zack tried lifting. He pulled out his knife and cut the thick paper cover from the box. Zack looked inside the box which was barely half filled.

"That will only just fill one of our guns for its first round. Where is the rest, we will need more than this if we are expected to fight and kill them? At some time. we will have to fire on the run for cover, closer to the House or Train Station," Zack said getting annoyed.

"Like I said in the other boxes," Robin said and lifted another box and put it on top of the seat opposite. Once again, he used his knife to open the paper top. This time the ammunition was filled to the top of the box with ten clips for their Glock handguns. Robin picked out an empty clip and loaded it with fifteen bullets.

"Andrew, bring me one of those new handguns please." Andrew picked one of the boxes out of the secret department. Walked down the bus handing it to Robin who handed it to Zack.

"Take it out of the box and look at it, ensure its brand new. You're lucky to get these, normally we get you the Polish handguns and machine guns, this time we have upgraded you all. Andrew, get two bags and we'll give the men as many handguns as we have in our bus.

"Ethan, go to Ken's bus, get all the Glocks and take them to bus 2. Wait there until they all have a gun. Tell them you'll be back soon with some ammo, then return to Ken's bus, take their ammo box down and tell them the other guns will come down later. Tell Ken we are handing out the Glocks why we are waiting for bus 1 to get running again, shouldn't be long now."

"Okay boss, on my way," Ethan replied. He stood, put his thick fur-lined coat on then walked past Robin and Zack, then off the bus.

"Sorry about that, soon everyone on the first two busses will have their handguns and will be able to load their clips. I do not want anyone showing off pointing their Glock to a passing police car, is that fully understood Zack?"

"Of course, Robin, I'll inform everyone on bus one and two."

"I have too much rolling on this, I need to get away from Ken before he kills us all. Are you happy with the Glock?"

"Oh yes, if they are all like this, we'll be fine," Zack replied looking once again at the gun.

Robin took one of the clips from the ammunition box and Zack watched him load the clip with bullets from the box which he had just opened.

"Can I have your gun please you can have it back in a minute?" Robin asked.

Zack handed him the gun then watched Robin as he inserted the loaded clip into the gun. Robin handed his own Glock to his wife.

"Zack, do you remember I told you Ken was sure you would all be killed?"

"Yes, what are you planning to do, kill me here and now?"

"That might be a good idea," Robin replied.

Zack took a step back, thinking he could jump out of the doors, but they opened to the inside of the coach.

"You had better get back from us, this might get a little messy and I don't want his blood over you."

Robin watched his wife move four seats back then he raised the gun and pointed it at Zack's head. "At least you won't have to go into the gun fight with this," Robin said laughing then pulled the trigger, not once, but he moved the gun up and down Zack's body pulling the trigger time after time. The sound of the gun going off seemed to echo around the coach and some of the women were putting their hands up to cover their ears, and closed their eyes, as their husband's, held them tight in their arms.

Finally, Robin pulled the trigger two more times, finishing the clip he had loaded into the gun.

"What in Hell was that all about?" Zack demanded to know. "Is the firing pin broken off on all the guns?"

"No, they are all brand-new guns and haven't been doctored at all."

"The bullets are blanks?" Zack asked a few seconds later as he thought the problem through.

"Yes, I'm afraid so. The open box over there, is full of live ammunition, which you will load into your guns, for as many clips as the bullets will fill, no more than two for each of you. When your two clips are empty and let's be honest, some men will switch to auto and hold the trigger until it stops firing.

"They load the next clip and fire every bullet hitting nothing, missing their objective, they will go on to say this box of bullets are duds, and load another two clips from another unopened box while some people take their time, firing one bullet then another as they get closer to men returning fire. When they fire their full clips, they will feel the kick of the gun, then stand running forwards to kill one of Gabrielle's men and he will be shot himself, as he is firing blanks," Robin explained.

"In that case, we won't stand a chance and I suppose all the machine guns are the same, all blank bullets?" Zack asked.

"You have hit the nail on its head. The only live ammo is in the half full box. He wants you all to die for some reason, perhaps there being no more money, he wants to skip the country with what he has in his bank accounts. If he paid you all what you were expecting, it would have had to come from his bank accounts, with you all dead, he doesn't have that bill and you won't know if your wife has been paid or not," Robin explained.

"I have checked and double checked the men on all these buses, are all the men he has left, there is nobody else to come behind us.

"I noticed Lucas and Neil, Ken's own bodyguards, took small suitcases to the bus and had them put in the holds beneath the bus, and Ken had a case in there as well and took his briefcase onto the bus. I have an idea do you have your bank card on you?"

"Yes, what are you intending to do?"

"Give me your card." Zack took it from his wallet and handed it to Robin who sat at his laptop, opened a bank account and transferred ten million to Zack's bank account. Now, I suggest you ring your wife, don't worry about clothes, tell her to get on the next train to London. Tell her you'll meet her at the Rothchild Hotel, Baker, street and a double room has been booked for you both, just bring your Passports. Tell her you'll meet her around seven this evening, it's ten thirty now, tell her to buy herself some new outfits, underwear, pretty and sexy nightwear." Robin was smiling.

"We won't get to London now until twelve. We'll stay here another half an hour, let some of the traffic go. Oh, what's your wife's name?" Robin asked.

"Charlotte," Zack replied. He was just checking his bank account, sure enough, there was the ten million, from Interstellar Communications. "Thanks for the money."

"There is more to come, in two million over the next ten hours. If I can sort things out quickly, I'll get you another bank account and you'll pick your bank cards up tomorrow. You'll need a briefcase do we have a spare Andrew?"

"Yes, we have six spare all with your company paperwork in it. Do you want one?"

"Please. You'll have to take this to the bank with you and your passport, so make sure your wife has them on her."

"Does this Interstellar Communications company really exist?"

"Oh yes, it has been going for just over ten months, when George was recruiting men to do jobs, and paid a lot of money for what you had to do.

"Time is passing leave your Glock here, you won't need it where I'm sending you. Take this clip board, here is a pen. Get the people on bus 1 to give you their names and bank details Tell them they will each get half a million each in their bank accounts before you return. I'll come to your bus just before we start off again and explain what will happen. I know you were going to get your driver to turn the bus around and return home, this way, they will get something for the bus ride. I still have a few things to work out, so say nothing about your payment or what you are doing. If they ask if you have had any money, say half a million," Robin ordered and handed him the clip board and pointed to the bus door which was now open letting in the cold air.

As soon as he was off the bus the driver closed the doors as Robin returned to his seat with his wife next to him and the small table on the seat in front, pulled down with his laptop on it.

Half an hour later, he had given everyone on bus 1 their half a million-pound payment for the day. He was now on bus 1 talking to the men telling them what they would do when they arrived in London. He also had four men from bus 2 on bus 1 so he didn't have to repeat himself.

When he got off bus 1, he hopped onto bus 2 and took the clipboard which had everyone's bank account details on it. As soon as he was back on his bus, the busses started to move, and eventually, they got into the first lane and continued their journey at 40 mph, often dropping to 30 mph.

At one thirty they finally arrived in London and all the busses stopped in a coach and bus park. The first two busses were soon empty of men, as they headed, walking over the crisp white snow, towards the shops, most of all the expensive jewellers. The men on bus 3, got off their bus and followed the others into London.

Robin was counting the close friends of Ken he counted twenty men and heard the doors close, and the driver get off the bus. The rest of the men from busses four and five, were now walking towards the shops by another route. Most of them were speaking to their wife as they got closer to the main shopping centre.

The men in bus 6 were cleaning it up and Ken was getting fidgety. They had arrived in London far too early, they should have arrived in the dark, then the men would not be seen.

"Ken, it's obvious we arrived far too early. Could I suggest, without getting my head blown off, that we all go for something to eat and drink. There are loads of cafés and proper restaurants here in some of the larger stores we are intending to blow up tonight. It might be a good idea to have a look at them before this evening, I know that's what Robin and a few of his men are considering doing, especially inside the shops so they know where to hide the explosives," Oscar suggested.

"Damn good idea Oscar, I'm getting famished myself. Yes, if we bump into any of our men, or see them, we do not acknowledge them, is that clear?" Ken asked.

Everyone agreed as they stood putting on their thick, warm coats. "We'll walk off in groups of five, I will walk with my bodyguards. Now, let's go," Ken said.

Within ten minutes, they were in different restaurants, either waiting for their food or getting it.

Zack was with Robin's group, he had spoken to his wife and told her where to meet him, he was on his way there. As he put his phone away, he noticed one of the CCTV cameras placed high on the shop front was pointing directly at him, He looked for another camera, just over the road on another shopfront was also looking at him. As he looked forward, high up for another camera, he saw one which was moving slowly in their direction. Two more cameras were watching them, that is when he spoke to Robin.

"Robin, look directly at me while I'm talking, do not under any circumstances, look up. The cameras on the shops either side of all of us, are following us, I just looked at two cameras which were looking directly at my face. How long until we meet our wives?"

"Good spotting Zack, we go to the end of this road, turn left and we'll meet them part way along the road. Elliot, can you ring Ella and ask her where they are or if they are in the right place, can they walk closer to the end of the road, not around the corner and wait for us.

"Make a big job of meeting your wife, kiss her, hug her and generally stay by her side. They will love it anyway. We'll all head off for lunch in groups of four and each group will visit one of the shops we are going to attack tonight," he said holding his wife close and looking into her face as close as possible. Then they kissed for the cameras. The other five women in the group kissed their husbands and held their hand or put their arm through his and the six couples walked together in the group until the rest of the men met their wife.

Charlotte ran to meet Zack, her arms wrapped around his neck with a couple of shopping bags dropped to the pavement. They kissed each other, mouths rotating around each other, tongues intertwined, licking each other. Zack's hands were running up Charlottes side as he held her close to him.

"We are now heading off to lunch there are really too many of us to go into one restaurant, so we'll split up into groups of four and meet up later about three pm, its one forty-five and there are some big department stores around the corner so we can look in those," Robin said aloud.

After lunch, the two women dragged their husbands to the dress department and both women were looking at dresses then tried some on getting each other's opinion, then asking their husbands if they liked it. Buying three dresses each, they moved off to the blouses and skirts, while the men walked downstairs to the men's section and bought two suits each with shirts, tee shirts and a thick jumper each. After they paid for the clothes, they were trying to carry in their hands, they walked over to the underwear for men got what they wanted, then picked out a new pair of shoes.

When they met their wife, they went to the jewellery department. The men bought gold presents for their wife, while the women were buying new watches and rings to go around their wrists. Zack found the camera department and looked at the Nikon cameras and lenses. It took him twenty minutes to select what he wanted with the assistant's advice. Charlotte took Shirley to look at the high heeled shoes. They may need one or two pairs to accompany their husband to a meeting or two, they were saying to each other as an assistant was now close to them helping another woman.

After paying for their shoes, carrying more bags around the store, the women were looking at handbags. Ella had a shock when a security man put his hand on her shoulder.

"Take your grubby hand off my wife's shoulder. Come on dear, have you picked your handbag and new purse yet?" Elliot asked his wife.

"Yes love, can we pay for this and leave? We can look in another store."

"Ella let's leave the store, we can look elsewhere for new bags and pursers. I was hoping to get everything in one store, but I don't think they want our money," Charlotte said in fluent French.

"That sounds like a very good idea," he replied also in fluent French. Ella looked at her watch seeing the time was just past three.

"It's time we were off anyway. Put the small bags into the big ones. Let's walk away from this man and go out of the main doors," she spoke again in fluent French and looked at the man who was still standing by the handbags.

"Do you want us for anything now, we have paid for everything in our bags and if you stop us from leaving, you can give us our money back, I'll get my clothes in another shop," Ella said again in fluent French.

"I will be wanting all my money back as well. I don't want it if your hands are going to touch it," Charlotte replied in French.

"You will return everything I've bought as well. I have spent over three thousand pounds myself here and my wife has spent about a thousand pounds. I want all this money back in cash, not returned to our bank cards," Zack said in Fluent French, stunning the man.

"I will also join them, you can return all the money my wife and I have spent, we'll go elsewhere."

A woman who was also shopping in the store had two large bags on her arm and they looked very heavy, with the clothes she had inside.

I think this is disgusting, I saw both women pay for all their clothes, I was behind them in the queue. They put all their clothes on the counter and one of your girl's folded them all up and put the items into your store bag. We come here from France to your beautiful country and get treated like this in an English store it's not right. I think I should make a complaint to your manager," the woman shouted in French.

"Thank you, madam for your support, we French should stick together and not allow these English people to walk all over us. Thank you very much," Zack replied in perfect French. Zack replied with no pausing or wondering what she had said, because she was talking fast.

"I apologise, I think I have made a mistake, you are free to go," the store detective said. having not understood a word they had said, and he was going to France the following summer, I had better learn some French he thought to himself as he walked away from the two couples, not looking back.

The man in the security office got what he wanted, but these people were not the people they were looking for, he would have to keep looking.

As they entered the next store, both women started to look for the handbags and purses which were on the ground floor. After another shopping spree, they returned to their hotel and dropped all their bags off. Zack suggested they have a look at the jewellers in Hatton Gardens and Bond Street.

"We need to look like the people we are supposed to be directors of Interstellar Communications," Frank said, "and you two women need to look like a Director's wife and wear expensive clothes, like millionaires wear. I know the clothes you bought are lovely, but we need to find an expensive, clothes shop for where a dress costs a grand or more. We'll go by taxi, that way we will not be seen again by the street cameras."

Soon they were on Bond Street in Barton's diamond shop. They were all stunned by the different designs of necklaces and diamond rings. Ella was looking at a diamond bracelet which she tried on her wrist and showed it to Charlotte.

"It's beautiful, really beautiful and expensive, Can I try that one please?" Charlotte asked the woman serving them.

"Of, course Madam," the woman replied and handed Charlotte the diamond bracelet. It fitted her exactly and although the design was slightly different to Ella's, it looked just as beautiful with a beautiful price of twelve thousand pounds.

"Yes, I'll take this one please," Charlotte said to the woman.

"And I'll take this one," Ella added.

"Thank you, that will be."

"Oh, we haven't finished yet. I want a diamond necklace," Charlotte said then they were both looking at necklaces, new engagement rings and eternity rings. And plain diamond rings for the other hand. Finally, they were looking at diamond watches, and their husbands were looking at the most expensive watches. Both men were trying on a Vatch Vachenon Constantin watch,

"I can't believe you have two of these watches, do you have a woman's watch similar to this?" Zack asked the man serving them. The man moved away from his position and went to the counter where the women's watches were kept. As he unlocked the cabinet Ella saw the watch, he was just pulling off the shelf. Could I have a look at that please?" Ella asked.

"By any chance are you two ladies married to those two gentlemen further along?"

"Yes, we are, is everything alright?" Ella asked.

"Of course, they just asked me to get this watch so they could look at it," he informed the women.

"Elliot, are you and Zack looking at women's watches?"

"Yes, come here, look at my watch."

Both women went to see the watch and loved what they saw, then they looked at the woman's watch which they both fell in love with. Ella put her watch on, it looked slightly different on her wrist.

"Excuse me, but by any chance do you have another of these watches and, do you have a diamond strap to go on it instead of the Alligator strap?" Charlotte asked.

"Elijah, what is happening here? You are only supposed to be serving one customer at a time, now it looks like you are dealing with four," his floor manageress demanded to know of him.

"Grace, yes, can you help us please? These ladies would like to know if we have another watch like this one, and do we have a diamond watchstrap for both watches, so the watches are the same as their husbands?" Elijah asked, hoping Grace would see the amount of goods they were considering buying.

"We have another watch. They are pretty, aren't they? I have found two diamond watchstraps we'll have to see if they fit you. If they are too big, I can take links out, if they are too tight, we'll need to send it away as we don't have any diamond links. Let me see your wrist please," she said to Ella.

The girls got exactly what they wanted. With their bags in hand, they looked in other shops and found an expensive dress shop. They went inside and came out with two dresses three thousand pounds each, and a suit each for the men at four thousand pounds each which also included four crisp white shirts and three silk ties.

They were just about to return to their hotel when they saw an expensive menswear shop. The four of them entered the shop, looked around, picked out three four-thousand-pound suits each.

The wives picked out four expensive ties for both men three white silk shirts and while they waited for their trousers to be adjusted in the leg slightly, they looked around at different diamond tie pins and diamond-encrusted cufflinks. As soon as their trousers were altered, they paid for everything and left the shop.

"I don't think we should join the others tonight," Elliot said to Zack, when they were in the taxi.

"I would like to see a film or go to a show instead. I've never been to London before; it would be nice to see a show or film."

It was now 4:15, nobody should be returning to their coach yet. Zack got out his phone and commenced to ring a few of the men under his command who he knew he could trust. He gave the orders then hung up. He made another call trying to save as many lives as he could.

"You said it, so get out your phone and start looking at what shows are on here, I bet you have to book in advance," Zack said as he started to write then copy his text. He sent the four messages and hoped the people would do as he asked, or they wouldn't see the light of day tomorrow. He was thinking about his next text message and who best to send it to as the driver pulled up outside their hotel. There was another shop front camera opposite them, but it was looking the other way as Zack paid the taxi driver.

As soon as they were in their room Zack told Elliot to find a show and ask how many seats were available. Both women were getting changed into their best evening dresses, made sure they had their diamond earrings on and helped each other with their diamond necklace. Their diamond watch bracelets were difficult to fit the clasps together so again they helped each other. Their diamond bracelets were on the other arm.

It was now 5:20, Zack had finished his calls and sending text messages. Elliot also finished making his calls.

"What are we seeing tonight?" Zack asked him.

"Pretty Woman at the Piccadilly Theatre. The show starts at seven and ends at ten fifteen with a short interval. I've booked four seats in the upper circle, what do you say to a late meal after Pretty Woman. There is a place with excellent reviews Café Royal in Regent Street, it's not far from the theatre."

"That sounds very good, if we can walk there, it's even better," Zack replied.

"I'll book a table for four, for about ten forty-five." "That's fine with me," Zack replied.

Both men changed into their new suits and put on a crisp white shirt, tie new gold cufflinks black socks and new very shiny shoes. Zack took four drinks from the fridge and poured two of them into glasses, as they only had two glasses. Elliot went to his room next door and grabbed two wine glasses.

They had their drink, and the two girls took Ella's clothes next door to hang up and put away. When they returned to Charlotte's room, Zack was on the phone, Elliot was sat down beside him. Five minutes later, he had an incoming call, he spoke briefly and hung up.

"Shall we leave?" Zack asked, getting up.

"Yes dear, we're ready," Charlotte replied.

When they arrived in the reception, Zack went over to the reception desk. "Can you call us a taxi please?" He asked the receptionist.

"Tim our doorman will call you one over, we always have a taxi stand up the road and always have four taxies there for our guests," Cloe explained.

"Thank you," Zack replied and walked back to his wife. Outside, Tim got them a taxi and once again, Zack made themselves known to Tim so he wouldn't forget them, the time they left the hotel and where they were going and the name of the restaurant they were going to after.

When they arrived at the theatre, once again he made themselves noticed and the time they arrived and made sure they got the taxi driver's name. Zack was talking to him all the way to the theatre.

At eight, Zack was looking at his watch keeping an eye on the time. At nine there was a terrific explosion which shook the lights in the theatre, allowing some of the captured dust to fall on the people below. Zack and his party were lucky, they were not sat directly beneath one of the lights.

Everyone at the same moment shouted "Ooohhhhh, what was that?"

Even the cast were stunned and didn't speak for a minute or two. The stage lights went out and a voice came over the speakers scattered around the theatre.

"Please, everyone keep calm, it was an explosion a few streets away. We are okay, it was just the shockwave hitting us. Anyone who was covered in dust from the lamps, please remain seated at the end of the show and we will come and speak to you. The show will resume in five minutes, the cast were shaken up as well," the man told everyone.

Zack's phone pinged with a text message which he read, then deleted. He looked over to Elliot, as everyone was still talking, and several phones were either receiving a text message or receiving a phone call from worried friends and families.

"Did you get any dust on you?"

"No, we were lucky we were not under a light," Elliot replied.

Zack was looking at the news reports of the explosion on his phone. "It seems like the explosion was a truck or some vehicle, was carrying explosives when a firework was let off and it entered an open window and must have landed on some of the explosives which blew up the lot. They say the vehicle was heading towards one of the large construction sites when it blew up killing the driver three streets from us on some open ground, designated for a new road to the M4 and M25," Zack told Elliot, with at least six men leaning over the back of their seats, trying to hear what Zack said.

After the show, as they walked to the restaurant, police cars were everywhere. Fire engines were still playing their hoses on the fire. There was one ambulance there for the possible driver if he got out alive.

One of the firemen had managed to get close enough to the driver's side to see in through the blown out front windscreen. He confirmed the driver was dead, the bones still strapped into the seat belt. He was either knocked unconscious and burned alive or the explosion killed him, and his body was burnt. They would not be able to retrieve the remains of the body until the fire was put out and they had cooled the van down enough for them to be able to work inside it.

The police told the ambulance driver to leave and then called in a Coroner's black van to take away the remains of the man and a Recovery Lorry the police used in accidents they were involved with. To the police, it looked like the rocket was set off from a few streets away, where a wedding party had ordered fireworks to be sent up during their dancing when the couple left for the evening, going to Heathrow airport for their plane to France, where they would start their honeymoon. It was a professional firm that set up the fireworks and let them off in a controlled order. It was just bad luck one of the rockets came down on the truck and entered an open window.

The Police were now treating this as an accident and the way the rocket entered the van, An Act of God. The police had now discovered where the rocket had come from and spoke with the couple who were just married and the man who was letting off the fireworks from his computer control station.

Zack got a call from Reggie, who was the driver of the explosive's truck. "Hi Zack, it's Reggie, just confirming everything went as planned. I picked up a tramp, put him in some good clothes, made him put an overall on, took away his bottle of drink, gave him two hundred quid, got him into the truck, and drove to the proper place.

"I told him to stay exactly where he was. I got a takeaway cup of coffee, got back to the van, He handed me the new half bottle of whiskey and watched as I threw away the coffee and poured the entire contents of the bottle into the extra-large paper cup. His eyes were bulging as I handed it to him and within a few minutes, he had downed the lot. It was a good job I had a second bottle on me.

"I filled the cup again and he started drinking as soon as it was in his hands. It was the strongest whiskey I could get at the time. He wasn't used to drinking it that strong especially with eight soluble Paracetamol in it. He downed the whiskey as fast as he could and a few minutes later he was sound asleep and would feel nothing of the explosion or the fire after," he said.

"Well done, did anyone turn up at the shops?" Zack asked.

"No, not that I could see. All our team went to their hotels, booked a last-minute ticket for four to New York. Others got on a train to the southwest and about ten of the men and their wife's wen to France via the Channel Tunnel. So, everyone in our group is gone, and we didn't blow up any stores," Reggie said proudly.

"Where are you going?" Zack asked him.

"The misses and I are off to Dubai. Our flight leaves in thirty minutes, we should be boarding the plane in about five minutes," Reggie replied.

"How long are you staying there?" Zack asked.

"Two weeks, then we'll be off to another country and make our way to Australia, where we'll stay for a very, long time. It's a huge continent to explore."

"It sure is. Have a great holiday, see you when you get back," Zack said, just in case anyone was listening to their call.

Reggie knew instantly, something was not quite right, he had used the code which told him the police were near him and to hang up so he turned his phone off and turned it back on fifteen minutes later, when they would hopefully be on the plane and in the air flying, with no contact to the land phones.

Zack had noticed two uniformed officers enter the restaurant, looking at the people who were eating and those waiting for their food. One of the police officers went to the place where you ordered food. He waited there a few minutes, then his mate walked over to him and collected their midnight lunch break. They both left with a bag of half a chicken and chips and a capped mug of cappuccino,

As soon as they left, Zack and Elliot breathed a huge sigh of relief, just as their meals were placed on their table. A waiter brought a bottle of wine to their table and filled the four glasses, after Zack had tasted it and said it was fine. He knew he would have to learn a lot more about wine, if they were to mix with other multi-millionaires.

When he called Reggie, they were already seated on the plane and just waiting to take off. They talked briefly, wishing each other good luck as Reggie lost his phone signal as the plane was in the air.

During their meal, Zack had twenty text messages, each message was the same. "Hi, we're off on holidays, see you when we get back." He deleted each one, and the call to Reggie. He was glad Reggie was away, he thought he was their weakest link. They had another bottle of wine with their dessert, a different one this time, a dessert wine. The next call was from Robin.

"Zack, we heard the explosion, was anyone hurt?" He asked.

"No," Zack simply replied, trying to keep the conversation short.

"Did everyone in our team get away?" Robin asked.

"Yes, were on our way to the airport right now, we're flying to New York."

"That's good because Ken is furious no buildings were partially destroyed. Then his explosive men were gone."

"Hold on are you with Ken now?" Zack asked. Eliot stopped eating and looked at Zack taking a sip of his wine.

"No, I managed to get away from him with twenty-eight other men including, Theo Baker Bus 3 and one of Ken's bodyguards Lucas Simms. They are right now meeting their wives with two suitcases filled with all new clothes for them both.

"They are all going on a package holiday to Florida in Texas, it's close to Cape Canaveral, where they have a business tour arranged for Interstellar Communications, based in the UK at Manchester near the Radio Telescope. In Australia, near SKALow, CSIRO's Radio Astronomy Murchison Western Australia. was their head offices and research rooms. All their wives were at the two-night stay Hotel in London.

They had arrived in London last night, checked into their hotel and went shopping with two million pounds to spend. They had purchased new expensive dresses and a skirt three-piece suit and four white satin blouses. More expensive skirts and tops, blouses, cardigans and two jumpers in case it got cold. New expensive underclothes, tights and stockings and then into shoe shops looking for four-inch-high heels and a low two-inch heel. last was a Sports Shop, and Nike TN's Trainers. They bought two pairs for themselves and two pair for their husbands.

Next, they went to a shop that sold expensive trouser suits in different colours. They bought their husbands two three-piece suits and four white shirts. They also bought them a warm expensive jacket underclothes then four pair of shoes and a pair that would grip the ice and snow in New York and the UK.

All their clothes were put into the two suitcases then back to the hotel, to try and pack it all, then realised they would need another suitcase.

The women were surprised when their men arrived at two fifteen. The men met their wives at the prearranged shop, going straight to the top floor to have a hot drink and something to eat. All they talked about was their flight the following day.

During their time on the bus coming down to London, they knew they would get paid by Ken, because they were his top men, he could rely on. He had even paid them half their money in advance, two million each. All they had to do, after the men on the first two busses had finished fighting and killed all of Gabrielle's men and hopefully captured both women. They would thank whoever was left, take the two women and two men would wait for their bus, as it would be parked a long way off. While the bus was on its way, the men would be looking to get paid by Theo or Blake, Ken had both men in his bus and spoke to them before they went out for the afternoon and early evening, meeting their wives for a meal.

"Theo, Blake, I'll have all the money I owe you now, so we're squared up," Ken said and looked at their bank numbers on the top of the list on the paper in his hand. He took out his phone and transferred eight million to both of their bank accounts.

Can you check your accounts please? Ken asked them. It didn't take long to check it, but Theo was having a little trouble and was touching his phone's buttons as fast as he could. He had made another account with his bank and was now transferring the whole eight million into the other account.

"Sorry Ken my account wouldn't open because it did not accept my face and I had to look up the passcode. It's done now. Yes, the money is in my account, thanks."

"Right Theo, return to your bus and get our men ready to leave. We'll all leave together as there are not many of us, we will not look out of place when we meet our wives. Blake, take a seat, I need to give you a list of the men's names and their bank account numbers so you can pay the men when they are done, you will also give the man or men who capture the two women, two million pounds."

Ken waited for the bus door to close properly before continuing. Theo walked away from bus 6 and down to bus 3. He ran between buses 3 and 4 and keeping low, ran as fast as he could up the road to coach 6.

"Just check Theo is not here," Ken ordered, as Theo left the bus. Blake looked down the road seeing Theo by his bus and getting onto it.

"Theo's on his bus," he lied, he knew exactly where he was heading. "God, it's stuffy in here, do you mind for a few minutes if I open the window just a bit to get some fresh air in here?" Blake asked Ken with his hand on the window opening handle.

"No that's fine," he replied.

Blake pushed the window open a bit and saw Theo outside the bus, right under his open window.

"Take a seat Blake." Blake Sat down under the window he had opened.

"Blake, I have something to tell you and I don't know how to soften the blow, so I'll just spurt it out. You were with me at Base one with all the kids we had in there."

"Yes, have they all suddenly returned?" He asked smiling.

"No they've not returned. Do you recall I split the money up between a number of metal safes?"

"I was wondering how you managed to get it all out and into your bank accounts."

"I didn't when I returned to the house, it was completely gutted, even the top floor. It fell onto the second floor when the roof gave way. I went to every safe and they were all open, the firemen had put out the burning money, I could see it washed away. I went to the big safe which was open before I got there. I could see the door had buckled by the heat of the fire. The left side of the safe was also buckled and the outer safe panel, was buckled and flat on the floor. You could see the inside of the safe through a few places where the other metal case had buckled and warped.

"The door was the same and levered open, probably by the firemen. The money must have caught fire in the safe and they needed to extinguish the fire in case it set off another fire.

"There was just over twenty million in that building and when the tiles fell off the roof, they killed nearly all my fish, but a fireman fell into the water and was bitten by the fish. The man started to scream for help, a copper heard him, raced around to the back of the building which was still on fire and slipped on the wet path between the house and the pool. He fell straight in and was attacked by at least thirty small fish they went for his face and neck, and he was killed three minutes and fifty seconds later, the fireman said.

He managed to get out of the pool with help from another fireman. His hands and legs were bitten to the bone. He ended up in short trousers and a jacket with short sleeves. He's in one hell of a mess, nothing to do with us though. Shouldn't have got anywhere near the pool.

"So, all the money is gone from Base one, twenty million. The money I stashed in base two, is also gone. There were only four people working there, repainting the inside of the base and they had all the materials and paint brushes they needed. The safes were locked and sealed by Theo he even sealed my office. The door was opened, and the seal broken. I had forgot they had to paint my office as well.

"How much did you lose there?" Blake asked.

"Not too much, about eight million. I was lucky, when I went to the base, to bring everyone to base three and put all the money in the bank so I could transfer it to you lot when the time came.

"I was lucky I suppose, I took two million in the four by four with both bodyguards and the money stashed neatly in about nine boxes each trip. Then I had to make a third trip to get the full two million to the bank. It took two cashiers and a manager with another accountant watching them, an hour to count all the money, put it in their safe and arrange for a security van with an armed police escort to take the two million to another bank, with a much bigger safe,

"The two million I gave you before we left, was that two million. When I went to Base three in Manchester, I assumed there would be some cash there as I had personally with both my bodyguards put twenty million, enough to pay the men for today, into three large safes.

"When we arrived, the place was deserted. Nobody had broken the seal on the front or back door, and we checked all the windows were closed from the outside. When, we got inside, before we went to the safes, we looked and checked every window was locked closed, then we went to the safes. None of them were open and the seals were still in place. I was the only person who knew the codes to open the safes and I was the only one to have a key to the safes.

"I opened each safe in turn, the money was gone from all thee safes. God alone knows how or where it went, but it didn't go into my bank account."

"How much did you lose there?" Blake asked.

"Ten million, that was the last of George's cash. It's all gone. Now, I won't lie to you, I have thirty million in my bank account so I can give you both an extra five million each. That will leave me with twenty million to pay the bills for today and the guns I had on approval.

"When you start to get the men to the shops, this afternoon, nobody is to carry a Glock or machinegun. When the men get back in the dark, you will tell them you have left three holdalls full of machine guns and a fourth bag with the explosive in right next to the House wall."

"I wasn't planning on giving them the machineguns. They'll just carry their own Glock."

"Surely, they will have machineguns to use?" Blake asked.

"No, I don't want them used, that way I'll get all my deposit back. We'll need it to give the men some extra money and pay all these men off."

"Are you referring to the men in the back of the bus?"

Ken turned around, he thought they had gone to bus 3 and were now walking into the city or still on bus 3. "Have they been there all the time, heard everything we have said?" Ken asked.

"Yes, to both questions."

"There were seventeen men sat at the back of the bus looking at Ken and Blake. Blake pulled his gun from behind his back and held it in his hand by his side, he wasn't worried about Ken, it was the others he was worried about.

"Look men, I'm not sorry you heard that, I suppose you needed to know. What if I give you half a million each just to keep this to yourselves and you don't have to fight at all, no matter what happens? You can go off and meet your wives and have fun in the city. I have paid you all three thousand each so far and another half a million to have a bus ride, enjoy a couple of days in London. I've already paid for two nights in your hotel, I'll give you another two nights for free, I'll pay the hotel bills. What do you all say?" Ken asked.

Some of the men were playing with their guns and pointing them at Ken and Blake.

"Come on men, stop playing with your guns, someone might get hurt, then I would have to kill one or two of you," Blake said. Everyone knew Blake was one of the best shooters in their entire group, so they put their guns down and Blake put his back from where he got it.

"Okay Ken, we'll do as you suggest. Give us an extra three quarters of a million each. And then we'll get right out of your hair. We'll also take the extra two days at the hotel as well."

"You're asking for a lot of money with the two extra nights, let me see, there are seventeen of you, that will cost me around one hundred and two thousand pounds."

Ken looked at the list of names and started to pay the money they asked for, rather than pay another eleven no he thought, twelve men to do a job a few men could do themselves.

"Can you please check your bank accounts?" Ken asked.

"Did you transfer any money to me?" Blake asked.

"I'm sure I did can you check again please?" Ken asked. Blake looked again at his bank account and started to count in his head as his fingers tapped over the small keyboard that would transfer money from one account to the other. One of the men at the back realised what Blake was trying to do, probably for Theo.

"Ken, the money didn't go into my account either," Jayden said.

"Me too, mine went in and then went out. It was taken to another bank account," Charles said sounding annoyed.

"What's happening here Ken replied," shouting at Jayden.

"Here you are Blake, is it in your account now?" Ken asked him.

"Yes, it's there now thanks Ken."

"Come up here Jayden, Nathan." While the two men made their way up the coach to Ken, he too was touching his computer, getting the money back from their phones, including the three million they had to start with. But it was gone, it wasn't anywhere in their account, neither was the money he thought he had sent them.

"Hugo," Ken shouted at the driver, turning in his seat, so he could here Hugo speak to him.

"What can I do for you Ken?" Hugo the driver asked.

"Oh yes, just a minute guys, Hugo, can you call up all the other drivers at the same time?"

"Yes Ken."

"Good, tell them all to start their engines and drive slowly into the centre of London, where we'll all get off."

"Yes, of course Ken," Hugo replied and started his own engine as he spoke to the other drivers passing on their orders.

"I want to see your bank account open so I can see any savings you have and the check account open, so I can see the balance. I also want to see what has been paid in and paid out, in the last twenty-four hours."

As their coach moved off, there was no sign of Theo, he obviously ran back to his bus as soon as Ken told them about transferring their extra money to their bank accounts.

They were now travelling towards inner London, getting closer to where the stores they were going to blow up that evening. They turned to their left and entered a bus and coach park. Hugo turned his bus around and reversed into a parking space, then shut off his engine, and put the break on.

"Here, let me see," said Ken, taking Jayden's phone. He looked at his bank account and when he checked the in and out boxes, he could see there were no transactions over the last twenty-four hours. There was seven hundred and fifty pounds in his Checking account and a hundred pounds in his savings account. He was right, the money had not been paid into his account, so what happened to the two million he was given, the day before?

"I'm happy with your bank account, it looks like the transfer either didn't happen or it went to another account." Ken looked at the account details and called them out to Blake who was now helping him.

Blake listened to the account numbers then stopped Ken, here was a wrong number third from the end. Ken snatched the phone from Blake and checked the account number on the phone to that on the paper. He could see there was a difference, when he looked again, there were another five accounts, where some of the account numbers had been crossed out and a different number inserted. There was one account that was completely scratched out by pen and re-written again and again. Six accounts had the first six digits wrote down wrong and scratched out, then a different set of numbers was put in above the scratched out, ones. The page had ink smudges and was a right mess.

"Who did I get to do this simple job?" Ken asked.

"I'm sure it was Niel, but he was ill that day and in a lot of pain when you shot him in the thigh, just to see what impact the Glock bullet could give a man. He had to go to hospital to have the bullet taken out of his thigh then you made him walk around getting bank numbers from people with a fractured hip. He should have been resting and I warned you he might not be well enough to fight tonight," Blake said.

"That's why I put him with the explosives team. He wouldn't be walking about much," Ken replied and snatched Nathen's phone from him. He checked the number himself and shouted again, that Neil had messed up again."

"Is there anyone else who has not got their money?" Ken shouted to the back of the bus.

Two people put their hand in the air, having altered their account. They walked up to Ken, let him see their accounts and Ken agreed they were not paid and apologised.

He quickly transferred the money to the four accounts, including the two million each they should have had the previous day.

"Now all of you go and meet your wives and buy them something nice, you have roughly five hours, I'll see you all back at the first store at seven pm," Ken said. When they had all departed. It just left Ken his two bodyguards, Benjamin and Jaxson. They watched the men walk off, following the other men into the main shopping centre.

The last three men left the coach and Hugo shut all the open windows, then shut the front doors and locked up the bus. He too went to meet his wife and like the other drivers, were given a million pounds each to never repeat what they heard on the bus. They were intending to have a good shopping spree in the main London shops.

As the men from bus 6 and 4 split up, some of them got into a group and spoke briefly to Blake and Theo.

"We don't want to blow up the buildings and kill people, that's not us. Destroying these six stores and killing maybe a thousand or more men women and kids, plus all the staff, mainly women, who if lived, would be badly scared for the rest of their lives. This is nothing to do with Gabrielle and Lynda Grayson, or their bodyguards," Ronnie said as he was the spokesperson for their group.

"That's fine we don't want to fight either. The men from busses 1 and 2, the men who are to fight Gabrielle's forces tonight, do not wish to fight either as they will not be paid. Watch out, Ken doesn't try and take the money he has given to you back. Send it to your wife's bank account, I'm sure you were all told to get your wife to open a bank account," Theo said quietly.

"If you are staying in London tonight, go to another hotel and go to the cinema or a show. Most of all, make yourselves known to the hotel staff, what time you leave and return. If you go to a restaurant after, make yourself known to the staff. Time you arrive and leave, if possible, get names of people who you talk to, so they can tell the police where you were if you need an alibi. Either get out of the country as soon as possible, by boat or train or get a train to the southwest," Theo told them then walked on to meet his wife.

The group of men moved on, talking to each other and ten minutes later met their wives. They decided to book a train to Paris the following day. At least they would have already booked the train before anything happened, and hopefully they would not be missed until they were supposed to meet at the buses. They decided they would go to different shows, and shop for the rest of the day and tomorrow they would board their train to Paris.

Like the others, their wives went shopping, buying expensive jewellery, watches gold necklaces and other items. The men had changed from their working clothes into the suit their wife had bought them the previous day and a clean shirt and new shoes. They had even surprised their husbands with an expensive gold watch.

Everyone had to buy an expensive briefcase that had good locks and a top of the range laptop, they would have to use for their job, as that would be the only way they could contact each other. They would have to buy the laptop in the UK and make sure they took it with them.

The first shop many of the men visited was a good, tailors to try and get an off the peg, three-piece-suit. If they needed any alterations, they would only have until the following day at midday.

Theo paid two thousand pounds for his suit which only needed the legs taken up two inches. He managed to buy another two three-piece suits and four crisp white shirts. They went to a tie shop recommended by Alex, who sold him his three suits, which he would pick up at six that evening.

Imagen, Theo's wife, picked out six expensive silk ties, and six standard ties, all of them with a matching handkerchief for the top suit jacket pocket. With his clothes all sorted, they looked for a computer shop.

A short time later with two laptops, a Nikon camera with ten short and long lenses, as many different filters as the shop had, a small camera for Imagen, and eight camera memory cards, for both cameras, they never knew when they would be able to upload the memory cards before they got to their final destination in Western Australia.

Theo and Imagen returned to their hotel, dropping off all their bags, including the three suits, Theo picked up at six. They were now hanging up in the wardrobe, He looked at the other suits Imagen had purchased the previous day, one was grey the other blue, the one he was wearing dark blue. Imagen changed her dress, for the evening out and put on some of her new diamond jewellery, brushed her hair when they were off, getting a taxi to the theatre showing Cats.

Halfway through the performance, they heard a huge explosion that rocked the theatre. Dust was falling from the large lights. A woman was screaming as some of the stage parts and props, fell on her and her husband. The house lights came on. The actors and actresses were running from falling wooden and metal beams that were holding scenery up.

A group of people were removing wood and two metal beams full of dust and upper debris from the man and woman, who turned out to be Aaron and Hannah, Aaron was on bus 4 earlier, in the day, but was now in a lot of trouble. The people helping them were also from the busses.

It took eight men some on the stage, despite bits of falling debris, which they were used to when they blew up buildings and smokestacks. Aaron had a huge lump on his head, still getting larger as the time passed. The first metal beam was now off

Aaron's head, which they placed in the last isle right against the wall, so it was out of the way. The second beam was still heavy as they lifted it from Hannah's left shoulder, allowing a gush of blood to get over herself and her husband.

"Come on, they need a little back up," Theo said to Imagine. He took hold of her hand, guiding her down through the gangway to the accident below.

"Hello boys, I didn't think I would be seeing you lot here tonight. Where is Hannah bleeding from?" Theo asked.

"It looks as if it's from the side of her neck," Leo replied.

"We have to get it off her, so, here is what we'll do." Theo looked around and saw just what he needed. Theo moved away from the bar and turned to face a woman in the seats behind them.

"Excuse me mam, can I borrow your scarf please?" "It's covered in that dust from up there," she replied.

"That's okay I'll give it a shake, can I borrow it please, it's for that woman with the girder on her. It's crushed part of her neck and it's bleeding badly. Until a paramedic arrives, we will have to make do."

"In that case, here you are young man," She removed her scarf and handed it to him.

"Thank you so much," he replied and was back with Imagen.

"Imagen, can you get under the beam and when they lift it off her, I'll slide this scarf over her head and you will pull it down to where Hannah is bleeding from when you have it covering the bleeding area, hold it in place and I'll tighten the scarf this side of her. Just press it against her neck for now and I'll have a quick look at it. Lily, while Carter helps the others lift the bar off Hannah, for now, can you hold his head still and let me know if that bump gets any bigger. I wish we had something to cover Aaron's head with," Theo said.

"Excuse me, here is all we have of a first aid kit. There isn't much, one small bandage and a couple of pads of some kind," the young girl said.

"Thank you, I'll have a look inside." He took the green box, opened the lid and sighed. "You were right when you said there wasn't much inside." His right hand went inside the box and pushed what was there about. Then he smiled. He removed two large three by five-inch cotton thick pads. There were just four large plasters, which he took out and handed them to Phoebe.

"Hold on onto those for me please Phoebe."

"Evie," Theo called quietly. "Is Hannah conscious yet?"

"Yes, she's just coming around. I'm holding her hand, she opened her eyes just now, then closed them."

"Try not to worry, it's probably the amount of blood she's lost, and I think the beam must have hit her head as well. When she comes around again, try talking to her, maybe you can pull her awake."

"Okay Theo, I'll do as you ask," Evie replied.

"Lily, take this please and just hold it over the bump on Aaron's head."

Theo moved to Hannah who was still unconscious like her husband. He took the scarf from Imagen and handed her the thick padding.

"When they lift the girder from her, let them get clean away over your head and my head so they can get rid of it. Put the pad over the bleed and hold it there, I'll pass the scarf over her head, grab it and pull the scarf down and put it over the padding. I'll tighten the scarf my side you make sure it's not too tight."

As soon as the girder was lifted from her neck blood spurted over Imagen, making her new dress blood red. She pushed the pad over the area that was bleeding and managed to stop the flow of blood. Theo passed the scarf loop over Hannah's head and Imagen pulled it down over the side of her neck and placed it around the padding Theo pulled it tight and inserted his folded up hankey beneath the scarf, where he was going to tighten it his end. A few minutes later, the pad was held in place and no longer bleeding. Theo made sure everything was alright with Hannah and the scarf was not tied too tight. Aaron was just coming around, as Lily gently rubbed his bump with her pad. Aaron's eyes just opening as he slowly lifted his right hand to his head and felt a woman's hand holding something in the centre of it.

"What happened, whose there?" he asked.

"It's Hannah you have a large bump on your head, does it hurt anywhere else?" she asked.

"Okay, I don't think I hurt anywhere else; but I have a really bad headache," he replied to her question. "What's going on here, what happened?" he continued.

"It's Lily now, you took a blow to your head when an iron beam came down after the explosion. Hannah is coming around now, a second beam fell which you took the brunt off, it slipped off your shoulder onto Hannah's shoulder and it cut her neck, Theo thinks it cut her archery," Lily said, checking him over for other cuts or bruises.

"Theo should know he is after all our Paramedic."

"It's good you can remember that Aaron," Lily said. as she took his hand and placed it on top of the pad on his head. She walked around to the front of him and started to remove his suit jacket. When it was off his right shoulder, she could see his white shirt was covered in blood and there was a pool of fresh blood near his shoulder. She pulled the shirt off his right side as gently as she could. When she looked up, she saw the theatre seats were slowly emptying of people as they were ushered out of the building. Finally, two paramedics and ambulance crews arrived and took over from Theo after he explained what he had done to Hannah and Aaron. Lily and Carter said they would go with them and let everyone know if they would have to stay in hospital and for how long,

"Nathan, Violet," Theo called to them as soon as they were with him, Lilly and Imagen were still with Aaron and Hannah.

"There are two ambulances, I want you two to go with one of them in the second ambulance. If they must stay in hospital for a few days, get them into a private hospital. I don't want any of Ken's men he has left, finding out where they are and kill them. I'll cover the costs."

The group waited with Aaron and Hannah who were now fully conscious as they were put onto stretchers and taken into the ambulances. Those who were accompanying them also left and after a few words from Theo, they all left the theatre at the same time to a host of photographers, and a news crew who were all shouting questions at them.

It took a while for them to get into the four taxies Theo had ordered and with the least of words said, they managed to leave with unanswered questions. They returned to their hotels and Theo spoke to them later after he had spoken to Zack.

Everyone who could get out of London, were told to get out as soon as possible. Eventually, they would all meet up at NASA's nearest hotels in Florida, Texas.

Theo had a text from Trever, who was still getting the rooms ready in the House, as more beds had arrived.

"Theo, Zack, Ken's men are just arriving over the hill, there do not appear to be many of them, I count ten men, including, Ken. They have multi round machine guns, grenades around their belts and a handgun. They are looking for hiding places. The explosion helped a lot."

"Thanks Trever, I hope you can overpower them Theo."

"Zack, only a few couples left to leave London. There was an accident in the theatre we all happened to be in. Aaron and Hannah are now in hospital, I will let you know how they get on. I treated them as best I could with what we had, the two Paramedics, said I did a good job. Both will require a CT scan and X-rays. I'll keep you informed as to how they are doing Theo."

"Zack, Theo, Ken has started the engagement, Gabrielle's people returning fire. Two of Ken's men are down and not moving.

Both men killed by ours in the House. Another of Ken's men down. it leaves seven men; Ken is moving them forward firing his machine gun. Have to go, Trever."

Chapter 18

Gabrielle and Lynda were holding hands, watching the men shooting at them in a hap hazard way. They were using machine guns which looked as if they were pointing directly at the Train Station, but the bullets were missing them, either going to their left or right, a few guns were even firing into the air and they could see the men in the House, were getting good hits on the men as they did not assume anyone would be firing from the House.

One man decided to try throwing a hand grenade, but as he stood and pulled the pin, he was just putting his hand behind his head, getting ready to throw it, when Isaac shot him in the head. The man dropped the grenade and seconds later it exploded, lifting the body into the air and broke his body apart. His arms and legs were flying through the air and one leg hit the man closest to him.

The man was knocked off balance and when he stood; instead of crouching, Mike put a rifle bullet right between his eyes. The six men left were firing at the House, allowing their bodies to be face on to the unseen gunmen looking through the side windows of the House. As three rifles fired at the same time, twice each killing three men who collapsed to the green, snow-covered grass. Just as they turned to face the Train Station, under Ken's orders, Craig, who was on the top floor of the House, looking out of the window through his telescopic sight, managed to get a clean shot on Nigel, one of the new Bodyguards to Ken. As his dead body fell to the ground, it hit Ken on his side and right arm.

Ken was angry on losing so many of the men he had left, after the others absconded. He hoped, the loud explosion was at least two or three stores being partially brought down, but it was further from the truth. With his anger growing, he removed his Glock from his side pocket. Looked at Nigel who had by now made his final slide down Ken's side and was now laying in the snow. Ken held the Glock in his hand and fired three times into Nigel's dead body and one bullet into his head.

"Well Henry, I had hoped we would have had many more men with us, but I suppose as they were not going to be paid, due to lack of funds, I'll pay you now, Let's sit down on the snow a moment, while I pay you your bonus, you have already had four million put into your bank account which your wife can access any time she likes."

Ken took out his phone and looked at his first bank account which should have had twenty million in it, which he was supposed to pay his men with, but he thought better of it, most of them he knew would die when they loaded the blank ammunician into their guns, so why pay them?

He couldn't believe his eyes as he looked at the account. It was empty of all cash. He moved to another of his six accounts, that too was empty, so was the third account and the fourth. So far, he had lost seventy million pounds of George's money, which was supposed to have been his pension for himself and his wife, Darcy. He had previously transferred, twelve million into her account two weeks ago, and he had seen it in her bank account, so in the event of his death, he knew she would be okay.

Ken's heart was pounding as he hoped whoever had skimmed the money from his accounts, would not keep it all to himself as he wanted to, but spread it out between all the men, who were now alive when they should be dead.

He opened the last two accounts, one was empty, the last account had ten million in it. He looked over at Henry and saw him reloading his Glock and his machinegun with new bullets from the ammunician box he had just opened. His mind was still going frantic over the lost money as he thought who might have access to his bank account and know the passwords. A few people's names came into his head. Then he thought of his wife, would Darcy, really have taken all the money from his accounts? Then he thought, if Darcy had taken the money, perhaps she was thinking of him? If anything happened to him, she would at least have most of the money to live out the rest of her life in a different country and start all over again from scratch.

With that thought in his mind, he started to open the file that would allow him to transfer money to another person. He found Henry's name and clicked on it. He was thinking how much he should give him, but he knew very soon they might both die, but he would try and talk himself out of it. As he was concentrating what to give Henry, Henry was loading another Glock and machine gun with new ammunician, so they would be ready to go out killing as many people as they could. He placed Ken's gun by his side and his machinegun back to the place he took it from. Ken was still thinking of the amount to give him when five million was taken from his account. He quickly clicked on Henry's name and was about to tap in three million when a dark shadow came over them both. Henry was the first to look up into the eyes of two bodyguards John and Alan.

Behind them was Gabrielle and Lynda, flanked by another four bodyguards, Tina, Noah, Isaac and Geraldine. Henry was on his feet, Glock in hand with fifteen new bullets ready to take them all out, including Gabrielle and Lynda. He wondered if he would still get the ten-million-pound bonus, for killing both girls.

"Well, who do we have here? No other than Ken Maximillian himself," John said answering his own question.

"Who are you?" Alan asked looking at the man now standing, his gun in his right hand. "Well?" he asked again.

"You talkin' to me?" Henry replied.

"Do you see anyone else left alive here, except of course, Ken, your boss?"

"Tell them your name," Ken said quietly.

"I'm Henry, the last of Ken's men. You would have heard the loud explosion earlier, that was some of our men blowing up the fronts of three multi story stores in central London. If nothing else, we would have killed over two thousand people who were in the three stores at the time and other people caught up in the explosions and debris from the front of the shops as it fell to the pavements and road below," Henry boasted.

"I'm sorry to tell you, but that didn't happen. The vehicle carrying the explosives was diverted to another road to get it away from the city centre, primarily, Bond Street. It was parked up on a pavement and a narrow road behind the very shops you were hoping to blow up," John explained.

"In a totally freak accident, there was a wedding party, going on two roads away. One of the big rockets, which was set off by a professional firework display firm, went up and came down, entering an open window in your vehicle. The rocket started its huge explosion of smaller rockets and stars, which should have happened high up in the air. Instead, the small rockets and stars, flew into your boxes of dynamite which blew up, one box after another then all the bottom layers of boxes were lit by the first layers of dynamite, and blew up the van, killing the driver.

"Your four-by-four vehicle, exploded on a derelict piece of land behind the stores where only four windows were damaged ...." John told them.

"No. No, No, that couldn't have happened, the shops must have blown up," Henry shouted, and lifted his Glock pointing it at John, then Alan. "No, you will not get away with this, Alan saw that he was about to pull his trigger.

Alan's gun was out in a second, as too was John's. They both fired at the same time as Henry's gun gave one bang then he fell to the floor dead. Both men were looking at each other wondering who had been hit.

"If I were to put money on it, I would say that was a blank," John said looking to Alan. Henry was now laying in the snow, blood coming from the two bullet holes in his head.

Ken was now standing, Glock in his hand, not realising what Henry had done to it.

"Ken, we finally meet each other, you were the last man George put in charge of all his money for you to pay his men to come and get us," Gabrielle said.

"You tried hard Ken, but you didn't get your hands on me, the one person you wanted back, to finish off what you had paid for when I was with Ian. How does it feel now, to be on the other side of our guns? You were one of George's top men, the one man he trusted the most to take his revenge on Gabrielle and myself?" Lynda added.

"You chased us around the world, killing innocent people at times, but we slipped through your grasp every time, and most of this was with the grateful help of John and Alan, our bodyguards. Of, course our other bodyguards helped us when times were getting hard," Gabrielle told him, holding her wife close to her.

"Do you have any last words to say to us before you die, as you would have tried to kill us?" Lynda asked, holding a Glock in her hand.

"I don't believe it, all this time you did have a pair of balls, and now you're going to use that Glock to try and kill me, but I also have a Glock in my hand. I'm fast, just as fast as John or Alan, and you for that matter. I guess at some time, we'll all meet each other again in Hell and we'll have a lot to talk about. Now Lynda, Gabrielle, prepare to meet your maker, whoever that may be," Ken said, holding his gun firmly in his hand facing Lynda.

The last thing he heard were four Glocks, all firing at the same instant. His body was pushed back and forth, then back again as the bullets hit his head and chest. His own Glock unfired, fell to the floor. His body was now crumpling to the cold snow below him, which he entered face down. His body no longer moving, he was finally dead.

John walked over and picked up Henry's gun, he saw all the bullets he had ejected from the clip and new ones he had put into it. John looked around held the Glock firmly in his hand and pulled the trigger four times the gun barrel pointing to the snow. There was a loud bang from the gun after every shot, but nothing hit the snow.

"He was firing all blanks and that box down there must be full of blanks as well. I just wonder?"

John picked up Ken's gun and fired it four times into the snow, but not one bullet touched it.

"Well, that is odd, do you think he knew Henry had changed the ammunician in his gun as well?" he asked the others.

"I doubt it, he was on his phone at the time Henry changed the bullets. He wouldn't have known anything about it," Lynda told the others.

"It's all over with now at long last, we can tell the police Ken is dead and most of his men left the coaches they were on and boarded any train they could to get them out of London and if possible, out of the country. It will also give us a little longer to get the House completed.

"Can a couple of you change your Glocks to your lance's please, and destroy what is left here, including the guns and that box of ammunition?" Lynda asked.

"Hold on a moment," Gabrielle said. She pulled out her phone and took photographs of the dead men and several different shots of Ken.

"Right boys, you can now clear the combat zone," Gabrielle said feeling proud that they had managed to finally kill the man who had chased them around the world, throwing man after man against them and all his men in those gun fights were now dead as well. At least some of his men got away.

The London sky was once again filled with electric blue lights, for a short time as the dead men were turned to ashes and the ashes to dust. When the removal of the dead men was completed, the electric blue lights stopped illuminating London, possibly never to be seen again for many years.

The following day, several lorries arrived with various loads of blankets, bedding, soap, perfumes, makeup and makeup brushes and everything which was needed in the shower rooms and toilets. Twenty of the girls were helping in the House, taking up boxes of everything they would need in the shower room and toilet. Once the number of correct boxes of items were on the top floor, they started again to move more of the boxes to the fifth floor. Another group of girls were on the top floor, unloading the boxes and putting items in each bedroom on the un-maid beds.

Another group of girls were taking up all the bedding and duvets from the Train Station with matching pillowcase and a single sheet to the top floor in each bedroom. There were four double beds on the top floor and four on the fifth floor and one double bed on the fourth floor. The bedding for these beds, was in another box marked double beds. Two girls carried the box up to the fourth floor and left the bedding on the one bed on that floor and moved up to the fifth floor and finally the top floor. As the girls finished one job, there were more jobs to do.

The rest of the duvets had to go to each room that did not have one. The girls unpacked them from their box, unpacked the duvet cover and sheet, then put the duvet cover onto the duvets and made the bed, leaving the pillowcase at the head of the bed. When the girls had managed to make all the beds, some with one pillow others with none, the next items were the pillows, which had to be removed from their packing had the matching pillowcase put on and moved on to the next bed.

There would be two pillows to each bed and the double beds would have four pillows. A group of twenty girls were in the basement putting a single pillowcase, to the send pillow. All the pillows once made were left in the basement, until a group of younger girls had finished taking the towels up to each room and left at the bottom of the bed. Once finished, they took all the pillows and loaded as many as they could into the lift and sent it to the top floor where two girls were waiting to unload the lift. With the lift empty it was returned to the basement when it was filled again and sent to the fifth floor.

Margarette showed ten girls, where everything went in the shower and toilet. Then they were off setting out the things as they had been shown. They quickly moved along the top floor, down to fifth, fourth, third floors, then the second and first, floors with extra rooms which they were sure were not there a day ago.

The other girls were following closely behind, putting the pillowcases on and then the duvets into its cover and moved on. Another lorry arrived with large boxes of toilet rolls. Gabrielle and Lynda dropped the boxes off, four to a floor. They also took up, all the remaining towels for each floor to the large stoor room.

Then they took the spare bedding to each floor's storeroom. They also took up boxes containing the lamps for the desks. Then they took all the lights which would go by the side of the bed.

Twenty men were working on the third floor, putting furniture up together and placing the wardrobes from the Train Station which Gabrielle and Lynda, were moving to individual rooms and being secured to the wall. Then they took the last of the chest of drawers and put them in individual rooms. The girls would have to spend another night in the Train Station, unless by some miracle, they managed to get everything completed in the bedrooms, office, hospital rooms and Triage room. There was also the basement and kitchen to complete as well.

The Train Station was now devoid of all the girls who were working in the House putting two toilet rolls in each toilet, the remainder went into the large storeroom. which was now filled up with spare duvet sets, sheets pillowcases and four spare duvets in case of accidents, with eight spare pillows.

It was the same for each storeroom on every floor. The towel sets were now being hung up in each shower room. One of the women was slowly moving along the top floor, putting the names of the girl or girls onto the door, all in the same position. The room numbers had been put near the top of the door in the centre by the carpenters when they rehung the doors and it needed a little shaved off the bottom of the door to get over the carpets, which were thicker than the ones they had before.

The next three large items to arrive, were the raised seats for the film rooms. Normally they would arrive in parts, making it easier to get into the rooms, then they would have to fit them together, but these were made up, the seats added to the frame with all the drink holders and footrests fixed by each seat.

"Gabrielle how do we get these into the House, let alone into the cinema rooms?" Trever asked.

"Have you worked out how they actually fit into place?"

"Yes Gabrielle, it's quite easy, its secured to the floor by twelve large bolts, which are supplied with it and fourteen large screws at the back into the wall."

"How many men will it take to fix it in position?"

"At least four," he replied.

"Let me know when you have four men with their powered, screwdriver's and they have all the packets of screws opened ready to use. Then call me, I'll be in the basement, helping to unpack all the chairs. Perhaps when your men are free. They could go to the basement and help the other men put together all the dining tables and benches."

"Yes, that will be fine Gabrielle, I'll speak to you again soon," he replied, and went off to find four men who would know what they were doing when it came to fixing the raised seats. Thirty minutes later, Gabrielle and Lynda were taking one complete set of raised chairs they hoped they could get it past the doors with them and dropped it into position. It took them ten minutes to move the seats from outside the House, into the three cinema rooms.

Trever kept an eye on his men who were fitting them, ensuring all the double washers went onto each screw before it was screwed into the floor or back wall.

An hour later, after finishing the jobs they had been working on, eight men Trever had from other jobs arrived in the basement with the four men who secured the seats in the cinema rooms and got straight to work on making the dining tables. With two men to each table, they were all on their legs and being put into their positions ready for breakfast.

Other men and four girls were quickly moving all the chairs to their allocated positions and four of the bench seats were now up together and at their correct tables; one chair and a folding three step ladder with a square flat tabletop attached to the steps so someone could put heavy bags of flour or sugar onto it allowing the woman to get it down safely then take the heavy bags from the top of the steps.

With the basement completed, and the kitchen, full of food and milk, with butter, jams and yogurts in the fridges, it was ready to serve breakfast to those who wanted it in the morning. The last room to complete was the reception and office.

Most of the items had already been built, all it needed now were chairs for visitors to sit on, two reclining and swivel office chairs in brown leather and set up the computer which also controlled the outside lights and turned on and off different monitors in the room. The printer had to be set up and loaded with white paper. There would also be twenty reams of white paper put into one of the floor cabinets and everything else that would be needed in the office.

On the ground floor a small room held four large colour laser printers, already set up, would now need paper, pencils, and colouring pencils with other items and folders the girls might need for their homework. The printers were one to each floor. The girls on each floor would input the name of their computer when they wished to print something then they would have to go to the ground floor to collect it, but it was the easiest way to do things. The last of the televisions and their wall brackets finally arrived and eight teams of two men, fitted the last of the brackets to the wall in each bedroom and the office and two televisions in the basement.

Then they fitted the TVs to the brackets, plugging them into the socket beneath the TV and fixing the two cables the TV company had rigged up and put the TV Channel box on top of the bookcases. Last, they had to set the TV and the channel box up. When completed, they left the TV and TV box remote controls, on top of the bookcase, next to the TV Box.

The men split themselves into pairs and went to every room from the sixth floor to the third new floor, ensuring each TV and box had been set up and were working fine.

Suddenly there was a lot of commotion outside, as girls were running around looking into large boxes, packed with boxed, top of the range laptops. Lynda and Gabrielle took three large boxes of boxed laptops to each floor.

The girls were then let lose, they ran up the stairs to the floor they had been told to go to and took the boxed laptop out and put the box in each bedroom on their floor. Then they unpacked the laptops, plugged them into the socket and moved on to the next room.

The six IT men who arrived in two cars, went to the top floor and started to install the computers, making sure the wireless Internet worked for each floor. They also installed the designated laser printer for their floor.

At long last the girls were allowed into their rooms.

All the girls on the top floor were having their photos taken by their computer and installed.

The technicians were still working through several problems some girls were having getting the laptop to take their picture and install it. Realising how long this job would take, one of the technicians rang his office and asked for as many men as they could get to help install four hundred and fifty laptops, and three full size computers in two offices and a further two medical computers in the Hospital unit.

The man was told to carry on as best as he could, help would be on its way. With twenty technicians working in the House, it still took four hours to set them all up and got each one fully operational. Everything worked and the last twenty rooms had their beds made and the rubbish thrown onto the ground outside the House.

As Gabrielle and Lynda walked hand in hand with John and Alan following them around the House, looking into each room and store cupboard, seeing that everything was completed, they declared the House was open to their girls and staff.

The girls were overjoyed to be in their own rooms and in their new beds. Simon was also pleased to be able to return to his house, with his wife and get a good night's sleep. As the lights went out all over the House, except the two nightlights on each floor and the night lights over the stairs the morning shift, for the first night, slept in the staff bedrooms.

Gabrielle and Lynda walked out of the House and looked up at the stars. Gabrielle pointed to a star far away.

Gabrielle took Lynda's hand in hers as they looked at the bright star over five thousand light years away.

"It's Gravilous, with its five planets and three Gas Giants."

"Yes, we went there a few thousand years ago, the Planet Lover's End, is so beautiful and ever so romantic. Do you think we could go there again on our next trip?"

"Wrong way I'm afraid, but there is the planet Romance Never Ends, in the Trinity star system, we could go there once we are on our way and everyone is settled down, including us, my love," Gabrielle sighed and taking Lynda in her arms, they kissed under their new moon.

Their mouths rotated about each other as their tongues met kissing each other, looking forward to the time they would have together and the wonders of the universe they would see on their next journey.

They jumped together into their large apartment, the, bodyguards were already there, drinking hot chocolate which Wendy had made them. When the girls arrived, Wendy made another four cups of hot chocolate as she saw their mother enter the door behind them. There was a young man behind her younger looking body and face.

"Hello everyone, I was out this evening and I bumped into Charles, we met a few years ago, had a few dances and got to know each other, and so we have met again tonight. Gabrielle, Lynda, I would like your permission to let Charles stay here tonight, with me. I'm a lot younger now and a younger woman has needs as well as young men."

"Mother, you have no need to ask us, this is your apartment as well and you have your own suite. Welcome to our apartment Charles, do you have a last name?"

"Yes Gabrielle, you look prettier every time I see you. Hello Lynda, good to see you again." Lynda was still wondering who this man was, then it dawned on her. Brenda would never bring another man into the house unless her husband was with her. For now, he was calling himself Charles. but it would soon be…"

"Dad?" Lynda asked stepping forward to the man.

"Who else would it be?" he asked her and stepped forward kissing her face and giving her a hug.

"You're looking good for your age dad," Gabrielle said and kissed his face all over, hugging him tight against her.

"What gave me away?" he asked.

"Mother would never bring just any man back here unless you were with her, and not to sleep with her, no matter how many years had gone by. Welcome home dad," the girls said together.

"It's nice to be back," he replied and held his hand out to his wife. She naturally took it into hers and held it with all the love she had for him. He gently pulled her towards him, and they kissed, as passionately as Gabrielle and Lynda.

Wendy came in with their hot drinks and placed them on the coffee table. She stood and looked at Charles.

"Mr Grayson, it's so lovely to see you again, may I?" she asked.

"Of course, Wendy, come over here and it's Charles for the moment." They hugged each other and kissed.

"It's so nice to have you finally home and you look very nice in your new body, a proper young gentleman," Wendy said.

With the welcome home talks over, everyone went to their bedrooms, Gabrielle and Lynda, stayed in the lounge a few minutes longer to welcome their father back home and to tell him all their news. Seeing they were both wishing to get to their room, Gabrielle and Lynda said goodnight and retired to their own suite.

For the first time in a few days, they undressed each other and got into bed naked. They kissed, passionately, holding each other close, their breasts touching, their hands all over each other, touching, feeling, caressing, and loving each other.

Gabrielle kissed Lynda again on her lips, before moving down her neck, kissing it all the time, then she moved down to her breasts, kissing licking them, sucking her nipples and kissing them, as her right hand rolled down the front of her body and her fingers gently played with her clitoris, then into her vagina, caressing her vagina walls and finding her G spot, rubbed it until she had an orgasm which ran over Gabrielle's hand.

She brought her hand up and played with Lynda's breast, rubbing her orgasm over it, then she licked her damp breast, making her nipples become erect, then they were kissing their lips again.

Lynda was now doing the same to Gabrielle as she had done to her and soon brought her to an orgasm. Smiling at each other as they lay side by side, they kissed, their eyes turning bright green and lighting up their room. Each time they kissed their eyes grew brighter, as they talked mind to mind, telling each other how much they loved each other and where they would go in their future, how they would spend their time with friends, many of whom they had known all their lives.

Lynda was slowing down, getting tired, finally ready to go to sleep.

"My love, it's three fifteen in the morning and we have a lot to do tomorrow. I think you are tired and want to go to sleep," Gabrielle said as she held Lynda in her arms turning her on her side, then onto her front. Gabrielle's arms went around her back, holding her tightly in place. She looked at her and knew Lynda had already fallen asleep.

Gabrielle closed her eyes and woke up at six thirty. Lynda was smiling down on her, with her arms around her back.

"Good morning my love, the love of my life, I couldn't think of spending another lifetime with anyone else but you. Now, shall we carry on from when I fell asleep on you?" she asked, smiling at her then kissed Gabrielle's lips.

Holding each other, they were soon in the positions they were in a few hours before. They made love twice, then got up, showered together, dressed each other and did each other's makeup. They decided on what jewellery to wear, put it on, then went up to breakfast.

The day flew by as Gabrielle and Lynda, with Sarah, Jenny and Penny, took all the girls shopping to buy four new dresses each, four skirts and different tops and a white ball gown, with underskirt, tights and everything else they would need for a long trip. They tried on more two-inch heels and had two pairs each. Finally, they went into a sports shop and bought three pairs of expensive trainers each.

When they returned to their rooms, there was a huge suitcase for their clothes and a smaller case for all their makeup, brushes and jewellery. There was also a reinforced red bag to hold their laptop and power lead, which would soon have a new plug attached to it.

Over the following six evenings, forty-three girls at a time, were taken to three different schools who, with an input of money from Gabrielle and Lynda, the schools allowed decorators in to create a ballroom. The boys who would be dancing with the girls, were each given a new suit, white shirt tie and new shoes, to keep once their job was finally over.

All the girls loved, it and thanked Gabrielle and Lynda for setting it up for them. They said it was strange at first, dancing with a boy, and them now a girl, dancing backwards at times as the boys led the girls around the ballroom. The boys were also glad to have the girls there, as they had been learning to dance for two years and now, they had their time to show off their skills. They didn't think holding a girl close would feel quite so good and the girls were so easy to talk to as they listened to what their partners had to say and were thinking of doing in the future.

For the girls it was a fantastic view of what being a woman meant and how they felt dancing with a boy, who would be holding her close, and maybe expecting or hoping for a kiss at the end of the evening.

The 60 boys aged sixteen to eighteen who were still sat in their coaches, were dressed in their new school uniform and slowly woken from their long sleep. The boys woke to find themselves wearing a dress. They got off the coaches four at a time and with Gabrielle and Lynda holding hands around them, they were turned into girls and asked if they would like to live forever as a girl and travel on a large spaceship to the stars. Of course, everyone said yes, and the two girls made them immortal.

When they were all changed, they were taken shopping for clothes. They were split up into three groups and for some of them, it was the first time they had ever gone out wearing a dress and now, being a proper girl, something they had wanted all their lives, was now here. They all made friends very quickly as they picked out their clothes.

Each girl had ten dresses, ten skirts and different tops, jumpers a small jacket for school and an overcoat. They all had seven pairs of two-inch heels and eight of the older girls wanted a three-inch heel. Gabrielle was delighted some of the girls had tried to walk in decent high heels. The last shoes were three pair of the most expensive trainers in the shop.

When they returned to the House, ten girls of different ages were there to meet them and take them to their rooms. The new girls were astounded when they looked at their room, they were large like all the other rooms, had a shower and toilet of their own, there was a forty-inch TV on the wall and like all the other rooms, the Channel box was on top of the bookcase. On their desk was a top of the range laptop, already fully charged. The large suitcase was also in their room with the makeup and laptop case.

More girls came down from upstairs who were currently not in lessons and helped the girls settle in, now one to one with the girls already in the House.

Over the following five weeks, they had special tutors come in to teach all the girls astrometrics, astronomy, names of stars, not the Earth names the humans had given the stars and planets. The stars had special names that meant something and the habitable planets in the star's solar system, were all given names that meant something that was happening on the planet below. All the Gas Giants in each solar system, were also given names that had a meaning to them.

The Gas Giant planets were in nearly every solar system, nobody knew why they were there until one engineer from the planet *EnGenius Engines*, in the Praxcis solar system. Phase Instrum, realised he could make an engine that would work on helium, which once its temperature was altered, it could drive a large Moonship through space and the three or four mile long, ships, would be able to pass the speed of light and create wormholes so they could travel through space much faster.

The ships would be able to stop at any Gas Giant, enter the solar system, and suck the Hydrogen into the storage tanks after the Hydrogen had been altered as it entered the ship's engineering area. That is how space travel continued to this day. Ships visit different star systems, load up with fuel, and sometimes meet new species, who they welcome into their family if they are peaceful.

On planets where the inhabitants fight each other, drop bombs on each other, they are left alone until the inhabitants have grown up and come to live in peace. Then they were asked to join the peaceful Intergalactic Space Farers.

During the day, all the girls, including the new girls, had to learn Astrometrics, Astronomy, names of planets, in the new language, then how many different classes of ships which were out there. At night, before they went to bed, they put their wireless earphones in their ears and started to learn a new language, not spoken on Earth. Galactic Unior.

Gabrielle, Lynda, Sarah, Penny, Jenny, John and Alan also taught Astrometrics and Astronomy in groups of fifteen girls each in the larger classrooms on the first, second and ground floor. Four teachers, who just seemed to arrive, saluted Gabrielle and Lynda, they talked for a moment, at ease with each other, then took their bags of clothes and teaching equipment down to the basement.

They knew their way and Gabrielle followed them a moment later, kissing Lynda on her lips before they parted. Lynda was extremely happy, she was smiling and laughing as she returned to her class on the second floor.

The four tutors went to their rooms, knowing exactly where the secret door was and how to open it. They changed into a blue tunic which had a brown sash across his shoulder. At the end of each tunic arm were two gold rings. This denoted he was a Pedologist, working in the science of soils on different planets and the soil they carried aboard their ship to grow food.

Maclain had a pale brown skin colour, six feet tall and thin. He had short blond hair with vibrant blue eyes and had something like a watch on his left wrist.

Cervas was dressed in the same blue tunic, with a red bar across his shoulder and three red stripes on his tunics' wrists. He was shorter, five foot seven but again thin. with blond hair down to the back of his neck, His stripe and rings denoted him as a Surgeon in the ship's hospital.

Resbanche, from the planet *Flowers Delightful* in the *Happacious* star system, five feet eight tall, pale yellow skin, vibrant blue eyes, which all the people aboard the ship had except Gabrielle and Lynda, due to the various radiations that as on Earth, passed through it, called Background Radiation.

She had light blond hair halfway down her back and one and a half inch long fingernails on all six fingers on each hand. They were painted white, with planets and stars on them in different colours. She also had six toes with short toenails also painted, white, then with a different planet on her left foot, different stars on the right foot.

She was wearing open toed, three-inch high heels, a pale blue dress down to just above her knees, with long sleeves. On her shoulder was a light blue and pale-yellow double coloured bar across her left shoulder and two rings the same colour as her shoulder bar, near the bottom of both arms. Then a Gold fluorescent glimmering ring above them. This denoted she was a Commander, in her discipline.

The dress was tight fitting in a breathable material that was lightweight to wear. She also wore a tight fitting Pale blue Jacket with her rank within her discipline at the end of her sleeves. The same, coloured bar was also on the left shoulder of the jacket. The back, front and sleeves of the Jacket was coloured in star systems, the Gas Giants had a slightly moving orange and yellow colour. The Stars all shimmered in interior lighting, as did the red and orange radiation waves, that were passing through planetary star systems. On its front were four large planets with blue oceans and green land areas on them. The rest was a dull grey background with hundreds of yellow, red, and blue stars on them.

This denoted she was an Astrogator, plottng the course the ship should take to see the most beautiful stars and planets as they travelled sometimes just below the speed of light, if they were coming to a highly populated star system, or light plus one, when their course was clear.

Her face makeup was of red, green and blue planets on her cheeks, bright orange eye shadow over her eye lids and light green eye shadow, above it, which swirled around and down the side of her face to her long ears. Her eye lids were painted blue for the colour of her planet's sky.

She looked very, beautiful and had a curvaceous body. At the top of her right arm, was a blue **M** to show she was married to a male abord the ship.

Cervac had a red **M** on his right shoulder, denoting he was married to a female aboard ship.

Chaasichole, from the planet *Well Fiddle Me*, in the *Muishess Doh* Star System. She was five foot six tall, pale-yellow skin, vibrant blue eyes, again with six fingers and toes. Her fingernails were an inch long, painted with a white background and different speakers and transmitters on every other nail. Her toenails were short but painted the same as her fingernails.

She had blond hair down to just past her shoulders her eye lids were coloured bright blue and just above them a bright orange sliding down her face close to her hairline and stopped at the bottom of her long ears. Her cheeks had a pale orange base then black transmitters on each cheek. She also wore a pale orange lip stick.

She was wearing Tan coloured tights, three-inch blue high heels, a light blue pencil skirt down to two inches above her knees. A tight-fitting white blouse, and a pale blue waistcoat, which had a silver bar across the left top and two silver bars, two inches long, close to the bottom of the waistcoat and a gold bar above it, denoting she was a Commander in her discipline of Communications.

She also had a light blue jacket with a silver bar across her left shoulder and the same rings around her sleeves, there was also a red **M** near the top of her tunic on the righthand side, denoting she was married to another woman aboard the ship. On the back of her jacket, were different ariels the ship used, and two loudspeakers near the bottom in bright blue, with silver squiggly lines coming from them which glittered and looked like they were moving in the light.

This was the crew's uniform, which they wore in their day, which was twenty hours long, and ten days to a week and ten weeks to a month. They didn't count the years they were travelling through space, as it was in their thousands on a Moonship, which was one of the most important ships in the Galactic fleet, as their missions last hundreds of thousands of years.

The crew would also wear their uniforms when a ship visited them, or they were going down to a friendly planet who knew of them.

Although the four crew members were going to teach the girls one of their space lessons, they were here for another task, to see if any of the girls would like to learn any of their four disciplines. The girls only had two weeks to make up their minds as during the third week, their uniforms would be made to measure, and grow with them.

The new teachers would be wearing their uniforms all the time during the hours they were teaching. At night they could wear what they liked, in the evening or day, whichever shift you were on, you could wear casual clothes and meet up with friends, loved ones, and go to a club to dance or the cinema which shows different films that are transmitted from planets and into space where the signals go on and on.

There are plenty of other places to go in the ship; or take a walk outside with your lover to look at the stars and new star systems the ship passed through. They erect a small force field over the surface where you are going to visit.

Every member of the ship has a tracker inserted into their arm, so the ship's computer, Grace, can keep track of where you are aboard the ship or on a planet. If you have a double injection of devices, another micro communication device inserted into the base of your skull, you can talk to Grace and hear what she has to say. She can tell you where you are if you are lost, or the fastest route to where you need to be.

The four travellers spoke to Gabrielle for a while. When they left the secret bedrooms, which would be secret no longer, it was ten in the morning when they walked out into the basement. Clayton was teaching Astrometrics, to the girls, precisely how to find yourself, if you go off course in your joy rider, a small craft that could take you down to a planet or to collect space dust and other Interplanetary gases.

Everyone in the class of sixty looked across at the four new tutors, dressed in their best uniforms. Gabrielle looked over to Clayton.

"May I just introduce our new guests?" Gabrielle asked.

"Of course, Gabrielle, please all of you come over here."

"They all walked slowly, looking at the class, seeing their faces, with makeup that would soon change when they joined the ship, and Claasichole, knew they would love it. A new programme was just being written especially for the humans.

Gabrielle stood slightly in front of her guests, smiled at the girls sat before her. Most were smiling, others, slightly apprehensive.

"Girls, when I asked you if you would like to travel in the Universe aboard a Moonship, you all said yes, possibly without even thinking about it. Clayton who has been teaching you now for four days is also from our ship and would normally wear the uniform of an astronomer, a commander in his discipline. You will hear these words a lot from now on and aboard the ship. Clayton is from the planet *Prime Force* in the *Zephier Star System*, the name of its Blue Star is *I'm on my way*.

"You have all been told the stars and planets have their own names with meanings of who they are within a star system, and you are already learning our universal language and I am extremely pleased how fast you are progressing. In some of your classes from tomorrow onwards, our guests will speak to you in our Universal Language, asking you questions of what you should know and what you have learnt so far. It would be good for you all to answer him or her in our Universal Language, as they will help with the pronunciation of words and phrases.

"Right, introductions, beside me is Resbancha, from the planet *Flowers Delightful* in the star system of *Happacious*. The name of the bright yellow star is called *I'm So Happy*." She put her hand up and waved to the girls.

"Next to her is Maclain, from the planet *Forever Watching* in the *Astro Star System*, the name of the star *Astro Pics*." He put his hand in the air waving to the girls.

"He said Hello Girls of *Utopia Prime*, in the *Starlight Star System*, the name of your star is *Solitude Abobold*. You didn't know that? Shame on you Gabrielle for not telling your girls where they are from *Earth* sounds so lonely but, is what I study, and a great many of us on our ship, are scientists and researchers. I'll see you all again later," he said smiling.

"Thank you for that introduction," Gabrielle said smiling.

"Next in line is my very good friend Chaasichole, from the planet *Well Fiddle Me* in the *Tenner Star System,* the name of their star *Maishesse Doh*."

She waved to the girls and added. "It's great to be down on *Utopia Prime* again. I was here a few centuries ago during your early exploration of your world in ships which sailed across oceans. It's a privilege to be here again, not many of our people get a chance to visit your planet, which is the most talked about planet in the Galactic Unior."

"Thank you Chaasichole," They smiled at each other as mouthed a word to each other as if they were long lost lovers somewhere in the thousands of years that separated them.

From the middle of the room, Megan and Lexi stood holding hands.

"I am Megan."

"I am Lexi." They then spoke together.

"Welcome to our planet *Utopia Prime*, in the *Starlight Star System*. We welcome you all to our House and we hope your time on *Utopia Prime* will be Happy and Joyful. We look forward to meeting you separately as you teach us what we need to know. May God move with you and be with you always," they said together in Galactic Unior then took their seats.

The four Travellers applauded them, not thinking they would be able to speak their language so well.

"Thank you. Megan and Lexi. I think I can see a red M going on each of your dresses, skirt sets and Jackets, no matter which discipline you choose," Chaasichole said smiling and clapping them.

"I think that would be an affirmative Chaasichole, Lexi replied in Galactic Unior.

The Travellers all laughed and applauded her again. As she took her seat.

"Thank you, girls. There will be a meeting for everyone at five, just before your evening meal at six in the Train Station. If you have any questions. comments or concerns write them down and bring them with you. We will all speak in *Utopian*, English for the meeting, Gabrielle said and led the Travellers off the small stage, a raised wooden box turned upside down.

Claythos brought the class to order. "Well girls, what did you think of our Travellers? Even from different planets, we all look the same, even here on *Utopia Prime*, you have people with different coloured skins, just like we have in the known Universe. What I would really like to know is if you like the uniforms, especially the women? Can we have a show of hands I think this is the easiest way? Up for yes, down for no or not sure." All the girls put their hand in the air.

"Is anyone against?" He asked. No one put a hand up.

"I see you are all in favour of them, I am so pleased you like them, they are so light to wear. I can assure you all, the men the same age as yourselves, and the men a little older, love the look of them too. I think they like the skirt set best because you can also wear stockings with them. That is not to say that there are many girls aboard who love and marry girls as well. Some boys and men also get together. It's the way love falls upon you.

"Now, where were we? Ah yes, what happens if you fall from the Moonship, practically impossible. But, not from a small scout or pleasure ship. Can anyone tell me where.........?"

Chapter 19

When five pm came around, all the girls and staff of the entire House, were seated in the Basement, waiting for Gabrielle and Lynda to bring in the new Travellers.

They were all stunned when Chaasichole entered the room alone and stood on the larger stage.

"As you can see, I am here by myself, that is because, the House is now once again, part of the ship and our two Captains, every Moonship has two Captains, one to command the interior of the ship, the other commands the exterior, which includes all the craft which leave the ship and return, dealing with anyone, especially the people from a planet they orbit and protect. Helping the people to move forward through their early years onwards and helping those who need their dedicated help, because these problems are all over the Universe, in nearly every planetary highly populated star system. Being born into the wrong body just like you girls.

"The Captain responsible for the exterior of the ship, is also responsible for retrieving the engine nacelle's, a very delicate job indeed and seeing them being deployed when the ship is about to leave orbit, The Captain is also responsible for refuelling the ship from a Gas Giant.

"Our ship needs refuelling before we go on our merry way, so we will stop off at Jupiter or Saturn to refuel. It is customary to introduce our two Captains before speaking in numbers, even if it is only a few of us, to any species we meet our two Captains have come down from our ship to officially meet you and speak to you.

"Therefore, it is my honour to introduce our two Captains and some of our crew who have come to visit you and help you learn more about ship life."

A lot of the girls thought Gabrielle and Lynda were the two Captains, or at least high up in their command. Everyone turned to their right as they heard the sound off shoes on wooden stairs. The two captains were holding hands, as they led their other officers along the pathway to the stage. When they were all on the stage, the girls could clearly see the two Captains were wearing the Skirt and Blouse set. As the others, it was pale blue with Gold bars across each shoulder and four gold rings around the jacket's sleeves. At the top of their jacket sleeves, was a picture of their ship and beneath, the name of the ship, Exodus Prime in gold. On their right shoulder was a red **M** denoting they were married to another female aboard their ship.

Their makeup was beautiful and romantic at the same time. On their cheeks was a pale blue base, with two dolphins in jumping position, backs curved out of the blue ocean facing each other mouths ajar, as if ready to kiss each other.

Their eyes were painted bright blue with a pale green upper brow above the eyebrow, which slithered down to the bottom of their normal sized ears. Both had light brown hair, to halfway down their backs. Across their brow, were nine planets, different colours and in an arc, which followed the curve of their hairline.

Their fingernails were a quarter of an inch longer than the end of their fingers. Which were painted with a light blue background and on her left hand, dolphins as they were on her face looking to the right, and on her right hand, the dolphins looking towards the left.

On the third finger of their right hand each Captain wore a mauve coloured diamond cut from Rysamic stone, the most valuable stone in the Galactic Universe, forged because the stone was so strong, set into a blue gold band forming the Captain's Ring. On their wedding finger, they each wore a blue diamond encrusted Eternity Ring, a large diamond solitaire Engagement ring and a band of gold with three red diamonds pushed into a gold band, Wedding ring.

Their toenails were short to the end of the toe. They were painted the same as their fingernails.

Both Captains wore tan stockings and three-inch blue high heels. On the back of their jackets, was a picture of *Utopia Prime*, with nine planets in an arc above it; around both pictures were stars of different colours, which shimmered under the lights. The thing they noticed, was on their jackets all the planets were now rotating and the makeup on their face had also come to life, with the dolphins jumping out of the water and kissing before they returned to the sea then jumped out again and kissed.

"Ladies, gentlemen I introduce to you *Captain of the Interior* and responsible for all the souls on our ship, *Captain Gabrielle Grayson* of the planet Love Aloud in the *Romantic Star System*, the name of their star, *Loving People Here.*

"Next to her, her wife, *Captain of the Ship's Exterior* and the souls that travel away from the ship, until they return, *Captain*

Lynda Grayson of the same planet and Stellar System Chaasichole said. Both *Captains* waved to the people in the room.

"Next to them are all the crew members that were introduced to you earlier. Now, Captain Gabrielle Grayson, being Captain of the Ship's Interior, if you would please explain why this meeting has been called," Chaasichole asked.

"Thank you Chaasichole, well it is very, nice to be properly introduced to you all. I sincerely hope you like our uniforms, or working clothes, as I hope many of you will be wearing them too.

"You have all been told about our Moonship, but we, Lynda and I have heard questions from some of you querying surely the Moon cannot be a starship. If it left orbit, it would be disastrous for the *Earth* and many of the people would die. Our Moon our Moonship, has been in orbit for a number of millenniums and we, Travellers, have been walking about on your planet for all or most of its time we have been in orbit.

"We were not the first Moonship to be here in orbit, we replaced the Moonship, *Well I'm Here, Finally*. This was a slightly bigger Moonship to ours, but we were covering an era of calmer seas and less Volcanoes and Earthquakes, the Land masses were different back then and Captains Joanne Harris and Kathleen Harris married to each other, watched *Utopia Prime,* with their crew of two hundred and fifty thousand, as the planet moved its Land Masses twice taking thousands of years, a short time for us, to reach their new positions.

"The land masses will move once again very soon, due to Climate Change. We cannot interfere in Climate conditions, unfortunately, we do not have the correct equipment. and this is only the second planet this has ever happened to. We can, however, help them in one area, the Oceans, before we leave orbit, we will clear the Oceans and seas of all kinds of plastic and destroy it. We want the Oceans to be as they were once before, when our friendly mammal fish swam in the Ocean's, to their hearts' content. Not getting caught up in your plastic waste.

"We have taken you from your families, in many cases, because you were abused for wanting to be a woman. Others came to us with their parent or parent's pleasure as you made them understand you were born into the wrong body. You would have had two operations, one a major operation, to change your sex to female, but they could not give you a female voice without another operation or long-term therapy with a speech therapist.

Neither would you have your figure of a girl or women's bone structure and curvaceous body, like we have given you. Most of all, I think, is that you would not have a woman's brain, wired just slightly different than a man's brain. The female's job is to bear children, to keep your species living or replace lives that were lost in wars.

"The woman is the home maker, men can build a house, but women make it a home. They have a great deal of patience, most of the time, patience to allow their baby to feed from their breasts, caring for the baby, caressing it, loving it, teaching it as the baby grows into a girl or boy and finally, a woman or man, when it will leave its home at some time. Her mind can be faster than a man's mind, girls are ahead in school subjects and when at Universities. They are good at solving puzzles as life can often be a puzzle, and it needs a woman's touch or input, to solve it.

"Men have their good abilities, they are strong, able to carry heavy loads on their backs or shoulders. They have become good at making things work and solving problems in the building industry and making rockets, they will eventually get into space properly and no doubt at some distant point in their future, join us. If you decide to join us, our five tutors will be helping you to decide what discipline you might want to be in. A complete list of disciplines will be sent to all your laptops at the end of this talk.

"There are over fifty disciplines as some are broken into two or three sections. Some disciplines are primarily for women, but some men do the discipline as well. Our five guests; are here looking for talented girls who might like to join their discipline and learn from them, what is involved in what they do.

"Do not join their discipline just because they have pretty uniforms, there are many different uniforms aboard our ship, and we try to make them all beautiful and interesting. For each discipline named on your computers, will be accompanied by the general type of uniform and jacket with a picture on their back. You can ask any of the tutors what their discipline is like or another discipline mentioned on your laptops.

"By the end of next week, we hope to have your decisions made for two reasons. First, we are leaving very soon in four weeks. Another Moonship is currently in orbit around Jupiter, taking on fuel for its long watch over *Utopia Prime*, which will very soon be getting new carers to its surface.

"Several civilisations have asked if they can visit the planet, land and make themselves known to the *Utopians*. We have agreed for the present time two species can land on *Utopia Prime*, after the new crew have settled in and taken control of all the Houses and homes of lead officers, with their bodyguards, all armed with the dual Glock and licensed to kill in any country.

"You too will meet many new species on our trip to our next destination, the planet *What's Happening?* in the *New Move* planetary system, their star's name *Changes Happen.* It is roughly nine hundred light years away, and it will take us eleven hundred years to get there, giving a decade or two, as we will be visiting several other star systems to see how the species are coping and sending globe ships to the surface with people to do different jobs, taking air samples, soil samples and many other research jobs. One or two of you may even speak with a few of the species on their planet, that for us will mean learning a new language we have to overhear and listen to recordings of the species, that is where our linguistic teams come in, deciphering their language into ours, so we can learn it.

"There are many other things to do on our way, which includes taking ships out as a couple or signally, or even more people aboard a larger ship, flown possibly, by one of you.

"We do have a few fighters aboard, not for battle, but for killing stray asteroids that get in our way that will not be delt with by our force field. A Moonship is extremely large and takes a long time to make course corrections, so the fighters sometimes have to either move an asteroid to miss us or blow it up. Sometimes we have our people land on the asteroid and drill into it, which is where our Geologists come in, to find the best place to drill and that means flying out to the asteroid to take readings of it, so you send our men out to drill three holes and insert explosives and blow it up.

"We have other jobs to do like mapping different sectors of space, any gravitational distortions. There is so much to do, and you will always be kept busy and meet many new friends during your time off as the clubs and dance halls café's, are open all hours. This is another Discipline you may choose. It is certainly one way to meet all the crew. There is no alcohol aboard the ship. You may only drink it when you are planetside and do not get drunk and show yourself up.

"When planetside you represent the ship. Even if we did do battle here when you live on a planet for over a thousand years or more, you may help the residents if you ask your commander.

"I apologise for not giving you very much time to make up your minds, but in four weeks, we have to leave and there are a great many things to do. There will be no more University or school, you'll have your special lessons here. You must learn certain things, you are in space and in small ships it is easy to go off course, and you need to get back to your ship. If you are unsure of which way, you are to go, talk to your friends or come to one of us, we may be able to help you choose. Are there any questions?"

Cloe was pushed off her seat and helped to stand by Orla who was sat next to her, one side, and Summer on the other.

"Cloe, I see by the way you were helped to stand, you are the spokesperson for your fellow students. What is it you all wish to know?" Lynda asked.

"Lynda, do we still call you by your first names?"

"It's fine here, but when we're aboard our ship, it is Mam for Gabrielle and me. When we are talking generally, you may call us by our forenames. However, that was not what you have been told to ask me, so please, ask away."

"Everyone wants to know, as we have little time to make our choice, and I want to come, is, what happens to us if we decide not to go?"

"A very, good question, which we should have covered. It is simple, you know how we changed you from boys to girls, we do something like that again? Have no fear, we would not be so cruel as to change you back to boys. You will have no memory of what you have seen and heard of the last few weeks. You will forget us, and we will put a false memory into you, that you are all here in a children's home waiting to be adopted. Margarette has several couples who will care for you and you will be adopted within two days, by then we will be gone.

"I know what you are thinking, we would put you into groups and have John and Alan use their Lance on you and you'll all be vapourised. That will not happen I promise. You will continue to live your lives until you die of old age. You will not have the gift of immortality we will take that from you. Does that answer your question?"

"Does anyone else have a question referring to if you wish to stay here?"

Sophie stood looking at Lynda. "Mam, can we all still go with you after you answered that dumb question?" she asked.

"Sophie, it was not a dumb question, and you all need to know what happens to you if you say No," Lynda replied.

"In that case we all wish to join you. Grace and I would both like to discipline in Astronomy and Interstellar Photography. We both took Astronomy as an extra course, and both excelled in it and all our exams were A plusses and we even used the large telescope at Greenwich and the hundred-inch reflector telescope in Rome. We were taken as a class to see Joderal Bank Radio Telescope and see what the dish showed us on the large two-hundred-foot dish.

"We both excelled in photography getting A plusses again in all our exams. We did very well in all our exams getting A's and A plusses," Sophie said hardly being able to stop talking.

"Of course, you are all welcome aboard our ship. and I'm pleased, to hear Grace and you have chosen a discipline. Astronomy is indeed done using a three-hundred-foot dish which is deployed as soon as we leave this solar system under my control. External cameras are used to collect some photographs of distant stars and planets, and of course, stray asteroids.

"You can all choose your discipline as soon as you like, and after your main studies on astrophysics is over, by the end of this week, you can begin studying your discipline," Lynda replied as she took hold of her wife's hand, so happy they had all agreed to come with them.

"Now, it's almost six, or eighteen hundred, so off you go to your evening meal. Don't forget all the disciplines will be on your laptops and phones from now on. Enjoy your meal we'll join you in the Train Station."

The Travellers turned and spoke to each other about the girl's decision to join them which was the main objective of their trip. Two weeks later, everyone had chosen their discipline, and were now getting some lessons by holographic tuition from officers aboard the ship.

Gabrielle and Lynda were doing the last of their packing with Sarah's help. Sarah had completed her packing using four large trunks for herself and Alan.

Gabrielle and Lynda chose what necklace to wear beneath their blouses. They quickly chose the diamond hearts, because they had so many memories of wearing them and they both loved them so much. Their diamond encrusted watches would go aboard the ship, they would only be able to wear them when they had two hours of their day off duty, but they were always on call even in their night's sleep period.

Gabrielle and Lynda used fourteen large trunks between them, to take all their fine dresses and other clothes, Hats and Bags & Wraps, which would very soon be in the hands of another man born into the wrong body who would meet his wife, as they had arranged and continue Gabrielle and Lynda's work all around the world.

They had wondered what to do with all the cash. Gabrielle and Lynda had already transferred ten million into each of their bank accounts and with John and Alan, were counting parcels of fifty thousand pounds for each of the men to flutter away.as they worked so hard for them.

All the men were transferring to the House next to their House. They would be well paid by the new man, who would be taking over both Houses, The Train Station and Gabrielle and Lynda's new apartment. Those who wanted it, were given the choice to have long life with their loved one if they so wished. Five single young men in their early twenties, wished to marry one of the girls they had worked with and protected. Gabrielle made all the arrangements, leaving Lynda to help with the five brides dresses and those of their bridesmaids, who were some of the girls from the House.

There were a further forty large trunks from the other members who used the apartment, which would very soon be handed over to the new man of the House. Wendy and Walter had decided to stay; but were given long life and looked a lot younger than they were to look after the new tenants, who would also have armed bodyguards. The last thing they were given was two billion pounds put into their bank accounts. They would need all this money if they wished to travel and they were also given John and Penny's two-million-pound house for them to live in and three cars, one of them a four by four.

On the Wednesday evening of the third week, a Sphere landed in Gabrielle and Lynda's back garden. All the trunks, large and small, were taken aboard the Sphere and one trunk from the ship containing all the new crew's uniforms and the new uniforms of the crew who lived in the apartment.

With one stop completed, the pilot took his Sphere to Train Station Two and took aboard all the crew's normal clothes and the new uniforms for the crew who lived in the House and their large and spacious apartment. Ms Sophia, who had worked for

Gabrielle for years, was also invited to join the crew and decided to discipline in Communications, interior and exterior.

When the Sphere's crew of six had loaded all the trunks and handed over another large trunk and a small trunk as there were more new girls and extra staff who had been invited to join the crew. The Sphere left and a few minutes later landed at Train Station Three. More large trunks of the crew caring for the girls and boys were loaded aboard the Sphere and two medium sized trunks were offloaded with uniforms for everyone.

The Sphere was off again, heading for Train Station Four in New York. With the job completed it was off to Train Station Five in Texas. Finally, with its loading bays almost full, it flew to Train Station Six in Australia.

Janet and Tom ran Train Station Six and the large House. They had girls and boys from all over Australia who had been born into the wrong body. Some of the older girls and boys aged seventeen and eighteen, had, had their sex change operations completed and were happy they were now a woman, but they still needed further surgery for their voice and another clinic appointment to remove their facial hair, but they were stuck with their big bodies.

Janet and Tom did exactly what Gabrielle and Lynda did, put their arms around them, in two's, let them decide the colour and length of their hair and size of their breasts. Then their Electric Blue eyes lit up sending blue bright light around the room. By the end of the transformation, they were real girls, with a girl's voice and a girl's figure, with smaller arms and legs, hands and feet. There were no longer any operation scars on their bodies and all their body hair was gone forever. and they could now if they wished, get pregnant and have a baby. This really made them extremely happy.

They spent a day transforming all boys into girls and some of the girls into boys. They were all given long life and the brain pattern for each sex. Finally, as they had left it so late to change them, they were given the new language they would speak to the crew aboard the ship, and languages from ten different countries on *Utopia Prime*.

There were fifty new boys and three hundred and ninety new girls in their House. They had a hundred and fifty square miles of land and all the boys and girls were taught how to fly a helicopter and small planes, to oversee their three thousand sheep. They had a flying school where all their students passed their flying exams and test flights, with A plusses. Now, they could all fly the jets, Janet and Tom had and fly the other aircraft in formation, so these people would make fine pilots for the Moonship. When the Sphere landed, everyone had a look inside and at the controls. Many of them knew what each control did as they had been studying the ship's external craft.

They begged and begged until finally the crew caved in and allowed five girls to take off, fly the ship around and land. Each girl who flew the Sphere managed to fly it safely and land it without bumping or damaging anything.

They spent eight hours letting as many of the new crew fly the Sphere. When they ran out of time, those that had not had the chance to fly the Sphere this time, would get a go next time they dropped in, which would be in a few days. Their pilot who took them up in his Sphere Rathmare, said he would try and get two Spheres to train in.

Aboard the Moonship, several men and women watched how the young girls handled the Sphere. They were extremely proud of them and let the entire crew see what they were seeing. It is just what they wanted, new pilots to replace those who had requested permission to change disciplines.

They were getting another forty new Vipers and thirty replacement Spheres, they would also get replacement Launches, Rescue Ships and thirty pleasure ships. The last ships were forty new Transfer Ships, for moving the population of *Fall in Love Here* in the *AquaLea Solar System.* These ships would come via the next Moonship, *Agraffe Keeper* now slowly moving through the solar system towards *Utopia Prime.*

When the *Agraffe Keeper* got to *Mars*, Pilots were flying back and forth changing over the new ships for older ones, which for the present would remain on the *Agraffe Keeper.*

During the last weekend of week three, all the crew from

Gabrielle and Lynda's apartment put on their uniforms, the women all chose the skirt and blouse, with tan stockings They all wore a Diamond encrusted Eternity Ring, a large diamond engagement rings and a band of gold wedding ring. They also wore their expensive most loved jewellery over their blouse.

On Saturday, they had the weddings for the five couples who helped get the House back up together, now wanted to be married and join the crew. The nine pairs of girls in love with each other, would also be married. As the girls had little or no money, they couldn't afford a wedding ring each and there was no time in which to get them one now. They were all dressed in their white wedding dresses, which Lynda paid for, in the basement where the services would be performed. With a ring tab from a drinks can, ready to exchange for each other when they said their vows. Gabrielle and Lynda entered the decorated basement and found the eighteen girls who were getting married.

"Hello girl's Gabrielle said, are you all happy?" she asked.

"Yes, do you think it will be okay if we use these tin pull rings when we exchange vows?" Sofia asked, holding the pull ring in her petite fingers.

"I'm sure they will. And here lies another problem, for now, just for a few days, could you put the rings on the next finger to your engagement finger. We need to put another special ring on your fingers as you are really below the age of getting married. The three-tier system will only monitor the amount of love you have for each other. You can remove them in three days. You will all get a lot of money in universal credits which you can spend on anything you like."

"We'll transfer a million credits into all your bank accounts as soon as your weddings are over. Ten UK pounds are roughly one UV Credit. Items on the planets we're visiting, will be a lot cheaper than those on *Utopia Prime.*

"If you will just hold your rings and close your eyes as there will be some very bright green flashes of light." Lynda told them.

The girls did as they were told and each couple in turn held their left hand out. They felt something narrow pushed along their engagement finger. Then another object was pushed along their finger. After it was adjusted, Gabrielle and Lynda moved to the next couple and the next and the next until all the girls had two parts of the item on their fingers. Then Gabrielle and Lynda moved swiftly down the row of girls removing their pull tab from a can and pushed another item onto the wedding finger of their left hand, which was only pushed halfway down.

When the last pair of girls and the last of the five couples had an object put on their engagement finger, they both stood back and held hands.

"You can all open your eyes now," Lynda told them.

As soon as they opened their eyes and looked at their fingers, they started to scream with pleasure, then held each other, all trying to say, "Thank You," to Gabrielle and Lynda.

"You all have the same Eternity ring, which is yellow gold encrusted with real diamonds. Your engagement rings for each couple are just slightly different in appearance and shape, but they are all six carat diamond solitaires. Your wedding rings are all eighteen-carat gold," Lynda told them.

"Ohhhh thank you, thank you so much, we never dreamed we would get anything like this. So, thank you so very much, you have made our day," Summer and Jessica said together, tears falling from their eyes.

"We could not allow you not to have a proper wedding ring each or an Eternity ring and Engagement ring, which have come from the shop that we use all the time to buy our diamonds and gold chains. Nothing in that shop is under thirty thousand pounds, we wish you well in your married lives aboard ship and of course, you have double quarters aboard our ship, which we have just been told by Grace, the ship is to have a new name, for a lovely big, new family, *Odyssey Prime*, which will also be our call name.

"That's a lovely name for our ship," Zoe said.

"Let's get on with your weddings, we've held the service up for a while," Gabrielle said laughing, holding Lynda's hand with all her love. The vicar from their local church walked into the basement, and standing before all the couples, and the entire new ship's crew and everyone who worked on the house watching as each couple were individually married.

"With all the wedding vows said, everyone walked over to the Train Station, which had been decorated for their weddings and instead of individual wedding cakes, Christine made a long four tier sponge cake with thick white easy to lay, white icing with all their names on it in gold piping at the bottom of the flat surface and at the top, Congratulations. Along the middle of the flat top, were fourteen small cupcakes, with red and gold icing placed equally along the middle of the cake with a single gold candle in the middle. As the new married couples arrived, with Simon's help, they lit all the candles.

Photographers from their own House, were taking photos of everyone and especially as they blew out their one candle using their new Knokin 3D camera with sound. Ultralight strong body made of Zulcration metail with ultralight lenses. With the Superblaz Treedlic lens, you can see planets and stars up to six lightyears distant, with crisp clear views of the planets and buildings on them. Made on the planet *Long Way to See* in the *Clasicolec Star System,* the name of its blue star *StarBright.*

They were all given the camera to for their own and use aboard ship or planetside. They only had them three weeks ago and Eshamiel, from the planet *Long Way to See,* came down from the ship to give the photographers instructions on how they operated, as all the printed instructions are in *Galactic Unior.*

They partied until late into the night including all the workers before returning to their rooms in the House. When each couple got to their room, as they opened their door, they were photographed as they carried each other over the threshold into their room and greeted with red rose petals over their bed and a large bouquet of flowers on their dressing table.

The five women of the adult couples also had a diamond encrusted eternity ring a little more expensive diamond solitaire at eight carrots and a gold patterned wedding ring. Their husband had the same slightly wider and thicker gold patterned wedding ring. The five men were also given a small box which had been gift wrapped. They would give the small package to their wife when they were in bed.

All the photographers were using their own Knokin 3D camera as given to them by their tutor and would be allowed to take them with all their other lenses and the large telescopic lenses with them. All the matt and silk photographic paper they had, eight-hundred reams, of five hundred pieces of photographic paper per ream, would all go to the ship, with all their large lenses and large camera bags, with another five hundred reams of different sized photographic paper, matt and gloss, would go to the ship the following day, with their packed cases. The wedding girls would have all their beautiful dresses put carefully into one large trunk.

This time, when the sphere landed there were only four trunks to go from Train Station One with almost five hundred individual suitcases, all marked with their names, Train Station Number, the name of their planet and Moonship. Ten men from the House and the six men from the ship, loaded everything as fast as they could.

To get the Sphere off their grounds, back into the air and return to their ship before the police came looking for the UFO.

There was now one Sphere to each Train Station as there would be a lot of luggage to take to different rooms on level 656. When the Sphere was completely loaded and checked, the pilot took the Sphere into the air, when it was a short distance away from Train Station 1, the co-pilot, switched on all the Sphere's external lights and slowly moved at three hundred feet over London and Buckingham Palace, taking night-time pictures and films of the capital city below them. When two RAF jets raced towards the Sphere, it moved between both aircraft as the Pilot and Co-Pilot, waved at the men in the aircraft. Then the Sphere went straight up and left *Utopia,* making their way home.

Gabrielle and Lynda jumped back to their home and their bedroom they had shared for twenty years with two timelines. They were naked in their bed, something they had shared from when they first met, again.

They held each other close and kissed each other's eyes and lips, their tongues intertwisting before they made love time and time again until four in the morning when Lynda was falling asleep.

They had to be up early, there was a lot to accomplish the next day. Gabrielle lay on her back and gently, rolled Lynda on top of her, put her arms around her holding her safe in her position then fell asleep.

They woke at six thirty, kissed each other, said "hello I love you with all my soul and heart for all time to come." They kissed again, looked at the clock and made love again until they both had an orgasm. Forty-five minutes later they were both in their uniforms with their diamond hearts below their white blouse both wearing a pretty-red bra and tan stockings.

They had to do their own makeup for now, but aboard ship, they would use the face makeup computers and foot and finger computers which painted their toenails and fingernails to the design they wished. Making sure there was nothing left in their bedroom, they put on their engagement rings, before their band of gold wedding ring and walked up to the dining room.

Wendy had breakfast ready for them with a hot pot of coffee.

"Have you had breakfast yet?" Gabrielle asked Wendy.

"Oh yes, we had ours at six, when you two were making love," she replied laughing.

"Only you could say that to us, our room was soundproofed, and we will be having our suite aboard *Odyssey Prime* soundproofed as well," Lynda added smiling and placed her hand on Wendy's.

"Why don't you sit down with us one last time Wendy?" Lynda asked.

Wendy poured herself a black coffee then added a spot of milk, just to give it a colour.

"You could change your minds and come with us if you like," Lynda begged pressing her thin, beautiful hands together in prayer.

"Yes Wendy come with us, you really will enjoy the nine-hundred-year flight and the planet we will be going to is in about the same timeline as it is here," Gabrielle said. "Please, you know you want to go," Gabrielle said softly holding her wife's hand.

"Well, my dear daughters how could I let you alone on your ship which has been upgraded during the last hundred years. Your mother and father wouldn't cope without us. We'll both be in the Catering discipline.

"John is going to pick us up in a few hours, while we change your bed for Kenneth. I have already set up a new couple to look after and care for Kenneth and his future bride, and the gunslingers," Wendy told them.

"Well done and welcome aboard *Odyssey Prime.* Later this morning, Sarah, Jenny and Margarette will be implanting the Trackers and Tracers into the girl's arms and neck, then they won't get lost on the ship, I don't think they have really taken in that the interior of the ship is the interior of the Moon."

"They'll love it I'm sure," Wendy replied.

After everyone had their parts injected into their left arm and just below their right ear. They were all talking to Grace and loving it.

At sixteen hundred, those leaving, boarded the Train a mile beneath them. *Odyssey Two*, the Train had been renamed after it talked to *Odyssey Prime.* The four lifts took everyone down to the train after saying farewell to those loved ones they left behind.

Once they had boarded the train and had the last small trunk loaded with the last bits of clothes they were changing into, mainly underwear.

At sixteen fifteen, *Odyssey Two* left Train Station 1, taking them out of the UK, under the English Channel and down to Paris; where the girls and a few boys, with their staff boarded the next section of the Train, behind the crew from Train Station One.

All the crew, new girls and boys, were wearing their new uniforms with a coloured bar of their discipline on their left shoulder and sleeve. showing they were a trainee in the colour of their discipline.

The Train moved off to Train Station Three, picked up more crew from Rome, then headed for the coast. They didn't realise the Train was moving at its fastest speed beneath the Atlantic Ocean. When the Train arrived at Train Station Four, they brought aboard four hundred American girls and fifty boys all wearing their new uniforms. There were also two doctors and two nurses who also joined them.

The Train moved on to Train Station five in Texas and brought aboard another four hundred and fifty girls and thirty boys, again all wearing their uniforms and mark of their discipline.

Now it was under the South Atlantic Ocean and into Australia and a few hours later, arriving at Train Station Six, there were eight hundred girls and sixty-three boys wearing their crew uniforms with their discipline bars showing. Odyssey Two eventually arrived at the underground Train Station six.

The crew were allowed off in sections. Gabrielle and Lynda's group were the first to board the four lifts that would take them to the surface and into the basement of the Australian House.

Holding hands all the way to the surface, Gabrielle and Lynda finally held each other close and kissed, just as they reached the surface. As the lift doors opened, everyone left the lifts, wondering what would happen next.

Gabrielle and Lynda saw their sister and brother-in-law. They hugged and kissed each other, talking nonstop until the French then Roman and Italian crew arrived. Tables were full off bottles of water, tea and coffee even bottles of different juices. It was still hot, very, hot, even in the darkness off night.

Above them the sky was crystal clear, showing millions of stars and planets. Some of the girls were taking photographs of the starlit sky as they would more than likely never see it again. It was now a New Moon and totally Black.

As the last of the crew arrived on the surface and got their bearings, taking in the late-night air. All the girls from every Train Station, who were interested in photography, were carrying their own Knokin 3D camera with a second short telescopic lens. In its material case tied securely to the bottom of her handbag.

Although it was short, when it was on the camera, they could extend the lens to four lightyears bringing the small planets in the dark night sky closer to them.

"Crew of *Odyssey Prime*, if you look closely, just above our Moonship, you can see the pale outline and final approach lights of *Agraph Keeper*, which are all green. To the right of our ship are two large Spheres. Crews from Train Station One three and five will board Sphere One, the rest will board Sphere two. You can now see a third Sphere, this is the crew that will be taking control of all the Train Stations, Houses, and apartments, which we have all left behind.

"Here come Spheres one and two, don't get caught in the group of adults who will be getting out of Sphere three as fast as they can so they can say they were on *Utopia Prime* first. Take a last look around at this huge continent of Australia, you'll never see this continent ever again.

"Our Spheres are ready, let's get aboard and take your first steps of being a space faring crew on a Moonship," Gabrielle said calmly.

Girls, boys and adult crew got aboard Sphere One with the three small trunks. Gabrielle and Lynda waited until they saw Kenneth.

"Kenneth," Gabrielle called. He looked over at the two beautiful women holding hands, smiling at him.

He walked over to them and was just about to say something stupid to them, then he realised who they were. He stood to Attention and Saluted the two Captains who returned his salute.

"You will be taking over our Apartment, House and the House next door. You will have a good bunch of helpers, treat them well and please, look after everything. We do not wish to hear it has all been destroyed, you will hear us both even a thousand light years away," Gabrielle said sternly.

"Are you joking? This is *Utopia Prime,* the most talked about planet in the entire Universe, and we are here, at last on, what is it called? *Terra Firmer*?" he asked.

"I do believe it is," Lynda replied.

They kissed each other goodbye and left him to go down to the Train that would take him back to Train Station One in London, where the staff were getting everything ready for their new owners. Gabrielle and Lynda got aboard their Sphere and it lifted off with the other two Sphere's following in its wake. Two fast response jets flew over the Train Station and tried to follow the alien ships into the air, to see if there was a Mother Ship there.

Their Mother Ship was right before their eyes, they just couldn't believe it was really there.

However, some people at NASA and a small number of astronauts had spoken with Lynda when she told them to get their tiny ships off her large Moonship and never come back. Four large Spheres and six fighters flew over their Apollo craft and landed right in front of them on the ridge.

She had given permission for the men to remain at their landing site to carry out a few experiments, so they would be able to return to their Mothercraft and return to Earth to give their message to NASA leaders and they also carried two discs which Lynda showed them how they operated. Wearing her uniform and walking on the Moon like she owned it and the two men by her side, again in their uniforms, were armed.

At the end of the holographic message, was a joint message from Gabrielle and Lynda.

"Mr President of the USA, and those people in charge at NASA and Russia. Do Not send your tiny Moon spaceships here again, you are making our people concerned for you and might come on the surface and start firing at your craft. We have Purchased your planet fair and square. The deeds to your planet were put up for sale and you should have gone to *Alpha Centauri* to stake your claim. As you did nothing, we purchased your planet from the *Planet Masters* many thousands of your years ago.

"The Egyptians managed to get into space and even started to Colonise Mars, so why haven't you continued with their spaceship designs? Too damn busy fighting each other instead of moving forward. We own your planet, the true copy of the deeds, we have sent with your astronauts back to *Utopia Prime* and stop calling it *Earth* it's not a pile of soil. Call it by its proper name, *Utopia Prime*," Paul then a man said.

"Oh, leave our Moonship alone or we'll just leave orbit, then you will be in serious trouble. The next ship that lands here, I'll have it destroyed and your men will have to stay with us until we deem to return them to you.

"When we do leave, and we will, another Moonship slightly larger than our ship will take our place and you will have a new set of Master's, who have the right to evict you all from your planet and put a new species in your place.

"Just before we leave, we'll return all your junk you have left on the exterior of our ship back to NASA. We will also have to do one other job for you, we cannot leave our Oceans in the state you have got them in," Lynda added, appearing to look at the President of the USA and NASA Chiefs.

True to her word Lynda had the entire surface cleared of the human's junk and had engineers check the exterior of their ship once again for any damage.

One large sphere landed at NASA's Headquarters in Washington DC and with two armed guards standing next to the men who were carrying the six Apollo Moon craft out onto the car park outside their building with hundreds of people seeing the craft they had not seen in decades returned to Earth along with their flags and other rockets they had sent to the Moon. One man even carried a Moon vehicle out of their craft and dropped it next to all the Apollo lower launch pads.

A message was left for the President. It simply said.

"Told you so, we'll be off tomorrow. More of your Rubbish on its way," Captain Lynda Grayson.

As everyone returned to *Odyssey Prime*, six of their largest Spheres, with fighter back up, and these fighters could also hover in the air, just like the Sphere's they were protecting.

The Sphere's moved over each Ocean and sea, moving all the plastic waist into one location. Most of it was vaporised but a section of plastic twenty metres square was dumped in the front garden of the White House; so, everyone and the press could see it and the notice on it, painted in large black letters on the multi coloured plastic.

We just Cleared your Oceans and Seas of YOUR PLASTIC waist. Most of it is vaporised, now you destroy this. We're leaving *Utopia Prime* tonight. Captain Gabrielle and Captain Lynda Grayson wrote onto the plastic waist.

Do not throw your plastic into the sea and oceans.

Chapter 20

When the Spheres landed on *Odyssey Prime*, their Second in Command, Commander Orizen, organised a Guard of Honour to welcome their two Captains back home.

The new recruits were taken to a huge viewing gallery where they could watch the final ceremony of changing the watch, which only happened every hundred and twenty- thousand years give a millennium or two.

Gabrielle, Lynda, John, Alan, Sarah and Tina were taken by an open hover launch to their State Rooms. John and Alan's staterooms were either side of Gabrielle's and Lynda's stateroom.

Sarah shared Alan's Stateroom while Jenny shared John's Stateroom. Once inside, they were all stripped by their dressers, and put into their Ceremony Uniforms, that did not see the light of day very often. The two Captains wore a skirt with light tan stockings with a gold line on the outside of the stockings.

Their skirt was now a vibrant electric blue colour, with gold trim at the bottom of the skirt. An Ocean of blue and green waves were rippling around the botting eight inches of their skirt, with Dolphins jumping in and out of the sea. They wore a bright red bra beneath their Satin white blouses and puffed-up collar. The Waistcoat was also in a Vibrant Electric Blue, covered in gold buttons and trim of thc waistcoat. They had Gold bars on both epaulets, with a bright red M at the top of the right side of the waistcoat.

On the back of the waistcoat, was a picture of Utopia prime, with the Oceans, swirling about, waves hitting the shores of land masses in green and brown. Dolphins again could be seen jumping in and out of blue and green oceans.

They put their Jacket on to check the fit, then stood before the makeup computer. Their previous makeup was removed by one of the dressers. When they put their face into the mould that went around the sides of their face, which would be the hair line, one of the dressers started the computer and ten seconds later, Gabrielle's face was made up, complete with intricate eye makeup, moving waves, and two Dolphins facing each other, one on each cheek, their tails moving left and right, their heads with blinking blue eyes and mouths open talking to each other. Below the tail of the Dolphin was a moving Ocean of blue sea down to the bottom of their face.

Their fingernails were again cleaned and new moving pictures of Dolphins with a moving blue sea background. It was then they put on their Jackets and had them buttoned up by a dresser. The front had gold large buttons, with their Moonship pressed into the middle of each button.

Gold trim on the edges of the jacket, Gold Bars on both epaulets and four gold rings at the bottom of their sleeves. A rotating picture of their Moonship was on both front panels of the waistcoat and just below the epaulets on each of Gabrielle's arms was a picture of the Interior of the ship, while on Lynda's arms was a picture of the exterior of the ship.

They each had a red M below the picture. Their now blond hair was made into ringlets that came down the sides of their face and the back of the hair was put into two inter twined ponytails with gold material tied into a small bow on each ponytail. The front of their hair was cut in a straight line, just above their eyes.

Last they put on their gold three inch open toed high heels and stood facing each other. They wanted to kiss each other, but couldn't mess up their makeup, so they thought to each other and kissed, holding each other in their arms.

"Is that it?" Gabrielle asked.

"Not quite, we must still put on your ceremonial swords, slightly shorter than a man's, but it looks fantastic on and glitters in the light. You also have all the planets in this solar system, on the sleeve of the scabbard, all moving of course, and the giant gas planets look brilliant shooting fires into the stary background," Maria, their final dresser said.

Two girls lifted the bottom of their jackets to slide the brown and gold wide belt around them and buckle it up, so the scabbard was on their left side.

"Are you both going to wear your medals from the Queen?" Jezebel asked.

Gabrielle looked at Lynda who smiled and nodded. "It's something Christine and Kathline will not have, yet." Lynda suggested.

"Fine then, we'll have our medals on then, do you know where they have been put?" Gabrielle asked Jezebel.

"Oh yes, we have them out already and are placed on your dressing tables. Here let me put yours on," Jezebel said and took the Dames medal from its box and started to put it on the left side of Gabrielle's jacket.

The door chimed and automatically opened with a single word from Lynda.

John and Alan entered their very, large suite, standing to attention.

"Good afternoon, Captains, you both look very beautiful, but your medals need altering Monica, the Dames medal is upside down," John informed her.

"I'm so sorry, I was so excited I forgot to check which way it went," Monica said, trying to hide her embarrassment.

"That's okay, with your permission Mam, I'll put your medals onto your jacket," John said.

"Of course," Gabrielle replied.

Alan stepped forward and picked up Lynda's Dame medal.

"With your permission Mam?" he asked Lynda,

"Yes of course Alan, you do look beautiful in your makeup, and I love how your fingernails are painted, blue sea background and a wooden ship moving on the waves, with ships facing the opposite way on the other hand," Lynda replied.

"Thank you, Mam, we both decided to keep to our traditions, all our men wear makeup, it makes our face more attractive to the females aboard ship," Alan replied.

"Stand back both of you," Gabrielle said.

They both stood to attention and took two steps back from their respective Captain.

"Yes, they do look beautiful in their new uniforms swords Lance and especially their makeup," Gabrielle said to Lynda.

John and Alan were wearing their new vibrant electric blue trousers, waistcoat and jacket with a white silk shirt and gold wide tie with their Moonship on and rotating in space.

A gold line went from top to bottom of their trouser seams and gold trim around the edge of their waistcoat and jacket. On their epaulettes both shoulders were a gold and red bar with a red line going down the front of each sleeve to a red ring above three gold rings at the bottom of each sleeve.

On each panel of the jacket, was a picture of a gunslinger on the right, firing his Lance towards the left panel, where a little of the electric blue light hits a man who falls to the floor dead, holding his heart. Both pictures move and the light from the Lance flickers.

On each side of their arms at the top is an image of the ship rotating in space and below, a red M denoting they are married to a woman aboard the ship.

Their face makeup was a bronze background with a gunslinger on each cheek at an angle facing each other, twirling their Lance around a finger.

Gunslingers standing on a dust and pale green floor, to the bottom of their face. Their eyelids, bright blue with a blood red filler on the upper eyelids, sliding down each side of their face keeping close to their hairline, down to the bottom of their ears. An electric blue line was at the bottom of their eyes on the lower eyelid. Their eye lashes were coloured electric blue which sparkled in the light. Finally, was their red lipstick, which they could touch up during their twenty-hour day.

Their hair was now dark blond, and they both just had a trim. Their makeup was put onto their face by the same makeup computer the girls used, with a different programme.

"Turn around guys, let's see the back of your jackets," Lynda asked.

They both turned around so they could see the moving picture on the back of their jackets.

Their pictures were the same, a sandy colour at the bottom of the jacket then a sky-blue background above. A single gunslinger was turning his gun on his right-hand finger, then with the Lance facing forward, fired it, and electric blue sparkling light left the Lance. "I love it," Gabrielle sighed.

"So do I, it's fantastic. Your Lances look brilliant, and I love your swords and the picture on the scabbard, our ship and the planets in this Solar System, almost like ours. That reminds me, Megan, where are our swords?"

"Just here Mam," she picked up Lynda's sword and slipped it into her scabbard and did the same with Gabrielle's sword.

"Alan, is our Commander ready?" Lynda asked.

"As always Mam, she will be joining us now, apparently."

The door chimed and Lynda said, "Open!" and the doors opened. Sarah was standing outside with her new uniform on and her makeup just like the Captains.

The girls were all dressed the same, except Sarah had a half gold bar and a dark blue background, with a starfield over it, which sparkled in the light. At the bottom of her sleeves, were three gold rings and a dark blue ring with a starfield going all around it.

At the top of both arms on the outside, and in the centre was a circle of gold and their ship in the middle. Just below the picture on her right arm was a blue M, designated she was married to a man. She too wore her Dame medal, and the Victoria Cross the Queen gave her. She was also wearing, as too the boys, the blue and red medal for worldwide TG's.

She too was carrying a sword and scabbard, with identical patterns as the others,

They walked outside their suite and boarded the first of the two open inner launches. The wives of the gunslingers and the rest of the gunslingers in their group got into the second launch, except Tina, who sat next to Sarah, dressed in her skirt and top, new uniform.

Sarah was clutching her hands together, shaking slightly. This would be the first time she had took this office and although she had rehearsed it a thousand times on *Utopia Prime*, she was now losing a little confidence in herself.

"Sarah, if you mess it up, just make something up, you know we'll all back you up," Gabrielle said to her.

"I know, but I don't want to spoil it for us and the other crew," Sarah replied.

When they arrived at deck 1092, they got out of their inside launches and walked the short distance to the main hall which was decorated with planets, stars, ships and behind each party, a large moving picture of their own Moonship.

Music started, from an Egyptian era. As they moved slowly to the round table between them, the music changed to a more modern time and Venus, the bringer of Peace, from the Planet Suite by Holst was played until they arrived at the table and chairs. The four Captains sat at the same time; their chairs slipped in behind them as they were sat by their gunslinger.

Then Sarah and Georgina took their seat opposite each other. Senior officers from both ships, took the remainder of the forty chairs, in the hope that it would make the people who had to speak more comfortable. This ceremony was being filmed, and watched by every member of both crews, wherever they could find a viewscreen. It was also being sent to other Moonships, up to fifty thousand light years away and each ship would send the signals on to Moonships further away.

This was the fourth time the ceremony was viewed like this from *Utopia Prime*.

Sarah stood and looked to her own Captains, then across the table to the other two Captains, who were also married to each other.

"Captains Commanders of the crew of the *Agraffe Keeper*, welcome to our Moonship, *Odyssey Prime*, orbiting the planet *Utopia Prime*. Captains, Commanders, welcome to this auspicious Ceremony of the Change of Guard.

"We have been here for one hundred and twenty, thousand years and we have watched the humans grow from Homosapiens to the current day human. It has been a truly magnificent history to live through.

"Now we give the Command of *Utopia Prime* to Captains Christine and Katherine Devalon and the crew of their Moonship *Agraffe Keeper*. We have enjoyed ourselves here and kept the planet free of intruding species, who will not wait their turn to visit *Utopia Prime."*

"Captains Grayson, would you care to talk to Captains Devalon?" Commander Sarah asked.

"Yes… please," Gabrielle replied.

"Captains Devalon, May I introduce my wife, Captain Lynda Grayson, is responsible for the exterior of our Moonship."

"Good evening, Lynda, we have heard great things about you," Christine replied.

"Gabrielle stood, with Lynda holding her hand firmly in hers.

"Captain Christine and Captain Katherine, welcome to our Moonship and this Ceremony. We have come to love the people in this time period although they still fight a lot, it is not as bad as it used to be.

"They have many Space Agencies, but still lack the skills and understanding to build a large spaceship which would leave Utopia Prime and head for planets further afield. There are currently four designers who have come up with an idea to build what they call a World ship, three miles long. It is well worth helping these three men and one woman, a TG we have helped get to live the life she was really meant to live but was born into the wrong body.

There are still another nine hundred humans to change to women. I have already spoken to Kenneth, who is taking command of our latest task of helping people born into the wrong body. Once they have changed sex, we find they are much happier, and their creative side comes through, and they come up with some brilliant ideas for building starships and world ships.

Kenneth should get these TGs changed as soon as possible and get them in groups aboard your ship. We fear when the people of *Utopia Prime*, will need their help, it will come from these people, who their species have shunned. *Utopia Prime* will need these TGs to help them in the not-too-distant future design a ship.

"My wife, Lynda and I would request you allow Kenneth to remain planet side and continue the work we have started. Is there anything you would like to add my love?" Gabrielle asked.

Lynda stood and felt Gabrielle's hand on her left thigh then moving up and down her satin stocking, giving her all her love.

"Unfortunately, there was an altercation, some years ago when the humans' sent men to our Moonship to see what it is made off. They had damaged some delicate machinery and instruments, forcing me, as Captain of the Exterior to go out on the surface in my official uniform, with a body forcefield on.

After I spoke to two men who returned to *Utopia Prime,* some months later, they sent three men, to our Moonship, but only two men landed, while the third remained in the mothership. The astronauts said it was their Moon, so I called for several ships to show themselves; a few fighters came as well and all our ships landed quietly on a ravine, overlooking their craft.

"As they refused to stop what they were doing, I kicked them off our ship and told them never to return, which they did not do until a few years ago."

Katherine stood applauding her and shouted, "Hurray well done for that, they just can't arrive and start trying to dig a hole in the outer hull of our ship. I will therefore be keeping a close eye on the humans," she said.

Everyone applauded her and suddenly it was not as official as it should have been, people were talking to each other across the table, laughing together.

Sarah looked at her counterpart, Amanda Breish. They mouthed words to each other then, both stood.

"Captains, Commanders, although this is wonderful to see both crews mixing so well at this time, our time is quickly running out and the *Agraffe Keeper* is waiting to take the place of *Odyssey Prime*.

"The *Agraffe Keeper* is currently drifting towards us, even though it is ten miles away, if it gets any closer, we will give the humans, a brilliant electrical storm over their planet as the magnetic fields of our ships act against each other.

"I am afraid we will have to continue with the Transition of authority and transfer of deeds of *Utopia Prime,*" Amanda shouted into the room, her words echoing off distant walls."

"You are correct Amanda, but we have melded together, and during those few minutes, made close friends. We should move along quickly to get the Transfer of Orders and Transfer of the Deeds to *Utopia Prime*. What say you Gabrielle and Lynda?" Christine asked.

"We agree," said Gabrielle still seated. "Jenny, can you please bring in the Change of Deeds to *Utopia Prime* please.

"Pauline," Katherine called, "Can you please bring over the *Transfer of Orders* and the Certificate to show, we legally own *Utopia Prime*, and *Transfer of Carers please*?" she asked.

Pauline, the wife of Paul Devonshire, Bodyguard to Katherine Devalon, dressed in her new uniform, held a tube, with scrolls inside, moved as Jenny moved, she too was carrying a tube with scrolls inside. As she walked up to the table Penny removed the scrolls from the tube.

Gabrielle took the scroll for *Transfer of Carers* from the table and took the pen from Penny.

Gabrielle read the Scroll three times and passed it to Lynda before writing anything on the Scroll.

"Yes, I agree to this," Lynda said.

As Gabrielle was filling in the Scroll, Christine was doing the same for *Transfer of Orders*, which came from the *High Council* of the *Galactic Unior*.

Both women passed their Scroll to their wife who signed it as well. The Scroll was read and countersigned by Sarah. After the Scrolls had been exchanged, everyone hugged and kissed each other as their Interior Launches arrived.

An hour later, both sets of Captains and Commanders were on the bridge of their ships. Gabrielle was one side of her bridge giving orders to the crew at their docking stations so they could help move the ship in the right direction, up.

Lynda too was giving orders to the engine room. The engineers had tested the engines twice to ensure they still operated as they should.

"Deploy the six engine nacelles please," Lynda said clearly through her head and mouth set.

When the engines started, their blue Hydrogen exhaust gases could be seen coming from the Dark Side of *Odyssey Prime*. It was being watched and recorded as the white ring of the

Moonship rose higher into the sky. Already, its movement was causing a reaction to the oceans, which were rising with huge waves crashing down onto the shorelines of different continents. Gabrielle noticed, from her side of the bridge the world's oceans were now being pulled up rising higher as Odyssey Prime rose higher into space. Other people entered the bridge taking up positions that had not seen any use for over a hundred and twenty thousand years.

"Lower pushers deploy shields to ninety degrees," Lynda ordered and when green lights indicated the pushers were ready to work. Lynda gave another order. "Pushers to half power and engage."

Nobody felt the ship move, but it was moving, rising into space, still increasing the impact it had on *Utopia Prime's* oceans.

"The Atlantic, and Pacific Oceans have risen by thirty feet, with high impact waves hitting the shorelines. Winds increasing to Gale force around the world. A lot of their rubbish they discarded into the Oceans is now on the surface of the seas and oceans, being drawn by the strong tides, towards the shores," Gemini said from across the bridge as she sat at her station watching her large screen, showing what damage was happening, to the planet below, which was out of their hands.

"There is nothing we can do about it right now; the ship has to rise a lot higher allowing *Agraffe Keeper* to take our place and return the oceans to their former levels."

As *Odyssey Prime* moved higher into space, it pulled the rubbish and the seas over the coastlines. When they had increased their height by another twenty miles, the oceans were a mile inland depositing all the rubbish that was close to the bottom of the Oceans, and a few wooden wrecks, in one piece, full of gold and gold treasures in their holds.

Another twenty miles altitude from the *Agraffe Keeper*, with all Odyssey Prime's external lights blazing, sent pure white and electric blue light to the surface of *Utopia Prime*.

As *Agraffe Keeper*, got lower and a little to the right, it started to influence the oceans itself and they slowly lowered the oceans and the waves got weaker, until eighteen hours later, the oceans were back to their normal height less a great deal of rubbish and at least four hundred wooden sailing ships still in one piece, scattered over different coastlines.

Christine, as Captain of the Exterior, showed her wife, who was hugging her close and kissing her neck what was happening on *Utopia Prime* which they now had to take care off.

"Later my love, I bet Gabrielle and Lynda are doing and thinking the same as us," Katherine sighed.

"But look at the people below, some are struggling to stay above the waters as they are now receding into the oceans." Christine said pointing to her screens which were now magnifying what was happening below.

"This happened because of the Change of Ownership of *Utopia Prime*. It's not very *Prime* at the moment, can we do anything?" Christine asked her wife, then they kissed, their bright electric blue eyes lighting up the bridge, talking together about the problem below.

"I suppose we could deploy our new Sphere's with an escort to pick up people who are in trouble and drop them off deeper inland," Katherine suggested.

"Good, I concur. Attention please," Christine said, as her voice was heard throughout the ship. "We will carry out a rescue mission to help those people on *Utopia Prime*, who are still in the seas and oceans. All pilots to their Spheres, all crews to their Sphere's deploy when you are ready. Go down and pick up everyone you can and drop the people off further inland do what you can for them.

"All fighter pilots to their fighters, deploy in pairs and give cover for each Sphere. You have permission to shoot any aircraft down that attempt to fire at our Spheres. Crew of the rescue ship, deploy now, two fighters for escort shoot to kill, maintain orbit around Utopia Prime to help any crew in trouble," Christine said enjoying the thrill of her first orders of deploying her ships with a fighter escort.

"All surgeons and nurses to the main hospital on new Textra deck," Katherine ordered. Katherine and Christine were in the middle of their bridge, so they could be together, hold hands and kiss when nothing much was happening.

The *Agraffe Keeper* had special orders that would change *Utopia Prime* forever. It had spent a year in space docks around the planet *Everglow*, in the *Repairs Forever* Steller system. The Moonship had been given stronger and faster engines, two hundred new decks, powerful and deadly exterior guns, extensive force fields covering the entire ship. There were twice the number of Spheres and fighters, that could now fire on a ship from other species. The hospital ship could land vertically onto the Textra deck where injured men and women could be taken straight to their new upgraded hospital.

Everything on the Moonship was updated including the bridge. The ship and crew were not just changing carers of the species of *Utopia Prime*. The species living there, despite the help from Gabrielle and Lynda to push them into space flight, did not listen to them or the people they suggested should help them. They had not managed to get to *Alpha Centauri*, to reclaim their planet from the *Planet Masters*. It was therefore decided to upgrade *Agraffe Keeper* and turn their ship of peace to a ship that could defend itself if attacked. It had a special job to do, that was not carried out very often. Eviction!

"I will send a message to the UK, USA and Russian leaders, telling them we are helping those in the sea and stranded on the coastlines which are still under deep water. I will send them a copy of our ownership of their planet *Utopia Prime*, I will also inform them our Sphere's will soon be cleaning up their atmosphere and stopping the Climate Change," Katherine suggested.

"I think now is the time you should tell them of the *Galanese* people who will be occupying part of their planet mainly Australia, New Zealand and all of Africa. It will give them time to organise themselves before we tell them we will give them six years' notice to vacate their planet," Christine suggested to Katherine, hoping to give a little protection to their pilots and crews.

"I think you should also tell them if anyone tries to fire on our ships the offending ship and its crew will be vaporised. While we change their atmosphere, not one of their ships are to be flying as they will be destroyed by the system, we have to use to clean up their atmosphere, they should not have got it this bad in the first place and asked for help to clean up their atmosphere. We could have arrived a few years earlier and took the place of Captains Gabrielle and Lynda Grayson who are the two people in charge of *Odyssey Prime*, their Moonship. Katherine suggested.

"Michca, can you please open a channel that will allow everyone on Utopia Prime to hear our message please. Can you ensure the heads of all Countries can hear us and not stop our message getting through to everyone please?" Katherine asked.

Michca had ten of her communication operators helping her to do this job. New antennas were being ejected from inside the hull to the outside, where the dish could be deployed to send messages through space.

They were also using *Utopia Prime's* communication satellites to assist them. send their message to everyone, via Tv's and mobile phones. The message would be automatically recorded and could be played back any number of times.

"We are now ready for you Katherine, everyone on *Utopia Prime* can hear you," Michca told her Captain from two sections behind her.

"Thank you Michca, you may as well deploy all our communication dishes and aerials. I think we will be talking to these people for many months to come," Katherine said with a long sigh.

She held her wife's hand in hers as she got herself ready to give the people below their first orders.

"Good morning and good evening to everyone on *Utopia Prime* as it will now be called. *Earth* sounds like a pile of dirt, your planet has a proper name for itself, *Utopia Prime,* use it. Your new Moonship is called *Agraffe Keeper*. Please acknowledge us with this name. Our call name and frequency to use to speak to us is attached to the end of this message.

"My name is Katherine Devalon, Captain of the interior of our Moonship."

"My name is Christine Devalon, Captain of the exterior of our Moonship. I am also in Command of all our Spheres and escort ships. You would have been told by Captains Gabrielle and Lynda Grayson that you are to have a change of Carers and Moonships.

"We all apologise for the swelling of your seas and oceans, the last time this was carried out was one hundred and twenty thousand years ago, when Gabrielle and Lynda arrived here in their ship to take over from another Moonship.

"The last time this happened, it did not matter about the people below, they were on a completely different continent to the way *Utopia Prime* is laid out now. We are therefore deploying some of our Spheres to assist your people in the sea and oceans, getting them back onto dry land. Please do not fire upon our Spheres, their escort will return fire and all our Sphere's will return home; leaving your people to rescue everyone.

"Like Gabrielle and Lynda, we will not tollerate any of your puny ships landing on our outer hull and setting up experiments. Our Moonship is now off limits to any of your ships from any land launch sites. There will be many more. notices or orders we will give you over the next few weeks.

"The first is you must not allow any of your aircraft large or small to fly while we use some special equipment to clean up your atmosphere and return it to what it was before your people created Climate Change. Again, you did not listen to one person in the UK that told you what was causing Climate Change and you could have stopped it from progressing if only you would have listened to her or asked for help. I will tell you when we are going to clean your air which may take several days.

"Gabrielle and Lynda helped you so much to try and get your species into space properly. Their Moonship did not have the equipment like we do to clear up the mess you made of your atmosphere, but Gabrielle did send us drawings and designs of the equipment needed to do the job, which you could not have made. So, thanks to them we have it with us and can accomplish the job using our ships.

"We will leave it a few of your days before we do this job, while we settle in here and take over some of the apartments and houses we own. We already have ten thousand people on your planet and none of them are to be interrogated by your people, we are just like you with the same problems.

"All our important people have armed bodyguards to protect them, and we are at the moment just setting our people up in the buildings their predecessors owned. We are not going to kill any of you as long as you do not fire on our ships or people on Terra Firmer.

"If you think you cannot get on with different races because you don't like each other. You will all be getting on with other species from different planets, who would like to come here and stay for a while.

"All of the people are mainly like us, and yourselves, some of us are yellow, others brown or red, it just depends on the colour of the star we live under. We all live in peace and speak *Galactic Unior*, so we all understand each other. That is over a hundred thousand different species who all live in peace and work together in harmony.

"Our Galactic species move about a lot and welcome new species to our large family. We suggest you all learn *Galactic Unior*, quickly. This will help your own people understand each other on Utopia Prime. Christine and Katherine out for a while for a cup of refreshing tea I have attached a copy of our language

Galactic Unior and how to speak it. The system will just attach itself to your mobile phones, televisions, computers and any other sound recording equipment."

"Very good dear, very, good indeed. Do you think it is the time to inform them the Galanese ships will arrive in six months?" Christine asked her wife.

"Yes, my love but let us do that next week, we will see if they are attempting to learn our language first. Give them most of the bad news first, then when the real bad news hits the planet, the people below will not be so frightened, when we tell them they must leave *Utopia Prime*, because it was sold to the Galanese people and they now wish to live on it, all of it," Katherine added smiling.

"Good evening and good morning to the people on Utopia Prime. I am Katherine Devalon, Captain of the interior of our Moonship. My wife Christine was speaking to you yesterday. We have five hundred and fifty thousand souls aboard this Upgraded Moonship, and like you, believe in one God. I would like to inform you all some more of the cleaning up the crew of Odyssey Prime carried out before our arrival.

"Teams from Odyssey Prime have worked hard to remove all the radioactive containers you have dropped into the Oceans and cleaned up all your test bore holes for nuclear bombs. Then there are your warships and aircraft from your first and second world wars and other wars through this time period. All of the wreckage has been vaporised, including deep sea scientific research dwellings. The crew were brought aboard their ship and given a tour of the Ocean floors and into the Mediterranean Sea. They worked hard cleaning the Mediterranean Sea of all its rubbish. There were iron warships, English and Roman warships French and Spanish ships made from wood.

"They vaporised all these ships after taking out all the gold medallions, items of jewerllry and larger items for trading with. All this gold was dispersed to the people who needed it the most and they now own it, as there are no Heads of State alive today to return it to. They also removed the plastic in all the oceans and seas. We will not tollerate the oceans being treated like this. The beautiful fish and large mammals wish to swim in clean water with no fear of being caught in large nets or fishing lines or plastic. So, no more fishing even for sport, you must have respect for this species, they were here an extremely long time before humans.

"The people on our Spheres are quickly rescuing your people, getting them warm and dry, mending any broken bones. or other illness they are suffering from, we have cured it. People in their hundreds, are being taken further inland and dropped off.

"We will be able to help you all a great deal with your health problems, we can even re-grow lost arms or legs. We will help those people who are going blind and have no water first. We will deploy eight hospital Spheres and a Hospital ship to those countries who need us the most," Katherine told everyone on *Utopia Prime.*

The new carers for *Utopia Prime* were seen and talked about, there was nothing the world governments could do about it after Katherine and Christine spoke to everyone on *Utopia Prime*. The new *Carers* had made their first mark on the planet below their ship.

As *Odyssey Prime* made its way to Jupiter, Lynda and Gabrielle walked about their ship, devoid of their swords. Alan and John followed them, walking before them towards the refuelling stations, they would need enough gas to get them over halfway to their destination.

Mitch, a top Astrogator, had worked out a course for them to get to their new destination, eleven point eight seven lightyears away, *The AquaLea Solar System* with three planets, *I'm Clean Now, Fall in Love Here, Ready to play:* and two Gas Giants, *Pure Love* and *In a Heartbeat*. They would orbit the second planet which was already in *The Galactic Unior.* and a peaceful race, for a short period, of only fifty thousand years.

They had a lot of problems with people being born into the wrong body and they would have to bring these people into space flight and build five different World Ships, as their Star only had seventy thousand years left before it turned into a Red Giant and their planets would be destroyed by their star as it expanded.

They were to find a new star and planet for the people to live on which meant lots of trips to other star systems to find a new planet. The Girls from Australia would be very, helpful doing this research.

Their course would take them close to the *Pride Star System*, with nine planets and three Gas Giants. The most populated planet, *I'm clean as a new pin*, is in the *Galactic Unior* and would be a good place to stop for a month or so and let some of the new crew, see another planet and another friendly species.

All three Gas Giants had Rings, which would not cause a problem as they were refuelling at the third Gas Giant *Self Esteem*. Their star was yellow, called *Pleasure*, but gave enough heat and light for the people to survive there, although they too were looking for another planet and a ship to take them there. This would be another job for the Australian girls, travelling around local star systems looking for a good planet for the people off *I'm clean as a new pin.*

Arriving at Jupiter, they deployed the suction pipes, which would take in the Hydrogen gas and through their fuel system, change it slightly, so it would power their ship at least for the next five hundred years. It took fifteen hours to refuel and once the fuel was settled and their equipment retrieved from Jupiter, they set off again.

Gabrielle and Lynda had been holding hands wherever they went and ensured their new girls and boys were in the discipline's they had requested. The girls from Australia who could fly a Sphere, were now in simulators learning to fly like their tutor wanted them to fly, safely.

Every night Gabrielle and Lynda were in their large suite, a hundred by two hundred feet, eight feet high. A king-size bed, walk-in dressing room, two dressing tables and a computer makeup artist, toenail painter and dryer, fingernail, painter and dryer.

An air shower, for two, was on the far side of their bedroom with two toilets which vapourised their food waste and water was sent, to the water recycling tanks. They had two sinks which used water which was also returned to the recycling tanks.

They had a meeting room for talks with other crew members, two offices, side by side with windows they could open so they could talk, hug and kiss each other when they had a moment to spare.

Their breakfast room was large fourteen by twenty feet, with six, five feet high-backed chairs, with a hologram of their ship on each chair back. They had a round breakfast table, which could be enlarged if they were having a breakfast staff meeting. Sliding automatic glass doors separated every room, but the glass doors to their bedroom were frosted with holograms of their ship on each door.

As per Lynda's thinking ahead, some members of the crew worked hard getting their Stateroom soundproofed as Lynda had asked.

While their ship flew out of their old solar system, everyone was looking at a large viewer as the rear large cameras, showed their solar system laid out with all the planets, *Utopia Prime,* sending its TV and Sound signals far into Deep Space. Mechanics and engineers were installing the hot and cold-water system throughout the ship. For those couples that wanted a wet shower. Other engineers were installing the latest defence guns and shield harmonics to bring it up to date with *Agraffe Keeper*.

A week after setting off for their new destination, Gabrielle and Lynda had calmed down a lot, their love making had been rushed over the previous few days because there were so many things to do, meetings to attend, separately and together, but they ensured they could spend the night sleep period, whatever time it was, together in bed.

A few weeks later, with everyone settled in and most problems now sorted out, they slowed down a great deal. Gabrielle and Lynda were in bed, both naked beneath their warm duvet. They played for a while, made love passionately then lay in each other's arms, happy and glad to be back in space, journeying for hundreds of years at a time, doing what they were good at. Helping people who have been born into the wrong body.

As they lay together arm in arm, breasts touching, they thought back to their time on Utopia Prime. They had been separated by jobs which took years at a time, sometimes, decades and they would not meet again until ninety or more years later.

This time they knew they would not leave each other's side, no matter what had to be done, they would do it together.

Laying in each other's arms, breasts touching, their green eyes grew bright as they kissed, giving each other all the love they had. They curled up together, bodies touching each other, legs around each other and arms wrapped around each other snuggled up together, warm, deeply in love with an eternity to look forward to, exploring space, holding hands.

They both fell asleep, dreaming about each other and their long lives they had before them.

About The Author

Sarah Henley is a Transgender and has written other books in the past under her former name of Terence J. Henley or TJ Henley. She is disabled, formerly an electrical engineer, until she had to retire in 1993 after she developed an Epidermoid Cyst inside her spinal column. After three major operations on her spine, she now spends her days writing from her wheelchair in chronic pain.

Sarah enjoys writing, as she can get into it and it distracts her from some of the pain. Sarah told me this was a hard book to edit as there was so much more she would have liked to add, especially near the end.

Sarah enjoys films mainly SF, but she also enjoys Harry Potter and some Romance films. Now she has changed from male to female, she is changing her preferences in the type of films she is watching. She still likes her music mainly classical and is an amateur astronomer and a Fellow of the BIS (British Interplanetary Society). She follows the space programme with keen interest and hopes to see the first humans walk on Mars.

Sarah has written this series of books especially for TG's to read and enjoy. She has already started another book on Covid 19 which will be published later this year. She enjoys writing stories and her mind is filled with them, ready to put down on paper for TG's and others to enjoy reading.

Sarah hopes to meet many of her followers when she does a book signing, starting in Bristol then to other cities and towns throughout the country, including visiting the North of England and Scotland.

Sarah sends her love to all her readers and will hopefully meet many of you as she travels around our country with her laptop at hand, continually writing her stories for you all to read.

Sarah was married to Angela who was very, happy to live their lives as lesbians. Angela died in 2015 with a large cancer brain tumour which left Sarah upset for three years, after which she decided to have a sex change. Sarah is determined to write many more books in her new name.

Printed in Great Britain
by Amazon